AF361274

JACOPO CAVICEO'S *PEREGRINO*

JACOPO CAVICEO'S *PEREGRINO*

Jacopo Caviceo's *Peregrino*

Annotated English Edition and Translation

SHERRY ROUSH

UNIVERSITY OF TORONTO PRESS
Toronto Buffalo London

ISBN 978-1-4875-0575-2 (cloth)   ISBN 978-1-4875-3261-1 (EPUB)
                                   ISBN 978-1-4875-3260-4 (PDF)

Library and Archives Canada Cataloguing in Publication

Title: Jacopo Caviceo's Peregrino : annotated English edition and translation /
   Sherry Roush.
Other titles: Peregrino
Names: Roush, Sherry, author. | Container of (expression): Caviceo, Jacopo,
   1443–1511. Libro del Peregrino. English.
Series: Toronto Italian studies.
Description: Series statement: Toronto Italian studies | Includes bibliographical
   references and index.
Identifiers: Canadiana (print) 20220441685 | Canadiana (ebook) 20220441863 |
   ISBN 9781487505752 (cloth) | ISBN 9781487532604 (PDF) |
   ISBN 9781487532611 (EPUB)
Subjects: LCSH: Caviceo, Jacopo, 1443–1511. | LCSH: Caviceo, Jacopo,
   1443–1511. Libro del Peregrino. | LCSH: Italian fiction – 16th century –
   Translations into English. | LCSH: Romances, Italian – Translations into
   English. | LCGFT: Romance fiction.
Classification: LCC PQ4617.C7 P3313 2023 | DDC 853/.3–dc23

We wish to acknowledge the land on which the University of Toronto Press
operates. This land is the traditional territory of the Wendat, the Anishnaabeg,
the Haudenosaunee, the Métis, and the Mississaugas of the Credit First Nation.

University of Toronto Press acknowledges the financial support of the
Government of Canada, the Canada Council for the Arts, and the Ontario Arts
Council, an agency of the Government of Ontario, for its publishing activities.

Contents

Acknowledgments

I first came across Jacopo Caviceo's *Peregrino* in my search for examples of ghosts among Renaissance Italian narratives, the object of research eventually published in my 2015 monograph *Speaking Spirits: Ventriloquizing the Dead in Renaissance Italy*, also with University of Toronto Press. Caviceo's use of Giovanni Boccaccio's voice in the proem of the *Peregrino*, as well as his couching of the entire work as a romance told from beyond the grave, was worth mention there. However, I was beguiled by Caviceo's book for so many other reasons that I knew I had to circle back to it at some point.

The *Peregrino* has languished in relative obscurity since the Cinquecento, perhaps because it intimidates for all kinds of reasons. It is long and a romance, so it tends to fall into the less serious genre category. It is by a relatively obscure author of unrespectable moral character. The language is not standard Florentine, but a northern Latinate courtly Italian that necessitates, even in the 1993 Italian edition for native Italian readers, a substantial glossary. It seems oddly quaint, almost quixotic, to dedicate years of toil in today's world to a mostly forgotten romance about romances. At crucial junctures three colleagues shared knowledge and encouragement, and I thank Konrad Eisenbichler, Suzanne Magnanini, and Christopher Nissen from the bottom of my heart.

I gratefully acknowledge two 2020 grants received from the National Endowment for the Arts in Literary Translation and the National Endowment for the Humanities in Individual Faculty Research, which, along with a research sabbatical in 2020–1 from my Department of Spanish, Italian, and Portuguese and the College of the Liberal Arts at Penn State University, permitted me to complete this translated and annotated edition. I thank my department and college for supporting its publication with a subsidy. Sections of the Introduction appeared in earlier published iterations. Besides the aforementioned *Speaking Spirits* (from pages 118–31), these include the articles "When a Pilgrim Is Not a Pilgrim: Subversions of Allegory and Allegoresis in Jacopo Caviceo's *Peregrino* (1508)" in *Italian Quarterly*, and "Dante Ravennate and Boccaccio Ferrarese? Post-Mortem Residency and the Attack on Florentine Literary Hegemony, 1480–1520" in *Viator*; and the encyclopedia entry on "Jacopo Caviceo" for *The Literary Encyclopedia*. I also presented papers on Caviceo or his *Peregrino* at a 2015 Interdisciplinary Symposium at the Ohio State University titled "Pointing at Shadows: The Procedures and Complexion of Allegory in Medieval Art and Literature," the 2018 Sixteenth-Century Society and Conference in Albuquerque, and the 2020 and 2022 Modern Language Association conferences.

Although I could draw on my previous experience of producing translated editions (my *Selected Philosophical Poems of Tommaso Campanella* was published in two volumes by the University of Chicago Press and Fabrizio Serra Editore in 2011), Caviceo's *Peregrino* was an entirely different kind of challenge. Here I am not offering a facing-page translation with the original text. I also knew I did not want to hew as closely to a word-for-word rendering of Caviceo's rapid-fire prose as I chose to do for Campanella's philosophical concepts and metred density. Caviceo's genre, mode, tone, vocabulary, everything required that I go back to school to study the translation of humour in its various forms, and my Summer 2017 experience at the Middlebury Bread Loaf Translators' Conference offered precisely what I sought. I practised translating into English the range of jesting voices in works by Piovano Arlotto, Ludovico Domenichi, and Nicolò Franco, and I thank the advanced workshop leader, Maureen Freeley, and all of my fellow literary translators, who offered valuable feedback.

My thanks also go to colleagues and friends: Bill Blair, Anne Coldiron, Mike Edwards, Marco Faino, Paola Gambarota, Linda Lee, Deena Levy, Laura Marshall, John W. Moore, Jr., Kristina Marie Olson, Michele Rossi, Arielle Saiber, Michael Sherberg, and Johanna Rossi Wagner. I thank my parents, Rodger and Mary Roush, for their loving support.

Months of isolation in 2020 due to the coronavirus brought an unanticipated boon: hearing my husband, Rick Weyer, read aloud a chapter or more of Caviceo's text in translation each day. It allowed me to catch countless infelicities, but also to experience literature in a mode that is relatively rare today. *Grazie infinite.*

Tackling the many drafts necessary to represent the *Peregrino* in English was not unlike learning to play the violin – practice, practice, practice, until it finally doesn't sound quite so squeaky. Tuning the translation involves approximating the tone and timbre of Caviceo's authorial voice. Campanella's voice was so different from Caviceo's, and neither writer's voice was anything like Arlotto's or Domenichi's or Franco's. Needless to say, none of these have much in common with my own. Despite the assiduous practice, a version can still feel "off." In the end, I recognize that there are countless potential renderings, but publication is the equivalent of a nerve-racking one-time performance.

I could not have done this without the editorial guidance of Suzanne Rancourt, Judy Williams, and the team at the University of Toronto Press. Of course, any views, findings, conclusions, or recommendations expressed in this publication do not necessarily reflect those of the National Endowment for the Arts, the National Endowment for the Humanities, Penn State University, or anyone else but me.

JACOPO CAVICEO'S *PEREGRINO*

Introduction: Jacopo Caviceo's *Peregrino* (1508)

Jacopo Caviceo's *Peregrino* "may have been the first novel specially written for women."

– Letizia Panizza in *The Cambridge History of Italian Literature* (159)

The *Peregrino* was a European bestseller in its day, as evidenced by twenty-one Italian editions and at least thirteen printings in French and Spanish in the half-century after its 1508 publication. Jacopo Caviceo's novel or sentimental prose romance appears in English translation for the first time here. He dedicated the work to Lucrezia Borgia, the new Duchess of Ferrara, who was actively seeking to remake her own image, including as generous patron of the arts, after the deaths of her father, Pope Alexander VI (Rodrigo Borgia), in 1503, and her brother Cesare Borgia in 1507, who would be praised for his ruthlessness by Niccolò Machiavelli in *The Prince* in 1513. Caviceo's love story features an array of complex female characters asserting agency in a society in flux. The book transports the reader to a vastly different world of physical danger, reputational risks, and erotic intrigue, a vision that nonetheless also invites the reader to compare and contrast its social dynamics with those of today, offering abundant source material for scholars focusing on domesticity, the urban setting, and comparative Mediterranean studies. The Italian Renaissance emerged from a period that witnessed the discovery of new worlds, the rise of revolutionary new technologies from the printing press to explosive weaponry capable of destroying cities, the turn away from feudalism to test the efficacy of modern republicanism, and changing definitions of nobility, all against a backdrop of war, pandemic, and a crisis of faith and religious institutions. Moreover, Caviceo's work offers great insight into this time of change and astounding innovation from the perspective of historical and fictional characters from vastly different walks of life – from monarchs to servants, prostitutes, diplomats, lawyers, Muslims, hermits, children, and parents.

Caviceo's *Peregrino* relates the story of a courtship between two young lovers in the city of Ferrara: Peregrino and Genevera, from hostile families of equal stature. The reader must face from the outset of the work that the narrative will not be simple or straightforward, since it is told mostly in the first person from the ghost of the work's namesake, and it unfolds in three books told in dream visions during three consecutive nights.[1] The first book chronicles how twenty-two-year-old Peregrino fell in love in church on May Day (1 May, the day "dedicated to lovers") with Genevera, six years his junior, and the increasingly daring attempts he employs to woo this clever girl of a rival clan. One of his many ploys, hiding inside a life-sized hollow statue of St. Catherine of Alexandria, allows him to breach Genevera's domestic walls, an idea he admits he takes from tales of the Trojan Horse. The consequences of this action, however, also prompt the only actual pilgrimage for this character whose name means "Pilgrim," when Genevera insists he seek the saint's forgiveness on Mount Sinai.

The second and third books recount Peregrino's return odyssey and subsequent search for Genevera, during which he endures many more tribulations out of love for her, including abduction by pirates, captivity as a slave, and a journey to the Other World, while she must resist the suitor her parents choose for her and withstand a period of cloistering in a convent when they attempt to persuade her to take the suitor as her husband. After plot twists that feature cameos of dozens of Renaissance celebrities and other historical personages, the bumbling protagonist and his beloved celebrate marriage and succeed in doing the one thing that eluded young lovers in so many more famous romance narratives, including that of the Montagues and Capulets: convince their parents to accept their will and broker peace between their families without resorting to suicide.[2] Nevertheless, this work defies the classical definitions of both a comedy and a tragedy: it does not culminate in the couple living happily ever after – at least, not in this world. The saga does not end before their three weddings and two funerals, then a reunion in the Elysian Fields.

In the process, the characters of the *Peregrino* reveal a level of psychological development transcending anything present in earlier romances. Aspects of Caviceo's work recognizably echo Giovanni Boccaccio's love laments (most notably from the *Filocolo*, the *Filostrato*, and the *Elegy of Lady Fiammetta*) and Dante Alighieri's otherworldly interactions in *The Divine Comedy*, while anticipating Ludovico Ariosto's mock-heroic quests in the *Orlando Furioso* (1516 in its earliest version), and Benvenuto Cellini's humorous mode of self-representation in his *Vita* (written between 1558 and 1562), since aspects of the *Peregrino* amusingly exploit autobiographical episodes from Caviceo's life.[3] Moreover, the *Peregrino* shares with Francesco Colonna's *Hypnerotomachia Polifili* (1499) and Jacopo Sannazaro's *Arcadia* (c. 1480, publ. 1504) the distinction of being among the most influential literary examples of non-Florentine Italian vernacular literature at the turn of the sixteenth century. This English edition and translation invites critical and comparative studies on a broad range of literary and cultural interests currently on the rise in early modern studies, since the *Peregrino* serves as a kind of treasury (its tone ranging from homage to parody) of popular and learned literary modes, including reinterpretations of Greco-Roman mythology, epic and romance contaminations, early fictional epistolary writing, dream visions and Renaissance interpretations of Macrobian dream theories, ghost stories, intersections of law and literature in the representation of courtroom dramas, philosophical love debates, pilgrimage accounts, fictional redeployments of autobiographical narratives, and the emergence of early modern feminism in what has been termed the *querelle des femmes*. Implicit in the courtship are disturbing attitudes concerning an exchange of risks and benefits articulated quite deliberately as an economic *quid pro quo*, and a mutual testing of feelings by the threat of death, which are worthy of deeper critical analysis. The result is also a profoundly enjoyable romance of wicked wittiness.

The *Peregrino*'s Setting, Title, and Characters

The 219-chapter work is set in Ferrara, though its protagonist will travel widely around the Mediterranean world and beyond. The fictional narrative takes place over the course of approximately six years, but it is not possible to specify a corresponding historical timeline. Many of the actual events described in the narrative occurred in the 1480s, including Bernardo Bembo's sojourn in Ravenna, Princivalle Mantica's festive gathering in 3.24, and the conflict between the pope and the Holy Roman Emperor Federico III. However, some characters, such as Ercole Strozzi (who does not die until 1508), are represented as already dead, and others, including two of the consulting lawyers in the trial in 1.18, Alessandro Tartagni of Imola and Felino Sandeo, were not active in their profession at the same time. Caviceo's composition is thus more focused on the literary impact that namedropping certain historical figures might have on the narrative or on its author's potential advantages in life than it was on historical precision.

Peregrino is the fictional protagonist and narrator, who also represents aspects of the author's own experience. Peregrino is seemingly the only son of well-to-do parents, the late Antonio and widow Camilla (though an unspecified number of sisters accompany his mother to meet his new bride in 3.78). He is educated, though not especially studious. Charming, well-connected, and extroverted, he enjoys interactions with powerful social groups and inclines toward adventure and new experiences, verging on recklessness. He demonstrates little authentic spiritual piety, at least in the first books, but acknowledges that he grows in virtue through his relationship with Genevera. He dies because he cannot go on living after Genevera's passing and her spirit's call for him to join her in the next life (3.96).

Caviceo presents much of Peregrino's development as a series of textual and symbolic interpretational challenges, which the protagonist repeatedly fails.[4] These tests frequently appear as lessons from mythology. For example, when Peregrino falls in love at first sight in 1.1, Love wounds him with the same weapons he used to strike unhappy Phyllis. In Ovid's *Heroides* 2, Demophon abandons the Greek princess Phyllis, who hangs herself for love and consequently undergoes metamorphosis into an almond (or, according to some sources, a filbert) tree.[5] This mythological allusion is only one in a series with unacknowledged moral lessons in the *Peregrino*'s first chapter, including the reference to Jove striking down an overweening Phaeton. The author seems to imply that his protagonist should exercise caution and not overreach in his love objective, but Peregrino will nevertheless persist. In succumbing to the power of his lady's beauty, he also compares himself to Acteon: "I seemed to resemble miserable, lacerated Acteon, and I pitied and upbraided myself, saying: 'O Peregrino, see how low Love has brought you! Where's that mind of yours so determined to resist temptations?'" ("mi parse vedere il misero dilacerato Acteon, e di me stesso facto pietoso e riprehensore diceva: 'O Peregrino, ove sei reducto? ov'è quella deliberata mente a resistere?'" 1.1). Moreover, if these multiple mythological warnings were not sufficient, Peregrino receives yet another caution against falling in love. He spies a sentence from an open book in Genevera's lap, which declares, echoing Matthew 22:14: "O mortals, I call all of you, but save only a few" ("O mortali, tutti vi chiamo, ma puochi ne reserbo"). The excerpt strikes Peregrino as a "cruel passage" ("parola crudele"), a "damning text" ("damnosa scriptura"), and an "ill-omened" beginning ("principio infausto"). He calls to mind the disastrous loves of Hercules and Achilles. All of these warnings Peregrino receives, but he does not interpret them in such a way as to circumvent his destiny.

Peregrino's inability to heed lessons from texts proves true for his incapacity to understand symbolic messages as well, particularly Genevera's encouraging gift to him of the ivory box containing the greenery and a living lizard in 1.12. These difficulties, along with his improper deciphering of *interpretatio nominis*, keep him on his wayward path in Book 1. In one episode, he is hunting with companions when one audacious peer shows off an object, boasting that it is a gift from his lady after a night of love-making. It is a falcon's hood, decorated with twined juniper branches.[6] Peregrino immediately interprets those branches as ones that signified "the name of my lady" ("quali representavano il nome de la mia signora," 1.25). Peregrino flees from the hunting scene in a fit of jealousy, but soon learns that the junipers depicted on this falcon's hood have no connection to his Genevera. His hermeneutic struggles will only be underscored when Genevera subsequently gives him a belt featuring the same decorative motif.

Caviceo's work joins a company of books that feature a primary protagonist whose name is Pilgrim or something similar, and allegorically hints that this *romanzo* might also be an account of Everybody's journey through life with an eye on the afterlife.[7] The work features isolated instances of a typical medieval moralizing allegorical mode, such as when Anselmo explains the punishments in the afterlife (in 3.11, for instance). Indeed, the reader might expect that Caviceo's own high clerical position might favour this interpretive mode. However, he figures his protagonist Peregrino as largely dismissive of these correspondences between sin and *contrapasso*-style punishments, with the exception of his curious inquiry about the realm of lovers. Once he witnesses that punishment, Peregrino is far from discouraged, naming a clique of modern luminaries there in much the same pathos-driven language he will employ in remembering the story of Hero and Leander, for example, in 3.1. In the end, the work's explicit pedagogical strategy (that is, instructing others through Peregrino's example on how to avoid the snares of love) insists on a method of reading and interpreting that seduces its readers on precisely the eros-charged quest against which it purports to warn. The *Peregrino* thus presents itself as a go-between (or Galehaut) between the author and his readership. By extension, I would like to argue that Caviceo's *Peregrino* should be seen as a kind of Italian *Celestina*.

Like the title of the Spanish near-contemporary masterpiece attributed to Fernando de Rojas, *La Celestina* (1499), the title of Caviceo's *Peregrino* may ultimately best be left untranslated.[8] Both are eponymous titles for the works' protagonists. Moreover, both titles suggest in their original languages personal traits or potentially allegorical characterizations that readers are invited to see (or more readily not see) in the characters themselves. Thus, "Celestina" might once have described a celestial or heavenly lady, but the more common definition in Spanish after the success of Rojas's work is "procuress" or "bawd," thus suggesting a certain irony in the old matchmaker's name. A similar potential for irony insinuates itself into the title of Caviceo's romance, based on the male lover's name and the scope of his "pilgrimage,"[9] which in turn illuminate the techniques the author uses to complicate and explicate his potentially allegorical meanings, his treatment of the sin that prompts the main character's nested pilgrimage to Mount Sinai, and the role of the otherworldly perspective of the *romanzo*'s dream narrative.

The name of Peregrino's beloved, **Genevera**, undergoes even more deliberate etymological scrutiny and interpretation within the text: "Genevera – a name which signifies to me nothing less than 'the true genetrix of every human created thing'" ("Genevera, che al iudicio mio altro significare non vuole, se non che de ogni humana cosa creata egli è vera genetrice," 1.2). The identification of the *genetrice* with the Virgin Mary is acknowledged by the reflection of Genevera in a painted image of Mary, "genetrix of the true Messiah made man" ("la genetrice del verohumanato Messia," 1.2). Caviceo effectively shifts the true genetrix from the Virgin Mary to the object of Peregrino's lust, who tellingly will die as a direct consequence of the act of generation: while giving birth to the fruit of their sexual union. The child's name, **Alexandro**, acknowledges the role played by the saint from Alexandria.[10] The birth results in a living son, but the genetrix generates paradoxically in the same act her own death, and subsequently the death of Peregrino, who succumbs to broken-hearted grief.

Physically, Genevera embodies the aesthetic ideals of the time: golden hair, bright, limpid, flashing eyes, pale skin with blushing cheeks, a high forehead, red mouth, straight white teeth, etc.[11] Intellectually, she is portrayed as having learned exceptionally well a course of humanistic study from her tutor Violante. She appears to be the only daughter of a family blessed with several sons (Timoteo, Hippolyto, Galeotto, and Genevera's unnamed brother who is stabbed to death in 1.46), and they dutifully protect the family's honour while thwarting her wishes. Nevertheless, she is mindful of her virtuous reputation, patient, and prudent. Once she commits her feelings to Peregrino, she is devoted, and understands that she must delay her parents' initiative of contracting marriage with Galeazzo, the suitor from Reggio Emilia. While at the convent in Ravenna, she takes the name of Hippolyta and appears to inspire genuine spiritual devotion in the nuns there. Genevera demonstrates capability in managing her maid and other servants to her advantage. She is also quite calculating; like the characters around her, she prevaricates when it serves her purposes.

Genevera succeeds in preserving her virginity until her wedding night and, on her deathbed, articulates an exemplary course of the young woman who dies well (corresponding to a popular literary genre of the time primarily associated with men). In a moving and memorable speech, Genevera faces her tragic, unavoidable death at a young age with fortitude, equanimity, and magnanimous courage, accepting God's will for her while teaching, comforting, and encouraging those in despair who surround her (3.88–9).

Although the novel moves forward through the interactions of the two young lovers, their represented relationships with other characters significantly enrich the plot. **Acate** is Peregrino's closest companion, who shares the same pre-eminent quality of faithfulness that his probable namesake, Achates, displayed toward Aeneas in Virgil's *Aeneid*. Acate is obedient and steadfast to Peregrino, even at the risk of his own imprisonment and slavery; nevertheless, he possesses a far more three-dimensional personality than did Virgil's Achates. Acate does not shrink from articulating moral values decidedly more conservative than Peregrino's. Indeed, Acate regularly lectures his friend, with the ensuing result that he manages to get Peregrino to consider the consequences of his actions before causing irreparable harm to himself or others in several episodes, especially when Acate prevents Peregrino from impulsively killing the Duke's male relative in church out of a fit of foundationless jealousy (1.2). Acate's discussions with Peregrino on the nature of love and duty illuminate a more pragmatic, ethical perspective than Peregrino's more classical- or courtly-love-inspired abstractions. Moreover, Acate becomes the architect of Peregrino and Genevera's marriage(s) in the third book, through his initiative to swipe the letters exchanged between Genevera's father and the Abbess of the convent in Ravenna, then substitute forged letters of his own. He is also in Peregrino's service, though this does not become discernible until late in the work. The way Acate demands payment of the ring off the widow Violante's finger (in 3.62) would be incompatible with the *noblesse oblige* expected of a man of Peregrino's own social rank and wealth. Moreover, when Peregrino dictates his will (in 3.98), he specifies that Acate, along with Violante, be provided with clothing and support from his household.

Violante is the fascinating and enigmatic figure described as once Peregrino's wet nurse and now Genevera's tutor. Her connections suggest she is a quintessential "violator" of boundaries, such as those between warring households or socio-economic classes. One is tempted to project onto her something of the Nurse for Shakespeare's Juliet or characters in earlier romances, but Violante is far more psychologically complex. The experienced widow perceives the strengths and weaknesses in both Peregrino and Genevera equally well and loves them both for who they are, at times seeming to suffer a conflict of loyalties.[12] Her teasing of Peregrino for being the slower witted of the two at the outset of the courtship is particularly keen. Compared to Genevera's mother, Anastasia, or Genevera's personal maidservant, Astanna, Violante is a more positive female figure, with the intelligence, courage, and authority to undertake the voyage to Ravenna in the third book in order to resolve the work's overriding conflict.

Astanna comes closest to exemplifying the stereotype of the greedy servant; however, she also proves, particularly in the growth she displays during the encounter with Peregrino in the afterlife, that she is a more dynamic character than the stock type. She's described as Genevera's *secretaria* (secretary), but since Genevera writes her own letters, rather than dictating them, Astanna appears more properly to function as a personal serving maid. She is employed by Genevera's parents, whom she reveres and fears. Genevera sees her relationship to Astanna at times as "the kind of rapport ... that is more like that of a sister than a servant" ("È stata tra nui una continua conversatione non servile ma sororia," 1.9), and at other times Genevera speaks to Astanna in less flattering terms: "Off with you, you hopeless thing! Summoning you mules is like harnessing an ass. What brain, what intellect can reason with you? Nothing of worth can be found in a servile heart. It is useless to trust your feral and perfidious lot with any secrets" ("Vapulate, ve desperate, come mule preghate, siete asine imbarate. Qual cervello, qual ingegno se puoteria col vostro conformare? Nel cuore di persona serville cosa alcuna integra se ritrova. A questa ferrina e perfida stirpe cosa secreta non se li può commettere," 2.11). Astanna's actions, such as when she dumps a vat of lye on Peregrino (1.13), nearly precipitate the tragic end to the love story, but she also ensures that Peregrino is the first pilgrim to be admitted to Genevera's house for completion of the girl's penance (1.27) and conceals Peregrino in the wine cellar, among other actions favouring their love. Astanna has a cousin, Lena, who also plays an intercessory role in the love story (first mentioned in 1.9, then in 1.58ff). Astanna acknowledges that Genevera's household has nourished her; she also accepted the gift of a ring from Peregrino (1.9). Thus, she is seen as a traitor when she does the only thing to avoid her own violent death – she follows the command of Genevera's parents to call the male members of the household to arms in order to search for Peregrino, rather than escort him out the door of Genevera's house in 2.43. The comparison between her ingratitude and Rome's ingratitude toward Scipio Africanus (2.45) must therefore strike the reader as wildly out of proportion. Astanna accompanies Genevera to the convent in Ravenna, then dies shortly thereafter of a persistent illness (earlier in the narrative, she is repeatedly described as *valitudinaria*, ill). When Peregrino encounters her shade in the afterlife (3.13), she expresses regret for her behaviour toward the lovers and provides the information concerning the convent in Ravenna that Peregrino needs to relocate Genevera.

Lionora is Genevera's neighbour and friend. She is also young, unmarried, and attractive, named among the pre-eminent female marriage prospects in the city, and she takes part in Genevera's retinue of ladies on the fishing expedition (1.38). Lionora's maidservant Gasparina complicates the lovers' plight by obeying Anastasia's order to deliver the pilfered belt (2.27); subsequently, Gasparina confesses her regret concerning that action to Peregrino (2.43). She thus appears a more positive, if perhaps duller-witted, servant than Genevera's Astanna. Ultimately, Lionora will be remembered as the girl deflowered by Peregrino, who believes he is in bed with Genevera (1.52), while she believes she lies with her beloved, Galeotto, who never makes an appearance in the story – unless he is to be identified with one of Genevera's brothers, a not inconceivable possibility given the two households' proximity and consonant social standing. During the trial, Peregrino basely but effectively defends himself by arguing that Lionora imagined a sexual act in a dream because she secretly wanted it. Her father, Petrutio, accuses Peregrino of being a thief, not Lionora's corrupter. Petrutio insists that she is pure, still virginal, a traditional stance of the *pater familias* wishing to protect his clan from any taint of immorality. The reader learns no more about Lionora's destiny, even after Petrutio brings Peregrino to judgment before the Duke another time. In the real world at this time, her compromised reputation would presumably have given her few options besides the convent or a life of prostitution.[13]

The space Caviceo dedicates to the characters representing the parents of Peregrino and Genevera also greatly enhances the narrative. The reader never learns the origin of the hostilities between the two families, which is telling – there is simply a habit of persistent, irrational, vengeance-seeking hatred. Genevera's parents, **Anastasia** and **Angelo**, and Peregrino's, **Camilla** and **Antonio**, offer remarkable insight into the nature of intergenerational dynamics at the time. Genevera's mother, *pudicissima* Anastasia, is the most visible because of her role in rewriting the significance of the pilfered belt in the second book, which represented the love bond between the young lovers. Anastasia is sickly, and the repeated threat of her death propels the plot at crucial points. She fears her husband because he rules as absolute head of the household, possessing a notorious temper. She also ultimately recognizes, however, that a wedding between Genevera and Peregrino could reconcile the longstanding feud. She is thus conflicted, and we learn she has distant family ties to Camilla (revealed near the end of 1.18). Indeed, the women seem less interested in ancient honour hostilities than in finding ways to maintain relative domestic peace in the present. *Honestissimo* Angelo is hot-blooded, violent, and, like Petrutio, eminently concerned with his role as the *pater familias*. More than from any other household head, we perceive the complexities of the role from Angelo, who seems ever to be dealing with wine inspectors or delivery boys with provisions or hay for the stables, supervising the continual traffic of pilgrims and servants, marshalling assistance for an ailing wife and a son stabbed to death by a love rival, negotiating the terms of a prospective marriage for his daughter, or writing letters to the Abbess in Ravenna.

Camilla is Peregrino's mother and a widow. Although Peregrino is frequently identified as "Peregrino, son of Antonio," we do not learn much concerning his late father. Camilla makes dreadfully clear the vulnerability of her position (in 3.77). She runs the household while Peregrino spends much of his time adventuring. She possesses wealth from her dowry and threatens to leave Peregrino to return to live with her own brothers, should Peregrino try to force her to submit to his choice of bride from a hostile family. She is equally quick to accept a worthy match for her son and civic peace, and shows remarkable generosity in her gift to her daughter-in-law.

Caviceo tends to represent disparagingly those characters associated with his real-life spheres of influence: religious vocations and jurisprudence. The **Abbess** of the convent of Sant'Andrea in Ravenna is Genevera's aunt, too pious and people-pleasing for Violante's taste, who laments her "damnable foolishness" ("dannosa sciocheza," 3.58) and in 3.62 describes the Abbess even less charitably. **Friar Dominic**, the priest whom Acate distracts to permit Peregrino his first opportunity to speak with Genevera while she is in the confessional, represents a stock type – "sophistical, verbose, and curious about everybody's business – both the living and the dead" ("sophista, verboso e curioso di voler intendere che faceano vivi e morti," 1.23). **Sister Ruffina**, the nun in the convent of Sant'Andrea in Ravenna, is a charitable, credulous simpleton (3.33). Moreover, Anastasia's arguments to her daughter to abandon any thought of taking vows in 2.23 underscore many of the worst assumptions concerning conventual life. In fact, the *Peregrino* repeatedly appeared on the Church Inquisition's *Index of Prohibited Books* (in Spain, 1559–83; in Portugal, 1581; and in Rome, 1590–6) – not so much for the work's licentiousness, as some might assume, but rather for its anticlericalism, sacrilegious contaminations, cavalier treatment of the cult of relics, and representation of the magical arts as more effective than prayers to God.[14] Plenty of examples from the *Peregrino* leap to mind, from Peregrino's consultation of fortune tellers (3.1) and **Anselmo**'s capacity to access a classical Other World a few chapters later, to Peregrino's violation of the icon of St. Catherine and the faux relics he enumerates for Sister Ruffina (3.34).

Caviceo casts aspersions a bit more subtly on those in the law professions. The **Duke of Ferrara** is seen almost exclusively as the intimidating legal judge, praised as thorough, thoughtful, and just, though he is far more indulgent toward reckless young men than toward women in relatively powerless positions. Although the Duke is accorded due respect, his authority is effectively undermined in 1.18 when the clamouring of the populace overturns the death sentence he had conferred on Briseida, for instance. The lawyers, as well as Peregrino, who speaks in his own defence at his three trials, do not seem to uphold any search for truth as their primary endeavour. Their emphasis, instead, falls on the capacity of rhetoric to move the affections of the judge and others in attendance, and to leverage legal technicalities, such as whether Peregrino's actions, recounted in 1.18, took place during the day or at night, or whether there are precedents in classical texts for women making accusations based on their dreams (1.54).

Caviceo's attitude toward other contemporary cultures (particularly in Africa and the Middle East) appears at least superficially negative. Peregrino stereotypes Muslims as a "tumultuous, indiscreet, lazy lot" ("la tumultuante indiscreta poltronesca turba de arabici," 2.1). With Acate, he experiences under a Muslim master that early modern Mediterranean form of slavery marked by temporariness, reciprocity, and the possibility for recurrence in the life of an individual.[15] Nonetheless, Caviceo depicts diplomatic relations between Italian states and Muslim nations, and in various episodes of Books 2 and 3, Peregrino notes the charity he received abroad from non-Christians. Caviceo also places Mehmed I in the same realm of the afterlife with historical Christian leaders in 3.12. The *Peregrino* is a work deserving re-examination by specialists of interconfessional Mediterranean interactions.

A plethora of historical people figure as minor characters within the fictitious narrative, whom I identify in the endnotes of the translation: **Bembo, Lazzarini, Mantica, Elisabetta Malatesta, Galeazzo** and **Gian Galeazzo Sforza, Federico da Montefeltro, Isabella d'Este Gonzaga, Antonio Leuto, Giovanni Maria Riminaldo, Felino Sandeo,** and **Matteo Bosso,** among many others. The author likely wanted to lend a degree of recognizable verisimilitude to his characterization while paying compliments to people who helped him in the past (or to powerful individuals who might be able to help him in the future). By the closing chapter of the work, the two fictional protagonists, Peregrino and Genevera, now deceased, arrive at the Elysian Fields and meet a number of notable historical figures there, including the murdered **Ercole Strozzi** and **Filippo Beroaldo the Elder** (d. 1505), the renowned classicist and professor of rhetoric and poetry in Bologna,[16] as well as **Giovanni Pico della Mirandola** and **Marsilio Ficino.** Through the juxtaposition of real and imaginary characters, Caviceo fashions other juxtapositions, particularly between the relatively obscure and significantly non-Florentine figures (like Strozzi and Beroaldo) and the major voices associated with the Florentine *Accademia* (Pico and Ficino). By figuring these four writers on the same narrative plane with the spirit of Boccaccio and his own embedded life story, Caviceo likely seeks to write himself into a literary genealogy with them. What is more, Caviceo may even emphasize the potentially more authoritative status of his work as "dead literature" by feigning its telling through a departed shade. The afterlife, according to Caviceo's description of the Elysian Fields in the proem and in the final chapter of the *Peregrino*, is a kind of literary limbo, akin to the one described in Dante's *Inferno* 4, but with more modernized interlocutors. The souls of the literati remain in a highly mobile state of exile, never achieving the stasis of eternal rest. The geographical non-fixity of literary giants, such as Boccaccio, Pico, and Ficino, has particularly significant consequences for Caviceo's purposes. He can signal what he perceives to be a new direction of literary development outside of Florence by making some of its most notable literary representatives wander through the Elysian Fields or praise Ferrarese pre-eminence.

Some personifications also almost come close enough to being characters in their own right in the narrative, including **Death**, **Love**, and **Fortune**. Death is evoked in ways that effectively take away its sting – not because it heralds an eternal blessedness, but because it seems hardly to differ from life. Peregrino describes the Elysian Fields in 3.7 as a place of reunions where people don animal costumes, a scene uncannily repeated among the living in the description of his third wedding ceremony's social festivities and attire (3.81). In the proem, both the spirit of Boccaccio and Peregrino-the-narrator tell their stories from beyond the grave and both also make a point of highlighting this fact. Boccaccio's ghost emphatically contrasts verbal tenses: "Living I *possessed* the body of Boccaccio … *Now I am* made a citizen" ("Vivendo *informai* il corpo di Zanbochacio da Certaldo. *Hora son facta* cittadina," proem; my emphasis), and Peregrino's first words are a cry whose tone hints at both the melodramatic and the slapstick: "Mercy, by God, that dead or alive I'm still dead!" ("Mercè per dio, che morto e vivo sempre sto morto," proem).

Love is not quite Dante's Lord *Amor* in the *Vita nuova* dictating poems and commanding the lover, but nevertheless is sometimes Peregrino's master, sometimes a childlike, mischievous Cupid. Fortune, whose wheel raises the lowly and casts down rulers, is a "most powerful goddess" ("dea potentissima," 3.58), described as "unpredictable" ("dubiosa," 3.61), "cruel and envious" ("spietata et invidiosa," 3.90), and so forth. Moreover, these three "characters" of Love, Fortune, and Death effectively undermine the work's overt message urging readers to avoid the snares of Love, since the individual is presented as not entirely capable of exercising reason to opt out of love; furthermore, Fortune will unpredictably overturn the circumstance of any decision, and Death comes to mortals in the end in any eventuality.[17]

Genre and Gender

The single term of *romanzo* in Italian covers a great deal of semantic ground in English, from the notion of romance as a mode to what is called the genre of the novel. Women have long been associated with reading sentimental fiction, from Chrétien de Troyes's lady, who read a romance aloud to her companions, to Dante's Francesca da Rimini, who receives eternal damnation after emulating the lovers' acts she textually perused.[18] Spanish humanist Juan Luis Vives (d. 1540) would be among the male writers who would enjoin chaste sixteenth-century ladies to avoid romances and texts by Boccaccio, Ovid, Sappho, and Propertius.[19] Among the great patrons of romances and translations of romances would be Lucrezia Borgia and especially her competitive sister-in-law Isabella d'Este Gonzaga. Caviceo's Genevera pushes the boundary of propriety, especially, but not exclusively, in her reading habits.

More generally, Caviceo's *Peregrino* insists on a nuanced vision of female perspective and agency. The work is told from a male author's point of view and refracted through a male narrator's point of view. The character perspectives that readers hear most authoritatively, particularly where the law is concerned, are also male – from Peregrino, the arguing lawyers, Petrutio, and the Duke of Ferrara, who makes the judicial pronouncements. Nevertheless, the fictions the men present during the trials do not wholly obscure the parallel account of what actually happened within the narrative, and the truth, *la verità*, is recurrently gendered female. Lionora's perspective proves the true one: she welcomed the one whom she believed to be Galeotto into her arms; now she is no longer a virgin and scorned by lover and father alike. Moreover, as improbable as Briseida's testimony seems to the Duke, her version – not Polidoro's or Nicolò's – conforms most accurately to the actual course of events. More than perhaps any Italian prose work since Boccaccio's *Elegy*, Caviceo's *Peregrino* presents a perfectly recognizable and compelling female perspective, though Caviceo cleverly does so by nesting nuanced narrative levels of women's truth within a fiction of a fiction.

While it may be tempting to assume from some of the women in Caviceo's *Peregrino*, who are literate and well educated or manage roles of political power, that they enjoyed self-determination, one must remember that this fictional work presents a mere fantasy for the vast majority of Renaissance women. While Isabella d'Este Gonzaga, Lucrezia Borgia, and Elisabetta Malatesta, for instance, are highly cultured and at times make consequential political decisions, their roles and authority ultimately depend on the men around them. Caviceo fashions Violante as an eminently capable tutor of the liberal arts and Genevera as an outstanding pupil. Even so, both female characters run risks to their very lives for the decisions they make, and Anastasia, Astanna, Gasparina, and other women quake in mortal fear of disapproving or controlling men, or indeed even armed boys, in the case of the threat from Genevera's brothers.

Moreover, readers of this book can see clearly the dilemma of the parents of a girl of this socio-economic milieu: How can they keep her chaste so she has the potential to receive a good marriage match – and as soon as possible? Otherwise, she faces the fate of the convent, which, despite Genevera's praises of Sant' Andrea, represents a far less attractive option, ultimately because it obviates the family's investment in the female child as having the potential to bolster the family's social or political ties through marriage and progeny. Maintaining a daughter's chastity remains a constant challenge, especially if we consider that Briseida and Lionora face unanticipated intrusions in their own bedrooms. The reader retains the impression that a proliferation of ladder-toting, sword-wielding, *farseto*-clad young men prowl Ferrara for sexual adventure on any given night – not merely Peregrino, but also Polidoro, Cesare, and Genevera's stabbed brother, among others.

The sexual encounters and attempted sexual assaults in this work offer a great deal of material for further study. While this Introduction is not the place to present critical essays, I would nonetheless like to raise two directions for potential development: the uncomfortable proximity of rape in the presentation of this courtship, and the articulation of love development as an economic exchange; I shall start from the latter.

It is difficult to overlook in this romance the frequency of economic vocabulary, particularly in expressions emphasizing the *quid pro quo* between lovers. I do not mean to suggest that earlier understandings of love were not predicated on an exchange. Andreas Capellanus in his *Art of Courtly Love*, to mention only one example, distinguishes carefully between love relationships between people of different socio-economic classes, as well as what recompense corresponds to particular acts of love service. Nevertheless, there is a notable difference in the context of mercantile Renaissance Ferrara. Generosity stands out as a pre-eminent virtue to which both Caviceo-author and Peregrino-character aspire, and a varied vocabulary describes this quality (not merely *generoso*, but also *affluente/affluentia, magnifico, amplio/amplissimo/amplitudine, celsitudine, copia, demostratione, donare/donata, divitie, honestare, hospitalaria, liberale, largità, locuplectissimo, magnificere, munificare/munifico*, etc.). Genevera provides a clear articulation of the love exchange and its consequences in 1.30. She says to Peregrino:

> Constant love and the accumulation of gifts beyond what is proper spoil the man and make him believe that anything proceeding from the sincerity of his spirit obliges some constant remuneration. Therefore, it is always prudent to proceed slowly when interacting with an unmindful man. You are generous in your actions on my behalf, but I am not stingy in return. Any faithful and virtuous lover should be content with this reciprocity. However, it is a clear sign of a covetous soul with wicked intent to seek to grow one's holdings

to another's ruin. You do not consider just how out of balance we are and how predatory our age is, though we live virtuously. It is time for you to think about how scorned we will be when people start talking about us. You should be very protective indeed concerning a good that once lost can never be reacquired.

Il continuo amar e lo accumulato donare più di quel che convenga fa l'huomo insolente e presta materia di persuaderse che tutto quel che prociede da sincerità de animo sia per eterna obligatione. Però è meglio consulto andare retenuta, quando se ha a fare cum huomo scognoscente; e se del buon volere me sei liberale, de quel medemo non te sono parca; e de questa vicissitudine contentare se doveria ogni fidelle e virtuoso amante. Ma l'è signo manifesto de [il]liberal animo e mal disposito, di volere ampliare le cose sue cum l'altrui ruina. Puocho consideri quanto siamo balestrate, e quanto è periculosa questa nostra aetà sempre insidiata, anchora che honestamente viviamo. Hor pensa, quando fussemo denigrate, quello che si diria. Se vuol essere ben cauta a la conservatione de quella cosa che, una fiata è perduta, mai più rehavere non se può.

In expressing his hopes for Genevera's affection, Peregrino also resorts to terms of exchange: "Death or mercy I beg of you, yet still you are slow in offering the aid you owe" ("Morte o mercede te adimando; e pur lenta sei al debito socorso," 1.63), and Genevera will echo in "What is deferred is not denied, however, if the will of the free giver saves it to disburse at a more appropriate time" ("quel che se differise non se remove, perhò, da la voluntà del libero donatore, qual a più commodità di tempo lo reserba," 2.15). Genevera will also use the same economic reasoning when she urges Peregrino to marry Lionora: "[Lionora] has been generous in offering you her honour and life, so you cannot be stingy in offering her your hand" ("Et se liberale t'è stata a donarte l'honore e la vita, non gli essere scarso de attendergli la fede," 1.64). Both protagonists appear to understand moral virtue in terms of measurement, though their standard does not appear to be the same, thus provoking varying accusations of generosity or stinginess.

Peregrino's deathbed speech in 3.99 helps to clarify what may be intended by this moral measurement standard and the one he prefers:

In all your actions may you be imitators of the geometers more than the arithmeticians. Geometers consider the merits of each person and are always thoughtful of an equivalent proportion of the merits of the individual, thus rendering to each one, according to what is due. Arithmeticians consider how much to give, according to what is given, without respect for the present or the past, because they are focused only on number, weight, and measure. Their nature is evil, awful, ungrateful, adulterous, escapist, and detestable.

Et in ogni vostra actione siati imitatori più presto de geometri che de arismetrici. Li primi son consideratori de li meriti de ciascuno, et sempre cogitabondi de una equa proportione che de' meriti a meriti, et rendeno a ciascuno, per le loro fatiche è debito. Li secundi considerano tanto de donare, quanto li viene donato, senza altro rispecto né presente né preterito, per essere il loro cogitato de numero, pondo et misura: la costoro natura è mala pessime ingrata adultera, fugienda et detestanda.

His message – presented in starker ways in other works, such as Shakespeare's *Measure for Measure* – seems to rest on a notion that to err is human and we should have compassion for those trapped in the snares of love/lust.

One term I have found especially beguiling is *humanissimo*, which in many instances in the work is an antonym of "stingy," therefore meaning "very generous." Typically, it implies, as its etymology suggests, a human or humane way of behaving. However, when Peregrino applies the same adjective to Genevera, the term takes on somewhat different connotations, implying a judgment on how welcoming she is or how freely she is behaving in their courtship progression – and its contrary thus becomes something more akin to "exceedingly prudish." From this vantage, Genevera is accused of ingratitude by Violante (in 1.7) even before Peregrino in his impatience subsequently weighs in. In the seventh chapter, Genevera learns that a man, a complete stranger and an enemy to her family, has taken a fancy to her. She finds herself immediately thrust into the role of debtor because she now owes him some response. Not to replicate, according to Violante, would make Genevera an ingrate:

Now consider the state your wretched admirer finds himself in out of love for you. You've made yourself haughty by ruining him … You can free him from such great suffering only by letting him see you … When Peregrino learns you're shunning him, he might be overcome by some melancholic humour and announce, even against his better judgment, the reason for his suffering. Genevera, take heed you do not incur divine judgment, which harshly punishes ingrates …

Ora considera ove il misero per te amare è conducto. Tu sei facta altiera de la sua ruina … Sol cum la tua vista, di tanto affanno il puoi librerae … vedendose il tapino da la tua bona gratia alienato, ch'el se occupasse de qualche humore melinconico, che contra a sua voglia annuntiare li facesse la causa del tanto martyrio. Guarda, Genevera, che la divina iustitia, quale acramente suol punire l'ingrati, non descenda sopra di te ...

Because she is noble and beautiful, those qualities entail the specific virtues of clemency and compassion, according to Violante, and she asks her, "If it's true that the soul's qualities correspond to the body's, how is it that you've adopted this ingratitude ...?" ("Ma se vero è che l'anima segua la complexione del corpo, come puoi tu usare questa ingratitudine ...?"). Peregrino will drive home the point (1.19) when he floats the foolhardy plan to Astanna to sneak in the back door of Genevera's home: "Given her generous nature, I suppose she won't be stingy about freely welcoming me then" ("Genevera, qual essendo humanissima mi persuado non me seria avara d'una libera e grata audientia"). Genevera subsequently acknowledges that she would prefer "to be considered ignorant rather than ungrateful" ("patirò essere reputata ignorante cha ingrata," 1.24).

Precisely the threat of being considered an ingrate compels another woman, Briseida, to come forward during the trial over Cesare's death in 1.18: "Since I believe there's no greater plague among humanity than ingratitude, I couldn't contain myself. Almost against my will and unable to quiet my conscience, I came all the way here to testify to the truth" ("Non me parendo ne le cose humane la più pestifera nota, quanto è la ingratitudine, quasi contra mia voglia, spenta da la mia interna consciencia, per rendere testimonio a la verità, non me son potuta contenere de venire qua oltra"). Moreover, the ladies' debate during the fishing excursion centres on whether the successful lovers owe anything to the pretender who conceded defeat, and Genevera's summary judgment hinges on what the loser suffered: "The youth really should have learned from this faultless example and followed it. Then if he suffered because of it, he would be worthy of our commiseration" ("Questa infalibile doctrina dovea imparare e sequitare il giovene; e puoi se violentato fusse stato, di commiseratione era degno," 1.43).

When love's language is not set in explicitly economic-moral terms, it nevertheless can tend to reflect a competitive undercurrent. What we might think of as a disposition to be open to falling in love, these characters understand as the entrance into Love's arena in which they will be tested. As we might expect, the young man prevails by extracting sexual favours or moving the erotic relationship along faster, while the young woman's moral mettle is proven by how well she preserves her chastity. However, even more interesting engagements are the trials of cleverness between young lovers. Elisabetta of Ravenna offers one example in her *facezia* in 3.22. The intelligent girl who inspires a boy to become a philosopher by deferring his sexual reward until he learns one more thing is characterized as "the sort who believed that to fail was a shame, so to give in to him would be as good as death" ("La donna, a cui il fallire era vergogna, il compiacere la morte"). When she asked him about the nightingale's mating habits, moreover, he "wanted to die, even more so because a mere girl seemed to surpass him in his vaunted studies in natural science" ("se volse exanimare, e tanto più ché pura fanciulla ne le cose naturale, dove faceva manifesta professione, lo superasse"). Elisabetta applies the moral of this nested narrative to Peregrino, a lesson he at least partially takes to heart a few chapters later during a discussion with Genevera (3.50):

> P: "We shall take up this debate again in a few days."
> G: "You will still lose it."
> P: "Whoever learns never loses."

> P: "Fra pochi giorni disputando il vederemo."
> G: "Sempre perderai."
> P: "Chi bene impara mai non perde."

Moreover, it appears that certain rejoinders based on the economic exchange rationale wield such power or cut so keenly that they have the effect of shutting down dialogue altogether, including Genevera's retort when she refuses to permit Peregrino to dry her tears following her "confession": "It is not the custom of the business dealer to offer valuable merchandise for little profit" ("Non è costume di negotioso mercadante per piccol lucro exporre la faticata merce," 1.24), or Anastasia's insult to Genevera as she pilfers the belt that serves as a symbol of love between Genevera and Peregrino: "The merchandise gives a clear indication of the merchants" ("Gli segni manifestano li mercadanti," 2.18). In sum, it seems the erotic tension heightens through continued flirtatious one-upmanship, but perceived disparities in expectations and rewards can tempt intemperate or impatient men to resort to force, an issue to which I now turn.

The term "rape" arises in the context of the first trial before the Duke (1.18) when Briseida denounces Cesare for attempted rape and asserts that she killed him out of self-defence. In a subsequent episode, a woman of Lionora's household decries Peregrino as a "nefarious rapist" (in 1.52, "nephario stupratore"), though rape will not be the official charge at the next trial. In another episode, Peregrino wields his unsheathed knife over a sleeping Genevera (2.37). It is a shocking scene, given the lack of narrative foreshadowing that he might suddenly stab her to death[20] – on the contrary, Peregrino has offered countless declarations of love toward Genevera. Nonetheless, Peregrino shows just how embittered he feels.[21] He has completed the requested pilgrimage to Mount Sinai to beg the saint's forgiveness for violating the womb of the virgin martyr's icon. He has endured years of slavery and uncertain suffering in foreign lands. The jealousy that Genevera cannot clearly communicate to him over their belt, which she believes has become an engagement gift from Peregrino to Lionora, prompts rage in Peregrino, a rage that derives from the perception of an unfair lack of compensation for the feats he has undertaken on her behalf. He thus seeks a way to re-establish the balance of power in the relationship. Nearly stabbing her thus becomes a symbolic threat of rape by means of his "flashing knife" ("fulgente coltello").

Rape and issues surrounding the notion of consent will remain awkwardly implied precisely at the consummation of Peregrino and Genevera's first marriage (3.52–3). After the wedding feast, Genevera is out of sorts and arranges herself on her nuptial bed as if it were the Trojan princess Polyxena's funerary pyre ("non altramente se cercava de collocare la mia signora nel pudico lecto, che facesse la vergine priameia quando al sepulchro achileo imolata fu"). Peregrino takes advantage of her unconsciousness, when sleep "tricks" Genevera. The ensuing wording in 3.53 is at once sexual and martial. Genevera notes: "No one is so vigilant who can guard against a domestic traitor" ("Da traditore domesticho non è così oculato che guardare se possa"), and Peregrino's act of deflowering is described as "The enemy rushed in in a fury and rummaged around all bloodied, as if wanting to avenge a patricide" ("Et l'hoste intrato tutto furente e sanguinolente vagava, come se de patricidio vendicare se volesse"). Barely beneath the veil of romance lurks the horrific consequence of the marriage between hostile families – the virgin girl is sacrificed to absorb sexually the vengeance of a patricide previously committed by her male relatives; in this case, presumably on Antonio, Peregrino's late father, or some other forebear in the annals of not quite forgotten or forgiven Ferrarese familial vendettas. Peregrino represents the besieging force taking her fortress by guile, a point that will offend Violante when she learns the details in 3.62 of how he not only "broke down the door" but broke Genevera's walls, as well ("Rupe la porta et il muro"). Genevera defends Peregrino's actions, but Violante confronts Peregrino in 3.67: "That captain who took the castle through stealth was vile" ("Vile fu quello capitaneo, che a tradimento la rocha ne tolse"). Genevera, whose "raw garden [was reduced] to the cultivation of better fruits [by Peregrino's steely plough]" ("cum lo arratro de fino aciale incommenciai ad excollere il rudo giardino, per redurlo a la cultura de megliori fructi," 3.53), must defend him again, this time with pseudo-legal arguments implying that his act could not be considered rape, since she anticipated the assault. Under the guise of *pudico* or *honesto amor*, this romance actually offers a deeply disturbing portrayal of the culmination of a courtship.

Certainly, Peregrino commits a violation of a different kind during his invasion of the life-sized, three-dimensional, hollow icon of St. Catherine

of Alexandria in the hopes of ending Genevera's siege of amorous resistance.[22] Caviceo's selection of this particular saint could not have been a
coincidence, since St. Catherine of Alexandria was the Christian model
of female learning and the patron saint of women scholars. According to
her hagiography, when the noble Christian virgin refused to adore the
pagan deities, fifty of the greatest (male) philosophers were summoned
to persuade the girl, but she succeeded instead in converting all of them
to Catholicism. Her cult was peaking just as Caviceo was penning his
romance. Bonino Mombrizio (d. 1482) wrote a legend of St. Catherine
for the Sforza family, dedicating it to Bianca Maria Visconti, the wife of
Francesco Sforza. Jacopo Filippo Foresti included St. Catherine in his
1497 catalogue of famous women, dedicated to Beatrice of Aragon and
published in Ferrara, as "an all-inclusive model of learning, able to master the liberal arts and the Holy Scriptures as well as many languages."[23]
Among the many dramatic confraternity productions of Catherine's life
performed during the fifteenth century, at least one is available in English in *La festa et storia di Sancta Caterina: A Medieval Italian Religious
Drama*. Venetian Pietro Aretino, known for a much different vein of literary production, would also write a work of hagiography titled *Santa
Caterina Vergine* around 1540. Visual arts scholar Marta Ajmar cited various scenes from the life of St. Catherine painted by Masolino between
1428 and 1431 (257), and Correggio's subsequent depiction of *St. Catherine Reading* (1527–8) and Giovanni Sogliani's painting (in the Pinaco-
teca di Brera in Milan), featuring "Catherine holding a book with the
inscription 'HAEC EST VIRGO SAPIENS'" (254). However, the most famous
rendering of St. Catherine disputing the philosophers is by Pinturicchio
in the Borgia Apartments of the Vatican, painted between 1492 and 1494
(257), and Lucrezia Borgia herself is most often identified as the model
for this St. Catherine.[24]

While Caviceo's narrator declared in the proem that this romance was
not intended be the *exterminio de Troia*, Peregrino opts to re-evoke precisely the same stratagem in the St. Catherine episode. Although Peregrino genuinely seems to want to pursue the story of a chaste love with
Genevera, he nevertheless succeeds in communicating to her a diametri-
cally contrary allegorical message. In constructing a statue in which he
violates the inner recesses of the virgin saint of Alexandria, he suggests
to Genevera that his intentions may be far from honest and chaste. This
impression is only reinforced by Peregrino's next escapade: to try to enter
Genevera's house by another means, that is, through the sewer system,
when he enters her neighbour's house by mistake. These are just some
examples of the possible avenues for critical interpretation that this novel
offers.

Caviceo's Life and Works

The author's life was almost as adventurous as that of his fictional protagonist, though not all of the details have passed down to us. Lorenza Simona's 1974 biography of Caviceo (*Giacomo Caviceo: Uomo di chiesa, d'armi e di lettere*) remains indispensable for understanding Caviceo's life and works, since it presents the fruits of her extensive archival research. She relied in turn on the biographical sketch by Giorgio Anselmi, a contemporary of Caviceo, also from Parma. Anselmi's apologetic *Vita de Iacobo Cauicaeo* was frequently printed along with the text of the *Peregrino*, beginning with the 1513 edition.[25]

Caviceo's ancestors enjoyed wealth and status in Parma, until Caviceo's grandfather, also named Jacopo, was exiled around the turn of the fifteenth century for political reasons and worked as a merchant upon returning to his homeland. The author of the *Peregrino* was born in Parma in 1443 to Margherita and Antonio Cavizzi, a *magister* (teacher/tutor) at the Santissima Trinità parish, and was the eldest of three sons. He passed his childhood and adolescence in Parma, subsequently adopting the Latinized humanistic dignification of his family name.

Biographers uniformly emphasize Caviceo's quick temper, which must already have been ingrained by the time he left Parma to pursue studies in letters and law at the university in Bologna. He had to drop out before finishing the regular course of study toward his degree in order to avoid official expulsion for a series of fights and nighttime brawls. Back in Parma, he utilized the library in the Franciscan monastery of Santa Maria Annunziata, which may account for the favouritism Caviceo accords to "temples" dedicated to "the *Serafico*" in his *Peregrino* and his close associations with the Friars Minor throughout his life. Caviceo pivoted to an ecclesiastical career path in the early or mid-1460s. He went to Rome for a year of study and returned an ordained priest praised for excellence in preaching. Evidence of a sincere spiritual vocation, however, is not readily apparent. Simona's supreme tact comes to the fore with her understated description of a long period in Caviceo's life as "this parenthesis that is not so very flattering."[26] Caviceo established a pattern of resisting discipline and authority. He also seduced a nun (a "vergine Vestale," in Anselmi's words) under his protection, and gravely wounded a man in an altercation, likely precipitated by his uncontrollable temper. Arrested, Caviceo faced charges, but opted for voluntary exile, or going on the lam, travelling to Verona, then to Venice, and as far as Byzantium.[27] Caviceo's three-year odyssey ended around 1469. He continued to pursue his studies under Ilario Anselmi, the canon and archpriest of the Duomo of Parma.[28]

Caviceo was again detained following a dispute with Bishop Giacomo Antonio Della Torre. This time, Caviceo's friends assaulted the bishop in the process of "liberating" Caviceo from custody. Caviceo begged mercy of Pope Paul II (Pietro Barbo), claiming self-defence. However, according to Anselmi, the bishop plotted with the Duke of Milan, Galeazzo Maria Sforza, whose men seized Caviceo and locked him in a more secure prison in Alexandria. Cicco Simonetta, the Calabrian statesman serving in the Milanese ducal chancellery, may have been the unnamed influential friend who successfully intervened for Caviceo's release in the first months of 1471.

Caviceo's patron Pier Maria Rossi II Count of San Secondo sent him to Venice as a diplomat representing the Rossi family and secured for him lucrative benefices, including that of the Cathedral of Parma.[29] In Venice, Caviceo made influential friends, including Doge Marco Barbarigo. The Doge's brother, Agostino Barbarigo, succeeded him upon his death in 1486; relations soured, and Caviceo left Venice in 1489. Between 1489 and 1491, Caviceo composed his first literary works in Latin: some brief works of praise for his Rossi patrons, another inspired by a noblewoman of the Lupi family, titled *Lupa* (She-Wolf, thereby punning on her name), and his *De exilio Cupidinis* (On the Banishment of Love).

In 1491 Doge Agostino Barbarigo ordered Caviceo expelled from all Venetian territories. The charge is left unspecified, but the expulsion is due to his "awful nature and evil ways ... Jacopo Caviceo should be made to remain elsewhere, since his return would be like that of a deadly plague."[30] Caviceo went to Pordenone, a city then under Austrian rule, joining friends, including Lazzarino Lazzarini and Princivalle Mantica, both of whom will figure as characters in his *Peregrino*. The Holy Roman Emperor Frederick III conferred on Caviceo the title of Doctor of Law (*doctor utriusque iuris*), and Lazzarino helped Caviceo to secure his position as Vicar General of the Diocese of Rimini, which Caviceo held from 1492 until 1494. It was a position of considerable authority and responsibility; the vicar general is second only to the bishop or archbishop and typically oversees judicial matters and governance for the diocese.

Caviceo served as Vicar General of the Diocese of Ravenna under Archbishop Filasio Roverella from 1494 to 1500. It was during these six years that he wrote the greater part of his *Peregrino*, while he resided in the creative literary cultural hub of Ferrara. Caviceo subsequently became the Vicar General of Florence under Archbishop Rinaldo Orsini (d. 1509), then, by the end of 1510, had been transferred to Siena, and served between Siena and Montecchio until his death on 3 June 1511. He was laid to rest in the Cathedral of Parma.

Lacking a portrait of the author, we can form only a tenuous idea of Caviceo's physical appearance from Anselmi's description of him. He was tall, almost gaunt, and possessed a wiry strength. In his prime, Caviceo sported a head of thick curly hair, although he went bald in his later years. His brows, bristling and *torvi*, that is, surly or threatening, overshadowed relatively small beady eyes. However, Caviceo's rosy cheeks on a face quick to amusement balanced the effect, according to Anselmi, imparting to Caviceo an air of majesty and decorum.

Caviceo was fastidious in his grooming habits and dressed splendidly and conspicuously. He preferred to frequent men of culture and refinement, disdaining the "dull-witted, plebian rabble" ("indocile e roza multitudine," *Vita*, cccxlii).[31] Anselmi stressed Caviceo's generosity in all of his actions, a trait that will be noted and praised in a variety of characters in the *Peregrino*, culminating in Peregrino's own desire to be remembered as generous when he speaks from his deathbed: "Up until now, I have made every effort to render myself such in this world that I am not reputed to be useless, lazy, or anything other than a generous man" ("Io, in fino ad hora, ho facto ogni conato per renderme tale al mondo, che l'essergli stato da altro non sia deside, ocioso né mancho de quello, che ad huomo generoso conviene, reputato," 3.99). In the end, Anselmi urged his readers to remember the good in Caviceo, a comment that, in itself, indicates that doing so would not have been the first inclination for at least some of his readers.

Caviceo's *Peregrino* distinguishes itself among the other works he authored for its significant length and its composition in the Italian vernacular. The work runs to 364 pages in Luigi Vignali's unabridged 1993 Italian critical edition. Given the number of sixteenth-century Italian editions printed in Parma, Milan, Vercelli, and Venice, it clearly sold well and to a broad readership.[32] The French translation appeared in at least nine editions, published in Lyon and Paris. It was produced by François Dassy (or D'Assy), who served as secretary to Henri d'Albret, King of Navarre, and Louise de Valentinois, the daughter of Cesare Borgia. This bloodline connection might explain why Dassy chose to translate and include the original proem and dedication to Lucrezia Borgia, at least until Jean Martin began to annotate and edit the French version of the work, beginning with the 1528 Parisian edition. The Spanish version, translated by Hernando Díaz under the title *Libro de los honestos amores de Peregrino y Ginebra*, first appeared in 1516 in Seville and was reprinted at least four more times.[33] Even though the broad lines of Caviceo's plot and many of his chapters are translated word-for-word in the Spanish version, Hernando Díaz neglected to acknowledge Caviceo as the original author.[34] Moreover, Díaz did not include the dedication to Lucrezia Borgia, changed geographical references, rewrote the epitaphs of the two protagonists in eight-line *octavillas*, and left out entire Italo-centric chapters and the final section of the last chapter that provided the otherworldly *cornice*, among other alterations. He presented the Spanish version as a single book containing 208 chapters, instead of three books containing a total of 219 chapters. For these reasons, some scholars have termed Díaz's work an adaptation rather than a translation of Caviceo's *Peregrino*, making the identification of the Spanish republications even more challenging.

Caviceo's minor works, composed before the *Peregrino*, are all written in Latin and are relatively brief.[35] The only work scholars can definitively attribute to Caviceo after the *Peregrino* is a confessional handbook: *Confessionale utilissimum* (Parma, 1509).[36] It was dedicated to Cardinal Ippolito d'Este, brother-in-law of Lucrezia Borgia, and it treats the sacrament of confession as an exemplary dialogue. Anselmi cites two more works he attributes to Caviceo, which Simona was unable to confirm: some "Dialogues on the Wretchedness of Members of the Curia"[37] and a commentary on Ovid's *Heroides*. In this regard, Caviceo's curriculum does not differ substantially from those of contemporary authors who pen a breakthrough work in the vernacular among other comparatively neglected Latin writings.

Literary Antecedents of the *Peregrino*

Summarizing the literature that Caviceo draws upon to compose his *Peregrino* is no small task, since the romance integrates the immense wealth of the literary cultural inheritance for a turn-of-the-sixteenth-century vernacular readership.[38] What some critics have disparaged as an unevenness in the tone of Caviceo's romance, I prefer to see as the author's intentional choice to embellish his fictional world with an astounding array of allusions to previous literary works. Caviceo pieces together his metaliterary novel with the aesthetic craft of patchwork. On one level, he might seem to overwhelm his audience with the book's amassing of verbal juxtapositions and allusions. On another, though, the work gives an impression of cohesiveness in its overarching design, bringing together disparate sources with such complementarity and cleverness as to delight the mind's eye of the discerning reader. What follows is an overview of some of Caviceo's most important points of reference.

From the proem of the *Peregrino*, Caviceo acknowledges and pays homage to his foremost authorial model: Giovanni Boccaccio (d. 1375).[39]

One of the Three Crowns of Italian Literature, the writer recognized for prose appears here, figured as a blessed spirit honoured by other souls in the Elysian Fields in the work's narrative frame. Caviceo employs the rhetorical figure of *eidolopoeia*, a subtype of personification in which the ghost of an esteemed historical figure lends authority to a controversial, taboo, or aesthetically arbitrary position by ventriloquizing the author's own opinion. As I previously argued in *Speaking Spirits: Ventriloquizing the Dead in Renaissance Italy*, Caviceo represents Boccaccio's ghost in the *Peregrino*'s proem as shifting his association to Ferrara from his birth city of Certaldo and from his adopted city of residence in Florence – not even mentioned by name. In doing so, Caviceo asserts the pre-eminence of Ferrarese culture and, by extension, the non-standard (non-Florentine), courtly vernacular language in which he writes. Caviceo also leverages Boccaccio's authority as the compiler of lives of famous women in the *De mulieribus claris* to praise his own female dedicatee.

Many previous scholars cite Boccaccio's *Filocolo* as the reason for Caviceo's gallant figuration of Boccaccio's spirit in the proem. Without a doubt, Boccaccio's elaborate retelling of the French tale of love between Floire and Blancheflor in the face of parental objections and the protagonists' peregrinations around the Mediterranean have some correspondences in the *Peregrino*. Both long prose romances also offer embedded stories, set speeches, and love *quistioni*, articulating the nature and dilemmas of love. Scholars have been less quick to see, however, just how divergent their narrative matrices are; the *Peregrino*'s love story is far from that of the two youths born on the same day and raised together by the King and Queen of Spain, Florio the heir to the throne and Biancofiore the adopted girl initially believed to be of low birth. Comments such as the ones suggesting that the *Peregrino* is a "heavy and lascivious imitation" of the *Filocolo*, or that it is only a "very elaborated version of the story of *Flores y Blancaflor*," are all too frequently repeated.[40] Anyone who takes up the *Peregrino* anticipating another version of the *Filocolo* may be left utterly bewildered.

Caviceo's frame for the *Peregrino* is, in itself, an homage to the great composer of the complicated *cornice*, especially as it is presented in Boccaccio's masterpiece, the *Decameron*. This mid-fourteenth-century work of one hundred *novelle*, many of which are tales of love and lust, trickery, or verbal cleverness, contains a pragmatic, down-to-earth treatment of sexuality, death, and Catholic religiosity.[41] The *novelle* are packaged within a frame in which ten Florentine youths tell tales during the bubonic plague of 1348 for diversion and entertainment over the course of ten days. The *Decameron*'s subtitle, *Prince Galehaut*, highlighted the status of the literary work as an erotic go-between, named for the one who set the meetings between Queen Guinevere and Sir Lancelot in the Arthurian cycle, and immortalized by Dante's character Francesca da Rimini in *Inferno* 5, to whom I shall return. Boccaccio's famous appeal to women readers in his *Decameron* is thus echoed by Caviceo, lending further emphasis to Letizia Panizza's assertion in the epigraph that Caviceo's *Peregrino* "may have been the first novel specially written for women." Caviceo gives a signifying nod to the ladies in the remark by Boccaccio's spirit, acknowledging that in Ferrara he now contemplates "an extraordinary beauty" ("una non più vista belleza"), and his appearance effectively authorizes Caviceo's project of writing another vernacular prose work to entertain an audience, which includes female readers.

In the author's foreword of the *Decameron*, Boccaccio admitted he offered his tome to women in love:

> It is women who timorously and bashfully conceal Love's flame within their tender breasts; and those who have had experience of it know well enough how much harder it is to control the suppressed than the open flame. Moreover, circumscribed as women are ... they spend most of their time within the narrow confines of their bedchambers ... And if Love's craving leaves their thoughts tinged with sadness, they are condemned to remain gloomy unless such thoughts are driven out by some fresh distraction ... If a man is down in the dumps ... he can go out and about at will, he can hear and see all sorts of things, he can go hawking and hunting, he can fish or ride, gamble or pursue his business interests. The effect of such activities will be to improve his spirits ...[42]

Because Boccaccio received compassion from others when he suffered the dissolution of a love affair, he states that he wishes to offer consolation to others, and he singles out ladies, who may not have access to the worldly distractions available to men.

Caviceo's envoi to his book will also be familiar from Boccaccio's works: "Book of mine, if ever you should be scorned or rejected, you could say: 'Reader, not the destruction of Troy, the fortunes of Rome, or the wanderings of Ulysses do I seek to tell, but rather a story of chaste love'" ("Libro mio, se aspernato o reiecto fusti, dire poterai: 'Lectore, non l'exterminio de Troia, non le fortune di Roma, non li errori de Ulyxe, ma de uno pudico amore la historia porto e narro'"). The words echo with slight variations versions of the romance rejection of *epos* in Boccaccio's *Filocolo* (1.2) as well as the Prologue of *The Elegy of Lady Fiammetta*. In these first words, Caviceo-author speaks directly to his book and dictates how the book may defend itself as it circulates in public, and he does so by adopting Boccaccio's formulation. It continues: "And if you are asked about the writer, you can say: 'Jacopo Caviceo of Parma, faithful reciter, lives and sends his regards. He wrote what he understood'" ("Et se del scriptore parole intende, respondere poterai: 'Iacomo Cavicaeo da Parma, fidele recitatore, vive et vale. Et, come intese, scripse'"). The *Peregrino*'s author thus emphasizes both his role as *recitatore*, that is, reciter or actor, and his role as scribe, one who writes simply what he hears and understands. In donning the masks of his distinctive roles, he also implies his unreliability as a narrator.

Lady Fiammetta in Boccaccio's *Elegy* declares that she tells her story to "noble ladies, and if possible, to awaken pity in you, in whose hearts love perhaps dwells more happily than in mine."[43] In this much briefer work of prose, Fiammetta mourns the dissolution of her love affair. It is a deep and nuanced, first-person, psychological profile of a female character by a male author. In it, we see the expressions of hindsight (i.e., "Oh, how much happier than any other woman I could call myself, had such love lasted in me forever!"), the lamentations of "Fortune's hidden snares" (4), the reference to dream visions and the interpretations of their "foolishness" (6), the couching of Christian terms in classical ones ("the sacred temple," 6), and so many other elements that Caviceo will emulate in his *Peregrino*. The hypothetical conjecturing that plays out in the earlier work returns in Caviceo's more sympathetic portrayal of Genevera, as she ponders her options, such as when she debates with herself if she should answer Peregrino's letter in 1.10, or when she wonders if it is truly Peregrino who has arrived at the convent in Ravenna and spoken with Sister Ruffina in 3.36. Incidentally, Caviceo will also reverse the gender roles, when Peregrino fears, during his sojourn outside of Italy, that Genevera may already be wed, reflecting the pain that Fiammetta experiences at hearing the erroneous news that her Panfilo has married.[44] Boccaccio's *Elegy* is also widely credited with inspiring the genre of the *novela sentimental* in Spain, even before it was translated and printed in Seville in 1496, and the borrowings and implicit accusations of plagiarism in the translation of highly profitable prose romances across Europe, including Caviceo's *Peregrino*, have been the focus of others' scholarly investigations.[45]

Much has been made among critics of Boccaccio's conflicting attitude toward women – in some passages offering praise and admiration for the gentle sex, and in other passages meting out the vilest insults based solely on gender. The misogynistic elements of Boccaccio's *Corbaccio* colour certain passages of the *Peregrino*, such as Peregrino's tirades against Genevera or Acate's debate arguments with Peregrino about foregoing any love relationships with women, or Matteo Bosso's reminder: "See how base it is to commit your body and soul to the command of a woman who always lacks reason" ("Vedi de quanta viltà è de commettere il corpo e l'anima ad uno muliebre imperio, quale sempre fu de ragione privo," 3.19). At times, even Caviceo's female characters parrot this language, considered degrading to their sex, such as Violante's assertion: "There is nothing in this world as soft, squirming, mutable, fleeting, and confusing as a woman's love, which always discourses without reason" ("non è cosa al mondo tanto tenera, flexibile, mutabile, fugace e varia, quanto è il muliebre amore, quale sempre senza ragion discorre," 1.8), or Camilla's arguments against welcoming Genevera as her daughter-in-law: "you'll see what we get from accepting women from other sides. Their houses harbour the most voracious plagues that only lead to utter ruin! It's impossible to gratify, control, or govern them! Those women always side with their children. They never devote themselves to anything except what can gratify their unquenchable appetite!" ("e vederai che utilità ce apporta il contracto de le donne de diverse opinione, quale ne l'altrui case sono peste voracissime e del tutto dissipative. Né mai se possono gratificare, né loro regere e gubernare: sempre legeno la posteriora, né de altro fano capitale, se non quanto prociede da uno inexperato appetitto," 3.77).

Beyond Boccaccio's fictional books, his encyclopedic texts – especially the aforementioned *De mulieribus claris*, his *Genealogia deorum gentilium* (*Genealogy of the Pagan Gods*) and *De casibus virorum illustrium* (*The Downfall of Illustrious Men*), as well as his vernacularizations of passages from Livy's *Ab urbe condita* (*History of Rome*), Valerius Maximus's *Factorum et dictorum libri* (*Memorable Deeds and Sayings*), and Ovid's *Ars amatoria* (*Art of Love*)[46] – serve as the reference sources for so many of the Greco-Roman classical examples of women, mythological figures, and men impacted by Fortune within the *Peregrino*'s debates and discussions. For all these reasons, Caviceo acknowledges Boccaccio's legacy by figuring his spirit's appearance in the *Peregrino*'s proem.

In addition to acknowledging Boccaccio's example, Caviceo reiterates recognizable aspects of Dante as a literary precedent. Dante's *Commedia* received a sumptuous new edition in 1481 by Florentine luminary Cristoforo Landino. The phrasing of Landino's proem ("But with such eloquence he did not write the errings of Ulysses, nor the battles of Troy, nor the arrival of Aeneas in Italy ... in which we see Homer and Virgil so exert themselves ...") will find a distinct echo in Caviceo's presentation of the *Peregrino*, as well.[47] The *Peregrino*'s first book opens with the protagonist meditating on the difficulty of remembering past joys. While his fate cannot be changed by the listener's suffering or advice, Peregrino will nevertheless tell his story: "Just as the memory of pleasant times lends consoling delight to the soul, so the repetition of sad ones afflicts and consumes the spirit. Although I believe the intensity of my memories will cause me to relapse into grief, I am resolved to bear every pain in order to please you" ("E come il rememorare le cose piacevole et ioconde presta a l'anima consolata letitia, così il repetere le triste et odiose afflige e consuma il spirito. E ben che io creda per la intense memoria recidivare in doglia, ogni extreme delibero patire per te gratificare," 1.1). These words call to mind another lover in Dante's poetic masterpiece who was anything but chaste – Francesca da Rimini. Her words spoken from beyond the grave also emphasize the fact that retelling her story will cause her pain, though she wishes to please her listener:

> There is no greater pain than to
> remember the happy time in wretchedness; and this
> your teacher knows.
> But if you have so much desire to know the first
> root of our love, I will do as one who weeps and
> speaks.[48]

Moreover, the *Peregrino*'s proemial characterization as a chaste love story is quickly called into question as the reader subsequently faces various accounts of the protagonist's almost unrestrained lust, which include an unabashedly erotic description of the protagonist's escapade one night not to Genevera's bedroom, as he had planned, but by mistake to the house of Lionora, her neighbour.

Even though the *Peregrino*'s frame is set in the pagan Elysian Fields, rather than Dante's Christian afterlife, Peregrino's trip to the realm of the dead in the third book contains many of the same figures from Dante's *Inferno*, including Cerberus, Charon, and Minos, and Caviceo re-articulates a Dantean notion of contrapasso, although Caviceo substitutes his own unique correspondences for the sins those souls committed during life.

Dante-author's physical place of burial will come up repeatedly in Caviceo's text. Dante died in 1321 an exile from his Florentine homeland and received burial in Ravenna. By the 1470s, his tomb was, by all accounts, neglected and shabby. Landino urged "the Florentine people [to translate Dante's body] back to his homeland and honor it with a tomb worthy of such a poet,"[49] and a contingent of Florentine officials made concerted efforts to do this. When the Venetian ambassador Bernardo Bembo attended Florentine humanist Matteo Palmieri's funeral in 1475, Lorenzo de' Medici leaned on Bembo to arrange the repatriation of Dante's remains, and Bembo vowed to do so. Nevertheless, between 1481 and 1483, when Bembo served as *Podestà* and *Capitano del Popolo* in Ravenna, he instead set in motion the long-needed renovation in Ravenna of Dante's resting place. Guy P. Raffa pithily summarized this action: "Bernardo did not just renege on his promise to have Dante's bones returned to Florence. Seen in the harshest light, he rubbed salt in the wound by improving the conditions of the poet's gravesite but not the reputation of his 'native shores.' The refined tomb and chapel further enshrined 'the rights of Ravenna's people' to keep Dante in their city, his final refuge after being cast out of Florence."[50] When Caviceo's Peregrino mentions seeing Bernardo Bembo in 3.33, the detail imparts no particular impetus to the *Peregrino*'s romance plot. What it does accomplish is to situate Peregrino's fictional arrival in Ravenna within a verisimilar Ravennate setting. In the process, Caviceo emphasizes a well-publicized cultural news event that, even decades later, would resonate keenly in the minds of Caviceo's readers.[51]

There are countless other borrowings from Dante's works in the *Peregrino*. The trope of the young man who falls in love with a girl during a church service was made famous by Dante's account of his love for Beatrice in the *Vita nuova*. The crucial contrast Caviceo underscores between the spiritual, *beatifying* force of love for Dante and the sexual, *generative* force of love for Peregrino depends on the reader's familiarity with the Dantean precedent. Much of the language Dante employs in his early prosimetrum to clarify the nature of Amor – the dictator of his life story, his *Dominus*, the prophet-bearer of Beatrice to heaven, etc. – is deliberately reworked in the *Peregrino*. Peregrino may be in Love's service, but his master is a Cupid armed with bow and arrows in whose arena lovers are tested. Significantly, Peregrino's post-coital exaltation in 3.54 claims he has fought the good fight and triumphed over this cupidity to secure marital love dominion.

Besides its references to the works of Boccaccio and Dante, Caviceo's *romanzo* incorporates elements from the corpus of the other crown of Italian literature: Francis Petrarch. His version of falling in love with Laura during Good Friday Mass offers a different set of references for the love story origin, its psychology, and the inspiration for his vernacular lyric poetry. The most recognizable Petrarchan poetic commonplaces – such as the lover who freezes in summer and burns in winter (1.3 and 2.16) – are subsumed into Peregrino's declared experience of love for Genevera. However, it is Petrarch's humanism, in particular his focus on Scipio Africanus, which plays out in intriguing ways in the romance. On occasion, Scipio is celebrated as the quintessential Roman hero who demonstrates compassion toward Masinissa (1.18), protects the virginity of captive women (1.53), leads an army (2.20), etc. Nonetheless, the perceived ingratitude that Rome displayed toward Scipio late in his life, which Petrarch bemoans with such pathos in his *Africa* (2.547–8), among other passages of his works, becomes the almost absurdly incongruous point of reference for Scipio's ghost in 2.45 to lend support for Peregrino's condemnation of Astanna and the ingratitude servants in general show their masters. It is one example of Caviceo's implicitly satirical treatment, if not of Petrarch specifically, then plausibly the crowd of Petrarchists taking part in the poetic style most in vogue at the time.

Allusions to Petrarch's *Secretum* in the *Peregrino* are also detectable, especially in as much as they inform the structuring of the romance and the overarching concern with what constitutes virtuous love. Petrarch's "secret book" unfolds as a conversation between "Franciscus" (who stands for Petrarch the author) and "Augustinus" (the spirit of St. Augustine of Hippo) over the course of three days, during which Petrarch dramatizes his inner turmoil concerning, among other topics, the questionable virtue of his love attachments. Petrarch's example displays a more personal, vulnerable tone than Caviceo's *romanzo*, a tone that will be taken up more explicitly by Caviceo in his *Confessionale utilissimum*, in which a character, significantly named "Peregrinus" (or "Filius," standing in for Caviceo the author), acknowledges to "Pater" (a priest and father figure) his sexual and other erring in the work published on the heels of the *Peregrino*, in Parma in 1509. As such, the *Confessionale* may have had some palinodic intent for Caviceo vis-à-vis his *Peregrino*.[52]

Other Italian authors, especially those in the novellistic and dialogic traditions, offer models for different scenes represented in the *Peregrino*, most recognizably in the courtly *brigata* storytelling episodes embedded within the text of the romance. Examples include Genevera's fishing trip with her lady friends, when Lucrezia poses a love question for debate in 1.40, and when Elisabetta of Ravenna tells a *facezia* at her lunch party (in 3.22) concerning how a wise, chaste girl puts off an over-eager suitor. From the anonymous *Novellino* (composed in the late thirteenth century) and after Boccaccio through the works of Franco Sacchetti (d. 1400), Giovanni Sercambi (d. 1424), Giovanni Gherardi da Prato (d. c. 1446), and Leon Battista Alberti (d. 1472), among others, the *Peregrino* illustrates the ways in which this social, entertainment tradition continued to be an integral part of life for a certain economic class of Italian Renaissance social gatherings.

Caviceo's *Peregrino* has long been likened to the *Hypnerotomachia Poliphili* (*The Strife of Love in a Dream*, ca. 1499) and Sanazzaro's *Arcadia*. In fact, the *Peregrino*'s most significant excerpted twentieth-century publication was in the authoritative 1952 Einaudi edition by Enrico Carrara, which showcases portions of the three works together in the *Opere di Iacopo Sannazaro con saggi dell'"Hypnerotomachia Polifili" di Francesco Colonna e del "Peregrino" di Jacopo Caviceo*. Thus, for decades, the *Peregrino* was remembered almost as an afterthought to two works with which it has little in common beyond its composition concerning love in non-standard Italian around the turn of the sixteenth century.[53] In addition to the opening and concluding chapters of the *Peregrino*, Carrara chose to excerpt the *questione d'amore* that Genevera's retinue discusses during the fishing expedition (much of 1.38–44), Peregrino's infernal vision (3.1–3.13, heavily redacted), and the description of what he terms Peregrino's and Acate's "Viaggio in Grecia," trip to Greece, which concludes with the encounter with Matteo Bosso on the island of Diomedea (abbreviated passages from 3.17–19). This means that, until Vignali published Caviceo's work in its entirety, Italian readers who did not have the benefit of access to the sixteenth-century printings may have had little impression of the narrative scope of the *Peregrino* or the contemporary, verisimilar interactions among its primary characters, since the isolated excerpts they received in Carrara's edition were an embedded and highly stylized love debate and two of the more fantastical episodes.

Even though Sannazaro's *Arcadia* follows the love tribulations of a male character, Sincero, who stands in for the author, Caviceo's *Peregrino* is quite different from the prosimetrical pastoral escape in almost every way. In fact, Caviceo's romance insists on its connections to real-world urbanity almost as exaggeratedly as Sannazaro's protagonist seeks to flee from Naples. While it may seem that Caviceo's work shares more in common with Colonna's – particularly in their flaunting of erudite references – Peregrino and the lover of Polia are also quite distinct. One obvious divergence is Caviceo's relative lack of focus on ekphrasis. While the *Hypnerotomachia*'s obsessive attendance on the details of art, architecture, design, and their potential for allegorical interpretation makes the work slow going for readers today, Caviceo does a far better job of integrating sparse artistic descriptions into the flow of his narrative. Connoisseurship in the visual arts would likely have been a *sine qua non* for courtiers in the circles in which Caviceo circulated,[54] and even though there is no evidence that Caviceo had particular aptitude in this area, I suspect that he wanted to incorporate some elements of these discussions into his romance pastiche. Nods to ekphrasis occur most prominently in the description of Peregrino's icon of St. Catherine of Alexandria (1.45) and in the ruse Caviceo employs in having Peregrino and Acate find a statue of Venus or Helen of Troy, which serves to introduce into conversation the ancients-versus-moderns debate as it pertains in particular to the ideals of beauty (which begins in 3.17).

Other Italian prose romances of note did not appear until well after Caviceo's.[55] For example, Lodovico Corfino (d. 1556) composed his *Istoria di Phileto Veronese* in the 1520s (and it was not published until 1899), and Nicolò Franco's *Philena* appeared in Mantua only in 1547. Unfortunately, neither of these works is available yet in English. Besides romance *novelle*, epic poems featuring romance plots and motifs will dominate the literary landscape of Caviceo's day.[56]

In terms of the love debates, Marsilio Ficino's commentary on Plato's *Symposium* (1474) likely precipitated the early Renaissance debates concerning love that readers see in many passages of the *Peregrino*, as well as the *De mulieribus* (1501) by Mario Equicola, and the *Asolani* (1505, dedicated to Lucrezia Borgia) by Pietro Bembo.[57]

Up to this point, I have limited my considerations of Caviceo's literary antecedents to his most proximate Italian references. Some mention must now be made of the recognizable classical precedents and borrowings from other national literary traditions. Already from the work's proem, Caviceo acknowledges Homer's epic. Here Caviceo relies more heavily on the romance qualities of the *Odyssey* than on the war narrative of the *Iliad*. He also draws on "the Mantuan Homer," that is, Virgil, in a similar way, emphasizing the dalliance of Aeneas with Dido and the protagonist's journey to converse with the spirit of his dead father over the overarching narrative of war, exile, and the founding of Rome in the *Aeneid*. Many other classical and medieval authors figure into Caviceo's amalgamation. On myth, the epistolary tradition, and love, Ovid's *Heroides* and *Metamorphoses* figure prominently; on love, Andreas Capellanus's *De amore* (*The Art of Courtly Love*, c. 1185) stands out, as well. Livy, other classical historians, and the encyclopedists offer a multitude of exempla recounted by Violante, Genevera, Peregrino, and Acate in support of their arguments in the work's debates. Macrobius's commentary on Cicero's dream of Scipio and other dream theorists serve as a point of reference for Peregrino's legal defence in 1.54, as well as his interpretation of Genevera's dream in 2.39–40.

Of course, the reader will identify Caviceo's phrasing from the Bible throughout the work. Even though Caviceo had first-person experiences of travels around Italy, the Mediterranean, and the Middle East, some of his geographical descriptions also resemble medieval travel literature, such as the narratives by Florentine Cristoforo Buondelmonte or by Ciriaco d'Ancona, and pilgrimage accounts. The didactic medieval compilations of exempla frequently used by preachers, such as the *Disciplina clericalis* (*Scholar's Guide*) of Petrus Alfonsi, likely lend their tone, if not the precise references, for such passages as Acate's comparison of Peregrino to Don Domenico da Treviso, the priest who prays for his life when God had not even granted his lesser petition, the capacity to pass urine (in 3.43). It is difficult not to see an allusion to Augustine's *Confessions* in, for instance, the page in 1.1 with a message that should prompt conversion in the reader, but in Peregrino's case, does not.[58]

Even more popular in Ferrarese theatre were the erudite comedies having, as Donald Beecher asserted, the "salient characteristic [of] formal and procedural allegiance to the plays of the two ancient Roman playwrights,

Plautus and Terence."[59] These works, originally set in Rome, played out in Caviceo's day against the backdrop of Ferrara and treated themes that Caviceo would also develop: "frustrated lovers and wily servants, blustering soldiers and chatty maids were only a few tweaks away from becoming contemporary plays in all but name, for they reflect in their ways the universals of the human social condition," and Beecher noted that there were "some twenty-two productions of Plautus and Terence in Ferrara between 1486 and 1505" and "no less than five Plautine plays were performed for the festivities celebrating the wedding of the crown prince, Alfonso, to Lucrezia Borgia" (8). Ariosto offered his *Cassaria* (*The Coffer*) in 1508 and *I suppositi* (*The Pretenders*) in 1509:

> Moreover, in choosing to depict the desires and tribulations of members of the mercantile class, we face "issues": the conflict between generations and between the moneyed and the serving echelons, between the "housed" and the "unhoused," as well as matters of propriety, the consolidation of wealth, marriage mores, manners and status, knavery and foolishness, all of which may be reformulated into themes. But of greater importance is the order of laughter that prevails around escape, deliverance, rewards, the incongruous, and the ridiculous. (*Renaissance Comedy* 13)

Caviceo appears to tap into this diversionary *zeitgeist* when he translates these concerns from the public stage to the intimate world of his novel.[60]

It is also plausible that motifs from Hellenistic or Alexandrian romances, such as those by Achilles Tatius and Heliodorus, were finding their way into the Italian literary milieu. The *Metamorphoses* by Apuleius (c. CE 125–80) had already been translated by Boiardo (c. 1440–94). However, most of the more popular versions were not printed until after Caviceo's *Peregrino*.[61] The same was true of Italian translations of the most in-demand Spanish romances. Lelio Manfredi, a humanist at the Ferrarese court, translated Diego de San Pedro's *Cárcel de amor* (Seville, 1492) into Italian, publishing it as the *Carcer d'amore* in Venice in 1514. Manfredi is also the likely translator (under the pseudonym of Lelio Aletiphilo) of Juan de Flores's *Grisel y Mirabella* (*Amorosa historia di Aurelio e Isabella*), which saw six Italian editions between 1528 and 1548, and *Tirante il Bianco* from its Catalan original, which was published in Italian in 1538, although it was evidently completed in 1519.[62] Lucia Binotti noted the editorial success of the *Carcer d'amore* and asserted:

> although these kinds of works may have originally been addressed to a rarified readership preeminently preoccupied with the cultivation of courtly ideas and behaviors, they quickly attracted a much more heterogeneous

public composed not only of noblemen intent on discovering the emblems of a longed-for world which was swiftly waning, but also of a bourgeois audience who found in these texts the elements of a behavioral code that could improve their status. (85)

Caviceo's *Peregrino* took part in this trend of attracting readers far beyond its deliberate dedicatee and courtly audience, perhaps especially intending to reach readers with ambitions to rise in social and educational status.

Thus, Caviceo employed a wealth of literary antecedents to craft his book and suggest how it signifies (in positive agreement by means of homage, for instance, or in negative contrast, via parody or satire). What remains to be addressed is: What attitude did Caviceo have toward the mass of masterpieces he and his peers inherited in the early 1500s? I believe that Caviceo offers us an indication of how he might answer this question. The issue arises in 3.17–18 during an ancients-versus-moderns debate between Acate and Peregrino. They have unearthed a beautiful statue representing Venus or Helen of Troy. Acate does not merely idealize the artwork's aesthetic quality but also proceeds to extend his argumentation, which favours the ancients, to praise the Golden Age's prowess, knowledge, faith, and customs. Peregrino boldly replies: "Acate, every age finds fault with its own time, bemoaning with cries, shouts, and laments its current suffering, cruelty, greed, ignorance, and foolishness. Not everyone back then was a demigod, as history likes to sing" ("Achate mio, ogni età al tempo suo se è lamentata, et in superhabundantia hebbe pianti, stridi, lamenti, affanni, crudeltà, avaritia, ignorantia e sciocheza. Non son stati tutti semidei, como la historia canta"). Peregrino acknowledges that the age of old may be remembered better, thanks in greater measure to their poets than to heaven. He goes on to say that history "contains the hazy recollections of writers who favour elevated and expansive themes" ("ma il fu uno vago pensiero de chi tende ad alte e generose cose"). If we as readers are taken by these stories from the past, that is not necessarily so bad, "since it can spur posterity to emulate virtue" ("aciò sia uno sperono a la posterità di emulare virtù"). Then Caviceo's protagonist, who speaks for the author himself, adds: "perhaps what's been laborious to us will be a delight to posterity" ("Et quel cha a nui serà laborioso, a la posterità renderà dilecto"). It is as if Caviceo casts aside here the Petrarchan saw of according absolute reverence to classical culture in order to deliberately plant the seed in the minds of his readers that his own work might mean something more to future readers than its relative idiosyncrasy of genre at the time in Italy might have foretold.

Critical Reception of the *Peregrino*

Caviceo's modern biographer, Lorenza Simona, has rightly noted that "studies and assessments of this literary work by Caviceo are almost entirely lacking."[63] Martínez Morán, in the introduction to his 2014 edition of the republished adaptation by Díaz, called Caviceo's book "a practically forgotten work" ("una obra prácticamente olvidada," 13).[64] Of those critics who pause to assess the *Peregrino*, very few find something original to praise, often reverting to the entrenched, mistaken belief that the work is a mere elaboration of Boccaccio's *Filocolo*. Panizza is among the few exceptions in her presentation of the work in *The Cambridge History of Italian Literature*.[65]

Nonetheless, the vast majority of critics delight in finding much to criticize. Luigi Callari acknowledges that the *Peregrino* was wildly popular in Caviceo's day, though he stands alone in insisting that Caviceo's little imitations of Plautus and Terence in Latin dialogues were "certainly more important than his romance" ("certo più importanti del suo romanzo," 2). Albert N. Mancini stated in "The Forms of Long Prose Fiction" that Caviceo "gave this narrative form a breath and fullness previously unknown," but ultimately, Caviceo is "[i]ncapable of a sustained effort in long narrations, feel[ing] more at ease in dealing with his privileged topic of love" (23).[66] Moreover, Marcello Turchi disdained Caviceo's situation as one of a writer who aimed to elevate himself toward a courtly humanistic world he recognized as superior to his own, though he did not quite have what it took to succeed, instead offering something amateurish and popularizing.[67]

Michele Pierantoni opted to excerpt just one chapter (3.22) from among the romance's 219 chapters to republish as a stand-alone *novella* for inclusion in a series of examples of the genre by various authors. Then he apologized quite sheepishly:

> By republishing this *novella*, we do not intend to offer a good read, only to present to the fans of such compositions a little piece to add to the many examples of its genre. The *novella* is taken from the third book of the romance by Jacopo Caviceo titled *Il Peregrino*, which once had its admirers, though today it is reputed with good reason to be exceedingly boring.[68]

It would be futile to dispute matters of taste, but my view contrasts sharply with the negative bias associated with these longstanding assessments of Caviceo's book as presenting a needlessly lengthy and tiresome narrative. The ways Caviceo draws out the process of achieving narrative climax and closure are deliberate, aiming to keep his readership engaged and ultimately, I dare say, gratified.

Some critics have cited the mixture of historical and fictitious elements as a reason that explains the *Peregrino*'s popularity at the turn of the sixteenth century. Without contesting this possibility, I would argue that what truly distinguishes Caviceo's romance is the degree of psychological complexity and sociological insight that he incorporates in portraying the machinations of his characters' thought processes. The author allows the reader to peer into the minds of not just the male protagonist but also his beloved lady and many of the other characters as well. A crucial instance occurs when Peregrino weighs the potential outcomes of making his presence known to Genevera in the earliest stages of their courtship when she awaits a priest so that she can partake in the sacrament of confession (1.23):

Now I know how easy it is to frighten the hearts of young ladies by startling them, so at first I hesitated, unsure if my next move should be to speak or remain quiet. If I spoke and she jumped, I'd surely be discovered hiding in there; then wouldn't that be worse than death? What defence or excuse could I offer for my actions? Dishonouring religion and scandalizing a lady's honour could destroy a man's reputation. What should I do? If I didn't speak, how could I be heard? Love and fear battled within me.

I said to myself: 'Genevera is wise; she won't make a sound. Even the most prudent, though, fail by mistake. And if she did, how would that be her fault? May any consequences befall me; Fortune favours the bold!'

Comforted by Love, I said in a humble voice, "Have mercy, lady. I am your servant Peregrino."

Io, che scio come facilmente ne li giovenili pecti paura se ingenera, non scio deliberare qual più mi conduca, o il parlare o il tacere. Se parlo e se spaventasse, sì che qua entro fusse ritrovato, non seria questo peggio che la morte? Che apologia, che excusatione mai faria per me? La relligione deshonestata, l'honore de la donna scandelizato gravariano ogni bona et optima conditione. Che debbo io fare? Se non parlo, come serò exaudito? Amore e paura combateano insieme. Dico tra me istesso: "Genevera è savia: la non farà moto. Anche gli prudenti per errore faliscono; e quando errasse, che colpa seria la sua? Hora sia cum mi lo affanno. Fortuna a gli audenti presta aita." Confortato d'amore, cum humil voce dico: "Mercede, signora. Io sono il tuo servo Peregrino."

Another important instance is in 3.36, when Genevera/Hippolyta hypothesizes the identity of the new arrival at the convent in Ravenna:

Ruffina went out, leaving Genevera in no less turmoil than Caesar must have felt when he cast the die and crossed the Rubicon. She feared some trap or new deception, which could denigrate her reputation or destroy her social standing.

She asked herself: 'If this man is Peregrino, how did he learn where I am? Astanna is dead, and Lena is captive here. Anastasia would never breathe a word about this, and the other sisters know nothing about me.

'Maybe Peregrino is dead. Perhaps his spirit has taken another body; and in whatever form passion possessed him while living, he must now do penance after death. But if this were true, what would become of me? What happened to so many other ladies! Was there ever a more unfortunate one? Of course, it's no great tragedy to lose what one never possessed. And yet I hope ...

'Perhaps he is not dead.'

Partita Ruffina, non mancho angoscioso restò il pecto de Genevera di quello che fusse il romano dictatore quando del Rubicon il traiecto vetato li fu. Dubitava de qualche versutia e novo commento, quale la fama denigrare li potesse, o vero deteriorare la sua bona condictione. Et poi diceva: "Se questui è Peregrino, como di me ha notitia alcuna? Astanna è morta, Lena è qui captiva, Anestasia in questa parte è muta, a le vestale sono ignota. Forsi è morto Peregrino. Il spirito suo ha revestito un altro corpo; et ove vivendo la passione lo informò, morto ne farà penitentia. Et se fusse il vero, che fia di me? Quel che è facto de le altre. Fu mai al mondo la più sfortunata? Si bene non è gran iactura a perdere quello che mai non se possesse. Era pur in gran speranza. Forsi non è morto."

In other cases similar to these two, the reader can absorb the scope and potential dangers or rewards of individual action. By implication, we understand the gravity of transgressions, which flesh out otherwise stark statements, such as Genevera's in 2.12, "Even if our love is equally shared [between the sexes], infamy certainly is not" ("se lo amore è equale, l'infamia non è tale"). Machiavelli's advice to princes, and Baldassare Castiglione's and Giovanni Della Casa's descriptions of proper behaviour in society, all appear in the decades following the publication of the *Peregrino*. In Caviceo's work, readers can already foresee the consequences of behavioural choices – for example, in exploring a love match, dealing with intergenerational conflict, or negotiating with servants – and from varying perspectives.

Sometimes it may be easy to miss the complexity this work offers. For example, Antonio Scolari expressed exasperation concerning Genevera's claim to have seen a vision of St. Catherine of Alexandria (1.70) in his article on "Un romanzo veronese" (which argues Corfino's approach to romance vis-à-vis Caviceo's): "one cannot fathom why out of some strange whim Genevera, pretending to be ill, sends our poor hero to the ends of the earth!" ("non si sa bene per quale strano capriccio ... Ginevra ... fingendosi malata, manda il povero eroe ... ai confini del mondo!" 76).

On the one hand, Caviceo's frank and relatable language lays bare the urgency of sexual desire. Falling in love causes individuals to forget their responsibilities, grow impatient for replies to letters, and even dare actions against which reason might rightly caution (such as sneaking into a church confessional or the home of an enemy family). As detached readers, we are perhaps drawn to share in Scolari's vehemence. On the other hand, however, Caviceo's novel emphasizes the flip side of desire – fear – and it does so especially well in Genevera's reaction. Briseida's situation in the legal trial of 1.18 offers ladies a sobering reminder (however superfluous) of the mortal risks of entering Love's arena. She found herself in a love triangle, wishing to devote herself to Polidoro while extricating herself from Cesare's attentions. Nevertheless, Cesare pursued her even to her bedroom at night. Briseida suggests that the classical model she may have been expected to follow would be Portia or Cornelia, or even Lucretia – the virtuous Roman matron who committed suicide after Tarquin raped her in her own room. Not surprisingly, Briseida seems implicitly to assert the need for updated exempla for sixteenth-century Ferrarese maidens to emulate. Genevera likely perceives the same desperate mortal fear.

It is not inconceivable that Genevera might want to bide her time in order to reason through feelings without the constant presence and pressures of Peregrino. She loves him, but she has also repeatedly requested that he moderate his feelings. Prey to the urgency of sexual desire, Peregrino demonstrated at least as many times that he was quite incapable of slowing down the pace of his courtship. We must recall that Peregrino inundated her with letters and riskily involved various go-betweens in their communications. He got himself arrested for lurking around a hostile clan's laundry facilities. He surprised Genevera in a church confessional, showed up at her house in pilgrim's garb, stayed on to do some chores, returned to her house to squabble on Annunciation Day when the rest of her household was out, tagged along with her to Polyxena's house, stalked her girlfriends' fishing outing, successfully entered her house through a hollow statue, and nearly succeeded in coming through the sewer system to accost her in the dead of night in her own bed. The perceptive reader can sense just how quickly fear accompanies desire in this psychologically probing narrative and, thus, how imperative it is not to shut down the discussion of love, as Scolari implies, by exclusively favouring a quick resolution for desire.

The Language of the *Peregrino* and a Note on This Translation

Linguistically, this work challenges the translator, not just for its northern non-standard Italian vocabulary but also for its Latinate syntax, which I decided had to be reflected quite differently in a twenty-first-century

English translation. Vignali dedicated sixty-eight pages of his 1993 Italian critical edition of the *Peregrino* to a glossary, necessitated by the "peculiarity of Caviceo's vocabulary" ("peculiarità del lessico caviceiano," 382), in addition to separate articles and a monograph he wrote on the subject of Caviceo's language. I do not intend to marshal nearly so much detail here. Suffice it to say, I am enormously indebted to his work and the resources he used, especially the *Grande dizionario della lingua italiana*, various Italian etymological dictionaries, and glossaries for the works of Colonna, Sabadino degli Arienti, Luigi Pulci, and others. I also found John Florio's *A Worlde of Wordes* (1598) enlightening for crucial passages.

Many of the most difficult semantic translations, I believe, do not involve an obscure *hapax legomenon*; instead, the hardest terms to translate are those words that recur with maddening frequency, but with varying meanings, such as *alto, amplissimo, arte, dubitare, exemplarità, fluente, habitaculo, honestare, humanato, iactare, ingenuo, libertino, machina, mercede, officio, remettere, sentimento, simulacro, sobrio, studio, virtù, vulgare* ... Taking just the first example, *alto* can mean "high," "noble," or "elevated," but also "profound" or "deep." In Caviceo's work, the exceedingly common word *e/et* ("and") is also sometimes used to signify "or"; *con/cum* ("with") can also mean "without," even when a negative is not expressed. This indicates how some passages present significant interpretive challenges because they might mean one thing or precisely the contrary.

Caviceo participated in a trend very much in vogue in an age of the rebirth of classical culture: he liberally adopted classical terminology for his settings. A church was a "temple" (*phano*), a ship, a *bireme* or *trireme*; noblemen were *senatori* or *semidei*, priests, *sacerdote*, and so forth. As I previously mentioned, the *Peregrino* was published in the same year that Ariosto presented his *Cassaria* for performance in Ferrara, modernizing the language, plot, and set pieces, pushing humanist emulation of the Roman comedy into the realm of "a new genre in the making."[69] In visual art, renderings of mythological gods and heroes were portraits of contemporary men and women. There is more to this *contaminatio* than cultural fashion, of course. In a time of crushing wars on the Italian peninsula, socio-economic upheaval, and East-West clashes, reminders of classical exemplars who overcame similar challenges or whose fame endured precisely because they faced those difficulties must have offered inspiration and some modicum of consolation.

In my translation, I opted to keep the "buskins in the Greek fashion," which serve to identify Peregrino as Petrutio's home invader, but I pared down many of the other obscurities or anachronisms for the sake of narrative coherence. Although something may be lost without a much more word-for-word rendering of the text, my interpretive iteration skews more toward the pleasure of the reading experience of a novel than any mere linguistic transference. Emphasizing literalness may only serve to keep the remarkable cache of early modern romances relegated to a niche of academic specialists.

In terms of his verb conjugations, Caviceo frequently uses the third-person indicative when one would expect use of the first person. For example, Genevera in the first chapter turned to see who was looking at her, and the narrator relates: "e *vide* uscire de li ochi suoi uno splendore, che più presto il core me trafisse" ("*he/she/it* saw flash from her eyes a splendour that more quickly pierced my heart than ..."). Other times he swaps third-person singular for third-person plural. Object pronouns also do not always accurately reflect the gender and/or number of their antecedents.

I chose not to slavishly respect Caviceo's verb tenses in my translation either. I recognize that the author may be shifting tenses for the same reason storytellers informally do in English. For example, at the outset of 1.8, Peregrino was waiting anxiously for Violante to return to him with an answer from Genevera. Caviceo wrote: "Amor, timor, speranza e gelosia al debil cuor *havean posto* il campo, quando cum demissa faccia la *vedo* ritornare. *Facto*gli incontra, gli *adimando* ...," which might read: "Love, fear, hope, and jealousy *had taken* their place on the battlefield of my weak heart, when with a downcast face I *see* her return. [*Went*] up to her, and I *ask* ..." The use of *see* and *ask* in the present tense are likely there to give the impression of immediacy in the retelling of past events. However, I found the temporal whiplash from past perfect (or in other instances the remote past perfect) to the present to be too much to sustain in English translation.

Facto in this passage also raises one of Caviceo's most pervasive linguistic tics, the (over)use of the past participle as a modifier, and it is not always obvious what it is modifying. Instead of debating whether "having gone up to her" or "going up to her" would work better, I more frequently rendered the phrasing in a parallel construction, i.e., "I went up to her and said ..." Further consideration of a longer citation of the above-mentioned passage from 1.1 might help the reader to discern just how complicated this verbal construction can become: "*Firmata* la vista per mirare chi fosse quella che cum tanta modestia e gentileza a la dolceza divina così intenta audientia prestasse, *voltata* forsi per altrove mirare mi risguardò, e vide uscire de li ochi suoi uno splendore, che più presto il core me trafisse che non fece la sagitta de Iove Phaetonte" (literally: "*Stopped* the gaze to see who was that girl who with such modesty and gentility to the divine sweetness so intently lent hearing, *turned* perhaps somewhere else to look she looked at me, and saw leave from the eyes a splendour that more quickly my heart transfixed than did not do the arrow/bolt of Jove Phaeton"). Context helps me to understand that *firmata* and *voltata* do not refer to the same subjects. The male narrator notes that he paused in his looking around and rested his eyes on a girl who was listening intently with much modesty and gentility to the sweet divine word, and she, perhaps to look somewhere else, turned and caught sight of him. In that instant, he saw a splendour issue from her eyes that pierced his heart quicker than Jove's thunderbolt struck Phaeton. In translating so many examples of this construction in Caviceo's prose, I have tried to imagine what is happening in the text and then describe it in English; it sounds easy enough, but it involves subjective interpretation, which carries significant risk of error. Any misinterpretations are not deliberate, and for them, I beg the reader's pardon.

Caviceo is a great aficionado of epithets, in further emulation of the classics. On first mentions of mythical symbols or characters, I frequently insert identifications (such as "Dawn" and "Ulysses") to go along with his naked epithets ("amica de Titone" and "figlo de Laerte" respectively). Subsequently, I typically go with a simpler identification.

Part of the fun of translating Caviceo's text comes in rendering his word choice in another language. He is fond of clever puns – *amanti/amenti* (1.8), *effecto/affecto* (1.41), etc. He includes a number of proverbs that I have not reworded because their meaning is discernible, while conveying a sort of wisdom of the common man: "You damn the doves and excuse the crows" ("damni gli palumbi, et excusi gli corvi," 1.31); "I am rounder than an egg" ("Io, più tondo che ovo," 1.66); or "A hearth that holds smoke is no place to live" ("camino che tenga fumo non è da habitare," 2.39), for example. Despite all the refined references to ancient myth and classical histories, there nevertheless coexists within the text this mirthfully folksy, far less aulic tone.

Of course, literary translation involves far more than word choice or interlinguistic turns of phrase, and issues of tone and extraverbal cues demand the translator's constant attention. In this regard, I should say something about how I rendered Genevera's language. Caviceo represents Genevera's character as both exemplary and fallible, leaving it difficult for readers not to admire and sympathize with her. Her coming of age in this book is portrayed through her negotiation of new and messy feelings in the context of thorny social and romantic situations. As I pondered how to render her voice, which admittedly lurks beyond the letter of the Italian text, I sought to tap into the psyche of a fifteen-year-old "good girl" endeavouring to please the man with whom she is smitten and bridge what must seem monumental disparities in age and experience. After all, here is an adolescent seeking to assert her voice for the first time in the world of adults – with an enticing man, but also with strict parents and a sapient tutor, as well. I wanted her dialogue with adult characters to reflect a sense of formality and boldness in her articulation, which I signalled in English at a basic level by rendering her direct speech without the use of contractions. I also resisted smoothing out her sometimes relatively elliptical argumentation (for instance, 1.67 offers an example of how her teenage mind moves from one point to the next while endeavouring to come across as logical, knowledgeable, and well read). Translator interpretations like those concerning tone cannot be easily highlighted through direct comparison with an original text, and yet translation demands the rendering of tone in tandem with the semantics.

I have taken liberties with the punctuation. In the sixteenth-century *edicio princeps*, most chapters, whether a few sentences or a dozen or more pages, were presented as a single paragraph. There were no quotation marks or separate lines for separate speakers. Statements, exclamations, and questions tended to run together. In this edition I have further distinguished between when characters are praying aloud or talking to themselves (indicated by single quotation marks) and when the characters are engaging in standard dialogue (indicated by double quotation marks). The epistles and epitaphs were not formatted distinctly, as they are in the present edition. Moreover, some Italian sentences contain too many subordinate clauses or parallel constructions to be rendered at all effectively in English. Quite a few of the final words of a chapter break off in mid-sentence, so I adopted ellipses not in the original. The vagaries of early modern printing mean that the numbering of books and chapters in different editions of the *Peregrino* may differ, though typically not as drastically as Díaz's Spanish adaptation of Caviceo's work. Suffice it to say that both the format and punctuation of this edition wish to conform more closely to today's norms in English than to anything in the earliest page layouts. I also made quite a few deliberate decisions for elements of style in this edition, following some of Margaret Sayers Peden's choices in her translation of Fernando de Rojas's *Celestina* (such as keeping the interjections beginning with "O," however tiresome they can admittedly seem at times).

Please also note: the rubrics in italics that summarize each chapter are my own. I offer them to assist readers in navigating this unabridged, complex work, emulating many recent editions of long Italian works.

I am fortunate to work in an era of great English literary translations. Emily Wilson's translation of Homer's *Odyssey* appeared in print while I laboured on an early draft of my *Peregrino* translation. My work is far from the feat in iambic pentameter she produced, yet the issues she poses concerning artifice, register, and gender have given me pause: "There is often a notion, especially in the Anglo-American world, that a translation is good insofar as it disguises its own existence as a translation; translations are praised for being 'natural.' I hope that my translation is readable and fluent, but that its literary artifice is clearly apparent" (82). In elaborating an aspect of this point, Wilson stated, "All modern translations are equally modern. The question facing translators and their readers is whether to try to disguise this fact, through stylistic tricks such as archaism and an elevated, artificially 'literary' register, or to underline it, and thereby encourage readers to be aware that the text exists in two different temporal and spatial moments at once" (87). Wilson underscored in her translation the "linguistically distinctive, even odd" (87) terms that deliberately draw attention to themselves; in calling serving women slaves, as opposed to domestic servants or maids, Wilson's choice was shockingly effective. However, the same choice would have seemed off in mine, despite the fact that Astanna's or Gasparina's or Violante's expressions of mortal fear are no less understandable.

Wilson goes on to state:

> It is traditional in statements like this Translator's Note to bewail one's own inadequacy when trying to be faithful to the original. Like many contemporary translation theorists, I believe that we need to rethink the terms in which we talk about translation. My translation is, like all translations, an entirely different text from the original poem. Translation always, necessarily, involves interpretation; there is no such thing as a translation that provides anything like a transparent window through which a reader can see the original. The gendered metaphor of the "faithful" translation, whose worth is always secondary to that of a male-authored original, acquires a particular edge in the context of a translation by a woman. (86)

In my case, Caviceo's text, with its unfaithful narrator and unfaithful protagonist, veritably begs for a faithful unfaithfulness. My own twisted satisfaction might be in precisely that outcome.

Another perspective at the forefront of my mind is Karen Emmerich's 2017 monograph *Literary Translation and the Making of Originals*, which squarely challenges the notion of any original text, arguing that some degree of instability remains, including at the (mythic) source. Even an *editio princeps* had previous drafts; its later printings or editions, with or without the input of the author, may very well improve (or not) on the supposed original. Whether wittingly or unwittingly, translators are forced to posit the source text for their work: "each translator creates her own original, fixes a particular text as the 'prior' text to be translated – fixes it sometimes before translating, and sometimes during and even by way of the process we tend to think of as 'translation proper.' So-called originals are not given but made, and translators are often party to that making" (13). Just as translations are derivative, Emmerich argues, so too are so-called originals.

What she asserts is particularly applicable to Caviceo's *Peregrino*, with its dozens of editions, translations, and excerpted passages. While I have accepted the 1508 edition as the primary basis for my translation and edition ("Each new published text in translation is both a translation *and* an edition. Editing and translating are mutually implicated interpretive practices that further the iterative growth of a work in the world," Emmerich, *Literary Translation*, 8), I have not been immune to the transmission history of the text in Italian, as well as Spanish and French. In offering the pioneering English translation, I perceive a frightful responsibility in erecting another original, while wanting very much to build upon the solid foundation of a source text. It is unmooring for a translator who endeavours to be doggedly *rigorous* not to hew so closely to a word-for-word correspondence as the blueprint for the English construction. But on some level, it is inevitably an illusion, or at best, a building that will, at some point, invariably require renovation, as all material and textual ones do. I am inexorably drawn to Emmerich's questioning non-question, her invitation to address: "What might it look like if we, as translators, gave ourselves the freedom to engage in forms of citational correspondence whose goal was not to reflect or represent but to grow, to mess around, to destroy the pieces, to magic poetry forward in excitingly non-original ways?" (189). As arresting as this statement is, it is equally inspiring in a resonant translator-spirit.

NOTES

1   At certain junctures of the plot, the ghost of Peregrino reminds the reader that he is retelling what happened to him during his life. For example, in 3.85 (that is, in Book 3, Chapter 85 of the *Peregrino*; all references to Caviceo's work will appear in this format, rather than page numbers, in order to facilitate consultation of the Italian), Peregrino has just awakened from a disturbing dream and three horsemen arrive to inform him of what he mistakenly assumes is Anastasia's death: "but woe is me! It turned out to be my own!" ("ma misero me, che fu la propria mia"). This is to say, the news of his beloved's death would precipitate his own passing into the realm from where he relates his tale. Nevertheless, the narrative also presents many chapters as direct dialogue or as the text of epistles, and other times, when the character of Peregrino is not present, it is told in the third person.

2   The theme of two young lovers divided by family hostilities is likely much older even than the classical example of Pyramus and Thisbe in Ovid's

Metamorphoses, which derives from a far earlier etiological myth. Even the familiar version from William Shakespeare's early seventeenth-century play *Romeo and Juliet* came from precedent source texts, four of which Nicole Prunster traces in *Romeo and Juliet before Shakespeare: Four Early Stories of Star-Crossed Love by Masuccio Salernitano, Luigi da Porto, Matteo Bandello, and Pierre Boaistuau*. Moreover, blood feuds were common in Italian city-states in Caviceo's day, lending a verisimilitude that would have been immediately relatable to his readership, and Caviceo will make reference to one in Bologna between the Bentivoglio and Canedoli families within his text (1.18).

3 Riccardo Bruscagli asserted in "Ruggiero's Story: The Making of a Dynastic Hero" from *Romance and History* that Ariosto's story of Ruggiero and Bradamante was "the first example I know in Italian literature of a true romantic story: that is, a story that traces a substantial character's development, along the curve of an emotional progression, displayed over a protracted stretch of time, through a carefully described series of significant situations" (166). For these same reasons, Caviceo's story of Peregrino and Genevera might entail that we revise this understanding.

4 For a more detailed analysis of this issue, I refer readers to my article "When a Pilgrim Is Not a Pilgrim."

5 Simona indicates in her entry to the *Dizionario biografico degli italiani* that an earlier Caviceo biographer, Giorgio Anselmi, mentioned that Caviceo may have prepared a commentary on Ovid's *Heroides*, although there do not seem to be any extant copies.

6 The most famous depiction emphasizing the connection between the juniper tree and a variant on the name is by Leonardo da Vinci in his portrait of Ginevra de' Benci (1474), with a juniper tree in the background and the depiction of a juniper branch on the reverse side of the wood panel.

7 The notion of the *homo viator* is discernible at least since St. Augustine's *Confessions*, and exists as the archetypal wayfarer. Even when the name is not as obvious as John Bunyan's protagonist in *The Pilgrim's Progress from This World, to That Which is to Come* (1678), for example, it is inherent in that of Romeo, whose etymology points to Romers, penitents bound for the Eternal City. "Viateur" is the narrator in Diego de San Pedro's 1492 romance *Cárcel de Amor* (*Prison of Love*). Luigi da Porto (1485–1529) will pen a novella in 1524, published in 1531 under the title "Hystoria novellamente ritrovata di due nobili amanti, con la loro pietosa morte, intervenuta già nella città di Verona nel tempo del Signor Bartolomeo della Scala" ("A Story Newly Relocated of Two Noble Lovers and Their Piteous Death, Which Occurred in the City of Verona during the Time of Lord Bartolomeo della Scala"), in the frame of which we learn that the one who relates the tragic tale of Romeo Montecchi and Giulietta Capelletti is none other than "Peregrino": "Peregrino was handsome and always in love, perhaps more so than became his years. This greatly enhanced his worth, since he delighted in telling the finest

stories, particularly those dealing with love" (*Romeo and Juliet before Shake-speare*, 28). However, this storyteller must not be confused with Caviceo's, since he was described as a "most agreeable man" of approximately fifty years of age, originally from Verona and an expert archer who served with da Porto in the war of the League of Cambrai. Some critics, according to Vignali in his introduction to the *Peregrino*, have suggested (and contested) that the protagonist's name might allude to Pier Maria Rossi's love interest, Bianca Pelligrini. See his summary of the debate on page xvii of his edition, especially n22.

8 The title of Caviceo's work first appeared as *Il libro del Peregrino*, but evolved by the Venetian edition of 1559 to include a subtitle *Il Peregrino: Opera ingeniosa nella qvale dottamente, et con leggiadria si ragiona del vero modo di honestamente amare*. In the 1527 Spanish adaptation of the work by Díaz, the work was titled *Libro de los honestos amores de Peregrino y Ginebra*. In the 1527 French translation by François Dassy, it was rendered *Dialogue tres elegant intitulé le Peregrin*. The French version seems to leave open the possibility of calling the work "The Pilgrim," though the Spanish makes it clear that "Peregrino" refers to the protagonist's name.

9 There is an allusion to the explication of Peregrino's name in Book 3.3 when an unnamed shade in the afterlife asks, "Weren't you called Peregrino in your native land?" ("Como così nativamente te adimandasti Peregrino?") and Peregrino answers, "A presage of my sorry fate!" ("Fu de la mia mala sorte uno presagio").

10 It may also be a compliment to the work's dedicatee, since Lucrezia Borgia's father took the same name when he was raised to the papacy.

11 Descriptions of her in 1.1, 2.38, and 3.52, for instance, echo aspects of the debate between Peregrino and Acate on female beauty in the classical statue they unearth in 3.17, or such debates in contemporary works by Pietro Bembo, Baldassare Castiglione, and others. This work's dedicatee, who was also the dedicatee of Bembo's *Asolani* in 1505, possessed many of these qualities, according to Allyson Burgess Williams in "Rewriting Lucrezia Borgia": "The appearance of Lucrezia in this painting expands upon the ideals of beauty (straight nose and rounded face) discussed in terms of her portrait medals. Like many depictions of sixteenth-century Italian women, she has white skin, rosy cheeks, smallish curved lips, curly hair (unfortunately, no longer the ideal blond), smooth high forehead, arched eyebrows, large clear eyes, and soft shoulders. These characteristics are derived from the Petrarchan tradition of love lyrics, in which the female beloved was described in these ideal and set terms" (86). Moreover, Williams continued, "Beauty was inextricably linked to goodness in early modern gender ideology; a woman's beauty was seen as having a direct relationship to her virtue" (87).

12 Although Dennis Romano focuses his sociological analysis on Venetian household servants at the time, what he asserts in *Housecraft and Statecraft*

seems to hold true for Violante's role as well: "With this new respectability [getting married; Violante was already widowed] came new responsibilities and a measure of prestige within the household. Some married female servants became wet nurses and governesses and as such had responsibility for the most prized possessions of elite households, namely, the children. This responsibility was reflected in part in the higher salaries paid to wet nurses. In addition, wet nursing and raising children fostered strong emotional attachments between servants and their nurslings. Many wet nurses took special interest in and developed lifelong attachments to their 'milk children.' Shared concern for the children could also lead to closer relations between mistresses and nurses. As a consequence of all this, the faithful nurse held a special place in many elite households" (165).

13 According to Diane Yvonne Ghirardo in "Marginal Spaces of Prostitution in Renaissance Ferrara" in *Phaethon's Children*: "A young woman who succumbed – with or without force – to a man who promised marriage often found herself abandoned. She thus forfeited her honor, the one asset that could enable her to contract a respectable marriage. Whatever the cause, relocation to foreign cities [in order to work as a prostitute] appears to have been a common practice" (94).

14 See Sergio Cappello's "Astuzia e inganno nel *Peregrino* di Jacopo Caviceo," 33.

15 Nancy Bisaha's *Creating East and West* offers various historical examples.

16 Caviceo could not have meant Filippo Beroaldo the Younger, the Tacitus scholar, Latin poet, and prefect of the Vatican Library under Pope Leo X, who also receives mention in Ariosto's *Orlando furioso* (46.13), since he was still alive when Caviceo imagines the ghostly encounter in 1508. The younger Beroaldo outlived Caviceo, dying in 1518.

17 Of course, the same constellation of Love, Fortune, and Death had appeared in Boccaccio's commentary on the figure of Thisbe in his *De mulieribus claris*: "Who will not pity the two young people? Who does not shed at least a single tear for their tragic end? … To love while in the flower of youth is a fault, but it is not a frightful crime for unmarried persons since they can proceed to matrimony. The worst sin was Fortune's, and perhaps their wretched parents were guilty as well. Certainly the impulses of the young should be curbed, but this should be done gradually lest we drive them to ruin in their despair by setting up sudden obstacles in their path. Passionate desire is ungovernable; it is the plague and the disgrace of youth, yet we should tolerate it with patience. Nature intends us, while young and fit, to feel spontaneously the procreative urge; the human race would die out if intercourse were delayed until old age" (*Famous Women*, trans. Virginia Brown, 29–30).

18 Lucia Binotti, in "Humanistic Audiences," rightly reminds us, however, that "the reading of sentimental fiction, far from being relegated to feminine

audiences, was a practice that bonded male courtiers and schoolmen in a quasi-liturgical performance of masculinity" (70). Of course, romance was also associated with an adolescent male audience. Marjorie Curry Woods in *Weeping for Dido: The Classics in the Medieval Classroom* offers a thoughtful analysis of the ways medieval boys read and identified with female characters in literary works, following on Augustine's admission in his *Confessions* that his memory for his studies was aided by the association with strong emotions. One cannot help but think that Caviceo shared an emotional connection to many of the same passages: "The allure of stories full of pathos, fantasy, danger, and death may be one of the most important aspects of the longevity and success of this aspect of the classical tradition, an attraction illustrated by the other parts of the *Aeneid* that Augustine liked most when he was in school, all found in Book 2: 'the Wooden Horse with its armed men, and Troy on fire, and Creusa's ghost' (*Conf.* 1.13.22) … soldiers hiding in the Trojan Horse and the burning of Troy might be expected schoolboy interests no matter what period. Creusa, however, was another woman abandoned by Aeneas: his Trojan wife inadvertently left behind during the escape from Troy at the end of Book 2 of the *Aeneid*" (22–3). See also various interventions from *The Premodern Teenager*, edited by Konrad Eisenbichler, especially Marian Rothstein's "Teen Knights: Interpreting Precocity in Early Modern Life-Stories": "Many years ago, I was taken aback in a graduate seminar when the distinguished medievalist teaching it brushed aside a question about repetitious, formulaic romance plots saying that these things were read only by adolescents anyway. That answer may well have been constructed off the cuff largely for its shock value, but once the question of the intended audience of medieval and Renaissance romans en prose is raised, one is led to note that teen-aged youths often do have a much larger place than might be expected" (173).

19   The list of reading materials to be avoided is considerably longer, according to Vives, whose *Education of a Christian Woman* is edited and translated into English by Charles Fantazzi. For specific recommendations, see the pages following 74, where he inveighs: "I marvel that wise fathers permit this to their daughters, husbands concede it to their wives, and public morals and institutions ignore the fact that women become addicted to vice through reading." Vives prefers the Bible, works of the Church Fathers, and "the advice of learned and sensible men, [such as] Plato, Cicero, Seneca" (78). Ruth Kelso's *Doctrine for the Lady of the Renaissance* offers insight into the ideals of womanhood around the time of Caviceo's work, referring to advice manuals on rearing daughters, works of etiquette and comportment, educational treatises, medical references on female sexuality, clerical works on counselling the confessions of girls, humanist theories of love, and arguments from both sides of the *querelle des femmes*.

20 One glimpse of foreshadowing, however, does appear in 1.8, when Peregrino
    says: "I would do best to kill this cruel one with my own hands. Otherwise,
    I'll never regain my freedom" ("per la salute mia conviene che sta crudele
    mora per mane meie; altramente a la mia libertà non me puosso restituire").

21 Caviceo seems to encourage his readers to interpret character emotions in
    his work, and I would be remiss if I did not underscore Peregrino's po-
    tential as an object of further analysis in the intersection of early modern
    Affective Studies and Masculinity Studies. Peregrino embodies an affective
    tension between the performance of violent masculinity that ignores female
    subjectivity, on the one hand, and the possibility of a rapport with Genev-
    era that acknowledges her potential as partner or ennobler of his nature on
    the other. Along these lines, see Todd W. Reeser's "Approaching Affective
    Masculinities."

22 It may be tempting to link this hollow statue of a holy virgin to actual ex-
    amples of *Vierges ouvrantes*, typically depicting the Virgin Mary in three
    dimensions as a sculpture that opens to reveal Christ. See, for example, the
    depictions and accompanying critical discussion in Elina Gertsman, *Worlds
    Within*. However, every indication in the romance is that Caviceo is more
    focused on the literary motif of a hollow object implemented as a ruse to
    access a defended space than on its potential artistic or devotional sculptural
    antecedents. Of course, in the Boccaccian novella tradition, a lover inside a
    hollow wooden object (such as a barrel) is the consequence of coitus inter-
    ruptus and the attempt to avoid detection by a spouse. But I am also intrigued
    that the verb Caviceo uses to describe the Greeks' act of hiding within the
    hollow form of the Trojan Horse ("informono," 116) is the same one used by
    the ghost of Boccaccio in the proem to refer to the relationship between body
    and spirits ("Vivendo informai il corpo di Zanbochacio da Certaldo," 3).

23 According to Marta Ajmar in "Exemplary Women in Renaissance Italy"
    (254). Moreover, Agostino Strozzi employed Catherine as a model of virgin-
    ity and learning for young women to imitate in his *Defensione delle donne*,
    which was written in Isabella d'Este Gonzaga's court in Mantua in 1501.

24 Images are available at: http://www.museivaticani.va/content/museivaticani/
    en/collezioni/musei/appartamento-borgia/sala-dei-santi/disputa-di-santa-
    caterina-d-alessandria.html.

25 My citations of Anselmi's *Vita* are from the version published together with
    the 1520 Milanese edition available online.

26 "questa parentesi così poca lusinghiera" (Simona, *Giacomo Caviceo*, 55). All
    English translations are mine, unless otherwise noted.

27 Nineteenth-century scholar Luigi Callari, who found and attributed to Cav-
    iceo an unpublished dialogue, preferred to characterize Caviceo as a boldly
    adventurous man. In "Un dialogo inedito di Iacopo Caviceo," Callari ex-
    cused Caviceo's behaviour as that of a "uomo avventuroso, audace" (2). He

is not incorrect in his observation that Caviceo "had that combative kind of personality that was common among a large part of the literary scholars and thinkers who lived at the turn of the sixteenth century" ("ebbe quel carattere battagliero che fu comune a tanta parte de' letterati e dei pensatori vissuti a cavaliere del secolo XVI," ibid.). For example, between 1433, when the great humanist Francesco Filelfo's face was slashed and disfigured, and 1570, when Nicolò Franco, the romance writer of the *Philena*, was executed at the Castel Sant'Angelo in Rome after his relentless provocations, scores of Italian intellectuals came to blows and blades in the streets. Not even churches were sanctuaries, given the case of poet and de facto ruler of Florence Lorenzo de' Medici, known as The Magnificent, who survived the attack in the Florentine Duomo by a conspiracy led by the Pazzi family, which killed his brother Giuliano in 1478. For further context concerning the violence committed by authors during this time, please see Hugh Bicheno's *Vendetta* and Jonathan Davies' "Violence and Italian Universities during the Renaissance." Less convincing, however, is Callari's assertion that Caviceo was a "a tranquil pessimist who did not despair about things" ("pessimista tranquillo, che non disperò delle cose," "Un dialogo inedito," 3).

28 According to Simona, Ilario Anselmi was likely a relative of Caviceo's first biographer, Giorgio (*Giacomo Caviceo*, 58n16).

29 After Rossi died in 1482, Caviceo continued to serve his son Guido Rossi, who had been named governor of Pontremoli and Lunigiana in 1478.

30 "pessimam naturam et modos malignos … Iacobi Cavicaci istic comorantis, et quod dum istic permanebit nomisi ab eo potest provenire nisi pestilens morbus" (Simona, *Giacomo Caviceo*, 96–7).

31 The biographer offers a series of anecdotes no doubt intended to illustrate Caviceo's wit and social grace. I offer two of them here. In one, an archdeacon wished to cast aspersions on Caviceo's financial spending habits, underscoring the author's precarious patrimony. He scoffed that Caviceo must have spent more than a hundred *libbre* on books; with that large sum of money, he would have done better to buy a vineyard. Caviceo readily retorted that a vineyard would suit the archdeacon well, since he was uneducated and incapable of tending anything but vines; Caviceo, however, boasted that he knew how to make better use of books. In another anecdote, a man asked Caviceo in jest if there were greater numbers among the living or the dead. Caviceo replied that there were more among the living, of course, because the dead were no more.

32 There were at least twenty-one, and possibly as many as twenty-five, sixteenth-century publications. These editions are listed in the bibliography. There is no evidence, however, to support Carlo Vecce's assertion that there was a 1507 publication of the *Peregrino* in Parma ("La crisi dell'Autore nel Rinascimento," 8).

33 Francisco José Martínez Morán in his 2014 edition of the work identifies four
distinct editions, all published by Cromberger in Seville; he lists the others
as 1527, 1544, and 1548. Javier Gonzalez Rovira in "El *Libro del Peregrino*
de Giacomo Caviceo y la traducción de Hernando Díaz" had previously
suggested that there was another edition by Cromberger in 1520; he also intimated another printing by an unnamed publisher in Salamanca in 1548 (52).

34 According to Gonzalez Rovira, "the translator hid the name of the original
author because he believed that he was creating a distinct work, among other
reasons" ("el traductor oculta el nombre del autor original, entre otras ra-
zones porque considera que está creando una obra distinta" ("El *Libro del
Peregrino* de Giacomo Caviceo y la traducción de Hernando Díaz," 53).

35 They are (in rough chronological order): a life of his early patron Pier
Maria Rossi (*Maximo humanae imbecilitatis simulachro fortunae bifronti
vita Petri Mariae de Rubeis viri illustris*, published in Venice between 1485
and 1490); another encomiastic work in honour of Pier Maria's son, Guido
Rossi (*De bello Roboretano*, or *Amicus quisquis es tam latinus quam grecus
liberum me scito, huiusque mei lucribrationes* [sic] *laboris solus habeto sum*,
1487); *Lupa* (*Beltrando de Rubeis Parmensi Guidonis legionis uenetae ducis
filios*, 1489); *De exilio cupidinis* (or *Nicolao Preiulo Maphei filio patritio
veneto Corneliani pretorem gerenti in exilium Cupidinis Iacobus Caviceus,
Grecus, Latinus*, 1489, On the Banishment of Love), now available in a
2013 edition by Pietrino Pischedda; a dialogue on Mary's virginity (*Sever-
ino Calcho regulari canonico benemerenti*, 1489); an unedited anti-Semitic
screed titled *Libellus contra Hebreos* (in the codex G. VI. I of the Biblioteca
Comune di Siena); a work in praise of Maximilian I (*Sex urbium dicta ad
Maximilianum Romanorum regem*, 1494), who would be proclaimed Holy
Roman Emperor in 1508; and a dialogue published in Rome in 1494 on the
abduction of a girl (*De raptu filiae*, or *Antonio archidiacono Urbevetanensi
dialogus de raptu filiae*).

36 Unlike Caviceo's other minor works, this one received another sixteenth-
century printing (in Venice in 1529). The *Confessionale* was edited, translated
into Italian, and annotated by Pischedda, published in 2014.

37 Callari makes the claim in "Un dialogo inedito" (2) that the Plautian satirical
comedy Caviceo presents under the title *Dialogus de moribus nostrae aetatis*
should be considered one of these dialogues.

38 In focusing on the literary antecedents, I largely leave aside historical sources.
One starting point for this approach may be Aeneas Silvius Piccolomini's
Europe (c. 1400–1458). In her introduction, Nancy Bisaha rightly notes, "*Europe* found a large audience because there were so few Renaissance works
like it, and readers were hungry for the richness and breadth of information
it offered in one convenient package ... *Europe* was viewed as an unsurpassed
general history of quattrocento society" (18).

39 It is not inconceivable that Boccaccio was also an exemplar for Caviceo on
a more personal/biographical level, given that he also studied law and was a
reluctant cleric. Moreover, both men demonstrated enthusiasm for Greek culture beyond the recuperation of literary works, if we consider, for instance,
Boccaccio's propensity for Greek or pseudo-Greek etymologies for his character names, and Caviceo's specification that Peregrino dresses unusually in
Greek buskins (1.52).

40 The first characterization appears in Alessandro Luzio and Rodolfo Renier's
La coltura e le relazioni letterararie di Isabella d'Este Gonzaga: "una pesante
e lasciva imitazione del *Filocolo*" (202–3), which in turn was summarizing
Adolfo Albertazzi's characterization of the work in *Romanzieri e romanzi
del Cinquecento e del Seicento*, 13–33. The second description, by Javier Gonzalez Rovira, appeared in "El *Libro del Peregrino* de Giacomo Caviceo y la
traducción de Hernando Díaz": "una versión muy elaborada de la historia de
Flores y Blancaflor" (51).

41 An anonymous reviewer of this project rightly pointed out that Caviceo
seems to recast his protagonist as various Boccaccian characters: "Like Ma-
setto (*Decameron* 3.1), Peregrino disguises himself as the convent gardener;
like Frate Alberto (*Decameron* 4.2), he is associated with angels (he stays at
the Inn of Angels); and like Fra' Cipolla (*Decameron* 6.10), he offers up an
absurd array of relics to Ruffina." Indeed, this is the kind of literary comparison that the *Peregrino* insistently invites.

42 "E chi negherà questo, quantunque egli si sia, non molto piú alle vaghe donne
che agli uomini convenirsi donare? Esse dentro a' dilicati petti, temendo e
vergognando, tengono l'amororse fiamme nascose, le quali quanto piú di
forza abbian che le palesi coloro il sanno che l'hanno provate: e oltre a ciò,
ristrette da' voleri [di altri …] il piú del tempo nel piccolo circuito delle loro
camere racchiuse dimorano … E se per quegli alcuna malinconia, mossa da
focoso disio, sopraviene nelle lor menti, in quelle conviene che con grave
noia si dimori, se da nuovi ragionamenti non è rimossa. [mentre per gli in-
namorati uomini] se alcuna malinconia o gravezza di pensieri gli affligge,
hanno molti modi da alleggiare o da passar quello, per ciò che loro, volendo
essi, non manca l'andare a torno, udire e veder molte cose, uccellare, cacciare,
pescare, cavalcare, giucare o mercatare: de' quali modi ciascuno ha forza di
trarre, o in tutto o in parte, l'animo a sé e dal noioso pensiero rimuoverlo
almeno per alcuno spazio di tempo, appresso il quale, con un modo o con
altro, o consolazion sopraviene o diventa la noia minore." From the edition of
the *Decameron* by Vittore Branca, 7–8. The English translation is by Guido
Waldman in *The Decameron*, 4–5. Genevera's words to Peregrino in 3.50
obliquely echo that passage: "You men distract yourselves by toiling and
thinking about lots of things, and you act in such a way that your days and
nights pass tranquilly. But we women are wretched and captive, so we are

never free of this one constant burning, and we can think or speak of nothing else. Thus, the experience of love is different between men and women" ("Diversamente ve affaticati, variamente pensati, e destinctamente ve adoperati, sì che facilmente il giorno e la nocte ve passano tranquilli. Ma nui, misere e captive, a questa perpetua fiamma emancipate, de altro non possiamo né pensare né parlare. Perhò, vario è de lo amare il studio tra vui e nui").

43 From the Prologue of the edition and translation by Mariangela Causa-Steindler and Thomas Mauch (*The Elegy of Lady Fiammetta*, 1). The citations in English that follow also come from this edition.

44 On the consequences of the potential gender roles and the gendering of compassion, which is the declared reason that the spirit of Peregrino recounts his story in the first place: "to have compassion for those who struggle and suffer in life and in death because they love too much" (1.1), please see Alessia Ronchetti's essay "Reading Like a Woman: Gendering Compassion in the *Elegia di Madonna Fiammetta*" in *Reconsidering Boccaccio*, 109–32.

45 For a recent overview of the *Elegy*'s inspiration of Spanish prose romances, please see Filippo Andrei's contribution, "The Tragicomedy of Lament: *La Celestina* and the Elegiac Legacy of Boccaccio's *Fiammetta*," in *Reconsidering Boccaccio*, 365–402. On the intricacies of copyright infringement related to Caviceo's text, see William Kemp's study, "A Complex Case of Privilege Infringement in France."

46 On the attribution of these *volgarizzamenti*, please see Alison Cornish's contribution to *Boccaccio: A Critical Guide to the Complete Works*, 255–61.

47 Landino, *Scritti critici e teorici*, 1:151: "Ma con tale eloquenzia non gl'errori d'Ulisse, non le battaglie troiane scrisse, non la venuta d'Enea in Italia … nelle quali cose veggiamo Omero e Virgilio essersi tanto affaticati."

48 "Nessun maggior dolore / che ricordarsi del tempo felice / ne la miseria; e ciò sa 'l tuo dottore. / Ma s'a conoscer la prima radice / del nostro amor tu hai cotanto affetto, / dirò come colui che piange e dice" (*Inf.* 5.121–6). The English translation is from *The Divine Comedy of Dante Alighieri* by Robert M. Durling. For a more detailed examination of the Galehaut reference, please see Valerio Fermi's "Galeotto: A Prologue by Way of the Proem."

49 Landino, *Comento*, 2:908, cited from Guy P. Raffa's *Dante's Bones*, 51.

50 Raffa details the state rift that festered over the claims to Dante's corporeal remains in "Florentine Remorse," his third chapter of *Dante's Bones*; this passage is cited from page 58.

51 In fact, Violante will treat Dante's renovated tomb as a must-see tourist destination in 3.67, when she sends her brothers to visit it as well as Classe and the Basilica of San Vitale.

52 According to Giuliana Giallella, who writes in the preface to the 2014 edition of the *Confessionale*, it was "probably written to make up for the fuss raised by the *Peregrino*, published in the previous year" ("probabilmente scritta

per emendare lo scalpore suscitato dal *Libro del Peregrino*, pubblicato l'anno precedente," 9).

53 Both of these works have already been translated into English. The first complete English translation of the *Arcadia* was by Ralph Nash in 1966. The *Hypnerotomachia* was completed by Joscelyn Godwin in 1999.

54 Indeed, Biagio Rossetti, the famed architect and urban designer, was in the midst of a massive civic beautification building project during Caviceo's time in Ferrara, and it would be a crucial component of what UNESCO determined to preserve in its 1995 inscription "Ferrara, City of the Renaissance, and Its Po Delta" (https://whc.unesco.org/en/list/733/).

55 Medieval Italian chivalric romances, including the *Tristano Riccardiano*, the *Tristano Veneto*, or the *Tavola Ritonda*, seem to impart scant traces to the *Peregrino*.

56 The *Peregrino* appeared after Luigi Pulci's *Morgante* (1483) and Matteo Maria Boiardo's *Orlando innamorato* (published in stages between 1483 and 1495), but before Francesco Cieco da Ferrara's *Mambriano* (published in 1509) and Ariosto's *Orlando furioso* (published in its first version in 1516).

57 Subsequently, similar *querelles* appear in Castiglione's *Book of the Courtier* (published in 1528), Leone Ebreo's *Dialogues of Love* (published in 1535), Tullia d'Aragona's *Dialogue on the Infinity of Love* (published in 1547), Bartolomeo Gottifredi's *Specchio d'amore* (Mirror of Love, published in 1547), and Agnolo Firenzuola's *On the Beauty of Women* (published in 1552), among others.

58 Intriguing is what little we know about the performance in 1494 in Ferrara of *Augustinus*, a play by Florentine priest Pietro Domizi del Comandatore (d. 1518), which was based on Augustine's *Confessions*. Its performance would have been a civic event that the vicar general might very well have attended. Even if it is not possible to trace specific references to the play in Caviceo's *Peregrino*, we might believe that Caviceo, newly arrived in Ferrara and intending to compose a romance, might pay careful attention to the kinds of entertainments that this citizenry enjoyed.

59 *Renaissance Comedy: The Italian Masters. Vol. 1*, 3. See also Louise George Clubb, "Staging Ferrara: State Theater from Borso to Alfonso II," in *Phaethon's Children*, 345–62.

60 According to Karen Sullivan in *The Danger of Romance*, "Whereas families tended to gather by the hearth to listen to moral or religious works together, beginning in the sixteenth century, young people preferred to retreat to their bedrooms or boudoirs to read romances and, later, novels by themselves ... Alone, they experienced their encounter with these works as unmediated, to the point where they could become entirely absorbed into their world and their characters' minds. Both men and women read novels, but women were seen as especially susceptible to this private, inward-directed state and to the

amorous fantasies to which it could lead" (27). In contrast, Beecher notes
that female roles in the theatre were limited: "until the stories could be represented indoors and actresses could take over from the amateur male actors
who played their parts (as opposed to the professional boy actors of the Eliz-
abethan theatre who specialized in female roles), women would continue to
be more spoken about than heard" (*Renaissance Comedy*, 1.25).

61 Agnolo Firenzuola modernized the work by Apuleius between 1515 and
   1525, though it would not be published until 1550 in Venice under the title
   Asino d'oro (*The Golden Ass*). The *editio princeps* of an Italian translation of
   Heliodorus's *Aethiopica* (c. CE 230) appeared in Venice in 1559. According to
   Albert N. Mancini in "The Forms of Long Prose Fiction in Late Medieval and
   Early Modern Italian Literature": "Niccolò Machiavelli (1469–1527) wrote
   a poetic version of Apuleius's novel during the last years of his life, leaving it
   incomplete. Francesco Angelo Coccio (no sure date) rendered *Leucippe and
   Cleitophon* by Achilles Tatius into Italian in 1551 ... The translation-adaptation
   of the *Daphnis and Chloe* of Longus the Sophist (c. AD 160) by Annibal Caro
   (1507–66) was published posthumously in 1786, but had circulated widely in
   manuscript form long before that time. The novelist Giovan Battista Manzini
   (1599–1664) published another rendition of Longus's novel, *Gli amori innocenti
   di Dafni, e della Cloe* (The Innocent Loves of Daphne and Chloe) in 1643" (27).

62 Lucia Binotti traces the complicated intersections of Italian and Spanish romance commerce at the time in "Humanistic Audiences"; here I am referring
   to the research she presented on pages 74–5. Emily C. Francomano edited and
   translated the *Grisel and Mirabella* in *Three Spanish "Querelle" Texts*.

63 In her entry on Caviceo for the *Dizionario biografico degli italiani*: "Mancano
   quasi totalmente studi e giudizi sull'opera lett[eraria] del Caviceo."

64 Moreover, "since the second half of the sixteenth century, the novel has seen
   itself relegated by critics and readers to a state of almost total ostracism, perhaps, one might hypothesize, as a consequence of its inclusion on the inqui-
   sitional list of prohibited books' ("desde la segunda mitad del siglo XVI, la
   novela se vio relegada a un casi total ostracismo para crítica y lectores, tal vez,
   cabría aventurar, como consecuencia de su inclusión en la lista inquisitorial de
   obras prohibidas," *Libro de Peregrino*, ed. Martínez Morán, 14).

65 After suggesting that it "may have been the first novel specially written for
   women," Panizza continued: "It is full of eloquent, usually deeply melancholic lovers' set speeches ... Autobiographical elements are present, too, for
   the travels of the pilgrim to the Near East describe the author's own travels, and place the romance firmly in realistic contemporary settings ... [I]ts
   very diversity, and mixture of styles and genres, open up new directions for
   narrative fiction" (159). On the opening up of new avenues of prose fiction
   in Spanish literature, see Martínez Morán's introduction to his edition of
   Díaz's translation, especially pages 47–8, where he notes similarities between

Caviceo's work and subsequent Spanish works by Contreras and Lope de Vega. J.A. Garrido Ardila attributes to Francisco Delicado's *El retrato de la Lozana andaluza* (1528, "The Portrait of the Lusty Andalusian Woman") the first appearance of narrative elements that appear in Caviceo and other earlier works: "The author appears in the text, talks with the characters, and even observes others and takes notes for his book. For the first time, perhaps, and eight decades before *Don Quixote,* fiction and the real world come together, and both the actual author and the verisimilar characters co-exist on the same level" (5). Caviceo speaks to Peregrino's spirit in the work's frame, and his historical and fictitious characters interact on the same plane within the text. In terms of the *Peregrino*'s influence in the French literary tradition, see especially Magda Campanini Catani's "Le *Angoysses douloureuses* di Hélisenne de Crenne e il *Libro del Peregrino* di Jacopo Caviceo."

66 Francesco Flamini, in his 1897 survey of the literature of *Il Cinquecento,* mentions Caviceo's *Peregrino* in the same breath as Nicolò Franco's *Filena*: he stipulates that in both there is the same fusion of classical, Dantean, and Boccaccian elements, but that they both also lack inventiveness and plot development. Anna Ceruti Burgio echoed his finding, calling the *Peregrino* a sort of *summa* of all the literary commonplaces of his time and the preceding ones. "Il *Peregrino* piacque ai suoi contemporanei forse proprio perché divulgava motivi in genere trattati a più alto livello, e quindi meno accessibili ai lettori comuni, contrabbandandoli mescolati con gli ingredienti romanzeschi, assumendo l'aspetto quasi di una specie di *summa* di tutti i luoghi comuni letterari del suo tempo e dei precedenti" ("Strutture narrative e modelli culturali del *Peregrino* di Iacopo Caviceo," 54).

67 Marcello Turchi, "Composizione e situazione del romanzo umanistico di Iacopo Caviceo," 16: "una prova dilettantesca e divulgativa." In the context of French reception through Dassy's translation, Silvio Ferrari weighed in rather ponderously: "Caviceo, a weak imitator of the motifs and themes dear to Humanism and the beginnings of the Renaissance (which stoked so much passion in the French court), hides behind a plot that has been elongated to excess and is ever ready to fall into a convolution of conceits, revealing that the structure of his reflection is particularly scant. In this, we can distinguish his tendency to collect and list the experiences and fates of others, more out of a pedantry and courtly devotion than out of any authentic and articulated assimilation" ("Il Caviceo, debole epigono dei motivi e dei temi cari all'Umanesimo ed al primo Rinascimento (che tanta passione suscitano nella corte francese) cela dietro un discorso dilatato a dismisura e sempre pronto a cadere nel concettuoso, una riflessione che si rivela di struttura particolarmente scarna. Si individua qui una disposizione a compendiare esperienze e risultanze altrui, più per pedanteria e devozione cortigiana, che per autentica e articolata assimilazione," "La traduzione francese del *Peregrino*," 346–7).

68 "Col ristampare questa novella non intendiamo di offerire al lettore una
     buona prosa, ma solo di presentare agli amatori di tali componimenti un li-
     bretto da aggiungersi ai tanti dello stesso genere. La novella è tratta dal libro
     terzo del romanzo di Iacopo Caviceo intitolato *Il Peregrino*, il quale sebbene
     oggi si reputi con ragione noiosissimo, pure ebbe in antico i suoi ammiratori."
     These words appear in the preface to the *Novella di Iacopo Caviceo Parmi-
     giano*, on page 3, and while the introductory note is unsigned, and there is no
     indication of the identity of the editor on the title page or elsewhere in the
     publication, I found the attribution of this novella to Michele Pierantoni in
     the *Archivio storico italiano*, ser. 5, vol. 25 (1900): 6.
69 According to Beecher in the introduction to *Renaissance Comedy* 1.40.

Bibliography

Italian Editions of Caviceo's *Peregrino*

Caviceo, Iacopo [Jacopo]. *Il Peregrino*. Parma: Ottaviano Salado, 1508.
– *Libro del peregrino novamente impresso e redvtto alla sva syncerita cvm la vita de lo avtore.* Parma: Octauiano Salado & Francisco Vgoleto, 1513. [Includes for the first time the *Vita de Iacobo Cauicaeo* by Giorgio Anselmi]
– *Libro del Peregrino nouamente impresso …* Venice: [publisher not specified], 1513.
– *Libro del Peregrino nouamente impresso …* Milan: Iohane angelo Scinze[n]zeler, 1514.
– *Libro del Peregrino nouamente impresso …* Milan: Minutiana, 1515.
– *Libro del Peregrino novamente impresso …* Venice: Manfredus Bonum de Montis Ferrato, 1516. [https://books.google.com/books?id=1EhcAAAAcAAJ&printsec=frontcover&source=gbs_ge_summary_r&cad=0#v=onepage&q&f=false, accessed 8 October 2020]
– *Libro del Peregrino novamente impresso …* Milan: [publisher not specified], 1518.
– *Libro del Peregrino nouamente impresso …* Milan: Augustino de Vicomercato, 1520. [https://books.google.com/books?id=IWMeeQOywhUC&printsec=frontcover&source=gbs_ge_summary_r&cad=0#v=onepage&q&f=false, accessed 8 October 2020]
– *Libro del peregrino, diligentemente in lingua toscha correcto, et novamente stampato et historiato.* Venice: Georgio di Rusconi, Nicolo Zoppino, e Vincenzo Compagnadi, 1520. [https://reader.digitale-sammlungen.de/en/fs1/object/display/bsb10165971_00131.html, accessed 8 October 2020]
– *Libro del Peregrino nouamente impresso …* Venice: Bernardino de Lisona Vercellese, 1520. [https://books.google.com/books?id=TRc8AAAAcAAJ&printsec=frontcover&source=gbs_atb#v=onepage&q&f=false, accessed 8 October 2020]

– *Libro del peregrino nouamente impresso* … Milan: Augustino de Vimercato, Nicolo da Gorgonzola, 1522.
– *Libro del Peregrino nouamente impresso* … Venice: G.F. & G.A. Rusconi for N. Zoppino e V. Compagni, 1524.
– *Libro del Peregrino diligentemente in lingua Thosca correttto* [sic] *et nouamente stampato & hystoriato.* Venice: Helisabetta di Rusconi ad instantia sua, e di Nicolo Zopino, 1526.
– *Libro del Peregrino.* Milan: [publisher not specified], 1526 [according to E. Carrara, *Opere*, 400].
– *Libro del Peregrino nouamente ristampato & alla sua pristina integrita ridotto.* Venice: Moise, 1527.
– *Libro del Peregrino nouamente ristampato & alla sua pristina integrita ridotto.* Venice: Francesco Bindoni & Mapheo Pasini, 1527.
– *Libro del Peregrino nvovamente revisto.* Venice: Bindoni e Pasini, 1531. [https://books.google.com/books?id=kAxbqZyjxjAC&printsec =frontcover&source=gbs_ge_summary_r&cad=0#v=onepage&q&f=false, accessed 8 October 2020]
– *Libro del Peregrino nouamente impresso* … Vercelli: I.M. de Pelipariis, 1531.
– *Il Peregrino. Nuovamente revisto.* Venice: [publisher not specified], 1533. [https://books.google.com/books?id=PP1XAAAAcAAJ&pg=PA1&dq =editions:OCLC645552612&source=gbs_selected_pages&cad=2#v =onepage&q&f=false, accessed 8 October 2020]
– *Il Peregrino.* [No city or publisher specified by Simona], 1535.
– *Il Peregrino nuouamente ristampato, e con somma diligenza corretto, et alla sua pristina integrita ridotto.* Venice: Pietro di Nicolini da Sabbio, 1538. [https:// books.google.com/books?id=-_A5AAAAcAAJ&printsec=frontcover &source=gbs_ge_summary_r&cad=0#v=onepage&q&f=false, accessed 8 October 2020]
– *Il Peregrino nuouamente con somma diligenza reuisto & ristampato.* Venice: Pietro di Nicolini da Sabbio, 1547. [https://archive.org/details /imageGXIII222NarrativaOpal/page/n519/mode/2up, accessed 8 October 2020]
– *Il Peregrino.* Venice: [publisher not spcified], 1549.
– *Il Peregrino: Opera ingeniosa nella qvale dottamente, et con leggiadria si ragiono del vero modo di honestamente amare.* Venice: D. de' Farri, 1559.
– *Il Peregrino.* Ed. Luigi Vignali. Rome: La Fenice, 1993.

French Translations of Caviceo's *Peregrino*

Caviceo, Iacopo. *Dialogue tres elegant intitulé le Peregrin.* Trans. François Dassy. Paris: Nicolas Couteau for Galliot du Pré, 1527. [https://gallica.bnf.fr /ark:/12148/bpt6k1517765k, accessed 8 October 2020]

– *Dialogue tres elegant intitulé le Peregrin*. Trans. François Dassy. Lyon: Claude Nourry, 1528.
– *Dialogue tres elegant intitulé le Peregrin*. Trans. François Dassy. Paris: Galliot du Pré, 1528. [Annotated for the first time by Jean Martin]
– *Dialogue tres elegant intitulé le Peregrin*. Trans. François Dassy. Paris: Couteau, 1528 [and/or 1529].
– *Dialogue tres elegant intitulé le Peregrin*. Trans. François Dassy. Paris: Alain Lotrian, 1531. [https://gallica.bnf.fr/ark:/12148/bpt6k131964j, accessed 8 October 2020]
– *Dialogue tres elegant intitulé le Peregrin*. Trans. François Dassy. Paris [or Lyon: publisher not specified], 1533.
– *Dialogue tres elegant intitulé le Peregrin*. Trans. François Dassy. Paris: [publisher not specified], 1535. [https://gallica.bnf.fr/ark:/12148/bpt6k15212428, accessed 8 October 2020]
– *Dialogue tres elegant intitulé le Peregrin*. Trans. François Dassy. Paris: [publisher not specified], 1540.

Spanish Adaptations of Caviceo's *Peregrino*

Caviceo, Jacopo. *Libro de Peregrino*. Ed. Francisco José Martínez Morán. Trans. Hernando Díaz. Alcalá de Henares: Universidad de Alcalá, 2014.
Díaz de Valdepeñas, Hernando. *Historia nuevamente hecha de los honestos amores que un cavallero llamado Peregrino tuvo con una dama llamada Ginebra*. Seville: Cromberger, 1516.
– *Libro de los honestos amores de Peregrino y Ginebra*. Seville: Cromberger, 1520.
– *Libro de los honestos amores de Peregrino y Ginebra*. Seville: Cromberger, 1527. [https://books.google.com/books?id=iRRfAAAAcAAJ&printsec=frontcover&source=gbs_atb#v=onepage&q&f=false, accessed 8 October 2020]
– *Libro de los honestos amores de Peregrino y Ginebra*. Seville: Cromberger, 1544.
– *Libro de los honestos amores de Peregrino y Ginebra*. Seville: Cromberger, 1548.

Excerpts of the *Peregrino*

Carrara, Enrico, ed. *Opere di Iacopo Sannazaro con saggi dell'"Hypnerotomachia Poliphili" di Francesco Colonna e del "Peregrino" di Iacopo Caviceo*. Turin: Einaudi, 1952.
Caviceo, Jacopo. *Libro primo del Peregrino*. Milan, 1514.
– *Novella*. [Ed. Michele Pierantoni.] Lucca: A. Fontana, 1855.

Primary Sources

Bembo, Pietro. *Gli Asolani*. Trans. Rudolf B. Gottfried. Bloomington: Indiana University Press, 1954.

Bigolina, Giulia. *Urania: The Story of a Young Woman's Love and the Novella of Giulia Camposanpiero and Thesibaldo Vitaliani*. Ed. and trans. Christopher Nissen. Tempe: Arizona Center for Medieval and Renaissance Studies, 2004.

Boccaccio, Giovanni. *The Decameron*. Trans. Guido Waldman. Intro. and notes by Jonathan Usher. Oxford: Oxford University Press, 1993.

– *Decameron*. Ed. Vittore Branca. Turin: Einaudi, 1987 [1980].

– *The Elegy of Lady Fiammetta*. Ed. and trans. Mariangela Causa-Steindler and Thomas Mauch. Chicago: University of Chicago Press, 1990.

– *Famous Women*. Trans. Virginia Brown. The I Tatti Renaissance Library. Cambridge, MA: Harvard University Press, 2003.

– *Tutte le opere*. Ed. Vittore Branca. 10 vols. Milan: Mondadori, 1964–98.

Bunyan, John. *The Pilgrim's Progress from This World, to That Which is to Come, Delivered under the Similitude of a Dream*. London: Nathaniel Ponder, 1678.

Caviceo, Jacopo. *Confessionale utilissimum*. Ed. Pietrino Pischedda. Intro. Giuliana Giallella. Milan: La Caravella, 2014. [The *Confessionale utilissimum* was first printed in Parma in 1509, then in Venice in 1529.]

– "*De bello Roboretano.*" In *La guerra veneto-tirolese del 1487 in Vallagarina: Fonti narrative del XV e XVI secolo raccolte e tradotte da Pio Chiusole*, 8–25. Comune di Calliano: Accademia Roveretana degli agiati, 1987.

– *De exilio cupidinis*. Ed. Pietrino Pischedda. Villanova di Guidonia: Aletti, 2013.

– *Dyalogus de raptu filiae*. Rome: Johann Besicken, 1494 [1500].

– *Lupa*. Venice: Bernardinus Benalius & Matteo Capcasa, 1489.

– "Un dialogo inedito di Iacopo Caviceo [*Dialogus de moribus nostrae aetatis*]." Ed. Luigi Callari. *Archivio storico per le province Parmensi* 3 (1894): 1–26.

– *Urbium dicta ad Maximilianum Romanorum regem*. Venice: Bernardinus Benalius & Matteo Capcasa, 1491.

– *Vita Petri Mariae de Rubeis comitis Berceti*. Venice: [publisher not specified], 1490. [Ed. Edoardo Alvisi. Parma: Ferrari e Pellegrini, 1895.]

Collected Ancient Greek Novels. Ed. B.P. Reardon. Foreword J.R. Morgan. Berkeley: University of California Press, 2008 [1989].

Colonna, Francesco. *Hypnerotomachia Poliphili*. Ed. Marco Ariani and Mino Gabriele. 2 vols. Milan: Adelphi, 1998.

– *Hypnerotomachia Poliphili: The Strife of Love in a Dream*. Trans. Joscelyn Godwin. New York: Thames and Hudson, 1999.

Corfino, Lodovico. *Istoria di Phileto Veronese*. Ed. Giuseppe Biadego. Livorno: Raffaello Giusti, 1899.

Dante Alighieri. *Dante's Vita Nuova*. Trans. and essay by Mark Musa. Bloomington: Indiana University Press, 1973.

- *The Divine Comedy of Dante Alighieri.* Vol 1: *Inferno.* Trans. Robert M. Durling. New York: Oxford University Press, 1996.

d'Aragona, Tullia. *Dialogue on the Infinity of Love.* Ed. and trans. Rinaldina Russell and Bruce Merry. Chicago: University of Chicago Press, 1997.

de Rojas, Fernando. *Celestina.* [1499] Trans. Margaret Sayers Peden. Ed. and intro. Roberto González Echevarría. New Haven: Yale University Press, 2009.

de Maulde la Clavière, René. *The Women of the Renaissance: A Study of Feminism.* Trans. George Herbert Ely. New York: G. Putnam's Sons, 1905.

de San Pedro, Diego. *Prison of Love.* Trans. with intro. and annotations by Keith Winnom. Edinburgh: Edinburgh University Press, 1978.

Diario ferrarese dall'anno 1409–1504 di autori incerti. Ed. Giuseppe Pardi. Bologna: Zanichelli, 1928–33.

Dizionario biografico degli italiani. Istituto della Enciclopedia Italiana fondata da Giovanni Treccani. https://www.treccani.it/catalogo/catalogo_prodotti /grandi_opere/biografia_nazionale/dizionario_biografico_degli_italiani.html#.

Ebreo, Leone. *Dialogues of Love.* Trans. Cosmos Damian Bacich and Rosella Pescatori. Toronto: University of Toronto Press, 2009.

Equicola, Mario. *De mulieribus.* Mantua: [publisher not specified], 1501.

- *Libro de natura de amore.* Venice: Lorenzo Lorio da Portes, 1525.

La festa et storia di Sancta Caterina: A Medieval Italian Religious Drama. Ed. and trans. Anne Wilson Tordi. New York: Peter Lang, 1997.

Firenzuola, Agnolo. *On the Beauty of Women.* Trans. Konrad Eisenbichler and Jacqueline Murray. Philadelphia: University of Pennsylvania Press, 1992.

Florio, John. *A Worlde of Wordes.* Critical ed. with intro. by Hermann W. Haller. Toronto: University of Toronto Press, 2013.

Franco, Nicolò. *La Philena: Historia amorosa ultimamente composta.* Mantua: Ruffinelli, 1547.

Fulgentius. *Fulgentius the Mythographer.* Trans. Leslie George Whitbread. Columbus: Ohio State University Press, 1971.

Gottifredi, Bartolomeo. *Lo specchio d'amore, dialogo nel quale alle giovani s'insegna innamorarsi.* Florence: Doni, 1547.

Homer. *The Odyssey.* Trans. Emily Wilson. New York: W.W. Norton and Co., 2018.

Landino, Cristoforo. *Scritti critici e teorici.* Ed. Roberto Cardini. 2 vols. Rome: Bulzoni, 1974.

Palmieri, Matteo. *Vita civile e De optimo cive di Bartolomeo Sacchi detto Il Platina.* Ed. Felice Battaglia. Bologna: Zanichelli, 1944.

Piccolomini, Enea Silvio [Pius II]. *Commentaries.* Ed. Margaret Meserve and Marcello Simonetta. The I Tatti Renaissance Library. 3 vols. Cambridge, MA: Harvard University Press, 2003–18.

- *Europe (c. 1400–1458).* Trans. Robert Brown. Intro. Nancy Bisaha. Washington, DC: Catholic University of America Press, 2013.

– "Historia de duobus amantibus." In *Novelle del Quattrocento*, ed. Gioachino
  Chiarini, 131–237. Milan: Garzanti, 1982.
– *Tale of Two Lovers*. Trans. Flora Grierson. London: Constable and Co., 1929.
  (Also at: http://www.forumromanum.org/literature/piccolomini/hist_e.html.)
Renaissance Comedy: The Italian Masters. Vol. 1. Ed. and intro. Donald Beecher.
  Toronto: University of Toronto Press, 2008.
Rodríguez de Montalvo, Garci. *Amadis de Gaule*. Trans. Anthony Munday. Ed.
  Helen Moore. Aldershot: Ashgate, 2004.
Romeo and Juliet before Shakespeare: Four Early Stories of Star-Crossed Love by
  Masuccio Salernitano, Luigi da Porto, Matteo Bandello, and Pierre Boaistuau.
  Trans. with an intro. and notes by Nicole Prunster. Toronto: Centre for
  Reformation and Renaissance Studies, 2000.
Sannazaro, Jacopo. *Arcadia and Piscatorial Eclogues*. Trans. Ralph Nash. Detroit:
  Wayne State University Press, 1966.
Shakespeare, William. *The Norton Shakespeare*. Gen. ed. Stephen J. Greenblatt.
  New York: Norton, 1997.
Sverzellati, Paola. "Per la biografia di Nicodemo Tranchedini da Pontremoli,
  ambasciatore sforzesco." *Aevum* 72.2 (1998): 485–557.
*Three Spanish "Querelle" Texts: "Grisel and Mirabella," "The Slander against
  Women," and "The Defense of Ladies against Slanderers" by Pere Torrellas and
  Juan De Flores*. Ed. and trans. Emily C. Francomano. Toronto: Iter and Centre
  for Reformation and Renaissance Studies, 2013.
Valerius Maximus. *Memorable Deeds and Sayings: One Thousand Tales from
  Ancient Rome*. Trans. Henry John Walker. Indianapolis: Hackett Publishers, 2004.
Virgil. *The Aeneid*. Trans. Robert Fitzgerald. New York: Vintage Books, 1984
  [1981].
Vives, Juan Luis. *The Education of a Christian Woman: A Sixteenth-Century
  Manual*. Ed. and trans. Charles Fantazzi. Chicago: University of Chicago
  Press, 2000.

Secondary Sources

Ajmar, Marta. "Exemplary Women in Renaissance Italy: Ambivalent Models of
  Behaviour?" In *Women in Italian Renaissance Culture and Society*, ed. Letizia
  Panizza, 244–64. Oxford: Legenda European Humanities Research Centre,
  University of Oxford, 2000.
Akbari, Suzanne Conklin. *Seeing through the Veil: Optical Theory and Medieval
  Allegory*. Toronto: University of Toronto Press, 2004.
Albertazzi, Adolfo. *Romanzieri e romanzi del Cinquecento e del Seicento*.
  Bologna: Nicola Zanichelli, 1891.
L'arme e gli amori: Ariosto, Tasso and Guarini in Late Renaissance Florence. Acts
  of an International Conference, Florence, Villa I Tatti, 27–9 June 2001. Ed.

Massimiliano Rossi and Fiorella Gioffredi Superbi. 2 vols. Florence: Olschki, 2004.

Baron, Hans. *In Search of Florentine Civic Humanism: Essays on the Transition from Medieval to Modern Thought*. Vol. 1. Princeton: Princeton University Press, 1988.

Bearden, Elizabeth B. *Ekphrasis of the Self*. Toronto: University of Toronto Press, 2011.

Beer, Marina. *Romanzi di cavalleria: Il "Furioso" e il romanzo italiano del primo Cinquecento*. Rome: Bulzoni, 1987.

Bell, Rudolph M. *How to Do It: Guides to Good Living for Renaissance Italians*. Chicago: University of Chicago Press, 1999.

Benedetti, Andrea. "Dame pordenonesi del Rinascimento in un passo del romanzo *Il Peregrino* di Giacomo Caviceo." *Il Noncello* 7 (1956): 23–38.

Bernardo, Aldo S. *Petrarch, Scipio and the "Africa": The Birth of Humanism's Dream*. Westport, CT: Greenwood Press, 1962.

Bertoni, Giulio. *L'"Orlando furioso" e la Rinascenza a Ferrara*. Modena: Umberto Orlandini, 1919.

Bicheno, Hugh. *Vendetta: High Art and Low Cunning at the Birth of the Renaissance*. London: Weidenfeld and Nicolson, 2008.

Binotti, Lucia. "Humanistic Audiences: *Novela Sentimental* and *Libros de Caballerías* in Cinquecento Italy." *La coronica* 39.1 (2010): 67–113.

Bisaha, Nancy. *Creating East and West: Renaissance Humanists and the Ottoman Turks*. Philadelphia: University of Pennsylvania Press, 2004.

Boccaccio: A Critical Guide to the Complete Works. Ed. Victoria Kirkham, Michael Sherberg, and Janet Levarie Smarr. Chicago: University of Chicago Press, 2013.

Bognolo, Anna. *La finzione rinnovata: Meraviglioso, corte e avventura nel romanzo cavalleresco del primo Cinquecento spagnolo*. Biblioteca di Studi Ispanici, I. Pisa: ETS, 1997.

Bongrani, Paolo. "Restauri quattrocenteschi." In *Le tradizioni del testo: Studi di letteratura italiana offerti a Domenico de Robertis*, ed. Franco Gavazzeni and Guglielmo Gorni, 133–46. Milan: Riccardo Ricciardi, 1993.

Brooks, Peter. *Reading for the Plot: Design and Intention in Narrative*. Cambridge, MA: Harvard University Press, 1992 [1984].

Brown, Peter, ed. *Reading Dreams: The Interpretation of Dreams from Chaucer to Shakespeare*. Intro. A.C. Spearing. Oxford: Oxford University Press, 1999.

Bruscagli, Riccardo. *Studi cavallereschi*. Florence: Società Editrice Fiorentina, 2003.

Burgio, Anna Ceruti. "Strutture narrative e modelli culturali del *Peregrino* di Iacopo Caviceo." *Aurea Parma: Rivista di Storia, Letteratura e Arte* 62 (1978): 42–54.

– *Studi sul Quattrocento parmense*. Pisa: Giardini, 1988.

Callari, Luigi. "Un dialogo inedito di Iacopo Caviceo." *Archivio storico per le provincie parmensi* 3 (1894): 1–2.

The Cambridge Companion to Allegory. Ed. Rita Copeland and Peter T. Struck. Cambridge: Cambridge University Press, 2010.

The Cambridge Companion to Medieval Romance. Ed. Roberta L. Krueger. Cambridge: Cambridge University Press, 2000.

The Cambridge Companion to the Italian Novel. Ed. Peter Bondanella and Andrea Ciccarelli. Cambridge: Cambridge University Press, 2003.

The Cambridge History of Italian Literature. Ed. Peter Brand and Lino Pertile. Cambridge: Cambridge University Press, 1996.

Cappello, Sergio. "Astuzia e inganno nel *Peregrino* di Jacopo Caviceo." In *Les pas d'Orphée: Scritti in onore di Mario Richter*, ed. Maria Emanuele Raffi, 29–42. Padua: Unipress, 2005.

Carrot-Maciejewski, Élisabeth. "Métaphores animales dans le *Peregrino* de Jacopo Caviceo (1508)." *Italies* 12 (2008): 261–84.

Catani, Magda Campanini. "Les *Angoysses douloureuses* di Hélisenne de Crenne e il *Libro del Peregrino* di Jacopo Caviceo: Due romanzi a confronto." In *Il romanzo nella Francia del Rinascimento dall'eredità medievale all'Astrea*, 165–78. Fasano: Schena, 1996.

Cavallo, Jo Ann. *The Romance Epics of Boiardo, Ariosto, and Tasso: From Public Duty to Private Pleasure.* Toronto: University of Toronto Press, 2004.

– *The World beyond Europe in the Romance Epics of Boiardo and Ariosto.* Toronto: University of Toronto Press, 2013.

Ciavolella, Massimo. *La "Malatia d'amore" dall'Antichità al Medioevo.* Rome: Bulzoni, 1976.

Copeland, Rita. *Rhetoric, Hermeneutics, and Translation in the Middle Ages: Academic Tradition and Vernacular Texts.* Cambridge: Cambridge University Press, 1991.

A Corresponding Renaissance: Letters Written by Italian Women, 1375–1650. Trans., ed., and intro. Lisa Kaborycha. Oxford: Oxford University Press, 2016.

Coudert, Allison P. "Sewers, Cesspools, and Privies: Waste as Reality and Metaphor in Pre-modern European Cities." In *Urban Space in the Middle Ages and the Early Modern Age*, ed. Albrecht Classen, 713–33. Berlin and New York: De Gruyter, 2009.

Daniels, Rhiannon. *Boccaccio and the Book: Production and Reading in Italy, 1340–1520.* London: Modern Humanities Research Association and Maney, 2009.

Davies, Jonathan. "Violence and Italian Universities during the Renaissance." *Renaissance Studies* 27.4 (2013): 504–16.

DeJongh, W.F.J. "A Borrowing from Caviceo for the Legend of Romeo and Juliet." *Shakespeare Association Bulletin* 16 (1941): 118–19.

Doody, Margaret Anne. *The True Story of the Novel*. New Brunswick: Rutgers University Press, 1997.

Early Modern Prose Fiction: The Cultural Politics of Reading. Ed. Naomi Conn Liebler. New York and London: Routledge, 2007.

Emmerich, Karen. *Literary Translation and the Making of Originals*. New York: Bloomsbury Academic, 2017.

Everson, Jane E. *The Italian Romance Epic in the Age of Humanism: The Matter of Italy and the World of Rome*. Oxford: Oxford University Press, 2001.

Fahy, Conor. "Three Early Renaissance Treatises on Women." *Italian Studies* 11 (1956): 30–55.

Fermi, Valerio. "Galeotto: A Prologue by Way of the Proem." In *Women, Enjoyment, and the Defense of Virtue in Boccaccio's "Decameron,"* 13–26. New York: Palgrave Macmillan, 2015.

Ferrari, Silvio, "La traduzione francese del *Peregrino*: Echi della cultura ferrarese nella Francia del Cinquecento." In *Alla corte degli Estensi: Filosofia, arte e cultura a Ferrara nei secoli XV e XVI*, ed. Marco Bertozzi, 345–53. Ferrara: Università degli studi, 1994.

Flamini, Francesco. *Il Cinquecento*. Milan: Francesco Vallardi, 1897.

Fletcher, Angus. *Allegory: The Theory of a Symbolic Mode*. Ithaca: Cornell University Press, 1964.

Foley Di Silvio, Patricia. *Orthographic Reform and the Questione della lingua in the Sixteenth Century*. Chapel Hill: University of North Carolina Press, 1979.

Fragnito, Gigliola. *Church, Censorship, and Culture in Early Modern Italy*. Cambridge: Cambridge University Press, 2001.

Francomano, Emily C. *The Prison of Love: Romance, Translation, and the Book in the Sixteenth Century*. Toronto: University of Toronto Press, 2017.

Garrido Ardila, J.A. "Origins and Definitions of the Picaresque Genre." In *The Picaresque Novel in Western Literature*, ed. J.A. Garrido Ardila, 1–23. Cambridge: Cambridge University Press, 2015.

Gaio, Raffaella. "Sur la voie du roman: Le *Libro del Peregrino* de Iacopo Caviceo (1508)." In *Formes et imaginaire du roman: Perspectives sur le roman antique, médiéval, classique, moderne et contemporain*, ed. Jean Bessière and Daniel-Henri Pageaux, 37–48. Paris: Champion, 1998.

Gertsman, Elina. *Worlds Within: Opening the Medieval Shrine Madonna*. University Park: Pennsylvania State University Press, 2015.

Ginsberg, Warren. *Chaucer's Italian Tradition*. Ann Arbor: University of Michigan Press, 2002.

Gómez Redondo, Fernando. "De Boccaccio a Caviceo: La conexión italiana de la ficción sentimental." *Cuadernos de filología italiana*. Special issue (2010): 109–28.

González Rovira, Javier. "El *Libro del peregrino* de Giacomo Caviceo y la traducción de Hernando Díaz." *Studi Ispanici* (1994–6), 51–60.

Greiner, Frank. "Le *Libro del Peregrino* de J. Caviceo et sa fortune française." In *Rapporti e scambi tra umanesimo italiano e umanesimo europeo*, ed. Luisa Rotondi Secchi Tarugi, 203–22. Milan: Nuovi Orizzonti, 2001.

Grieve, Patricia E. *"Floire and Blancheflor" and the European Romance.* Cambridge: Cambridge University Press, 1997.

Griffin, Clive. "Giacomo Caviceo's *Libro del Peregrino*: The Fate of an Italian Wanderer in Spain." In *Book Production and Letters in the Western European Renaissance: Essays in Honor of Conor Fahy*, ed. Anna Laura Lepschy, John Took, and Dennis E. Rhodes, 132–46. London: Modern Humanities Research Association, 1986.

Hieatt, Constance B. *The Realism of Dream Visions: The Poetic Exploitation of the Dream Experience in Chaucer and His Contemporaries.* Paris: Mouton, 1967.

Hollander, Robert. *Boccaccio's Two Venuses.* New York: Columbia University Press, 1977.

Honig, Edwin. *Dark Conceit: The Making of Allegory.* New York: Oxford University Press, 1966.

Italian Storytellers: Essays on Italian Narrative Literature. Ed. Eric Haywood and Cormac Ó Cuilleanáin. Dublin: Irish Academic Press, 1989.

Kelso, Ruth. *Doctrine for the Lady of the Renaissance.* Urbana: University of Illinois Press, 1956.

Kemp, William. "A Complex Case of Privilege Infringement in France: The History of the Early Editions of Caviceo's *Peregrin*, 1527–1529." *Bulletin du bibliophile* 1 (1992): 41–62.

Kirkham, Victoria. *Fabulous Vernaculars: Boccaccio's "Filocolo" and the Art of Medieval Fiction.* Ann Arbor: University of Michigan Press, 2001.

Knapp, James F., and Peggy A. Knapp. *Medieval Romance: The Aesthetics of Possibility.* Toronto: University of Toronto Press, 2017.

Kolsky, Stephen. *Courts and Courtiers in Renaissance Northern Italy.* Aldershot: Ashgate, 2003.

– "Lelio Manfredi traduttore cortigiano: Intorno al *Carcer d'Amore* e al *Tirante il Bianco*." *Civiltà Mantovana* 10 (1994): 45–69.

Lewis, C.S. *The Allegory of Love: A Study in Medieval Tradition.* New York: Oxford University Press, 1961 [1936].

Looney, Dennis. *Compromising the Classics: Romance Epic Narrative in the Italian Renaissance.* Detroit: Wayne State University Press, 1996.

Luzio, Alessandro, and Rodolfo Renier. *La coltura e le relazioni letterararie di Isabella d'Este Gonzaga.* Ed. Simone Albonico, intro. Giovanni Agosti. Milan: Sylvestre Bonnard, 2005.

Machosky, Brenda. *Structures of Appearing: Allegory and the Work of Literature.* New York: Fordham University Press, 2013.

Mancini, Albert N. "The Forms of Long Prose Fiction in Late Medieval and Early Modern Italian Literature." In *The Cambridge Companion to the*

Italian Novel, ed. Peter Bondanella and Andrea Ciccarelli, 20–41. Cambridge: Cambridge University Press, 2003.

Mazzoni, Guido. *Theory of the Novel*. Trans. Zakiya Hanafi. Cambridge, MA: Harvard University Press, 2017.

Medieval Cautionary Tales. Trans. Peter Speed. New York: Italica Press, 2003.

Michaud, Monique. *Roméo et Juliette: Intertextualités*. Poitiers: Maison des sciences de l'homme et de la société, 1999.

Moretti, Franco, ed. *Il romanzo*. 5 vols. Turin: Einaudi, 2001–3.

Niccoli, Ottavia. "Rituals of Youth: Love, Play, and Violence in Tridentine Bologna." In *The Premodern Teenager: Youth in Society, 1150–1650*, ed. Konrad Eisenbichler, 75–94. Toronto: Centre for Reformation and Renaissance Studies, 2002.

Nissen, Christopher. *Kissing the Wild Woman: Concepts of Art, Beauty, and the Italian Prose Romance in Giulia Bigolina's "Urania."* Toronto: University of Toronto Press, 2011.

Orth, Myra D. "'The Prison of Love': A Medieval Romance in the French Renaissance and Its Illustration (B.N. MS fr 2150)." *Journal of the Warburg and Courtauld Institutes* 46 (1983): 211–21.

Orvieto, Paolo. "Boccaccio mediatore di generi o dell'allegoria d'amore." *Interpres* 2 (1979): 7–104.

Osborn, Peggy. *G.B. Giraldi's "Altile": The Birth of a New Dramatic Genre in Renaissance Ferrara*. Lewiston/Queenston/Lampeter: Edwin Mellen Press, 1992.

Outi, Merisalo. "Translating the Classics into the Vernacular in Sixteenth-Century Italy." *Renaissance Studies* 29.1 (2015): 55–77.

Panizza, Letizia. *Women in Italian Renaissance Culture and Society*. London: Routledge, 2000.

Parker, Patricia A. *Inescapable Romance: Studies in the Poetics of a Mode*. Princeton: Princeton University Press, 1979.

Pavel, Thomas G. *The Lives of the Novel: A History*. Princeton: Princeton University Press, 2003.

Perry, B.E. *The Ancient Romances*. Berkeley: University of California Press, 1967.

Phaethon's Children: The Este Court and Its Culture in Early Modern Ferrara. Ed. Dennis Looney and Deanna Shemek. Tempe: Arizona Center for Medieval and Renaissance Studies, 2005.

The Premodern Teenager: Youth in Society, 1150–1650. Ed. Konrad Eisenbichler. Toronto: Centre for Reformation and Renaissance Studies, 2002.

Psaki, F. Regina. "Chivalry and Medieval Italian Romance." In *The Cambridge Companion to Medieval Romance*, ed. Roberta L. Krueger, 203–17. Cambridge: Cambridge University Press, 2000.

Quilligan, Maureen. *The Language of Allegory: Defining the Genre*. Ithaca: Cornell University Press, 1979.

Raffa, Guy P. *Dante's Bones: How a Poet Invented Italy*. Cambridge: The Belknap Press of Harvard University Press, 2020.

Reconsidering Boccaccio: Medieval Contexts and Global Intertexts. Ed. Olivia Holmes and Dana E. Stewart. Toronto: University of Toronto Press, 2018.

Reeser, Todd. W. "Approaching Affective Masculinities." In *The Routledge International Handbook of Masculinity Studies*, ed. Lucas Gottzén, Ulf Mellström, and Tamara Shefer, 103–11. London and New York: Routledge, 2020.

Richardson, Brian. *Print Culture in Renaissance Italy: The Editor and the Vernacular Text, 1470–1600*. Cambridge: Cambridge University Press, 1994.

Romance and History: Imagining Time from the Medieval to the Early Modern Period. Ed. Jon Whitman. Cambridge: Cambridge University Press, 2015.

Romano, Dennis. *Housecraft and Statecraft: Domestic Service in Renaissance Venice, 1400–1600*. Baltimore: Johns Hopkins University Press, 1996.

Rothstein, Marian. "Teen Knights: Interpreting Precocity in Early Modern Life-Stories." In *The Premodern Teenager: Youth in Society, 1150–1650*, ed. Konrad Eisenbichler, 173–88. Toronto: Centre for Reformation and Renaissance Studies, 2002.

Rotunda, D.P. *Motif-Index of the Italian Novella in Prose*. Bloomington: Indiana University Press, 1942.

Roush, Sherry. "Dante Ravennate and Boccaccio Ferrarese? Post-Mortem Residency and the Attack on Florentine Literary Hegemony, 1480–1520." *Viator* 35 (2004): 543–62.

– "Jacopo Caviceo." *The Literary Encyclopedia*. http://www.litencycl.com.

– *Speaking Spirits: Ventriloquizing the Dead in Renaissance Italy*. Toronto: University of Toronto Press, 2015.

– "When a Pilgrim Is Not a Pilgrim: Subversions of Allegory and Allegoresis in Jacopo Caviceo's *Peregrino* (1508)." *Italian Quarterly* 51 (2014, copyright 2018): 36–55.

Sacchetti, Maria Alberta. *Cervantes' "Los Trabajos de Persilles y Sigismunda": A Study of Genre*. London: Tamesis, 2001.

Scolari, A. "Un romanzo veronese dedicato ad Isabella d'Este." *Giornale storico della letteratura italiana* 84 (1924): 75–83.

Sebregondi, Ludovica. "Clothes and Teenagers: What Young Men Wore in Fifteenth-Century Florence." In *The Premodern Teenager: Youth in Society, 1150–1650*, ed. Konrad Eisenbichler, 27–50. Toronto: Centre for Reformation and Renaissance Studies, 2002.

Shemek, Deanna. *Ladies Errant: Wayward Women and Social Order in Early Modern Italy*. Durham, NC: Duke University Press, 1998.

Simona, Lorenza. "Caviceo (Cavizzi), Iacopo." *Dizionario biografico degli Italiani* 23 (1979). http://www.treccani.it/enciclopedia/iacopo-caviceo_(Dizionario -Biografico).

– *Giacomo Caviceo: Uomo di chiesa, d'armi e di lettere*. Bern: Herbert Lang, 1974.

Stanivukovic, Goran. *Knight in Arms*. Toronto: University of Toronto Press, 2016.

Sullivan, Karen. *The Danger of Romance: Truth, Fantasy, and Arthurian Fiction*. Chicago: University of Chicago Press, 2018.

Tartaro, Achille. "La prosa narrativa antica." In *La narrativa italiana dalle Origini ai giorni nostri*, ed. Alberto Asor Rosa, 43–140. Turin: Einaudi, 1997.

Tentolini, Renzo. "Un 'best-seller' del Cinquecento: *Il Libro del Peregrino* di Iacopo Caviceo da Parma." *Parma per l'arte* 11 (1961): 3–9.

Thompson, S. *Motif-Index of Folk Literature*. 6 vols. Bloomington: Indiana University Press, 1957.

Tissoni Benvenuti, Antonia. "Libri e letterati nelle piccole corti padane del Rinascimento: La corte di Pietro Maria Rossi." In *Le signorie dei Rossi di Parma tra XIV e XVI secolo*, ed. Letizia Arcangeli and Marco Gentile, 213–30. Florence: Firenze University Press, 2007.

Turchi, Marcello. "Composizione e situazione del romanzo umanistico di Iacopo Caviceo." *Aurea Parma: Rivista di Storia, Letteratura e Arte* 46 (1962): 9–19.

– "Iacopo Caviceo o del compromesso tra avventura e retorica." *Aurea Parma: Rivista di Storia, Letteratura e Arte* 44 (1960): 145–56.

Tuve, Rosemond. *Allegorical Imagery: Some Mediaval Books and Their Renaissance Posterity*. Princeton: Princeton University Press, 1966.

Valla, Elena Ceva. "Libro del Peregrino." In *Il dizionario Bompiani delle opere e dei personaggi di tutti i tempi e di tutte le letterature*, vol. 6, 394. Milan: Bompiani, 1983– .

Vecce, Carlo. "La crisi dell'Autore nel Rinascimento." *California Italian Studies* 1.2 (2010): 1–17.

Venier, Matteo. "Caviceo, Iacopo." In *Dizionario biografico dei Friulani*. http://www.dizionariobiograficodeifriulani.it/caviceo-cavizzi-iacopo/ [accessed 2 September 2020].

Vignali, Luigi. *Il Peregrino di Jacopo Caviceo e il lessico del Quattrocento*. Milan: Unicopli, 2001.

Vinaver, Eugene. *The Rise of Romance*. New York: Oxford University Press, 1971.

Weaver, Elissa. "Dietro il vestito: La semiotica del vestire nel *Decameron*." *La novella italiana: Atti del conveegno di Caprarola 19–24 settembre 1988*, 701–10. Rome: Salerno Editrice, 1989.

Williams, Allyson Burgess. "Rewriting Lucrezia Borgia: Propriety, Magnificence, and Piety in Portraits of a Renaissance Duchess." In *Wives, Widows, Mistresses, and Nuns in Early Modern Italy: Making the Invisible Visible through Art and Patronage*, ed. Katherine A. McIver, 77–97. Farnham, Surrey: Ashgate, 2012.

Williamson, Edwin. *The Half-Way House of Fiction: "Don Quixote" and Arthurian Romance*. Oxford: Oxford University Press, 1984.

Wood, Diana Sylvia. *Literary Devices and Rhetorical Techniques in the Works of Hélisenne de Crenne*. Madison: University of Wisconsin Press, 1975 [1946].

Woods, Marjorie Curry. *Weeping for Dido: The Classics in the Medieval Classroom*. Princeton: Princeton University Press, 2019.

Zumthor, Paul. *Towards a Medieval Poetics*. Trans. Philip Bennett. Minneapolis: University of Minnesota Press, 1992 [*Essai de poétique médiévale*. Paris: Editions du Seuil, 1972].

Jacopo Caviceo's *Peregrino*

Proem and Dedication

Jacopo Caviceo introduces his work, mentioning himself by name and presenting his character as sleepy and scared by the sight of a ghost. Giovanni Boccaccio's spirit introduces itself and praises Lucrezia Borgia, the work's dedicatee. After the ghost compliments the ruling family of Ferrara and some of the most esteemed ladies of Italy at the turn of the sixteenth century, Caviceo remembers an earlier dream that he had when he first arrived in Ferrara. In that dream, another ghost – of his fictitious protagonist Peregrino – appeared to him and promised to tell his story, which will unfold over the course of three nights, corresponding to the work's three books.

Book of mine, if ever you should be scorned or rejected, you could say: 'Reader, not the destruction of Troy, the fortunes of Rome, or the wanderings of Ulysses do I seek to tell, but rather a story of chaste love.[1] Thus, I proceed confidently because love and pity escort me.' And if you are asked about the writer, you can say: 'Jacopo Caviceo of Parma, faithful reciter, lives and sends his regards. He wrote what he understood.'

Proem of the *Peregrino* by Jacopo Caviceo of Parma to the Illustrious Lucrezia Borgia, Duchess of Ferrara.

The restless swallow Procne heralded with her chittering song the arrival of Tithonus's beloved Dawn. I was still captive of sweet drowsiness when I seemed to see a shade whom the Elysian Fields honoured. Scared and trembling like a man who suffers cold while feverish, I wanted to scream,

---

1   This sentence echoes Giovanni Boccaccio's own words in the *Filocolo* (I.2) and in the Prologue of *The Elegy of Lady Fiammetta*.

but from my wretched lips there issued merely a mumble. The pain in my suffering heart grew inversely to the same degree that my cry became faint. Ever so quietly I mouthed: "O blessed shade that did not disdain my crumbling abode, tell me please what you are, so that oppressed by fear I am not compelled to give up my spirit."

It spoke: "Living I possessed the body of Giovanni Boccaccio of Certaldo. Now I am made a citizen and resident of the wise city of Ferrara, where I contemplate an extraordinary beauty who sees, delights in, and discourses on everything. If I were to tell you all about her in detail, a full year would not suffice. She is wise, intelligent, decorous, and beautiful, born to people more than patrician and near to regal in degree. She comes from a glorious country, nurtured on the joys of literature and fine customs, and a family line that regularly produces Roman pontiffs, dukes, barons, and nobles, and soldiers who would not yield to Mars on the battlefield, nor to Caesar in fortune, nor to Pompey in glory. What aid this singular Phoenix could give to your declining muse if you found yourself under her happy patronage! It could not be greater considering her sacred marriage to Alfonso d'Este, unparalleled duke, son of that Ercole who excelled even the other three Hercules.[2] And still more grace accrues to them by the continual company of Cardinal Ippolito d'Este, the most refined censor of orthodoxy in the church militant."

So, Lucrezia, between your husband and brother-in-law, you can consider yourself blessed in every way. Adding to your excellence is the light that cannot be extinguished of the true mortal goddess Isabella d'Este Gonzaga, Mantuan princess, whom the Muses revere.[3] With her

---

2   Alfonso I d'Este (1476–1534), Duke of Ferrara, was the son of Ercole I d'Este (1431–1505) and Eleonora of Aragon (1450–1493). His first wife, Anna Sforza, died in 1497; Lucrezia Borgia was his second wife, and their wedding was celebrated in 1502. Together Alfonso and Lucrezia had four children who survived to adulthood (Ercole II, Ippolito II, Leonora, and Francesco); Lucrezia died from complications ten days after another birth (that of Isabella Maria d'Este, who died the same day she was born in 1519). Ercole is the Italian form of Hercules (Heracles). Cardinal Ippolito d'Este (1479–1520) was the younger brother of Alfonso, and thus Lucrezia's brother-in-law.

3   Isabella d'Este (1474–1539), sister of Alfonso I d'Este, married Francesco II Gonzaga Marquess of Mantua by proxy in 1490. She was the mother of eight children, a prolific letter writer, celebrated patron of the arts, and head of the state of Mantua in her widowhood. Among those honouring Isabella were the artists Leonardo da Vinci, Andrea Mantegna, Perugino, Raphael, Lorenzo Costa, Dosso Dossi, and Giulio Romano; authors Ludovico Ariosto, Baldassare Castiglione, Mario Equicola, and Pietro Aretino; musicians Bartolomeo Tromboncino and Marco Cara; and many others. An outstanding online resource directed by Deanna Shemek on Isabella is available at: http:// isabelladestearchive.org.

go Taurella of the Trivulzio family line of Milan, Greece, and Latium; Violante di Pii da Carpe, splendour of good letters and saintly religion; Bianca Rossa of the Riario line; and the poetess Cassandra, who honours Venice, as well as Padua.[4] Let all the rest of Italy fall silent now because nobody can surpass or equal you, Lucrezia. Among us you will be a perpetual Phoenix.

To render you, praiseworthy spirit, some token of my thanks, I say that Phoebus was passing by the horns of Taurus to increase the light of Venus's month, when I was summoned by Filasio Rovorella, most generous pre-eminent man of Ravenna, to undertake spiritual matters in the noble city of Ferrara.[5] On the day I arrived there, the first night, in that hour when Mercury usually circles man's head with rosy oblivion, I heard a cry: "Mercy, by God, that dead or alive I'm still dead! O exalted God, come to my aid! I suffer great pain that heaven, free will, or human ability cannot extinguish. O too blind world, O transient form of ours, where have you led me that I can no longer breathe?"

Shade of mine! I sense the light of Tithonus's beloved touch the first horizon of the ocean, so pay attention, and you will hear the whole story from me.

---

4   Taurella is Damigella Torella Trivulzio (d. 1527), Countess of Montechiarugolo, a noblewoman in the Estense court who read Latin and Greek; she will also be mentioned in the fourth octave of the final canto of Ariosto's *Orlando furioso* in its definitive 1532 edition. Violante di Pii da Carpe is identified by Luigi Vignali in the Introduction to his edition as Iolanda dei Pio da Carpi. Bianca Rossa Riario (d. 1522), the eldest child of Caterina Sforza with her first husband Girolamo Riario, was Marchioness of San Secondo by marriage to Triolo I de' Rossi and regent of the marquisate when her husband died in 1521; she is the mother of Pier Maria III de' Rossi (d. 1547), not his wife, as Enrico Carrara indicated in *Opere*, 405. Venetian Cassandra Fedele (d. 1558) was one of the most celebrated female scholars of her day, particularly in oratory; Politian is among those who, in a letter to Lorenzo de' Medici (known as The Magnificent), praised her for her poems in Latin and Italian, although only some of her letters and three orations have passed down to us.

5   Filasio Roverella (Sismondo Filiasus Roverella, d. 1521) was archbishop of Ravenna during the period that Caviceo served as vicar general for the same city, though residing in Ferrara, 1494–1500.

Peregrino Book 1

Book 1. Chapter 1.

Peregrino's spirit begins to recount his story to Caviceo in the hopes that his listener will avoid the snares of Love or have sympathy for those who, like him, could not. At twenty-two, Peregrino believes that Love can have no dominion over him, but he finds himself conquered upon seeing Genevera in the Franciscan church of Ferrara. Peregrino describes her and reads an ominous message from an open book.

This much is certain: no assistance or advice from you can lessen in any way the pain I endure. Nonetheless, to satisfy your very understandable desire, I will not hide anything from you. Envious Fortune, thankless luck, and love of a woman have brought me to this point. I am called Peregrino. My ancestral homeland was Modena; now I reside in Ferrara. Just as the memory of pleasant times lends consoling delight to the soul, so the repetition of sad ones afflicts and consumes the spirit. Although I believe the intensity of my memories will cause me to relapse into grief, I am resolved to bear every pain in order to please you.

What a joyous beginning now turns out to be an inauspicious day! Woe is me! Silence is burdensome, but to speak is to suffer. Love, my Lord, if you lack power over the substances, which have been separated from the body, please lend me some recourse. Once I was blessed, and most blessed I would be if – after the trials I endured – you had washed me in Lethe's sacred waters, which take away life's memories. But since immutable heaven has willed otherwise, I shall hold my peace forevermore.

I am moved and won over by your persuasive entreaties to tell you all that happened to me, so that you'll know from my example how to guard yourself from similar passions, or at least to have compassion for those who struggle and suffer in life and in death because they love too much.

At twenty-two years old I was convinced I had complete command over myself, and nothing was so strong or trying in all the world that I couldn't overcome or slip free of it according to time, place, or necessity. Confident in the strength of my determination, I paid no heed to Venus or Apollo, believing the heavens held no power to bind me. I even wanted to test myself a bit to probe what might defend against Love. I believed I could not only overcome Love's power but confound and dissipate it, too. Love was offended by my lack of respect, though, and like a subtle and ingenious hunter, he spread at my feet a net far cleverer even than the one made by Jove's craftsman, Vulcan. When Love saw that I left my sails so loose in impetuous winds, he seized and bound me, keeping me his captive and slave unto dust, as you shall hear.

On the first of May, the day dedicated to lovers, I entered the Franciscan church without the least suspicion. The great preacher Dominico Ponzon was imparting the Gospel lesson. Because it was the feast day of the apostles Philip and James, the material was as delightful as it was arduous, and when he proved to the congregation that Father and Son was a single essence and omnipotent, even the great Plato or Theophrastus would have yielded the floor.[1] I had been entirely absorbed by that lesson when Love's messenger made me aware of a secluded nook where a lady sat to hear the divine word. From that moment, she would be the Empress who ruled over me. Love lay in her lap, girded with those weapons he used against tragic Phyllis. I stared, trying to understand who listened to the divine sweetness with such rapt attention, modesty, and nobility. She turned, perhaps to glance elsewhere, and caught my gaze. From her eyes flashed a splendour, which transfixed my heart quicker than Jove's lightning bolt struck Phaeton. I received a lethal shot. Without a further thought, I stashed Love's arrow deep in my soul, assuming I could withdraw it whenever I wished.

Bewitched by her sweet glance, I began to admire each quality of that lady who was extraordinary in her actions, grace, appearance, and liveliness. She was fifteen years old, proud yet of humble mien, with elegant and refined gestures, and a knowing glance from lucid, wise, moist, and calm eyes. She appeared tentatively inclined to pleasure, with a wide and pleasing brow adorning her forehead, a clear and subtle complexion, and admirable proportions. I recognized that this lady was formed in such a way that she could depose the heavens and raise the earth, cast a shadow on

---

1   Fra Domenico da Ponzone (d. 1499), who is compared here to the greatest of pagan orators, was an itinerant Franciscan priest noted for preaching against the Dominican Girolamo Savonarola during Lent in Florence in 1492. For another literary allusion to this particular feast day of the apostles Philip and James, please see William Shakespeare's *Measure for Measure* 3.2.205.

the sun, give light to the Underworld, dry up fountains, rivers, and the sea, raze the mountains, sublimate the damned, and cast down the blessed.[2] In that instant, an invisible and unknown force was at work in me. I was separated from myself, and her image was transferred deep within my bodily organs not unlike how an infant will display some birthmark as a sign of the mother's craving for a glass of wine while pregnant.[3]

I suspected some occult enchantment. My heart fluttered timidly and happily, first cold then hot. Many contrasting sensations followed, depending on the lady's glances, charitable one moment, and less hospitable the next. I was conquered, chained, and enslaved. I seemed to resemble miserable, lacerated Acteon, and I pitied and upbraided myself, saying: 'O Peregrino, see how low Love has brought you! Where's that mind of yours so determined to resist temptations? Where's the promptness of your free will? Where's that strength you believed would conquer the gods? If you are captured by a single glance, which you're not even sure was intended for you, what would you do if you felt Love's full effect? It is preferable to turn away from harmful and shameful things when you're in the first throes and repent, rather than persist, then still need to repent! While you yet have your wits, change your ways and seek pardon for this plague-like death.'

Instead, I drew much closer to my fire, and I saw between her and the Lord Love a little book open to a page that read: "O mortals, I call all of you, but save only a few."[4] O cruel passage, O damning text, O ill-omened

---

2   This description is an extended version of others of romance heroines. Cf., for example, the qualities of Lucretia in Aeneas Silvius Piccolomini's *Tale of Two Lovers*, which I cite from the 1929 English translation by Flora Grierson, available online at http://www.forumromanum.org/literature/piccolomini/hist_e.html: "The lady was taller than the others. Her hair was long, the colour of beaten gold … Her lofty forehead, of good proportions, was without a wrinkle, and her arched eyebrows were dark and slender, with a due space between. Such was the splendour of her eyes that, like the sun, they dazzled all who looked on them; with such eyes she could kill whom she chose and, when she would, restore the dead to life. Her nose was straight in contour, evenly dividing her rosy cheeks …"

3   On the beliefs and so-called old wives' tales circulating in this period concerning conception and birth, see Rudolph M. Bell's *How to Do It*, especially pages 86–97.

4   The text is similar to Matthew 22:14, "For many are called, but few are chosen," though the contexts are different, raising the possibility of parody. In the Italian text, Genevera is sitting in Love's lap here, whereas three paragraphs ago, Love was sitting in her lap. There may simply be a mere lapse in gendered pronoun usage. In my translation, I resist the call to emphasize any shuffling of intimate positions on a church pew. Nevertheless, how the reader imagines the personification of Love admittedly plays a key role. My first impression of Love as a Cupid figure with bow and arrow, small enough to hide in a girl's lap and carry out his mission secretly, is far different from the imposing *Dominus* that Dante describes in the third chapter of his *Vita nuova*, for example, in which Love conveys Beatrice in his arms to heaven.

launch of a battle that can never be won by anyone! O too daring hope, O misguided human presumption! The one who places too much confidence in himself is wretched indeed.

I was reminded of Hercules, Achilles, and the handsome Trojan Paris, who wrongly chose Venus. But if even those great heroes could not resist the fires of love, what can I possibly do, parched tinder and sapless branch that I am? If they were taken captive and brought low by Love, what can I hope for? These words struck my breast with such terror I nearly dropped dead.

Book 1. Chapter 2.

Peregrino returns to the church, where his closest companion Acate prevents him from jealously killing a male relative of the Duke of Ferrara who happens to be sitting in a pew adjacent to Genevera's. Peregrino follows her home and realizes he has fallen in love with a girl belonging to an enemy clan. Love prompts Peregrino to seek out Violante as a go-between. She attempts to dissuade Peregrino before urging prudence: he should write an anonymous love letter to determine if Genevera might be open to love.

The day of love's first spark, the fire spread, consuming my marrow like imbibed hemlock sap. I began to neglect all my public and private affairs, and I felt lost and besieged like a hunted beast. Laughter turned to weeping, speech to silence, and social grace to scornfulness. The night teemed with anxiety, such that every spirit of hell must have rested easier than I. Through tears I cried out: 'Cruel destiny of lovers! Life more miserable than death! O untended wound of love, conceived quite unintentionally! It's not Love's arrow that hurts you, but your own thoughts. It is easy to conquer a person who puts up no resistance. Wretched man, see where your overconfidence has driven you! Has Love tricked me by means of a girl's disregard? O my Lady, how can I go on living without you? O light of my eyes, mirror of my lost soul, guiding star that never errs, look on the man whose life depends on you.' These and similarly confused laments accompanied me all night long.

When the sun rose again, I went alone back to the place where Love assailed me to try to recall my lost wits. Without noticing anything else, I saw a relative of the illustrious Duke Ercole sitting directly across from my lady. Love and jealousy seized my heart in that instant with such force that I couldn't bear to see more. My face paled, and I heaved such deep sighs that I nearly revealed what Love's laws demand everyone must keep concealed. Ablaze with choleric blood, I fled the church, resolving to seek revenge on that youth, although he was blameless. If it weren't for my faithful Acate, who guided me back to reason, the life of that youth would not have been safe. I banished those wicked schemes.

From some distance, I followed my lady all the way back to her residence. I sought to peer into the front of her house, the back, and then the side window, anywhere I thought I might find comfort from a glimpse of her sweet light. Suddenly, I realized this was Angelo's house, and I began to fear my newly conceived love would meet with little success, given the hatred that long divided our families. But then, reflecting on the fact that the lord of Love is the great reconciler of the world, capable of repairing all differences, I took heart. With prudent determination I learned the name of that lady – Genevera – a name which signifies to me nothing less than 'the true genetrix of every human created thing.'

Afterward, I went about covertly gathering information about her household servants, specifically the woman who served her most closely. With almost suspicious ease, Love made my lady aware of me. When she chanced to offer some sign of affection to me, I could not have felt any greater happiness in the world equal to or surpassing it. See now what the life of miserable lovers depends on: the look of sweetness, not distaste, from the beloved lady ruled and governed by Love. I felt conquered and with such force constrained by another's power that I immediately quit all my advantageous and honourable pursuits; instead, I indulged those silly activities I had learned at a tender age, that is, singing, making music, dancing, and amusing myself night and day, without regard for my reputation or that of my household. In these distractions I wasted my life, my reputation, and my potential. I acted boldly, socialized freely, and gave generously to anyone I believed had taken risks in words or deeds on my behalf. There wasn't anyone in Genevera's household who didn't owe me for the little gifts I bestowed, but at that time I did not find anyone so bold as to facilitate the slightest assault on Genevera's most tenacious virtue. Between false hope and burning passion, I began to feel faint. O God, O heavens, O forces favourable and not, what kind of life can ours ever be? What cold marble or even hardest diamond could withstand so many forces pitted against it? When hope is in the air, fear takes hold; when one's friend is far away, the enemy lurks at the door. What can I do? Asking is shameful, continuing like this risks ruin, and praying falls on deaf ears. O Venus, ruler of the third heavenly sphere, do not let me perish in this agony!

My heart verged on utter stillness when I noticed a small window through which I saw my lady resting without care or suspicion. Displayed near her was a painted icon of Mary, genetrix of the true Messiah made man. Given my good upbringing, I reverenced it by bowing my head. My lady, assuming I greeted and honoured her, reciprocated with the slightest of smiles before she withdrew.

When I received that boon from her, I said to myself: 'Give thanks to heaven, soul, which today has interceded on your behalf!' Not long after that, Love showed me a way to easily end my suffering – or so I thought. I once had a wet nurse who, because she was well versed in the liberal arts, also served as tutor to my lady, so she frequented her house, typically accessing it by the garden adjoining their houses. My heart rejoiced, and the memory still brings me comfort and happiness. When the opportunity arose, I went directly to the house of my former wet nurse, whose name was Violante, and she welcomed me with eagerness and affection. After the usual exchanges, I divulged as faithfully and accurately as I could the state of my calamitous life. Moreover, I made it clear to her that if I didn't become her next act of charity, she'd have the nearest vantage to see my life wane. My words, accompanied by hot tears and profound sighs, undoubtedly lent truth to my suffering.

Violante, moved by motherly pity, compassionately asked what flame burned so hot in me. She reminded me to guard myself against the assaults of love, this world's universal plague: "Love is a kind of insomnia full of terror, errors, ills, stupidity, arrogance, inconsideration, petulance, cupidity, malevolence, desire, crazed poverty, and a lack of modesty. It is wordy where there's no mystery to expound and holds its tongue when it should not. It is without order, time, or place, an incurable disease from which is born a neglect of God and oneself, a waste of time, loss of honours, infamy on households, an offence to relatives, the squandering of wealth, unchecked lust, discord, contentions, rivalry, arguments, fights, envy, slanders, feigning, dissembling, false insinuations, exile, murders, poisons, mysterious deaths, obsessions, destruction of the body, and damnation of the soul. In the end: nothing good.

"Suppose this lady you burn for loves you in return, what then? If she's a lady of higher nobility or a princess, you'll never be secure in her love and may risk losing your head. If you love someone of low station, then you can never hope for honour, leisure, or a good end. If she's your equal, and you just want sex, why so much drama? Leave this burning to the perennially dissatisfied. You once dedicated yourself to the study of literary and spiritual works, but now all you want to do is indulge childish distractions that repulse those who prefer to ascend Minerva's throne. Such pursuits befit only those who adore Venus, Bacchus, and Ceres. Don't waste yourself, my good man, on these wretched habits, for once they are established in your soul, they cannot be uprooted without extraordinary difficulty."

The more Violante talked, however, the more I burned. I wept and kept begging her until she promised to help in whatever way might be possible in a case in which trustworthy and beneficial advice could not overcome eager desire. Finally, with a loosened tongue and open heart, I disclosed to her my secret: the lady I loved more than all others in the whole world was Genevera, daughter of Angelo.

As soon as she heard the mention of Genevera's name, Violante's expression changed, verging on disbelief. At that, my indignant soul suddenly felt its innermost vital powers flee my poor body. I collapsed against Violante as if I had died.

Compassion extinguished her next thought, and she sought to bring back my wayward soul with sweet expressions of comfort, saying: "Peregrino, you must be very careful. She comes from a patrician household. Her father is scrupulously upstanding and her mother most chaste. Genevera is exceedingly modest and well educated. Although still a girl, she displays maturity beyond her years. I'm sure my affection for her doesn't lead me to exaggerate what I say about her in any way. I love her effusively because her virtue and condition merit it, and the more carefully I observe her, the more lovingly I can commend her.

"If you proceed, you must pick your way discreetly. You have opened your heart far too quickly to Love's burning pain, suffering, and crazed desperation. What sailor would be so foolish as to set his course on uncharted seas without careful consideration? If you wish to venture forth with greater wisdom, remember what is often said: the man who barely assesses his circumstances does not last long. If you act too hastily, your end will come in pain, and if you do not act with greater prudence, you'll reap little fruit from your plans. Nevertheless, I remain willing to serve you."

She judged my situation as nearly impossible, given the longstanding animosity that divided my household from Angelo's, which prevented any contact, to say nothing of a relationship based on true love. Moreover, Violante did not want her actions to tinge Genevera's reputation in any way.

Violante: "Nonetheless, if I should learn that she returns your love, I'll do everything in my power to please her. So, before we go divulging this secret, we should somehow sound her soul and determine if she's disposed to love. From this answer we'll learn how to steer our ship. My advice would be for you to write her a letter leaving out both your names. I'll pretend to have found it by chance and make her a copy to hear her impressions of it. If I see she is moved by reading it, I'll encourage her with whatever words seem apt. If it should produce the contrary effect, though, I don't want us wasting our efforts trying to sow infertile soil. Please take my sound advice and write with enough cleverness that if some disaster impedes your plan, you'll be able to extricate yourself while wisely salvaging your honour."

The urgency of her words stuck in my mind so forcefully that I decided to follow this wise path to learn what Love might do in an inexperienced breast. I composed the following letter, dictated by Love and Violante, and this was its gist …

Book 1. Chapter 3.

Peregrino writes an anonymous love letter following Violante's advice.

My Letter,

You are the only one who knows my secret suffering. May our Lord grant you the same happiness he gave to the Trojan refugee Aeneas when He put Cupid in Dido's lap. Go propitiously and unseen to my lady, whom only you can identify, and reverently say to her: 'Lady worthy of every act of courage and excellence, may my unexpected arrival and the stirrings of your heart not startle you. If Helen's beauty was powerful enough to launch the forces of Asia and Europe, can anyone wonder if your appearance, no less worthy, attracts, conquers, and captivates a man born to this world only to serve you?' This, O lady, is heaven's inherent virtue bestowed on man: to love what is noble, honest, wise, and beautiful, just as you are. Therefore, welcome me, and read me when you are alone, calm, and at your leisure, so that you do not inadvertently cause a cruel or violent death to another. If this came to pass, you'd feel pain to the depths of your soul.

Rest assured you are loved by a man of equal station. Don't waste the flower of youth feigning rejection or lukewarm feelings because doing so would only denigrate your most noble condition, made for love from its conception. Before divulging my feelings, I shall follow the ancient and celebrated Persian custom never to appear before an exalted ruler empty-handed, a tradition that exists not because the ruler is greedy, but because the petitioner is reverent. Since my patron possesses no object truly worthy of your honour, he sends me to entrust to you as your perpetual servant what God could not outdo in granting to mortals – that is, his soul. I beg you to accept it along with his heart, which he offers to you.

I know the greatness of your peerless spirit would never suffer being surpassed in love, since you have proven superior in every other act. Believe me, my lady, there's nothing in the world that warms the heart of a splendid and discerning giver more than the great spirit of one who accepts him, since a grateful receiver is no less virtuous than the one who freely gives. So, lady, take and cherish this offering in proof of your spirit's splendour, and vouchsafe the true service of the man who loves you above all others, including himself. This wretched man lives for the light of your eyes that he may never give cause to annoy you. At the first sight of you, my lady, he was left without his spirit and free will. He lives, though he dies of too much love; he cries out and remains silent; naked he burns and shivers in a burning fire; and he dies in spirit and lives on merely in his flesh.[5] He rails against those who never offended him, and trusts those he has never even met. His hope doubts, while his martyrdom is certain. When he feels pain, Echo accompanies him; if he cries, he weeps alone like Orpheus. If he remains silent, the tongue held in check cannot expect a reply. If he divulges his passion, he finds no confidante.

He has told me many times: 'Blessed and ever blessing letter, if you are received humanely by those heavenly hands, you'll be worthy of Empyrean if you get a smile from her mouth when she reads and rereads you with sparkling eyes, or you'll be exalted above Jove if you earn being hidden at her candid breast where Cupid and Venus rejoiced on the day of her birth. If – woe is me! – you should be rejected, power shall pass from Love, life from this letter's writer, and humanity from you, lady. But if, as I hope, you return to me with good news, I will proclaim to all posterity your sacred name, whose memory of new happiness continually sparks me.'

Faithful letter, since I trust only in your diligence and precision, carry out your task and return right away.

Book 1. Chapter 4.

Peregrino gives the letter to Violante, who meets with Genevera.

Once I had written the love letter – and not without shedding copious tears – I sealed it and gave it to wise Violante. All the while my heart burned ardently. I begged God it not receive a less welcoming audience than the clever speech Ulysses made when he convinced Achilles to join the victorious cause. Violante accepted my letter with downcast eyes and bowed head, as if in regret. Weighed down by all the thoughts she conjured in her head, she made her way toward Genevera's palace.

Genevera greeted her affectionately. After exchanging the typical pleasantries of women, Violante paused in reticence, which suggested she held back words concerning a very serious matter. At last, she heaved a heartfelt sigh, and from her poor lips poured out what follows.

Book 1. Chapter 5.

Violante pretends that she found an unsigned letter during that morning's Mass. Genevera insists that Violante entrust it to her and directs her to find out what she can about its author without arousing suspicion.

---

5   The series of oxymorons present in this language is reminiscent, of course, of popular Petrarchan topoi of the time, perhaps verging on parody.

Violante: "Genevera, my dear, if love and trust in our close confidence did not bolster my heart, I wouldn't choose you – out of all the people I know who love and protect me – to hear, console, and advise me on this matter. But I believe what's needed is precisely your appraisal of the best course of action. Since it concerns a most urgent passion, though, I'm begging you, please do not breathe a word of it, so harm or shame does not follow.

"Woe is me! I'm so anguished I hardly hope to regain any peace or rest. I don't know if I am tormented today by some cruel influence from heaven, an evil star, or some sin of my own, but … This morning I was offering my prayers at Mass, as I always do, when I found this letter, all folded up in my prayer book. The church was full of people of rank. I was so surprised that I immediately wanted to show it to someone, but holding off a bit, it seemed better to keep it to myself. Before saying another word about it, I wanted to have it read and considered with the utmost discretion to prepare for its fires of incipient passion, although I do not believe the letter is intended for me. My wrinkled face, advanced age, and low station all make me sure on this point. On the other hand, I fear the scandal that might bring shame to my chaste and modest life."

That said, Violante drew the letter out. With a tearful expression of dread, as if she were facing imminent death, she handed it to Genevera, who, with a daughter's compassion, sweetly comforted Violante. Before reading the letter, she urged Violante to stand strong, resist the world's deceptions, and be of good cheer, for a devout conscience deserves neither suffering nor penance. Eternal God would not permit such a terrible wrong.

Genevera: "Since time is short, though, please allow me to keep this letter, and trust that I would never knowingly allow a living soul to hear of it. Go, and see if you can learn anything about its author, not to bring him grief, but so that we can act more cautiously."

As soon as Violante left, Genevera withdrew to the solitude of her room and opened the letter. She read it and reread it many times, and, moved by so much love, she said sighing …

Book 1. Chapter 6.

Genevera reacts to the letter, and when she speaks with Violante again, she expresses compassion for the writer's plight. Violante meets with Peregrino, bringing him hope, and Peregrino begs Violante to talk to Genevera again.

Genevera: 'O how fortunate this rival of heaven! The poor youth has discovered the first stirrings of love, at least there is no mystery there. But he certainly was forgetful if he could not remember the place where his beloved lady always sits! I believe he must fear being discovered.

'O God, how is it possible that a man can be so enflamed by a woman, as this letter makes clear? This wretched man, through nobody else's fault, could end up dead because of his own suffering. What is so bitter, harsh, or uncouth that the mind might not incline to it out of love? Blessed is the lady loved so greatly, and fortunate the man introduced to her by heaven!'

Genevera passed the time in these thoughts until Violante returned. As soon as she saw her, she smiled and said, "My good Violante, sins committed without deliberation and malicious will are worthy of pardon. The writer of the letter you found is so anxious that he neither lives nor dies, and to vent his misery he wrote this, believing it would fall into the hands of the lady he can no longer live without. Do not torture yourself over it. Leave others to their passions. If you are asked anything implicating your virtue, you have the option to respond or remain silent."

Violante was reassured, and after offering some typical words of response, she came back and encouraged me to be strong and go on living because she hoped to bring about the happy outcome my initiative heralded.

That day and the following night passed for me as if I were the sentinel on guard against an approaching army. My thoughts veered in all directions. I worried that Violante put too much trust in Genevera, whose great beauty and tender age made me doubtful; and the rift with her household also tormented me. Between love and fear, sleep and wakefulness, I emerged to face a new day.

I cancelled all my other obligations so I could steal away and beg Violante to return to Genevera. She did, and after talking over topics typical of women, Genevera very cleverly inquired if Violante happened to have any news of the letter writer's identity. More through her silence and gestures than by her voice, Violante gave her to understand that she did. When Genevera realized this, she warmed even more to the subject (and thus became curious about her future undoing). Genevera beseeched her not to deny any detail about the man who loved so ardently. Violante made as if to speak, but then held back. Between these two contending actions, she did nothing but increase Genevera's desire to know (what would have been better for her to ignore).[6]

At long last, Violante capitulated …

---

6   The two parenthetical expressions in this paragraph foreshadow what is to come from the perspective of the now dead spirit of Peregrino, who tells his story to Caviceo, who sleeps and dreams.

Book 1. Chapter 7.

Violante reveals to Genevera that the letter writer is Peregrino, and Genevera is the lady he loves. They debate what to do next, marshalling support for their arguments from classical mythology, Roman histories, biblical passages, and exemplary tales that they have studied together. Violante favours prompt and unequivocal communication between the two young people, preferably face to face, while Genevera expresses fear for her reputation if she meets a stranger in person.

Violante: "O Genevera, it is natural for ladies, especially young ones with little experience in cases like these, to readily blurt out every passing triviality that passes through their heads, given their gullibility or awkwardness in governing their anger, disdain, or overwhelming joy. That is why smart, circumspect people don't rely on them to keep a secret because there's little reason to trust them. However, I know you to be an intelligent and self-respecting young lady, so I will share with you my great secret. If you consider it well, you will realize God is taking special care of you, just as I love and respect you, which you know from experience."

Genevera hastened to reply: "Violante, everyone knows the inconstant nature of the female sex tends not to protect those matters worthy of the highest confidentiality, unless she has gained this capacity by discipline or upbringing. If you call to mind your ceaseless efforts and those of my parents, as well as the exacting path of my life, you will see that such girlish whimsy is quite foreign to me. I shall always give thanks for the high regard you have for me. Although I may not always live up to it, under your tutelage I shall strive to preserve every secret entrusted to my ears without any cause for doubt. So, enough of your fears: tell me already!"

This made Violante bolder, and she said while sighing: "I speak to you not because I'm convinced you have any lustful inclinations, nor because I scheme to divert you from your chaste, virtuous ways, but only because I care for your honour and continued well-being. Do not be annoyed by the words you are about to hear. Cruel indeed is the person who deprives another of life, but cruellest of all is the one who has the potential to rescue another through honourable action but refrains. Nature has determined that our sex always inclines toward mercy and meekness. I believe it's tragic when a girl's self-control is so unyielding that she harms someone else. After all, how would heaven and earth carry on if Love did not govern and reign over them with sweetness? From the time we are created in this world – pure and immaculate as doves and without guile or greed – we ought to dedicate ourselves to delightful pleasures and rejoice, showing compassion for the trials and tribulations of others.

"The letter you saw was written by the most ardent and respectable lover under the sun. When I think about the pain and suffering of his life and the torments he has endured for love, I could die of pity. I wonder how his body can go on living without its soul. It must be like the chronically feverish who subsist, even without consuming food, because they are nourished by their deeply rooted suffering. Similarly, poor lovers must feed on their own pain."

Genevera, moved by her inner virtue, exclaimed: "Oh my, who can it be who suffers such a sad fate because he loves?"

Violante: "The writer of the letter I found."

G: "His name, if you please?"

V: "I fear …"

G: "There is no need of that for one assured salvation."

V: "This is true."

G: "Well, the time has come to free me from this suspense!"

V: "It was Peregrino, son of Antonio."

G: "How did you find out?"

V: "I'll tell you. He heard I was the one who found his letter, and he came to me begging for mercy, crossing his arms in penance over his chest. He wanted to die. Moved by compassion without understanding the cause of his desperation, I promised him any proper assistance I could give. The poor man remained silent, then broke down in tears. Eventually, he confessed he was doomed because he loved too much. I asked him which lady prompted such passion in him, and he said it was Genevera, Angelo's daughter, and he wished to be joined in marriage to her more than to any other woman in the world. He hoped I would foster his desired objective when I saw the opportunity."

G: "So he burns for me?"

V: "For no one else."

G: "But how could this be?"

V: "The light of your eyes has captivated him."

G: "I give thanks to Love for remembering me."

V: "Would you like to respond in a way befitting your nobility and his trust?"

G: "That would be impossible."

V: "Then you are not free to offer him your love?"

G: "No, not for that reason."

V: "Then change your mind."

G: "What would you have me do?"

V: "Write him a few words so he can understand your thinking."

G: "It would be very foolish of me to write someone I do not even know. If he loves me so much, he should have tried a different way."

V: "He didn't trust it was possible."

G: "The one who delivered the letter could have said more."

V: "I was afraid."

G: "On my account?"

V: "Yes."

G: "Why?"

V: "Your age and lack of experience gave me pause."

G: "No, I do not believe that was the reason. My fate is in your hands. Rather, I believe it was because you do not entirely trust him whose sex is always eager to cheat and bend the rules in order to get what it wants, then beg for more."

V: "Not true! I don't think there's a more faithful man in the world. You can certainly trust him."

G: "Violante, how difficult it is to place one's hope in another! Legions of ladies whose faith has been betrayed go about in the world all forlorn and miserable. Recall the examples among the ancients and moderns. At every turn you will find them tearing out their hair and regretting that they ever put their faith in a man. Only liars and fools find pleasure in this world. Any man who possesses the dubious capacity to deceive others is considered blessed. Instead, heaven grants to our unfortunate lot the continual threat of being stripped of honour and life. Believe me, these nice-sounding words are more like fables, legends, and gossip – they can be forgotten with the same ease they are uttered. See how varying and changeable the human condition is: the whole world buzzes about feigned and dissembled infidelities. It seems no vice exists that one might easily overlook in oneself to indulge some little fantasy or other. Think how many misfortunes, injuries, damages, suffering, calamities, ruin, deaths to the body and soul, and losses to reputation are experienced by those who trust too readily. Really, if the whole world weeps and wails over these kinds of evil, what can I possibly hope for as a young girl of no experience? Nonetheless, I do not want you to think it annoys me to be loved by a virtuous and noble man, only that you understand the human condition and man's nature."

V: "How else can I prove that Peregrino loves you sincerely? He would rather die than prove false."

G: "Most of the time love and pity fool those who are too trusting."

V: "Rest assured on this account. If ever there were a man who loved faithfully and for whom posterity would be able to render eternal thanks, Peregrino would be that one to whom Love and every devoted lover were obliged. He's the one in whom true piety reigns with freedom, faith, and the highest integrity. To serve you he scorns wrath and hatred, and he refuses to take part in public and private animosities; to love you he would give up time, resources, even his own life. To serve you he would respect any person who pleased you; and to obey you he would put heaven, the world, and every created thing after you. He awaits nothing more than your command, acknowledging life or accepting death.

"Genevera, do not allow this man to suffer so much because his begging, weeping, nothing can sway you. Please save the man whose heart is eager and whose soul is ready to suffer any extreme for your well-being and honour. Behold the ark of faith, Genevera; behold the man for whom every act is easy except betraying you.[7] Soften your harsh attitude a bit; put aside this ferocity, which doesn't befit an innocent girl. Don't you see that the virtue of meekness comes from nature? Even when we see our enemies caught in extreme circumstances, we incline toward pity and gentleness, and if we feel this way toward those who hate us, how indeed must we treat those who endeavour to care for us?[8] If Publius Horatius's tears for his son, who killed his sister out of excessive piety, were capable of moving the consuls to free him, what must I do for you, whom I love so much that I endeavour to protect your honour and seek information for you? Genevera, don't deprive this man of your grace, for his reputation and experience prove he wouldn't yield to any living person. Besides, I want you to understand he is rich in everything under the moon, except faithful friends. You would do well to show him you are one of these by your actions, one who prefers to live morally and ethically and not listen to the barking of those fools who act out of cowardice."

G: "While your wise and affectionate arguments delight and edify me, and I am inclined to agree with you, it is still prudent to follow the good sailor Ulysses' example and plug one's ears against the siren's song, so that we are not attacked while sound asleep when we should be on guard, thus sacrificing our honourable life in pursuit of some fleeting sweetness. So long as a man pursues integrity, he merits good will and love. But if he languishes, it suggests his love is flawed, since a life guided by virtue does not languish or perceive overexertion.

---

7 Violante recommends Peregrino to Genevera by describing him in words incongruously similar to Pontius Pilate's *Ecce Homo*, presenting the scourged Jesus, crowned with thorns, or Dante's emblematic figure of fraud, Geryon, in *Inferno* 17.1–3. Subsequently, she will attempt to ply Genevera with pleas to have mercy on Peregrino, which take a form that resembles the anaphora of the Litany of the Saints.

8 Cf. Valerius Maximus's *Facta et dicta memorabilia* 5.1 and Dante's version of the words between Peisistratus and his wife in *Purgatorio* 15.103–5.

"Be careful, Violante, that your words do not misrepresent Peregrino's intent, which would be a clear sign that your friendship is less than true. However, if I determine that his intentions toward me are sincere, I shall make every effort to satisfy you. Still, it would make sense for you to speak to my parents about it, since they have the say in what happens to me. This way, our relationship can be properly governed to preserve my good name and our everlasting love."

V: "Now is not the time for that conversation."

G: "Why not?"

V: "Because of the hatred dividing your families."

G: "Is loving not less of a burden than hating?"

V: "Yes."

G: "So once a new friendship appears to them, they will put aside their stubborn hostility."

V: "Focus first on your feelings and leave the rest to me."

G: "I will always be quick to follow your instructions."

V: "If his sweet words and feelings were to find some correspondence in you, then no man in this world would be happier than Peregrino. But I fear he has been lured into a labyrinth of false hopes, where there are two hundred threads, but no useful assistance. Taking your time to act upon hearing news is a just and praiseworthy response, according to models in Roman history, among the Argonauts, or the Pontic king Mithridates. But in matters concerning love, speed earns greater praise. Your sweet words could cure a dying man through their virtue, validity, keenness, sublimity, generosity, elegance, purity, deeper significance, and precious value. I wish you would act more decisively. Democritus used to say that a lean, fit body utilizes calories and maintains itself better against a wide variety of attacks. Genevera, while we have the time, let's think about how to perpetuate your good love so that fortune, adversity, or any other evil cannot take it away.

"How many glorious love stories vanish into thin air because of belaboured delays or lukewarm reactions? I'm not trying to convince you to do anything your virtue doesn't permit. You'll merely be acting without everybody knowing about it. Believe me, it's not worth airing Peregrino's secret when he's just asking you to help him understand how much he's in your good favour. You could write a letter, or better yet, you could meet in secret so he could speak to you directly and disclose the inner stirrings of his heart, which perhaps might not be properly conveyed through an intermediary. He can dispel your doubts and will obey and carry out your every wish because you're more precious to him than every treasure. Decide then which option seems best to you, so long as it is quick and prudent, and his presence doesn't bring harm to you or shame to me. Please, this is all I ask of you."

G: "What could be so far from my true intention or so contrary in its effects from what the Punic, Thracian, and Syrian believed they could do? How could I ever freely desire what repulsed my mind? I do not want to sell to another what would be harmful to me to buy. Those who have occupied themselves with continually pretending and keeping secrets cannot plan or carry out any honourable action, but instead always exhaust their bodies and souls with doubts, and in the end, they confuse both themselves and others. If I am especially protective of my honour, I know it cannot displease you, because in behaving this way I prove myself to be the rightful offspring of my parents and worthy of your teachings, which I always seek to satisfy through my disciplined, chaste way of life. I do not go biding my time, if not to put off what I would never set out to do. I only want to work for the continuation of a life that is just, virtuous, and praiseworthy, which, if that is also what pleases Peregrino, will enable our hearts to be joined in equal and enduring love.

"From what I have understood from you, he has secrets of serious consequence to communicate with me. I cannot think of a better means to convey them than a letter, or perhaps a spoken message, to a person like you in whom he can certainly trust. These secrets are Love's stratagems to trick those who fall easiest into damning gullibility, a ruse that has corrupted many famous ancient and modern heroines, as you can read in history."

V: "Genevera, my dear, if there were no other benefit to lovers except the exchange of words from a distance, they'd never get together, nor would they waste so much time pining for one another. It's right for a reasonable spirit to consider, debate, and plan carefully before launching the most expedient plan of action, since neither Marcus Furius Camillus nor Quintus Fabius Maximus, not Horace or St. Paul has ever defended their homelands with mere thoughts. You are preaching to me about virtue as if I suggested a move that would strip it from you. You live like those who are guided in both body and mind by the rod. You consider it a wicked inconvenience to lend an ear to a man of worth, love, and faith. But really, would you ever refuse to speak to a servant, a manual labourer, a gravedigger, anybody at all? And if you grant this privilege to the lowliest of men, why must you deny it to the servants of Love? Perhaps your heart fears because I told you to meet in secret? But these words, innocently spoken, do not suggest any evil intent, only the means to maintain love, as well as honour. If you just accepted these words as coming from a sincere heart, there'd be no need for so many explanations. Peregrino loves you effusively and entirely, and he yearns for your good as his own. So, prepare yourself to set up a time and place when he can communicate to you his ardent desire. Now, please, grant me the favour of an answer corresponding to the virtue I have observed in you."

G: "In my opinion, Euripides' judgment was false, unjust, and wicked. He said, according to the great Cicero, that if sworn faithfulness is about to be violated, one can break faith in order to lead. Who could have believed the pure-minded Romans would commit the rape of the Sabine women entrusted to them to satisfy their sensual appetites? No one wants to be under a lord or master with the only hope of rescue being whatever the next day brings. If only Leda's daughter Helen had been a little less gullible, then a Greek would never have ruled the famed city of Troy; and if Dido Queen of Carthage had not granted Aeneas an audience, she would have been praised eternally for remaining faithful to the ghost of her beloved Sychaeus. Women who ruin their reputations because they do not resist a moment's longing deserve their unhappy wretchedness, and more so those women who lose their high rank because of their own sin. Women would do better to weigh their options cautiously. How many stories have we read or even seen in our own day of unhappy damsels and matrons who fall, losing their honour and their country because they were too trusting? But if a mere glance of desire is considered a sin for our sex, what must it be when others find out we have spoken of it?

"It thus makes good sense to extinguish this passion. Do not get upset if I do not stoop to your will. Youth, inexperience, and unease are my excuses. Do you believe I lack the discipline, courage, or faith in Another to resist an encounter with a man of this world? Or that death would not be sweeter to me than life if my actions or presumption caused me to be discovered? Think about it: I am saddled with a strict mother, a proud father, ambitious brothers, unreliable servants, and untrustworthy maids, in a noble house on a public street and walled in by this garden. What can I do on my own? Even if I assented to your wishes, my weak power could not bring it about. Those passions, which always make things worse, must be quashed, because any medicine that does not cure the sick must be considered useless. Let us hope the future brings more salubrious diversion than trying to pick fresh roses from arid ground. Nevertheless, in order not to seem ungrateful for so much love, I will acknowledge him, if I can figure out a way, since I love him as virtuously as my own life."

V: "If fertile Greece had as many true accounts as it abounds in fictions and legends, it would be called the kingdom of heaven. But the true passages are so mixed up with false ones that even many well-educated and discerning readers cannot distinguish between them. Genevera, this equivocating response of yours seems decidedly bitter to me because it contains nothing solid, no true convictions. If I can speak frankly from the heart, I can only understand you have a bad opinion of me. It's certainly not the custom of a noble lady to reward her faithful servant with such an earful of ingratitude. Now consider the state your wretched admirer finds himself in out of love for you. You've made yourself haughty by ruining him, since if you pause to consider it carefully, he can't breathe without you. The poor man is asking you to grant him either a sweeter destiny or death. Otherwise, when he sees you in public, he'll prostrate himself at your feet and take his life by his own hand. Afterwards, you'll be sorry because you're generous by nature. You can free him from such great suffering only by letting him see you. Cimon could only regain his senses by the sight of an attractive lady. When Peregrino learns you're shunning him, he might be overcome by some melancholic humour and announce, even against his better judgment, the reason for his suffering. Genevera, take heed you do not incur divine judgment, which harshly punishes ingrates, entailing a perpetual penance of withstanding the public complaints of a rejected and embittered lover who was captivated and devoted to you, but then was wretchedly destroyed through your thanklessness.

"Well, Genevera, given you show no respect for God or the world, think at least about how deserving of punishment you are because you have cultivated an arrogant, disdainful, and incorrigible character at such a young age. Consider what you are refusing, Genevera. You are his goddess, the pitter-patter of his almost lifeless body; you're the seat of his soul. His heart suffers for you, cruel one! How can you shred his heart without any reason other than that he has offered to serve you, and his soul was born to this world to love and obey only you? What greater inhumanity could you foist upon a cruel enemy? Do his ceaseless efforts merit this reward? Is this the mercy he should receive for his continuous struggles? Are these the riches his vigils warrant? Genevera, try to imagine the hot tears piercing his heart; such pity would bend the will of hell. I'm certain you'll change your mind, because if you don't, you'll lose your good reputation, and you'll see worthy Peregrino come to a bad end."

G: "When the Titans, offspring of Gaia and monstrous beings, chose to contend with mighty Jove, the first war was over before it began, and no trace of them can be found today. I like to believe I am the kind of person unharmed by made-up lies, even if they should have the face of truth. This is my nature, formed by good habits. I know words spoken in the heat of the moment carry little weight. But if that poor lover were unfortunately predisposed to ill humours, one would sooner attribute any fault in this matter to his sinful nature than to my virtue. There are men in this world who are so melancholic, irksome, and spoiled that they immediately want to die as soon as things do not go their way. This clearly denotes lustful ones rather than true lovers, not men of integrity who would be as thoughtful of another's honour as their own. Even though he would unjustly stain my reputation, his shame would be the greater, because a bad reputation follows the perpetrator more than the victim.

"I cannot imagine what kind of detractor would be so bold of face and heart that he would denounce me while supposedly loving me and proclaiming my virtue, as you say. Sallust first praised Cicero to the skies then damned him, and for this wavering he was reputed to be a man of little substance and inconstant mind. I am convinced Peregrino will not want to deviate from his good nature, which has always been noble, modest, well-mannered, and prudent. I know a corresponding cowardice cannot co-exist with virtue. I pity his excessive amorous passion and forgive him. Love incites him more than it should; lust carries him away, and where desire waxes, reason wanes. Given his dignity and experience as a man, he is responsible for safeguarding my age and condition much more than his fleeting and erring appetite. If I were ever lacking for true advice, I would need to turn to him.

"Violante, rest assured everything has its appointed time. I do not have the power your request demands, nor are you patient enough to wait for the mercy that virtuous Love typically prepares for his followers. Do you believe an impatient man will go far, and only the one who lives in lust can be called miserable? What wise man who desires mercy would not wait for the proper time? If you believe the burden of love is unbearable for him, then however such a notion entered his mind, it should be able to come out again. Sudden desire cannot be cured without time. Life on this earth demands it. Consider that the things that begin with sound advice usually turn out just fine, while any wind that blows the precipitous sailor is not favourable. I beg you now, please stop your fretting and give my weak life some rest."

V: "Genevera, the virtue to resist an inner passionate love is not human, but divine, and there's no patience so great it can withstand greater effort at the final breath. Take Cato of Utica or Mithridates, sworn enemy of the Romans; consider proud Hannibal against pitiless Nero; take another look at Dido, Sophonisba, Phyllis, Medea, Deianira, Phaedra, and Sappho, who in trying to get away from wickedness sacrificed their own lives. I understand Peregrino's state: he won't be able to live bereft of the hope he anticipates and the mercy he believes proper now. Even though he might want to carry on, he might not have the power to do so, since his soul has already suffered for his ardent passions. But seeing you want to console him for the death you are generating for him, he'll gladly accept it. Perhaps in place of his living body you'll take his soulless corpse. Once his life leaves him, you'll be moved to weep for him out of natural compassion, and the infamy of this senseless death will besmirch your name. In public people will denounce you saying: 'There is that cruel woman whose overly harsh response caused the death of the most faithful lover under the moon.' And you, grieved to the point of desperation, will bring death on yourself.

"If love for him doesn't sway you, think of yourself. You're born of the most noble blood and with divine beauty, which entail exercising the corresponding virtues of clemency and compassion. If it's true that the soul's qualities correspond to the body's, how is it that you've adopted this ingratitude, which would hardly be appropriate to the flesh of a beast? You must know besides: if I hadn't seen your inclination to love from reading the letter, I would never have set myself up for long debates and toils, which have only brought annoyance to you, exhaustion to me, and death to Peregrino. If you want him to live, you must change your mind. Fortune has blessed you with such a great beginning; don't squander it, else you'll suffer what was written about the she-wolf: it always moves toward the saddest plight. If you lose the flower of your first beauty, trembling, sobs, and weeping will follow you the rest of your life, and you'll rue your lost chance to the depths of your soul because no one by nature has the power to go back and choose differently. If only God had given me your body or given you my mind, then every disagreement between us would cease. So, Genevera dear, beware time's flight and accept as your everlasting servant him who adores you on earth through our eternal God."

G: "The one who tries to escape suffering through death is very wretched indeed. If Fabius or Coriolanus had done so, then Rome would not have triumphed. We read also how Jove transformed himself in various ways out of love, but not one chose death. Only frantic and thoughtless types tend to go to such lengths for a cure for amorous passion. So, Violante, do not try to confuse the virtue of the truly magnanimous and courageous with your improper examples. The wish to depart this life because of sensual passion is an act of cowardice, because human virtue is not so deeply rooted that there is no means to defend against its adverse effects. What thing is so serious that it causes Peregrino's death? You might answer: it is love. But if love's nature is all ease and comfort, how can it cause such contrary effects? Remember what happened to the Roman matron who tried unsuccessfully to kill herself upon hearing the news of her dead son? After a while, she got over it and died happily. Maybe that will be true in Peregrino's case, too. Considering that if he had everything he wanted from me, his heart would burst with such consolation it would be unbearable, and he would still wish for death. Believe this, Violante: the body is lost to anyone who lives lustfully. Most of the time it is an act of cruelty to show pity. You are not giving me any material that can worthily save me; I refuse to trust malicious smooth talkers. I have placed all my hope in One above, and in time you will see that my honour and reputation are in your hands."

V: "Genevera, if the eyes of Jove watched vigilantly over the health of Augustus, who ruled over a peaceful world for fifty-six years, I don't believe he'll be less clement toward me. One who has never dreamed of anything but what is honourable shouldn't be unjustly attacked because divine justice will have its revenge in the end. Since I see I'm wasting our time here – the weary sun is about to set – I'll put an end to annoying you, begging your forgiveness. I yield humbly; have compassion for my long service.

"Ah, Genevera, have mercy on that suffering man!

"For the light of your eyes, have mercy.

"For your divine brow, worthy adornment for your celestial lights, have mercy.

"For these becomingly plaited tresses, have mercy.

"For this heavenly visage, have mercy.

"For your holy little mouth, have mercy.

"For your thin, straight nose, have mercy.

"For these coral lips, have mercy.

"For your ivory teeth, have mercy.

"For your divine gracefulness, have mercy.

"For your ladylike gentility, have mercy.

"For all that is seen or hidden, have mercy.

"For whatever keeps your poor lover ablaze, have mercy!

"Look upon your devoted supplicant with your usual thoughtfulness and calm mind. Remember: less drama turned Mithridates to the Romans, Masinissa to the Carthaginians, Hannibal to Fabius, and Gylippus to Nicias. Genevera, won't you deign to meet with him, hear his sufferings, perceive his hot sighs, see his sad face, consider his pallor, succour his sad heart, and gaze on his body and soul ready to serve you? Genevera, if he seems so unworthy of your mercy, focus on the greatness of your character and not on his current condition. But as his sole master and queen, be generous. Your glory and everlasting reputation derive from this.

"If the sun looked again on human suffering, it would not lose any of its splendour by shining on the myriad dreary and fetid places here. Rather, it would maintain its prim light in its heavenly abode. It would give its favour to miserable mortals without diminishing its clarity by loaning us its rays. What would it be to you, Genevera, to satisfy him with a single audience? What damage, what infamy, what tribulation could befall you? Your house is large, your servant good; night is dark, and I am nearby and at the ready. Peregrino is on guard at night, an intrepid warrior, magnanimous and eager. What harshness or insipidness or wicked thoughts could thwart such passion? Nothing better commends man than generosity: this is truly attested by every single tongue, keen spirit, celestial intellect, indeed every blessed thing. Genevera, your will holds every present and future satisfaction and disaster. If your good grace accepts him, he'll live a happy life; otherwise, he'll give up living altogether. Don't be less honourable than the nobles of antiquity who before losing their reputation would castigate the ardour of their lovers. Genevera, Peregrino is your prisoner – he has already confessed that. He begs you for his life, which can't be denied even to an enemy when he begs. Ashamed, he waits for his messenger to return with news of your ultimate sentence for him: life or death."

G: "Do not let it pain you, Violante. The suffering that turns man toward the good is a blessing. Seneca the moralist confesses himself more indebted to the toils and tribulations he endured than the dalliances of his youth. From struggles come patience, endurance, and greatness of spirit; from licentiousness one acquires death of body and soul and the loss of one's reputation. When I listen to your words, I imagine what it would be like to face Peregrino, so I am going to speak more freely with you than I would in his presence, where I would be completely speechless. How could Peregrino ever endure a great blow, if this newborn passion of his completely overpowers him? If the love he shows is true, then I judge him to be small-spirited; if it is feigned, then he is an expert in frauds and deceptions, which do not befit free men. One should recall again when Andromeda was kept in the tower, Medea in Colchis, Helen in Mycenae, and then see if love is so easy. Anyone who chooses to follow Love must possess manly patience and tolerance and practise those things that offer the prospect of a blissful life and glorious end. The wise and prudent man would sooner keep fighting than be killed so as not to suffer the effects of lust, which include torments, toils, desires, and complete destruction. It is not enough to have a fetching body if the heart, eyes, and tongue are not properly restrained. If one chooses not to listen to damning tales, and to gird the spirit for better tasks, then this deadly lust will pass into oblivion, and eventually all suffering will be in the past. It is best to die one's own death, not somebody else's.

"At this time, who is tormenting him? Who makes him suffer? Who is killing him if not himself? This proceeds from his thoughts, which are vain. Nobody in this world is at fault other than the man who chooses, because of his inconsiderate passion, to live, suffer, and die.

"Violante, go in peace, and may a sudden breeze carry his weak boat to a better port. Note that the things most urgently desired give great annoyance before they come to their desired end, then after more thought are rejected. In the proper satisfaction of appetites, true love always increases self-love, not sickens it. If he so loves me without appearing before me, what would he do in my presence? Perhaps I would be less pleasing to him? Therefore, in order to strengthen his ties to a perpetual love, I am resolved to keep as much distance as possible between us with the firm intention of not depriving him of deserved mercy when the moderator of heaven sees fit to give it. Tell him to stand determined in the field because to the strong warrior great hope grants the victory. Go in peace."

Book 1. Chapter 8.

Violante reports back to Peregrino. When he learns that his letter has not bought about the desired result, he loses his composure. After Violante calms him, he decides to take her advice and write Genevera another letter and meet Genevera's maidservant, Astanna.

Never has a ship whose helmsman has abandoned both sails and rudder ever been as agitated as my mind was while waiting for Violante. Love, fear, hope, and jealousy had taken their places on the battlefield of my weak heart, when I saw her return, her head hanging low. I went right up to her and asked, "What news does Love bring me?"

"You're about to find out," she answered. "Sit down, and I'll tell you everything."

Racked by uncertainty, I retorted more like a rabid dog: "Cruel destiny of mine, pitiless heavens! Blessed is the virile seed that never reaches conception ... twice blessed the infant whose mother's milk is poison ... but most blessed the one whose crib is the grave! Indeed, heaven smiles brightest on the man who never knows the flames of Love! I am uncertain what my life holds, but very certain it amounts to suffering. My thoughts pull in all directions; I don't know where life leads, but suffering is a given! Anxiety so seizes my soul that it careens from one thought to another without reprieve.

"O God, if I die, may my death come without fame! If I go on living like this, bitterness and pain, stronger than harsh death, will always accompany me. Lord of Love, I see you bereft of all power and punished with your own weapons. Solace of my life, faithful Violante, come to my aid!"

Violante: "Medicine is useless on an incurable wound. How can you want help when you scorn advice? It's a true saying that goes, 'He who lives poorly never begins to live, since the life he leads is always unrealized.' You number among that herd of lovers (or rather lowers). Your single-minded pursuit of sensual pleasure makes you live like swimmers flailing upstream against a river's rapids. You're all just carried away, unable to go where you want. One swimmer is held back by an eddy; another washes up on shore. One is submerged, while one clings to life half-dead, and another one flops his exhausted spirit on the sand. These are the life paths for wretched lovers. You fools lose your lives before they even begin. It pains me to say this to you: There is nothing in this world as soft, squirming, mutable, fleeting, and confusing as a woman's love, which always discourses without reason."

Peregrino: "Violante, if nature, fortune, or fate has guided me toward a bad end, what can I do about it? Heaven determines every man's destiny. Who was ever so wise or careful that he could temper this flame? It's possible to catch this disease without intending to, but not to shake it. Leave me. I was born a wretch, and it's fitting I die one!"

V: "Inept childishness! What nonsense! How could we be lords of ourselves if our will were not free? How could we deserve the name of truly rational beings if we didn't give reason its place? In you there still exists a kind of pusillanimity that caves at every challenge. Sweet nothings, with praises and cloying hopes carried by lying messengers, represent themselves in your mind as some sort of virtue and piety, and they're what you cling to and hold close to your heart. You embrace the bad as good, fearfulness as a strength, sloth as moderation, timidity as deliberation, and desire as easy rest. These are the arts your intellect invents, the knots you always tie yourself up in. It isn't nature or fortune that forces misery on you; it's your own imbecility. Save yourself, pardon this little detour of your life. Follow your nature, which offers you simple rules that are sweet to follow. Any more vain and raving speeches and you'll wind up infamous, suspect, or forgotten by muddling just ethics and holy living. So, moderate your life. It's easier to change your ways at the outset than at the end."

P: "Violante, you're killing me. How can I impose an end on my own overwhelming torment?"

V: "A mind may free itself with the same ease it chose its shackles."

P: "Violante, every created thing desires its good, whatever path it might take. I have come to understand clearly that for my own good I would do best to kill this cruel one with my own hands. Otherwise, I'll never regain my freedom."

V: "O accursed Peregrino! Is this the great love you offer Genevera? Such words ring dishonourably in the mouth of a powerful man, since vengeance on a girl is hardly the act of a noble spirit. Pardon her and harm yourself, since you're undone by your own lust. I know with certainty you couldn't feel so wounded that you'd arm yourself to attack her in any way. So, for the sake of your honour, guard against uttering shameful words like the wicked ones you said just now."

P: "Violante, it was because of her reply."

V: "On the contrary, she answered with modesty deserving of praise. And don't you see the other big sign? She willingly and patiently listened to what you said, which means she hasn't given her heart to another man. If her reaction seems a bit cool in your view, her facial expression was nevertheless relaxed and happy. Had you seen her, you'd easily have interpreted her heart by the emotion in her voice. Besides, it isn't proper for prudent ladies to trumpet when they fall in love.

"Maybe you don't trust me. To prove it to you, I'd like to lean on other intermediaries. Ah, no, don't despair. You've tried one way, now try another: write a letter expressing your feelings much more clearly this time and approach her maidservant Astanna to deliver it. Do not show anger or stubbornness. It is the woman's place to be begged, after all. If she realizes you love her, she will welcome you with open arms. She is young and beautiful, made of flesh and blood like you, and her pitying look still promises what you desire. You'd thus do well to take comfort.

"You men are so impatient and pushy, and in your lust, you have such one-track minds that without any light of reason or propriety you demand an execution before the sentence. What obligation, what bonds of friendship, what closeness does Genevera have with you that she is bound to capitulate to your whims? When good sense returns to you, you should realize you cannot cast aspersions on a family of such high regard just to satisfy your appetite. What wicked enemy, what hired assassin, what known pillager who destroys and burns in his wake does not have respect for virginal honour? Inconsiderate man, temper your fury, because it must be faithful service that makes you worthy of her love.

"I must maintain my good reputation with Genevera and her family, so I can continue to do as I wish. I wouldn't want my frequent meetings with her to raise her mother's suspicions; she is especially observant where her daughter is concerned. From this vantage, I can still be very attentive to your needs and opportunities; but for more frequent access, I'll introduce you to Astanna, her secretary. Come back here to me early tomorrow morning, and make sure your visit doesn't arouse any suspicions. Bring the letter I told you to write, and when I ask you questions tomorrow, be sure to answer calmly, so Astanna can see what kind of man you are and will be able to faithfully relay to Genevera your modesty and integrity."

Violante's affectionate admonition produced its effect. I was comforted and eager to carry out her wish, even though it was a bit like subjecting gravely ill patients to theories of therapeutic music. Mindful of her advice, however, I wrote in this way …

Book 1. Chapter 9.

Peregrino writes his second letter to Genevera and takes it to Violante's house, where he meets Genevera's servant Astanna. Astanna agrees to assist Peregrino, especially after he bribes her with the gift of a ring. Astanna meets with Genevera, offering her a convoluted explanation of her meeting with Peregrino. Astanna's delay in delivering the letter prompts Genevera to condemn the entire class of servants.

My Lady,

Since God, Fortune, and your virtue have made me your servant, I hold you in the regard your dignity requires. You are sublime; I am lowly. You're the lady, and I your attendant. Nothing befits you more than offering recompense for faithful service. I've marshalled all my forces and committed myself to your highness. You may deem they amount to little, still I beg you to treat me not as just any other citizen, but as my lady. Though my efforts seem slight, my ardour to serve you is great because I want to be appreciated by you more than to achieve anything else in this world. I live in your good grace and, if ever it should falter, I'd prefer to die than continue to suffer. If my prayer finds any favour with you, please allow me to speak briefly with you. It would be the greatest satisfaction of my weak life, the continuance of which I beg you to consider.

Once the letter was written, I signed it and took it with me to Violante's house at the arranged time. It was already mid-morning before Astanna arrived. As soon as she saw me, she turned away and would have left if Violante had not held her back on the pretext of some errand. All three of us stood there speechless, they out of embarrassment, and I weighed down by apprehension.

Finally, Violante broke the silence, "Peregrino, it is not the custom of young men to loiter about like this. Though silence can be a mark of good character, we would sooner have lighter company. Don't be like the melancholic man who drains all the life out of us."

Then I replied, "Violante, from my time in the crib my wretched body has nourished itself on that food of melancholy, and I don't foresee a change for the rest of my days."

Violante: "Why do you complain so?"

Peregrino: "I don't know."

V: "What kind of man suffers without knowing why?"

P: "My heart is overwhelmed."

V: "Share the cause of your anguish; and if I can't do anything to help, at least my compassion will accompany you."

P: "You are responsible, because from the first moments of my birth my development has been in your hands."

V: "So tell me already."

P: "I'm in love."

V: "So ardently?"

P: "Much more than I can say."

V: "With whom?"

P: "I'm afraid to say."

V: "Then you don't trust me?"

P: "Yes, but …"

V: "Tell me right now."

P: "I burn for Genevera."

V: "Which one?"

P: "Angelo's daughter."

V: "Why her?"

P: "Her extraordinary beauty has captivated me."

V: "Oh my, watch what you say, because this woman here is her faithful servant."

P: "I shall obey anyone who serves my lady, and I can't believe this would give her cause for offence."

Then Violante turned to Astanna and said to her: "Now don't pitch a fit over what you've heard. It's what young people do: they fall in love. I'll be there for you if you find the occasion to serve either of them, knowing well that the condition of servants is uncertain and ever changing. If you should get in a fix, you can count on Peregrino, too. So, with due consideration of your honesty and honour, I'm asking you please to support their courtship."

Astanna listened and answered: "It'd be difficult for me to attempt anything of the sort. I'm under the impression that Genevera's nature inclines elsewhere."

P: "Where? Can she possibly be in love with another man?"

A: "I didn't say that. She just prefers to keep to virtuous activities for noble ladies."

P: "If you understood my goal, then nothing would be dearer to you."

A: "I'm at your service then; and whenever you ask, I'll faithfully carry out your wishes."

At that point, I responded: "Astanna dear, my sad soul rests in your will. Please have the same sympathy for me you would wish for yourself if you ever found yourself in a similar situation. I ask only one thing: speak well of me when you see Genevera, give her this letter, and please encourage her to respond with those loving words you'll find fitting. As a token of our new friendship, please accept the gift of this ring."

She took the symbol of our pact and returned home, and I went back to mine. Left alone with my thoughts, I cried without interruption, "Pity, O heavens, have pity on me whoever can! My heart burns like a raging fire; everything in me melts like iron in a furnace. Have pity, since I can't go on living like this, and I curse anyone who's an enemy to pity to carry on without it!" My mind was racked by all manner of doubts. I worried about the maidservant – maybe she'd forget or find every excuse that each passing moment wasn't the right opportunity. Or what if Genevera was already corrupted, and she showed my letter to some sweet lover? I also fretted about some other accident that might put an end to our love in an instant. Tormented in this way, I tried to bear my life.

When Astanna made her way back to the house, Genevera welcomed her with a caring expression, inquiring what cause had prevented her from returning sooner. Putting it as a silly joke, Astanna prudently replied: "Genevera, if I didn't have such heartfelt love for you, I'd quit your service this very day."

Taken aback, Genevera said: "Oh my, why? What hassles have I ever caused you that you wish to quit so speciously? I have always enjoyed the kind of rapport with you that is more like that of a sister than a servant, and I am unconvinced you could find anyone else who offered you more affection. If you need anything, just tell me, and I will do whatever my honour permits to satisfy you."

Astanna: "Genevera, it is my nature to serve, and I'll always do so. I can't say I've ever felt compelled to serve you, so much as I've freely chosen to do so, and I've benefited from your generosity whenever I've asked. It's just … I'd rather not get mixed up in something I'm blameless for. I've never been one to indulge wicked thoughts. This is why I considered leaving."

Genevera: "I do not understand you. What scandal is afoot that you want to quit without taking your leave of this house? If you make such a request, you will be denied. If you flee, you will be suspected of something. You may even put your life in peril. So, if you can, please explain yourself clearly."

A: "I don't care if that happens to me."

G: "Your refusal to talk can be perceived as having an evil intent as much as a virtuous one, especially if it concerns acting secretly at some place and time on matters of honour or scandal. Yet if your plan was to free yourself of your place as a servant, you did not need to tell me, since you came into our service even before I came into this world. If I have offended you in any way, just tell me freely, and I will listen to you with patience and affection. You have always been able to tell me what is on your mind, so that I can put at your disposal whatever you might need."

A: "Genevera, my every act of gratitude toward you pales when compared to your generosity toward me. But it's better to remain silent than blurt out something inappropriate. Still, before I leave you, I'll tell you in secret why I believe I must depart right away. I know the keenness of your intellect makes you well aware of your parents' nature, how they are so easily prone to suspicion and quick to anger and how they can cruelly turn on their servants. I don't want to suffer unwarranted punishments because of someone else's audacity. However, while all is well, I'll take this chance, even if the thought of losing your good company kills me. Wherever fate leads me, I'll always be faithful and obedient to you. Now you'll see how wicked Fortune besieges me …

G: "By God, I pray you get on with it! It took less time to tell the story of the fall of Troy."

A: "Okay, I'll begin."

G: "Now, please!"

A: "Thanks to you I was given leave to visit my cousin Lena, but not finding her, I sat down, as much out of tiredness as to keep company with her seven-year-old daughter, who was sitting there. While I was waiting, Peregrino, son of Antonio, entered without so much as a knock at the door, and with caring concern indicated he wanted to speak with Lena. I informed him she wasn't there. He said he had a matter to discuss with her, so he'd wait. Then we started talking about different topics, and he asked me about my situation and service. When he learned I serve you, he sighed and said, 'Happy service, indeed, to be praised more than every liberty!' He said nothing more and collapsed in his seat as if he'd given up his spirit.

"After a time, he began to ask me about you, always praising your beauty, modesty, and generosity above all other young women. In the end, he said he didn't know another God in heaven or on earth than you, and he made a pact with me, that for every favour I did for him there would be a correspondingly greater reward. He begged me to speak well of him to you, give you his letter, and let him know clearly if you loved him, too, or not.

"When I heard his plan, I was beside myself and on the verge of fleeing or screaming at the top of my lungs as if he were some kidnapper or rapist preying on people's chastity. But out of fear of infamy or some worse scandal, I held back in a fraught silence. To free myself from his anxiousness, I promised him I'd do everything possible to satisfy him; and he made me swear to it.

"So, you see, for my soul not to fall into eternal perdition, I had to tell you everything so you wouldn't think I was leaving you out of some impetuosity. I know I won't be able to resist his constant pressures, and when the rest of this house hears word of this, there'll be hell to pay. It's better you know why I'm going, even if it brings you some displeasure, rather than I stay here facing such danger."

G: "Astanna, you have never spoken to me like this before. It seems like you have lost your mind. I have never met this man. What does he want from me?"

A: "A great deal, you understand?"

G: "I cannot and should not."

A: "Far be it from me to beg you or force you."

G: "What kind of demeanour did he show you?"

A: "Sweet and sad."

G: "What words did he use when he asked about me?"

A: "Very respectful ones."

G: "How did he act?"

A: "Humbly."

G: "What did he promise?"

A: "All he could."

G: "Do you believe he was lying?"

A: "No, I don't think so."

G: "Why not?"

A: "He's a noble man, inclined to love."

G: "How do you know?"

A: "Everything about him indicates he's in love."

G: "What did you do with the letter he gave you?"

A: "I left it at Lena's house."

G: "That was not your smartest idea. Why not bring it with you?"

A: "I didn't want to offend you."

G: "It is a greater offence to have left it there. What if it should fall into the hands of some evildoer? What would you have to say for yourself? O God, how many evils are caused by the ignorance of servants! Go now and bring it back, and with the absolute secrecy necessary in matters like these. What is more, stop your racing thoughts, and be at peace. Put aside your worries, because no suffering comes to those who serve faithfully … and I mean faithful not just in words, but you must also be calm in your actions, gestures, and all your movements. If you do so, things will turn out well. I believe the letter may contain some words of reconciliation between our families, which I would be happy to support. So, focus and go."

Astanna, ever ready to please her, went to retrieve the letter from her stash and, when the time seemed about right, showed it to Genevera.

Book 1. Chapter 10.

Genevera reads Peregrino's second letter and eventually resolves to answer him.

Genevera took the letter and went to her room where she could be alone. She sat down, rested her palm under her blushing cheek, and stared at the floor. She stayed that way lost in thought for quite some time before opening the letter. Love and fear stirred in her inexperienced breast. She could not tell which way her soul inclined and said to herself: 'If I read this letter I have accepted, then not to reply would be downright cowardly. Really, what archenemy when begged so insistently and pitiably would keep silent? Even though hate has long held sway over our houses, perhaps our love can convert it to benevolence. See how Love wields power and control over men? While Julia lived, not rivalries, calumnies, nor even the potent speeches of great Cato could break the bond between her husband Pompey and father Julius, no matter the rancour gnawing their hearts. How many men do we see reconciled by Love's sacred flame who become the dearest of friends? I do not believe Peregrino would lull me into any circumstance less than proper, because love burns as a virtue unique to keen spirits who have stamped out every impurity. Now I should read the letter, so its contents do not suggest that my thoughts are more wicked than what the man wants.'

After she reasoned with herself at length, Love presented the sign of my promise to her, which was my heart. Little by little her girlish innocence warmed to love. She became more anxious and fearful after she read the letter than before, unsure of whether she should write back, agree to meet, or press her maidservant to deliver a spoken message. 'Writing always attests to a fact nobody can deny. This would be risky, a pawn on my liberty. If it fell into the wrong hands, it would provide definitive proof of corruption and an indelible stain on reputation. However, I have learned from wise authors that people are esteemed by managing their own affairs …

'So, what now? Are you going to allow such licence to youth as to invite a stranger whose motives are iffy – an enemy of your family – to meet with you? What woman, other than a prostitute, would stoop to that filthy madness? It would be much safer to have Astanna thank him. Keep focused on the end you seek, Genevera. However, servants do not always stick to the task they are assigned, because by nature they are variable, unstable, scornful, and greedy. They are so dimwitted that they relish proclaiming, sermonizing, or commenting on subjects they cannot even wrap their heads around. And if they are so eager to bandy about their own affairs, what will they do when they hear of another's? If anyone accuses me of these things, what am I to do? What advice does urgent necessity offer me? Ah, the beginning is supposed to be the most important step; blessed is the one who considers the consequences of every action.'

After fretting over many potential objections (posed, I believe, to free herself from my pressures), she resolved to write me back, and this is what her letter contained ...

Book 1. Chapter 11.

Genevera pens a brief reply to Peregrino, whose initial reaction is sheer desperation: commit suicide or leave his homeland forever. Upon further thought, he decides to test the girl's resolve by writing another letter.

Whoever You Are,

Greetings. Love, according to what we read, is a passion of the soul, which we have no power to accept or reject. Nevertheless, it can be governed with prudence, moderated by reason, and overcome with effort and proper behaviour. Please take care to regain control of yourself, so that Love does not lead you along its age-old, predictable path of unhappiness. In this state, the whole world weeps, complains, and howls. If this beginning seems sweet to you, the end shall be bitter. You will be reputed blessed, if you reset your pursuits on more modest goals, following the examples of others.

When I am of an age to consider setting foot in the arena of Love, I will make you the first of any contenders in our city. But for the present, I am determined to stay as far away as I can from his arrows, which harm indiscreetly and cruelly. Use me as a model to correct and discipline your life, since from what I can tell, you are more anguished and afflicted by the unbearable burden of Love than is fitting to a wise man. I pray God give you rest and peaceful happiness.

When I read what she proposed, an anxiety worse than the greatest human torture wormed its way into my heart. It was so all-consuming that I determined then and there to deprive myself either of life or my country. But before I took this extreme, I opted to test how long this stubborn cruelty could hold out in the breast of a delicate girl. I convinced Astanna to deliver another letter of mine in which I begged God either to foster the beginning of true love or put a definitive end to my life.

Book 1. Chapter 12.

Peregrino composes another letter, requesting a face-to-face meeting to clarify where they stand. In response, Genevera sends him a symbolic gift: an ivory box containing a living lizard in a bed of greenery. Violante helps him to decipher its meaning and what he should do next.

My Lady,

We mortals cannot accept or possess divine things unless it pleases the Creator of all in Whose faculty rests the power to persist, forgive, or change. I know the weight on my heart from your harsh resistance will be the cause of my departure from this world. I can feel pain but find no remedy. Since cruel luck has destined me only to languish in perpetuity, my remaining comfort is to be subject to one who judges with modesty and clemency.

If the thought of my final hour should occupy your thoughts, I beg you through your divine beauty to agree to meet briefly with me before I yield so unhappily to nature. At least I'll be content ever after, whether I'm dead or alive. What disastrous prospect keeps me from expressing what I feel in your presence? I'm certain your consummate gentility, untouched by the uncouthness of common folk, will move you to compassion. I'm not asking you to grant the impossible, but only to offer mercy for all I have endured, and an audience with you would be that.

What lady was ever so coy when it came to love that she refused to admit a servant to her presence? Following the examples of others doesn't lead to vice. Many ancient and modern ladies of high, middle, and low station have been discreet and affectionate toward their servants. Even if you didn't love me as much as my faithful service warrants, you must still consider and have respect for the splendour of your reputation. And what I haven't earned through my own efforts, you might concede to me out of your grace.

If you wish to withdraw from our venture, I beg you – for your honour and my salvation – do not rely on any living person other than yourself to communicate it. You may hope by doing so to cool my ardent heart, though it doesn't seem you'd find pleasure in my death. My weak hand would like to write more, but I lack the necessary powers to do so. Remain in peace, flower of gentility.

My faithful and ever diligent servant saw to delivering the letter to its rightful recipient. Love, who had yet to strike Genevera's tepid heart with its golden arrow, tested me further by allowing her caprices to wander wherever her youthful feelings took her. Moved by fear and anxiety, she decided to put in motion a clever puzzle of a plan, which only left me more confused, given the tumult of new love I was experiencing.

She had a living lizard caught and a note tied around its neck. Its message consisted of these words: "Learn the way. Prudence reigns. Time moderates all." She had it placed in an ivory box she tied and sealed. This is what she sent to me in answer to the letter I wrote.

Before I opened the box, I humbly accepted the generous gift, offering profuse thanks. I wanted to preserve the celestial boon in my memory forever as the true beginning of our love story. I admired the artful packaging, adorned with no less magnificence than the chest in which Darius kept his copy of Homer's *Iliad*. Overcome by joy, I heaped effusive thanks on the lord of Love who had made me the worthy servant of so great a lady, because nothing in the world confirms one's innermost hopes more than to receive a gift in response to those thoughts.

I went to my room, sat down, and rejoiced over that divine reward. I considered it a sacred object worthy of great veneration. Finally, impelled by curious desire, I unwrapped it very lovingly and carefully.

Suddenly, I glimpsed that leashed little beast on its bed of grass! It showed its sharp teeth and bi-coloured limbs and sought its well-being by means of escape. Its menacing aspect frightened me. Had I startled a poisonous serpent lurking in the grass I would not have been more dumbfounded. What it presaged was hard to understand, but most difficult was its underlying significance – an almost indecipherable riddle. I set out to learn any information I could about these creatures, which, it turns out, are chameleon-like, uncertain, unstable, and solitary. I sought to unravel if Genevera intended to refer that thing's nature to me, or rather to convince me to act more like it did, or instead to inform me that a woman's love is like that. I considered the season, which was cold and dry – already the ground was covered with a white mantle – which made any interpretation even more obscure to me. My heart armed itself with ire and disdain. Blood flowed to my extremities with such urgency and abundance that I almost went mad. I detected scorn; I noted a womanly cleverness, and I condemned my own frank ways. Communicating is shameful but remaining silent is damning.

Without recourse to other advice, I sought out Violante, who had faithfully kept secret my feelings. I showed her everything, and she smirked at me, saying: "O Peregrino, you haven't gleaned much from your studies of the natural sciences. Laurel, ivy, boxwood, and similar plants are the habitat and food of little animals like this one. You should investigate if these plants grow near Genevera's palace or the walls or outbuildings around it. If you give some thought to the place, you should be able to comprehend its significance."

Heavy with fretful cares, I wandered around Genevera's house. Behind it was a pathway that skirted the walls of the old city. It was so out of use that even its nearby inhabitants seemed little aware of it anymore, and it would've brought infamy on a man of high regard to be seen beyond it. I considered this timeworn place. It teemed with those kinds of plants, and among these were a thick green ivy, which covered the ground up to the roof of some sort of outbuilding and concealed a small entryway and a tiny window, not directly visible from Genevera's house. (I surmised it might have been purchased by a man wanting to avoid detection to have his way freely.)

Stupefied, I marvelled at her cleverness, and I put away all my sad thoughts, reassured of Genevera's love. I returned to Violante and asked her to speak with Astanna to find out what was in store for me.

Book 1. Chapter 13.

Arrangements are made for a meeting at what turns out to be Genevera's household laundry facility. While Peregrino furtively waits outside, Astanna dumps a bucket of cleaning lye on his head. He cries out, drawing the attention of the city's watchmen on the lookout for a man wanted for stabbing a love rival to death. Peregrino is arrested and locked in prison to face trial and execution.

Two more days passed before Love deigned to give me an invitation from Genevera. Astanna informed me that the outbuilding I had seen was used for washing clothes. Genevera would sometimes gather there with the household servants for some company, where they would pass the time discussing various topics of interest to women. Genevera would be there that evening for a few hours.[9] Astanna did not say another word before leaving me with so little to go on.

When the appointed hour came – happy and propitious above all others – I felt I had waited far too long. So, I took off toward the meeting place wearing only my *farseto* and with my unsheathed sword in hand.[10] I kept close to the wall, using my free hand to feel my way along it hidden under the ivy. Once I reached the building, I did not neglect to praise Genevera's ingenuity and venerate the power of lord Cupid. Contemplating my happiness, I sat down there to wait for my lady to come out to me.

Fortune, deemed a goddess by our blind world, has a wheel that always turns unpredictably toward another man's gain or convenience. At that time, Fortune ordained that another youth in the act of meeting up with his beloved be discovered by an insidious, foolhardy rival and stabbed to

9   Time specifications in the text seem to follow neither the traditional canonical hours
     nor modern standard time, which was not established before the nineteenth century.
     Here Caviceo indicates that the women will be at the outbuilding from the third *vigilia*
     of night until *meza nocte*, which may mean they gather some evenings to wash clothes
     while there is still some light around dusk and talk into the first hours of darkness.
     Subsequently, especially in 1.18, I offer approximate times according to today's norms.
10   The style of the *farseto*, or doublet, a tight-fitting vest that typically fell just below the
     waist, certainly varied over time and according to the occasion or regional location.
     Ludovica Sebregondi offers some descriptions and illustrations in "Clothes and Teen-
     agers." See also Elissa Weaver's "Dietro il vestito." Readers of Caviceo's text should
     assume that Peregrino is inadequately dressed for his evening venture.

death. Shrieks pierced and echoed throughout the neighbourhood, and the terrible news of the committed murder reached the ears of the city's ruler. He dispatched the night watch to investigate the whole area with strict orders: when the nefarious disturber of the peace was apprehended, he should be hauled in without delay to face the death penalty.

Completely unaware of what was afoot, I crouched like a hunted beast between the plants and the door. The cold had already begun to seep into my bones. I had already passed the point at which my whole body went numb, when I thought I heard Astanna murmur vaguely: "Let's go; the time has come." I glimpsed some comfort for my fleeting hope and tried – beyond my own powers – to recall my bodily spirits, which due to the cold had fled my heart. Just then, I heard the little-used window of the washing house creak open. Believing I was about to have my much-anticipated audience, I lifted my head to see what new vision would appear. I made out in the darkness a shadow, which I guessed was the font of my well-being and happy peace. It turned out to be Astanna, however. She leaned out the window holding a cauldron full of hot lye and, without looking, dumped it unceremoniously on my head. Completely soaked, I thought I might drown, and I was in such terrible agony I couldn't even manage to exhale and inhale. I remained more or less like a soulless cadaver.

In that state I heard Astanna reach the gate, where the night guards were happening by. They heard something, thought it might be the one who had perpetrated the homicide, and rushed in to find me prostrate on the ground. They hauled me up. Hearing this, Astanna abandoned the idea of coming back to tell me of some unexpected change of plan. She fled in terror, and I was bound over to be judged just as the ruler had decreed.

I felt overwhelmed by fear and disorientation. I was not entirely conscious. The executioner had already placed a noose around my neck as he had been commanded, but the chief of the ducal guard, who had known me for a long time, took pity on me. He untied me and had me sent to a cell reserved for those awaiting execution for treason and high crimes.

After quite some time had passed, I came to, but I began to have doubts and questioned if I were really myself or not. I couldn't see the sun or light of any kind, nor did I hear any screaming. My feet were tied and my arms were in chains, so I began to convince myself I couldn't possibly be me. Then I shouted, cried out, and moaned so much that the guard at the door turned toward me, fury rising in his voice: "Peregrino! What wickedness or hostile fortune has landed you here?"

I couldn't reply at first, given my pain, but in my anguish and affliction, with a tremulous voice, I ventured: 'Woe is me! Have I been metamorphosed? Is Phoebus taking his revenge because I love someone worthier than I deserve? Has Jove picked me as his rival, such that he has destroyed my chance at true love? Did Cupid regret having given more than he kept for himself? Cursed Cupid, may your bow be broken in half, your power blasphemed, and your fury exhausted! O how miserable anyone is who puts his faith in you!

'O Peregrino, you recognize too late Love's snares. You have forgotten yourself and your condition. Are these the first fruits, the outcomes, the just rewards of your years of toil? Is this how you'll make your late father proud? And you leave an inconsolable mother. Mother, why didn't you abort the seed you received; why didn't you cast it to the dogs, so I'd never be conceived? O womb, fertile only in grief for me: why did you bring into this world such a shameful burden? O ill-omened nine months, O cruel midwife: why didn't you kill me at my birth? O thankless age for a son toward his parents. O heavens, O earth, O higher bodies, O wandering spirits, O disquieted souls, why didn't you conspire at my birth to make me stillborn? Cruel Fates, why have you kept the thread of my miserable mortal life intact for so long? O Charon, why doesn't your boat take me from this bank to your other shore, which would be a sweeter realm for me? O Fortune, more inhumane than Hydra, more mutable than a tiger, more violent than the lashing southern winds, more bitter than a Harpy, more uncertain than a breaking wave, now I know your pains and deceits! Who can lend any aid to my unhappy state? Has a more unfortunate man than me ever lived? Without any reason, without guilt, I'm condemned. O God, in what country do we live where Astraea, goddess of justice, is wholly exiled?

'Some men poetically sing their elegies in fragrant cypress groves or among the most cultured salons, others in verdant woods or in a delightful shade. Me? I get to weep my sorry destiny in a dank and dreary prison! Highest Rector of heaven in Whom justice and mercy find unequalled application, You freed the innocent Hebrew woman from the fire;[11] look with that same eye on my innocence. I know Your goodness won't permit evil to vanquish my purity.'

I passed a bitter and pitiless night raving in that way.

Book 1. Chapter 14.

Peregrino learns why he's been arrested. He experiences a vision of Genevera encouraging him before he faces judgment.

---

11   The reference to the Hebrew woman here is unclear. Although Rahab the harlot is not Jewish, she helps the Israelite army to take Jericho, and she and her family are consequently spared the burning of the city (Joshua 6:23–5).

The guard in that sorrowful prison sympathized with me by shedding tears of pity, and although he could not offer any other aid, he revealed the reason for my arrest. Because not much time remained, he exhorted me to accept death patiently or mount my defence bravely.

Then it seemed as if I saw Genevera in her actual form. She reassured me by saying: 'Not distance, suffering, or punishment will ever separate me from you.' After these words, the vision vanished. Because there's no message with greater impact than the one from an oracle, I convinced myself it was a message from heaven. So I gave thanks saying: 'My lady, even the most dire torment will seem slight now because your salvation and blessed appearance in this vision emboldens me to suffer and face whatever comes.'

Fame, the daughter of Gaia, had already flown about the city disseminating the news of the committed homicide and my capture. At sunrise the people gathered, the magistrates were called, and I was taken bound and in chains surrounded by officials and guards. The city roiled with discontent. I was presented to the ruler, who said out of sincere piety …

Book 1. Chapter 15.

Duke Ercole I d'Este of Ferrara acknowledges his authority as ruler of the city to judge legal proceedings and addresses Peregrino.

Duke: "Only the one who excels all of his subjects in probity, industry, and integrity is worthy to rule, nor should anybody else administer public goods or judge another, according to philosophical writings. For this reason, Alexander the Great of Macedon, when asked by friends and associates about who should inherit his command after him, said 'the best one.' That is a pronouncement truly worthy of a great king: to prefer someone better to his own sons, successors of his kingdom by right. Thus, it is said, according to the judgment of divine Plato: Blessed are those governed, corrected, and preserved by prudent men dedicated to wisdom. Therefore, it is necessary for one who is elected by divine commission to lead others; otherwise, all matters would be confused by the infamy of rulers and bring harm to the righteous. It is far better to punish rigorously than adopt too much lenience; the former encourages disciplined living, but the latter leads to licentious behaviour and constant sinning.

"I proceed with the utmost seriousness to judge this criminal case. On the one hand, I acknowledge the private nature of your love, the piety due to your aged parents, the tears of those present, and the sobs of your relatives. On the other hand, I have a duty to determine justice for the woeful tragedy of spilled blood, which moves me. I cannot, nor would I, do otherwise than rule for you to be punished for the crime you wilfully and rashly committed, once your defence, which has no recourse, shows it to be fitting. You should accept it for your own good with the same patience and inevitability. So you can better understand, listen patiently to the just accusations of your accuser, who is present here."

Book 1. Chapter 16.

Nicolò accuses Peregrino of stabbing his son to death.

Nicolò: "I see your eyes fixed upon me, great ruler and all of you here present. Pain and heartfelt grief compel me to appear in this exalted place, which is more appropriate for accomplished orators and civil defenders. Though I have long sought to avoid what goes on here, perhaps my changed behaviour will prompt admiration in you, not scorn for my commonness, if I must set aside my quiet honest pursuits to confront this criminal matter.

"As my rotten luck would have it, this wicked man, rife with lust, cruelty, and arrogance, has corrupted, confounded, and destroyed everything. O God, help me, so I don't perish along the way! What bounty of prayers could I offer? Whose tongue could eloquently tell this case? What man could hear it with patience and put up with such cruelty? Unconquered ruler, I appear before you moved by paternal grief, throwing myself on your mercy: Do your duty to set good examples and carry out the laws – both human and divine – to uphold your reputation, authority, and dignity. I know this wretched case seizes your heart with no less suffering than it does mine.

"Woe is me, the outset of life is difficult, the midst toilsome, and then only death looms! O great God in heaven, who would be so cruel and inhumane as not to feel piety and come to my aid? Who doesn't share my tears and incline in my favour? I see our city dishonoured and our free life destroyed when the accused can wander about putting a knife through the breasts of the innocent! Given that the risk of danger he poses affects everyone, his defence cannot benefit him alone.

"See, Your Grace, it doesn't matter if he is patrician or plebeian, this destroyer of liberty is captured and shackled; he stands before you, and his nature is more depraved than that of Sulla, Marius, Catiline, or Nero! Last night, this man threatened our lives and betrayed every debt he owes humanity. Armed, in violation of the city's laws, unprovoked, and against reason, this man stabbed to death my only son. Lord, look on this cruel spectacle, which would be impossible to endure even for the most Stoic thinker facing a great enemy!

"O heaven-born son who bears my face, who will see your prowess now? Your life, which began so well, has been cut down in the first flower of youth. Your Grace, please look at that prisoner: do not allow his personal tyranny to denigrate your state! Note the yellowish cast of his downturned face and his shameful silence. His clothing and sword and the place and time of the committed homicide all render clear testimony. Consider, ruler, and judge his past life: you can't believe this is proper behaviour for this day and age! How many homicides we don't know about, how many thefts and arsons have been committed by this deranged bloody beast? Why could nothing restrain this wicked killer, not God, reverence for you, not fairness, friendship, faith, piety, nor the honour due to country? Isn't it fair for him to die as he has lived?

"Your Grace, wicked ones prefer sinful pleasures more than well-founded reasoning. Thus, if he sinned willingly, let him be punished against his will. If he's deprived of life, no great harm is done, because his death isn't some favour granted in response to prayers but is carried out through necessity to quiet our suffering and misery. He'll receive the just reward for his actions and evil life, finding satisfaction, according to the law, your honour, and the highest God, Whom I pray preserve your state forevermore."

As soon as my accuser spoke these words, the entire family of the dead man cried out before the Duke, saying: "O God, where are we? Where do we live? What kind of magistrate do we have? O ruler, order justice to be served, or move that we be exiled from this land. It'd be better to live as a vagabond in peace and tranquillity than as a resident of a city harbouring such iniquity! As long as this obdurate disturber of the peace and enemy of virtue lives, no one can pursue a good life path or correct its course. So, for your honour and the preservation of this state, order that justice be served!"

When their bitter shouts finally subsided, and there was a mournful silence, I responded in the following way.

Book 1. Chapter 17.

Peregrino defends himself against the accusation.

Peregrino: "Highest ruler, not even the greatest painter could through his art express such raw pain. This is why Agamemnon stood mute, wrapped in his mantle, believing silence expressed the extremes of so much grief better than launching into vain speeches. I would more readily incline toward silence in my anguished state of mind if I didn't know you to be a true assessor of man's character, a supporter of virtue, the maintainer of justice, and an unhesitating exterminator of vices. We therefore worthily place our public and private goods in the care and universal trust of your integrity and greatness.

"This age of ours is golden and blessed because under your leadership all our crazed, sinful, hateful, and detestable acts worthy of punishment are eradicated and destroyed. It's also the age, however, in which wild fury in an impudent shadow of a man attempts to destroy it, though your authority and wisdom will put him in his place. Even if my defence is tenuous, bare, and weak, the divine justice in your presence will make it acceptable. The declamations of my false accuser cannot be so sordid, rustic, prolix, exaggerated, base, uneven, indecent, fictional, insane, fastidious, hateful, or vulgar that they inflame your highness, justice, or the great God against me. You will clearly understand his speech to be nothing but tearful malice, heated invention, and calculated deception. Nonetheless, so that I am not considered anything like him, I'll control my emotions and express what reason dictates, so as not to annoy this great audience, which always recoils from hearing people whine. I'd rather be damned for honourable silence than praised for garrulous chatter.

"I know the nature of stray dogs is to bark more than bite, calculating that they can frighten others just by making noise. First of all, Your Grace, I praise your holy premise – to preserve your state through justice such that man may more readily turn to the magistrate than the magistrate go after man, and to temper justice with mercy so you can truly be considered lord and not tyrant. Among all the traits of body and soul given to man, one alone was uniquely ascribed to Caesar, that is, equal justice. You are an example. Antonius Pius, the philosopher and most thoughtful emperor, was moved by this to write to Faustina, 'No other thing can commend a Roman emperor nor gratify his people more than clemency.' So, my lord, temper justice with mercy, and you will find your love joined in me. Do not let the voice bandied about accuse me of spilled blood, or your justice is vain.

"Highest ruler, just as innocence can to some degree be passed down through men and render them magnanimous and intrepid in the most serious matters, so can iniquity make them timid and pusillanimous. Therefore, trusting in these fundamental points, I do not doubt I can counter the base and malicious insinuation of my accuser.

"A major argument in these cases concerns the past life of the man accused. If one may deduce such a thing, then I can say without fear that I have never committed any act so evil, nasty, impious, wicked, and worthy of capital punishment. Why must I be lumped together with similar filth? Duke, consider who has the more just reason to complain: the dead hoodlum or the living innocent man? The first had his life justly taken away; the second is dishonoured without cause.

"Now consider what one has wrought for the other. What man of good sense and prudence can deny that a rightful stabbing has taken place? He was like the man who boldly samples every illicit pleasure; he must've taken advantage of some virtuous girl's chastity and gotten caught and killed. What can I do about that? Who has greater licence to go out armed at night than I do? Is the law not equal for all? If in breaking the law he died, was he not the transgressor? Since this is the way it was, what does this man have to complain about, if not to excuse his son's evil and depraved life by casting infamy on others? Has a more impious, stupid, wicked, and inconsiderate suggestion ever been uttered – unlike any well-weighed judgment – than that a living man should die for a dead one? O insipid arguments unworthy of this hearing: that is the insinuation, and that is the man who uttered it.

"The suffering one glimpses in another's face doesn't prove a homicide has been committed. What man, if he were not a lunatic, would show any sign of joy in this context, facing a trial like this one? Silence is shameful, unless what must be heard is plain infamy. My clothing at the time was appropriate. The sword itself is evidence: have you ever seen the blade of a killer without blood? A just and level-headed sentence wouldn't accept similar remarks and unfounded hints, which indicate his malice more than thoughtful reasoning.

"Then you said, probably with the intent to inflame the ruler and the people here present against me, that I committed this cruel homicide during the night, unprovoked and without any reason. Really, what man in all the world (except Diomedes King of Thrace and Boursiris) would take pleasure in killing a man? I've got nothing against the dead youth, no family connection; I don't know him through friends or associates. There wasn't anything between us, no love jealousies leading to fights, nor any bad blood as a result of public or private matters between us. I can't imagine what wild delusion has caused you to rail so brazenly against me.

"Moreover, if the night watchman had been more dutiful, he would have carefully questioned me at my capture. But there are certain men who are so self-righteous they do not care to do what is right, only make a big show of doing something. However, it is proper for the one who wishes to govern others well to proceed with great prudence, especially in criminal cases, and process and weigh all considerations. You know how little thought the Roman procurator Gessius Florus gave while people wept for the burning of the holy city of Jerusalem.

"Woe is me! Fortune persecutes me more than the truth of any committed homicide. I do not see my longstanding honour impugned in any way. I'll offer a brief example so that you can understand how much I am worthy of esteem. Achilles' mother Thetis warned him that if he took revenge on his companion's killers, he would die shortly thereafter. The hero responded that a death with honour would be preferable to a life of shame. Ruler, I realize my dire circumstance; I have been captured without cause. Do not perpetuate a false accusation. Reason, justice, and honour are on my side. You who know this and can carry out your will, make your judgment accordingly. In me you will always find a man readier to obey you than to live."

Book 1. Chapter 18.

In the longest chapter of the "Peregrino," the Duke assigns esteemed jurists Antonio Leuto and Giovanni Maria Riminaldo to argue whether Peregrino violated a nighttime prohibition to carry arms or was licitly circulating during the day.[12] The Duke is about to pronounce his verdict when the trial is interrupted by Briseida and Polidoro, each claiming to have killed Nicolò's son, Cesare. Briseida convinces the Duke that she killed Cesare to protect her chastity; she must face the executioner. The populace of Ferrara objects, however, and the Duke shows mercy toward her and absolves Peregrino.

Nicolò: "Highest ruler, I do not know if your long silence is due to true conviction through reason or because you are moved by his vehemence. Maybe you're overly inclined toward good will, or his fiery speech has left your head spinning. Perhaps, however, you're ready to purge the earth of wicked men to satisfy a just one with every right to complain and grieve. In my view, a wise and necessary sentence would say something more significant about you than a thoughtless act of mercy might.

"Even if his cleverly invented defences might appear to you to have some semblance of truth, you should not believe them so readily, since

---

12 Leuto will defend Peregrino by arguing that the action in question took place during the day; Riminaldo will argue for the prosecution that the murder took place during the night, consequently warranting the death sentence. The time of contention is *l'hora septima*, or the seventh hour of darkness, or sometime close to four a.m., as it is specified in the Spanish adaptation ("Cuasi a las cuatro," in Martínez Morán's edition, 159). It is a time when the sun is not shining (indeed, the wee hours of night, according to Nicolò's understanding), but almost when the rooster's crow will herald a new day and some workers are beginning to circulate around the city. By emphasizing the minor detail of defining the time of day, Caviceo, who studied law, may be implicitly critiquing the profession's preference for following the letter of the law over getting at the truth. Another possible criticism of the legal system comes when the Duke is compelled to reconsider his sentence in response to the tumult from the Ferrarese people; that is, justice depends on popular appeal.

they cannot obscure what happened to my son. He wasn't born of oak or rock – his death deserves justice! Although he could have been more careful, consider the reputation of our city; it should be a free land where everyone might live with honour.

"Duke, your hesitation is shameful because the law dies when those in power are slow or late to exercise it. Too much mercy is also damaging because it proceeds from either cowardice or greed, traits of the most despicable princes. Since your mind is righteous and sincere, you must consult it in such a way that no one wonders if you shirk assigning guilt. O ruler, I fear that man is about to launch into a disputation over some minutiae, which might waste two lifetimes. Thus, I would prefer to limit us to the one thing no one can deny or try to explain away: for the sake of your own virtue, order the execution that has been prepared in accordance with the statute language, which doesn't permit contradiction. I'm certain you have the utmost integrity and consideration in every one of your actions, so I know you will appreciate one candid piece of truth over a thousand masked lies. Do not let yourself be swayed, O ruler, by the loose living, depraved habits, and wicked customs of the city, but rather consider your sublime condition and remember that through your mother's blood, your upbringing, and your relationships, you are the one ruler of all, and true judgment is your innate virtue.

"In civil matters, one should proceed according to the customs of that land; but in criminal ones, only pure justice can be followed. Command courageously, O ruler, that reason have its place, which concerns not just private convenience but also the public good, and see to it that you do not lose in one hour through a pull at your heartstrings what your ancestors acquired with virtue and hard work over many centuries. Three main things can incite people to crazed violence: starvation, too much preying on other men's women, and neglect of justice. If you diligently preserve these things, you'll worthily be numbered among the gods."

I saw in the Duke's face that he was moved, determined to rule against me. I eagerly and intrepidly interjected: "Unconquered Duke, not even the Maker of the heavens can separate pleasure from pain; the end of one already includes the beginning of the other. Just now I was summarily attacked by his false, unfounded, and disputed accusation, motivated by ill will more than reasoned judgment. Now, God willing, freed from it, I will be consoled, not so much because my life is saved than because our social order is restored. Moreover, to the glory of your reputation, others will understand you rule virtuous men, not wicked ones. I give eternal thanks first of all to God for the grace He has bestowed on me thanks to you, Duke, whose honest and most prudent consideration saved me in my innocence. I also thank my accuser, who was confused, but through reason recognized his error. At this point, ruler, you can dissolve this wearied assembly since justice has been served.

"You see, my accuser admits I am not guilty, but asks that the statute be followed in a similar case, a riddle whose meaning may be interpreted only with more time. The poor man, who isn't terribly sharp, does not seek its enforcement. Like one who trots along an unfamiliar road and stops at the most frequented spot, even if it is a pitiable one, he has taken after those insipid wet nurses who nastily smack a whimpering baby before they figure out the cause of the child's suffering. This man has discoursed with a cursory eye and a distracted mind on what he doesn't comprehend at all. In order to clarify this matter, I will follow reason and patiently explain what fate holds for me. Please do not be annoyed, but listen with your usual clemency and prudence to what I argue, because I won't deviate from the truth in any way. If I should lie, may every light blind me, may curs and beasts tear my dead body to pieces, and may my cursed spirit wander the dark shores in perpetual restlessness!

"I know magnanimous souls do not excuse their tiny faults by contrasting them to extreme examples, which comes easily to over-eager storytellers. A sincere promptness and a virtuous and courageous heart in word and deed – even if it should appear reprehensible – can be excused according to the quality of individual, if he is more likely to sin out of meekness than cruelty, which has always been abhorrent to God and the world. If I go against my wont and become wordy, it is due to my young age; please pardon me in this case.

"O highest ruler, everyone knows about the hatred between the Bentivoglio and Canedoli families in Bologna. Witness the spilled blood, the exchanged threats, the diminished focus on anything else, the recent killings, and the ongoing persecutions, both in secret and out in the open. Now Canedoli influence is everywhere; there isn't a house, church, or any hideout they haven't taken over.

"Because I am determined to increase my patrimony, which should be a welcome activity to all of my fellow citizens, I was thinking about investing in Giovanni Canedoli's farm. He lives out where he fears every day may be his last. We agreed by letter to meet yesterday morning just when the gates opened to sign the contract in the house owned by Petronio, his relative and faithful merchant. As the appointment time drew near, the weather was quite foggy and dark. Out of an abundance of caution, even though it was day, I grabbed my sword. In the clothes I had on at the time, I set off, and I had not even gotten halfway there when a vat of hot water was suddenly dumped on me from a high window. I fell to the ground, incapable of proceeding any more than I could return the way I had come.

In that instant, your worthy guards took me captive and brought me here, as you see."

Possessed by fury and rabid frenzy, my accuser interrupted: "O impious and cruel soul, O wicked opinion, O nefarious audacity, O most truculent beast, O proud daring! What would that rogue do, say, or think, if his capture had been hidden when he makes such excuses out in the open? O God, will such a farce accomplish more than plain truth? O ruler, a slick lie should not curry so much favour. I know you aren't so unseeing that you can't distinguish light from the shadows. He has an impudent mouth, a lustful look, and a vain mind and speech.

"Answer this: if it was day, why was he walking around in his doublet? If it was night, how did that liar get through the gate? Ruler, sometimes a man doesn't want to confess what is most important. He must belong to a group of thugs, given the time of night they were gathering to prey on our city. O God, prevent it! Ruler, be prudent. A domestic threat rises; seek the truth here with every diligence. This case seems so important that it could destroy your state and our livelihood. His capture interrupted some evildoing; and that other man had some insidious plan, since he doesn't seem to respect our walls. How regrettable a similar breach was to the founder of Rome is attested by his brother's blood. This striving age does not shirk any danger to realize its desires.

"Two traits cause one to disregard faith and precedent: a desire to seize the reins of power and the opportunity to satisfy one's lust. Be careful, Duke, that your overindulgence of mercy doesn't come back to harm you. You can avoid this risk by toughening your stance toward justice, so he is made an example to the whole city to keep within the bounds of what is proper. The Roman consul Titus Manlius Torquatus deprived his son of life for a far lesser crime, and Emperor Trajan, renowned for his justice, dedicated himself to avenging the death of a poor woman's son as an example to his people.

"Duke, time passes, and your people are agitating. The law must be upheld. It's just like an evildoer to try to get out of this: he who is rich in time is poor in options. Take care that a clandestine conspiracy does not interrupt your virtuous thinking. Caesar cried for nothing more than that his case be settled with efficiency and promptness. This man's guilt is apparent, and the law is clear. Only his execution remains."

At that I responded: "O thief of another's honour, O man envious of my success and thirsty for the blood of the just! Cruel, arrogant, rash, and presumptuous, you were born to this world only to commit evil. Consider, ruler, what kind of youth came from this shadow of a man who even beyond sixty years of age says not what a mature, honourable man would say but what only the filthiest beast would let fall from its mouth. You see how cleverly he tries to arm you with anger against your most faithful citizen and impinge his false character on me. Clearly, I would not have been up to such a task had I not been helped by another, which is nevertheless allowed.

"O my fellow citizens, why do you stop now? Here is the wicked one entrenched in vices, he calls you all traitors: let arms, fire, and stones be your response to him. Hunt down and exterminate this sewer of vices, so he won't corrupt our bond with his convictions.

"Duke, new ideas sometimes spring from similar accusations. This pretender with his crafty scheming wants to lead you to hate your people, which I understand you were close to doing. Still, I would have been more faithful to you than ever. This Sinon deserves to have his perfidious and garrulous tongue corrected. Ruler, pardoning these extremely wicked types only strengthens the audacity of evildoers. To distinguish myself from them, I prefer reason to defend my innocence, rather than lies.

"In order not to leave any confusion, I will respond to your queries. The time was fitting when I could properly go about in these clothes because by that hour all of the nocturnal adulterers, whoremongers, and rapists – like your son! – had already returned home without raising the suspicions of the night watch. Much of the time, these guards mill about dissatisfied with their thoughts; they delight in making bold boasts, and when they catch someone, they usually become even crueller where there's no guilt. Preferring not to suffer their harassment, I cautiously went the way I did. Giovanni came through the gate, which is left open at apt times for the benefit of farmers from the countryside and merchants, like we are, whose contributions are felt near and far. Why should we be denied this privilege?

"Duke, what remains is for the truly wicked one to be punished for his iniquity, and I should be justly liberated."

Nicolò: "Duke, command so that our faith in the law find its correspondence in your actions. First: consider his arrest, then inquiries about Giovanni's arrival can follow."

Duke of Ferrara: "Guard!"

Guard: "Here I am."

D: "Tell the truth."

G: "I cannot deny it, nor would I want to do so."

D: "What time did you pick up Peregrino?"

G: "Around four."

D: "What was he doing when you found him?"

G: "He was prostrate on the ground."

D: "Where exactly?"

G: "In an alleyway."

D: "Why did you go there?"

G: "To search for the killer."

D: "What led you there?"

G: "A ruckus in the area."

D: "Where were you?"

G: "At that hour, in my house."

D: "Then how did you get there so quickly?"

G: "It was almost time for the changing of the guard."

D: "Is that the way it is typically done?"

G: "That is how I believe it has been observed."

D: "Be sure you tell the truth."

G: "You can ask others about it."

D: "Now go. You, Peregrino, how did you find yourself in that out-of-the-way place? I believe you behaved as a hunted animal, escaping to the first hiding place you came across."

P: "That was not the case at all. I took that route only to go with greater discretion."

Nicolò: "Ruler, these excuses have no substance! The open gate and the guard on break … They make sense only because the gate is open all night and the changing of the guard must happen at some point. And yet, it was still nighttime! It was still pitch dark at that hour on the first day of May, if I must declare the date.[13] From the confirmation of his capture, the time of it, and the fact he was armed, he must be punished. Executioner, do your duty; settle this account."

It seemed I had no time to waste. Almost in a faint, I said, "Duke, when cruel Nero faced a capital punishment decision, he said he wished he did not know how to read, so he wouldn't have to consent to put another man to death. If that impious emperor had such clemency, what must a man of mercy and discretion do? In similar cases, ruler, it is far better to be upbraided for taking your time than for acting too hastily. Paris did well,

---

13 Peregrino saw Genevera for the first time in church on the first day of May. Since then, the narrator has made a point of indicating that the sun has risen and set a number of times, though my impression is certainly not another full year. I cannot explain the insistence on the first of May as the night when Peregrino is arrested. It would also be unusual in Ferrara to see a mantle of snow or frost on the ground, such as Peregrino described when he set out that night. Issues of chronology will continue to beguile the reader who takes them too literally. Duke Ercole's feast day is 26 October, mentioned in 1.22. Not many days pass when 1.30 opens with the specification that it is the Feast of the Annunciation, celebrated on 25 March. Caviceo likely wishes to associate developments in his narrative with cultural celebrations specific to Ferrara at the time (including the holiday celebrating the Duke) or with symbolic links to his story (the day "dedicated to lovers" may wish to link Peregrino and Genevera's story to Polidoro and Briseida's, for instance).

before he made his decision, to ask to see the goddesses naked, so he could assess every detail carefully before making his judgment. If any doubt remains in your mind, it would not harm to sift the details of legal matters.

"Divine Plato was not ashamed to hear Euclid's full explanation. Although you are very wise, you will only become more so by listening to others. If I am condemned properly, I will blame nobody. There are men of high intellect, who happen to be present here to determine the border between our lands and Bologna's: Giovanni Maria Riminaldo and Antonio Leuti.[14] Ask them to interpret the statute, and you will understand that the hour of my capture was not during the night. Or if my accuser objects to them, then Felino Sandeo and Alessandro of Imola,[15] renowned for their integrity and knowledge throughout Italy."

A trial convened straightaway with the reading of the law, the words of which stated: "The armed man who is apprehended during the night is to be hanged without delay."

The ruler, persuaded by compassion, said: "You, Giovanni Maria Riminaldo, advocate for death, and you, Antonio Leuto, defend the side of life. The greatest difficulty seems to consist in whether the hour in question falls during night or day."

The two assigned parties remained silent for quite a while. But after much time had passed, it was like watching two starving lions contend over the prey. Each one honed his eye, wrinkled his brow, bared his teeth, lashed his tail, and stepped forward to take the field with a sudden, violent rush to puff out his chest. Each believed the statute clearly favoured his own side. Everyone took sides; places were designated; and the two jurists were commanded to argue their cases.

Because Antonio Leuti represented the defence, he was first to speak, which he was on the verge of doing when my accuser let out a cry, which was louder than what is usually screamed by a person who spots a serpent nearby. Nicolò shouted: "The navigation of Colchis is more straightforward, and the building of Crete happened with less effort, compared to the immortal intelligence necessary to comprehend this legal intrigue! Nothing is what it seems here! But you want their disputations to lead the mind where nothing can

---

14 Gian Maria Riminaldo (d. 1497) was professor of civil law at the Studio di Ferrara and diplomat on behalf of the Estense court. Antonio Leuto (or Antonio dai Liuti) lectured in canon law at the Studio di Ferrara.

15 Felino Sandeo (or Sandei, d. 1503) hailed from Reggio and taught Canon Law in Ferrara and Pisa. He was named Auditor of the Sacred Palace in Rome and rose to Bishop of Penne and Atri, before becoming Bishop of Lucca. Alessandro of Imola is Alessandro Tartagni (d. 1477), the famed Italian jurist and professor of law in Ferrara, Bologna, and Padua.

ever be found? I set aside the most glaring evidence so as not to drag this out, but if it had all been presented, this killer would doubtless deserve death.

"Even so, there is no way to avoid outright execution. I return to the words of statute, which are clearer than the noon daylight, before they get lost in the twists and turns of their argumentative maze. This man was found to have cheated another of his greatest good. Say black is white, and pervert rightful justice. What is the law, then, if not lies, pains, thefts, and betrayals? Only people who readily turn to lies and deceptions consider it wise. The law functions only as well as it is compensated: it checks the hands before the feet.[16]

"I am a poor, sick old man; my enemy is rich, healthy, and young. For this reason, not only are men against me, but the law itself as well. O unhappiness of ours, O once blessed age when we were content with common sense! If you wanted to justly decide a case as plain as this, you should have dispensed with the legal predators, those greedy, quibbling liars. It would be more praiseworthy to have a hard-working baker's opinion on whether that hour was day or night. Woe is me! I'm made fun of by everyone here!

"My son, my only consolation, is dead! Now little remains to me, all I have to depend on in my old age is gone. I see your intent, but now I must be silent … In the name of just vengeance, I call on Acheron, Minos, and the three Fates whose judgment is incorruptible!"

That said, he fell to the ground as if dead – perhaps feigning it or actually overcome with grief. Everyone seemed to be quite moved, which left me embittered. But when things quieted down, Antonio Leuto said: "After Cicero divorced Terentia, ruler, he was implored to speak on an extemporaneous case. The prudent orator replied he had been without his books for three days. I am tired, weary, and exhausted, and I have gone a whole month without the use of any library. How can I speak on a case as rancorous and dire as this?

"What calculating man of Odyssean cleverness, Nestorian experience, or Chalcas-like prophecy would not quake in fear before so many esteemed men, to say nothing of the judgment of one to whom the law would yield? If I did not fear causing displeasure, when I prefer to serve and obey, I would refuse this imposed role. I trust in the one who said: 'When you are in the presence of kings and authorities, do not worry what you will say; you will be given the words to answer any query.'[17]

"Therefore, I will begin with the law's wording, assuming it is true as stated and the arrest was not the issue. The words of the statute are

---

16 That is, the lawyer looks to the hands or seeks a bribe before investigating any basis of truth.

17 These words echo various biblical passages on the theme. Please compare Exodus 4:12, Matthew 10:19, Mark 13:11, and Luke 12:11–12, for examples.

copulative, that is: he who is arrested at night *and* while armed is to be executed. One side asserts the action took place at night, and the other denies it. I say, the objection is well founded.

"Those who distinguish the hours of night after midnight designated them as day, and many figure among these, including Varro, Macrobius, and the Roman jurists Quintus Mutius Scaevola and Julius Paulus Prudentissimus. The work titled *On the Days* confirms what they say and accords with the customs of Rome, which this city follows, and what Cicero says in the *Philippics*, and the Cordovan poet writes in the first of his *Histories*.[18] Moreover, our orthodox mother Church, whose true Creator made the heavens and does not err, offers ulterior, unshakeable support: the Gospel parable warned all virgins to go out to meet their bridegroom at precisely midnight.[19] He must mean day, since he would otherwise be contradicted by the verse: 'He who walks by night hates the light,'[20] and hating the light is an act of a depraved conscience, which is not proper to those who incline toward the kingdom of heaven.

"Our well-known morning prayer reads: 'Lord, lead me not into temptation this day.'[21] That is surely something we would not say if it were night. One can corroborate this on the authority of the trembling Psalmist who said: 'After midnight I rose to confess your sacred name.'[22] How could we believe these men were inspired by the divine spirit if they had said anything less than what is true?

"Moreover, the Church decrees how everything is determined by its time. If we speak of the Liturgy of the Hours, the day goes from matins to vespers; but judgments are made from the rising to the setting of the light of Phoebus. If a truce is declared, it is in effect from morning to evening. If we observe corporal abstinence, that goes from vespers to vespers. If we speak of contracts, they go from midnight to midnight. None of this was displeasing to the Roman orator Julius Paulus, nor to the one whom Bologna honours.[23] If you add, since the law is honourable, just,

---

18   Vignali identifies the Cordovan poet with Lucan. In this case, the *Historia* would be his *Pharsalia*, otherwise known as the *De bello civili*. A case might also be made for identifying the poet with Lucan's grandfather, Seneca the Elder, who composed a magnum opus on the history of Rome, frequently referred to as his *Historia*, which, however, is no longer believed to be extant.

19   See Matthew 25:1 and following concerning the Parable of the Ten Virgins.

20   Cf. John 3:20, John 11:9, and John 12:35.

21   See Matthew 6:9–13 and elsewhere.

22   This may be a reference to Psalm 119:147–8.

23   Julius Paulus worked during the third century BCE. The one whom Bologna honours may be identified with one of the twelfth-century *Quatuor doctores bononienses*, Bulgarus, Martinus Gosia, Jacobus de Boragine, or Hugo de Porta Ravennate.

and sacred, what has been compiled, said, and written for the benefit of mankind, nothing would be prohibited to this man, nor would we concede that he has committed any nefarious crime. Given that it is possible to negotiate a contract after midnight, we understand its signing occurs that day. Infallible wisdom teaches us about that with clear words, not silence. Hear the divine voice that intones: 'I announce to you a great joy; today is born the Saviour of the world'; and that hour was morning.[24] It is thus truly considered day. Furthermore, the great migration of the Son at His divine conception confirms this; after all, how could Eternal Wisdom have prompted an elderly Joseph to accompany a young virgin Mary to foreign lands by night?

"If legal and spiritual reasoning does not satisfy you, let us consider the evidence concerning the sun's movement, which I have never known to play tricks. Phoebus in the present month and day stables his shining horses for a respite at one. That is the hour when all activity among mortals ceases, a time apt to oracles and sacred visions. After the horses feed on ambrosia and nectar, the sun chariot tends toward our hemisphere with great speed. We call this period *gallinicio*, or the time before we expect the rooster to crow. When the sun's path matures toward us, humidity closes in. This time is called *conticinio*, because man rests most peacefully in the cool air. At this point Phoebus is almost about to crest the horizon, which is around four o'clock. Then the other spheres receive so much light that it soon separates completely from the shadows.

"But when everything is dark, Phoebus sees to the horses, refreshing them with new food, before mounting the chariot again to push toward the horizon. This is the hour when Juno sends Iris to industrious mortals telling them not to wait for Phoebus in their bedrooms. These next hours seem shorter than the previous ones. Virgil seems to ratify this understanding when, in the sixth book of his divine *Aeneid*, he sings: 'Humid night withdraws for a better path, when great Orient with its ardent horses begins to blaze its rays,' and then following he writes more clearly: 'Night passes in a great hurry; and we will count the hours weeping.' This is how the poets declare it, that the last hours pass faster than the first ones, which the lawgiver explained in the Old Testament. Thus, we can conclude that the hour in question is certainly not intended to be included in the city's statute.

"Highest ruler and wise members of this assembly, it takes patience to delve deeper into the meaning more than the mere words. I interpret the statute as firmly establishing the need to punish insolent and lustful men,

---

24 See Luke 2:10–11.

so everyone can live within the bounds of virtue and justice. Since this is the case, there are no interpretive difficulties in the laws or statutes. Peregrino has lived an irreproachable life up to now; he should not be punished according to the full extent of the law for one possible mistake – if indeed there was any mistake – since harshest penalties were intended to punish only awful rogues and evil men.

"Once, divine Plato was walking through his city and happened upon a young man who played a bit too rambunctiously, perhaps to ease his stress. When Plato saw him, he castigated him. The modest youth, raised on pleasant diversion, objected to such harsh admonitions, pointing out that this was the first time he had played that game, and he had no intention of doing so ever again. Then Plato said: 'Well, in that case, I will not insist. I feared you had formed the habit of regularly playing these games.'

"Now see, ruler, if the first peccadillo, accompanied by the promise not to fall into it ever again, is worth the same degree of punishment as a very serious threat to the republic. Ruler, send away this crowd and release this innocent youth. I am sure this is a universally satisfactory solution and the greatest contentment to my father, who is a teacher and peer in these matters. That is all I have to say."

Giovanni Maria Riminaldo ruminated on all that Antonio Leuto had said for some time, then he prudently replied: "Sovereign Duke, I call to your mind an example. The greatest painter in terms of his elegant representation of figures was commissioned for a portrait of Alexander the Great. It was said that this artist had previously refused to produce works of other praised rulers, although perhaps that was just a calumny. Nevertheless, because the ruling authority demanded his work, owing to the rarity of its beauty, the artist did not want to disobey, nor could he do so. I, who have in the past been assigned to evil, despicable criminal cases, also cannot object, nor can I reject your high commands. I can hardly temper my inner compassion for the lifeless body of a man. I will try to say neither too little nor too much, so as not to offend justice, since I know you to be a most consummate interpreter of the law. Moreover, I will ready myself for this task, which I see tends toward a difficult point of interpretation, but especially because my respected colleague Leuto is arguing, whom even the lyres of Amphion, Orpheus, and Apollo would reverence. To satisfy you, O ruler, I will counter his reasonings with clear arguments, and in order not to bore this great assembly, especially since the hour grows late, I won't reiterate, but simply show how truth rests with the other side of this debate.

"First of all, I say that Varro's great contribution, and that of Paulus and the other writers of old, introduced Roman customs, which differed from those of outsiders, that is, the Athenians, Babylonians, Umbrians, and Egyptians. The Athenians considered day as the time between sunrise and sunset. The Babylonians calculated it from dawn to dawn, the Umbrians from noon to noon, and the Egyptians from the beginning of night. The Romans, however, believing they knew best, determined that the day went from midnight until midnight. They intended a natural day encompassing twenty-four hours, and during all this time, man may virtuously go about his business according to his needs. Lawgivers and the rigorous Thomas Aquinas agree. Moreover, this number of hours – twenty-four – must be appropriately distributed. Specifically, the first portion of the day we should dedicate to God, the second to work, the third to bodily sustenance, and the last, which is night, for as long it lasts, set aside for the rest of body as well as the spirit. No one can prevent man from seeing to his proper needs at any time. Indeed, the letter and spirit of the law – both natural and recorded – aim to preserve the individual.

"However, when two things produce conflict, if one is allowed, the other must be prohibited. For example, when business negotiation is permitted, then the possession of weapons is prohibited, since the latter involves menacing action. And even if common law permitted it, a municipality could still restrict, moderate, and inspect the arms, according to the conditions of that place, its customs, and its risks. Eastern people live in a hot, dry climate, so drinking wine is forbidden in the hopes of quelling rampant thirst. Instead, this city's sins are prompted by choleric humours, so we prefer to limit the carrying of weapons, especially during those times when, without oversight, they would more likely be used to sin. In our present case, arms are restricted when the sun is not over our hemisphere, which it was not by many degrees when Peregrino was apprehended.

"Don't you think that what lacks substance should lack a name? Darkness is proper to night, just as light is proper to day. Now can you see how they fit together? If day begins at midnight, what do we call the other time? If this were the case, it would seem the great Creator did not make everything perfect, unlike what is written in the holy book of Genesis.

"Second point. Since the virgins called to meet the Bridegroom were warned to prepare in advance by making sure their lamps contained sufficient oil to last through the night, this is also a sign that it was not daytime.

"Third point. Since we mortals are prone to sin at all times, we need to be reminded to pray for our faults, an act we must do without interruption, if we follow what the apostle says.[25] Otherwise, the mind wanders, prompted by evil. It doesn't focus on the potential for damage or the

---

25 These words possibly reference St. Paul the Apostle in 1 Thessalonians 5:16.

consequence of being excluded from divine blessings. Therefore, we cannot conclude it is day. It may seem to the examiners of clever things that it is preferable to square the time of natural day by the point of midnight than by another hour because then its motion is still. But only at the dawn of light do we render thanks to God for bringing us another day.[26]

"Fifth point. Nobody objects to a man working whenever he needs to. Paulus and others have noted the specified extreme cases, calling notaries' attention to how to determine when time begins and ends: at midnight, is it considered almost precisely the end of one day, only in the instant that it lasts, or the beginning of the next? For this reason, extreme cases have not been determined according to the strictest significance of daytime.

"Sixth point. The Lord's nativity was announced at the hour of true prophecies when we tend to hear such pronouncements most receptively, so that hour was very appropriate for that message.

"Seventh point. The Holy Family's migration did not occur without sacred mystery, so it was hidden to the whole world but three wise men. God came in the flesh; He was made man and performed human works, so humanity could see what comes after death. Who still has any doubt that if He was born from a womb without an opening, He could be moved without being seen by humans? He did not want to reveal Himself then, but instead when a truly tranquil hour could bring joy to human souls.

"Final point. If it is more wearying to ascend than descend, as Virgil seems to attest, why do the last hours of night seem shorter than the first when the sun is setting, if everything in nature appears to contradict that? He rightly states, 'Humid night turns at the midpoint of its course,' and he makes distinctions between nocturnal hours according to their qualities. When the sun sets, the masses of earthly vapours are exhaled and rise, and the earth is left warmer. We give thanks that, with its splendour and heat, the sun chases the vapours down toward the earth, which is why during that time of night it seems to get colder and more humid. Although Virgil appears to complain when he says: 'Night flees in a hurry,' this is just the illusion of Phoebus, who, in returning to us, shines on inferior bodies, making them diaphanous and transparent, apt and born to receive the light of the sun. It is not because in this hemisphere there is an artificial day. It is obvious the name given to day after night has passed is when the light originates.

"Therefore, one can conclude Peregrino's arrest to be in accordance with the law and compelled by the penal code. Duke, the law must be upheld

---

26 There is no fourth point indicated in Caviceo's 1508 Italian text, nor did I find it in the subsequent revised editions I was able to consult, such as the 1531, 1538, and 1547 editions.

where licit, approved, and ethical matters are concerned. It must also deter as much as possible any evil, wicked, and hateful actions. If irrational animals can stay in their dens until dawn, why can a man with the capacity to reason not do as much? One must not favour a bad act, otherwise it may lead to your own downfall. Mercy usually fosters licence, and licence leads to insolence, insolence to calumny, calumny to evil speech, evil speech to blows, blows to injuries, injuries to death, and death to the depopulation of the earth. Allowing too much licence is the perpetual infamy attributed to lords, as we easily understand from when the Roman empire was brand new. Blessed is he who corrects his ways based on others' examples. I urge you not to pardon similar delinquents, for your honour and the salvation of your land."

The Duke appeared quite troubled by Riminaldo's forceful arguments. I saw his eyes flash both pity and justice. Deeply conflicted, he called on Felino Sandeo to offer his view. He was moved by this sad case to begin in this way: "Most modest ruler, Gaius Marius and Catullus were revelling in the glory of their triumph when, from among a crowd of excellent men, they were elected proconsuls – not because they were the only men up to the task, but because everyone held them in high esteem. They also accepted that the ones they found guilty be freed. I am not unaware of the great integrity and knowledge presented by my esteemed colleagues here, who easily clarify every difficult and complicated point. I thus offer my view not out of arrogance or self-confidence, but only to satisfy the one who can do what he wills of me.

"I believe it is possible to resolve this case without further injury. It is natural for each individual's instinct to incline toward its goal by the most convenient means, which, when achieved without ruining or harming others, is considered virtuous. From what I have heard debated and disputed, it seems that Peregrino's life, leaving aside the question of Cesare's murder, is quite sober and contradicts the accusations. But tempted by the thrill of a new pursuit, like many men of his age, he did not give heed to the time, which might fool even a wiser man, given that this city is situated in a low, humid place. He is worthy of pardon, considering that the gate was open and the guard was absent, which clearly suggest it was more day than night. This is my view, which I believe no honourable reason could contradict."

When Nicolò heard these words, though, he interjected: "Who are you with cleverness armed with proofs come to ruin me? O cruellest Felino! You show you favour Fortune more than truth. What reason suffers, what honour wishes, what piety commands, what description comforts, what conscience dictates, what law advises that so great a crime pass without penalty? Consider the quality of the man who died, the time it happened, and then judge if this is what he merits."

Felino: "It was not Felino who spoke, but the law that judged. The law must determine where evil is considered."

A new tumult was rising when we saw a woman appear in the Duke's presence. She was dressed as a prostitute, and she went straight up to him to whisper a few words in his ear.

He instantly called the guard, who brought in Polidoro, son of Brunamonte, subdued in chains as the killer of Cesare, son of Nicolò. Just after the homicide, Polidoro wandered like a mole into this woman's establishment, which was on a street near where the crime took place. When the wretch was interrogated about Cesare's death, he confessed he did it.

Fame, the disseminator of all news, spread the word that Polidoro was in prison for homicide, and all that awaited him was the death penalty. In mourning clothes, his father and relatives begged and pleaded through tears, throwing themselves at the feet of power, promising hefty tribute for the life of their son. But the Duke's heart fixed on justice for what had been debated at length.

He called Polidoro to account in greater detail about the time, place, weapon, and motive for killing Cesare.

Polidoro stated: "It was night shortly before three o'clock on a public street in the San Michele neighbourhood. With evil on my mind, I was armed with a sword and eager to use it out of jealousy: I blamed Cesare, who tried one too many times … To dispel that fear for good, I killed him without a second thought. This is the whole truth. Pass your judgment."

This was heard, written down, and noted. The ruler determined that Polidoro confessed publicly and spontaneously to homicide; for that, Polidoro deserved the death penalty.

This sudden move shocked the city. Each person spoke about it differently, with one saying: "That is where Love leads his servants"; and another said: "If you wish to love, do so modestly." While they shared different points of view, the executioner cleared the place and prepared the instruments necessary to his next task.

In that instant, this news reached Briseida, daughter of Pompeio, on whose behalf the homicide had purportedly been committed. She put aside her virginal meekness and innate modesty, barging in more like a priestess of Bacchus. With the lightning pace of a rabid bear, she threw herself into the fray in a fury with torn clothes, an exposed chest, and hair untended. Unaccompanied, she cried and wailed with her palms pressed together: "Pardon, ruler! Pardon the cruelty, the just blood! Pardon my necessary presence and pardon this utter haste! That poor, pusillanimous man, more considerate of another's life than his own, has confessed without torture to what he should not, indeed could not have done. Spare his life, concede the time to discuss it. He was examined superficially; he claims like a child what he does not understand, and likewise he will take back just as promptly what he confessed."

The Duke remained still as a marble statue. Stupefied, bewildered, and shocked, he marvelled that a girl of seventeen, well-proportioned, beautiful, genteel, well-behaved, with an esteemed reputation and from a high family, was appearing before this high court, and here her face would have been difficult to distinguish from the prostitute's. But so willed the sempiternal God Who for all ages is owed thanks for everything in heaven and on earth, and Who, according to His high law, moderates and changes human hearts. He lends His wisdom and when He wishes, He denies it. He makes the magnanimous and the pusillanimous, rich and poor, faithful and disloyal, truthful and lying, boastful and humble, beautiful and ugly, and … the living and the dead.

At that sight, all the women – from matrons to virgins – dashed about, as in the tribal assemblies in Rome, first blurting out one thing, then another. Pompeio, together with his friends, offered himself in service to the ruler, begging and exhorting him to think of his honour and that of his daughter, whom he believed to be possessed by some melancholic humour and out of her wits. He begged the Duke to return her to him.

Polidoro's father, Brunamonte, contradicted him outright. He denied she should be released until the cause for her arrival was settled, an outcome that might save his son's life and satisfy the lady.

The just ruler expressed his willingness to listen to the sides, so he called for Polidoro and Briseida and addressed them with compassion: "O unfortunate youths, you two are not so young, nor so lacking in experience that in those things concerning your life and honour, that you need me to remind you that you have offered yourselves up for criminal sentencing. I almost cannot help but greatly admire how you, O most chaste Briseida, wish to intervene in a conflict as shameful as this one to offer testimony without need or honour. Even if you could get some measure of satisfaction, you would not take anything away from this but an everlasting stained reputation. The female condition must be kept so pure that it is free from even the least suspicion. Even when you adhere to the strictest good life, it is still quite difficult to protect. Nature has bestowed on your sex no greater gifts than virtue and silence, which I am not seeing at all in you today.

"O how I fear that a wicked and unworthy end will come to the noble, innocent girl who ruins herself to excuse another. She corrupts her reputation, denigrates her house, brings suffering on her parents, afflicts her household staff, and becomes the object of gossip for the whole populace. Because we do not dominate our first instincts, I encourage you to recommit to more virtuous pursuits and learn to live more temperately. Even if you burned for some childish love at first sight, the passing of time and a change of context and place should help you get over it. It is the custom of young girls to love, but not to go mad, which is more likely in public women and prostitutes in whom burning lust triumphs over true love. Even though heaven has dealt you women a heart inclined to love, you should never let it tempt you from virtue and grace.

"Now you must be sorry for what you've done. Allow these ladies to accompany you back home, and may your return bring your parents more consolation than your flight did. Polidoro will remain here to face his sentence according to the reason and honour demanded of him. Go with God."

When Briseida heard the well-chosen and affectionate words worthy of a most generous lord, she responded bravely in this way: "O most generous ruler, among all the chaos of war, anguishes of the mind, passions of the body, wasting of time, consumption of goods, and changeability of fortune, our all-knowing God would not have reserved this seat for you if He had not clearly seen Hercules in you, you who exceed the rest of humanity in excellence to the same degree that God exceeds humanity. You possess a knowledge of letters and military science, as well as a conscience, which is just and free. You are more prudent than Argos, more vigilant than Phoebus, more prepared than Mars, more benign than Jove, more eloquent than Mercury, and more loving than Venus. Anyone who adored you as a god could not be thought a heretic. O blessed people – twice blessed – who have such a ruler to preside over you. This is the judgment; this is the sentence, which will bless you today with everlasting immortality among all your other divine, unique virtues.

"Please grant me an audience no less welcoming than the one Dido offered Aeneas. I know once you understand precisely everything that happened, what others might consider lustful you will esteem as prudent, since you more than all mortals weigh matters with deliberation and experience.

"I do not come before you to defend Polidoro out of voluptuous infatuation, or an illicit ardour. The flame that burned in Myrrah, Byblis, and Cleopatra has not been sparked in me. Instead, I was faced with the same situation as Lucretia, Portia, and Cornelia. I certainly regret the unjust damage done to my reputation. However, I should not be condemned for rebuffing the petulant advances of that impudent dead man. I did what I had to do – and quite willingly – so posterity could understand clearly that the hearts of young people still cherish constancy, love, and faith.

"O famed ruler, for many years now Polidoro and I have persevered in virtuously maintaining the secret flame of our love. In that state, we wanted sweetly living to die or dying to live, if it were not for that most arrogant man, no less nefarious than he was indecent. I am speaking of the late Cesare. He brazenly tested my most tenacious virginity by various means, which were improper, annoying, and increasingly offensive to God and the world, and I never encouraged him.

"O ruler, heaven rejoices, the earth celebrates, love laughs, every lover makes merry, and our whole neighbourhood gives thanks to God that his sin is extinguished! O the dirtiness of that wicked man! O rabid and untamed dog never to bark again! It won't stalk me anymore, and our love will be free. He is cut down like a useless tree trunk, and by the hand of a woman! There is no kind of death in this world that can frighten or annoy me, now that I have demonstrated my true love.

"O ruler, Cesare made so many vile attempts that I finally lost my patience. I told Polidoro about him during one of our evening conversations because he seemed to doubt my loving faithfulness. After we exchanged the appropriate expressions of affection, Polidoro continued to think long about it and said to me: 'Briseida, I have always been a faithful and modest lover to you, and even though I have eagerly and frequently sought your presence, it is not because I intend to take advantage of you, but rather only to satisfy the sincerity of my heart, which, besides wishing to remain in God's good graces, hopes only to remain in yours. However, at least from my perspective, you've always offered those graces sparingly to me. Nonetheless, an ardent fire usually gives off some spark, though your female nature might prefer to hide it, which would be worse to me than death. In order to allay my present and future fears, please accept me as your husband through these words now and the ring to follow. Should the name of husband displease you, I am content to be your servant. And if you should deny me this request, I will be forced to believe you have already promised your love to another, in which case, I want only to die! I remain concerned about Cesare's behaviour. Even though I trust you, the fact that your beauty attracts many men makes me suspicious. So, I beg you to accept this proposal: be joined with me in marriage.'

"Having said these words, he collapsed in tears, which would have moved even the cruellest archenemy to compassion. I, an inexperienced girl burning in love, could not deny what he asked so earnestly. With ready heart and holding out my hand to him I vowed to marry him. After that, it seemed time to search the house to see if any insidious person was lurking there.[27]

---

27 This translation reflects the ambiguity in this Italian sentence. "Fornita l'opera" (after that, or after the work is done) may mean that the two young people simply agree to be married, though it may imply that they consummate their marriage. Moreover, it is also unclear why Briseida suddenly believes it necessary to search her house. Other editions forego assisting the reader, including the Spanish, which states only: "Acabado esto, parescióme tiempo de buscar la casa, por ver si persona de peligro en ella estuviesse" (in Martínez Morán's edition, 171).

"The rooster had just crowed when I heard a little sound, some strange noise, and fear seized my heart. It wasn't long before I saw the head of someone on a ladder trying to enter my bedroom. I steeled myself, more out of necessity than my own willingness. And lo! There was the thief of virginity leaning his chest against my window on the verge of entering! Only then did I remember a certain weapon my younger brother had left in my room. I seized it and dealt the intruder a blow, which, more through divine justice than any ability on my part, stabbed his heart. He fell dead to the ground along with his ladder.

"Various thoughts assailed my mind in that instant. With what face, voice, or heart could I speak with Polidoro, who could suspect nothing but evil of me? Who would believe any man in this world would have the gall to go after women without their leave while facing such danger? Perhaps I might actually accuse myself in the act of excusing myself. If I admitted that I committed the act on my own, no one would believe it; if I were helped, there would be suspicions of a different kind. Perhaps it would just be better to keep silent.

"Meanwhile, some neighbours heard the loud crash of the fall. When they looked out their window, they saw the dead man lying in the road. Each one surmised disapprovingly what had happened. I knew I couldn't wait any longer. I told Polidoro everything, and he went pale with fright.

"After a few breaths, he said: 'O God, may our marriage be happy and propitious, though you might prefer to be honoured with an offering other than a human sacrifice. This was supposed to be the day to decorate the windows and walls with flowers and fronds and branches, not with mortal blood. My Briseida, your lovely, candid hands weren't made for such violent acts. But what's done is done. We must forget this matter by never speaking of it again. Now, since I fear the uproar raised by the neighbours, I'll slip out your garden's back gate.' We walked down together, and he seemed to me more dead than alive, which is proven by what happened next. He didn't trust the area; for cover he went to a nearby house of a vulgar prostitute who'd sell God for a coin.

"After he left, I began to feel bad for myself because I had pined for many years for a man who lacked courage. I told myself: 'Pusillanimity can be thought of in two ways: if it's bestowed by nature, then it indicates no defect in the man, or if he comes of it through piety, then it is quite natural, since anyone who lives honourably must be pious. Perhaps this poor man's young bride forces this role on him.'

"I kept turning the many possibilities over in my mind until the hour when I heard that Polidoro had confessed to killing Cesare and faced death. Since I believe there's no greater plague among humanity than ingratitude, I couldn't contain myself. Almost against my will and unable to quiet my conscience, I came all the way here to testify to the truth, so that once you knew what actually occurred, you might change your sentence. May it go as it can and should. This is the full account of the committed homicide. God could not recount it more truthfully or more incisively. You, lord, are modest and wise; judge according to what seems most just."

Once she had spoken these words, she set her mouth in silence.

Duke: "Your speech was elegant and precise, and it might satisfy me if only I believed it."

Briseida: "If you refuse to believe my words, consider the evidence."

D: "That death occurred is certain, but I remain in doubt about who perpetrated it."

B: "That is clear enough. Is there anything more believable than a true confession?"

D: "Too much love prompts you to speak, not the pursuit of truth. Why would Polidoro accuse himself, if his conscience did not torment him?"

B: "He is ashamed to accuse a girl in a criminal proceeding."

D: "That is not unreasonable, since shy maidens typically do not sport that kind of audacity."

B: "I cannot entirely agree. What unimaginable, wild, and insane situation wouldn't draw female fury to attack? Myrrha killed her father, Procne her son, Medea her brother and children, Clytemnestra her husband ... Myriad similar shocking examples have passed down to us through history. In truth even timid women would not acquiesce in especially terrifying or extreme cases."

D: "It is much more likely Polidoro did this deed than you."

B: "While Achilles slept, Thersites fought in battle. In all the time you fought alongside Aragonese, Angevine, Bolognese, Genoese, Florentine, and Venetian armies, haven't you ever seen a cowardly one rise to act more like a magnanimous one? I neither deny nor confess to you that Polidoro may have killed someone at some time. But of one thing I am certain: Cesare's death is my doing. Have the words of Polidoro's confession repeated to you, and you'll know what I say to you is true."

D: "Notary, read it."

Notary: "Last night at approximately three o'clock on a public street I killed Cesare, son of Nicolò, with a sword out of jealousy."

B: "Duke, you must see the childish insipidness. He wants to glory in an action he did not commit. Make him answer to the condition of the sword, and you will see clearly what I mean."

D: "Polidoro."

Polidoro: "Lord?"

D: "What sword did you have?"

P: "A long, large Epirus sword with a broad point."

D: "Where is it?"

P: "In the river where I threw it out of fear."

D: "And why did you hide?"

P: "I was afraid of capture."

Briseida: "Now consider, Duke, the suffering in the mind of this man who supposedly has just killed another and does not dare carry around a weapon. He says he committed this act at three o'clock. O ruler, question the woman about what time he entered her house."

D: "Albertina!"

Albertina: "Here I am."

D: "Swear you will tell the truth. What time did Polidoro enter your house?"

A: "Before two."

D: "What weapons did he carry."

A: "None."

D: "What words did he exchange with you?"

A: "He sighed and cried, like he feared capture because he had quarrelled."

Briseida: "Duke, have the dead body brought in, and you will see the fatal blow did not come from a sword, nor any lance or sharp arrow for that matter. You will find the weapon in my room all bloody still. At my window there is spilled blood. All of this can witness to the truth."

A diligent investigation was made, and an official confirmed it. Nothing else remained than to pass the final sentence: condemnation of Briseida to death.

Screams from among the throng of female onlookers cut through the air. Each one clamoured for her life. Then Briseida turned to the ruler and said: "Lord, justice cannot bow to grace. Do not permit this ruckus from women to break you in the least. Remain firm as a tower. I prefer accepting death to begging for a life in which I were judged unworthy by my country and my progeny. To go on living in disgrace is not an acceptable option for rational people. For the sake of your honour, though, let me remind you that in indeterminate cases one should not pass a final sentence before everything has been discussed. If you consider the full ramifications of justice, you will proceed carefully."

D: "Briseida, since God and nature have bestowed on you a clever intellect, you wish to sit in this seat and pass judgment."

B: "Lord, proper discretion requires great humility. I am far more content to be condemned by your judgment than liberated by mine, which would be considered unjust. If it went in my favour, it would be suspect; if it went against me, I would be called arrogant. But from you, it will be pure, just, and right. Thus, I urge you faithfully to carry out justice so that it is without fault. My honour is stained through no sin of my own; and Polidoro's life hangs in the balance. You know no communication could have since passed between us.

"Reason wills, the statute demands, and honour persuades you to deter others by setting an example: even though Cesare is already dead, you should still have him hanged to heap more shame upon him. First of all, he was found with the ladder, which suggests theft; second, the law demands you take this action; third, he made an attempt on virginal chastity, and in order to defend it, I was compelled to kill him. For that I deserve commendation. If Cicero, a man with every advantage, received so much acclaim that he was called the father of his country for having exiled Catiline, what do I deserve for having exterminated a much more wicked one than he? O ruler, if virginity cannot be kept sacred in one's own house, in its most inner recesses, what will it be on the public street? Your principal objective should be to suppress insolent men, not just their actions, but also their unchaste words. A just compensation for my damaged reputation would seem to me to be, first, you have him hanged as a thief, and then cut off his head as a would-be rapist. Second, confer on me all his material goods that do not pass legitimately to his inheritors, not because I have any need of them, but because a harsh judgment is demanded for my honour, and because what comes from his base nature does not merit any other end."

She had barely spoken these words when Nicolò interrupted. He was no less impatient than Achilles upon hearing the news of his dearest friend Patroclus's death. He looked this way and that, gesticulating wildly, like the man whose melancholic humours have overtaken him, and who has lost his natural wits. At last, he interjected: "O greatest ruler, I've always known and held this firm belief: the female sex possesses a well-attested boldness. If I were ever in doubt about it, this one's present action makes it abundantly clear to me. I see the lengths a wicked woman will go to satisfy her lust. She has confounded each one of you, and all good reason is vain. O impudent lust, O wicked desire, O rabid libidinousness, O wretched shame, in what way are you actually condemned here? O frightful news, O unhappiest of outcomes for parents, how did you conceive such a monster? I'm confounded by the repetition of this horrible case, and I cannot put on a good face when a girl confesses guilt to homicide during the night in order to save her lover, then when her lust is sated, prefers to give up her life rather than forego fornication. If only I were granted blindness and deafness from heaven so as not to see or hear our youth mired in the depths of such filth!

"Duke, you should focus on matters closer to the truth! Who could possibly be persuaded that a modest and civil young man in love would expose himself to the danger of losing his life by hauling a ladder and a weapon around unless it were at the greatest insistence of his lady? Love is none other than a shared pleasure. If you invited him, Briseida, why did you kill him? If you didn't invite him, how did you discover him so quickly? Typically, strange or unusual things scare us. If you feared a robber, you could've scared him off just by emitting one shout. But he was stabbed before he was seen, which is a clear sign of betrayal.

"Many details make you suspect. You are the only guilty one; you surely merit the heaviest sentence. You leave your lover alone in your house. You conveniently find yourself prepared when Cesare arrives at the appointed hour. You leave the window open. There just happens to be a weapon in the room. All was so silent that you could've spoken to him, thrown him out, or admitted him. You displayed such rabid lust that, in order to gratify your new lover, you became crueller than Medea or Myrrha or Eriphyle, the wife of Amphiaraus.

"What is more dreadful, inhumane, and unbearable in this world than a woman sopping with lust? Catiline ordered his son put to death for copulating with a woman, but you took the life of a true suitor in order to gratify your lover. If you wanted him for your husband, you should've spared the dead youth and saved your honour by letting him live. Don't you realize that the time of night and your clandestine location without supervision cast doubt on your marriage? Did you believe you had no one you could tell about what you did? Just as you willingly sinned and even boldly gloried in having done wrong, it is right for you to be punished against your will."

The Duke remained rigid, constant, and still, like Minos, and he seemed by his gestures to be inclined to come down with the harshest sentence, when Briseida spoke up in this way: "O highest ruler, he who condemns nature damns himself, since we all share her as universal mother. If our sex is openly generous, what can be done when it is practised in this world? It isn't just men who endure troubles, since suffering is a universal evil. For this reason, I am greatly pained to be taken to task with my whole sex by you, Nicolò, an uneducated, rustic, squalid, and boringly prolix man.

"You are the sort who becomes more insolent and beastly when reason is lacking, who eagerly seeks refuge in denigrating, insulting, and offending others, like those common crossbowmen who shoot first, then take aim. It must give you great satisfaction to shout out your weaknesses in public. In many impertinent matters, you exert yourself to excuse one whose actions clearly serve as his self-accusation. But I do not doubt judgment rests in a person who weighs truth so properly that your assertions won't stand.

"You should recall what Semiramis wrote to Stabrobates, King of India: virtue is determined by action, not words. It is not our place to argue here about what somebody else was thinking about doing, or in what state of mind she acted, or about what should've been done, but rather, we must acknowledge what was done, then act. The sentence must rest only on what happened. Suppositions are included in those cases involving unknowable circumstances, but when they are known, it is useless to proceed according to suppositions.

"God, nature, and reason do not permit one to be assaulted in one's own home, which should be one's haven. Whether my husband is more or less legitimate in the eyes of the Church is not, I believe, any of your business. So, answer, if you will, what reason prevents your son from deserving first hanging, then the amputation of his head, and then the confiscation of his goods? If we focus on this issue, our case should proceed quickly toward a conclusion."

Nicolò: "Duke, her arrogance more than her age should be taken into consideration. Here before everyone we have declared our sides: Briseida on her own behalf, and I for my dead Cesare. Let whoever loses suffer punishment."

The Duke approved that statement. They thus prepared their arguments, with Briseida intending to prove she had a right to kill Cesare, and she began this way: "O most just ruler, when Clodius called Cicero to account after Catiline's death, Cicero shamefully preferred to suffer bitterest exile than speak in his own defence. It seems our nature recoils from speaking of ourselves. Therefore, it is customary to find a lawyer who can defend his client dispassionately at trial. But confident in your great integrity, although I am but an unlettered girl facing a highly astute adversary, I shall speak, nonetheless, because I am better informed of what happened, not so much because the law favours me, but to let my true conscience shine. I hope God will assist me.

"I say it was my right and place to kill Cesare for the following reasons. First point: in divine law every commandment is just, honest, and permitted, and it states that killing is allowed and demanded for sinners and the wicked. So, putting Cesare to death was my duty. This first part is proven in the Book of Exodus; the second is obvious, since Cesare was armed and used a ladder by night.

"Second point: the sinning man is like a beast. Just as killing a beast is not a sin, neither was killing Cesare. The first is proven by the Psalmist; the second is clear.

"Third point: each citizen can do without punishment what is useful and honourable to the republic, and purging the earth of malefactors benefits everyone, so Cesare's death was a common good.

"Fourth point: divine actions exist so that we might imitate them. In one day, God killed twenty-three thousand people, so my act of emulated homicide is permitted. St. Paul attests to both the first and the second part.

"Fifth point: in order to preserve chastity, one may kill oneself or others, so says the law where adulterers are concerned. Since Cesare was among these, his death was therefore just.

"Sixth point: the killing of a nighttime thief is excused, as determined by those who legislate on homicides. Given that Cesare is clearly numbered among these because of the ladder, his death was warranted.

"Seventh point: one can kill another in self-defence without fear of punishment. It must be conceded that this evildoer was about to commit an act of violence. So, it was right and necessary to kill him without regret. I could cite infinite reasons to support my action, but in order not to annoy this great assembly, I'll content myself with the brief summary I have made."

Having heard these cited reasons, Nicolò interrupted, saying: "Most just ruler, I do not intend to imitate those who opt for damning exile over defending oneself, which indicates a depraved conscience scared or frightened of everything. The one who uses others' means to meet her own needs is frequently deceived. Some people are moved by various opinions or fears to speak, remain silent, or act according to what is right and proper, out of cowardice, greed, an evil nature, or a lack of experience. As for myself, I'll defend my side no less courageously and justly. Though it's superfluous in such obvious matters to draw things out further, I'll reiterate my position in order to better summarize the truth among so many variables, and I'll counter her apparent syllogisms.

"On the first point, I concede that, according to divine law, one can kill an evildoer. However, it can't be carried out according to one person's whim. Because this task isn't proper to you, Briseida, you're not excused from punishment.

"Second: although one can kill a wild and dangerous beast, it's absolutely not true that one can kill a domestic animal, which confers injury on one's neighbour. Even if a man is a sinner, he's not that much different from the good man, so the law must judge him, the purview of rulers, among whom you, because of your sex, are not numbered. So, his death was unjust.

"On the third point: every citizen can do all she can in good service to the republic, but execution is reserved to one specifically tasked to preserve the common good. Even though one may be a doctor, he isn't permitted to just cut off a limb of a sick patient he happens to see without express permission to do so. Because you are denied any special role or privilege, it wasn't right for you to kill.

"On the fourth: in every matter, God can do whatever He wishes whenever He wishes because He is the Lord of all. We aren't supposed to be imitators of Him in all things, only in specific acts. Now see if such a commission was granted to you by heaven that you can easily defend yourself against a committed homicide.

"On the fifth point: neither Gratian nor Aquinas conceded that one was permitted to kill oneself or others to preserve one's chastity, although some people interpret the law to allow death to adulterers. But they intend actual rapists. Our case concerns mere accusations, since it remains unclear what Cesare's intention was when he came to you.

"On the sixth: the nocturnal thief isn't always to be killed. It depends on whether he stole anything, and whether it could be retrieved without killing. If it were possible to get help by shouting to others, there'd be no need to spill blood. You can clearly surmise he didn't go there to steal anything, nor for any other ill intent. He was only there to satisfy loving desire, concerning which you should've shown some compassion, as you did for another. But a woman's nature is diabolical, always directed toward the worst goal. Now let us see what merits the privation of life and the scandal of death. He committed no theft, no rape, and no homicide, so his death was wrong, and you are the one who must face the executioner.

"On the seventh point, she has cited every law naively. I don't deny that to avoid death a person can use self-defence when there's no other recourse. However, the law doesn't apply in your case in any way, because, had he lived, Cesare wouldn't have done anything deserving punishment or infamy, to say nothing of condemnation to death. Only the satisfaction of your appetite with your waiting lover pushed you to commit such awfulness. For this, you deserve the death penalty.

"Duke, I've responded to her childish chatter more out of politeness than necessity, and her case remains confused. Command that the punishment be carried out on the one who deserves it!"

The Duke was ready to end the case with Briseida's execution when she insisted on countering.

Before she could open her mouth, however, Nicolò shouted: "Ruler, there's never been in this world such perfect cleverness nor such persistent boldness to equal the annoyance of a woman's garrulousness! If you want to act after so many words, let it come to pass in this lifetime! At this point the trial has concluded; your judgment is determined. Nothing remains but to carry out the sentence."

The Duke immediately summoned the executioner, who promptly stepped forward. He looked like a shade from hell. At the arrival of the minister of justice, the girl's beauty paled. She looked lost and wilted like a rose plucked four days earlier. She was led ever so slowly to the place where prisoners condemned to death for the worst crimes typically left their heads.

As she passed, she caught Polidoro's eye. He was still bound and under heavy guard. She said sweetly to him: "I was once a rose in bloom, but now I am a dry twig. I was born blessed, and I shall die happy. Love joined us faithfully together, and I now go in peace. Fortune varies, and in denying you justice, they make war on you. I call on God, the final judge who sees all, to reward you."

Without any further act to show that she was discontented, she exposed her candid neck to the executioner. Such great constancy moved the populace to pity her, and from one part of the crowd to another, urgent shouts rang out to spare her life.

It seemed I was watching Hector light the Greek ships on fire. Some said loudly and bitterly that Briseida deserved another defence.

To assuage the clamouring populace, the Duke ordered Briseida brought back to the place where judgment is rendered.

Briseida, displaying considerable composure, raised her eyes to heaven, then humbly lowered them saying: "Duke, perhaps you think you see Gnaeus Papirius Carbo, who after being commanded by the great Pompey to be deported to Sicily for his death sentence, was not ashamed to ask for more time to evacuate his bowels out of an eagerness to extend his short life, which is much more wretched than a happy death. Ruler, do you think that if I was bold enough to kill a man, I would not be equal to defending myself? Please do not be angry or lose your patience. May wrath come slowly, may you listen attentively, may your judgment be free, advice well considered, passions set aside, and justice ready. Then whatever happens will be the will of God Who observes all our actions with open eyes and an unsheathed sword. Now give me your attention and listen carefully anyone who will.

"The law states under the section on rapists that not only does violent rape warrant the death penalty, but also its attempt. Violence consists not only in the act, but also in the idea, words, and evil habits, which we have understood were all present in this shameful case. The dead youth was passionately rash, licentious, and armed, all characteristics that demonstrate consummate wickedness. His disposition must be considered more than the outcome because all he had left to do was to carry out his impious and wicked plan. This was no less a sin than a fact.

"My opponent suggests it should have sufficed for me to make some noise, but that senseless man does not consider the danger that posed to my life and Polidoro's. Nicolò wanted me to be deprived of life and honour before defending myself. Consider that, among the wisest men,

Dido is more praised than Lucretia: the first ended her life on a pyre out of reverence for chasteness; the other ended her life with a knife after her marital vow was violated. If I've imitated the famed virago, I feel no regret. Moreover, even if I had no other excuse, the terror caused by his unexpected arrival should save me from punishment, because no man behaves so calmly when he is trying to save his life by taking another. If Charon the boatman over the river Styx felt terrified at seeing an armed Trojan, what must such a sight be to me, a girl of shy nature and inexperienced in everything?

"Please tell me, lord, if an armed man attacked your stronghold by night, although yours is well fortified, what would you think, what would you say, what would you do? Can't you believe a wise girl would act as promptly to save her honour as you would to save your state? Every lost thing can be returned, but never violated virginity, which must be carefully safeguarded, particularly when there's no difference between the act and the fact, and the aggressor has nothing left to do to fulfil his evil plan. Let's assume he had come with pure intentions: that alone is worthy of death. When Caesar learned Clodius had seduced his wife, he immediately divorced her, and if it hadn't been that others overheard and pleaded for the favour of his life, Clodius would've been put to death. If the abductions of Io, daughter of Ianachus, and Europa and Medea had been punished, Paris would've been warier with Helen, the daughter of Leda, for whom Asia and Europe still suffer and quarrel. You who are wise, temper and moderate this case as you see fit." After she had spoken in this way, she closed her lips in silence.

After a long pause, Nicolò spoke: "Greatest ruler, I see well how much an ignorant tongue in a beautiful figure can do. Her loveliness coupled with smooth words has so beguiled these listeners that one can't put up any resistance to her Socratic insistence. I give up. I'm brought to the saddest extreme worst luck could offer. Little is to be gained, and everything lost. For my sake, make peace. Innocence is laid low, while malice rules. The law yields to favour, piety to impiousness, knowledge to garrulousness, and sincerity to wickedness. That's just the way my sad plight goes.

"O unpermitted impunity, O evil act impudently tolerated! Until the end of time there'll always be the precedent that a lustful girl can receive mercy for violently killing her faithful lover. Be careful, young men, keep in mind my poor son's case. He met the end you've heard because he eagerly carried out her bidding.

"And yet, Duke, if you still should wish to make amends for a man's death, consider that love was the cause, not villainy. Pardon his great affection, which led to this tragic end: the death of a son, parents left to grieve, and a house stained with infamy in perpetuity!"

After he said these words, he burst into tears hotter than fire and collapsed half-dead over the cadaver, an act that moved the whole city to pity him.

Fearing renewed tumult, the Duke called forward Peregrino, son of Antonio, Polidoro, son of Brunamonte, Briseida, daughter of Pompeo, and Nicolò, the father of Cesare. In a loud and reassuring voice he declared: "Peregrino of Antonio, because you are innocent, you are free of every infamy, both in act and thought, as if no mention were ever made of you in terms of this matter. You, Polidoro and Briseida, true spouses, may you be returned to the good graces of your parents. You are absolved of every legal punishment, and may you enjoy many rewards. May Cesare receive an honest and proper burial. And you, Nicolò, may you be free of every accusation against your house for the pain you've endured."

As soon as he finished speaking, he dismissed the assembly. In that instant, it was as if Cicero had returned to Rome and Scipio from Africa, such was the consolation I saw among the people. Sweet tears, gentle laughter, tight embraces, impassioned kisses, songs and dances demonstrated the shared rejoicing of the whole populace, not just for my liberation, but for everything else as well.

We were about to head toward our homes with the Duke's good wishes when Briseida moved as if she wanted to speak. She went up to that eminent place reserved for the greatest orators and said modestly: "Sovereign Duke, it was the custom, and not a base one, among the losers of war to adore those from whom they had received some benefit. If we are reunited in life, honour, and happiness through your greatness, how can we not owe you divine adoration? We're certain your modesty wouldn't permit it, but it seems too undignified to leave without offering some small thanks, since we are not sufficient to render the great thanks that's owed. Your fortune is sublime, your kingdom flourishing, your children blessed, your people most devoted, your reputation the highest; nothing we have isn't thanks to you. You are sincere, intelligent, modest, genteel, and wise. Through you every purposeful idea finds its good end. From the day of your birth until now we have seen your life rise by degrees. I fear, however, you would say to me what Aulus Albinus – the one who vindicated the imperial name in Gaul – replied when a poet offered him a book singing his praises. He urbanely castigated him saying that the commemoration of good deeds should be withheld until it can no longer be corrupted or changed. So, I pass over in silence what might disturb your mind, though I understand neither praise nor blame can ever bend your rectitude in any way. This echoes what is said across Italy: heaven gathered everything most excellent and put them in two Hercules – one a god and the other a hero – uniting them together in you, and these traits adorn both your body and soul such that you worthily take your place among the other two. Your kingdom rejoices in you and in it establishes this hope: every case, however complicated or criminally serious it might be, can find charity and forgiveness. Accept our thanks then, lord, with your rich heart and ready spirit, and we pray to remain worthy of the seat of your good graces. That is all."

The Duke listened with the greatest satisfaction and praised her words. He turned to the people and spoke in this way: "Just as amid the tribulations of shipwreck there is nothing more fitting than a quick and ready rescue operation, so the need is equally great for a circumspect assembly in weighty legal matters. For this reason, Virgil wrote, referring to Quintus Fabius Maximus: 'This is the man whose virtuous delay has restored liberty to our land.' So we do not seem ungrateful to God for the blessings we have received, it is my wish and command for everyone to put aside any rancour and disagreements and live together in civil harmony and brotherly affection. And you, Peregrino, who made a counter accusation, forgive Nicolò's charge, which was not made intentionally, also because your accuser has greater reason to complain of you than you of him."

He continued in this vein, offering to one side then another what his heart prompted, and with great clemency the ruler bid farewell to all. Friendly company escorted me back home. Even though my liberation and the great honour I received were most welcome to me, I was even happier that Astanna was present to see my success in all that happened. She returned to Genevera and told her I was well.

I went to my room and thought back on what I had been through. I marvelled to myself how rarely a happy beginning is accompanied by a good and prodigious ending. The Duke had just gently cautioned me, so I sought to figure out if there was some good way to save my honour and extinguish the fire that was immoderately consuming me.

I asked trusted Acate for advice, and he recommended I give it a rest for a little while. Perhaps with the passing of time, he persuaded me, I might forget love, "a pernicious force for those who adored it, as is clear from many examples of antiquity, from Gaius Silius for Messalina, Antony for Cleopatra, Achilles for Polyxena, Paris for Helen, Demetrius for Lamia, Leander for Hero … Infinitely large is the crowd of those who ended their lives in misery because they loved too much. So, it would be best, before anything else happens, if you take your ship back to port."

I confirmed and approved this plan in my good thoughts, and I arranged every one of my actions with this end in mind.

Then it happened that Genevera's mother, along with other noble ladies and Genevera herself, were strolling along the street and decided to visit and comfort my suffering mother. They wished to rejoice with her on my release, giving thanks to God. Anastasia was the name of Genevera's mother, and she had a bond with my mother through distant family ties, so sometimes they secretly visited each other.

Love was also present. Because Love won't suffer to see the number of his worshippers decline, we mortals must suffer Love's continual burning. He moved Genevera to express such pity and gentleness toward me, perhaps not equalled even by Scipio toward Masinissa. During the first of the ladies' visits, Love bound my heart with such force that my voice was broken to the point I couldn't utter a single word. I seemed to see everything transformed, and what articulation in words was denied me, I signified in gestures and emotions.

When my heart regained a bit of its tranquillity, I approached Genevera with tentative steps. She was resting at a window with Astanna, and I quietly begged her forgiveness. She, pretending to joke with Astanna, immediately responded: "Live assured, and be of good cheer. A letter will follow, and your recompense awaits." I didn't quite understand the emotion behind her words and was left entirely in doubt. But after a while Astanna clarified things for me, and I was consoled.

Book 1. Chapter 19.

Peregrino reflects on the emotions he feels knowing his love is shared. He proposes an audacious plan to see Genevera again, but Astanna advises him to write her another letter instead.

What inspiration so overflows from Helicon and Castalia and the wood sacred to Phoebus Apollo that it can express in words, learn in concept, or imagine through fantasy the sweetness born in my heart then? I banished every doubt, marshalled my forces again, and with every thought I committed to serve and obey Love.

O good God, what eloquent language she showed, what Virgilian rhetoric, what erudite learning, what elegance and dignity in her divine, concise, and conclusive words! To such a lady (no, to such a goddess!) all concede without a fight. She surpasses the gravity of Cato, the refinement of Gaius Lelius, the force of Demosthenes, the charisma of Caesar, the breadth of Horace, the keenness of Gaius Licinius Calvus, the promptness of Cicero, and the inventiveness of Aristotle. If God spoke in human language, this lady could easily and without blasphemy be considered God. Repeating to myself her good greeting with its promise of a reward, I cast away every thought of my earlier resolution, and I determined with all my might to fight the glorious fight, which alone can make man blessed. Moreover, whenever my body's forces flagged, I would make up for that with my imagination.

By subtle means I got Astanna to meet me at Violante's house, and after exchanging a few superficial words, I asked them what Genevera said and felt about me. Astanna answered me: not otherwise than lovingly and courteously. After I asked them for more specifics about Genevera's household, I continued: "Astanna, a bond of sacred friendship joins us, which can never be broken. I'm certain you feel the same for me, though if you should ever have a different opinion, I beg you to let me know."

When she heard these words, she replied: "Peregrino, I'm more perplexed than consoled, since your words imply you have little trust in me, though all my actions have up to now been entirely faithful. I don't understand your misgivings. From the first moment I agreed to help you, I've served you with the same integrity I would've employed had I been raised in your household, and I'll persevere in that upstanding service for the rest of my days! You shouldn't believe I need a longer lecture on this subject. If you ever believed I were unworthy to serve you, I'd still accept whatever you wished."

I couldn't hold back tears at the sweetness of her heart, then considering her capability, I told her: "Astanna my dear, I couldn't place greater trust in you than I've already done. As you know, you've been the protector of my life, as I believe you fully understand. I used those words only because I wish to involve you in an even more delicate plan, not to prompt your disdain or indifference, but only to signal to you a greater challenge ahead. You must know how I've requested a thousand times a brief meeting with Genevera, but I've been left guessing what she thinks of me. If you agree to my plan, my long suffering will at last find sweet peace."

Astanna: "What is it?"

Peregrino: "I'd like to enter her house secretly through the back door and hide somewhere there until you think it best to meet with Genevera. Given her generous nature, I suppose she won't be stingy about freely welcoming me then."

A: "Oh no! We'd be acting way too foolhardily, risking my ultimate ruin. How can you think it would be acceptable to see a man all of a sudden in your house? I'm certain you'd cause her death from fright and anxiousness. A much better plan, it seems to me, would be for you to write her again. I'll scrutinize her response and find a way to push her toward a firmer resolution."

P: "As long as it comes soon."

A: "I'll do my best. Since time is short then, see to your writing."

Won over by reason, I scribbled what follows.

Book 1. Chapter 20.

Peregrino writes another brief letter to Genevera requesting that they meet face to face.

My Lady,
The light of your eyes has been received by mine and being in your presence has sparked a fire in my heart. I am burning like a hot furnace and being consumed! No one can extinguish it but you. Please, for the sake of your divine beauty, which has made me its slave, gaze more sweetly on the one who lives or dies because of you. You'll learn the rest of my thoughts from this letter's messenger. May she act as quickly as she promised! Go with God and remember me.

I gave Astanna the letter, and she delivered it to Genevera, adding those words she thought might produce the desired effect. In the end, I merited this response.

Book 1. Chapter 21.

Genevera answers Peregrino's letter, and Astanna arranges another meeting at the outbuilding where the ladies of the house do the laundry.

Peregrino,
My heart has always tended toward you in virtuous reciprocity, as much as my age and circumstances have permitted. If my aid seems inadequate to your ardent desire, the fault lies in you, since your love exceeds the bounds. Please quell your potentially damaging passion, so we can maintain our love in equal measure and not become gossip for rude people. You'll hear more about your request from Astanna.

Astanna returned to me, and after I read and reread the letter, she told me there was nothing with enough force or authority to make Genevera veer from her chaste path. However, she did say that if I could return to that outbuilding signified by the lizard Genevera had sent, then she'd find a way to get Genevera back there. Astanna made me promise to be there and not make any other moves without including her. I accepted her terms and awaited the appointed hour that evening.

Impelled by excessive desire, I returned to the back door of the place covered in ivy. Inside all the girls of the house were talking and laughing together. It seemed there were a lot of them, given their commotion.

Book 1. Chapter 22.

Peregrino connects with Genevera. That night, Love's messenger informs him where he can see Genevera early the next morning. He does, and a sudden thunderstorm offers the occasion for another brief exchange, during which she tells him she will be his even after death. Anastasia becomes suspicious of her daughter's behaviour, and Peregrino must invent another way to see her, including the disguise of a "pilgrim," the literal translation of his name.

The back door near the wall was very old, almost crumbling and out of use, so I could peer through it. Lucina favoured our love, lending the splendour of her moonlight, and I could contemplate the flash of Genevera's eyes and the movements of her body quite easily. She possessed enough grace to prompt Charon to destroy his boat and Minos the gates of the underworld. The great concentration of words among the ladies, which fed the light in her eyes, could stop the coursing blood of a living body.

With remarkable finesse, clever Astanna managed to steer Genevera close enough to me so that I could greet her, which consoled me for all the pains I had endured. Without expressing any other words, though, we had to part again.

O joy of lovers, what blessedness, what contentedness can ever equal yours? What terrible accident, what mode of death even could scare you off? O happy present moment, O sacred encounter, O silence when loving words bloom: this is the chain the binds loving hearts together! This is true nourishment for the soul! My suffering was worth it, my martyrdom most blessed because it led me to this glory.

I went away in body but left behind my soul. Back in my room, I felt carefree and ready to indulge in some rest that might restore my limbs.

Suddenly, I heard a spirit say: "Deep sleep does not befit Love's servant."

I stirred, startled. "Who interrupts my sleep?"

"A messenger of Love," it answered. Without saying anything more, it made to disappear.

At this point, I was completely awake. I got up and heard it say: "This morning, not very far from the city gate, there will be a celebration marking the birth of Hercules whose labours will be performed. All of our city's nobility will converge there."

When morning came, I walked toward that place, and I spotted Genevera with many of her ladies. The crowd bolstered my confidence to stroll over and speak with them.

Phoebus, however, had not put much distance from earth and went into a frenzy at the sight of a greater splendour than his. He immediately withdrew his sun's rays. Heaven's wrath armed itself and sent a scout ahead with warning shots of lightning and the most frightening thunderbolts, accompanied by a superabundance of rain. We all felt as if we were experiencing a flood like the one Deucalion suffered. The shadowy air with its dark, threatening aspect seemed to announce none other than unleashed Chaos.

The young ladies made soft murmuring sounds like doves. Weeping, they commended themselves to God with humble hearts. Nearby were the ruins of a Roman arch that had been erected to mark military victories, and we fled there to escape the downpour. I moved among the ladies, reassuring first this one, then comforting that one. With greater boldness I made my way toward where Genevera had taken cover.

It seemed heaven favoured my every move. Without being seen or noticed by anyone, I brushed up to her and said, "My life, my sweetness, this day is to be celebrated more than any other since a single sweet word from you has restored me and makes me ready and willing to endure the hot fire that consumes my flesh."

She had a ready reply: "I was yours and always will be, even beyond the ashes of death." She said nothing more.

I perceived the slightest cinnamon-scented sigh escape from her tiny red mouth. Her tongue seemed to move with the sweetness of nectar. I murmured, "O my lady, I'm dying of sweetness for you. I'll lose my soul right now if you don't help me!"

In that moment, Phoebus donned again his sunny mantle. I beamed from receiving her great gift, and the earth's face also shone once again. We rejoined the happy festivities. All the while, Love stirred within us an incredible disquietude. We were at turns consoled, sad, pale, overly analytical, and lonely, to the point that we resembled shades more than human beings.

Anastasia became quite suspicious, given the new signs she was observing in Genevera. She scrutinized her eyes, counted her sighs, considered her potential suitors, called to mind how Genevera had behaved at home and with whom she had had the closest interactions. Anastasia began to keep Genevera under such close watch that she hardly permitted her to leave her bedroom.

I tried numerous times to disguise myself in order to see Genevera, once as a visitor from the countryside, another time as a porter, and once as a chimney sweep. But Love never deigned to give me any success. One foggy, rainy day, overcome with agony and unable to endure her absence any longer, I tried another guise – it was becoming a habit, after all: I put on the ragged sackcloth typical of a sick pilgrim and showed up at Genevera's front door when I knew her mother was out. I knocked and cried out for alms. A not-so-generous servant hurled angry looks and threatening words my way, commanding me to be off or my alms would consist of a sound beating.

Redoubling my insistent and humble prayers, I shuffled to a side door continuing to implore, when … lo! I caught sight of Genevera through a window. She rested one side of her head on her hand and didn't realize I was there. Steeling my nerve, I begged her in a low voice and with reverential gestures for mercy, and I didn't mean bread.

Shaking herself out of her reverie, she focused her heavenly eyes on me and somehow recognized me underneath my torn, lowly attire. I couldn't tell if she became more relieved or anxious because pity for me urged her forward while powerlessness held her back.

I was about to tell her more when her mother returned home. When Anastasia caught sight of me, she was moved to such pity by my apparent indigency that she made Astanna serve me enough food in one meal to nourish my entire life. The servant, who knew what I was up to, dawdled for as long as she could until Anastasia retired to her room, so she could speak with me of my more pressing concerns. We had a quick exchange about Genevera's occupations and feelings, the way she continually thought of me, why her mother was so suspicious, and if there was any mention of me concerning that. Reassured that Anastasia didn't suspect me, I was relieved and happy.

Then Astanna intimated to me that after vespers, Genevera and her mother would go to the Franciscan church dedicated to St. Jerome to make confession: "Now use your wits to take the place of the friar, whose name is Dominic. If you manage without him knowing, you can take advantage of the opportunity to speak with Genevera and put an end to our interactions. And may it bring an end to your languishing!"

Book 1. Chapter 23.

Peregrino gets Acate to distract Friar Dominic and succeeds in declaring his love to Genevera. The penance, which Dominic imposes after her confession, offers Peregrino another opportunity.

The chapel figuring a bearded St. Jerome comprised a space of four cubits between the Church's holy altar and the outer wall. There was a seat for the priest, and the rest of the space was occupied by the person kneeling in front of him. Considering all this, I decided to hide, enclosing myself behind the altar, so I could overhear what Genevera would say to the priest about me or learn if she was distracted by another love, or maybe, if the opportunity presented itself, to confide in her my thoughts. In order not to miss this last possibility, I communicated my entire plan to faithful Acate. I told him that, when he saw Genevera approach the seated priest, he should call to Dominic, pretending to have something urgent and very important to divulge to him. After all, the priest was sophistical, verbose, and curious about everybody's business – both the living and the dead.

Once we were clear, I withdrew behind the altar, where I'd be close enough to overhear any voices. I wasn't there long before my lady, peerless in divine modesty, placed herself at the priest's feet. My faithful friend carried out his task masterfully. The priest got up, abandoning his devotion to the sacrament, and launched into the heights and depths of disputations with Acate, leaving me time to carry out my plan.

Now I know how easy it is to frighten the hearts of young ladies by startling them, so at first I hesitated, unsure if my next move should be to speak or remain quiet. If I spoke and she jumped, I'd surely be discovered hiding in there; then wouldn't that be worse than death? What defence or excuse could I offer for my actions? Dishonouring religion and scandalizing a lady's honour could destroy a man's reputation. What should I do? If I didn't speak, how could I be heard? Love and fear battled within me.

I said to myself: 'Genevera is wise; she won't make a sound. Even the most prudent, though, fail by mistake. And if she did, how would that be her fault? May any consequences befall me; Fortune favours the bold!'

Comforted by Love, I said in a humble voice, "Have mercy, lady. I am your servant Peregrino."

She was stupefied and on the verge of crying out to relieve her fright. I saw her celestial face turn pale. A tremor agitated that virginal breast, not unlike the zephyr that blows across waves and rustles the trees and fields of arid grains. I didn't know whether to stay or go, to calm my wavering mind or to listen to things, which might sooner bring my death than life.

I faced that impending danger and tried again in a somewhat louder voice to say, "Lady, have pity on me! An excess of love has prompted me to hide in this place, as you can hear. My life and death are in your hands. You can no longer have any doubts about it. I'm your true servant who this morning appeared at your house as a beggar. Be still as a strong tower to preserve our shared honour."

Although I allayed her fear a bit, she stuttered in a cracking voice: "It is not in the nature of a thoughtful man to seek his pleasures at the expense of another's reputation. If love is shared, then this appetite should not be peculiar to one. Plus, it is one thing to offend men, much less God. Sooner or later, His hand will avenge our sins, even when we believe they have been forgotten."

Peregrino: "Lady, since you've already deigned to hear of my suffering through a messenger, please don't refuse to listen to me directly now."

Genevera: "The time and place do not permit it!"

P: "I can't find anything better."

G: "That is what happens to a lover who hearkens more to body than soul."

P: "Lady, time is short. Please listen patiently and don't waste this opportunity. I'm burning and come before you – who are colder than ice and the first snow – to convince you that my desire is to be with you honourably. The proof is obvious from the danger I face. If you should betray me now, I'd have every right to complain against Love and rue my many efforts. I realize this is not the time or place for these conversations, but for lack of better, we must make the best of this. Because it seems you doubt that I'm your true servant, I'm speaking in a louder voice from this confined place than I would if I were out in the open. If you call to mind the constant pleas Violante, Astanna, and my letters have made to you, you can be sure I'm undoubtedly Peregrino."

While I spoke in this way, her face began to show its natural colouring akin to garnet. Her initial terror dissipated, and she remained there devotedly reading and speaking, content to listen to me talk. And my soul (following its usual inclinations even while gaining new ones) obliged in this tenor: "Lady, like any faithful servant, I cherish your acknowledgment of my efforts no less than if I were regaled with prizes. I'm prepared to list here for you what I've already done out of my longstanding desire for you, although you're already aware of most of them because you possess a very keen intellect. Nevertheless, I'm the one who can recite them most faithfully to you. I believe it's clear to you how much love, benevolence, and respect I've always had for you, and if you consider it well, the facts provide conclusive evidence to the truth of what I say.

"You'll recall the clever ruse of the anonymous letter, which Violante feigned finding in order to discern your feelings about love, as well as the urgency with which I have hounded Astanna day and night while keeping things secret – only the divine intellect can imagine! You heard how I was seized, and if it were not for God's clemency, I would've been guiltlessly deprived of life. I won't repeat to you my numerous disguises because I needn't speak of those attempts beyond those you know of. If I could do more, I'd do it to free your mind of every doubt.

"If I had listened to Love, who continuously impels me forward, I'd already have found a way to abduct you by force or pressure, and it would've been worth it, since your person is greater than country, propriety, and my own life. You're my solid ground in the vast ocean, my sure strength in dangers, cooling relief in my fire, exceeding riches in poverty, and my health in sickness. I couldn't wish for anything more in you, though a virtuous drive for recognition continually spurs me onward. What could heaven offer that would be more welcome, accepted, happy, and proper to my soul than to be together with you? When that happens, I'll no longer fear anything from an armed and hostile world. If I believed I couldn't have you as my lady, I wouldn't have tolerated so much suffering; heaven would seem unbearable to the world, if I were divided from you.

"I've never sought for you anything less than the most virtuous reputation. With this promise may our hearts be joined together, as I desire our bodies be entwined. You came into this world as my lady and protector. I thank God for such a great and chaste lady. I loved you before I saw you, and I've always passed on every other interaction with women. Blessed is the hour in which you appeared to me in this very place, and from that moment, you've been so fixed in my heart that my mind hasn't been able to focus on anything else.

"If only Angelo had a friendlier or more accepting attitude toward me, I'd already have contracted our engagement. If you trust my words as I intend them, we can quickly accomplish ourselves what will be appreciated by all, given there's no man in this land who could make you a more honourable match. Since we can rarely converse like this, please use Astanna to inform me where we can meet again so your thoughtfulness can offer me some consolation.

"Here before you, Lady, are my lacerated heart, my inexperienced soul, my preoccupied mind, my conquered body, and my weak members, which can't be cured except by you. Lady, sweet is the fruit enjoyed at its peak. Too many demurrals typically tire the soul and rack the body. You are no less generous than you are beautiful. Your parents haven't given your qualities due consideration. Angelo is austere; Anastasia doesn't think much about your happiness, and your brothers don't care at all. It's up to you to plan and carry out what most faithfully accords with your will. You mustn't waste the flower of your youth waiting for what couldn't possibly be better in the future. I am yours, and I swear to you in the presence of God here I give you my vow of faithfulness. Do not reject me. Let us live according to this firm, constant, and consoling hope until the time when we can more openly attest to our actions. May God carry out what He knows, since He knows all."

I could not say anything more, nor wait for her reply, because the priest came back. I peered through a hole and saw her heavenly eyes glimmer with prayerful tears. They seemed two gems sparkling in that dark place.

After she entered the depths of the sacrament of confession, the priest imposed as penance that, in addition to other good acts of mercy, she feed a poor pilgrim who might seem worthy of her compassion, since there's no better and more welcome good we can do for God than share compassion for another's sufferings.

At that, I silently thanked that priest who, without realizing it, was providing for my well-being. After they concluded the rite, Anastasia came to escort Genevera home. Seeing Genevera with tears in her eyes, Anastasia was moved to maternal tenderness and comforted her, telling her not to doubt divine mercy, which is freely offered to anyone who seeks it with a faithful heart. Genevera, who was gazing elsewhere, praised the beneficial qualities demanded by penance, and she implored her mother for the space to offer the prayers she owed. The priest comforted her mother, and they left Genevera alone. After a time, she turned to face the wall and holding a small prayer book in her hands, as people do, she began to speak in this way …

Book 1. Chapter 24.

Pretending to offer penitential prayers, Genevera speaks to Peregrino, who hides behind the church altar. She asks him to be patient and prudent, and after giving thanks to God, Peregrino resolves to follow Genevera's advice.

Genevera: "Peregrino, if I do not know how to respond spontaneously to what you keenly propose, blame my tender age and guileless prudence, which makes me such an exception to my sex. When I consider I was born female, I despise my fortune because it deprives me of that virtue, which renders man immortal. Still, I will respond with greater equanimity, preferring to be considered ignorant rather than ungrateful.

"First of all, thank you for the efforts you have endured for me in the past and the present, and for the faithful love with which you embrace me. Nonetheless, I wish you did so with a bit less passion, since a burden carried without pause for rest destroys life without any consequential usefulness. Heaven does not permit our wishes to be fulfilled sooner or later than what is determined by the heavenly influences on our actions. Still, I will endeavour not to appear ungrateful, and if I get the opportunity, I will let you know my thoughts and plans through Astanna."

Her concise, serious, and pithy words ended, and she closed those rosy lips in silence. I didn't have the wherewithal to answer because, looking through the peephole, I was entirely mesmerized by the heavenly light of her beautiful eyes, adorned with tears, which made them look like oriental gems set in gold.

Graced with such light, I didn't respond in any way except with deep sighs, which signified how sweet and welcome her words were to me. But Apollo was beginning to hide his crown, and the waning sunlight urged Genevera to leave. Aided by the Lord Love, I spoke up: "Gentle spirit, your elegance, which I've always considered the worthy refuge of faithful love, together with your generous mien, born and disposed to pity, convinces me to freely become your servant because I am certain my service will be appropriately rewarded. Now I realize you have not been unfair to me, for which I give thanks to Love, and to nature, which has bestowed on you such a noble heart."

Out of embarrassment and tenderness, I asked her to allow me at least to dry with my own hands the many tears she had shed for me.

And she: "It is not the custom of the business dealer to offer valuable merchandise for little profit."

This wise and proper retort gave me an unshakeable belief that all my suffering would be rewarded. I tasted that pabulum, which was a foretaste of divine nectar and ambrosia, and I was content.

All the parishioners had left the church, the main doors were locked, and the priests were preparing for their meal, when I emerged silently from my hiding place and found a back door left ajar, which saved my honour and my life. I walked slowly toward Genevera's house. Even though I was denied Genevera's presence, I eagerly scanned, venerated, and adored the walls of her home. Then I returned to my place, repeating my lady's name at least a thousand times.

Rejoicing in the day's events, I proclaimed: "O happy day, O propitious hiding spot, O celestial pleasure! I don't believe even Jove enjoyed anything to equal or surpass this. O happy suffering and comforted torment, O divine prize, which Venus would yield to Mars. To be graced to see firsthand a lady's tears of compassion for a lover is worth a thousand blessings and more! Those glorious tears make up for all cares, cleanse all faults, and purge them from every stubborn heart!

"You, blessed eyes of mine, which saw liquid distilled from those celestial lights, what greater grace can Love offer you? What greater happiness can he promise? May you live happily now and your death be consoled! O holy God Who can bring the dead to life in one instant, do not be stingy or miserly in providing more days like this one, because nothing manifests Your divinity more than Your generosity."

I spent the night in this joyous state. I felt my ship had arrived at its much-desired port where with propitious winds it would be safe from any storm. It seemed right to rest a bit in the pursuit of love, so that it might grow during a short absence. After all, absence can foster fondness, while constant presence can sometimes become annoying.

Book 1. Chapter 25.

While hunting, one of Peregrino's friends, Cornelio, shows off a falcon's hood. Its decorative symbolism suggests to Peregrino that

Genevera has been unfaithful, and he denounces all women in a pique of jealousy. He retreats to a Franciscan convent and Sister Paula sets him straight.

The next day, I accepted the invitation of friends to meet at a country house to go hunting and trapping. We entered a dense wood and, following the dogs on the deer's scent, came to a spring in a delightful clearing. We were no less intent on our task than if we had been on the Caledonian boar hunt when Atalanta received its head in spoils. We marvelled at each other's prowess, since it seemed every young man was spurred by Love.

When we gathered in a circle, we broached the subject of love and who among us was most loved by his lady. One youth, more licentious than the others, set at the font's edge a falcon's hood, which seemed to me the handiwork of angels. He boasted that it was a gift after a night of lovemaking. I examined the object's artifice again and noticed it was embossed all over with twining branches of trees, signifying the name of my lady, along with a motto: "Two hearts joined in one desire." Given these details, I concluded it was a gift clearly made and bestowed by Genevera.

My heart instantly froze, my face fell, my legs gave way, and my tongue tied, as if I suffered a stroke or other tragic accident. Pretending an urgent matter had arisen, I took my leave of those companions as best I could, while they expressed great disappointment. They had no clue why I was so troubled.

Faithful Acate and I got back on our horses, and Jealousy, who was envious of my happiness, entered my weak breast as a worm bores its way into wood, consuming my heart with such rabid fury that I considered taking my own life. I complained to myself of my bitter fortune, thinking: 'O scattered ashes of these vast battlefields, O shades without the honour of burial, O spirits damned to hell, why don't you enter my body and destroy it? O infernal inhabitants, if you have any pity, rend me apart! O death, so troublesome and unwelcome to all mortals, how is it you don't come at my urgent call? Don't delay, please, I'm begging you, free me from this suffering and give the greatest relief to my sad soul!

'Ah, cruel woman, vase of impiety, home of betrayals, abode of iniquity, place of every fiction, falsehood, and fakery! Where are your sweet and thoughtful words now? Where's your vaunted modesty? Where's that virginal covering dearer to you than your soul? Where's the one who scorns all other loves? Where's your desire to live virtuously? What woman, if not a prostitute, is in the habit of giving gifts to lovers to mark their acts? Does it seem to you that I deserve to see a lesser man go before me with such licence to sin? Where is that tacit faith that only yesterday you promised to me? Why did you shed all those hot tears capable of shattering a diamond? Was there no better recompense for my toils?

'Woe is me! I realize too late – he who puts his faith in a woman loses his freedom. May heaven's fire scatter you all; may God's fury blast all you women! You see how in no time at all these ribald, wicked, and traitorous women change and change again. Among them there's no cause for trust, no humility, and no discretion. What wise, blessed, even sainted man wouldn't have trusted the sweet words of this cruel girl whose face is always composed to tell lies?'

Bemoaning my fate, I came upon the Franciscan convent and decided to vent my frustrations with a relative there with whom I had always shared a singular affection. She had a companion there named Paula, who was a most helpful and serious sort. She received me humbly and asked where I came from and why I was so pained. I replied I'd been hunting, and because she was curious to know all about where we went, what happened, and who was there, we came to the details of the hunters. I mentioned Cornelio by name, who was the one who boasted of his lover's gift. When she heard his name, Paula eagerly questioned me about whether I had ever seen the craftsmanship of a certain falcon's hood he had. Hearing these words, my mind was roused, and her company gave me the excuse to learn more about its provenance.

Paula said: "Our Mother Superior in Ferrara ordered it for our novices, so they could see that kind of craftsmanship and practise it themselves."

I immediately rejoined: "Then how did it end up in Cornelio's possession?"

Paula: "I'll tell you how. Not last night, but the night before, he was here to visit us because he's related to one of our sisters. The conversation took this kind of turn, and he wished to see our handiwork because he wanted a similar design as a decoration for his falcon hood. We agreed to do it out of loving charity in two days."

Peregrino: "Why is it decorated in this way with junipers, instead of other trees?"

Paula: "Because our cloisters are shaded by them, and junipers signify true repentance."

Peregrino: "I don't get the connection."

Paula: "Its virtue derives from its greenness and perseverance in its unripe bitter phase. Therefore, he who wishes to enter into something thoughtfully should welcome it, and blessed is he who finds himself the cultivator of this tree."

We digressed from this topic and entered into others (as is typical of women) until the time approached when we had to part. Acate and I offered them profuse thanks and got back on our horses. After we had put some road behind us, Acate turned to me and peevishly castigated me, saying …

Book 1. Chapter 26.

Acate takes Peregrino to task for so readily doubting Genevera's love and compares him to the many men ruled by their melancholic, choleric, and phlegmatic humours. In a fit of impatience, Peregrino condemns all women before ruing his outburst.

Acate: "Peregrino, it's no secret that men madly in love are good for little more than ruining their own business and everyone else's too. Look how quickly your pestilent tongue – the devil's instrument, consumer of the world, and dissipater of every good – ran without reason to put down and stain the modesty of such a lady. Thoughtless man of little worth, have you no shame? What venially wicked woman would be worthy of such accusations, imprecations, and execrations? Isn't man's fate sad, cursed, evil, and ungrateful, if he seduces a lady to give her his love without pure and sincere intentions?"

Peregrino: "That's not true. It was due to her imbecility."

A: "That's the harvest reaped by a servant of an ingrate!"

P: "It's just like a woman never to want a helmsman at the prow."

A: "Many times, yes, you made adjustments to your ship's mast. However, you still refuse to recognize the status of her house, while you childishly vaunt her as your patron. One type of melancholic man exists who convinces himself that everything he imagines in his fantasies is true, and he feeds his mind on his empty thoughts. Others so smoulder with choleric humours that they catch fright before seeing anything worth fearing. Still others are phlegmatic and foolish, so obtuse in their inexperience that they understand little, but nevertheless declare their empty pronouncements. Finally, there are those who are such good keepers of secrets that they never disclose any hint to anyone. You are very far indeed from this last praiseworthy disposition.

"That irksome, presumptuous youth Cornelio imitated the untalented painter who, in order to honour his less beautiful product, attributed it to the master of the art, so he could gain fame, if not through aesthetic achievement, then through the cleverness of having his work identified with that of an authority. How many statues, images, and paintings in the Troas, in Crete, Rhodes, Cyprus, and in the rest of famed Greece are attributed to Apollo, Zeus, and Lysippus, which were never made, carved, or painted by them? That arrogant youth had no better material to occupy his fantasy, so he boasted that the falcon's hood was a special gift.

He assumed the craftsmanship sufficient to endorse his reputation as an accomplished lover.

"And you! Since you don't dedicate yourself to better pursuits, most of the time you talk yourself into impossible undertakings. Don't you see you share the sad condition of those deluded men who assume that whatever they encounter, though it might be separate and completely unrelated, is the root cause of their little affliction? This is why even the representation of a juniper tree contributes to your delusion. The more of them you see, the more you think they all speak of her, as if no other woman in the world possessed the same name! O I see you mired in so many errors because you're an ungrateful, thoughtless, and perfidious man! You confuse God, the world, and hell. Behold the work accomplished by a rabid, poisonous tongue, which speaks evil and suggests even worse ways to act."

P: "Love makes me fear things not seen."

A: "If all you want to do is be afraid, then sure, but you can't make a decision without having relevant knowledge about it. What circumspect judge passes sentence before hearing the proceedings where evidence might be presented? For the sake of reason, temper your sudden and inconsiderate actions, and don't let yourself crumble because of your passions and appetites. Follow what is right, because the earth and the air are full of false reports and boasts."

P: "You are raving mad! That is the nature of women. They deserve to be kept under the strictest discipline. Even when they are wrongly accused by false men, they will develop the habit of following true men more easily. Not even what we say between us is safe from evil eavesdroppers."

A: "If it's true that the lover's soul lives in the body of the beloved, and she is capable of feeling all of our same passions, don't you believe Genevera – the true abode of your soul – understands what your evil opinion toward her is? The spirits we safeguard denote whether we live for good or evil. Peregrino, be careful your tongue doesn't deprive you of what you've worked so hard to establish all these years. The faithful lover must always serve, obey, and praise his lady. O unfortunate Peregrino, you – more than anyone else – make your path longer and lonelier."

P: "I'm humbled and will pray to Love in the hopes there'll be no consequence of my evil action."

A: "That is precisely what you owe: to put your words into effect."

P: "Lord Love, who dispels all anger with sweetness, reconciles every annoyance, and reunites all those who have disagreed, remember my long-suffering service. I know you have heard how I cursed my lady with a petulant tongue and an indisposed heart when I was overcome by excessive ardour. Take your vengeance out on me to the degree you think appropriate to a weary heart."

With these and similar words of supplication, full of jealousy and hope, we carried on until the time when Astanna came to see me.

Book 1. Chapter 27.

Astanna tells Peregrino that Anastasia has agreed to allow Genevera to satisfy her penance to feed a poor pilgrim, and Peregrino undertakes to play that part.

Astanna, faithful messenger and consoler of my heart, announced to me that my lady had persuaded her mother to agree to allow her to satisfy the conditions of her penance, which was to feed the first pilgrim who should knock on her door on Friday. "You must dress in a fitting manner and arrive early. I'll take care to admit no other before you. We'll be able to make further plans while you partake of your meal. Remain in peace and be mindful of me. I await you tomorrow."

When the day of the anticipated meal arrived, I forced myself to dress and look so downtrodden that I'd be deemed worthy of compassion. I went barefoot, and I scrubbed one leg and my hands with some water strongly infused with lime and soap, prompting my skin to produce an irritated moist sheen; I resembled a man suffering from leprosy. Never was a Persian bow pulled with such violent tautness as my skin, to the point I wasn't even able to move my washed limbs. My fake beard was straggly, chopped off, and tended toward a reddish colour. My brows were lacking, and my hair was arranged willy-nilly. Pater noster devotions dangled from my neck and wrists. I wore a mantle haphazardly stitched together containing more colours than Primavera.[28] One foot had a sock, and the other was bare.

Arrayed in this sluggardly, stinky get-up, unrecognizable and repellent even to myself, I rushed to the house before anyone else arrived. Astanna wept copious tears of compassion when she saw me. A whole crowd of beggars also came, but because I was the most pitiable of all, I was invited into the house and ushered to a place fit for a man far better than me – certainly not dressed like that – it was a spread for a king. I seemed to see Jove served by the cupbearer Ganymede. It was like a bolt of lightning seeing Genevera in that dining room. She bustled about with such modesty, readiness, grace, and clemency, entirely focused on her task of serving.

---

28 Caviceo probably did not intend a specific reference to Sandro Botticelli's painting *Primavera*, which was produced in Florence between 1477 and 1482, so I have not italicized it in the text. He may simply have meant that the pilgrim's mantle displayed more colours than we see during springtime.

Her strict mother came in and harshly criticized Genevera's solicitude, saying it was an affront to patricians to have to serve wretched, polluting, and wandering beggars. "It's right and proper for each person to serve according to one's class, especially young ladies who are most likely to suffer denigration to their reputations. Destitution of this kind is most often a result of poverty or pusillanimity. Therefore, daughter, attend to better and more honest tasks. I don't believe your life is so stained that wiping it clean should necessitate this degree of charity."

Genevera withdrew at her mother's insistence without offering any contradiction or resistance or demonstrating the least disappointment. Astanna followed her, and it was left to one of the many other serving women to show me out the door when I had finished eating. My appetite vanished, and I got up and left the house without taking my leave or offering thanks. My head drooped in shame, anger, and melancholy, all the while damning and cursing the beastliness and insolent haughtiness of that perfidious sex, which believes the whole world is at its perpetual beck and call.

Peregrino ruminated: 'Lend them something and you'll lose even more; believe something they say and they'll lead you farther astray; love them and they'll only be more offended. Because of her I've known nothing but suffering, sighs, and a bad lot; she doesn't even care that I'm her servant. Why? She is rich, though I'm not poor. She's noble, but I'm not plebian. She is beautiful, but I'm not ugly. She's young, but I'm hardly decrepit. She is healthy, though I'm not unwell. She's wise, but I'm not uneducated. When all of these qualities are added up, her heart should be elated.

'I must find a way to get out of this servitude. I have wasted more time serving her than a Hebrew theologian does in riddling the divine vision! I don't believe there's a man on earth who would do more for his beloved than I've done and was ready to do for her. I am resolved to quit her completely: she doesn't want a lover, nor am I lacking in ladies to love. I don't believe there's ever been or will ever be a man more obsequious than I. My constant faith did not deserve such stinting charity. I swear to God I'm never coming back where this ungrateful woman can see me!'

Although I had dictated and signed this irrevocable pronouncement, the very next morning I put on the same miserable disguise and went to her house under the pretext of begging for alms, though actually I intended to break completely from Genevera. Love, to better ensnare me, took away my power of speech, and without any forewarning, ushered her to that doorway. Because she took me for a beggar, she gave me some alms – not an ungenerous amount – with that same hand which opens and locks my heart. She conducted herself with no less dignity in that place than Jove practised in heaven's consistory. Then I became cold and timid, jumpier than a deer in flight; forgetting myself, I fell to my knees and like a man who fears justice and pleads for mercy, I opened myself to her ...

Book 1. Chapter 28.

> *Peregrino's speech to Genevera is interrupted by the arrival of her father, Angelo. Peregrino seeks advice from Violante, who tries to encourage Peregrino in his determination to break from Genevera by not seeing her again, but he insists on doing so in a face-to-face meeting.*

Peregrino: "Lady ..."

But before I could say anything more, Angelo appeared. I recognized his shadow as soon as Genevera did. She quickly withdrew with her companions and servants, as was proper. Angelo locked me out. In that moment I couldn't move, given the shame and scorn that pained me. I now imagined every step of our love was evilly presaged, and all my toils were destined for unhappiness. All this confirmed in me my resolution to break from her.

First, however, I wanted to hear Violante's opinion. I went to her and made her aware of my unhappy state, begging her to get Genevera to agree to speak to me by whatever industry, art, solicitude, and promises she thought necessary. Genevera's bedroom had a window opening onto Violante's garden, a fitting place for secret conversation. No matter what time she arranged, I was ready and willing to satisfy our shared aim.

Violante questioned me then: "What thing is so sensitive that you cannot write it to her in a letter?"

Peregrino: "I want to speak to her, as is right."

V: "Without her knowledge, you've gotten yourself trapped by Love; and without her, you can just as easily free yourself. But if you try to meet with her again, you'll only be more subject to her."

P: "My mind is made up."

V: "But that's not in your power."

P: "Why not?"

V: "You have behaved a bit too familiarly."

P: "It's easy to do what one wishes."

V: "So it might seem to you who have no experience in these matters."

P: "Our will precipitates toward its goal."

V: "Julius Caesar defied the Roman senate, fatal for him; and Alexander fled from ancient Babylon, but even so, heaven's will was done in the end."

P: "So even their actions were determined?"

V: "It would appear so."

P: "Who says so?"

V: "Take Apollo and Daphne. Do you see how one loves and the other does not?"

P: "That's just how it is with me! So I'll always serve and suffer."

V: "Peregrino, let me offer you some examples to the contrary to encourage you. After all, no other pursuit could be praised more highly. Let me speak, since I offer mere words. In the end, you, as a man, will do what you wish.

"Take Absalom, who fell in love so quickly that he was led directly to his end. There are infinite lovers who burn hot as fire one moment, then find themselves cold as ice the next. Although this vice is in all created people, it predominates in ladies. Once you realize you're not loved by this ungrateful woman, you won't want to abase yourself but seek to preserve your reputation. After all, abject servitude is not a lesser shame than the lack of gratitude in a high-born lady. Consider Samson and the great Hercules and how they became the object of gossip among the masses through their damnable submission. Thus, persevere in your determination with an unconquered spirit!"

Seconded by Violante's arguments, I resolved to do just that, but first I wanted to let Genevera know my thoughts so that in time she wouldn't think I broke faith. "Let me say what needs to be said. She is free, but I am bound, nor can I untie this bond if not in her presence. The sooner you can arrange it, the more grateful I'll be to you."

Violante was glad to leave and went to Genevera's house to pass the time. She found so many ladies and maidens there that day that she didn't have the chance to get in a word. Still, more with looks and gestures than spoken words, she gave Genevera to understand that she had an urgent, confidential message to communicate. As Violante was leaving, Genevera smilingly invited her back. The next day, she eagerly waited for Violante.

As soon as Violante arrived, she said: "Genevera, Peregrino sends his regards and wants nothing more than to love you. In truth, he is worthy of your love. So that you can understand fully what I attest and he demonstrates, he begs you for a brief audience to conclude what in the past days you have discussed. I don't know what that is, but since you are wise, you must know."

Book 1. Chapter 29.

Genevera sets a meeting with Peregrino for the following day through Violante, who communicates it to him. He passes the night playing out tormenting scenarios in his head.

Violante's brief words caused Genevera to marvel, and she began to wonder if something had changed. There were plenty of excuses she could offer to refuse his humble request, given that they were always in great danger of being discovered. Violante deftly reminded her of that garden window, but didn't say more. Genevera replied that to meet by night was dangerous. If Peregrino loved truly, he should spend his whole life wanting to make amends for his recent arrest. She would prefer to die rather than be the reason he might fall into a similar situation. If what he had to say was so important, there should be no reason he could not communicate it by letter, which faithfully transmits every intent.

Violante conveyed to her that I disagreed and wanted to put an end to so many messenger go-betweens. Then Genevera felt in her heart that I must be referring to a marriage proposal, so she agreed I should appear as a beggar at the courtyard gate, behind which she would listen humbly with Violante and Astanna present. I accepted the place, confirmed the terms, and named the very next day for the meeting.

But that night brought me no less torment than the fraudulent horse offered to King Priam. My uncertain mind imagined first one scenario, then another. Leave Genevera … that would be impious. She is quite beautiful, gentle, wise, elegant, and affectionate. But if she cannot love, how is that her fault? If she wants to continue: then this will prove my virtue, and may it bring victory! "Peregrino, leave aside these ruminations, which only foment extreme lust, the servant of every cruel vice. Follow reason. Consider: you're the dupe of this evil woman. If she loved you, she would have more respect for you. Don't you see she enjoys making you miserable? What greater torment could she cause for me, if I were a herder of her sheep! She's haughty, proud, scornful, and without faith. If this is how she is, how can you not leave her? You must be a coward. But I must understand her error. Isn't it true that only an insane person, when facing a fire, would look for every excuse to delay rather than find the means to put it out?

'But I believe this is the kind of situation in which I can enter like a lion, but come out like a lamb. Just one word, one laugh, one look, one tiny flicker in her eye, or some other show that she is happy to see you will bind you even more tightly to her than before. O change your mind, or don't go where your condition will only worsen!'

I passed the night in this kind of suffering.

Book 1. Chapter 30.

The following day, the Feast of the Annunciation, Peregrino and Genevera meet and bicker. When Peregrino sees Genevera, his intention to break up with her vanishes, and he begs for some favour from her. She argues that she has rewarded him sufficiently already and cites examples that support her assertion that all men seek to seduce then abandon women once they have got all they wanted.

The day arrived, which marked also the anniversary of the Annunciation when Mary, praiseworthy queen, learned that she would give birth to the Saviour. For this reason, everyone else was out of the house to take part in the celebrations. I presented myself, as I had been instructed, and through a sliver of space I saw her two lovely eyes flash, which deprived me then of life, speech, soul, and spirit. I almost wished I hadn't been so eager or daring.

In the end, I changed my mind and said: "Ah, lady, why are you so cruel to a dead body? Why do you demand so much of one who cannot feel? Why incite one who cannot move? Why do you continue to wound one who has no blood left? If you're so generous in giving your body and soul, why are you so stingy with my meagre request? Don't you know it's a sin for any master to be ungrateful? Clearly, you must see that my promptness of service with integrity of faith hasn't been adequately compensated. Why do you leave me languishing in such anxiety, lady? I don't know what more I can hope for. May God grant either an end to my misery or the beginnings of your good grace." After I spoke these words, I sat down in a snit.

With her divine tongue and a sparkle in her lucid, lovely eyes, which could've easily dispelled the shadows of Chaos, she replied: "Constant love and the accumulation of gifts beyond what is proper spoil the man and make him believe that anything proceeding from the sincerity of his spirit obliges some constant remuneration. Therefore, it is always prudent to proceed slowly when interacting with an unmindful man. You are generous in your actions on my behalf, but I am not stingy in return. Any faithful and virtuous lover should be content with this reciprocity. However, it is a clear sign of a covetous soul with wicked intent to seek to grow one's holdings to another's ruin. You do not consider just how out of balance we are and how predatory our age is, though we live virtuously. It is time for you to think about how scorned we will be when people start talking about us. You should be very protective indeed concerning a good that once lost can never be reacquired. Any other thing, whether good or evil, if taken away can be restored, but honour never. It is precisely this good that must be the faithful companion of every living person unto death."

Peregrino: "O how cruel you are!"

Genevera: "Cruel is not appreciating how vulnerable another's reputation is! If I reward you appropriately, why are you not content? It seems you will never be satisfied until you strip the honour of the one you pretend to love. Just read and reread the words of the ancients and moderns, and you will see what happens to wretched girls who accept great promises with unchecked faith."

P: "Well, my lady, I have freely given you every reason to trust me, not merely from words but also my actions. They attest as much to you in clear and sacred proofs. You would understand me, if you but listened to me! If this match pleases you, what are you waiting for? Otherwise, why are you killing me? I see well what your aim is. You are the queen, and I am your slave; you are free, while I am enchained; you are sublime, while I am cast down. You take pleasure in my suffering, and that saddens me. If I hurt, where is my comfort from you? If I die, where is your glory? If you abandon me, what praise will you earn? If I falter, what prize will be yours? If I beg for mercy for all I've endured, I am not insulting you. Change your thinking, lady, and remember who loves you above all else. Save your man, while you still can. Ah, most cherished is the gift that comes before its petition. Tell me, lady: isn't it a virtuous act to reward a man for his sacrifices?

G: "Yes, certainly."

P: "Who can ever be shamed by acting virtuously?"

G: "No one."

P: "Then you can't possibly fall into infamy for granting me what my faith and toils have earned."

G: "I accept that, but the recompense must equal the effort."

P: "I agree."

G: "My prize is everlasting, and your toils are temporary; whenever you like, you can quit your suffering and go back to more pleasurable pursuits, but I can never get back my prize once it is taken. Now do you see that the two cannot compare?"

P: "Oh, my!"

G: "Hush. This is no place to raise a commotion."

P: "I can't help it."

G: "Why?"

P: "You offend me to my soul."

G: "How?"

P: "With these harsh words."

G: "I do not believe it."

P: "Hear the reason then. If my heart together with my will are freely in your service, how can I take them back without your consent? What madman ever wished to suffer? What wretched man remains a captive who could be free? Since you have my will under your power, how do you go about preaching freedom?"

G: "How did I transform you so?"

P: "It was through the light of your eyes."

G: "How strongly?"

P: "So strongly my eyes, mind, and spirit have been blinded."

G: "Well, cool your ardour."

P: "That's out of my power."

G: "It is so great then?"

P: "I sweat in the snow and ice. Love has scorched me to the marrow, such that even if I swam all the sea, rivers, torrents, fountains, streams, rivulets, swamps, anything that might put out the heat, I wouldn't be cooled one tiny bit."

G: "O too wily flirtation, O feigned speech, O calculated attack! What resistance can one pose, if not gifted by some grace from heaven or endowed with exact knowledge of what the future holds? O mute shades, why do you keep silent? If chastity falls to credulity, how can you justifiably rest? Going along with you to appease social niceties would be a much greater affront to our sex. O how difficult it is to fool those who believe faithfully!"

P: "It's a much greater offence not to put your faith in one who has never told a lie."

G: "This is man's unique gift, bestowed by nature, always to trick others. Who in demanding mercy was ever humbler than Theseus? Then after Ariadne rewarded his powerful desire, he left her alone on a deserted shore, prey to wolves, the meal of bears, and food for the lions! What prayer was more tearful and insistent than Jason's? What greater recompense could a lady offer a man and with such prompt subservience than Medea offered him? In return, she was condemned to exile and had to beg to alleviate the suffering of her children. What tiger, what feral heart would not have been moved to weak compassion by the refugee Aeneas's pitiful tears, destroyed homeland, and recalled exploits? And see how he repaid the magnanimous Queen Dido? Consider Phyllis who loved. Who would want to tarry adrift on the high seas with these spurned ladies? It would be a fretful state of both mind and body. You men are all the same: bold in making promises, but not so eager to keep them!"

Genevera's words caused no little roiling within my spirit, which I sought to temper by replying in the following way.

Book 1. Chapter 31.

Peregrino counters Genevera's arguments with ancient and modern examples of men who loved faithfully and enduringly. Her family returns, and Violante and Astanna seek to hide Peregrino in the wine cellar.

Peregrino: "O how pitiable the one who complains without cause! Just see how far you're wandering into error. And people say a gullible man has little prudence! If you were to put that blessed reason of yours to good use, you'd easily conclude that Theseus could not have treated Ariadne any more compassionately than he did. The girl had her own reasons for arranging the clash between her brother the Minotaur and Theseus, son of Aegeus. She was so seized with passion for Theseus that, in order to satisfy her lust, she planned to run off with him. Once she made her lover victorious and his men were paid – they had gone to Crete to plunder it – Theseus sailed with her to Dia, the island of Venus. Since his queen could not endure the sea voyage, and because Theseus feared that the armed ship of Minos was closing in, he commended Ariadne to the island's inhabitants, and not just with words, but also with a good sum of money. Theseus had been travelling for so long he forgot to change his sails, and he caused the death of his father, who jumped into the sea that took his name. After Theseus regained possession of his father's kingdom, he returned to the island, where to his bitter grief he learned his beloved Ariadne had died after terrible suffering. To perpetuate her memory, he had two statues erected, one in gold and the other silver. Gathering the twin children from her one and only birth, which was the cause of Ariadne's death, he made his way back to his country. Now do you see how undeserving Theseus is of your recriminations?

"What faithful, patient, and virtuous man would suffer the servitude and cruelty of Medea, if not most pious Jason? During exile, he gave Medea no reason to carry out what she wrought: murders, fires, and her poisonous art. He deserves criticism or admiration for having shown clemency toward the poisoner Medea, rather than reprehension for having left her. Phyllis, a gracious hostess, terminated her life out of impatience through no fault of her lover, since human beings lack the power to influence gods. Moreover, if the sea didn't permit a crossing, why should Demophon suffer censure? Aeneas, as refugee, humbly begged Queen Dido to grant refuge in port so his weary men could rest, and she generously offered him the grace of her port along with her body. However, this act didn't earn the pious Trojan a perpetual stay in Carthage. Their love had the damning and shameful end its wicked beginning deserved because it wasn't love, but the satisfaction of her illicit lust.

"Don't you see, lady, how wrongly you blame their pure and unstained faith? You damn the doves and excuse the crows. But because it will take more time to reason through this, I beg you to listen patiently. There's no need to denigrate the male sex. I can show you through a review of ancient and modern stories how we men love more valiantly, tenderly, and enduringly, while your sex loves incomparably more faithfully and constantly.

"What more could the great David have done than what he did to honour his beloved Bathsheba? Or Hercules his beloved Io? Or Alexander the daughter of Leda? Demetrius exalted Lamia to the heavens. Antony accompanied his Cleopatra to the kingdom of Syria; Aristotle sacrificed for his Hermia. Since modern examples are clearer to you, though, let's speak of them. Triumphant King Alfonso of Aragon didn't overlook anything to uphold the dignity and glory of his Lucrezia. Francesco Sforza, glory of Italian rulers, exalted his Elisabetta, who is called Elisabetta dalle Grazie, above all others. Galeazzo, Duke of Milan, honoured modest Lucia beyond his forces. Federico of Urbino sang in prose and verse the praises of his Presupina, as did Sigismondo Malatesta his Isotta. Alessandro of Pesaro would not have lived happily without his Pacifica. The love shared by Roberto Malatesta and Elisabetta of Ravenna – praiseworthy example of married women – endured unbroken even beyond the ashes of his death. Pietro Maria Rossi, easily the pre-eminent prince of gentility and courtesy, celebrated the eternal memory on earth and in heaven of his Bianchina.[29]

"Given the quantity of faithful lovers for whom the mere thought of losing love would cause them to lose their wits, a continuation of this catalogue of many examples would be like hoeing the seas or planting rocks. Let us leave in peace all those men who have been mentioned in ancient texts and those who have been observed among the moderns. Never has there been a man in this world humbler and more respectful than I toward you. Human and divine generation could sooner pass into nothingness than my soul would not hold fast to you. I did not come into your perpetual service out of lust, but to be the true and legitimate possessor of your love in as much as conjugal status permits. So, take pity at last on me and accept with a sincere heart what accords to my faith."

We had concluded our discussion, and I was mostly satisfied with Genevera's audience. I was about to say, "I go in peace, O peerless goddess of mine," when we heard a large crowd arrive along with Genevera's brothers. I feared my presence might provoke them – young men are quick to take offence. Thus, urged by Violante and Astanna, I sought to hide by heading toward the wine cellar. I hadn't even set foot down there when I

---

29 Alfonso V King of Naples (known as The Magnanimous, d. 1458) loved a noblewoman named Lucrezia d'Alagno (d. 1479). Francesco I Sforza Duke of Milan (d. 1476) took a mistress, Elisabetta Robecco, who was also called Elisabetta dalle Grazie (of the Graces). Galeazzo Maria Sforza (d. 1476) had a mistress named Lucia Marliani, who left him a son (Ottaviano Maria Sforza) who became Bishop of Lodi and died in 1548. Federico da Montefeltro Duke of Urbino (d. 1482) is said to have loved Presupina. Sigismondo Pandolfo Malatesta (d. 1468) loved his young mistress (and later wife) Isotta degli Atti (d. 1474), who bore him four children. Alessandro Sforza Lord of Pesaro (d. 1473) took as one of his mistresses Pacifica Samperoli. Roberto Malatesta, the Italian *condottiero* and Lord of Rimini (d. 1482), loved Elisabetta Aldobrandini. Pier Maria Rossi II Count of San Secondo, *condottiero* and Caviceo's patron and protector (d. 1482), loved Bianchina Maria Pellegrini d'Arluno (d. c. 1480), for whom he had built the Castle of Torrechiara.

heard a voice say, "Astanna, relieve our thirst, and bring enough to eat that we can fill our hungry, rumbling stomachs."

Astanna replied with an austere look on her face, indicating that the cellar was not the place to receive anyone of status, nor was it a fitting place for Angelo to dine. They should go upstairs where they could eat in comfort. Still, he persisted, insisting Astanna set a small table there to accommodate their meal.

Terrified, she rushed to me, more dead than alive, and hid me between the wine jugs and the wall, where I stayed well hidden for so long I thought I'd leave my spirit there. After she had served the food and drinks and taken her leave, Astanna came back to comfort me. She exhorted me to take heart because one rotten day could herald the beginning of everlasting happiness. She had to pull me out of that tormenting hiding place by force, and she put me in a cask large enough I could at least stretch my tired legs.

Book 1. Chapter 32.

Peregrino hides in the wine cellar of Genevera's house precisely when Angelo insists the casks be prepared to receive the new harvest. Astanna covers for Peregrino, who is dressed as a begging pilgrim, by insulting him.

It was nearly the harvest season, when love and fear first hid me in that risky prison. Hours passed before Angelo rejoined his family in the house. While he mounted the stairs, though, he expressed his determination to have the casks prepared for the wine. His words pierced my heart like a poisoned arrow.

I remained half-dead, mumbling to myself inside the cask: 'O Peregrino, you are so cursed by the world and God that after being so careful today, you'll still end up in prison! What will become of your spirit if you're discovered? What excuse, what explanation could you possibly offer? What will you say, wretched man? I think some miserable destiny will be the fitting end to your life. If you confess your love for Genevera, you won't be believed. You should remember: when it comes to irrational motives, the more emotionally urgent they seem, the more bothersome and detestable they are. It would've been so much better had you kept closer to the chaste life, rather than follow your excessive appetites, which always end in unhappiness. Wicked one, know this: there aren't as many armed men in the whole world out to harm you as there are myriad, lurking desires. A man is blessed indeed who learns how to overcome them with prudence!

'Unfortunate one, you must see what will follow your capture: either execution or perpetual exile, which to respectable men is worse than death. Anyone would easily believe, given my pattern of behaviour, that I have come here either to kill Angelo or to stain his daughter's honour and distinguished reputation. God and the ruler of this city always incline where justice tends. This is the reward meted to the excessively lustful; this is the prize for insolent ones. This is the consolation you can expect, the outcome of your long suffering. These are the doleful days, and this is the joy of your rivals when you don't accomplish anything else!

'It is right for me to suffer for my sins. But what pains my heart is what I fear for you – my soul, my life, and the light of my eyes! You, unlucky lover, will undergo penance before committing the sin; your sentence precedes the crime; pain comes before the blow, and innocence will be punished as sad wickedness. O face of innocence, I see you disparaged because of my failing.'

My virtue was so moved and my passion so seized that I could not provide for any of my actual needs. While I tormented myself in this way, it was my bitter fortune that the workers were shown in who had to pour out the wine, which couldn't easily be done without the use of the empty cask where I was hiding. Hot water was already being prepared to wash it out.

Clever Astanna, seeing the risk to both of us, with the excuse of letting those workers taste some other wines first, took them outside the cellar and escorted them far enough away so I could get out of the cask. Just when I thought I was in the clear, she hurled insults at me in a show to those who might have some suspicion about my presence there, accusing me of laziness, reckless presumption, and boldness for begging so brazenly and disturbing the household servants' chores.

Book 1. Chapter 33.

Astanna puts Peregrino to work in Angelo's house, and Genevera teases him. Although he does not do the chores he is given, Peregrino receives a compensatory meal, during which Genevera sings, accompanying herself on a monochord. When he leaves, Peregrino receives his reward: a lazy dog and an invitation to return the next day.

My vital spirits were so scared and frightened by the inherent sweetness I sensed in my lady's presence that I didn't know where to turn.

At the ruckus caused by Astanna's words, Angelo was about to come back down to find out more. But she replied with a troubled expression on her face: "Some lazy beggar has gotten in without our permission. It seems he's done nothing else but sleep, so I can hardly contain myself from doling out a few good whacks. However, a more fitting penance might be to put him to work cleaning the casks and the small wine cellar."

Angelo answered with a smirk: "You should be incensed, Astanna. Do as you wish, and if he works, give him something to eat."

Without further ado, she led me to the designated cellar, which contained his most precious wines – one could worthily sacrifice to Bacchus there! In one breath she ordered me to do more jobs than ten servants could handle in a month.

Genevera saw and heard everything. When she realized I was out of harm's way, she turned toward me and whispered great consolation: "Work, good man, and you will be compensated as you hope." That news was keener and more penetrating than Jove's thunderbolt or an arrow to my heart. O great reconciler of so much suffering, who would believe one could forget such a great danger in an instant? O incomprehensible power of love, how quickly you live and die!

I was incapable of answering her tenderness; I didn't know what to do at all. I acted more like a hunted beast seeking refuge. I looked here and there for something to occupy my attention. Then my eyes happened upon a broom, with which I did nothing but go through the motions of sweeping the cellar.

Genevera assisted in her uniquely modest way, which would have compelled Jove to an even baser task.

Her mother, Anastasia, either because of her age or gender or country of origin, eagerly sought to indulge her greed. She said: "Given this poor man seeks nothing but a meal, we ought to keep him around the house two or three days to do some of our chores. Just look at how well he takes to this work! It seems he was born and raised for this task!"

Love and shame pressed Genevera. Still, she praised her mother's idea and had Astanna take me to an enclosure where the doves were kept in order to clean it out. I passed the whole day there. When the workers began to prepare for dinner, I was plied with food and drink, which was as satisfying as it was exquisite.

Genevera came to a window and began to play a song on the monochord, which began "Vedo quel sole che d'ogni tempo luce,"[30] with such melodiousness she would've bested Apollo on his lyre. After she finished that lovely concert, which restored my weariness, she had Astanna confer on me my 'reward': a lazy dog, which she made me swear on my body and soul to care for in perpetuity! Then Astanna begged me

---

30   "I See That Sun Which Shines at All Times" is reminiscent of Petrarch's poetry set to
       music, but I found no composition beginning with precisely these words.

on my lady's behalf to return again the following morning. My eagerness made me wish to carry it out, even before she finished extending the invitation.

Book 1. Chapter 34.

Plans change when Angelo must send Genevera to console her ailing cousin Polyxena. Peregrino tags along and, instead of returning home on his own, seeks refuge from the gatekeeper of Polyxena's household. Peregrino prays to Mary, and the gatekeeper associates the pilgrim's orations with Polyxena's miraculous recovery.

That great god who repays our every toil, the one who moved Neptune to hasten to offer a port to Hippolytus, transformed the fine health of Genevera's cousin into a grave affliction and with such fury that she didn't seem long for this world. Angelo, beside himself with worry, decided to send Genevera that very night to visit Polyxena to offer the family's consolation.

When I heard the plan, I changed my mind about returning to the place as promised and accompanied Genevera to the sick woman's house. When we arrived at her door, Genevera cast an affectionate glance at me and modestly whispered, "Go in peace, faithful companion."

Like a keen hound, I sniffed love in the air and, although I had been dismissed, I couldn't bring myself to leave. I approached the gatekeeper and begged him, for the love of our Lady, to grant me hospitality for that night, since I knew nowhere else to turn.

The good man was moved by my entreaties, believing he might placate God's wrath through the exercise of charity. So that I might be closer to his ailing mistress, he led me to a shed in the garden he maintained. From there I heard a constant train of doctors, relatives, and neighbours call on Polyxena, who had collapsed due to the rise in vapours from her stomach to her head. Her prognosis was grave. A crowd gathered round Polyxena in the hopes for a cure, while I was alone in the shelter offering my usual prayers to the Queen of heaven. As I was reciting them, the gatekeeper rushed in with word that Polyxena's state was improving. That simple man believed the hospitality he offered me, along with my prayers, had brought better health to the woman. Eager to explain his part, the gate-keeper went to Polyxena and told her humbly how he had been diligent in finding her healing because he had offered charity to a poor pilgrim whose devotions had placated divine will. Polyxena thanked him and insisted I not leave without seeing her, since she wanted to satisfy a vow she had made during her illness.

Genevera praised her cousin's opinion, adding that she would also like to communicate her spiritual thoughts with that beggar, which met with no resistance from Polyxena.

Book 1. Chapter 35.

At dawn, Genevera attempts to persuade Peregrino to moderate his feelings and consider the consequences of his actions to their reputations. Polyxena overhears them and cautions Genevera about strange pilgrims with less than virtuous intentions, and they send Peregrino away.

Apollo's swift coursers had hardly emerged from the ocean when Genevera went to her window, which took in the light of the lovely garden, and asked the gatekeeper to bring me there, which he did.

After some time, Genevera sighed and said: "Peregrino, it is not in my power to render to you those great rewards your efforts and serious suffering deserve. I wish you would put an end to them because I am certain your over-eagerness to serve me will eventually expose what you try so carefully to hide. If my parents should hear of this, consider what my life would become. My mother already suspects me of something. Just imagine what she would do if she had evidence to back up her imaginings. Believe me, there would be nothing in the world to crown this chaste love of ours then! When I see you mired in your current state of dissatisfaction, I cannot help but feel badly. Thus, it is our duty to return to a more virtuous course, so we do not become the talk of scorning townspeople out of some malice or mere silliness. Please, temper your ardour with modesty."

After she spoke these words, she made as if to withdraw, when I cried out after her: "Lady, be moved by pity and pause a while. This place permits it, and virtue has suffered to make it possible. Nobody can have any cause to suspect us. I'll be brief."

Genevera: "I cannot."

Peregrino: "You mean you don't want to."

G: "It is difficult to love one who does not want to be loved."

P: "I ask for nothing more."

G: "You flee from love."

P: "Tell me how exactly."

G: "Experience shows you go around indiscriminately begging and courting danger and disaster. These risks you take with their accompanying suffering do not incline toward honour or a comfortable situation for either of us. Actions must be fitting to the actors, otherwise such acts damage their reputations. Seeing you so wretched and shabby gives me even more reason to grieve. A man can legitimately have two reasons to be sad: when he is frustrated in his desire, or when he is deprived of something once possessed. Neither describes your situation. Moreover, whoever suffers because of himself cannot blame it on others."

P: "O cruel and unhappy destiny of lovers!"

G: "And still you persist in your whining! Make clear the cause, please."

P: "My heart wishes to be united with yours."

G: "This is as much as is permitted. I see clearly how you flounder in the depths of wretchedness and misery, which, when it splits from true love whose aim is virtue, causes you to succumb to lust. Leave aside your mindless rancour, which derives from the sensual appetite; renounce your overly ardent, useless pursuits, and regulate your mind under the discipline of true lovers, those who have acquired glory and fame. Love is nothing if not the contemplation of the beloved object, which gives greater delight to the mind than to the body in the physical act."

P: "Lady, if a man has ever had a legitimate cause to complain I am he, since two causes burn urgently in me together. The first is: I have been cheated in my expectations. The other is: I have been deprived of the one thing that should've been mine through faith and love. I would be grateful to know how it's possible to feel some type of intellectual joy unless it is a consequence of an external demonstration, which is actual and not merely simulated. Assuming your opinion to be without error, a man could be rich or poor, so long as he believed himself to be such. The problem with such thinking I leave you to ponder. If we never experienced delight in any other way than an imaginary or mental fantasy of love, there'd be no need to weary ourselves so much, because whatever man's condition, he could find satisfaction in his mind. Do you know what pleases the soul most readily? The memory of past pleasures. When I am sure your wish accords with mine, then I'll consider myself blessed and satisfied with my efforts.

"This recompense you owe me is not for some disordered fury, as you seem to believe. My response signifies that my love is true. Do you believe that Julia, Cornelia, Portia, and other famous women willingly faced such dangers and death out of some love only in the mind? You would be quite mistaken. Although it's true that when bodily acts cease, the mind persists in lending support by recalling them. Divine and invisible things are not loved if they are not enjoyed. Do not let this falsehood enter your mind that a thing of the mind can lend some effect to make it real. Make me worthy of your love with some kind of clear sign that you are mine as I am yours. Otherwise, I'll consider myself deprived of your grace."

G: "It is grave to place one's health in the hands of a poor doctor. You men do not stop to consider anybody else's honour for a moment because you have only one thought until your lust has extinguished itself. Only love accompanied by virtue as its end is truly sweet. Oversight must suffice where that is lacking."

P: "Water from the freshest fountain doesn't relieve the thirst of the feverish; instead, it only increases the desire to drink."

G: "To the one with fussy digestion, every food is unappetizing. First you need a good purgative before you go tasting anything else. Go in peace. There is Polyxena. I do not know if I can trust her."

P: "Stay where you are, leave her to me, and listen to me patiently. There is a psalm that states the starry heaven has a wondrous power to heal the sick …"

At this point, Polyxena came up to us, and Genevera greeted her affectionately and told her of my good reputation. Thus, comforted first by one, then by the other, I told them of the efficacy of many prayers. Polyxena marvelled quite a bit at my words and became suspicious; first she scrutinized me, then Genevera.

Pulling Genevera aside, she counselled: "Dear cousin, it is customary for one who wishes to maintain a good and true reputation to behave so as always to avoid not just the effects of blame but also the mere suspicion of it. You've spent time with this pilgrim, whose clothes are shabby, without knowing anything about him or his provenance. Don't you see how calculatedly he speaks, accompanying his words with apt gestures? Sometimes men like this one, under the pretext of holiness, come to corrupt our bodies as much as our souls. For this reason, it would be preferable if you lived more cautiously and mindfully, so you don't fall prey to foul tongues. How many innocent souls do you believe fall to false men who go about disguised as poor beggars, but who only intend our ruin?"

My close proximity to them permitted me to hear her arguments, but more so to see the change in colour on Genevera's face. I was then harshly berated and expelled from the house. It seemed more honourable to leave in silence than offer any defence. I left in a fit of disdain, anger, and pain.

As my weary body shuffled away, I said to myself: 'O Peregrino, which magical charms of Zoroaster or Beroso, which of Orpheus's mysteries, which Pythagorean secret or Socratic rite or Platonic ritual or Aristotelian cleverness could cure my dire case? O heaven, blind and deaf to my pitiful prayers; O gods, vigilant guardians of my every downfall; O times, ever eager and ready to curse me. Woe is me, to what end have I come? Now is the time for you to leave this world and make your next pilgrimage to your infernal resting place, since you haven't proven yourself worthy or prudent in preserving such a love.'

Ire and disdain crushed my heart; and compassion for Genevera more than for myself weighed on me. A thousand times I repeated: 'Destroyer of your own interests, why are you still alive? Why do you expect so much? You aren't worthy of love; the world refuses you; death only grants you more time in order to make you suffer more! What is to be done with you, you impertinent, annoying, crazy-headed, constipated, lost man with a lightless soul, inconsiderate mind, obtuse intellect, and body without a spirit, when through your own fault you most distance yourself from your lady without any hope of return?'

It seemed I was aboard the chariot of Regulus, because my thoughts were so conflicted. Projected thoughts of similar lovers' cases and others of high estate who fall into misery continually pricked my mind. Love brought me to such a low point that I fell into my bed as my final refuge with no hope of getting up again.

Book 1. Chapter 36.

Peregrino succumbs to a fever, and Genevera sends Astanna to him. Peregrino vents his frustration. After a few days, she returns to inform him that Genevera and Violante are planning a fishing excursion.

I passed a fitful night, no thanks to the conjunction between Diana and her brother, which wrought upon me a most insidious fever, affecting not just the arteries and veins but also my joints, digestion, nerves, bones, and marrow. It consumed me so cruelly that I walked to the boundary of death. I stepped across Persephone's threshold and looked about. My most elemental powers returned, and I thought I glimpsed in the depths of the night's shadows a lucid, shining sun. I went toward it and adored it, and it spoke gently to me: "Suffering is vile when it doesn't lead anywhere." Then it disappeared.

News of my poor health reached my lady's ears, and she was moved to send Astanna to visit me. As soon as I saw her, I cried out, saying: "O liberator of my anxiety, O restorer of my weak body, O aid for my poor little wandering soul, may heaven bless you! Astanna, my lady lives safe and sound while I carry on without my spirit! I rest without my head, eat without a mouth, taste without appetite, recline without life, and walk without moving. Love has brought me to this state. You're a most welcome sight. What good news do you bring me?"

She said to me: "Genevera is distraught over what has happened, and she sends me to tell you: the rudder not the sail must steer the ship. She also understands that your present woe stems from over-eager curiosity, and your cure is its contrary. You must be more considerate and respectful, because in an open garden neither flowers nor fruits can flourish for long."

She said no more.

I thanked her as best I could in my weak state. I made her solemnly swear to interpret truthfully Genevera's reason for sending me away.

Otherwise, I would ceaselessly worry that I had caused her some kind of grave offence. I also feared I wouldn't ever be compensated as human decency demanded, and as a faithful man, I'd never receive my reward. My tears, hotter than the flames of Mount Etna, followed these words.

If these first pangs were harsh, the next ones were no less so. In a growing fit of rage, I lamented: "Did Erysichthon suffer more at his own hand, or was Acteon more ravaged by his dogs, than I have been beset by anguishing pains? At least your death was quick, O desperate spirits! My suffering drags on and on. Furies besiege my body. Scylla and Charybdis are much calmer and more tranquil than I. What soldier, what rustic labourer, what sylvan shepherd, what sailor, mechanic, slave, servant in the convent, or overworked animal remains in as little peace as you? Traitor, die. I ask nothing more. Why do you tarry here then? To increase my pain!

"All the powers conspire in me to make me the laughingstock of every human misery. What Pelops, devoured by the gods, what Tydeus, who on the point of death demanded to drink from the skull of Menalippus, whom he killed, what Itys, eaten by his father Tereus, what Absyrtus, chopped into pieces by his sister Medea, what Pelias, killed by his daughters who believed they would make him young again, what Bacchic follower devoured by dogs, what cursed adherent has ever had more cause to complain than I have?"

The agony, lack of food, and the disquieting night had all brought me to this extreme, which nourished my sighs, trembling, and tears.

After a few days, Astanna, who had communicated through Violante, as she usually did, cautiously returned to me to tell me what Violante said, which went as follows.

Astanna: "Man must not govern himself by the sail, that is, the sensual appetite, but rather by the rudder, which is reason. This is especially true when appearances triumph over actions. Here man's prudence is demonstrated by choosing to live moderately and temperately, and by denying himself what does him harm. Therefore, you must shun destructive passions and dedicate yourself to the life of a grown man rather than a boy, because the suffering that must be overcome by this curative advice indicates a lack of resilience, which presages a man who is useless in every future need.

"You have seen that Genevera loves you as much as is proper. There's no mystery requiring a response that offends honour. That would be like trying to dry out the sea, sow the sky, eradicate the stars, lay waste to the foundation, and return to the previous chaos. If a modest life like hers appeals to you, and you seek to rejoice and follow it, you must not show yourself to be curious about matters, which will always be denied to you with good reason.

"You loaf about like this, thinking of nothing more than satisfying your rabid lust. Pull yourself together right now, and stop seeking so much destruction by letting your whims run rampant. Get up and marshal your wits, because a great, unhoped-for opportunity awaits you.

"Next Sunday, we have arranged to go fishing to relieve our stress. Dressed like a fisherman, you could blend in and take part in the company's pleasant diversion. If Fortune favours you beyond your expectations, you'll remain in her debt. But let me remind you: don't let your thoughts get stuck where you can be easily deceived, because consuming the spirit without any utility or honour can only be ascribed to pusillanimity. I look forward to seeing you. As much as I am able, I will offer encouragement. Whatever I have left out, Violante will fill in because she'll be present, too. May God give you the greatest comfort. Go with God."

Book 1. Chapter 37.

Peregrino relishes the fishing plan and recovers his health. Dressed in fishing garb, he sets out for the Rubicon's banks anticipating the fulfilment of his greatest desire.

O protectress sent from the Empyrean, O reason to hope for renewed health, O heavenly consoler, whether I live or die, I shall remain indebted to you! Your reminder is not without wisdom and love; it also contains truth, and something in its concealed happiness frees me from my woe. Once my forces of reason had returned, I was more consoled than before, and I begged Apollo infinite times to shine his rays on a faster course toward this occasion, since I longed to shorten the time until the day when he could offer me great blessings through sport. My heart held me in such eager desire that my newly born optimism didn't cause me to suffer as it had previously. How weak the one who is moved by every chance occurrence! I passed that short span between Friday and Sunday in various distractions because I knew the time would seem to fly quicker if my mind were seized by various matters instead of focusing on one particular thing.

The anticipated day of my highest expectations arrived. I donned the gear Astanna had recommended and went to the place where the Triumvirate Roman cast the die of tyranny over the world. I kept some distance down the river from where Polyxena and Genevera were expected to set up. There I sat alone with my self-critical thoughts, saying: 'See, Peregrino, your beatitude is nigh, your supreme fulfilment, and your true joy, which cannot be denied to you by heaven, earth, or bad luck! Blessed is the suffering that brings such a prize!'

Book 1. Chapter 38.

Peregrino sees Genevera in the company of her ladies. They elect Genevera as their empress for the day, and she encourages storytelling.

My mind wandered amidst these consoling thoughts when I spotted Genevera. She blazed like the sun among other bright stars, since many ladies accompanied her. She descended like a queen from a chariot. They all paused to rest a bit, but didn't remain there long; instead they began walking toward the glade that extended to where I was.

At that point I reminded myself: 'Peregrino, if heaven by grace should permit you to be seen, recognized, greeted, or touched, behave yourself! Please, tongue, speak your passions properly; eyes through which a great fire kindled your heart, moderate modestly your pressing desire; lips, open wide to virtuous speech; hands, remain reverently close, because such a divine creature must not be polluted; feet, don't be curious about anything that might offend or disturb my lady.' I lectured each of my members to adhere to its duty chastely as I moved among the fronds and grasses.

Then that lady who is the sole glory and praise of the female sex in all the world proceeded with a slow, modest, and proper pace, as would a unicorn among all the other animals. Her dress was purple; her hair thick and abundant, loose and cascading all about her divine neck. A crown of various flowers graced her sacred head, and as she passed by, she exuded an Arabian perfume that could have brought the dead back to life. She entered the clearing before the wood where I was. There the ladies followed, skirting a font of sweet water, clear as glass. Any viewer of this scene would have assumed it to be in the enchanted Elysian Fields.

The noble company gathered in a circle while some servants began to fish. They didn't waste any time in electing amongst themselves an empress at whose command they dedicated the festive day. The empress, Genevera, judged the time and place conducive to storytelling. Once the other maidens understood her request, they were as diligent as they were obedient. Lucrezia, who was second only to the empress, received the nod and began thus ...

Book 1. Chapter 39.

Lucrezia praises the empress before she begins her story.

Lucrezia: "Supreme empress, I am not unaware of the importance of oratory, which, as Demosthenes, Cicero, and Horace attest, is frequently lacking even in excellent minds. If I didn't believe that I would be accused of disobedience, I would have passed this duty to another, because I would more readily sit as listening pupil than as apparent teacher. But I know well that the greatness of our empress, in whose breast are lodged knowledge, customs, nobility, and generosity, will excuse the lowliness of my lesser mind, which also has the excuse of a lack of time to prepare. Deign, then, to grant me your attention, and you will hear how abundant our city is in modesty and the virtue of tolerance, which can stand as an example for many suffering spirits."

Book 1. Chapter 40.

Lucrezia presents the account of a recent love triangle.

Lucrezia: "Delicate companions, as I believe you are aware, just a few days ago in our city a noble youth of tender age fell hopelessly in love with the angelic visage of one maiden. He was so strongly in love he almost gave up his spirit. As he walked about, the afflicted youth seemed more like a ghost; and standing still, he might as well have been a marble column or statue, so little did he resemble a living man. Only when he looked around or sighed did he show his heartfelt suffering, which would be difficult to describe even in a thousand languages.

"The lady occasionally offered him some honourable and sociable encouragement, such that among a thousand deaths hope caused him to carry on his miserable life. Because the youth was reduced to this extreme, to the point he could suffer no more, he begged peace with his arms crossed in humility.

"He didn't remain long in that state before love found the breast of the maiden and kindled it with a new flame. She lost all memory of her old love and assumed the same semblance toward her new lover, which made the suffering youth conclude she was giving him a clear sign that their relationship had reached its end. Seeing that his luck had changed, he put an end to his suffering by setting his mind at peace. If so much virtue is possible in a youthful heart, what might be possible in the hearts of those who possess age, experience, and integrity? It is admirable, if I'm not mistaken, how quickly a miserable lover can be freed from grief. So, I ask you, generous maidens, if Love can be so easily given, is the couple indebted to the rejected youth?"

When she finished her delightful proposal for the love debate, noble Camilla, who yielded to no other lady in beauty and seriousness, responded in this way ...

Book 1. Chapter 41.

Camilla takes up the prompt of Lucrezia's love debate, arguing that the first suitor's weak character and lack of persistence do not deserve any acknowledgement from the couple.

Camilla: "Most noble lady in whose creation nature and God leant every care, I listened with great interest to your proposal, which doesn't lack for wise thoughts within its words. I cannot but gravely condemn the youth's insipidness, which prompted him so readily to give up his quest for love. If he had thought carefully before entering Love's arena, he would have remained more determined before exiting it. But as the trite proverb says: 'He who begins rashly, ends miserably.' These ardours of young men cool down as quickly as they heat up, and they can be extinguished with the same ease they can be lit. This is caused by their lack of stability at a tender age. If his love had been confirmed, then he would have received it and fixed it in his heart, and there would have been no way for him to eradicate it. He would sooner have suffered every torture than be deprived of his love.

"However, given the pusillanimity he demonstrated, I refuse to concede that anyone owes him anything, because love isn't for the timid, petty-minded type. The man in love must be solicitous, secretive, independent, curious, modest, magnanimous, and patient in adversity; he must not be arrogant, difficult, or obstinate, but instead sweet and flexible, according to the circumstances. One cannot entrust to a weak-minded man anything of great value, whether a public or private good. The mass of pusillanimous men leaves Love's power unrealized, ignored, or cast aside; and in an instant they can render love scandalous, exposed, dishonest, unworthy, and spurious. Moreover, this lack of courage can lead a prudent man to turn away from Love's arena, where he might triumph and acquire fame. For this reason, few men prove themselves to be true lovers.

"This not so experienced youth didn't understand that well-proven motto: 'Every great undertaking is difficult.' Even if his energies were insufficient to bring about what he sought, his will should never have been extinguished, because, just as the soul improves with age, so love that persists through suffering grows in strength and sweetness.

"We should more highly praise the wise doctor who anticipates an adverse side effect to his patient's health than the doctor who claims to be able to cure the person whose suffering he caused. Greatest of all in my estimation, however, is the army commander and protector who knows how to thwart his enemies' plan and action. The lover who knows how to anticipate ways of preserving his lady's love deserves no less commendation than the leader in maintaining his army. O how shameful it would be if an enemy took the commander without a fight! What injury did the youth suffer out of love that made him surrender so vilely? What justification does anyone ever have to give up so readily? Saving himself in that way is very shameful indeed, on par with retreat. Instead, death is considered happy if it comes as a consequence of proving the strength of one's spirit.

"But giving up is as disgraceful as when Caeneus transformed himself from a man into a woman! Who has ever seen anything lamer than a new lover quit his quest? This youth is thus owed nothing, certainly not her love! As a divine essence, Love isn't obligated to repay any human merit. The new lover remains subject only to the effect of Love, not Love's true affect. He was freely given what could not be traded. Moreover, the maiden isn't obligated to him in any way, because a loving lady, even if she loves tepidly, doesn't find delight in being abandoned. I find his desertion especially galling because she inclined her heart to offer him his due in good time. Therefore, I judge the lady as worthy of commendation and the youth as timid and reprehensible. If he is vile at this age, when he should be daring, when will he assert his greatness? If he was raised without facing fear, what would he do when threatened? What hope could his beloved lady have of him if he puts his own life in such danger?

"This poor youth should've suffered by keeping his love to himself before involving his lady; instead, he re-enacted the great refusal out of cowardice! He might've persisted with requests and prayers and begged her for mercy with open arms, which is never long denied to one who seeks it in good faith.

"After contenders face off in battle, don't we see how victors pardon the vanquished who bow down before them? If this is the way it is, what must we think of a naive, delicate, and beautiful girl, who could offer nothing but peace and comfort to the persevering lover, if only the youth had persisted? I'm convinced she would not have abandoned her first suitor. But what she did to him was for his own good, to incite him to greater valour. Thus, the fault lies not with the lady, but with the insipidness of the young man. We must also consider the infamy that accompanied the damage he caused, so he must be judged unworthy even of the encouragements he received, which aren't fitting to thoughtless men."

Angelic Lionora followed Camilla's words intently, not unlike the Queen of Carthage at the speech of pitiable Aeneas. Compassion for the abandoned youth rushed to her mind, and with grave modesty she replied in this way …

Book 1. Chapter 42.

Lionora counters Camilla by defending the youth as behaving properly in his pursuit of love, while criticizing the new lovers. Lionora then calls on Genevera to resolve the debate.

Lionora: "Not because my lips have ever sipped from the sweet fountain of Helicon or Parnassus, nor because Love has ever turned its ardent face toward me, will I speak, but because my judgment inclines toward where the sceptre of justice and clemency hold fast. O glorious empress, if I am long-winded or pose a contradictory viewpoint, may it not be ascribed to any mean intent on my part. After all, differing opinions do not break friendships.

"I naively concede that Love can burn, extinguish, move, and alter our minds as it will. But if the proper actions of the impassioned youth are not accorded everlasting gratitude, well, this would entail the scorning of divine justice. Natural reason, which teaches us about love, asserts that every action of our will is either a sin or a virtue. Supposing, as is credible and allowable, that the youth set out in the service of Love with the best of intentions and a dedicated will, and he persevered in his aim for as long as Love and his lady wished. If he yielded to their tacit commands, why must he, after his many toils, lose his recognition? After all, the alternative – contradicting her will – would be a vain and dangerous pursuit. Love cooled the girl's mind, and she shunned his service. It was not in the lover's power to rekindle her affections or Love's grace without their consent.

"For this reason, the youth is not at fault, because he never gave up on his quest until his Lord, the reconciler of all, drove him away. Therefore, there is no reason why the lover should not receive some recompense for all his suffering. Can we not see how the eternal God renders more generous rewards for our endured suffering than perhaps we deserve, not because He is obligated to do so, but simply out of a generous and well-disposed will? Why must this youth go without any acknowledgment or gratitude?

"This same reasoning can be applied against the lady who preferred the second lover to the first. Since she granted to one man priority of place and enjoyed something he had done for her, by rights she still owes him. It seems necessary to me to praise the youth's great constancy and virtuous action. The heirs of so much good, who gained it in peace while the other felt its contrary effects, remain in his debt.

"I do not dare, however, to seek to judge beyond what the keenest interpretation of our high empress deems fitting. Since daylight is waning – Apollo's first horse seems to now be reaching the far horizon – perhaps we should return the way we came. But first, for our shared satisfaction, let us hear what our just empress determines in this case."

Book 1. Chapter 43.

Genevera offers her judgment on the debate, siding with Camilla: lovers must be persistent.

Genevera: "Lovely, faithful, and wise maidens, you must know everything tends toward its end according to proportionate and fitting means. Love is an essence, which, in order to be enjoyed, requires trials, suffering, toils, and unbearable pains. Whoever languishes and suffers the most is judged worthy of victory, as the stories of Jove, Hercules, Mars, Perseus, and Leander show, and never was a prize given to a lazy or cowardly man. For this reason, Juno sent Iris from heaven to powerful Agamemnon with the message that sloth is never fitting to a man of deeds.

"If the youth, the subject of our proposed story, had prepared himself by all necessary means before entering Love's battle, he would not have quit before enjoying celestial delights. Even after a thousand trials and death, he should still have pushed back against the heavens to follow his quest, because ladies are not so cruel or impious as to refuse to lend satisfaction to the solicitous lover.

"But the fact that he got lost along the way meant he cared little for the lady's love. What fool ever lived in this world who tried to take a treasure from a sealed tomb without keen, probing, and clever planning, as our poet teaches concerning Acontius? We read how Helen yielded to Paris, almost against her will after persistent urgings. The youth really should have learned from this faultless example and followed it. Then if he suffered because of it, he would be worthy of our commiseration.

"However, if the lady flirtingly provoked him and strung him along, as in the accounts of Myrrha, Byblis, Phaedra, and other ancients and moderns, then Lionora's most perceptive viewpoint would stand. However, there are truly so many ladies of well-tested opinions who would sooner suffer death than be courted by an unworthy man; and even when they are begged and entreated do not enter readily into amorous relationships.

"Therefore, it is important to consider carefully one's first foray into love, so that our prize is not lost to excessive efforts over time. Lionora, when you say gratitude is appropriate to one who has laboured, I do not deny it. But do you not think the lover's efforts have been more than compensated already by the lady's thousand sweet glances and affectionate words, which might have restored health to a dead man?

"Now, my ladies, I see our servant focused on fishing, so let us pause our discussions about this story now, in the hopes that we can come back to it again later."

Book 1. Chapter 44.

Astanna makes Genevera aware of Peregrino's presence, and he experiences a moment's bliss before Genevera's brothers interrupt the interlude and he must steal away.

That angelic company rose from their sweet discussions and were strolling about the water's edge, relaxing, modestly laughing, speaking, commenting, and chastely discoursing on one topic or another. I had been following them in the guise of a fisherman without being noticed, and I consumed their virtuous lesson, which offered nourishing recreation to my soul. The sacred murmuring of their words seemed to be a divine thing, and I believe Love had dictated them. The ladies came back to where the fishing nets were being gathered, and they admired the hefty haul, which would have surpassed that of saints Peter and Andrew.

Meanwhile, Astanna made Genevera secretly aware of my presence, and with just one sweet, demure, and lingering glance, Genevera transfixed me to the bone, such that I remained still and rooted like a Herculean column in that dense wood.

I thanked Love, as the master, lord, and reconciler of all, who rules over and preserves the entire universe, and from whom all of our happiness proceeds: 'Please, be the master who teaches me, the ruler who preserves me, and the lord who loves me, since I'm ready at all times to do everything to serve and obey your power.' My mind wandered in sweet memory, repeating everything, and it seemed there could be no bliss to equal what I was experiencing.

In this state, I saw Astanna coming toward me, but she was striding purposefully as if she had some other aim. When she got close to me, she said: "Go with God," because Genevera's brothers had arrived with quite a few of their companions. Her voice imprinted itself in my breast with the same pain as when condemned men hear their death sentence from the executioner.

My soul retreated into itself. Given my acute pain, I forgot the pleasures I had received, as if I had been in Lethe's vestibule for years. Jealousy, tears, and sighs accompanied my departure; indeed, I was hardly capable of stumbling away. I didn't know how to force myself away from so much light, and I remained like a bat caught in the sun's rays.

Book 1. Chapter 45.

Peregrino commissions a hollow statue of St. Catherine of Alexandria, hides inside it, and has it put on display. Genevera's mother, Anastasia, confined to her home by illness, requests that the icon be brought into their house so she might adore it. Peregrino's attempt to breach Genevera's domestic walls goes according to plan, but before he has the opportunity to speak with Genevera, the household receives news that her brother has been stabbed.

Three days passed before I hit on the reward for my efforts: I remembered an oft-repeated story. Love embellished in my imagination a plan to overcome Genevera's great resistance by means of a clever contraption that might put an end to my suffering. Like the gift of the Trojan Horse dedicated to Pallas Athena by the Greeks, it was not without trickery and fraud. I pretended that the reason I was offering an icon of St. Catherine, the Virgin of Syria, was in gratitude for recovering from my feverish illness. The statue was tall and deep enough that I could comfortably sit in the hollow cavity of her womb. It had a little opening in its centre, fabricated with such artifice that it couldn't have been discerned, even with the eyes of a lynx. I had it placed on an ornately decorated cart, and the whole city sought to see and adore the saint whose endurance in both body and soul merited eternal blessedness.

At that time, Anastasia was quite ill, and more than anything else she wished to see the statue, believing the Virgin's intersession could cure her. She contacted my mother in secret and pleaded with her to arrange for some means to contemplate and adore this St. Catherine. I, who had sought nothing else, praised the request Astanna delivered and ordered it be done right away. I involved Astanna in my plan – but no other living soul – because I needed her to assist me in entering the statue.

Astanna sought to serve me as ardently as I hoped to be served. She squeezed my hand, promising to place me in some quiet room where I could rest without disturbances until a private audience with Genevera could be arranged. The necessary horses were convened to deliver the cart and its contents to Genevera's house, my mother none the wiser, and I was left at the appointed time where I had been promised.

Genevera's family, along with curious neighbours, adored the statue, offering profuse veneration. Someone climbed on the cart and moved from the front to the side and around behind, peering so close I feared I would be seen or sensed. Some onlookers praised the craftsmanship, others the artistic quality, and another offered highest praise to its designer. Once they offered their dutiful prayers, they all went back to their business.

That night, Astanna locked the door of the room where I had been placed and cautiously, in the utmost silence, opened the latch of the statue and pulled me out. We sat down together and strategized how we could trick Genevera into willingly granting me an audience in her bedroom. To Astanna it seemed wildly difficult, if not impossible, to spring such a demand on Genevera. Astanna thought it better to lead her to the garden window to talk beneath the starry sky, as is typical of girls who are in some kind of difficulty or wish to pray to the heavens to send them a suitor. I liked this astute plan so much that I forgot all of my previous suffering.

She led me out to the part of the garden directly underneath Genevera's bedroom window. Such an intoxicating fragrance wafted from there that it could've taken away the sense of smell from the best hounds. I was about to climb up to her barred window when I heard the most blood-curdling scream and menacing words of the worst sort. Such clamour came with pounding at the front door of the house. Some enemy could've breached the city's walls with less fury.

Utterly terrified, but also bitterly frustrated, I hustled back to my statue to be assisted by faithful Astanna. The roused family descended to learn the reason for the shrill scream: Genevera's younger brother, out of love for his girlfriend, had been stabbed and taken back to his home more dead than alive. The entire family wept in desperation at this tragic turn of events, issuing cries loud enough to echo to heaven. Each member of the household sprung to a different task: one to fetch the doctor, another the barber-surgeon, and another a priest; they all hastened to help the near-lifeless youth as best they could.

Genevera, with hot tears and affectionate prayers, prostrated herself before the statue and prayed for her brother, grieving bitterly for Fortune's overwhelming unpredictability. She declared: "O great Jove, I am not the one who with the giants besieged the fields of your sacred realm, so why do you punish me so? Was it not awful enough that you sent sickness to my mother that now you wish to take my younger brother by violent death? Saturn, I am not the one who deprived you of your father's paternal kingdom. Revered Venus, I was not the one who made the snares to entrap you with Mars. Bright Apollo, I was not the one who took your son's life. O Mercury, I never eavesdropped on your messages. O Moon, I have never interrupted your long nights of love. O guardians of hell, I have never lent aid to Hercules or his companions who despoiled your realm. Why do you all conspire against me? See how much suffering I have endured: a sickly mother, a grieving father, a dead brother, a disconsolate family, and I am denied every single pleasure! What must I do? O gods, take into consideration my tender years. In and of myself I am worth nothing – I do not know what to do nor how; and if you do not come to my aid, I will be even more shunned than Scylla, the daughter of Nisus."

Hecuba's laments fleeing Troy after cruelly being forced to give up her children were nothing compared to this. I listened to Genevera's tearful pleas, and my pain increased in proportion to my inability to offer her a consoling word. Instead, I remained like a dead man, stifling every movement so as not to give any indication of my presence. From the moment her brother's imminent death was announced until the hour when Phoebus's rays were gathered again, every relative and friend of some degree came to offer condolences at the house.

Meanwhile, I hid there with no less fear than did the men who were inside the horse waiting for the final cries in Priam's realm to cease. But given the news of both the tragic death and the presence of the statue, the house remained as crowded as Rome's Via Sacra during a parade of triumphal chariots. Lack of food and sleep along with the weight of sadness had exhausted me to the extreme. I could hardly breathe when Astanna, moved finally by some inner virtue, ordered everyone from the room and began trying to revive my body.

Book I. Chapter 46.

Genevera's brother succumbs to his wounds. Astanna convinces Peregrino to leave and write Genevera a condolence letter.

The sun was on the verge of setting again when frighteningly pale Death transfixed the heart of Genevera's brother with its lethal dart. Nature thus deprived the boy of happiness and a long life. Not in Troy or Sagunto, which witnessed Hannibal's first attack, nor in any land of massacred inhabitants did louder lamentations resound. All heaven reverberated with their wailing cries.

I could do nothing to comfort my lady, so I wept miserably alone in my confinement inside the statue. After burial arrangements were made, Genevera volunteered to hold vigil over the dead body by herself that night, so she could let her tears freely flow for her sad brother's soul without others' judgment. Silence had fallen on the house, and the statue was forgotten along with its author and the saint, due to the family's overriding pain.

Astanna hurried to me and urged me to slip away. After all, a lyre's love songs do not accord with grief. She reminded me that I could write Genevera a letter for Violante to deliver when she goes to offer condolences, and my consolation would be no less welcome to Genevera in words than in person. This advice seemed more necessary than optional to me, so I came around, and through Violante, who agreed wholeheartedly, I wrote to Genevera in this way ...

Book 1. Chapter 47.

The text of Peregrino's letter to Genevera endeavours to offer consolation through its many examples attesting to the immortality of the soul.

Peerless Lady of Mine,

Euripides concluded his discourse on the fragility of the human condition, saying that our life passes in less than an hour, and Demetrius of Phalerum reduced it to a fleeting moment. Virgil called our lives brief and irreparable; and Quintilian, the apex of eloquence, declared: "O wretched mortality of ours, what advantage is living for many years and holding fast our soul within its bodily prison when our life is but a day?" The Psalmist also very aptly expressed: "The days of man are like grass and flowers that dry out as soon as they're cut."

What well-instructed intellect would ever hold in high regard things that so quickly pass away? It is not Death we should fear, but rather any offence we have committed against God. Therefore, anyone who keeps far from sin is far from fear. We should fear only those things which oppose nature; but what is more natural to man than death, which divine Plato writes is the least of all evils? O God, what is more righteous, fair, and holy, and less worthy of castigation than death? Death unites what the world puts asunder; it is what equalizes all mortals. Facing death, we have no distinctions based on titles or social status.

St. Paul, the doctor of the people, referred to it saying, "I long for my end, so that I can be with Christ," for death comes through Him, and He is the true, certain, and anticipated way. How wise and prudent is the person who faces what is necessary!

After the fatal order of death takes us, what use are our complaints, regrets, grief, and tears? If they could satisfy our thoughts, then our tears would be more precious than oriental gems and pure gold. But by crying we offend three: God, first of all, Who established the laws of nature; second, the soul of the deceased person, because in doing so we seem to envy his blessedness; and finally, ourselves, because we become embittered, seemingly without any hope for a good end.

Lady, we can know Fortune as much as we can place our hope in her. Perhaps her instability would have brought your brother to an even more tragic death than the one you now grieve for him. Give thanks to God and to nature that they have freed you from this anxiety, which previously seized Agamemnon, Menelaus, Achilles, and Orestes.

If the absence of your dear brother still afflicts you, you should be consoled by the expectation of the true immortality of his soul, which every writing attests, both classical and orthodox religious ones. Sextus Pompeius summoned Gabienus from the Other World, who predicted for him many different events. Divine Plato admonished us not to offend other people so that the spirits of their relatives do not take vengeance on us. Writings attest that the souls of Lucius Cornelius Sulla's dead sailors entreated and disturbed him. And if you believe another tragedy, spirits of the dead prompted madness in Orestes. Polydorus was killed for his family's gold, although he tried to avoid cruelty and greed. Achilles demanded that the Trojan princess Polyxena be burned as a sacrifice of retribution at his sepulchre. Clear examples of the immortality of the soul are available in every ancient and modern text, so you should be comforted that the soul of your brother has been released from the dark prison of the body in order to come face to face with the One he has endeavoured to meet since his creation.

Lady, gather your strength, and do not let your grief ruin your beauty. Do not deprive your country of your fair appearance. Preserve your life for better applications and call to mind my service to you.

May the bearer of this letter satisfy for you what my heedless hand has not written, and I pray that God send her back to console me. Be at peace, my one and only lady. You are correct that a single soul unites our two bodies.

Book 1. Chapter 48.

Violante offers her condolences to Genevera's family and delivers Peregrino's letter to her.

After I finished writing this letter, I gave it to Violante, who went to Genevera's house as soon as she heard the news. She first offered her condolences to the mourning parents, then with a deft manoeuvre withdrew herself to one side where Genevera sat weeping. Speaking together about the terrible tragedy, Violante reminded her that she should take heart because this is the way of the world; nobody can cheat death. Then in a low voice, she gave her to know of the heartfelt sympathy I felt and that nothing could afflict me more than to see her consumed by tears and sobs, which are a sign of baseness because we have never read of a person of noble heart shedding tears for similar reasons. Therefore, because she is a lady of outstanding intellect, she should show herself equal to the resounding fame of her education and good deeds.

If she cared no more about that, she should at least take to heart in my faithful service, attested by this letter standing in for my person, which would've been dearer and more preferable. Given heaven's opposition to this honest desire, however, she should be content to read the voice of a living man, and when she resumes her life after some consolation, she should remember to share some part of that consolation with me.

Genevera gratefully accepted the letter of condolence and went to her room. After she read and reread it many times, not without tears, she replied to me in the following manner.

Book 1. Chapter 49.

Genevera answers Peregrino's letter.

My Dearest Friend,
Your sweet and well-written words could stem the wrath of Agamemnon, who fled the company of others, tore out his hair, and gnawed at his

heart in his dire pain, or transform Caesar's anger toward Quintus Ligarius to sweetness.

I have received much consolation from your letters, and I understand the public and private implications of your discourse. Your exhortations convince me to put an end to my weeping, as much as I am able to do so, because it is God's will. Alas, the constant expressions of sympathy by friends are a painful burden, as the examples of Phoenix and Chiron attest: they did not want to go on living after their beloved disciple Achilles died. And when the old Laertes saw his son Ulysses depart, he left the ruling palace and took to the fields. Sulla, who experienced bitter pain following the death of his wife Caecilia Metella, revised a funerary law so he could more honourably offer her homage. If these famous men have wept and given up their lives out of grief, how can I hold back my tears any more easily or not waver on this side or the other of life?

O bitter times, O ruinous day full of misery! O sorrowful, cruel, bitter, and impious Death worthy of every curse, why did you enter his body so prematurely? O elect spirits, do not scorn me when I may finally be content to join you and leave this unpredictable world in which one cannot build anything on firm foundations.

I thank you as best I can, and pray God gives you the comfort that befits a true and dear friend. Be well.

Book 1. Chapter 50.

Peregrino devises yet another plan: to access the wine cellar of Genevera's house through the city's sewer system. He consults one of the city's engineers and surveys the layout on his own.

When I received Genevera's letter, many thoughts came to mind. I began to fear something terrible might happen to my lady. After all, ladies have weaker hearts, and she could easily catch ill, especially if she were left alone with no one to offer her the consoling hope of happiness. I determined to try to find out what was going on in her house by some other means. I was not keen to over-involve Violante, since suspicions might be raised if she appeared unusually helpful. I hadn't heard from Astanna either.

Then and there I ordered my carriage driver to retrieve my statue of St. Catherine from Genevera's house and to take note of what they said about it. Perhaps because of the fervency of their hopes or their ardent devotions toward the icon, Anastasia recovered her health. I was no less celebrated for my act of charity than if through my battling I had brought victory to Olympia. I vowed to render perpetual thanks to that saint for her celestial grace. Although my driver reconnoitered the whole area around Genevera's house, he was not able to spot Astanna or Genevera.

Meanwhile, the mourning period for Genevera's brother had run its course, and Love rekindled latent flames of desire in me with such force that all the watery powers of Neptune couldn't have extinguished even a small part of them. Add to this, Astanna, whose faithful service I constantly relied on, was now abed quite sick. So, it was up to me to devise with even greater cleverness some other plan to permit me to speak at last with Genevera.

Turning over in my mind all the places where Love had led me in tests of prowess, I remembered Genevera's family wine cellar, where I had hidden in great peril. If my memory wasn't failing me, I thought a sewer line passed through there, conducting any filth out of the cellar. Where it went I had no clue, nor could I imagine it, since I have no aptitude whatsoever for geometry.

Pretending to resolve other matters, I went to a respected engineer. After discussing various issues, we eventually hit on the details of the sewers, which are the guardians of the city, and he told me that the line serving Angelo's home is the most complicated on earth, extending more than a stadium,[31] and terminating in the public cistern. He also told me how its gate was once opened and locked on a schedule, but these days it had come into disuse, and no one locked it anymore. The engineer spared no details in his descriptions, and during our stroll, we came to the place I recognized must certainly be the one that the engineer described to me.

Book 1. Chapter 51.

Peregrino ventures into the city's sewer system by night. He emerges in a house and stealthily finds his way to the bed of a young lady. They have sex, which Peregrino describes euphemistically in terms of a naval assault on a castle stronghold.

Night, a most apt and faithful companion of tricks and frauds, persuaded me to investigate the sewer. Dressed in buffalo leather, clad in my buskins, and with a sturdy lantern in hand, I called on the holy spirit of Love and set off in the hopes of discovering what kind of propitious end Love sought to impose on my passion.

At the entrance of the sewer stood an iron gate, which was not at all common, but rather quite in line with its ancient respectability. The muddy path, surrounded by walls, was about three cubits deep and a good bit

---

31   One stadium, the length of the lap of a footrace in ancient Greece, ranged in measurement from 607 to 738 feet, or 185 to 225 metres; in Roman calculations, it was typically set at 607 feet.

wider. The continual flow of humours through that channel had infused the place with the most fetid stench, far beyond my powers of endurance, and made my progress difficult and indeed unbearable. More than once I was tempted to quit my explorations. But comforted by thoughts of love and having made it that far, I eventually came to a passageway out, which I judged must be the one leading to my lady's house.

Reeking and filthy, I emerged from the sewer line. Unable to endure a moment longer the swoon-inducing stench produced by all that rot, I stripped off my buffalo vest, deposited my buskins, and dried off my sweat. I looked around to see if I could recognize this cellar as the one where I had previously hidden in great danger. But my sensual appetite, dominating every reason, didn't permit me to discern the truth. Without the least thought, I quietly opened the door to the house and began tiptoeing toward the stairs.

My heart beat wildly in its fear and anticipation, and it began to consume me, burning hotter than a furnace. First one feeling, then another, leapt to my mind's eye: jealousy, cowardice, daring, fear of scorn, lust, ambition, strength, wicked thoughts ... They made me so confused that I didn't know what I wanted.

I said to myself, 'What unheard-of rabid lust has ever held such sway over a human body and has ever had the power to lead a man to such iniquity as this? Foolish is the man who responds to a lady who doesn't call him! Without letting her know, you're daring to enter her bedchamber and try her virtue? What love wouldn't break, what friendship not dissolve, and what character not be stained? Whose patience could endure this?

'Genevera has always been rather reluctant to see you by day, so what makes you think she will be more eager at night? And where? In her bed? This plan is far too hastily enacted. It is indiscreet treachery!

'What if recent grieving for her brother doesn't permit Genevera to feel pleasure now? I must be cautious ... But how? I'll speak with Astanna. Ah no, she's sick, I know ... I'll just talk to Genevera, since she's cautious by nature. She'll be shocked with fright. But when she thinks it over, she'll excuse my actions as perhaps sinful, but understandable and necessarily brave. But ... what if I am overheard talking to her? No, I'll speak extra softly. What if I am spotted? No, the night is dark. What if I can't get into her room? Well, if there is nothing else to be done, I shall at least find a way to let Genevera know I have come this far so she'll know I'm not lacking in eagerness and fervent love.'

While talking to myself this way, I became scared, though I couldn't exactly say of what. My mind, which already foresaw something of the mess that would come of this endeavour, nevertheless prompted me to seek out that unknown danger.

The profound darkness made me bolder. I made it to the top of a marble staircase and crept into a large room where a number of chairs had been oddly arranged. I bumped one of them with my chest, causing it to scrape noisily across the floor as in an earthquake. I froze and waited to hear if anyone stirred in the house. I listened vigilantly, ready to flee at the first sound. But the hearts of the inhabitants, joined in sadness and sleep, didn't perceive this din.

Fear assailed me. Love rallied round, but all reason departed. My nerve began to falter, and a sense of futility swelled. Agitated in these various ways, I tried to convince myself to return the way I had come. But my feet carried me forward more than my good sense, and I passed into another room, which turned out to be where the ladies of the house were sleeping soundly without care or suspicion.

Pulling myself together, I began to perceive their sweet and gentle breathing. Slowly, I reached out my hands. I felt a bed! I inched closer to it. Inclining my ear near the face of the lady sleeping there, I could tell she was sleeping deeply. I patted with my hands ever so carefully, ever so delicately about. They alighted on two fleshy mounds, which seemed just as I had always imagined my Genevera's to be!

Not satisfied yet, I nevertheless rendered thanks to Love who had conducted me, almost out of my wits, to this long-desired place.

Then with a humble, low voice I murmured: "Stir now, my dear. Sleep no more. I am your faithful one. Wake now, spirit of mine ... Hmm ... Why are you sleeping so much? This is no way for one in love to behave, snoozing so deeply!"

I accompanied my words with sweet kisses and clasping embraces. Finally, I figured words were superfluous where actions needed to be swift. After all, girls typically deny that they desire what their appearance shows they clearly want. I stripped naked, got into the bed, and manoeuvred into her delicate arms.

I whispered, "O Jove, I hold in my hands my little turtledove, my sweet sparrow! Happy night, you've brought a dead man back to life. O marvellous mirror of my life! O joy of mine! O priceless treasure!" Going on in this way, I hoisted my sails to the wind and hurled my armed ship straight onto her cliffs, for it was indeed a difficult strait to pass.

The guard of the bulwark, realizing my ship was ready to fire, was roused in spirit – both in act and in potential – and turned to me, throwing her arms around my neck. She was about to say something when another girl in the room stirred and moved as if she had heard us.

Without the slightest sound, we clutched each other even more tightly, entwined like vines around a tree.

O unfathomable beatitude! You souls wandering the Elysian Fields, nothing of your former glory, nothing of your blessedness now even comes close to what I feel! This is the true harmony of the spheres! This is the shrine of every true and sure delight! Come to me, inconsolable souls, who without the fruits of love are left to nature, so that you may find comfort in my joy. May God grant you the well-being and peace my soul feels now!

Book 1. Chapter 52.

Peregrino realizes he is not in bed with Genevera, but rather with her neighbour Lionora. When Lionora recognizes she is not with her suitor Galeotto, Peregrino must flee for his life. He's identified by his buskins and must face trial.

The vain morning swallow was already chittering the advent of a new day when the lady covered me with more kisses, saying, "O Galeotto dear, you are my afflicted heart's only hope. Now make me content by satisfying your promise, I beseech you."

These words pierced my heart. In order to buy time before answering, I re-armed my ship and with strong embraces sailed her wide sea again. All the while I reasoned with myself: 'Can it be that Genevera is in love with another man? Or have I mistaken the room? If I speak, I'm discovered. I don't know where to turn. I can't remain silent, since she has asked me to speak. Ah, divine goddess who pined for Adonis, help my poor cause!'

The damsel – whose name was actually Lionora – insisted while pressing kisses between my lips: "Galeotto, why won't you speak? Why do you hesitate?"

So then, with a halting and cracking voice, I started to tell her some story. But even before I could form a proper word, she let out a loud cry of shock: "Woe is me! I've been betrayed!" And she escaped from me just as an arrow-studded deer flees a hunter.

The servant girl, hearing Lionora's lament, shouted at the top of her lungs: "Wicked corruptor of another's honour! Nefarious rapist of holy virginity who goes stalking so vilely the bedrooms of ladies! Get up, brothers, to arms, to arms! There's a thief in the house. Fire, fire! All is burning! Every man: rush to her aid! Get the traitor and tear him to shreds as his depraved life deserves!"

The entire household, though half-asleep, jumped to grab weapons and candles, all intent on seeking my demise. The house, in a horrendous ruckus amidst doleful laments, seemed as if Vulcan were erupting in every direction and crashing upon me.

Frantically scooping up my clothes, I fled from room to room tearfully calling on Love, who in so many dangers had previously come to my aid: 'O excellent guide of mine, domestic speculator of my heart, inseparable witness to my faith, holy tutor of your faithful servants, make me worthy of your favour! As you can see, I'm surely about to die. Lord who saved Leander so many times at sea and conceded Jason a happy return, who didn't forbid Orpheus to descend to Dis, and who freed the great Trojan Aeneas from the barbaric deceit, help me, too!'

I seemed to perceive a voice that said, "Love is your faithful guide." Heartened by the divine spirit, I took my sharp sword, and though I was dressed only in a shirt, I slashed here and there around me and created such a space without being wounded or recognized that I made my way back to the sewer. I dropped down into it in such a hurry that I left behind my buskins, while the rest I took with me. I quickly beat a retreat from my persecutors and disappeared.

However, the buskins, because they were in the Greek fashion (and the latest style), could be traced back to me, because I had worn them in our city where they were uncommon. In fact, little time passed before a servant of the family attested that I was the one who had been in the house.

Petrutio, Lionora's father, seethed with wrath, disdain, and offended honour. He cried to heaven and lodged a complaint against me before the supreme Duke. Summoning me to trial, Petrutio expounded his iron-clad case against me in this way …

Book 1. Chapter 53.

Petrutio accuses Peregrino of armed trespass in his house during the night and cites his evidence before the Duke.

Petrutio: "Just Duke, under whose power Astraea marshals all her forces, you distinguish yourself among the rulers of Italy, and wisdom and manly mildness proceed from your radiant, magnificent appearance. With your usual discernment, please consider the grave offences against your faithful subject and take the action required by the dignity of your reign, which I know makes no exception for any man, and which you could never be prevented from carrying out with diligence and integrity. Therefore, I can hold out hope that your harsh judgment will be in my favour. Most clement ruler, great love for my daughter inclines and obliges me to fear for my honour, because one easily believes what one dreads.

"This architect of fraud, sower of every evil, harbinger of lust, stalker of the public, stain of infamy upon your state, confounder of pure and virtuous living, universal pest to our young people, this rogue Peregrino, son of Antonio, I declare was spotted prowling inside my house last night, and he was armed! I do not know if he intended to steal or to leave his indelible stain of sin in some other way on my house. But the buskins he left at the scene attest to his entry and escape, as does the testimony of my servant, which in similar cases has been admitted.

"Moreover, sovereign prince, the homes of innocent men must be free not only from the consequences that such scandalous acts may cause, but also from the effects of mere suspicions, as Caesar himself testified against Clodius. Even though the wicked act he intended to commit and to which his libidinous desires were leading him was not consummated, that does not mean his intent should not be judged. Just as this man has disrespectfully put his desires before your honour, scorned the law, dishonoured this city, stained the neighbourhood, and violated a friendship, he must be punished to the same degree. What poisoner or hired assassin, what thief or glutton for whores, what adulterer or scandalmonger, what corrupter of minors or parricide could ever be compared to this miscreant?

"Just watch with what nerve he will maintain how scandalized he is at being accused of his attempt on virginal modesty. To him, petulance is virtue, incontinence modesty, fraud faith, betrayal innocence, and madness is clemency. O what preposterous impudence to invade another's home in the middle of the night with the intent of violating a virgin's bed! Honestly, what traitor or enemy to the state would not show greater pious respect?

"Hercules freed Hesione from a ferocious sea monster, then delivered her to her father. When Alexander vanquished Darius, he took pity on the virginity of the conquered man's daughters and humanely protected them. Moreover, Scipio Africanus forgave an obligation and conducted a captive maiden back to her new bridegroom without besmirching her virginity. But why should I cite a list of examples, which when compared to this spurious beast have no meaning whatsoever?

"Show the world, Duke, and make it known that in your state prevail prudence, vigilance, an esteemed court, a powerful and wise senate, arms, prison, and the fitting sentences and harsh punishments reserved for these kinds of villains. In this way you will demonstrate your splendour and greatness."

When Petrutio ended his remarks, the Duke turned to me with a face less than humane and said: "You there, do you think you can free and absolve yourself of that much turpitude? Or are you disposed to suffer the consequences of our city's laws as a deterrent to all who have so little regard for other men's honour?"

These harsh words, articulated eloquently, didn't permeate me so deeply as to cause my vigour for my own defence to falter in the slightest. Mindful of divine aid, I formulated my response with great humility as follows.

Book 1. Chapter 54.

Peregrino defends himself against Petrutio's accusations before the Duke of Ferrara.

Peregrino: "Great ruler, trusting in your fairness and my innocence, I need not fear the false accusations of delirious men. As God's grace makes me worthy, I seem to understand that Petrutio is dreaming. When he puts his hand to his heart, he will recall I have always respected his honour and sought his well-being and love. Instead, Petrutio is the one being inconsiderate. He is the one who has raised a groundless dispute, and he is the one responsible for any defamation. Just censure wouldn't adequately punish his tears and wild accusations.

"There are many occasions, Petrutio, when it would be better to close your eyes, turn your face away, and wonder, when speaking proves nothing at all. Wise David recognized when his daughter had been compromised and remained silent, and Tancred of Taranto followed his example. I shall not name modern examples so that I am not judged to be anything like you. Stifle your exclamations, shut your shameful mouth, and control your shameless tongue. Do not denigrate yourself, taint your house, bring infamy upon your posterity, and deflower the virginal sex, which must remain more candid than the sun. If I summarize part of your accusations against me now, I'll prove to you just the opposite and leave you without this opinion of yours.

"Sovereign Duke, I've always been a man of quiet peace and harmony, a reconciler and supporter of others, not a sower of new hostilities. And I possess the highest reverence for my elders. Up until now I've pursued a virtuous life, as your whole city can attest and which I call as my witness. Whoever does not know the rectitude of my life is a rustic outsider; whoever contradicts me speaks evil; and whoever spreads slander is detestable.

"So why, when you are usually wise and prudent, Petrutio, do you rave so deliriously now? What passion has overcome you, what frenzy has alienated you from your true character so that you and your entire household accuse me of such grave infamy? Haven't you yet learned how the sorceress Circe transformed presumptive lovers into various animals? How many times have we heard that someone takes the form and clothing of another in order to blame him for his own transgressions? Many people sin while hiding behind the shield of many innocents. Therefore, it is best not to believe so readily on the basis of some buskins.

"Most pious ruler, I do not recall anybody ever associating me with the profession of hardened criminal, since nothing could be further from my devotion to my country, life, household, upbringing, development, education, and daily business.

"Petrutio, have you so lost your good sense that you believe a lover should yield to the pleasures of his beloved by using his rightful name? Never has any corrupted official, cheater, nocturnal thief, or spy passed through a blockaded road giving his own name! To prove your error, you cited the uproar raised by the ladies, presuming, as is true, that furtive lovers don't cry out or sleep. If I had come as a lover, the lady would have kept quiet; if I had entered as an enemy, all there would be left of you is the remembrance of my hatred. Tarquin entered Lucretia's home and raped her, and a cry excused his awful violence. If a similar thing had happened to your daughter, she would be most worthy of our compassion, and the rapist of the death sentence. Instead, Petrutio, you really must believe that what happened was in a dream. Our soul can shift the meaning from the subject and change it into every conceivable form; and according to whether it finds the subject stable or not, it makes it fearful or happy. Take Dido, for instance. While she was sleeping, she wept and called out, 'To arms!' and roused all the people. She called for her sister, but when she was awakened, she asked, 'What cruel dream disturbs me?' The representations of our mind act in a way similar to thoughts and cogitations, since they appear to be only simulacra of what we desire to see.

"Petrutio, you must be absolutely certain because we always carry within ourselves two contrary spirits – one is the good conscience and the other evil – and they often confuse and contend with one another, not because of bad luck or nature, but only because they coexist in such close proximity. They try to lure us away from the good we seek to do. But what we see isn't real; it's in our detestable routine to follow bad habits. The apparitions conform to whether they find the person disposed either to good or evil. It's no wonder a spirit appeared to your daughter, which frightened her by signalling what her heart actually desired. Just as occurrences are signalled to us by signs and voices when we are awake, they appear through spirits to sleepers as images and oracles. The Platonic disciple Dion of Syracuse received a vision forecasting his death, and Caesar's spirit appeared to Brutus threatening: 'Tomorrow you will see me in the fields of Philippi.'

"Petrutio, it's typical of these forces to announce something true and false, which is why many people are deluded and confused by them, especially young girls and crazy people. Because of their imbecility, they imagine that whatever they see must be true, though it is not, and they become horrified and are nearly frightened to death. How many men are fascinated by ghosts and believe they must be tangible substances, when they are not? It seems you don't understand that it is possible to apprehend by the faculties a substance in another form. How many people die of fright fearing what they only imagine because the poison of what is only 'seen' infuses our mind and, without receiving any toxin, it is consumed? This mercurial illusion enchants our eyes and does not permit us to distinguish truth from falsity. Do you understand how many transformations the Egyptian magicians Jannes and Mambres made before the Pharaoh when Moses was sent to free the chosen people? Anyone without pure eyes couldn't have seen through them. How many times did Circe the enchantress change the appearance of Ulysses' companions? Orpheus, in order to get back his beloved Euridice, went to the underworld, where because of Minos, he was shown only a phantasm of her.

"Petrutio, your daughter has just as easily been tricked. Because she was moved by a repressed thought, she reported what her fantasy represented to her. When you cry out how I was glimpsed, I rebut that no one can trust what a domestic servant says unless she speaks against herself. Neither the law nor truth can permit her testimony in your favour.

"As for the buskins on which you base your accusations, although they may once have been stylish in their Greek way, they are now worn even by labourers and plebes. Perhaps some beggar who received them in charity sought a restorative draught from your wine cellar and forgetfully left them behind there. You could ease your conscience by announcing that they will be auctioned off, then allocating the proceeds to a very pious cause."

Silence fell, and the Duke, who had listened to me, pronounced his sentence with the utmost gravity.

Book 1. Chapter 55.

The Duke of Ferrara passes judgment, insisting in conclusion that the matter be kept confidential on pain of death.

Duke of Ferrara: "We are very much indebted to nature, whose straightforward principle of necessity means that everything is generated according to the endowments of its species, and I believe this to be common knowledge and clear to everyone. Moreover, if we wanted to debate its operations, we would judge in every particular not to have been cheated by nature. See and subtly consider what a fine lesson can be learned about nature from the example of the poor farmer who, unperturbed by foul weather, focuses his energies all year long on the cultivation of his soil. If he sees a weed germinate there in his well-watered earth, he uproots it with diligent determination, so he can eventually enjoy the best fruit of his labours. In like manner we are called to correct and care for our ladies, so they will produce children like us.

"Take, for instance, the admirable example of a Spartan woman whose son was sent away to defend the country. He missed his friends and returned home alone, believing she would accept him and appreciate more that he saved his life through flight. When he appeared before her, however, she hit him with what she had at hand, a rod, and took his life, saying, 'Go, bad seed, unworthy of your mother, as well as your country!'

"If every man must correct, protect, and oversee his small household to the best of his ability, what must we do who are responsible for a whole population? If we are lazy or slothful, we would be a poor match for diligent governors and vigilant subjects. It is thus necessary to consider this sentence in a way similar to how the great Emperor Constantine managed his succession, when he named Julian Constantius, the son of his half-brother, so that his rule would accrue honour and his people would be appeased. Two necessary means can bring it about: obedience and benevolence. These qualities foster good security and the safeguarding of high reputations. Helen used to say to Priam: 'Most beloved father-in-law, I love you and fear you,' because love must be neither presumptuous nor reckless, but rather always held in reverent and honoured esteem.

"Herein consist the glory and dignity of all rulers. Alexander the Great gave a reply, which was so fitting it is now celebrated like an oracle, and the emperor Julian Augustus followed it. When prodded by his overly interested dependants about where he kept his treasures and great holdings, he responded: 'With friends.' We read of the keen Roman senator and philosopher Helvidius Priscus, who when speaking in the senate concluded that true friends are instruments of good fortune. How many honest and illustrious men and powerful kings were reduced to extreme wretchedness through the malice and petulance of traitorous false friends? This happens more times than not because men are indulgent, tolerant, or too slow to pull out the useless weeds from their gardens. Just as justice, liberality, and fortitude of spirit are the virtues preserved by all monarchies, so too must levity, luxury, and intemperance be treated in the opposite way.

"Therefore, Peregrino, I address myself to you alone and say: 'What censure cannot do, let examples serve to instruct and satisfy you. For your good and honour, incline your heart to modest living, so you can preserve your dignity and modesty. Calypso, daughter of the Titan Atlas, begged Ulysses to remain her consort, promising him the prize of immortality in return. But the son of Laertes sooner chose to die a good death than accept the infamy that immortality would have ascribed to him. Moreover, Ulysses would have been briefer and more restrained in his bedsharing with Circe if he weren't constrained by the dire threat to his companions' welfare. If his remembrance of the faith he owed Penelope after so many years away from her was strong enough to temper his dallying with such a queen, how much greater must the faith we owe to our country be, given that we are only more indebted to God? I do not believe you have committed any illicit act. Be sure you continue to behave properly in the future because any hint of evildoing could leave you stained by infamy.

"To you, Petrutio, have pity. I know how heavy offended honour can be. But neither you nor your family has been denigrated in any way. You have reacted more through suspicion than in response to any cause's effect. Therefore, put aside your rancour so you can live more honourably. Remember: a man demonstrates the true magnanimity of his unconquered spirit while he suffers trials, tribulations, and slanders, which, in any event, we do not believe has happened here. Henceforth, if you should behave as if this matter went differently, then you will learn how, as we are a clement lord now, then we shall become the most austere judge and punisher. Learn to respect justice, keep your friendship, and love one another."

When the Duke finished, the death penalty was imposed on anyone who mentioned anything concerning this case. We left satisfied, each man returning to his own house.

Book 1. Chapter 56.

Genevera learns about Peregrino's latest escapade when Lionora's serving girl Beta visits ailing Astanna.

Envy – that sad and shadowy inhabitant of the lowest, squalid ward, which has never seen the light – spread her tongue with poison, and because she is always pained by another's good, most especially by my contentment, she harshly attacked Genevera's credulous heart. She did so by dispatching Beta, Lionora's servant girl, to visit Astanna, who was ill and attended by Genevera.

In the course of their conversation, intended to bring comfort, Beta told them she wished she could work for somebody else so as not to have to endure Petrutio's harsh treatment. After all, he had become impatient, unbearable, annoyed, choleric, and downright frightening, especially given recent events. She had barely finished this sentence when Genevera immediately questioned her about what had happened that was so terrible.

Realizing her mistake too late, Beta regretted it and refused to say more.

Genevera's eager curiosity grew in the same way that fasting stokes one's appetite. She begged Beta most insistently not to deny her the truth of what happened.

The servant girl replied that the matter was so important that she couldn't divulge it without putting herself in danger. But if Genevera were to promise to free her from Petrutio's service, she would tell her the whole story.

Genevera was so eager and impatient to know that she swore and reassured her she would, so Beta at last began to speak. Precisely three nights ago in the wee hours, a man was discovered in Lionora's room, and from what the servant Gasparina had heard, the man in Lionora's bed was Peregrino, son of Antonio, who had been identified by the buskins he left at the scene. It was a wonder he survived the chase that Lionora's defenders gave. Evidently, he escaped the way he had entered, but nobody could tell how that was exactly. Petrutio was so offended that if he could not get Peregrino to marry Lionora, he would kill him.

Beta's account, along with what Genevera had previously surmised, deprived her in that instant of all feeling. She fled from the devoted servant's company like a wounded beast and stayed away so long that Astanna, who immediately understood the reason, bid Beta farewell.

Genevera eventually reappeared to Astanna and, turning toward her with a threatening expression on her face, said …

Book 1. Chapter 57.

Genevera and Astanna try to make sense of Peregrino's actions. Genevera's mother, Anastasia, overhears some weeping.

Genevera: "Ah, see how eager we are for our own downfall – you in persuading and me in accepting! See how that perfidious and nefarious traitor pretended to love me faithfully and truly! See how his feigned service and all those empty words trying to convince me to marry him only led me along in his depraved and wicked ways. God of greatest good with His all-knowing judgment has seen the purity and sincerity of my soul, and He has kept me from falling into that damnable credulity that usually destroys ladies who trust too easily. Since what has passed can be more easily punished than remedied, we must tolerate with the greatest equanimity what destiny has dealt us. In the future, we must be more cautious about entering into dealings at our own risk!"

Then with tears in her eyes, Genevera raised them to heaven and said: "O highest lord of heaven, O exalted Jove, put an end, I beseech you, to such grave disasters and make it such that one sin brings the end and not the beginning of others. What misled lady deserves a moment's rest more than I? To me Fortune has always been bitter, adverse, atrocious, plague-ridden, and fierce. To others, suffering's end is the beginning of happiness, but I still languish. It is high time I exchange these devouring worries for something better. Help me, Astanna!"

Astanna: "Put away your anger."

Genevera: "It is too late for that."

A: "It's never too late to do what is right."
G: "You set me up to burn so all-consumingly."
A: "It has not been to any wicked end."
G: "Can you not see the effect it has on me?"
A: "You must believe otherwise."
G: "Letting oneself be captured is not without infamy in the long run."
A: "You have reached the end, and you can free yourself."
G: "Everyone likes to preach to others."
A: "So long as no damage is done, you can move on."
G: "Soap does little against a stain of the flesh."
A: "Do not torture yourself over what might not be true."
G: "The case is clear."
A: "What does she know about it?"
G: "You heard her."
A: "Her evidence was lacking."
G: "But obvious enough to anyone who was listening!"
A: "Reason does not concur."
G: "Why not?"
A: "What woman would be foolish enough to display her own wickedness?"
G: "It seems you do not understand: it was Gasparina."
A: "Was she aware of the situation, or not?"
G: "What do you mean?"
A: "If she was aware, then are they not both at fault? If not, it would have been just as bold to contradict something like that."
G: "Still, a man broke in."
A: "Not to my knowledge or understanding."
G: "What do you think it was?"
A: "Maybe it was a thief."
G: "But why then was Peregrino accused?"
A: "As a test."
G: "Of whom?
A: "Of you."
G: "Me?"
A: "Yes."
G: "Why?"
A: "To raise doubts."
G: "To what end?"
A: "About your marriage plans."
G: "But how would she have gotten wind of our love?"
A: "She may have feared it."
G: "I do not understand."

A: "Can't you see that Lionora is weighing two options? First, there's no person in the world who can frustrate her hopes more than you; and merely catching a glimpse of him by chance strolling by here would've raised her suspicions. In order to test that fear, she ordered her servant girl over here to relate to you these clever tales, which have absolutely no basis in fact. If you had only paid attention to her change in colour, the cracking of her voice, variations in her articulation, the lack of artifice, and her lowly gestures, you would've seen through her, too. She doesn't want to be so easily believed, either, but only make insinuations and enough suggestions that you change your mind.

"I'm not telling you this because I want to see you two reconciled. I only speak what reason dictates. I'm happy if you believe him a traitor, because in this case, you save yourself from further suffering and me from more hassles. If this story continues, I know I'll be the one to pay in the end. I know better than to encourage actions that might be toilsome, annoying, or burdensome, because they cannot end otherwise than in pain. You're aware that I have little experience in these matters, and I want you to free me from them, so I don't fall into a hole I can't get out of, since that's what happens to a poor woman who's born unlucky, as it has been for me from my conception.

"Now just consider if I've been so eagerly seeking your disgrace at the cost of my shame and infamy. If any word of this illicit matter ever came to light, I know it'd mean the end of my life. Meanwhile, you've governed yourself wisely, prudently, and humanely in your words, gestures, and expressions, and you've been exposed in no way whatsoever. So that I, a miserable wretch, may not suffer because of another's fault, please permit me to leave this anguished bed and find another place where I can carry on without suspicion. O violated faith, O human lust, O shattered integrity everywhere I go, O once happy face of mine, how you've been betrayed without cause! My dear Genevera, I weep with you over your bad fortune!"

She persisted along these lines for a while. Both of them produced a flood of tears. Then Anastasia passed by and was moved to great tenderness to remark …

Book 1. Chapter 58.

Anastasia assumes that Genevera's tears are still in grief over her brother. Meanwhile, Peregrino, ever eager to meet with his beloved, engages Astanna's cousin Lena to deliver another letter.

Anastasia: "Genevera, when are you ever going to put an end to your grief? You will not change God's will through your tears and trembling. Have pity on my advanced years and think of another way to console your soul over your brother's death, because so much ruminating only sparks more pain in the one who mourns rather than benefiting the object of grief."

Anastasia consoled her daughter in this way, then she left again without waiting for an answer because she was needed elsewhere.

Drying her eyes, Genevera said: "Astanna, it would be a far cry from piety to punish an innocent for another's failings. I know it was not your intention or sin that put me on Love's path. It was due to my misfortune and trusting too much. Whatever happens, I do not wish you to believe I do not love you, since I depend on your confidence, which is faithful, modest, and proper. If ever love or authority could sway you, cast aside any plans to leave, which would cause me no less suffering than the betrayal of that womanizer or the death of my brother. Now cast off every passion that might disturb clear judgment, and let us speak more about our habitual scourge."

Astanna: "Since you're now free of his sin of lust, stay far away from not just your meeting places, but also any occasion to speak, so that you don't reset a fire to a parched branch. Let's leave the wicked to their passions; let love be dead in you."

Genevera: "And yet, Peregrino has loved me for a long time."

A: "That's true."

G: "With great faithfulness."

A: "Very great indeed."

G: "Why then did he betray me?"

A: "That comes naturally to men."

G: "But there must be some faithful ones among them."

A: "Ah, let's stop this now, so we don't get mired in it any worse. I'm tired and exhausted. Go in peace, Genevera, and think about living."

I, who knew nothing about what they were thinking, tried to get word to Genevera about finding another way we could enjoy each other's company again. I moped about because Violante wasn't around – she was enjoying some recreation in the countryside. Astanna remained ill, and I certainly didn't want to entrust anyone else with my secret. It was difficult to remain like that for long, but too dangerous to get others involved.

Finally, I remembered Lena, Astanna's relative, who moved to our land from Nicosia in Cyprus after the downfall of King Zachus.[32] I got up then and there without the least hesitation and went to see Lena. I told her that I had letters from an uncle of Astanna addressed to her, and the return messenger was awaiting Astanna's response. I begged Lena not to put off going to Astanna as quickly as possible, so as not to lose the service of such a faithful emissary.

Lena, who was by her nature eager to serve, offered to do more if she could. I thanked her, and she delivered my letter, which was worded in this fashion …

---

32 Zachus is Giacomo or James II King of Cyprus, who died in 1473.

Book 1. Chapter 59.

*Peregrino's letter requests another meeting with Genevera at the gar-
den window. It goes unanswered, however, prompting in him even
more doubts and fears.*

My Lady,
   Those women who once offered the guiding light to our bond are now
unavailable to assist us. One is away, and the other indisposed by illness.
So, I found it necessary to use the service of this messenger in order to
obtain reliable news of your condition, since you govern and oversee us
both together. Because I must now tell you something of a most secret
nature, please let me know if you will agree to meet me in your garden
where the window will lend us the courage to speak. These bitter and
mournful times prevent me from just showing up at the designated place
in my usual disguise. As always, I will gladly accept most gratefully
whatever decision you make, because you are wise.

   I gave my letter to Lena with strict orders not to entrust it to anyone
in the world except Astanna, or in her absence, her mistress Genevera,
who was accustomed to read and write them. Lena promised to carry out
her mission as instructed. She went to Astanna, who was with Genevera,
and delivered it. Astanna accepted it appreciatively and asked Lena who
needed such an urgent response. Lena spoke freely, answering that it was
Peregrino, Antonio's son.
   Both Astanna and Genevera looked at the ground and didn't say another
word until they had sent Lena away. Then Genevera ventured, "What traitor is so bold to attack, rather than fear another, and sallies forth in the face
of his enemy's forces? I readily await your impression."
   Astanna: "You're wise enough to govern your own life without my input."
   Genevera: "I am not seeking your advice, but rather reasoning through
it with a confidante."
   A: "I believe the poor man must truly be raving mad if he wants to meet
you in the garden where the birds hardly have the space to fly around.
He believes that anything he sets his mind to is feasible. Love incites him,
madness guides him, hassles assail him, and desire holds him fast. He'll
deny it in writing. Any proof is risky, and a judgment is difficult. For now,
let his missives go unanswered. We'll see how he behaves once some time
has passed."
   Astanna dismissed Lena without another word. Lena returned to me
and said only that she delivered my letter. I was alarmed and baffled by
the resounding silence.

I began to suspect that Genevera might be in love with someone else, and I reasoned: 'The number of visitors to Genevera's house lately have estranged her from me. It's too difficult to hold onto what so many other men eagerly seek. Genevera is beautiful and disposed to love. Her house lacks proper oversight now. Whoever he is, he's sparking her interest under the guise of a social call; he'll speak to her familiarly and deprive me in a short time of what I've toiled at for ages.

'Or maybe she doesn't trust Lena. Or maybe she holds some grudge against me. If that's the case, there's nothing I can do, because an uninformed doctor can't possibly diagnose the right cure. It certainly is hard to serve a lady who changes her mind a lot. Women tend to think there's no one in the world to serve them properly because they're so fastidious, uppity, moody, and unbearable. I give up already! If Love doesn't come to my aid, I'll take my leave of this life.'

Weeping, I entreated Cupid in this way …

Book 1. Chapter 60.

Peregrino complains to his lord, Love, and decides to write Genevera another letter.

Peregrino: 'O Love, lord of my life, guardian against every ill-intended wish, propitious and generous father, tutor in the desire for every good, and my defender in the harshest dangers, I beg you through the faith I have in your power, deign to change Genevera's scorn into her usual clemency, and grant me such favour that I don't perish in my present ruin! Your glorious hand has freed and saved me from many fires, so don't permit my friends to seem more eager to do me harm than my enemies.'

I recited these words with my unexpressed longing, and I felt a certain happy peace spread within my heart, which offered me hope that a good outcome was possible.

Comforted, I wrote to her again in this way …

Book 1. Chapter 61.

Peregrino writes Genevera another letter, and once again Lena returns to him empty-handed.

My Lady,
    It is the duty of a true friend and servant to share in the joys and sufferings, according to the times and circumstances, especially with those

people to whom we are already indebted. If I have been eager to learn news of you by different means, please do not ascribe to it any evil intention, since it is a well-known fact that a man in love fears and always doubts. My curiosity prompts this letter, as it has others, to know if you will equal my affection by satisfying me with the possibility of contemplating your divine face on which depends the entire course of my life.

You are more beautiful than the moon, worthier than the stars, higher than Jove, more splendid than the heavens, more serene than the sun, more generous than the extravagance that violets symbolize, more fragrant than the carnation, softer than a swan's feather, whiter than the lily, purer than a dove, brighter than gold, more precious than an Oriental gem, and greater than all the world! I beg you through all of these divine qualities, make me worthy of my requested audience so I do not suffer the consequences of a sin never committed.

I wrote the letter out of great bitterness and sent for Lena again. I told her for Astanna's benefit not to waste the returning messenger, to deliver the letter addressed to her from her uncle. Lena wasn't easily convinced this time, but reassured by the fact I couldn't insist openly, she ultimately took it.

When she delivered the letter, Genevera read it with less anger this time and told Lena she would need to consult with Astanna before answering.

Lena came back to me without any news again, and I thought I would die. That would surely have been the case had Violante not returned. I sighed and made clear to her by weeping copious tears how bad my current state was. She was moved and without saying more returned to speak with Genevera and said …

Book 1. Chapter 62.

Violante speaks with Genevera, eventually convincing her to meet with Peregrino at the garden window. She then returns to inform Peregrino and upbraid him.

Violante: "My dear Genevera, I dislike seeing you in this mournful state. If my arrival has been tardy, please pardon my work, age, and my great pity for you; seeing friends suffer is a shared death. Nevertheless, when duty calls, one must gird oneself with patience. Adapting to the circumstance when there is nothing else to do is a supreme virtue. Still, I must remind you to think of your honour and place.

"You must be aware how a transplanted tree withers in most cases because its native soil is its most natural environment, not the strange new stuff. Peregrino once was planted in you as in his native soil, and there he set down his roots so firmly that no power will be able to eradicate them. According to the logic of love, you were obligated to do the same, and had you not done so, you would not have been worthy to carry on living in this world.

"But given that you are equally united together, why all the resentments, bickering, and hostilities between you two? What farmer is so sad that he delays chopping down a fruitless tree in his orchard? How do you believe you can proceed in sincere love if you two always become mired in this distress? It would take less time to restore Rome to the first glories of her empire than you waste in spats and sniping.

"Either you love him or you don't. Make known your wishes once and for all. It's much better for a hanged man to die than continue to dangle wriggling on the rope. It's time you clarify where you stand. Whichever side that may be, I'm ready to oblige."

Once Violante had spoken these words, Genevera thanked her for meeting with her, and she replied: "If his faith were where it should be, there would be no need to seek so many clarifications. It is a cruel situation indeed for a man to want always to be seen as the opposite of what he actually is. Peregrino is through the proof of his actions a traitor, although in words he wants to be considered faithful.

"Violante, you are fooled by the excessive affection you have for this man when you speak of him. My roots have not been moved from where I planted them, and nobody else will ever uproot them. But since going over distasteful matters only breeds greater annoyance, let us put an end to this."

Violante: "Then you would consider a friend to harbour some hidden hatred or traitorous intent when he is not around?"

Genevera: "Yes, when his sin is clear."

V: "And how did Peregrino sin, thereby earning your condemnation?"

G: "He is not a little boy. He can testify; let him answer you."

V: "You do not want to make peace with him anymore?"

G: "I did not say that."

V: "What do you want him to do?"

G: "What he thinks right."

V: "About what exactly?"

G: "He should examine his conscience."

V: "He is too guarded."

G: "Sure, when it comes to his misdeeds!"

V: "Well, what are we going to do?"

G: "What he has always done, probably continue to kill me."

V: "Oh, Genevera, just give him the chance to speak to you in person."

G: "Why? So, he can lie to me?"

V: "To hear him out, then you can pass your judgment and base his sentence on what he tells you. Just do it, please, if only to avoid the many issues that might otherwise arise. If you simply withdraw from him, it might indicate that you're moving on to a new lover. Even if you lived for a long time, do you think you'd ever find a man who loved you more dutifully than Peregrino? For this reason, he deserves this audience."

G: "For your sake I will listen to him."

V: "When?"

G: "Whenever he likes."

V: "Where?"

G: "Where he indicated."

V: "Speak more precisely."

G: "Tonight at the garden window. Now go in peace."

Violante was annoyed, because she sided with Genevera. Without any preamble and without mincing words she said to me: "Traitor, you have always been wicked and misguided! The fires that consume you are a punishment from heaven. Does Genevera's beauty, dignity, propriety, faith, or the love she has gratefully shown you warrant the vexation you cause her? I don't believe she's wrong in complaining against you. If you've harmed her, spare her your love. Otherwise, go and explain yourself in that place you have so insistently requested. Be there tonight at the hour that seems most appropriate to you. Whatever has come between you two, I'll wait to understand at a later time."

Book 1. Chapter 63.

Peregrino and Genevera argue at the garden window that evening.

Comforted by Violante's action and hiding my face from my dear mother, I donned my usual nocturnal garb and took the road toward the sewers. When I reached the wine cellar, I took off my filthy overclothes and hid them under a tub. I wiped my sweaty skin and rinsed with orange water, powder, and a musk-scented balm that I brought with me for such occasions. Then, I headed toward the garden, where I found the gate open. When I got to her barred window, which was ajar, I listened attentively for any sound of voices. I lifted myself up to the window and with a practised hand began to enter hesitantly.

I heard a murmur, and I wanted to whisper a proper greeting, when I heard, "Go with God. This is not the place for presumptuous men like you."

More humbly than a servant I responded, "Here I am, lady, remorseful and suffering beyond death with my arms crossed over my chest, kneeling on the ground, and head bowed. Death or mercy I beg of you, yet still you are slow in offering the aid you owe. Why such hardness, lady? Why so much scorn? Why are you so infuriated with me, and why the constant threats? Don't you know how much I tremble not merely in your presence, but even at the mention of your name?

"Woe is me! The fire I feel is too hot for me. I realize that I cry out to one who is deaf; I speak with a mute, and I beg from a stone. May this knowledge lend you something of the fire that burns and consumes my soul. If you feel wronged in any way, please make that clear to me so I can prepare myself more readily to take on your pain, which I'm willing to do on your command. However, if I've been faithful to you, why do you destroy me and keep me at a distance?"

Genevera, silently encouraged by Astanna to answer, indignantly said, "If your actions corresponded to your words, accompanied by these tears of yours, I would be as sincerely joined to you as I ever was. But your excessively wicked ways and depraved thoughts correspond to the change you see and experience. Therefore, do not waste your efforts. I will be deaf to all of your entreaties."

Peregrino: "Lady, if you persist like this, you'll kill me."

Genevera: "It would be a sacrifice worth celebrating, depriving a man like you of life."

P: "Oh, cruel one!"

G: "Not cruel, just."

P: "How are you just?"

G: "Your arrest and the evidence against you concerning your assault on Lionora offer clear and sufficient proof."

P: "Lady, I swear on your health, on the love of my mother, and on my reverence and faith in God, please give me the chance to satisfy you, me, and the truth."

G: "This would be like trying to recount all of the labours of Hercules! Since time is short, I will make clear to you where I stand."

Book 1. Chapter 64.

Genevera reveals her feelings to Peregrino – she pities herself for being luckless in love and rails against Cupid. In the end, she encourages him to do the right thing and marry Lionora.

Genevera: "I believe and am continually reminded that Love has sought to punish me from the moment when my eyes first chanced to read your anonymous letter. He transfixed my heart with his tormenting arrow, which carried maddening moodiness, jealousies, and erring spirits. If I had just one bit of common sense, I should not have put my faith in a little Cupid; instead, I should have scorned his power and found other ways to occupy my thoughts.

"How blind are our senses in seeking aid from what cannot provide it! What fool seeks to get water from a stone or blood from a dead body? Who would expect a long life in the halls of brave action? Who ever tasted sweetness in the essence of absinthe? Who has ever found true riches in the house of liars? Who would not waste away? After all, who is more destitute than this bitter Cupid? He goes naked and homeless, frail and wretched. He always flies to the ground and lies in wait at the doors of others. He is bold, impatient, an experienced trickster, partisan of missed appointments, enchanter of arguments, wizard, poisoner, and sophist. A thousand times a day he lives and dies. Bereft of every good, he is infamous and cruel; he shows glee at others' woes and sadness at their success. Using his cleverness and false promises, he leads everyone who trusts in him to the extreme of misery such that one cannot live in peace and tranquillity in his presence. Instead, each wretched heart feeds continuously on woeful thoughts and bitter tears. It is true: anyone who sets foot in the arena of Love experiences misery!

"I thought my life would be happy and calm when you made your vow to me – and the sacred altar where we spoke is my witness! – that no one else could come between us. Instead, my life holds little value for me since I learned that you were in Lionora's bedroom in the middle of the night! From this clear evidence, I know your love toward me was always feigned, false, and a mask for other covert overtures. God most pious has made manifest your cruelty and our shared shame to the whole city.

"We women are too gullible and weak! We abide in the unhappiest condition. Our damnable piety, which traps us in a net of faith, promises, tears, sighs, solicitude, and false vows, accepted and circumvented, then in the end wickedly renounced and forgotten. O heavenly Venus, you incite our minds too bitterly though your cruel son. If ever his barbs wounded your heart, too, I beg you to take pity on us through that suffering. Undo our knot, put out this fire, free us from so much worry, since faith and discretion are spent and dead in us.

"I weep for my unhappiness together with Lionora, whose love I praise and exalt, since she is a girl of the highest gentility. Given that your actions have been dishonest, her good condition must be rehabilitated through the marriage bond. She has been generous in offering you her honour and life, so you cannot be stingy in offering her your hand. If you do this, I shall truly be content, as if you were saving me, since what happened to her could happen to me or any other girl, given the shiftiness of men's faith.

"Since it is inherently human to have compassion for others,[33] I encourage you to refuse every other love and go to Lionora. I pray God leads you both aright."

After she said these words, she closed her lovely mouth. Then I said …

Book 1. Chapter 65.

Peregrino begins to defend himself to Genevera, emphasizing her ingratitude for his efforts to see her again.

Peregrino: "My lady, there is no greater happiness that nature can grant to a man than to see his service appreciated with the same good and sincere heart with which he offered it. Merely thinking about our love, upheld in holiness by your usual gracious detachment, couldn't possibly satisfy the debt you owe me, and I couldn't go on without seeing you. But Astanna was ill, and Violante up until now has been away. Committing Love's secrets to another is risky, since anything shared is weakened and languishes. Lazily biding one's time can also indicate ingratitude and baseness.

"Therefore, I determined that it would be a more praiseworthy response to seek someone else's assistance and lose my life in the process of demonstrating my appreciation to you than to go on living while trying to forget our great love. If I found a way to satisfy our common desire, what reason do you have to take me to task? If I sacrificed my honour before allowing any possibility of denigration to your reputation, why do you accuse me in this way? If I've magnified your reputation in my every action at the risk of my own life, what cause do you have to complain? Since I only want to nourish our love, do not be displeased. If I'm seized by too much passion, what recourse do I have? By God, if only you understood how much I've suffered out of love for you, you'd be as meek as a pure dove! You are so absolutely sure that your will can direct life and death.

"If I've ever done anything to offend you in any way, please tell me clearly now. Otherwise, if there's nothing else, no budding relationship you have, kindly deign to listen to me calmly and with an open mind about all that's happened to me in my attempts to serve your love and to comfort my afflicted soul."

---

33 Genevera echoes the famous opening line of Boccaccio's foreword in his *Decameron*: "It is inherently human to show pity to those who are afflicted; it is a quality that becomes any person, but most particularly is it required of those who have stood in need of consolation and have obtained it from others …," according to the English translation by Guido Waldman (3).

I had not begun in the way I wanted, but as I was able I continued in this manner ...

Book 1. Chapter 66.

Peregrino continues defending himself to Genevera, offering a version of what happened at Lionora's house, and affirms that his heart has never lied.

Peregrino: "If truth be told, my lady, in order to acquire some thanks from you, it would take longer than a lifetime to recount every way I've suffered (beyond what is already evident). However, to relieve your heart of what crushes and burns it, I'll get to the point, mindful of time passing quickly. If you wish to take your revenge on what you perceive to be my error, do as you wish, since I shall obey you as a humble servant. Heaven couldn't grant me a greater gift than seeing and feeling your heavenly hand spill my blood; I'd consider myself blessed among the angels, if your knife released my soul.

"But before you concede me such blessedness, listen to my explanation. In your wine cellar, my lady, there is, as you know, a drain to the sewers with a long duct ending in the public cistern. Hardly anyone knows about it. I furtively investigated the place, and I believed it could offer easy access to your cellar without anyone knowing. Once a plan crystallized in my mind, I put it into action.

"That night I hadn't been walking in the duct for as far as I believed. I became overpowered by the fetid stench in that foul place, so I took the first passageway I came to, believing it to be yours. After I emerged in the basement, I was buoyed along more by the anticipation I felt than by anything I could make out in the utter darkness of night. I reached – more by chance than any reliable knowledge – the room of Petrutio's house where the lady slept.

"Convinced she was you, I tried to rouse her, but she did not respond to any of my pleas. I then added somewhat louder words to my gentle whispers, intending to dispel her sleep, but she, not realizing who was disturbing her or why, let out a shrill cry for help. In that instant, her whole family took up arms and descended on me. If God in His justice hadn't come to aid my innocence, I would've suffered my last breath then and there without committing any wrong.

"After all, what bold corruptor or what fierce gladiator even would be so audacious as to commit such a crime in this ruler's territory? These days the likes of the Tarquins and Clodiuses are extinct. This is not the age of Jove's transformations or Mars in chains or Mercury turned into a shepherd.[34] What woman of this world would ever be so heartless and thoughtless that she'd shout out and basely betray a man whom she was expecting? Who sleeps so profoundly while waiting for the arrival of someone she desired? Who would cast him away, if she really wanted him?

"Do not believe that either of us enjoyed free consent in any way. Chance led me where there was no desire. You shouldn't condemn me because I was eager to see you and sought to do so in secret. That would be a grave insult to one who loves you most faithfully. You see my heart and how it clearly suffers pain without lies. Even if all the slanderers of the world rallied against me, they'd never have the standing to keep me from satisfying my duty to you, which I intend with all my heart to do, even if it means giving up my own life. In this you can be certain.

"But if a man who fights the good fight, who is ready and brave in the face of dangers, who is generous and strong of spirit, and who is unconquered in struggles to defeat his vile foe is worthy of immortal praise, then why not I, since I have defended a greater treasure than any held by Midas, Darius, or Alexander the Great?

"Believe me, lady, it's so much more fun to roll boulders, shoot arrows, clash swords and lances, gallop around, stab others, and test one's body in these ways, compared to what a sad lover must endure in mind and body. It isn't in my power to curb my efforts to win your heart, since my satisfaction rests in this. You alone are my lady and the ruler of my heart, you are the soul of my life, my spirit, and my vital force. So it's no great wonder if I strive with all my energies, but my error is in having to keep trying. I failed because I was tricked, and my pain comes from your suspicion that I experienced delights or pleasure with another lady. I've always prayed for heaven to grant me sufficient understanding so that I can conform to your will.

"But … O how tiring it is to pursue one who flees, to call for one who doesn't respond, and to speak with one who doesn't listen! Even so, let heaven, earth, and fortune do their best; I'm determined to serve only you, even if you deprive me of your grace. If I tarry in coming to you, you blame me; if I come too soon, you complain. If I'm far away, you're impatient; if I'm near, you refuse me. If I'm ablaze with desire, you laugh at me. If I beg you, you don't listen to me. If I swear to you, you don't believe me. If I'm silent, you assume the worst; and if I speak, you don't listen to me. What am I to do?

"Whether sweet or bitter, I walk, skip, run, and gallop to serve you, and doing so is never a burden to me, so long as I know I can satisfy you. Do

---

34 Of course, in addition to his lie of omission concerning the sex act with Lionora, Peregrino's argumentation here also pointedly differs from what he presented to the Duke in Chapter 45.

not be dismissive or contrarian without reason. Please, by that power of that God who gave victory to Apollo, intelligence to Minerva, leadership to Jove, craftsmanship to Vulcan, and returned a lost love to Orpheus, put aside your hardness of heart. What glory comes to you, my lady, in vanquishing the already conquered? More praise wasn't heaped on Apollo for flaying Marsias after besting him. What would it prove, my lady, if Achilles picked a fight with lame and bow-legged Thersites, or the Muses rallied about a farmhand? It would amount to nothing more than delirium.

"I've willingly become your servant, for what it's worth; don't exhaust your ire on me. You are like the Asian conqueror, and I the vanquished Lydian; you are Dorian, while I Phrygian: I yield to you in all things. Fortune has given you every power over me. If you abandon me, the shame will be on you; if you love me, greater praise. Does it seem proper restitution for all my service for you to feign baseless jealousy so as not to repay what you owe my efforts? When Cydippe showed her ingratitude toward a lover, Venus punished her harshly.

"How many times in speaking this way have I believed you to be entirely moved, then with bitter words you send me away, calling me unfaithful. Instead, in my integrity I am rounder than an egg! I have accepted your every command in order not to disturb affection's harmony, and just as many times I've had to change my opinions, according to your words."

In the end, disarmed by my constancy, she answered me with greater sweetness.

Book 1. Chapter 67.

Genevera begins by acknowledging her inexperience and jealousy, then expresses to Peregrino her anger and disbelief.

Genevera: "Peregrino, it takes no less virtue to maintain a bond than to acquire it. Given my exceeding naivete, you should not marvel if I overstepped propriety or used words with you which were not very polished. Love and fear are two qualities that derive from the same source, and they should be equalled by reason. But I fear more from you than you love in me. Thus, incited by well-founded jealousy and seeing my reputation threatened, I did not temper my reaction well.

"But really, who would believe a handsome, bold young man would be capable of taking such liberty to sin? You must be accustomed to passing off these apparent excuses of yours on lowly girls of loose morals, not on well-educated patrician ladies. Although we do not learn as much, it is enough to know how to avoid your traps. If you heard that your beloved lady had committed a similar failing, how would you feel? What reason, what excuse, what authority, what righteous swearing, what credible story could persuade you to accept the opposite of what you knew to be true? I never believed you were so foolish, so crazy as to confuse Petrutio's house with ours, since they are not terribly alike, unless you did it on purpose."

Peregrino: "It was dark that night."

Genevera: "There was not any light in your head either, if you thought you were coming to my bedroom ever so quietly, calling out, waking me up, begging, and pawing around!"

P: "I don't deny I believed she was you; but when she cried out, I realized she wasn't."

G: "She cried out, not to rally her household against you, but simply to call back after her own soul, which had abandoned its body in that moment of fear. Sometimes when a person is in a deep sleep, different kinds of phantasms happen to occupy the mind, and whichever one predominates in the dreamer's humour is the one that resonates as a true vision, even if it is just a vague dream. These powers can be so strong that they influence our virtue. It is no surprise, then, that the beloved lady cried out when you startled her, which was certainly against her wishes, because it is not in our power to hold back or repress the soul's passions when we do not have direct control over them, as it was in this case.

"Even if a person intends to stay awake but imprudently succumbs to sleep, that person would not be able to immediately carry out any other act but the one represented in the dream. Perhaps when she cried out she was complaining to you because you were making her wait so long; maybe she feared being denounced by another woman when she awoke. A thousand times we hurt others and ourselves without intending to do so. That poor girl in one instant hurt two people. And if heaven's goodness had not intervened to show you a clear path to safety, you would have been dispatched without witness to the realm of oblivion.

"When your excuses do not have the appearance of truth, you like to dress them up as best you can. You can harbour this happy prospect in your heart: what you have discovered concerning the secret passageway from the sewers can continue to offer you more delights and pleasures to equal the filthy functions for which they were originally conceived![35]

"In all the works of the world, the first step is the hardest part. Countless, seemingly hopeless love stories have been consummated from much

---

35   In my interpretation here, Genevera seems to be reassuring Peregrino that his secret concerning the discovered passageway to satisfy his lust is safe with her. In her disdain, she seems also to be suggesting that the delights and pleasures he gets from passing through the secret passageway are on par with the foulness for which the sewers were constructed in the first place (that is to say: waste = waste).

weaker beginnings. You were in Lionora's bedroom at night with the consequences you have admitted. None of that suggests a person with much forethought. If you did not have full knowledge of the situation, why would it not occur to you to take further precautions beforehand to discern things better? But since I see clearly now that it is too late to help my cause, I will be comforted if you occasionally think of me and give thanks that I was the propitiating force of your love for her.

"Ah, ruinous Fortune, with what authority and trickery have you led me, a wretched woman, into such suffering? It must have been that debt I owed our love that made me a participant in your latest scheme. You would not have fallen earlier into this error, but this situation has become more serious, so you must also be more accepting of your new beloved, on whose behalf I beg God through His grace to lend that glorious end He once gave to Procne and her sister."[36]

These were the words she hurled at me with such vehemence that I almost convinced myself they must be true from the way she said them. It seemed I had no time to waste in silence, so I ventured in this way ...

Book 1. Chapter 68.

Peregrino doubles down on his faithfulness to Genevera and insinuates again his belief that she must have a new lover. He concludes his speech by asking that she forgive both him and herself.

Peregrino: "My lady, if I have been unfaithful to you in any way, may God's wrath damn me altogether! If ever I were unfaithful to you, may I be deprived of the light of the sun and moon. If ever I were such, may every elemental power move against me, and may my every good hope turn into the worst grief. May a dank, dark prison be my perpetual resting place; and may what happened to Dathan and Abiron befall me, too.[37]

---

36 Why Genevera references the myth of Procne and Philomela here deserves further examination. According to Ovid (in Book 6 of his *Metamorphoses*, though there are other ancient versions of the narrative), Tereus is married to Procne, but lusts after her sister Philomela and eventually takes her by force. Genevera may imply that while she and Peregrino were committed, she knows he has taken sexual advantage of Lionora. Direct comparisons with other memorable passages of the mythical narrative (i.e., Tereus cuts out Philomela's tongue to preserve the secret of what he has done, but the tapestry Philomela subsequently weaves informs Procne of the truth; Procne exacts her revenge by serving the son of their marriage to Tereus as a meal, etc.) do not appear readily applicable.

37 The fate of Dathan and Abiram in Numbers 16:30–2 is for the ground to open its mouth and swallow "them alive down into the nether world, with all belonging to them."

May the Fates cut short my thread of life, and while still healthy and vigorous, may I be fed to lions, bears, and wild beasts!

"But if I've been faithful and loyal to you, why do you accuse me without cause? If your secret plan has been to leave me for a new lover, and pay me with the usual womanly ingratitude, you should at least have shown me a more consistent heart, because it would be much less painful to be simply abandoned now for another man than endure your fictional pretences. I'm not so thoughtless, however, that I don't realize you're worthy of a god on earth, not a mortal man. As your servant, I continue to dedicate myself with the firm intention to serve you even beyond the grave. If you followed me in sincere love, which my long and unbreaking faith deserves, you wouldn't be condemning me for my many efforts.

"Lady, believe me, even the most perfect horse dies from the asp's poisonous bite. What could your mind imagine, your heart desire, your appetite crave that I didn't do to satisfy you? Lady, if you consider it well, there's never been a man even of great cleverness or grace who hasn't at some point needed a friend. The fortunes of Pompey the Great were so reduced after the Battle of Pharsalus that he was forced to beg from others to meet his needs. Sertorius, Demetrius, Hannibal, and Nero all ended their lives in misery because they were abandoned by those they had trusted. Do not disdain, destroy, and denigrate the sacred name of true friendship, which must be defended by one's own blood.

"Who could you find in this wide world who loves you with greater faith? I am ready, eager, willing, and able to carry out your every whim. There is no imposition that wearies me, no obstacle to delay me, no danger to frighten me, no setback to discourage me, no situation to change my mind, no prison to contain me, and no pleasure that can separate me from you. By now your mind should be assured by so much evidence that no suggestion to the contrary should ever be able to strain our unbreakable bond of love.

"If you save my life, you'll harvest its fruits; if you kill me, yours will be the blame and the consequences. Think now, Lady, pause and refocus your erring opinion, and don't be such a subtle investigator of new arts aimed at torturing me, because every life is laid bare by sufferings and made lean and poor to pleasures. Consider forgiving yourself and me together now."

Book 1. Chapter 69.

Genevera reconciles with Peregrino and gives him a gift: a belt embroidered with the symbols of their names' etymologies, a peregrine falcon and juniper branches. Subsequently, Genevera learns from Lionora's servant Gasparina that Peregrino is to marry Lionora, and she falls ill. She barely has enough strength to meet Peregrino at the garden window the following night.

Cupid, who wounded himself through Psyche, sparked a new flame of love in Genevera. In remorse, she turned to me and began: "Peregrino, all the passions that are in our soul are derived from this essence of Love, and anyone who does not distinguish one from another will have occasion to suffer both the good and the awful. Although love is a passion that in its beginnings is quite delightful, over time it turns into suffering and unhappiness, which overtake intellect, prudence, and discretion as their rightful place, moderating my life, too, since I was not born for anything save to serve a true and chaste Love."

After she spoke these sweet words, she proffered with her celestial hands a gift that was a sign of her reconciled mind. It was a green belt, stitched in gold representing a juniper tree, which signified her lovely name, and a peregrine falcon flying over it and eating berries from the tree. I felt weak in my attempts to offer her thanks sufficient to such a divine gift. At a loss, I praised its inspired composition, along with its value and craftsmanship.

Already we could see Ursa Major yielding its space to Venus, which boded our parting, when in gratitude I said to her: "If all the goods from India were amassed together – the metals and silvers and golds – along with all those treasures possessed by the Great Genghis Khan,[38] I would not trade them for this gift. Now just let anyone be cruel to me who can find some new reason to insult me! I do not fear Fortune or her changeability any more. I imagine in my mind no tragic outcomes, no portents of doom or slanderers, no fear of death at each new day, and no evil words are possible now that I have returned to my lady's good graces."

After saying these words and exchanging our goodbyes, I left her in peace. With a tired body and a pained soul, I considered how difficult it is to maintain love, and I almost fainted at the thought. My mind, not being especially stable, was preparing for another bitter blow. My body had barely enjoyed a moment's rest before morning came. I was relaxing, strolling with some friends, when we came to the place that would mark my destiny. I saw Lionora's maid leave Genevera's house. My mind, anxious investigator of my woe, rehearsed all those things that could possibly hurt it. Even so, it didn't arrive by half at what was truly headed my way, which my servant lady innocently mentioned to me. She was related to Gasparina – because, as you may know, all the descendants from Dalmatia, Illyria, and Pannonia here call each other relatives and cousins.

---

38 Genghis Khan was the founder and first Great Khan and Emperor of the Mongolia. He died in 1227.

Prompted by her unbearable jealousy, Genevera called Gasparina back to her house with the excuse of some errand. After much discussion, she broached this question: What was Petrutio's attitude toward Peregrino, son of Antonio, given the recent offence?

Faithful Gasparina, who didn't know better to conceal her mistress's shame, answered her that she had heard talk among the city's pre-eminent men that there might be a wedding between Lionora and Peregrino.

When Genevera heard these words, she cut short the conversation and with prudent and courteous words dismissed the servant. The colour in her face changed. Possessed by a thousand furies, she suffered a fever and fell into bed. Bitter pain rampaged her loving heart like a wild boar tearing through the woods, poisoning her love. But her courage wasn't yet weighed down so much that she didn't act to put an end right away at this news of betrayal.

Astanna, using Lena as a messenger, kindly invited me to pen an answer to the previous letter, but before I could set my hand to it, I read that I should return to the same place and at the same time as the previous day to see Genevera again. I was frightened simultaneously by love and doubt, since I didn't know the reason for such an urgent and unusual request to meet.

At the appointed hour, I anxiously trod the sewer path once again to the usual garden window, where I encountered Astanna. She was a bit recovered from her illness, but sad, and her face showed a mix of weak hope and defeat at the same time. I greeted her, which she barely reciprocated before informing me that Genevera was in bed – languishing, complaining, and trembling – unable to speak as if dying.

I immediately erupted in tears, gulping down her speech and devouring her words with continuous sniffles. I cried: "O days of contentment, how brief and fleeting you are! O happy times, how quickly you pass! O Peregrino, you must be the unluckiest and most miserable of all men! O painful and bitter news! O infernal furies, the day has come to take me without delay. O heaven and earth, O sea and powers above and below, O fixed stars and orbiting ones, too, watch over my lady, since it's not in your power to create another one like her!"

While I continued to weep, my lady, aided by the use of a cane like an old woman, which moved me to such compassion it would take ten centuries to describe it, came to me and spoke just a few words with an expression of respect for God and the world: "Peregrino, forgive my failing voice. I am barely alive," and she said no more.

I inquired the reason for her current condition, but she remained silent for a long while. Then her lucid eyes brimmed with tiny tears, and she replied ...

Book 1. Chapter 70

> *Genevera doesn't mention her conversation with Gasparina. Instead, she tells Peregrino that she had a vision of St. Catherine of Alexandria. In it, the saint insisted that Peregrino complete a pilgrimage to her shrine on Mount Sinai to appease divine will on pain of Genevera's death. Peregrino bravely agrees to carry out the demands of the vision and departs. The first book ends with Peregrino's spirit suspending the story he is recounting in Caviceo's dream vision until the following night.*

Genevera: "O Peregrino, your meagre pity toward me has brought me to this precipice of life, as you see. It did not suffice to you to offend human matters; you also profaned spiritual ones to satisfy your fleeting desires. It is thus fitting for you to be deprived of satisfaction and me of life, if you do not make restitution right away.

"The holy virgin of Syria, whose icon you violated recently when you made her sacred womb a den of filth, appeared to me yesterday at the very end of the day, when I was alone and resting in my room. She took the form she had when she was martyred. In my shock I fell to the ground almost dead. She announced to me that I would soon be relieved of life if the perpetrator of the fabricated statue did not go in person to where her body was buried and placate her anger and the wrath of God. With great effort I have managed to come here to the window to tell you everything: this is the reason I summoned you.

"Now see how at every turn I am aggrieved, and I am much more pained by your affliction than my own, because if I yield to nature, I will be free of so much pain, but I will only perpetuate your torture. If you set off on the long journey, death will come first to one of us, then the other in absentia. If you remain, I will die. Do what you believe best."

Once she had spoken, she became as silent as the dead.

My heart was transfixed by the conflict within my soul. Through sobs I responded at last: "My lady, not any wanderings in the labyrinth of Crete, not the pains of a raging bull, nor the burning flames of hell, no pain can be found that is keener or causes a hotter fire in my lifeblood than the one that has caused your present suffering. I dedicate myself entirely to your freedom and salvation from cruel Charon, if what you just said or any other obligation prevents you from thriving in good health. Be comforted, lovely soul: you impose little or no effort on me compared to what I would wish to undertake. But first, give me your blessing on my journey. Give me a sign of some improvement, so I can go and return hopeful and thankful."

My lady raised her eyes to the highest heaven and said to me: "O starry heavens and great lord of Olympus, if your irrevocable design was to create me in this world as a helpmate, why did you not shield me from proud Cupid, whose great power is felt cruelly but never seen? Every other creature is blessed and content in its passion because when love's act is finished, its yearning ceases. But miserable human beings continually pine and are consumed without respite.

"Every other creature has its own happy song it sings at different intervals. The domesticated morning lark chimes its early tune; the cicada follows in its way in the afternoon. The tawny owl marks dusk, and the great horned owl shrieks by night, while the rooster heralds the crack of dawn. I alone tremble and sob all the day and night. What will my life become after you depart?

"Portia did not feel as much anguish for Brutus, nor Cornelia for Pompey, nor Laodamia for Protesilaus, nor Penelope for Ulysses, as I do for you. If only God could accept my prayers without you having to go there in person! Oh, who will be left to console me? Ah, death would have been so much easier to endure than having to live on without you here!

"But since the cure for my state has such power to move you that you are willing to pursue such a long and defenceless road, I render my everlasting thanks to you; and whatever is left of me, whether living or dead, will be yours upon your return. Go in peace with warm memories of me. Goodbye."

What lightning bolt from the sky, what rupture of the earth, what awful earthquake, what fire cleaving the air could have so much power in me as my lady's words? Moved by her sweetness, and with copious tears streaming down my face, I turned away without another word.

Persephone walked to the house of Cerberus, the three-headed dog, and Phoebus took his chariot across the zodiac, when Peregrino's sad shade said to me at the close of my first night's dream: "Tired and weary I have brought you to this point at last. If the sufferings you've heard have something in them to bring you pleasure, then I'm content to have satisfied you. Go in peace now until that time when the star of Jove returns to us. Then, if you're curious and wish me to continue, I'll keep my promise to you as I am able."

No other word was said as the speaking shade disappeared among the trees and plants. He left me no less saddened by his departure than Theseus was when he was forced to depart without Ariadne. But reassured by his promise, I gathered my energies to await the next occasion.

So ends the first book of Peregrino.

Peregrino Book 2

Book 2. Chapter 1.

Peregrino, accompanied by Acate, makes his pilgrimage to Mount Sinai in fulfilment of Genevera's vision. On their return, they fall prey to Arabs and become slaves to a Circassian.

It was late September (Apollo had already taken over the house of Libra) when I had at last gained my mother's blessing and sailed to Venice, accompanied by faithful Acate. There I arranged for passage on a trireme bound for Syria carrying merchandise. After I had amassed the funds for the trip and we had packed our things, we boarded the ship.

We arrived that same night with very favourable winds at the port of Parenzana, where Venetian vessels customarily stop for provisions. We stayed two days, which seemed a decade to me. Setting sail again, we passed Dalmatia, as well as all of Epirus and Macedon. Without any more stops on land, we reached the Gulf of Corinth. We passed the isthmus and skirted the lands once ruled by Saturn. Scouting the region, we got our fill of Crete, the site where Daedalus displayed his handiwork. The winds of Aeolus happily pushed us toward Cyprus, the island of Venus, where we spent two days relaxing. We set sail again and soon reached the city that takes its name from Alexander the Great.

I spent three tiresome days taking in Alexandria, a new and very crowded Babylon, rimmed by the fury of the Nile. Resting without rest, we set out again and continued toward the city of Salem, where we arrived after eight days navigating a lonely, harsh route lacking enough to eat. After we venerated and adored the holy place and the lands that were the abode of the true and only Messiah made man and worshipped at the famed temple, we saw the land of Joseph the elder and the kingdom of proud Herod, with exertion to both mind and body.

Fifteen days later, we ascended the mountain where the blessed virgin St. Catherine has her angelic sepulchre. The followers of St. Benedict welcomed us compassionately and hospitably, and I carried out the task my lady had imposed.

After ten days, we gathered our energies quicker than lightning flashes from the sky, offered our due thanks, and embarked on the return journey. We reached the Jordan River, where John performed the first baptismal rite, and we admired the ancient tombs of the Patriarchs before we reached that small plain, where we who receive the merited reward for our efforts will return in flesh and blood after the final coming. Picking up our pace, we made for Ramah, so as to learn if Rachel had sated her weeping.[1] We hoped to see the place where Herod sacrificed the blood of innocents.

When behold! A tumultuous, indiscreet, lazy lot of Arabs rushed toward us. They seized us and held us captive. We were shocked by their ingrained villainies. They attacked, beat, and stripped us, and we were sold as slaves to a Circassian, who with the Sultan maintained a duchy of one thousand slaves.

After they led us to their new Babylon, we were forced to perform household chores, including fetching water continuously from the Nile to that land using asses and camels. Alack! There can be no destiny more wretched for a master, nor duty that heaven and earth could ordain than to toil in a muddy, sweaty cesspool of scourges under a cruel, envious, greedy, drunken, impious, incontinent, supreme enemy of the faith and of every goodness, despiser of God, and discerner of little in this world, enduring an obstinate, obdurate, and unrelenting hunger and thirst with only the prospect of perpetual imprisonment or violent death.

Book 2. Chapter 2.

While they toil as slaves, Acate encourages Peregrino to face and overcome adversity in order to establish a reputation for greatness. Peregrino laments not receiving any acknowledgment from Genevera; the two friends debate the nature of Love and its effects.

Woe is me! That wicked slave driver became so insolent that he put us to the yoke like a pair of oxen to toil in a ceaseless, unbearable monotony. Many times my ribs absorbed bitter blows from a cane. My bare feet caked with dust. My clothes consisted of a sack cinched by a rope, and my head was half shorn. Food was little more than grain or stale twice-cooked

---

1   The episode is recounted in Jeremiah 31:15 and Matthew 2:18.

bread, and what water there was to drink was filthy. My bed? Maybe some straw, but most of the time, just bare ground.

We experienced such dejection in that suffering that there was little hope of health or consolation except the pious memory of my Genevera, whose absence had filled my soul with grief to the point that I spent the brief time left to me in weeping and trembling. And if my days were bitter, nighttime left me far more troubled.

My faithful Acate was pained by my suffering as much as his own. Seeing my soul's sadness and the weakening of my body, he consoled me with sweet words: "Peregrino, why do you waste your life and your spirit with so much weeping? Why do you weary yourself with anguished cries? Why do you destroy your manly, jocund face with useless tears? Why do you fill heaven and earth with vain laments? Why do you pound your chest? Why not save your life for better pursuits? We haven't fallen into such oblivion that God doesn't remember us!

"What anticipated triumph has ever been achieved without effort? The deeds and wandering of Ulysses earned him commendation; dangers and shipwrecks made Aeneas celebrated; the harsh and unbearable labours that Hercules performed made him a god. More heroes and demigods find their place in little Olympia than great, famed Greece can contain; more philosophers fill the villas of academe than great and famous Athens. Greek matrons knew no greater contentedness than to listen to the stories of suffering from their husbands.

"Once Love releases you from these pains that are intended to prove your mettle, a single glance from Genevera will make you forget them all. Pull yourself together then, because ultimately Love will grant you victory. When Fortune turns, man's virtue becomes clearer. Human ingenuity has never been tested in periods of long prosperity; less fortunate circumstances render man greater and more famous. Undoubtedly, Alexander the Great would've been more highly praised if in the first throes he had experienced misfortune. Misfortune challenges you, not in order to destroy you, but to perpetuate your practice of true virtue."

The more Acate tried to comfort me, however, the sadder I became, and I lamented: "Woe is me! No matter what, I see myself dead. I give up! O rope, O knife, O poison, O precipice, O shipwreck, may one of you be my refuge!"

Acate: "Peregrino, what is it that seizes your soul more than usual? Why are you crying? What causes you to take up lamenting again? Speak to me openly and calmly. Loving another isn't a defect of character, and you haven't cast aspersions on Genevera's chastity. Where these issues are concerned you are in the clear; and with just a little more patience, your desire will be satisfied."

Peregrino: "Acate, what oppresses me is not that I'm currently in a wretched state, deprived of my country, family, and servants, or that I'm the victim of a wrongful abduction and slave to an evil man, or that I'm locked in this harsh and bitter prison, bereft of friends and advantages, uncertain, as you see, of continued survival. I complain for one reason only: that for all of the effort I've expended, I haven't received a single reward, which should be a foretaste of my future contentment."

A: "Who do you expect to give you these rewards?"

P: "Genevera."

A: "When?"

P: "Now."

A: "How?"

P: "By means of letters."

A: "Delivered by whom? And where should they be sent to?"

P: "Wherever I am."

A: "Who can know that?"

P: "Somehow Penelope knew of Ulysses."

A: "If you think more on that, she had news of him quite late."

P: "If only I were certain Genevera loved me, I'd content myself with the rest."

A: "Wrongly you complain."

P: "If only God willed that to be the case."

A: "What is it that reassures man most reliably?"

P: "The reward he is given."

A: "But how many times has she told you as much in words and in deeds?"

P: "Infinite times."

A: "Then what do you fear?"

P: "The sun, the moon, and the planets that shine on her; the earth she walks on; the house that holds her; the clothes that cover her; the bed that gives her rest; the food she eats; the water that bathes her; the road she takes; everyone with whom she speaks … Everything conspires against me!"

A: "It's impossible to foresee all eventualities."

P: "It's impossible for me to continue living!"

A: "What has put you under such a spell?"

P: "The splendour of her eyes."

A: "But if you've received that splendour into your soul as a spiritual and invisible force, why doesn't it rest there without bitterness and tension, since it is the habit of the soul to offer contentment through memory, and not by other actions?"

P: "Acate, this is a habit that brings little enjoyment without the presence of its actual object."

A: "Then love isn't a habit?"

P: "It is a habit in as much as it can be acquired and comes from another."

A: "Since time is fleeting, let us get to the point and start from this premise: What is Love?"

P: "It is a mixed essence, that is, it's both human and divine, and in a subject."

A: "How does one recognize it?"

P: "By its workings."

A: "I don't understand."

P: "This power causes its effects visibly and invisibly. In one day, in one hour, or in a single moment, it can kill or give life to man."

A: "How?"

P: "Through a single glance, and in that instant a man goes from living to dead and from dead to alive. Here are the two representative and significant operations of two powers: one is mediated and the other immediate. And it's a weighty argument concerning the human and the divine."

A: "Peregrino, you aren't answering me about whether love is a habit or an accident. If it's a habit, you can enjoy it and not feel deprived of it; if it's an accident, you can free yourself from your desires. So, if the latter is the case and you want to free yourself, what are you waiting for?"

P: "Just as its power is mixed, so is its derivative."

A: "Then what must love be? It can't be a habit, since it varies; it can't be an accident, since it fixes its roots in the soul. How it stays in us, according to habit or accident, I want you now to make clear.

"Ahasuerus King of Persia lived to behold his dear lady, Esther. When she fainted, depriving him momentarily of her presence, he broke down. The Hebrew Amnon, son of David, fell in love at first sight and just as quickly fell out of love. If these were divine actions, no one could resist them; if they were habits, they wouldn't be forgotten so easily, since an ingrained habit isn't easily shaken. Dido and Phyllis ended their lives violently out of love. If love were an accident, they wouldn't have considered at length how to carry out such desperate deaths. And since by Athenian statute, it is not permitted to speak of things that cannot be proven clearly through reason, Socrates was condemned who was the oracle of wisdom.

"Believe me, your excessive affection makes you ascribe power to some filthy little Cupid. You lovers, consumed by passion, are like combative hens that out of some hope for victory seem to believe you have spurred talons for feet. You insist on making your madness and insolence a divine guiding light. What thing in all the world is more likely to draw you off the righteous path than that false god? Your love of beauty is nothing more than an oblivion of reason, which isn't fitting to a spirit with free will or a prudent man, because it disturbs the intellect, unhinges noble and generous character, denies healthful well-being, and makes man whiny, angry, over-eager, foolhardy, commanding, arrogant, withdrawn, annoying, insatiable, unbearable, always focused on evil, servile to things that lack honesty, and neglectful of God, the world, and himself.

"Love is an assassin that kills while taking away one's selfhood. In its place, man languishes somewhere between dying and getting well again. Your imbecility has given the name of a god to these vain and false idols of Venus and Cupid. Really, who is at once the lord of life and at death's door? Who can feel pleasure while seeking suffering? Who considers prudently while pursuing unhappiness? Do you believe that they are gods, though they constantly vary, while the divine order remains immutable? Don't we read of the toils, struggles, ardours, jealousies, rapes, and pandering of Venus and Cupid? It's an abominable insolence to attribute divinity to something that is nothing!

"Instead, love is a pleasure that at first is voluntary; you want something that's delectable in itself. But when you don't get it, pleasure converts into passion. It proceeds from a spoiled heart, which because of its sensory powers wants what it desires. Even if it comes to possess the thing desired, out of fear it doesn't turn away from it, but becomes its eager overseer, and that curiosity can't proceed without turning into a passion, which is without the order of reason. Moreover, to make his error more acceptable, man says that Love forced him."

A voice: "… You, over there! O sloths, O most abject slaves, get up from your hoes! Useless donkeys, your unbeaten ribs are numbered!"

P: "O Acate, who is that?"

A: "The Circassian, I suppose. Let's go."

Book 2. Chapter 3.

Peregrino and Acate continue their debate on the nature of Love. Acate denounces all women as lustful, greedy, and untrustworthy, and counsels Peregrino to give up his Love madness. Peregrino counters.

We jumped up from our brief respite and were sent to harvest an entire orchard, notwithstanding the objections of our backs. Just as the sun was setting, we had to pack the camels with empty jugs and drive them to the Nile River to fetch water for the family.

On the way, we went back to our previous topic of discussion. Acate continued by saying we could only be defeated by ourselves, not by any other power. "Hippolytus's stepmother Phaedra tempted, begged, and pestered him to lie with her. However, he never consented; thus, he was never forced. Penelope was pressured by a thousand suitors, but she lived chastely.

"You, lovers, are a flock of vultures seeking out cadavers. All these passions of yours amount to cowardly senseless submission, and the more you love, the more broken you become. Menelaus loved Helen; but she shamelessly fled from him. Besides, you know what happened to nefarious Clytemnestra's faithful husband. It's the nature of women to want whatever they see. Woman is a greedy, haughty, disdainful, lustful, and ever untrustworthy creature. Therefore, banish your resolution to follow Love because you believe it's a god. It's a poor and wretched thing, which among great men has no place or respect.

"I don't deny at all your point that this name, Love, is worthy of praise. Through it, we become aware of every beloved subject, and in loving, we ponder, and in pondering, we're able to deduce true sentiment through meditation and the memory of experience. Consider, Peregrino: the memory of acquired things that promote the good always prompts delight in the soul. They bring us joy every time we call them to mind. However, the memory of that vain love you two experience is always accompanied by tears, sighs, blame, and regrets. Why cry over something acquired with so much effort? Who has ever complained about the effort endured for something he really wanted? Who was pained by what he wanted most?

"The practical man searches high and low over the earth and across the seas, and faces infinite dangers to win his desired object, then happily and diligently endeavours to preserve it for himself. But you're different. You never forgive disagreements, and you never seem to want anything but to be estranged from what you've acquired, which, if you consider it well, has led you to be taken captive in Arab lands.

"Now for my sake, stop this nonsense! Don't suffer for someone who glories over your misery. You weep while she laughs; you suffer while she rejoices; you're captive while she's free; and you go begging while she abounds in wealth. The sun is about to rise again on another day after you left her behind. Because we kept our departure secret, everyone will assume we're dead because we haven't been seen in ages. She'll take up with a new lover, because in youth when a lover is out of sight for long, he's out of mind. Stop this madness, because you've already wearied yourself more than befits even a naive man. Only with your honour intact can you put an end to such awful affliction."

Peregrino: "Acate, with persuasive reasons you stubbornly try to deny the power of that god who reigns over all. First you try to confuse the issue with universalities, such as when you say that those things that can't be demonstrated with proofs through reason aren't worth considering, according to the Athenian statute. But now, if you account for the change in the times, you'll understand their writings. The Athenian people believed that Socrates' view of preferring an unknown god to their household divinities was very serious and objectionable, since it sought to introduce a new worship of the gods. Because the human intellect can't fathom a clear understanding of the divine essence through reason, the ignorant throng suspected that Socrates was raving mad. For that reason, he was condemned.

"But we aren't in the situation of having to prove new beliefs. Instead, we are simply confirming with evidence longstanding views. I know that love isn't a created spirit nor a separated substance, which one can assert by a demonstrable proof: this is God. It's better to hew to the tradition of the Fathers. You can't deny my point that love is an actual and necessary essence, which influences the whole universe, and it's said to vary, according to the myriad ways it's experienced. To love God is a specific subcategory called 'divine love'; to love what is of the world is 'worldly love'; and to love women is termed 'sensual love.' Moreover, even though different types of love exist, all of them derive from this category – Love – which is nevertheless a mere essence.

"The ignorant throng, following its own view, at times praises love and at other times condemns it, according to whether it's found to be pleasing or displeasing. But because in its essence it is a good, nothing bad can proceed from it. Thus, it follows that, no matter whether one defines it broadly or narrowly, love is not evil. Does it seem possible to you that love of a woman is reprehensible? Then you are greatly mistaken, because what is commended, celebrated, and honoured by all should never be besmirched, criticized, or misrepresented in its quality. If you speak rightly of it, love is the true blessedness, the greatest joy. Has there ever been a spiritual man, an inspired or wise one, who hasn't believed in its power? Who more than God was beloved by David, though he committed murder and adultery, in order to enjoy what he most loved? And David merited forgiveness. Who is wiser than Solomon, who wasn't ashamed under the guise of love to commit idolatry? He didn't adore his lady as a lady, but rather as an idol representing Love. Aristotle, the prince of natural scientists, adored Love through Hermia.

"Acate, how is it you have this fantastical notion that the whole world has been bewitched and fooled by Love? There are some well-schooled intellectuals who have attempted to show off to others some new theory to demonstrate their high learning and who have argued that love is detestable and must be avoided. But what thing pleases God more than the creation of souls, which is an act that proceeds necessarily from a woman through love? If it were ever stopped, then divine worship would also cease. If you consider this carefully, divine and human scripture command nothing but love."

A: "It must be within orderly bounds, however."

P: "In what way?"

A: "Love must not be precipitous, damaging, cruel, or lethal."

P: "If it had all of these qualities, it wouldn't truly be love, more likely an insipid friendship. Those who risk their lives for their country or friends and receive violent death are disordered lovers, but to speak of them might only confuse matters."

A: "I'm not referring to them."

P: "What then?"

A: "This mad love of a woman."

P: "But if you believe it's possible and virtuous for a man to give up his life for a friend, why not for a girlfriend who after all has the potential to offer him greater goods, since she is the giver of our very being?"

A: "One must die for a virtuous cause, not for a lascivious one."

P: "What could be a more virtuous cause of death than to maintain what is commanded by divine law? If these were only imagined fantasies and not heaven's impressions, they wouldn't have such force in themselves. They'd be transient and more like accidents. How many men and women, committed to each other, have tried to free themselves but never could succeed? How many died because of this passion, though no wise person ever seeks death? Do you believe it's possible to find a subject who isn't worth the grace bestowed upon her? How many people die abruptly and desperately? How many waste their seed? How many are eviscerated or have their hearts ripped out due to no defect of their own, but rather because their subject was wretched? For this reason, all things can usually be attributed to the patient, if he's disposed toward good or evil.

"But believe me, if love comes from its true source, then it establishes the kind of habit that makes us entirely incapable of leaving it. If the delight I feel for Genevera were simply in my imagination, then I could quickly get over it; but since heaven has created me this way, I'm resolved to follow my infallible influences. Let's plan our escape, since there's nothing else to be done."

A: "You implicitly take away my free will when you state that it isn't in my power to free myself of a passion that proceeds from my true disposition."

P: "Acate, the present subject matter is vaster than the ocean, and our boat is weak; the boatman is tired, and he doesn't trust he can sail in such a high tide. Still, if you want a short answer, hear this: I'm not denying you your free will in any way. Nevertheless, I'll say this: our will to choose yes or no at any time depends on the confirmation of our fixed habits. Much of the time, man feels as if he couldn't act in any other way, so he perseveres along a certain path. However, I do concede that if he were determined, he could – however bitterly – withdraw from every passion."

A: "There's nothing that could bind me beyond reason. O how nefarious and detestable those poets and physicians are who so presumptuously speak of some divinity to whom they've attributed lovers, sensual generation, emotional disturbances, erring, escapes, exile, and all those defects that befall a dabbler in lust. Now, see how serious, weighty, and unbearable this love is that ignorant men, depending on their appetites, sometimes figure as a god and other times as an empty vanity, according to whether they're having a good time or suffering. Whoever experiences satisfaction offers thanks to Love as a god through whom all our contentedness proceeds, but those who experience tribulations ascribe all the blame to Love. Don't you see how they make Love a god, then unmake it so, from one moment to the next? Therefore, I judge that you lovers most of the time don't even know yourselves, and I understand your love to be a bitter passion."

P: "It isn't so bad, but your experience of love makes it seem especially awful to you."

A: "Why?"

P: "Because of your dominant humour."

A: "So you're saying that melancholic types don't yield to love?"

P: "Perhaps not so easily. But if they're hooked, they can never get free of love. Consider how much strength it took those who tried to resist, such as Hercules, Plato, Aristotle, Virgil, and Sappho; or those who contended with it, including Hannibal, Sertorius, Demetrius, Philip of Macedon, and Lucretius the Epicurean, who ran toward death in a mad fury. Now you see what love can do in a melancholic subject."

A: "How does this love appear in human nature?"

P: "It is a passion very close to melancholy."

A: "Which men are most susceptible to it?"

P: "The choleric ones."

A: "Why?"

P: "Because of the heat inherent in that humour. Although these types are the most susceptible, they're also the ones who fall out of love the easiest. But the melancholic ones, like you, given the solid, earth-like quality of your humour, are lackadaisical and slow. You'd sooner die than leave love."

A: "At this age I feel more temperate, so I don't need to fear Love's arrows so much."

P: "Actually, old men burn much hotter than young ones through a cruel fascination. The eye of the old man latches onto a young one, who attracts him more than the glances between two youths. Recall how David, Masinissa, and Marcus Porcius Cato burned in old age."

A: "So, two types are especially subjugated to this power?"

P: "There's yet another that is also very much consumed by love."

A: "Which one?"

P: "Those who burn for illicit love. In this type, love is inherently dangerous, scandalous, and shameful, which accords it so much power that it becomes impossible to resist. Take Phaedra with Hippolytus, Canace with her brother Macareus, Myrrha with her father Cinyras, Byblis with her twin brother Caunus, and Semiramis with her son Nimrod. So, don't let yourself get too close to these kinds of loves, because it's a poison destroying both soul and body."

A: "Isn't there a cure for this malady?"

P: "Not really."

A: "Oh! What cruelty it was to create a malady for which there's no cure!"

P: "Just protect yourself from its initial contaminations."

A: "But isn't that impossible if it moves invisibly? How can one guard against it then?"

P: "I can only tell you what hasn't worked for me, nor is there any advice in the Scriptures. The Arab doctor Rhazes in his manual recommends engaging in physical exercise, parties full of revelry, and frequent copulation, because love is latent when sobriety is oppressive."

A: "O how many different effects – it seems impossible to me – proceed from a single cause! Who's ever heard that sobriety and revelry produced the same effect?"

P: "The sun is an essence. At one and the same time, it shines necessary light and is so hot it melts things. Leisure is a cause that can make one lean or fat."

A: "In the end, then, are people who've taken religious vows more inflamed to passion than secular ones?"

P: "Yes."

A: "Why?"

P: "Listen. The soul prefers to think most about what pleases it; the object of the soul is love. It follows then that it doesn't contemplate much that isn't near at hand. Those without much experience who fall under the aegis of love will burn and be consumed. Fittingly, one says that Dido, all alone and bored at home, wept and complained of excessive love."

Book 2. Chapter 4.

Acate summarizes his arguments for why Peregrino should quit Love, while Peregrino insists that Love improves man.

Acate: "It's time to put an end to our discussion, since the point is moot. Set your sights on more manly and praiseworthy action, and put aside childish thoughts. Otherwise, they'll denigrate both our souls, which if left to their worst habits, only learn and reinforce them. You don't want to be like the child at play, who twists his ankle on a rock, gets hurt, and remains on the ground. Instead of seeking medical help, he keeps crying and miserably wailing the time away, stuck in one place. O how irrational, lazy, sick, and unbearable it is to carry on in that way, which damages the body, torments the soul, and deprives one of immortality! Consider what's proper and fitting to man: temperance, modesty, common sense, gentleness, well-ordered habits, generosity, nobility, and strength of character. All these traits have been glorified by our ancestors. Avoid their opposites, which are lust, a disordered life, desire, cowardice of heart, and a wimpy character, all of which are better suited to children.

"Consider the sun. After it passes its highest point, its rays reflect back onto itself, so it appears much brighter illuminating our hemisphere, and the general consensus is correct in calling the afternoon sun a sign of serenity. Now you should examine more carefully the female sex. Consider her age and measure whether she compensates the great service usually rendered, then see if you'd be far better off freeing yourself or pulling back more on the reins of your galloping horse. What wise man ever pursued contrary ends as much as you have?"

Peregrino: "You've always prodded me to seek and love one similar to me, since it's an offence to be influenced by those who aren't worthy peers. But can't you see how well the poor go with the rich, the weak with the strong, and the doctor with the sick patient? Although they're dissimilar, these fit more aptly together than they would with their peers, as it'd be if the doctor always stayed with another doctor, or a healthy person with another healthy one, or the rich with other rich people. Common sense can offer you enough proof of this. See how what's dry desires the humid, how cold seeks heat, how bitterness needs sweet, darkness light, the vacuum something to fill it, blackness white, the fool someone wise, the servant his freedom, hate friendship, and war seeks peace. Now kindly permit me to continue in my ways, which aren't contrary or repulsive, as you wish to convince me."

A: "These things you claim to be contraries aren't desired by their dissimilars as contraries per se, but as what will perfect them."

P: "What renders man more perfect, what makes love either similar or dissimilar? If it's similar, it follows nature; if it's dissimilar, it follows greater perfection, according to your implication. Now let's consider love."

A: "Peregrino, man allows himself to be subjected to three things: nature, education, and discipline, sometimes following vice, and other times virtue. Please show me that you aren't subjugating yourself to vices, which your own nature would find repulsive, and do not allow a sad accident to corrupt your considerable talents, which God and nature have bestowed on you."

Book 2. Chapter 5.

The Circassian takes his slaves with his retinue to honour the Sultan in Alexandria. There, Peregrino recognizes a Venetian patrician, Girolamo Marcello,[2] who tries to help the two friends escape.

We had not presented all our arguments for debate before our master summoned us to accompany him to appear before the Sultan in Alexandria. After we deposited the water jugs, we were girded as slaves and marched before the Circassian's knights. When we reached the city, we saw that every foreign nation, including Venice, Genoa, Ragusa, and Ancona with the rest of the Adriatic states, had come to honour the Sultan.

Among these delegations, the Venetian one distinguished itself. On entering the castle I caught sight of a Venetian patrician named Girolamo Marcello, who was a man of the highest intellect and great discernment and with whom I had a longstanding rapport. I realized when I saw him that heaven was providing me with an unimagined favour. Leaving Acate under the watch of the Circassian, I followed the Venetian through the antechambers, trying not to raise the suspicions of that wicked and inhumane crowd. After I reached his rooms, I paused to make sure my mind wasn't playing tricks on me. Looking closer, I confirmed my initial impression and approached him. He assumed I was a beggar and put his hand to his purse to offer me a bit of jasper.

I refused him politely and, calling him by name, said: "I have a greater need of your aid."

He looked me squarely in the face and recognized me. With sweet tears in his eyes, he asked me: "O Peregrino, what foul Fortune has landed you in these parts? From what I see, you're a slave and on the run. Therefore, don't come any closer, but tell me your story while we walk together."

Strolling around the city's gates, I recounted to him all of my misfortunes. He shed a few hot tears, but told me only: "Go in peace, Peregrino, and heaven will show you the way."

I seemed to receive no more satisfaction in taking my leave of him than I had when I greeted him, so I returned heartsick. I told everything to trusted Acate, who comforted me to have strong resolve, because the

---

2   Girolamo Marcello (d. 1493) was a Venetian senator, then *Podestà* in Chioggia in 1490, before accepting in 1491 the nomination to serve as a special envoy to Constantinople. History documents Marcello's negotiation with the Ottomans for the release of a Venetian patrician. Marcello was accused of espionage and interfering in Turkish affairs and died in Zara on his way back to Venice.

Venetian's response was fitting in every way to the circumstances and his status.

While I bemoaned my bitter situation, the Venetian came back to me and added briefly: "Come to my room tonight, where you'll be furnished with everything you'll need to easily launch and complete your escape."

Taking advantage of the dark of night when sleepiness oppresses even the most valiant of men, trusted Acate and I went together to the designated place, where our friend in his great charity was not neglectful. He hid us among a shipment of cotton and spices so we could put the pagan madness behind us.

Book 2. Chapter 6.

A manhunt ensues for the runaway slaves, who are discovered and imprisoned. Marcello intervenes to negotiate their freedom. Peregrino sends Acate to Italy to gather the gold for repayment and deliver a letter to Genevera.

When Phoebus shone from his high balcony, not only the Circassian but his whole army together realized we weren't where we were supposed to be and set out to find us to take their revenge. Moreover, there wasn't one person among the throngs who'd refuse to denounce us. That tumultuous and mad rabble, united with the city's magistrates, zealously took up arms, and surrounded and attacked the Venetian's mansion, searching every corner of it. Death surely would've come to the owner of the house had his resourceful slaves not provided us an escape worthy of such a great man. That friend not only promptly offered his promise of aid but also risked his own life when he cleverly denied that there were slaves fitting our description among any of his men.

Heaven is always at odds with the wretched, though. While the Venetian was out conducting business, his young assistant brought in a foreign trader to sell some merchandise. Meanwhile, we believed we were finally in the clear and had reached the point of no longer being able to withstand the spiciness of the pepper, so, we raised our heads.

An Arab who accompanied the merchant and had eyes sharp as those of Argos noticed our wretched hiding spot and shouted out to the others, identifying us as the runaway slaves. They cast aside the spice sacks, seized us, and violently dragged us out, presenting and denouncing us before the magistrate. Right then and there, they threw us in a dungeon, where we expected to suffer our last.

My Venetian friend devised another clever plan, however, and implored the Sultan for a favour, which was that after we were flogged, we be freed from prison upon payment of two pounds of gold. Until then, he would provide the Circassian with hostages in place of us.

I had already endured so much on credit by this time that I insisted on repaying him. So, I got permission from the Venetian to send Acate home to fetch the gold needed for our release (and Acate was also to inform Violante of my condition). Once Marcello and I agreed, Acate boarded a ship bound for Italy from Alexandria. With propitious winds it sailed past Cyprus and Rhodes and arrived at Ancona, where he disembarked and made the rest of the journey over land.

Upon his arrival, our city gave Acate a warm reception. Downplaying his unannounced appearance all alone, he set about gathering the gold, and he had my letter delivered to Genevera, which was of this tenor ...

Book 2. Chapter 7.

Peregrino's letter contains the news of his completed penance and imminent return. Acate informs Violante and Genevera of his and Peregrino's release from slavery. Genevera at first resists the suggestion that she write Peregrino a letter in response, but then is moved to do so.

My Lady,
If my meagre action – willingly undertaken – has in some way placated St. Catherine, then I render everlasting thanks that you have reaped the benefit. Because I fear my prayers in her divine presence may have been inadequate, I have not dared return to you without first making certain your health has improved. Therefore, I send Acate, who will inform you of my news through Violante.

If some other reason remains for you to prefer my continued absence, it would be no less welcome to me, so long as I know I am in some part satisfying you. But if my faithful service has earned some approval, please do not allow the bearer of this letter to return to me empty-handed, which I would judge far crueller than every violent death.

Remember me. Live and be well.

Violante, who was most obedient and affectionate toward me, was overjoyed to receive my letter. She went straight to Genevera and with fitting words made her aware that she had sure news of my health and imminent return. In order to remove any doubts, she handed my letter to her.

At first, my lady seemed like an inexperienced swimmer saved from shipwreck who remains breathless and in shock. Eventually, she recovered her wits and with a voice cracking in pain, she said: "Oh, where is my Peregrino?" She kissed the letter and unsealed it, and she learned all about the promise I kept and the toils I suffered, including capture and enslavement.

She hesitated for a long time. Genevera wanted to avoid writing me back because she feared her letter would be intercepted and because not writing might prompt me to return sooner. But then after Violante's comfort, reassurance, and entreaties, Genevera finally began her letter as follows …

Book 2. Chapter 8.

Genevera writes to Peregrino, urging him to return to Ferrara. Meanwhile, Peregrino considers remaining in the Circassian's service, but once he hears from Genevera, he determines to ransom the hostages in his place and return home with Acate.

Peregrino,

The distance from your homeland, the long passage of time, all that you have endured, the tribulations, my eager anticipation, and the fact that you have a trustworthy messenger all indicate you might have sent me a massive collection of epistles, rather than just your brief note. I fear the scarcity of your communications proceeds from some indignation you have conceived in your mind about me, which causes you to believe that you have suffered more than I have in thinking of you. Or perhaps you are still embroiled in some dreadful situation of the body or mind that prevents you from writing to me as you once faithfully did. Whatever the case, I will understand it better if you are here in person than by means of letters.

Thanks to the saint and your most holy prayers on my behalf, I have regained my health. Since I can no longer benefit from your continued absence, I beg you to put an end to it. You have satisfied what I asked, and upon your return, I will find the means to thank you in a way that shall be most welcome to both of us. You can read about my other news through the letters I am giving to Violante.

Be well and prosper.

After she wrote the letter and sealed it in gold as usual, she gave it to Acate, who took a Rhodian ship back to me.

While I waited for him, I considered my situation. I knew from the experiences I had had that the Circassian was seeking in every way to keep me perpetually in his service. Besides, I was growing tired of Love's service and began to allow myself to consider a change in residence. These eastern lands offered their own delights and freer temptations. I also feared that my mission, which had kept me separated from Genevera for two years, had deprived me of her favours. After all, it's difficult enough to keep a prize that many want, even when one is present, armed, and vigilant. 'Just wait and see what has come to pass in my absence and without a trusted intermediary. It's easy to believe Genevera has by now been joined in marriage to some man more fortunate than I.'

In the midst of these doubts, I saw Acate disembark at the port. When he delivered her letter to me, not all the riches the world possesses, not all the treasures ferried across the sea or produced from the earth or promised by heaven would've delayed me from rushing back to Genevera.

Counting what little money remained to me, I freed my hostages and thanked my Venetian friend as best I could. Then I adored the gods and prayed for good fortune in this way.

Book 2. Chapter 9.

Peregrino prays for a safe return. A Venetian patrician, Angelo Iolim, hosts Peregrino and Acate on Crete before they return to Ferrara. Both lovers are emotionally overwhelmed at the reunion and can say nothing.

Peregrino: "Heavenly spirits, I beg you all to lend your aid in fulfilling my greatest wish. And you, unrelenting, powerful Fortune, put an end to your cruelty now! If, through your intervention, I should return home safe and sound, I'll make perpetual sacrifices in your honour. I've suffered so much; may your anger be appeased! Now you are the protectress of my freedom and the port of my salvation. I'll render all my thanks to you; I'll dedicate all the honours I receive to you, and all the sacrifices I'll make shall be on your behalf. I'll seize the unfulfilled promise of your forelock, Fortune, and I'll always adore your grim and menacing face. While I live and wherever I live, I'll witness to your glory and display an icon representing you in my home. You'll be my sustainer, my true joy and blessedness. I'll proclaim you all over the world, and I'll commend your name to posterity.

"Please, do not let the task of saving one man be a burden to you. After all, you rescued Phrixus on the back of the golden ram, you guided the poet Arion on the dolphin, and you saved Europa on a bull. You caused Jove to be transformed into a lowing ox, and you saved Cyrus King of Persia from being roasted in the vicious pit at a banquet for many people. You exalted the founders of bounteous Rome to the supreme ranks of a high empire. You preserved the Sicilian realm for Hieron, nourished by dogs, and you saved the boats of Abydos from shipwreck and kept Moses the lawgiver safe in a wicker basket. Since you have saved many people, do not disdain one who calls on you with faith and a pure heart.

"Queen Fortune, after such a long battle don't deny me a victorious return to my lady. I beg you by that sacred bond of Love, which you made in joining my spirit to my beloved lady, do not delay me. But if you should deny my safe return in order to quench your ire, at least spare me shipwreck and inhumane hunger, so that, punished, at least my corpse can squeeze sweet tears from her beautiful eyes."

I mixed my many prayers with frequent sighs. When I finished my petitions, Acate and I happily boarded a Cretan ship to leave behind for good our cruel and greedy master. During the passage Acate and I spoke of Genevera and her house and what he said about me to her. He told me what Violante had faithfully related to him, that Anastasia was still suspicious of Genevera, but of precisely what, Violante wasn't sure. The cause for her suspicion concerned a belt Genevera had crafted with time and great artifice. Genevera told her mother that the belt had been stolen when she thoughtlessly left it in her unlocked room. She implied it was her brothers' fault. Anastasia pretended to believe it all, as though it were news to her. But she was watching Genevera even more carefully for any indication that she had given the belt to some secret lover. Thus, it would be best to act very cautiously, so that nothing else could come to Anastasia's attention.

Discussing other matters along these lines, we disembarked on Crete, the island of Minos, where a Venetian patrician residing on the island, Angelo Iolim, generously welcomed us. When an opportunity arose to sail on a Ragusan ship with favourable winds, we accepted, and in fifteen days we crossed the Adriatic Sea and arrived in the port of Rimini, where we disembarked all alone.

When it pleased God and heaven, we reached our sweet homeland. Disregarding every other care, I went straight to Violante's house. As soon as she saw me, she collapsed into my arms, moved by heartfelt tenderness. Once her heart's strength revived, we fittingly celebrated my happy return. Since she agreed to put me up, I sent Acate to announce to my mother and relatives that I would return in four days' time. This way, I could pass the time with Genevera, if heaven granted me such a boon.

The sun was setting when Violante informed Astanna of my arrival. Astanna agreed that I should present myself at Genevera's door dressed in the Arab fashion and she would sneak me into the room where I had previously spent the night inside the statue. I chose trusted Violante to accompany me, and I followed her with tentative steps to Genevera's house. After we made certain no one else was around, Astanna welcomed me most affectionately. She showed me her left hand on which she wore the ring that signified our pact.

She hid me, and after just a short while, I saw through the window of that room that Astanna had gone to Genevera, who was on the balcony. They huddled together speaking in hushed voices. When they stopped talking, they moved toward the garden.

They came to the threshold of the room where I was waiting, and I heard Astanna say: "O once happy refuge for a man and a statue, now you are empty and without consolation."

Genevera: "That is how Fortune always treats lovers."

Astanna: "Anything is possible to those who love faithfully."

G: "I do what I can and must."

A: "Be of good cheer because heaven will help you."

G: "Yes, help me to suffer some more!"

A: "Desperation has never been slow in pursuing you."

G: "I am not worthy even of myself, I am so unfortunate!"

A: "On the contrary, you are most blessed."

G: "What consoling news do you bring me?"

A: "Acate has returned."

G: "That is nothing new."

A: "I mean a second time."

G: "How do you know?"

A: "I spoke to him at length."

G: "And you are just now telling me this?"

A: "It was for a good reason. I was waiting for the right moment."

G: "Any time is good to speak of happy things."

A: "That is certainly true for one who listens, but not necessarily for the messenger."

G: "Tell me, what did you talk about?"

A: "He arrived at Violante's house in a very good mood."

G: "You are weaving me a long yarn, O will you not free me! Did he bring any letters? Where did he leave Peregrino? Now I see that you are toying with me to spite me. You stir my blood with your useless gossip."

A: "Hold your peace. I will tell you everything."

G: "Out with it, please."

A: "He wants to see you."

G: "Me?"

A: "Yes."

G: "Why?"

A: "To console you."

G: "I do not like this news. If he has nothing to deliver to me, why was he sent?"

A: "If Peregrino came, would you receive him?"

G: "Where?"

A: "In this garden."

G: "Denying him would be cruel."

A: "With your permission, I will bring him here."

G: "Then he has arrived? You have been quite cruel to leave that part out. Since I am sure you will command me, do as you will."

Once they finished their conversation, they left. As dusk fell, Astanna led me to the usual place, and I went up to Genevera's window. When I heard it open, I felt my blood drain away. A sun had entered the room, a sun that could shine an aura of beauty on the Underworld. When Genevera saw me, she paled, believing she was seeing a ghost. She stood stock still, though she wanted to flee. If Astanna hadn't been there to comfort her, Genevera would've deprived me of this meeting.

I seemed like one straight out of Persephone's realm, and I had nothing fitting to offer her at this reunion, so I didn't dare speak. Astanna reassured Genevera, who moved closer.

At the first sign of battle, two great enemies appear: Love and Fear. Love rapped on my heart with his arrows saying: "Open up! You harboured me first." But Fear tightened its grip and became deaf to those words. If it hadn't been for my lady's gestured greeting, I would've fallen down dead. I was ambushed between those two great enemies, and I could not manage to produce any sound from my terrified chest.

My lady was mute, and I remained deaf and blind. The increasing darkness of evening caused my lady to bolt abruptly from her room.

I was left alone to ponder my life. I could come up with no reason for my existence, if that's what it was. My mind jumped from one thought to another like a bird going from frond to branch. I prayed heaven would guide me to a brighter destiny.

To console me in my state, Astanna came and plied me as best she could with happy reassurance, promising to give me all the time I needed to be able to reason rationally again. Then she swore to me that Genevera's heart never burned for anyone else but me and smouldered for me as much when I was far away as when I was near. She was as smitten now as she was before. Although her bitter suffering in my absence should have extinguished her love, instead it increased with each passing day. In short, Astanna persuaded me to cast aside every fear and doubt and rest assured that Genevera loved me more than any man was loved by a woman, and with greater fidelity and sincerity.

So that I could better comprehend how difficult my absence had been for Genevera, Astanna told me Genevera had vowed to God not to wear anything except her mourning clothes until my return, and she kept the same routine she had during the first days after her brother's death. Her pretext: she would never don colourful clothing or accept marriage until her slain brother's soul was appeased.

Astanna: "Now see, Peregrino, how loved and treasured you are! You would do well to take comfort and to offer thanks to Love."

Her caring and affectionate words made me feel much better. Astanna, who had prepared a lavish dinner, slipped out, in order not to arouse suspicion in the house. Fear of infamy, jealousy of love, and exhaustion of the body all waged war within me because my poor spirit was so afflicted.

Book 2. Chapter 10.

A sudden storm interrupts Peregrino's sleep. The downpour floods Angelo's house. Peregrino's hiding place is nearly discovered before the entire household retreats to an upper room. Peregrino then wanders the house alone and finds what he believes is Genevera's bedroom.

I felt as if I were smashed into a thousand pieces, to the point I wasn't sure what I wanted anymore. Once my belly was filled, satisfying its immediate need, I began to think about how I could direct my present circumstances toward a profitable goal, since continuing to languish in this kind of passion only indicates a lack of prudence.

Overcome by drowsiness, I finally embraced sleep. I experienced at once a frightening vision. It seemed I was snatched into heaven's Empyrean where Jove reigns and governs from on high, ever contending with his brothers. They were in such an uproar that the entire heavenly abode appeared in dark chaos. Phoebus did not shine, nor did Lucina the moon, nor any star of the zodiac – nothing cast even a sliver of light on the godly abode. Standing before this dread spectacle, someone came up to me (I don't know who) and angrily snatched me away to where he resided in utter resentfulness. My soul, agitated by this vision, caused me to stir.

I awoke in that moment and heard the god who carries the trident as his insignia. Neptune was no less disturbed now than when he killed many of its inhabitants of the land that Theseus wickedly conquered. Neptune struck the ocean with his fierce trident, summoning Triton and Palaemon, along with Peleus's wife and the virgin Panopea, and all his clouds. They immediately rushed to their duties, nor did Aeolus fail to offer his services. In an instant, such a dark fog obscured all of heaven, the air, and the earth that you would have guessed that both hemispheres had lost their fixed stars and planets. Rain pelted the house and threatened it, as if it were a dinghy unable to find refuge from shipwreck and dashed against a shoal.

As a last resort, Angelo decided to go down to the room where I was not-so-safely hiding. Astanna flew down to me faster than thunder from heaven and informed me the house was about to flood, so Angelo believed everyone would do well to gather where I was. Just as she was saying this, I heard the family's footfalls on the stairs.

Faster and blinder than a bat, I looked for a hiding place in the wine cellar. I crouched as best I could in an empty barrel. Then, to free myself from overwhelming anxiety, I called to mind the suffering I had endured in the sewer. Neptune was already beginning to occupy the doorway, however, sending ahead puddles as his scouts throughout the cellar. My barrel began to rise, and I felt as if I were atop Mount Olympus in the chest Deucalion had built to save the seed of man. I also thought back on my Arabian enslavement and my suffering in Syria, and they seemed to me preferable to my current predicament. How presumptuous is the one who is never satisfied with what happens to him!

I heard weeping and screaming throughout the city. It was as if Priam's city were contending with Nero's, or the Gauls were occupying the nest that would save Rome. Angelo turned about, barricading himself with his whole family in an upper room, which was on much higher ground and topped with arches, as if he expected to receive any minute the severed heads of his strongest enemies to plant there.

This gave me the opportunity to wander freely through the house because everyone else was confined to one room. I went up the stairs and found a door that opened onto a well-furnished room with a bed that I thought it must be Genevera's. I was torn – it was difficult to remain there, but death to leave. If I stayed, what would happen to me if I were discovered? Besides, that evening was unusually chilly, given the season, and I was dressed in lightweight clothes. If I left Angelo's house, where would I go? Who would guide me? Who would open a door to me? It seemed better for me to wait until morning to see what Fortune would bring me.

Book 2. Chapter 11.

The storm abates around dawn, and Genevera returns to her room, where Peregrino hides undetected under her bed. Genevera and Astanna argue.

Only around the time when Phoebus incites his horses from his lofty house did Neptune's horn herald the ocean's retreat. Genevera's family, wearied by the nocturnal vigil, hastened to return to their rooms for rest. As soon as I heard footsteps, I ducked under chaste Genevera's virginal bed.

She entered the room, heaved a deep sigh, turned to Astanna, and said: "O wasted efforts, O suffering in vain! Poor Peregrino must have been born under the unluckiest constellation in the heavens! Years have passed, and still he can find no delight or pleasure. He barely returned from his exhausting trip, and now his life is in danger again. Tell me, Astanna, where did you send him?"

Astanna: "To the wine cellar, where he would be safer."
Genevera: "But that was completely flooded!"
A: "Nor was anything else spared."
G: "Poor man!"
A: "It serves him right. Now let us get some rest as best we can."
G: "Rest is impossible for one who remains unsatisfied."
A: "What do you want me to do?"
G: "See if you can find out if he is dead or if he managed to get out."
A: "But it's day."
G: "Everyone is asleep, though, now."
A: "So it'd be if only you willed it!"

G: "Ah, it is a bitter life with you, worst of those born into service! Off with you, you hopeless thing! Summoning you mules is like harnessing an ass. What brain, what intellect can reason with you? Nothing of worth can be found in a servile heart. It is useless to trust your feral and perfidious lot with any secrets. Thus it is said – not merely among the common masses, either – that Jove deprived those who are subjected to servitude of a part of their minds. Just to be rid of you and your ceaseless whining, I shall deprive myself of Peregrino's love. Who has ever endured so many excuses and annoyances as I have from you? You shut him up in that cellar as if he were your slave. Now go with God. It is much better to go it alone than to be wickedly attended!"

A: "Genevera, you can't fault me for the weather! What more could I do? If I hadn't seen to it to move him when he was in danger of being discovered, where would we be right now? I've always served you with faithfulness and due obedience, perhaps indeed more than I should. If your parents ever learned of what I did and am doing for you, what would become of me then? You see, I've always put your wishes before my comfort, reputation, and life.

"Because I'm more concerned about you than my own good, you've vented your anger on me quite unfairly. Since it's far better to fall to earth from down here than from heaven, and since my loyal service earns only this reward, I beg your leave. Maybe another girl, more fortunate than I, will make better headway with you. I know how difficult it is for you to temper your emotions. You blame me for everything that overwhelms you or doesn't go your way. It should be enough for you that I willingly do the best I can. But seeing as I've fallen so far in your estimation, there can be no more peace between us. Be with God."

Book 2. Chapter 12.

Genevera and Astanna reconcile and try to figure out where Peregrino is. After he emerges from under Genevera's bed, they hide him in the adjoining room of Genevera's late brother. The lovers plot a way for Peregrino to return.

Genevera: "What moves me to speak of this with you is not the burning of lascivious love, which conquers pitiless stepmothers, tames lions, joins animals together, makes saints go mad, conquers the heavens, and imposes the law of the universe. Rather, it is the fear that such a fire could be ignited. So do not wonder if I have said more to you than I typically do. It has never been my intention, Astanna dear, to offend you in any way. If I have overstepped, do not ascribe it to malice on my part but only to the trust I have in our rapport. You are my consoler; you know my mind and body. Go forth courageously, since a noble spirit does not hold grudges. Go and seek out Peregrino so that a chance encounter with another does not bring evil upon him."

Astanna: "Genevera, if ever you believed I sought your happiness any less than you do, you'd be mistaken. Since experience breeds trust, I defer to your opinion. Oh my, here comes Angelo, and his face indicates he's angry. May God save us from him discovering Peregrino!"

In that moment, I heard Angelo shout loudly, "Astanna!"

Astanna: "Sir?"

Angelo: "Come down here to me, and I'll show you your good works!"

Ast.: "Oh, woe is me, Genevera. We're doomed!"

Genevera: "Go, and deny everything."

Ast.: "He'll figure it out."

G: "One piece of evidence cannot bring down a bold defence. Peregrino's usual cleverness will defend him. Leave the worrying to me; just see to it that one way or another Peregrino escapes."

When Astanna had left the room, Genevera called out, "Father of mine, what has happened now? Astanna is here with me to clean up my room. Come here and stay with me a bit, and you, Astanna, continue what you are doing."

Angelo: "I only need a pail, the sturdiest she has, since the downpour of water has increased and has battered the house as if it were a tiny boat. I would like her to take better care of our possessions, as I believe you do."

G: "It is not her fault."

Ang: "I know. The problem is the sewer, which I need to block off. Better a bit of inconvenience than a grave danger."

G: "You seem to me to be in a bad mood."

Ang: "Perhaps that's due to lack of sleep."

G: "Go and rest."

Ang: "And what will you do?"

G: "I will go with you."

Ang: "No, you stay there in your room."

G: "Go in peace.

'Ah God, how easy it is for a guilty conscience to cause shame. And how difficult it is to hide the inner workings of one's heart from others' prying eyes! I am ruined, undone, tired, and exhausted. I do not believe my erring soul can even recognize me, given my current fear. I am shaking all over! Any little hint and my guilty face will betray my wickedness. Now see what I have been reduced to!'

"Astanna, Astanna!"

Astanna: "What d'you want?"

G: "Come here right now."

Ast: "Here I am."

G: "I am dead."

Ast: "I'm not exactly brimming with life!"

G: "How are things going?"

Ast: "I haven't seen your man. The barrel is empty, and the sewer has completely flooded. All is ruined."

G: "Oh, my! Could he have drowned? Let us go and see if he is dead or alive."

Ast: "No, leave it to me. Put your spirit to rest, lock your room. I'll search the house, and if he's not here, I'll go to Violante's to see if he went there."

G: "Go then, and do what you say."

Once Genevera had locked her bedroom door, it seemed to me the right time to free my lady from her fright. Besides, beyond my wildest dreams I was being offered this chance to speak to her about our love.

I emerged from under her bed and got to my feet. Then I said to her ever so quietly: "Lady, here I am at your service."

A wolf's glance when it alights on man does not move us to act as quickly as my word effected Genevera. Shocked, she said: "It is not the custom to traffic so familiarly in the bedrooms of virgins! Even if our love is equally shared, infamy certainly is not!"

She slipped from her room to fetch Astanna (who had not really gotten far), and she had Astanna put me in the adjoining room, where her brother had died. She went back to her bedroom and she opened a little window, which I believe had been placed there so the siblings could share confidences. Now no one went near his room, so as not to be reminded of his violent death.

I locked the door, opened the window, and tried to calm my frustration, as we settled into seats divided in this way. I began to tell her what had become of my life. I had not arrived at the end of my long travails when tears began falling from her luminous eyes. In this way, she rendered eternal thanks for all I had endured. Indeed, that was a gentle reassurance to my soul, a true comfort, and an everlasting joy. If I were to recount our exchanged comments one by one, it would take more than a human tongue – a divine one on eternal time – to tell them all. Therefore, I think it best to leave it to the imagination of the listener than to attempt the impossible.

After a thousand and more words were broken off and taken up again, I began to consider some new way to reach Genevera, given that the sewer was now out of the question. As soon as I mentioned the sewer, I saw Genevera's face turn different shades of red, as she recalled what happened with Lionora, which I realized more through what she manifested outwardly than anything she said. Still, she held back, and I pretended not to notice. In order not to have to go down that road again, I glanced around.

Raising my eyes a little, I noticed a sturdy iron-clad square window that looked onto the garden. It was so high that nobody gave it a second thought, certainly not bothering to check if it was locked. I examined it more carefully. It seemed higher than Mount Ida and with other pitfalls to consider. But I burned for the challenge and sought solutions to the hypothetical dangers that arose, even infamy and death. It did not seem possible to me to overcome so much. Then I had an idea: Genevera could tie a knotted rope to the window, and I could climb and descend it without risk. We agreed, and with the help of Astanna, I happily passed the rest of that day on the subject of love. Then after many more sweet words and abundant tears, Astanna escorted me out the door.

Book 2. Chapter 13.

Peregrino celebrates his return with his mother, relatives, friends, and the Duke. At a banquet, he hears that Genevera's father has promised her in marriage to a young man from Reggio Emilia. Peregrino returns to Genevera by way of the rope ladder.

The city quickly learned of my return, so I could not keep my presence there a secret any longer. That same evening, I met up with Acate, and we spoke about Genevera as we walked together to my family's house. There my mother greeted me with the same loving tenderness and warmth that Lamia offered Demetrius. After I rejoiced with relatives, friends, and servants, the next morning I paid my respects to the Duke, who celebrated my return with no less enthusiasm than Menelaus did Ulysses when he recalled the destruction of Troy. All the city vied for my attention – it felt as if Roman assemblies had been convened.

A few days passed, and I went to dine with some relatives and friends. We were speaking about various matters between courses when I thought I heard it said that Angelo's daughter had been promised in marriage to a gentleman from Reggio Emilia. That news pained me as much as it did Tereus to learn that his son was his meal. My colour changed, as did my mind and heart, and I thought I would pass out. I could not say what cruel or unheard-of way to die had seized me. I slipped away from the banquet.

The next day, I marched to Genevera's house full of anger, love, and disdain. There I adopted every cleverness and secret sign to request a brief audience in the place where we had previously talked in order to find out if there was any foundation to the gossip. That night, armed with my knotted rope ladder, I went to Genevera's garden under the designated window. I found a string to which I tied my rope. It was hoisted and secured, according to our plan.

I stripped down to my *farseto* in order to make the climb. Never was there a dried autumnal leaf less securely attached to its branch than were my legs to the rope's knots. When I looked up, it was like seeing Aegeus awaiting his victorious son. As I hoisted myself closer and closer to the window, I felt as if I had traversed all of the kingdom of Dis, passing Persephone, Charon, and Cerberus.

When I finally reached the place in one piece, I took my seat where I could speak with Genevera. She welcomed me with a greeting more divine than ever Alcmena gave to Jove, or Venus to her Adonis, or Deianira to Hercules. No greater ardour was ever seen or expressed in caresses than the splendid greeting she gave me.

Book 2. Chapter 14.

Peregrino notices Genevera's dress, and he questions Genevera concerning the gossip about her engagement.

I am not sure why, but Genevera was wearing the same dress she had worn when she reassured me during her fishing outing with Polyxena.[3] Genevera had changed as a consequence of spending long hours alone in her room because of her mother's suspicions that Genevera was secretly in love. But I feared her appearance might also be influenced by her imminent marriage to another.

Considering the time and circumstances there, I broached our discussion by saying: "My lady, I don't believe it's necessary to repeat to you with more and different words or flatteries how much I have always loved you since the moment when you first appeared to me. You can see how much I've respected your honour from how I have been abiding, discreet,

---

3   The dress Genevera wore on that outing is described in 1.38. Here we learn that Polyxena must also have been in the group of ladies who accompanied Genevera, including the participants in the love debate: Lucrezia, Camilla, and Lionora.

and careful. Moreover, I'll happily accept anything you demand of me because I know you are wise, noble, and distinguished, and you wouldn't think to make an unfitting request. I'm sure you don't need me to swear on this to convince you. If your opinion toward me has changed, I beg you to tell me clearly, because I wish only to fulfil your will and pleasure. Moreover, if I speak briefly and to the point, please excuse me, because I don't know who started this story, but you who are better informed of the truth can correct or fill in any uncertainties with what is certain.

"Yesterday at dinner with company, I heard said that Angelo's daughter was soon to be married in Reggio Emilia. This news was a blow that drained me of blood and appetite, and I said to myself, 'O wasted efforts, O long and useless suffering! Where has it gotten me? O lady crueller than cruelty itself, how is it possible for your heart to tell you so insipidly to abandon the one who loves you above all else?' Even before I heard the gossip, I tried to learn the truth from you and remind you that our love depends on your will. Whatever has happened or shall happen, if you know some secret, I implore you not to hide it from me. If I've ever earned your trust, don't deny me an answer, because hiding things that are out in the open is not such a prudent act, but one that invites meddling, and I know you to be a lady of consummate prudence."

I spoke through tears and heartfelt sobs, and my lady took pity.

Book 2. Chapter 15.

Genevera tells Peregrino that she is going to Reggio Emilia to attend the baptism of her cousin's first child. She suggests that Peregrino approach her parents about marriage arrangements.

My peerless lady was poised at the window with no less majesty than Juno sitting on her celestial throne. In another corner of the room a candle of pure wax burned clear and bright. Whiter than new snow, it illuminated the room through the light of her eyes more than the power of its flame. Whenever she glanced up or down, the room brightened or dimmed. It was a heavenly marvel to see the blazing of her sublime eyes as she spoke; even the firmament would have yielded to her without a fight.

She absorbed my words and replied: "My answer will not seem mysterious if you listen willingly and love faithfully. Your love and faith through sufferings, the passing of time, obstacles, and manifest dangers have shown me clearly what you mean to me. It pains me not to be now what my heart desires, so you could understand how deeply I love and respect you. However, what is deferred is not denied, if the will of the free giver saves it to disburse at a more appropriate time. I have no knowledge about what you have heard, so I will not be able to answer you as fully as your heart desires. But I assure you, only God knows what the future brings.

"I prefer not to say now what I would do if obedience to my father should impose another on me. Nevertheless, if your heart burns on this subject, it would not be unheard of for you to take up the matter properly with those whose consent can increase our love and augment our reputation. In this way, we will show we behave with the proper decorum.

"Perhaps the gossip grew out of this: Three days ago, my cousin gave birth for the first time, and she invited me to the baptism, which will be celebrated next Sunday in the church in Reggio Emilia. Maybe some busybody, more intent on the business of others than his own, assumed my trip had some other aim. I will go, and since it cannot be otherwise, do not be vexed.

"Please do not think of coming along, either. Since the time when you were arrested, my mother has been suspicious of you, and you could harm your standing and mine, and give her a reason to object to what you so much desire. My mother frequently praises you when speaking to me in order to gauge my reaction, but the more she says, the more I remain quiet, so she will never guess my feelings. She has spied on my interactions with Astanna in a thousand clever ways, and all the while I behave properly and faithfully. She repeatedly asks, though, what happened to my belt, so I pretend it was stolen. She would never imagine, however, where it has been. Now keep the faith and do not doubt. Your toils have not been in vain."

Book 2. Chapter 16.

Genevera and Peregrino discuss the belt and their feelings.

Since we were on the topic of the belt, I wanted to put to rest any previous suspicions and pre-empt future ones, so I said to her: "My lady, I came to you as your servant; now I leave as your slave because the greatness of your spirit, which is founded on true wisdom, matches the outpouring of love you show me. The heavens may turn as they please, for in good fortune or in bad, I'll remain your ever-devoted servant. I thank you above all for the good opinion you've always shown in my regard.

"Since we've broached the subject of the belt, I'd like to suggest that, if you agree, you take it back. You could always say that it must've been hiding in some chest, which you chanced to find again. If anyone should imply something questionable concerning the falcon, you could always get a gem setter to remove it from around your trees, and you could hold close those gems to remind you of me, for which I'll always be grateful, because you've brought me from death to life."

After I said these words, she gazed directly at me, which melted me more than the sun does the snow, and she said, "Peregrino, I would always agree with your position when it is founded on solid reasons. But I believe that, if we did this, we would give more fuel to the fire of suspicion. That spark went out as soon as it flashed. If the belt were to reappear now, the coincidence of your return would give the strong impression that you had possessed it. Therefore, you keep it, and may it be yours always. But please be so kind to allow me to see it again, so I can give thanks that you have richly exalted a lowly object, which I had given to you, not for its dignity, but as a faithful memento of one who loves you."

So, I drew forth the belt and said to her: "I pray God that this belt binds and increases your passion to the same degree it did for me when you first gave it to me."

Modestly smiling, she said, "A rough and turbulent sea is not changed by higher winds." She took the belt in her lovely ivory hands and, examining it again, praised its fine craftsmanship, then she set it aside. I begged her to allow it to spend the night in her room, where her father would never enter. In the end, she didn't object to my persistent pleading. She moved the belt from the window ledge to her virginal bed. She returned to her place, and we remained in hushed thought.

Finally, she broke the silence, stating: "Peregrino, for God's sake, what is this? I feel such inner anguish!"

I, who was experiencing far greater pain, comforted her by saying, "These tremors, which manifest as sighs, arise from our soul, or perhaps from some star's influence. You shouldn't fear them, since they're empty and have no effect, something like sleeplessness. However, to make you aware of everything that might interrupt or change our love, I want you to be very careful not to give credence to anything negative anybody says about me when I'm not around. Our city is full of slanderers. Any one of them could make something up in an attempt to break our love, which, even through no fault of ours, could weaken our bond. So, be unreadable; make like one entirely deaf, plug your ears, and don't believe everything like a gullible sort. Even if you should doubt the solidity of our love's foundation in some part, you must not fear asking me about it, so that I can defend my innocence."

As I spoke, I was shivering in summertime and languishing without running a fever. I knew that fear was only an anticipation of evil, and although I wanted to reassure her, the blood to my own heart was beginning to freeze. Amorous words became hesitantly tepid between us; love was insipid, our sighs truncated, and our glances sidelong, such that Nature herself was left marvelling.

Book 2. Chapter 17.

Genevera's parents overhear weeping, and Anastasia enters her daughter's bedroom just as Peregrino ducks out of sight. Genevera claims that she grieves for her late brother. Anastasia sees the belt her daughter left on the bed and slips it under her robe.

The sun's gatekeeper was giving the first indications of Phoebus's arrival when we were warned by Astanna that I should leave quickly because Genevera's parents had heard our murmuring from their bedroom. We repeated our goodbyes with tears and sighs, accompanying them with humble, sweet words, blaming ourselves out of fear that our love had been discovered.

I wasn't quite ready to go when I heard Anastasia say, "Genevera, open this door."

I immediately closed the window and withdrew from it.

Who knows what maternal instinct caused Anastasia to veer from her custom and enter Genevera's bedroom? She found Genevera clothed, trembling, crying, and sighing. Startled, Genevera asked her why she had stormed in, since the dewy air was more conducive to rest than to anything else.

Her clever and suspicious mother replied that she had heard such weeping as to disturb her peaceful sleep, so she came to console Genevera. With curious and suspicious insistence, she asked Genevera what had caused her to cry.

Genevera answered that it was her brother's death.

Her mother retorted, "Seeing you dressed in colourful garments again with your hair done and awake at this hour contrasts sharply with grief for a sibling. You've been neglectful of good works, and such a lost, pensive expression doesn't accord with your young age. You eat and sleep very little, and flee to your bedroom, where you continually read and write of love. When I consider this, along with recent events, I have reason to believe your life has taken a bad turn, and if a rumour should get around, it could ruin our reputation, which would make your life worse than death. So, I'm here to encourage you to correct your ways and aim for the virtuous and modest goals you learned from me.

"If some little love spark has touched your heart, snuff it out, and don't believe in it, because it'll bring about our ruin. As your mother, I might sympathize with you, but consider the anger and violence it might arouse in your brothers. Please set yourself to extinguishing any wicked feelings, if you have any."

I could overhear Anastasia from where I was, halfway out the window with one foot on the ladder. By heaven's bad luck, Anastasia had abruptly entered the room before Genevera could hide the belt I had returned, which was lying forgotten on her bed. What's more, the belt contained one of Genevera's love letters to me, which I had saved out of the greatest tenderness.

Without Genevera realizing it, her wily mother swiped the belt and surreptitiously concealed it under her robe. After a while longer, she exhorted Genevera to lead a better life and fell silent.

Genevera, almost losing her patience by this point, responded in this way ...

Book 2. Chapter 18.

Genevera defends herself to her mother. Peregrino descends the rope ladder to leave, but is picked up by the night watchmen as soon as he emerges from the gate of Genevera's house onto the street. The neighbour, Petrutio, makes new allegations against Peregrino.

Genevera: "If my tender years have been modest and tempered, there should be no reason to think my more mature ones will be lustful and licentious. Just because I am a diligent and solitary reader, and well dressed, you need not attribute to me any evil, since these are the necessary and proper attributes of virgins. Because I have been chaste and modest, I do not believe that an evil opinion can harm me. By now my life is what it is, and shall not improve through praise or be diminished through baseless accusations. Even if evildoers and detractors conspired against me, citing some infamy, they would find in me neither its origin nor its end.

"You can vaunt that in this age, in which so many insolent youths have been censored and punished, I have acquitted myself most admirably. Even if I amuse myself dressing up or reading or singing or playing music, none of these constitutes a vice, since similar pastimes were attributed to Minerva and her companions. What strictly virtuous temple does not permit its vestals discreet and mild pleasures? Do you not know that a bow pulled too taut either breaks or becomes so loose that it is useless? Living in this way, between two extremes, I will preserve myself so as to cause you no shame and myself no harm. Rest assured of this."

Age had taught her mother a thing or two, and she had formed the impression from the rediscovered belt that her daughter's virtue had nearly been violated. Nevertheless, she gave no indication of this, preferring to squelch her daughter's boldness in another way. O how difficult it is to trick Ulysses, O how arduous it is to fool Argos, O how impossible it is with a lie to extinguish the truth when it shines like the sun!

As she was about to leave, Anastasia turned and said, "The merchandise gives a clear indication of the merchants. Be with God, and rest your mind and body."

Her remark pierced my heart, and I thought of the myriad disgraces that could befall me. Even with so many possibilities racing through my distracted mind, however, I could not discern how Anastasia had guessed the truth. After I heard her words, I began to doubt Genevera's youthful fortitude, and I became frightened. I did not dare climb back up or make my way down. Her mother could easily return, so that way was out for me; but if I descended, I feared Genevera might neglect to remove the ladder, or if she unsecured it too soon, I might end up falling. In the end, I thought it best to go back up to the window and make my presence known.

Genevera immediately came to me with great modesty, as soon as I reappeared. I reminded her to love and obey her mother and not undo the rope until she was sure I had reached the ground. Reassured by her promise, though not without great fear, I made my descent. Then I gathered the ladder and quietly left the garden, accompanied only by love.

On the street, I heard a group of men nearing Petrutio's house. The sun rose bright on a new day, indicating it was time for the night watchmen to return home. They spotted me just in front of Petrutio's gate, seized me, and tied me up with heavier ropes than those needed to secure the largest ship.

Meanwhile, Anastasia had the proof of our love, given my capture, the belt, along with the letter she read and other hints she had accumulated in the past, but she dissembled everything.

Instead, Petrutio armed himself with new defamatory accusations against me. I was led to a private trial with only the Duke sitting in judgment, and I laid out my unfortunate case to him.

Book 2. Chapter 19.

Peregrino convinces the Duke to pass a mild sentence on his actions.

Peregrino: "Greatest ruler, it is true that nothing is more fitting or worthy of higher commendation than protecting one's subjects, more so through clemency and generosity than rigidity and austerity, because we celebrate and admire mildness most among all the virtues, since it renders one most like God. This is an outstanding gift no matter where we live on earth: we should greet one another, pardon delinquents, and be indulgent to supplicants with mildness. If we are indebted to everyone out of piety, we are even more so toward those on whom we depend and with whom we have had longstanding, honourable social ties.

"I am convinced you are not so ungrateful nor such an unjust arbiter of things that you would disregard the great devotion and reverence I have for your position. If through my long service I have merited pardon for the most serious sins – not these bandied accusatory inventions – so much so that I accuse myself and confess to have inadvertently sinned, for this I deserve forgiveness. Any shortcoming arising out of piety, not out of wickedness, should not be considered a vice. Love is to blame for my capture. A rotten night, lack of pleasure, great danger, a heavy burden to carry, the quarrel I anticipate from my lady, and these last five years' worth of suffering all serve as my penance already.

"So, please, Lord, do not unleash your anger, which is the enemy of good counsel, and do not be too accommodating of false accusers who are the pestilential ruin not only of private affairs but of public and powerful matters as well. In this regard, divine Pythagoras commanded that the swallow – because it chitters incessantly – not be kept inside the house. Likewise, you have always rightly guarded yourself against garrulousness as the supreme enemy. Today there is no ruler in all the world with so much nobility, humanity, splendour of justice, rectitude, keenness in the good and best arts and in every other praiseworthy pursuit as you. Your dignity in judgment is as great as your generosity in pardoning. Therefore, be indulgent of a small mistake, since it amounts to a slight to reputation more than any indication of true wickedness in the soul.

"Decius Mundus, a Roman youth of the equestrian order, seized by vehement passion for Paulina, a Roman patrician and most chaste matron, succeeded in violating her with the assistance of the head priest of the Temple of Isis. The youth boasted of the adultery he had committed and showed in fifty thousand ways how he had behaved. The lady, along with her husband Saturnine, given the grave offence, complained to the emperor Tiberius, who after hanging the priests and burning the temple with its statue of Anubis, merely condemned Mundus to exile because he did not believe that Mundus's act, which stemmed from a rabid, urgent love, deserved any greater punishment.

"Ruler, since you have the freedom to change or reduce the sentence or the punishment, see to it that you allow me to feel you are my Lord, and I remain your servant."

With a happy and compassionate expression on his face, the generous ruler promised me a lenient and wholly affectionate punishment and left me in peace, knowing that the one who complained of me was not doing so without some bias.

Book 2. Chapter 20.

Peregrino insults Petrutio one more time before the Duke dismisses both of them. Acate walks Peregrino home, and the two men discuss the effects of love. Acate urges Peregrino to desist in his service to Love.

Although the sentence was passed satisfactorily with love and reason, vacuous Petrutio hurled accusations at me and complained how unfair and partial the judgment was.

Therefore, I boldly retorted: "O Petrutio, you vile-headed, wayward sheep! You toga-wearing vulture! Doesn't it seem just and reasonable for our ruler to consider my loyal service and virtue, then rule in my favour, when in similar cases among the gods they determined in much the same manner?

"Paris, conquered by a similar passion, awarded Venus the apple. Sometimes one person determines a course of action from impulses, which others deem precisely counter to what's right. The strong warrior Ajax saw poor Ulysses take precedence. Isn't that what great Hercules did among the illustrious Greek heroes when Palamedes was condemned with false insinuations? It's time you give your loose tongue a rest, and consider safeguarding your daughter's reputation. Think about it: it's certainly not in your power to prohibit all traffic on a public street, and even though your house is private to you, the street is common to all. My nocturnal stroll shouldn't concern you so much, since it wasn't aimed at evil ends."

The ruler exercised his authority to put an end to the exchange of insults, and each of us left his presence reconciled.

Acate walked me home. Along the way, he chided me gently, saying: "Peregrino, it is time to return the bow and arrow to cruel Cupid. Man should regulate his own life by living it not merely for himself, but also for the benefit of his city, household, parents, and friends. What glory, what praise can there be for you and your posterity if you carry on like this? Our ruler does well to foster reason, as well as good behaviour.

"Cato the Censor was no less useful to Rome than was Scipio Africanus's military prowess. If man only had to attend to his bodily needs, he'd be the basest animal in the world. Virtue, manners, and the well-ordered life are what distinguish rational creatures. Do you think love wreaks little havoc because it's universal? Its offences, which many people don't seek, can and should be freely avenged. O put aside this great infamy or you'll deprive yourself of life besides being a plague on us."

Peregrino: "Acate, if only you experienced one time how great Love's blessing is, you'd accept every suffering, even the most burdensome."

Acate: "Peregrino, what do my just admonitions have to do with your ravings?"

P: "I want you to understand how powerful Love is. When I entered Genevera's house, my mind was on the verge of being free of this fire."

A: "Why didn't you free yourself then?"

P: "I'll tell you. When my lady appeared, my insides began to roil, my eyes were dazzled by so much light and couldn't bear to look on her; the colour of my face changed more than once, and my tongue remained mute. I experienced what happens to the ashy remnants of a fire when it's relit: what seemed extinct immediately sparked again. And here is proof of our immortal God's power: Genevera's divine words of comfort and sweet laughter turned to joy every pain I suffered in Arabia.

"O God, how sweet it is that our small labours can bring about what feels like a rose garden in full bloom! Believe me, Acate, there's no punishment or suffering that can or should delay this joy or diminish it even a little."

A: "Peregrino, if you received an equal measure of pleasure and delight in exchange for the considerable sadness you endure in the course of your misguided pursuits, you could perhaps consider yourself happy. But what prudent, wise, and careful man would ever concede that the licentious and lustful life contained in itself any virtue?"

P: "Acate, we are greatly indebted to the Lord Love for the many graces conferred on us."

A: "Oh my, how flighty and delirious you are! What nonsense is this?"

P: "Love makes man prudently adapt as each situation demands to be keen, productive, generous, unvanquished, secure, refined, discreet, and tolerant."

A: "Didn't you realize when you were in prison as a consequence of pursuing her sensuality that these qualities weren't so constant and unconquerable as you represent them now? You're the type of man who gets burned as soon as he sees fire. O how much damage is done when you prefer your fictions to the truth in guiding your wicked undertakings, when all that's left are puffs of dark smoke!

"Do you see how shamefully you prefer shadows to light, death to life, ignorance to prudence, blindness to vision, misery to glory, cowardice to strength, poverty to wealth, servitude to freedom, aridity to fecundity, bitterness to sweetness, and the worst to the good? What holy, religious, just, pious, honourable, and worthy thing in heaven or on earth contains in itself these abominable passions of yours? Believe you me, only virtuous individuals have a share in heaven and earth!

"Do not believe that noble and famous men have wasted their time in similar pursuits and ascribed them to God, because what comes from this lustful desire is ceaseless daring and bitter disappointment; vehement indignation for the offence against God, one's neighbour, and oneself; wars, abductions, injuries, frauds, fires, and murders. Instead, in all things man sets himself against God, his soul, and his honour. This is the condition of impatient love, which always demands whatever it desires.

"The man who thinks of nothing but what he loves is without judgment, reason, discretion, and natural discourse, and even though it may be impossible to have what he loves, he has no clue how to console himself or find a remedy for his condition. When he feels certain longings, he grows agitated, breaks down, and destroys himself.

"Virtue, however, rises to heaven, resists vice, rejects the corruptive beginnings of matters poorly undertaken, and dissipates every malignity. This is the medicine for all the passions and sensory appetites; this is what consumes every sadness and confounds every form of cowardice; this is the true generation and creation of the high God; this is the holy and religious reward for endured suffering; and this is what must be venerated and adored by those who wish to love and embrace."

P: "Acate, as much as it is in my power, I'll adhere to your will."

A: "The will is born of advice, and willing and not willing proceeds from it. While you're still within sight of good health, seize it, because every good that's accumulated crowds out baser inclinations. It's better to keep yourself healthy than to need medicine and rest in order to get well again. The memories of the torments you've endured should be enough to frighten you."

P: "I'll respect what you say."

A: "Do not put it off."

P: "We've arrived home. Let's close here."

Book 2. Chapter 21.

Anastasia decides to seal the window Peregrino has used to access the room of Genevera's late brother by means of the rope ladder.

Although she quite regretted my capture, Anastasia tacitly acknowledged it was my own fault. When she was alone in her study, she began to admire the craftsmanship of the belt and its falcon, whose meaning she easily recognized. She put the belt away, concealed her outward anger, and went to Genevera's room.

There they were: disdain incited Anastasia, and charity calmed her; her cruelty waxed and waned. She was on the verge of speaking, then remained silent, and she gnawed from within. The prospect of an argument with Angelo weighed on her; but remaining silent would witness to her consent.

Sending Genevera to some nearby relatives' house was not a praiseworthy idea, she thought to herself. It was bad enough to have a sinner under one's roof, let alone spread shame to another's home.

After a long silence, looking again at that window that was my refuge, Anastasia said that it was too drafty and could easily bring sickness. So, she decided to have it renovated to face a direction that might draw more healthful air. To her words, she didn't delay adding action: she had it closed off right away with some old stone.

She also didn't wait to order everyone else out of Genevera's room. Then Anastasia moved closer to her daughter, and with a show of compassion, said …

Book 2. Chapter 22.

Anastasia breaks the news to Genevera that she and Angelo have promised her in marriage to a gentleman from Reggio Emilia, and she encourages her again to extinguish any flame of love within her heart.

Anastasia: "Genevera, dear, if perhaps you believe your father and I have been slow or lax in our concern for your comfort and honour, that is not the case. Instead, we're as attentive and eager for your happiness as ever. The problem is due to these wicked times in which it's impossible to carry out what God, nature, and our responsibilities demand of us, though we're encouraged by your virtue, education, and modesty. Therefore, just as we are understanding toward you, we believe you will be obedient to our wish.

"Although you deprive us of your usual sweet disposition, we're only too happy to look after your perpetual good rather than dwell on the lack of filial affection you show. So that you can understand what your future holds, I'll spell it out for you: we have promised you in marriage to a rich, young, wise, handsome, and well-mannered gentleman, who's beloved by all and considered the pre-eminent man in the city of Reggio Emilia, where you've been invited by your cousin for this purpose.

"Before we came to this happy decision, we carefully considered the status and quality of our city's prospects, because we wanted to keep you nearby for our consoling company. When we examined every case, however, we couldn't find here an eligible bachelor worthy of you. Aurelio's son Francesco has already exchanged vows and consummated marriage with the daughter of Cesare, as have Sigismondo's son Alberto with Galvano's sister, and Antonio's son Peregrino with Petrutio's daughter Lionora. There's no other man equal to your dignity here.

"We know these matters shouldn't perturb you much, since you aren't currently promised in body or mind to any living person. But even if some little flame sputtered in your breast, extinguish it, because a marriage with an unhappy beginning rarely leads to lasting love. This happens when wretched lovers bear jealousies and sufferings, and waste their time and thoughts in pursuit of love. They constantly remind and accuse each together, which is worse than death. I'm not saying this because I believe this is the case with you. As your mother, I'm simply reminding you of what could happen."

After she spoke these words, Anastasia squeezed her daughter's hand, gave her a kiss, and ended there.

Book 2. Chapter 23.

Genevera conceals her true feelings and instead divulges to her mother that she must refuse marriage because she was called to a religious vocation five years ago. Anastasia is surprised and counters with various arguments against the cloistered life.

Genevera absorbed her mother's words. Although her tormented heart squeezed keenly within her, she feigned dignified composure and replied: "If there was ever a person I was bound to obey, it is you for the motherly attention and great affection you have always shown to me. The suffering I feel at not being able to satisfy you is as great as the joy you were expecting from me. Since you have broached this subject, it pains me to tell you that I must reject your parental generosity in readily anticipating the needs of natural virginal inclinations. However, if I am not to break my vow to God, you must change course. What you thought would offer me great pleasure will instead represent for me a failure to uphold a vow.

"Five years ago, I was moved by a divine vision to restrain my soul, which was beginning to err from its principles. I began contemplating the dignity of the separated substances, which cannot be attained by any other means than by pursuing the glory of virginity. I so enjoyed the inspiration offered by contemplative study that I became convinced I would dedicate the remainder of my life to a religious vocation. Since you are wise, pious, and religious, you must reassure and strengthen me to persevere, because you know it is a capital sin to lie to God – as much for the one who falls short of fulfilling her promise as it is for the one who gives occasion for her to break it. Therefore, most patient mother, do not resist what is divinely inspired in pursuit of transitory delight. Countering what God has inspired would lead to eternal punishment. I am resolved to live according to this, my final, will."

Genevera's mother was thunderstruck at her prompt, well-composed response, displaying keen intelligence, graceful words, and seriousness of purpose. She understood clearly that nothing short of death could extinguish Genevera's love. Still, Anastasia tried with modest, sweet words to change her daughter's mind, reminding her how difficult, if not impossible, it would be to repress the burning longings of the flesh, ever contending with her spirit, but also to avoid the snares of Love, which abound in all places, both secular and sacred. The piazzas, streets, crossroads, and houses, indeed all the world burns with this flame of desire. It does not spare youths, adults, or even decrepit elders. It even inflames saints and consumes the heavens.

Anastasia: "Read the Old and New Testaments and you'll see how much those blessed souls suffered in trying to resist desire. Remember their vigils and their austere forms of discipline. You were born and raised with so much freedom. How will you so quickly change your ways? The thoughts you entertain in the leisure of your bedroom do not dictate what you imagine. Between thinking and doing, so much typically happens that a person can lose her way, if she doesn't lose body and soul together. Oftentimes a bad or sinister end comes from such seemingly virtuous promptings. Nature could not endow human beings with anything greater than freedom; and whoever deprives oneself of freedom is a rebel to God and Nature.

"O how grave it is for a person who is free and possesses an excellent character to live under the law of servitude! Among the Egyptians, the pre-eminent animal was the one with a lion's courage, a horse's speed, and a bull's strength. This creature didn't typically fall to any hunters' arrows, but was once captured by fraudulent means – a pit dug into the ground. When it fell into the trap, it remembered its lost freedom and quickly gave up its life. If beasts are so careful to protect their heavenly gift of freedom, what must humans do?

"These thoughts of yours are too choleric and disordered. Believe me, it was some evil spirit, feigning your well-being, which has convinced you to choose a way of life you'll come to regret. Of all the sisters we see in the cloisters, few ever reach that blessedness you suppose you can acquire through your dreams and fantasies. Who ever made a show of embracing childish notions so ardently? I doubt you are delirious enough that you'd choose to cure a small wound by drinking poison.

"O how wretched and misguided is the one who believes death can provide the sedative for one's pain! If you can't live with your virtuous and loving parents in this freedom, how will you live among a thousand vulture-like, scavenging, common, indiscreet, and ignorant women? The convents are stuffed with them, and a clear-sighted person has never set foot in there except out of immaturity, pusillanimity, or fear of poverty.

"What legacy will you leave for yourself if you enter one? We must give greater weight to others' praise or blame, rather than follow our own advice, because we're not very capable judges of our own affairs. If you think back and consider more carefully the first motivation for your decision, you'll realize you must extricate yourself from this notion. You'll only give many people fodder for reappraising your life, and if you fall into the gossip of the crowds, you'll wish you had never been born.

"Perhaps you should consider that among humanity's greatest calamities, the worst is the one that most afflicts the spirit, that is, poverty, which all virtuous acts resist. Is there a more ruinous plague to be found in all the world? How many delicate and noble souls choose this path of dissolution and death, or how many perish in servitude? Poverty has undone the world, prostituted countless naive bodies, dishonoured a thousand temples, and destroyed innumerable cities. This is the ruin of the universe, the violator of chastity. Poverty defeats honour and ruins virtue. Out of poverty a father will sell even his dear children in the public marketplace. This enemy of the religious makes them wicked; and poverty can always be found milling around meretricious and rapacious taverns.

"Obeying will be especially bitter and difficult for you because you're accustomed to command others. There is no greater calamity in this world than to obey one's inferiors who issue their commands more out of insolence than usefulness. You know how much madness great Hercules suffered by having to obey others. This unbearable, disdainful, and vile burden disgusts anyone of a high and worthy spirit. How many people of excellent mind, having lost their wealth, dignity, and titles, have been content with only their liberty? Human beings shouldn't seek anything more doggedly than to live and rejoice, and there's no closer means to do so than through the gift of liberty for which one can die with honour. If you subject yourself to strangers, you'll end up killing yourself out of desperation.

"Consider, poor dear, how many people have devoted themselves to religion by taking solemn vows to religion, then, scorning God and their honour, seek to escape to freedom again without any right. Therefore, my Genevera, do not disdain the great advantages you have or you may be forced to face a worse penance. Your condition doesn't grant you enough knowledge to take your vow without our consent. If some trifling matter has hastily pushed you to promise something you never should have, we can find a way for a priestly blessing to undo it for you.

"Now, change your mind, so you don't vex your father or bring sorrow on your house. Don't sadden your relatives, or deprive your old mother of life. I beg you to be content with your daughterly duty to marry because it's better for you to pursue the active life, rather than the contemplative one. In this way, you can contribute more, and more widely, and be commended by many."

After Anastasia finished speaking, she embraced Genevera tightly, encouraging her to put aside her stubbornness.

Book 2. Chapter 24.

Genevera counters her mother's arguments with many famous examples of chaste women.

Her mother's pleading lacked all power to sway Genevera's resolution. Although she was extremely tired, Genevera answered: "I do not believe human beings are so different that what is conceded to one cannot be accorded to another, since we all come from the same Creator. If it sometimes happens that one person is wiser, more modest, and more chaste than another, it is not due to any defect in God, the first Architect, who is a just giver and a most abundant dispenser of His graces. Instead, it is because the individual soul fails in its duty to control its own bodily prison from domination by the senses, which naturally make incursions among the weakest souls. However, when reason adheres to our principle, then what does not seem easy, even if others consider it difficult? Our will is not subject to that of others unless it has violated itself.

"So many famous ladies have put virginity before motherhood, and celibacy before conjugal union, since it is in each one's free will to choose the more pleasing option. If we wanted to peruse the historical tomes of the Hebrews, Greeks, and Romans, we would find more examples than stars in the sky. In order to preserve the dignity of her virginal state, Atalanta, the Caledonian virgin, pursued a life among the forests, thorny shrubs, glades, hills, and plains. Camilla, the Queen of the Volscians, courageously took up arms, and Turnus could not honour her with a greater title than by calling her a virgin. The Greek Iphigenia showed how much authority rests in chaste virginity by arguing against twenty adversaries. How many with this virtue have prophesied, including Cassandra and Chryse, Apollo's seer? This glorious name of virgin is included even among the signs of the zodiac in Virgo. How many Hebrew, Greek, Lacedemonian, Spartan, Theban, and Roman virgins have submitted to death in order to preserve their state?

"Other ladies have embraced chastity after repudiating marriage. What coerced that bright beacon of Roman chastity, Lucretia, to die, if not love for her lost virginity? This same preference for death extinguished Sychaeus's wife Dido. It would be a never-ending undertaking to recite the infinite number of holy ladies who put the virtue of chastity before every other pleasure. Catherine, the famous Queen of Cyprus, after the tragic loss of her husband, eagerly adhered to the celibate life with the greatest dignity, which she preserved for her kingdom. After the passing of her husband Amadeus, Violante of Savoy remained ever chaste, even though she was left alone at a very tender age. After Roberto Malatesta's death, Elisabetta of Urbino, though she was also still in the flower of her youth, refused every other union with a man and dedicated herself to the religious life with great patience and equanimity. Camilla of Pesaro, the mirror and jewel of all modesty, governed her life with manifest continence and clear virtue in devotion to the departed spirit of her Costantino Sforza.[4]

"If these noblewomen behaved in this way after their consorts' deaths, what must we do for God on Whom all our good depends? Their reach is not curtailed, nor the fervour of their inspired minds diminished, if one considers the good reason behind their objective; every suffering seems a delight. For this reason, I do not consider the urgings of the flesh to be a particular challenge, nor would I anticipate receiving a greater honour if I were killed to receive what my heart most desires: living chastely to the end of life. In this are the glory, praise, and prize of our actions. To the true athlete there is nothing more engaging than continued struggle, rather than sitting in idleness. What thoughtful person wishes to acquire the virtue of continence who does not flee its contrary, such as lascivious glances, improper conversation, and nefarious trysts? By these means a person arrives where her character tends."

Book 2. Chapter 25.

Genevera continues countering Anastasia's argument by citing admirable predecessors who triumphed over poverty.

Genevera: "What spirits of outstanding and excellent mien were ever frightened by poverty, whose burden you consider so bitter and unbearable? It is as if you assumed I wished to subject all the powers of Asia and Africa!

"It takes little to live according to reason, whereas no treasure can satisfy living according to one's appetite. If you consider it well, Lady Poverty is the foundation of cities and the repairer of all broken things. She

---

4 Caterina Cornaro, Queen of Cyprus (d. 1510), was married to James II, who died in 1473. Violante of Savoy (also known as Yolande of Valois, d. 1478) was married to Amadeus IX Duke of Savoy. Roberto Malatesta (d. 1482) had a mistress, Elisabetta Aldobrandini, previously mentioned in 1.31. This reference is probably to his wife, Elisabetta da Montefeltro, whom he married in 1475. After Roberto Malatesta's death, she took vows and lived out her life in various convents in Venice, Urbino, and Ferrara, until her death in the late 1520s. Costanzo I Sforza, Lord of Pesaro, died in 1483, and his wife, Camilla d'Aragona, served as regent for his illegitimate son, Giovanni Sforza.

is rich in grace, free from those who err, and the most deserving of praise in all the world. You know how Poverty was just to Aristides the Greek, benign to Phocion, encouraging to Epaminondas, very wise to Socrates, and discerning to Homer.

"Poverty erected the foundations of Rome's greatness. Gaius Fabricius, Gnaeus Scipio, and Curio so cherished it that they dedicated their daughters to serve the people's inheritance. Because of their poverty, Publicola, the tribute collector of kings, and Agrippa, peacemaker for the Roman people, had their tombs provided by the state. Marcus Attilius Regulus lived gloriously, although he cultivated his modest field in penury.

"Poverty is not what ruins man. Rather, it is man's insolent and greedy appetite that does so. Every good fruit comes from this holy root. Poverty is not the result of our shortcomings; it is a release from greed, and anyone who rejects greed is considered blessed."

Book 2. Chapter 26.

Genevera concludes her three-part speech, corresponding to the religious vows of chastity, poverty, and obedience, emphasizing the virtue of obedience, particularly obedience to God before parents.

Genevera: "Obedience, which you rebuke, is the mediator of all things, both created and not. Heaven, earth, the universe, men, and animals all willingly and naturally obey. If the world lacked this virtue, what would it be like? Serving God is not enslavement but a joyous freedom. Many are the philosophers and great men who have insisted on fleeing from the world in order to rest in the true liberty you call servitude.

"The Thessalian woman St. Anysia did not fear death at the hands of two Romans in order to gain life, which consists of service to virtue. I do not deny, nor am I ashamed, nor do I disdain being an obedient daughter to you. But I can say truthfully that even without your permission I can arrange all that pertains to my well-being, especially where it concerns reverence to the Divine, to which I am obligated more than I am to you. It is possible to secure a priest's assistance in cases of necessity. Although the active life is to be commended, the contemplative one is closer to my heart. So, please, quit your pleading; heaven has destined me for this."

Anastasia felt the full magnitude of Genevera's pain, and she already regretted a thousand times having resorted to a cauterizing iron as the first medicine for Genevera's condition. However, her pride prevented her from turning back now. Anastasia retorted that, were it up to her, she would accept Genevera's choice, but she first had to hear what Angelo determined.

O how difficult it is to feign a smile on a confused and suffering face! O how hard it is to imitate false joys! O how much evil comes to prudent, serious people from the actions and words of drunken ones! Anastasia did not know how to explain this matter to Angelo. She pondered to herself: 'If I mention Peregrino, that'll only fire up Angelo's temper again, though it might be possible to deal with that, as we've always done. If I tell him love has drawn Genevera away from us, he'll surely resort to an evil act. If I tell him I suspect some cause for scandal in her, he'll blame it on me. If I tell him God has inspired her to become a nun, he'll assume she's pregnant or has had some other mishap. If I say nothing, I fear she'll keep communicating with Peregrino because she's so much in love with him, and when Angelo discovers the truth, I'll still be made to suffer!

'What should I do? Who can advise me? Who will help me? This is what happens to anyone who tries to make things easier for others. Has anyone seen anything more obvious in all the world than that Genevera is in love? Who among the living is spared this flame of desire? She burns now, unfortunately, and by doing so, she manifests her nobility. Whoever loves most is worthiest of being loved. We should pardon her youth, her surroundings, and her permissive upbringing.

'If we permit her to go into the convent, then Love, subtle snoop that he is, will divulge it to Peregrino, and he'll follow her there. O how inadequately the convent is cloistered; its gates are never locked to love or gold! A thousand loafers, friars of little worth, spying gossips, washerwomen, gardeners, godmothers, people who claim to be relatives, scribes, doctors, herbalists, and plenty of good-for-nothings are found in the world who'd readily take on the role of wily, amorous go-between. One must always be on one's guard. If Genevera isn't safe under the watchful eye of loving parents in her own house, though, how can I be sure she'll be so under another's roof? The care of others is always more apparent than actual. I've never seen a person who dedicated particular attention to another's discipline. Even the Athenian Phocion, after serving Chabrias for so long, eventually chafed: see how quickly Phocion regretted taking care of Ctesippus after his father Chabrias died.

'Now I understand what I have often heard in the works of wise men: before resorting to weapons, all other recourses must be tried, since every wretched one tends to take desperation as the cure.'

Book 2. Chapter 27.

Anastasia decides to try to break the bond of love between Peregrino and Genevera by using the belt she pilfered to plant jealous anger

*in her daughter toward Peregrino and Lionora. Gasparina, Lionora's
maidservant, carries out the ploy.*

Anastasia: 'It's time to change tactics and make Genevera do out of disdain
what is the most difficult of actions. There's nothing more apt to break or
diminish a strong love than jealous indignation against which nothing can
resist. I must make the belt I found the cause of perpetual disharmony
between Genevera and Peregrino. Word is already out that love reigns between him and Lionora, which can be made to find some confirmation if I
can make Genevera see that Peregrino appears to give the belt to Lionora.'

Once Anastasia had formed this plan, she found the guile to pull it off.
Because Gasparina, Lionora's maidservant, had long been devoted to Anastasia, she had the habit of frequenting her house, where Gasparina was
received according to her status.

One day Gasparina was passing along the road outside Anastasia's house.
Anastasia quietly invited her into the garden and discreetly directed her
to its most overgrown area. They began conversing about various topics
there. Then, with stricken commiseration on her face, Anastasia brought
up Lionora's situation, supposing that if Lionora didn't marry Peregrino,
she'd be left to a spinster's fate, given that scandalous gossip about her was
already circulating. But if, Anastasia hinted, Gasparina could be trusted to
keep a secret, she'd tell her how things could be arranged to bring about
the desired outcome. The servant, who couldn't reason far enough ahead
to recognize where the betrayal was going, assured Anastasia that she
could entrust every secret to her because she promised to keep it safe.

Seeing that the servant was poised to follow in any direction she led her,
Anastasia said: "There is, from what I hear, a great love between Lionora
and a young man who's friendly with Genevera, Antonio's son Peregrino.
I want you to take this belt and go outside the walls of this house. When
you see Genevera sitting outside with me, make as if to pass us right on
by. When I call after you, make some excuse that you're busy with your
errands. Then, when I call you a second time, come, but reluctantly. When
I ask what you're carrying, speak to me through gritted teeth and tell me
you're taking a gift from Peregrino to Lionora."

The servant did as she was told without any excuses or second thoughts.
Gasparina saw the ladies outside as described, and Anastasia called after
her, asking if she would please pause a moment. Gasparina replied that,
as much as she wanted to do so, her other concerns prevented it. However, after being pressed most insistently, Gasparina satisfied Anastasia by
stopping. The clever older woman seized Gasparina around the waist and
demanded to know what she was carrying so furtively.

The maidservant promptly answered her, saying: "Forgive me! I can't tell or show you because it's wrong to divulge the aims of an errand when it concerns the affairs of others. I'd be glad to do anything else for you."

Genevera, distracted and unaware of her imminent upheaval, chimed in with a voice that far surpassed in grace that of any other woman. She warmly encouraged the servant to be persuaded so as not to waste any more time. With great insistence, Gasparina made them promise never to let on through signs or words to others what she was about to say.

After Gasparina received their promises of secrecy, she revealed the belt and told them how Antonio's son Peregrino was sending it – the dearest thing he possessed in the world – to Lionora, asking her to keep it until their engagement could be made public. After the maidservant finished, she pretended to have other matters to attend to and agreed to leave the belt with them for the moment, so that they could admire it.

Anastasia turned to Genevera and said, "Such a worthy gift, and by the worthiest of artisans! Lucky indeed is the lady to whom such a husband is given! Since he has already harvested her fruit, at least he's doing what is fitting to a man of faith. Lionora should be satisfied, for she has done well among the ladies of her age. Nonetheless, I can't admire the choice of adornment. To me, the symbolism doesn't seem proper to the one who sent it or to the one who receives it, since in their case there's no need for vague allusions. If I'm not mistaken, this seems to be the same belt you made with your cousin Domicilia, a most chaste nun."

Genevera: "May admiration not seize your heart. Since the sisters all work from a single pattern, there are bound to be similar copies. You know how their cloisters are full of these trees, so they are fitting to the place and people who do the work; nor is the falcon particularly unusual, since a noble bird is apt to graze on a noble plant. The belt that some wicked servant took from me was not as fine as this one, ornamented with gems like you see here, nor was my work as detailed, since it lacked gold as its true and proper colour, nor did the design of my first attempt completely satisfy me.

"But when God grants me to do what I so desire, that is, to join their secluded cells where I will have the opportunity to devote my time to the task, I hope to equal or surpass this work, not in the ornamentation, but in the grandness of the design. And I pray you allow me to serve that One on Whom my mind is serenely fixed without further delay."

Anastasia was more shocked by her daughter's determination than was Hecuba, the Queen of fallen Troy, when she saw her son Polydorus, a pledge for peace, returned a wretched corpse. Anastasia tearfully begged Genevera to change her mind. If she remained set on this outcome, it would bring about her parents' death.

The arrival of several matrons put an end to their conversation.

After Genevera got up from her place and went to her room, she collapsed in shock, not unlike Hercules after he donned the Nemean lion's pelt. Her voice cracked from drawn, delicate lips; her face paled, her eyes were weighed down by hindsight, her brow arched, and her hurried step was erratic, like that of a priestess of Bacchus. In the end, she made it to her bedroom. Through tears she wailed to herself …

Book 2. Chapter 28.

Genevera vents her anguish alone in her bedroom, but Anastasia overhears her. Anastasia demands that Astanna work to change Genevera's mind.

Genevera: 'Ah, what heaven, what riches, what sweet star can console me through all my anxious and uncertain days fraught with weighty blows? O death, the only refuge for the inconsolable, when will you alleviate my great pain? My star has been falling since my birth. I believe that on that day all the gods conspired against me. So promising was my conception, but my birth was monstrous, my life horrendous, and my end will be torture! O true traitor, was there no other way to satisfy your lust?'

At these words, Anastasia quietly approached, since she had already said goodbye to the group of matrons. She overheard some of these pitiable laments, and now she had the proof of our love. She was about to interrupt Genevera with a bitter scolding when the thought of Angelo's anger and that of her sons gave her pause. She decided to make use of Astanna's services, who she guessed was already well aware of Genevera's secret. Genevera could communicate her passions more familiarly and more trustingly with Astanna.

Resolved, Anastasia called Astanna. Setting aside her better judgment, Anastasia said with a sad and worried expression on her face, "Astanna, Angelo and I took pity on your poor, vulnerable state, and with great charity and compassion, we took you into our home and nourished you. I believe your experience has given you occasion to appreciate this. If your actions, which have long offered clear evidence to the contrary, had in any way corresponded to our pious offerings, we wouldn't be burdened like this: me with worries, and you with guilt for your part. But I hope your next acts will serve to console us both.

"I know you are aware where Genevera's precipitous feelings of love have led her, and what her progress has been in that arena, which in the end has led her to want to become a nun, a clear sign of desperation. When you first realized this, you could've more easily prevented further damage and avoided the suffering in which we now find ourselves. You, who know well what Angelo's temper is like, can suppose what would happen to your life and hers if he were to hear anything about this matter. You must find a way to change Genevera's erring decision. If you believe that distance might cool the stirrings of her obsession, we could try keeping her in voluntary isolation for two or three months. I'm sure that once she doesn't see Peregrino for a while, she'll change her mind. Or if you believe that she could be made to accept another man, speak to her freely and openly so she gets the impression she has options.

"I proposed a fine match to a nobleman to her, but she appeared disgusted, not out of religious zeal, mind you, but out of some secret vow she made of her own accord. If it can be discerned, then we might be able to take care of it. If her father or brothers should hear about this, though, louder wails wouldn't issue from any wounded beast ... which is what she would be. However, if her new religious calling should be sincere, I'll see to fulfilling it right away, if it means body and soul can happily find well-being. Now go, and act prudently, as I believe you're capable."

When Astanna heard Anastasia's words, she remained utterly beside herself, not knowing where to direct her thoughts. It would be senseless to deny the patently obvious. But changing Genevera's stubborn mind seemed like an impossible undertaking. Merely speaking about this matter amounted to a confession of a sin of omission. In the end, not promptly obeying her mistress's will meant risking her own life. When this thought occurred to her, Astanna's first impulse was to run away. Then, pulling herself together, she answered ...

Book 2. Chapter 29.

Astanna is unsuccessful in her attempts to persuade Genevera, who declares her determination to take holy vows. Anastasia confines her daughter to her bedroom, but gives everyone else to believe Genevera is on a spiritual retreat. Genevera and Astanna come up with a plan to deliver a letter from Genevera to Peregrino.

Astanna: "My lady, it'd be beyond my power to acknowledge all the graces I'm in your debt for. My heart's only desire is to repay you, which would extol you no less than it would be a relief to me. If Genevera is Love's captive, it isn't through any fault or knowledge of mine, and I'm not aware that she's transgressed to such a point that we must endure her absence rather than be consoled by her presence. If you think about how she spends her days, you know there's nothing to be found there that's worthy of even the slightest punishment. I suppose it could be that she was called by some kind of divine vision, which comes when the Great Maker wills it, and it'd be very wrong to try to oppose that.

"However, if you want me to sound her out, I could do so to make sure that no sins of hers might threaten us. But I also know that if you force me to take this on, I don't hold more sway than you to convince her to change her mind about anything she's stubbornly set on. But, as much as my cleverness allows, I'll use all of my forces so you'll know my service toward you. With your leave, I'll go and return this afternoon."

Anastasia: "Go and do what you can."

Astanna: "I think of nothing else but to serve you."

Ana: "What outcome do you anticipate?"

Ast: "Worse than you might think, because she's more unyielding than marble."

Ana: "If she doesn't change her mind, she will get a taste for death."

Ast: "But this is the glorious end of true lovers, that between torments and death they'll be made perfect and stable. This path might only confirm the ideas in her head, because love is nourished on similar food. Then again, if you think about it, being a nun is no different from living a perpetual death …"

Ana: "Astanna, these comments of yours are far too unsavoury to me."

Ast: "I speak to you in this way not to offend you, but only to remind you of what the habit of lovers is. Even so, I'll face the danger you command for me because in the moment, action and luck can accomplish more than rumination and prudence."

Ana: "Perhaps she will show you clearly what she keeps naively running on about to me. I realize I'm denying her what she most desires. I'm not so simpleminded that I don't know what lies beneath that pretext of the nun's vow she pretends to want. But if she acts guarded with me, I'll be scornful to her. And if she still perseveres in her fantasy, she'll earn some time to repent willingly in a cell. Now go in peace and quickly bring her back reconciled to me."

Astanna, whose chest throbbed with the anguish of overwhelming thoughts, pretended to be harried by some other chore while she directed her steps straight to Genevera's room. She entered without greeting Genevera in her usual way, but kept to her task at hand.

Highly indignant, Genevera said to her: "What has changed that you enter without any show of respect?"

Astanna: "That's the way of nuns. During this time of day, they keep silent."

G: "You are very prudent! It is not that I want to become a nun, but I would talk about it for a while with the sisters."

A: "But what would that get you?"

G: "It would give my heart some rest from this city, my parents, and that perpetual traitor."

A: "If my question isn't unwelcome, please tell me the cause of your desperation. I understand your words, but not what's behind them."

G: "Astanna, remember that what annoys only doubles my suffering because a punishment meted out to a blameless person causes even more offence."

A: "You're wrong. I'd rather be falsely blamed than truly judged. If the fault is improperly attributed, what pain does it really bring, when your conscience is pure?"

G: "We give advice and good words too freely. If only you felt what I am experiencing, you would determine otherwise. You know how passionately I loved that wicked man whom I dare not name. My heart has not been the same since he mentioned Lionora. I was bound to be betrayed, and yet I never expected to be betrayed so vilely. I never forgave him for it all because I wanted to understand what my heart meant to him. In all of his interactions with me, he was nothing if not loving, such that, even if God and the world had sworn to me, I would not have believed what I saw today with my own eyes."

A: "What happened?"

G: "Ah, my bones quake, my mouth clamps shut, my tongue refuses to speak of his cruel betrayal! That belt that in my delusion I made as a symbol of the love I had for him when I gave it to him ... Today he offered it to Lionora!"

A: "How do you know that?"

G: "Gasparina, Lionora's maid, confided as much to my mother, and in my presence."

A: "How is that? To what end? On what errand? What do your mother and Lionora have in common? This news tries the bounds of belief! I who am not a woman of many words can't fathom such behaviour. Could you read your mother's face? Did she know it was your belt?"

G: "She may have suspected it, given the rich adornment around its border. She muttered to me that it definitely resembled the one I had produced. Admitting it was similar, I denied it was mine, and she believed me. That silly rascal of a serving maid just happened to be passing along the road ... My mother demanded to know what she was carrying, and she explicitly stated it was a gift from Peregrino, son of Antonio, to Lionora. Now see if I am not right to refuse to live in love."

A: "Ah, Peregrino, how could you be such a rotten inept lover? This behaviour doesn't fit even the lowest rustic boor! Genevera, your brave heart can't fail now by withdrawing and renouncing every hope of living."

G: "Does that not seem a virtuous reason to die?"

A: "Maybe for him, yes, but not for you! Who's ever heard that the greatest peace, the most intense obsession, the wildest folly would make one wish for death in order to gratify an enemy? What's the difference then between love and hate if you invariably choose to suffer? There isn't a mind in this world that could think such a shameful thing, much less carry it out. Who'd ever pine for long suffering or death to gratify an enemy? What greater consolation can you offer Peregrino, if it's true he hates you, than to leave the city? Wouldn't that make a public confession of your wicked life? Isn't it more likely everyone will think that he scorned you? Do you believe he should get the glory? He'll always boast of having done more than was imagined, and when the whispering starts – that because of him you were sent away – you'll provide the weapons for both your families.

"Why not try instead to be a girl wiser than her years? What baser act than running away would we expect from prostitutes? I say, when a lover suffers for his beloved, it'd be something to praise only if the suffering between the two were equal, like true friendship. Where did you ever get this idea that one must triumph while the other suffers?

"But if love has joined you together, you must spend by the same coin. If you're still willing to follow my faithful advice, I'll show you the way to save yourself. And if his betrayal is true, you'll be able to confirm it easily, and the suffering will fall to the one who caused it, not to the innocent. It won't cost you much effort."

G: "Astanna, I would be content to follow your advice, but my soul is bitterly offended, and it cannot be consoled."

A: "Genevera, our soul isn't any different from a disposition, which is like an image we make out of wax, which we can alter or melt down at will. Our soul can get offended or rejoice just as easily. Our life is none other than an act of choosing; wherever you incline, that's where your soul will meet you. Now be like the good doctor and seek out your cure by following this different course.

"If Peregrino hates you, you can grant your love to another and in this way show your prudence. If it's true he's betrayed you, he won't pay any more attention to you. He'll move where Love urges him, and if he gets what's typical for him, he'll triumph. Every little bit of suffering you display will only push him to love Lionora more. But if you're serene, he'll quickly realize his error about her and you. If he loves you from the heart, as is likely, he'll do everything in his power to prove himself to you. Believe me, great intimacy was never without passion. You could write him a letter and tell him what an ingrate he is."

G: "O clever advice, O proven astuteness! But if he showed himself rather untrustworthy in matters without much likelihood to turn out, what can be expected of him when things are clear and proven? If he has given so much to Lionora, why would he deny her anything less?"

A: "What numbskull ever exposed his own turpitude?"

G: "Among wretched men, vices pass for virtues."

A: "That's true, just as much as the contentedness of a clear conscience."

While the women were reasoning together, they heard a voice that might've been Minos calling the three Fates to judgment. It bellowed: "Where is that wicked woman? Astanna, where are you?"

Astanna: "Oh, my, Genevera, I fear this dark cloud over me will never dissipate!"

G: "Go confidently, and if she speaks about me, feign ignorance."

A: "What good will it do?"

G: "What proof does she have otherwise?"

A: "God, one's face, and one's depraved conscience all testify to the truth."

G: "How have you sinned?"

A: "In no way."

G: "Then, why are you afraid?"

A: "I fear for you."

G: "Then you do not have enough work, if you take on the cares of others."

Anastasia: "Astanna!"

G: "Go now."

Astanna: "I'm coming."

Ana: "What were you doing?"

Ast: "What you commanded."

Ana: "What has stubborn Genevera decided to do?"

Ast: "She remains as before."

Ana: "O greatest rector of the heavens, why must I always be the one to fix things? Will I let youthful wiliness make a mockery of me? I'm going to divulge her every wickedness to Angelo right now, and what I've pretended to overlook so far, I'll now make clear."

Ast: "Anastasia, remember that she is your flesh and blood! You would certainly be considered cruel and thoughtless if you sought to go against your own issue. Every wild animal seeks to preserve its species, but you wish to destroy yours? How has Genevera sinned so?"

Ana: "She loves him."

Ast: "Doesn't God love, too?"

Ana: "God is modest, just, and holy."

Ast: "Nor is this love shameful."

Ana: "What do you know about it?"

Ast: "The proof is clear."

Ana: "How?"

Ast: "The entire city has an opinion about everyone. When one has a good reputation, that person is hailed as virtuous. Of course, in contrary circumstances, it's also made known. Our city is such that it would make no distinction for one or another if word got around. You know Petrutio. He's a highly respected man. But just look at how the gossip about his daughter spread from one impudent mouth to the next among the people. If that were ever to happen to Genevera, they would wag their tongues just the same. But because your daughter is prudent and wise, and everyone has this opinion of her, why would you want to defame her before God, the world, and your own honour?"

Ana: "You speak as soothsayers do. I renounce her as my daughter, and I repudiate all my previous efforts on her behalf. I am her mother no longer! It's a great disgrace to have conceived such a monster. Whoever hears good about her is quite separated from his wits."

Ast: "Anastasia, you made her, and you can reap what you have sown. I'm blameless in these matters. You rehearse comments in your imagination that go against any good judgment, and you do wrong by causing yourself and others to suffer. It's time for you to pause and rest for the benefit of our shared reputation."

Ana: "Astanna, so that you'll believe I'm not blathering lies, take this letter and keep it with you. Read it when you're alone, and you'll see if she offers any signs of girlish modesty."

Ast: "Oh my, then she has written to him?"

Ana: "Well, thanks be to God, your wits have returned!"

Ast: "I heard nothing about it."

Ana: "There, now you are entirely informed."

Ast: "What does the letter say?"

Ana: "You'll see."

Ast: "Who delivered it?"

Ana: "I'd like to know that."

Ast: "Who do you believe it was?"

Ana: "I have no idea."

Ast: "Even so …"

Ana: "I think it was delivered to her with the belt."

Ast: "I don't understand."

Ana: "Let's put an end to this matter."

Ast: "Now leave it to me. I want to continue my war of words with her."

Ana: "Go, and show Genevera the letter so she can understand the gravity of her error. But bring it back. Find out if this is the reason why she wants to become a nun."

Ast: "Anastasia, salvation is born of sin."

Ana: "Yes, if the heart is contrite."

Ast: "Which heart is inclined more than the one that wishes to leave the world for perpetual penance?"

Ana: "Do you think she'll repent?"

Ast: "I believe so, if she has sinned."

Ana: "Now you can see that for yourself."

Ast: "Heaven isn't judged by its colour. Well, in the end, what is it that you want her to do exactly?"

Ana: "Ask forgiveness and be obedient."

Ast: "Reason wants as much, and virtue commands it. I'll do my duty."

Astanna left Anastasia and went to Genevera's room. With a hint of a smile Astanna tried to cheer her and told her everything in great detail.

But Genevera then replied: "Now you see how I am wounded by my own arms and destroyed! I cannot deny the letter I wrote. Even wishing to fight this, I know the judge is conflicted, and I cannot expect my bad case to end well. If I ask forgiveness, I will declare myself guilty in perpetuity; and then in the guise of a thorough investigator, she will only want to spy on me more. Ah, too gullible faith! Where have you led me in my faithful service? Astanna, please help me."

Astanna: "Genevera, it's no less prudent to flee than hold your ground. Yield to overpowering anger, bide your time, and adapt to her wishes. She who can't do what she wishes should opt for what she can do. Fierce war usually ends in sweet peace. Perhaps this current disagreement will play to your favour because remaining ever dependent is a perpetual death. Don't you believe Anastasia wants your honour and comfort, just as you do? Be of good cheer and agree to her wishes."

Genevera: "I will never do so. I would rather die than break my promise. May God and the world do what they will. I accept my sentence."

Astanna realized this was the end of it. So, she returned to Anastasia, gave her back the letter, and told her Genevera humbly requested one favour: a month's time to decide what was best, since she wished to determine if her vision to become a nun came truly from God or was some kind of deception. "At the end of that time, she'll submit to your wishes and obey whatever you command of a good, meek daughter. Anastasia, as a mother, a noble lady, and a devotee of God, do not deny this requested favour, which would justly be granted even to those condemned to death."

Anastasia listened, not without tears. But still, she feared some kind of danger. She had all of the doors, gates, and windows secured, everywhere it might be possible for someone to enter or exit the house. She locked down Genevera's room and the one next to it where her brother had breathed his last, the room where I had been so happy. Then Anastasia put the word out that Genevera was staying in Ferrara's cathedral on a spiritual retreat, so she wouldn't be disturbed by visits from anyone.

Confined alone to her room and relieved of the burden of going to Reggio, Genevera set to conferring with Astanna. Before she began to write another letter, Genevera wanted to know who would deliver it and what would be gained from it.

In answer Astanna said: "I already told you, this way you'll learn the truth."

Genevera: "I do not like this plan. It is necessary to adapt to the changing circumstances. I will not have any news of Peregrino's comings and goings because I am confined, as you see. If he answers me, there will not be anyone to bring me his letter. I must hear a plan before agreeing to this, so that my second error does not outdo the first. You will need to consider it further, then we will talk."

Astanna: "As I see it, your mother has reached the point where she can't be any more suspicious of what you do, so there's no room for negotiations. It's not as if we could slip from prison on a hint of cleverness. I'll ask her for the time to fulfil a vow I made to heaven for regaining my health. On the way I'll give your letters to my cousin Lena, who'll faithfully deliver them where I tell her and bring news back to you."

G: "That sounds fine, but how will it end if you cannot go to see Lena or she you?"

A: "Don't worry about that. Heaven finds a way. Lovers who already know what to do have no need for instructions. It'll be easy to find a way either to speak or write."

G: "Then you will comfort me by reporting everything you discuss with Peregrino?"

A: "Yes, so you'll know the truth."

G: "That may be too much to expect, given his past betrayals."

A: "Let's leave future things to the future, and deal with present circumstances. I'll test your mother's leniency; and I'll leave your letters with Violante or Lena, whoever I reach first."

G: "Go, and may God lend you aid."

Without any hesitation, Astanna went back to Anastasia and told her: "If I understand correctly, you've decided I'm to share in Genevera's isolation. If this is so, I won't refuse your command; but if you please, first allow me to complete my penance to satisfy a promise I made to God for the return of my health. If you agree and subsequently permit me other duties in Genevera's regard, then I'll be forever indebted to you in life and in death. I ask you this not because confinement to her room isn't agreeable to me, but because I worry you don't trust me, though I adore you on earth like God in heaven."

Reassured by her flattery and perhaps also a tad guilt-ridden, Anastasia readily agreed to allow Astanna make her trip to the church. In fact, she almost released her from having to serve Genevera during her isolation, which was a most unbearable thing for Astanna, since she feared my absence from her. Still our just and clement God permitted me to persevere. After Astanna took her leave of Anastasia, she came with the letter Genevera had written, which was of this tenor ...

Book 2. Chapter 30.

Genevera writes a letter to Peregrino, which begins without any salutation. She claims to know his secret and advises that they put an end to their love before it goes any further. Genevera hands the letter to Astanna, who gives it to Violante.

I write to you not because I hope or believe I could ever trust you again, but only to make you aware of your faults. I hope God will either forgive them or give you what your faithless ways deserve. You have imitated the ancient custom of inciting the wrath of the gods such that they can be placated only by spilling another's blood, as we read in the stories of Iphigenia and Polyxena.

I have discovered your carefully guarded secret: to woo the woman you found by roaming the sewers, and in doing so, you ended up sacrificing your faithful beloved. I do not believe, however, that a person must hate his friend to gratify his enemy. If you will recall, because of me you were never punished in either a civil or criminal sentencing – you could have done at least as much for me. My efforts were not of so little worth (although I have received a sentence of house arrest) that you should bestow my gift to you on a lady who is my inferior.

There is a trait common to insolent ones: they believe they can use others to attain whatever passes through their fantasy. I thank God, who has preserved my glorious prize, which another licentious and lustful girl lost. Even though you do not want to deviate from the truth, as you have done from virtue, you cannot keep insulting me. You can and should put an end to this for the sake of your honour. It would be better never to pursue anything between us, since a small spark could ignite a raging fire far bigger than what Sagunto saw. I am not of such low birth, nor deprived of such loyal defenders, that I will endure being torn apart in this way. You should regret what is, what was, and what might have been, because truly I deserved more gratitude than you have shown to me. Exactly how, when, and why you offended me I leave to you to figure out. But since you are so stealthily prudent, I anticipate you will offer few words of apology and even fewer actions, if there is anything left to you to say or do.

As soon as Genevera finished writing this letter, Astanna did her duty. She had not even set foot in the church before contacting Violante, on whom she discreetly pressed the letter, whispering only two words: "Comfort Peregrino."

Astanna worried that servants might spy or take notice of her actions, so she said little and hurried to return home.

Book 2. Chapter 31.

Peregrino is so shocked by Genevera's letter that he catches a glimpse of the Other World. He shares it with Acate, then Violante. Violante tries unsuccessfully to discover how Genevera is doing. Acate hatches a plan with Peregrino to get him smuggled into the courtyard of Genevera's house on the cart of Faustino the wine-seller.

Ever affectionate Violante, eager to assist me in some pleasing and welcome way, tottered toward my house, her gait showing her age. As soon as she saw me, she smiled sweetly, saying: "Happy are you to whom Love yields! All obey you on high and here below. Love has put away his bow and arrow and kneels before you; Venus reverences and adores you."

I marvelled at her words and asked: "Violante, what good news do you bring me?"

Violante: "You will see for yourself," and she showed me Genevera's letter.

The ark of the covenant was never adored with more veneration by the Jews, nor the tomb of God made man by the Christians, than was that letter with the greatest reverence and humility when I received it in my hands. I gave thanks as best I could and sat down. My hands began to tremble along with my heart. Violante bade farewell and left me alone.

In my imagination, I seemed to be sailing a wind-tossed sea in a frail, leaky dinghy between Scylla and Charybdis as I unsealed the pain-filled letter. My soul bolted in the instant I began to read. I lost my mind. Crazed and terrified, I wailed: "O what traitor causes me to lose what I have laboured for so many years to secure? O seat of my true repose, O most reliable anchor for my little boat, O too credulous sex! O unimagined ruin, is this the comfort I anticipated? Is this how I hoped she would keep her promise?"

Weeping while reading, I was overcome by such a sudden, bitter bile that I didn't notice if Tisiphone and Megaera took me by the right or left hand to visit their father's realm. You see, the voracious dog Cerberus had already bolted free of Persephone's gate. Charon the boatman had already rowed to the shore and with a raucous voice and unkempt beard cried out to me: "Peregrino, I've come for you!" But the last elemental powers within me stopped just short of final death. Wretched Charon made the trip for naught.

I shook myself, like a man suddenly roused from deep slumber. I called for loyal Acate, who had come to me in this time of need to see what had become of me. He saw tears, but could understand nothing.

After some time, I gathered myself together and, raising my eyes to heaven, began: 'O queen mother and daughter of our resounding Lord, who without complaint brought salvation to a fallen world by giving birth, and through whose favour the universe is ruled and governed, by your grace make me worthy to live and praise your name and celebrate you forevermore.'

I had hardly uttered those words in the recesses of my mind when I was surrounded by a bright light that presaged my well-being. Had divine grace not favoured me then, I would be numbered among the spirits of Persephone's clan.

At this point, I was more coherent, and I continued to cry out: "O good God! What monstrous outcome is this, or what unexpected turn of Fortune?"

I faced Acate and asked him through tears what death was. Although it might be fierce and cruel to others, I imagined in that moment that it would be exceedingly tranquil to me.

Acate: "Death is a separation of a weakened body overrun by harmful spirits, in which all of the body's members, slowed in their operations, set themselves in opposition to the vital powers. When the body can no longer fend the spirits off, all vitality dissolves."

Peregrino: "Oh my, what body in all the world more than mine is weak and weary? And yet it does not dissolve!"

A: "Ah, wretched indeed is the one who asks for help by asking for death! But if heaven and nature refuse to gratify you with a girl's glance, how have they really strayed off course? Not only is it necessary that the body be weary, but also that it be overrun with spirits. Nature cannot go against this order."

P: "Then what kind of life will I have without Genevera?"

A: "Whichever one you choose."

P: "Can I continue to suffer because she is unhappy?"

A: "What can you do about that?"

P: "I'll free her."

A: "Is she perhaps in prison?"

P: "Yes!"

A: "How will you do it?"

P: "By force."

A: "You'll be punished by death, according to common and municipal laws."

P: "Love will defend me."

A: "As he did for Achilles and his followers?"

P: "Death brings glory to the one who dies virtuously."

A: "How is this virtuous?"

P: "I'm defending a friend."

A: "What's Genevera offering you?"

P: "Only true friendship. And, from what I can tell, she suffers mistreatment because of me."

A: "That's her father's concern."

P: "He'll kill her."

A: "She made this up."

P: "Still I want to help her."

A: "That's a heavy request; rescue is impossible."

P: "So it might seem to you who banish every thought of love."

A: "What are you complaining about?"

P: "That Genevera is badly in need."

A: "Who says so?"

P: "Her letter."

A: "Make me a copy of it."

P: "Here, just read it."

A: "I'll tell it to you straight: it doesn't matter if you're awake or asleep, you continually vacillate and take the first thing that comes to your mind as some divine omen. This lady claims you're a boastful, arrogant, and vacuous man. It'd be easy for your mad whim to hatch some mishap. Given the state of things, she wouldn't appreciate your attention. On the contrary, she'd shun it as a death sentence.

"Now, just consider if you can ferret out the cause of her complaint. If it's caused by a defect in you, resign yourself and put your soul at rest. But if there's another cause, try not to isolate yourself, which isn't fitting to a faithful man."

Just then Violante approached us. I went up to her and said: "O sweet Violante, my only hope, you couldn't come at a more opportune time! God save you."

Violante: "And you, as well, my Peregrino. Why such a distraught face? What direction are your love matters taking?"

Peregrino: "Read this letter, and see for yourself."

After she read it, she paled, wrinkled her forehead, and couldn't speak, given her keen pain. Setting aside all her other duties, she marched back to Genevera's house. She greeted Genevera's mother and spoke to her about various matters of interest to the women. After some time, she inquired after Genevera's health. She was told that, for the present time, Genevera was taking the country air, and Anastasia said nothing more.

Violante returned to me, lamenting: "O Peregrino, the miserable girl is imprisoned in her own home."

Acate: "Peregrino, every delay suggests cowardice now. Ah, Peregrino, let's summon brave and manly courage to attack her house tonight and search the rooms with our knives at the ready. May all those who sleep meet death, and those who resist be stabbed and suffer! In this way we can save Genevera and get her back."

Peregrino: "Dear Acate, here are my hands outstretched in tearful prayer. I beg you, through our true friendship, don't rescind your promised aid from me now. It's better to die than break faith."

A: "What if she has been sent away out of some suspicion or to punish her more, then what should we do?"

P: "Do not fear: cleverness favours the brave. Hercules, Theseus, Pirithous, Aeneas, and Orpheus all descended into hell to satisfy their desires, and they came back. We'll search every hiding place to the antipodes; we'll go beyond where Ulysses journeyed and even to the realm of Styx to find her again."

A: "O how difficult that'll be!"

P: "That is precisely what marks virtue. I believe it was much more difficult for Aesculapius, the inventor of medicine whose temple was consecrated on the Libyan mountain, to call back an errant soul and make it pose as a statue, turning it to stone in order to evade a god's attentions, than for us to have the free will to choose good or evil. But if man is author of the gods, can he not search carefully all created things? Love and necessity are twined together with interlocking knots. They'll make us bolder than we could ever hope. O great God, O highest Architect, help me, for otherwise I'll fall under this great burden of suffering!"

A: "Do not weary God with your long-winded prayer. He attends to the necessity of eternal reason, and is uncontradictable, unmoving, and indissoluble. Our situation concerns changing Fortune, which mixes in all earthly matters, and one must suffer it as it comes. Be strong and don't permit these sufferings to bend you. Leave this bed and your room, and embrace the mission that'll bring you happiness."

P: "And yet, I am weak."

A: "Rest then."

P: "I'm afraid my assistance will reach her too late."

A: "If Love has the power to transform itself and take other forms, how can it be that it fails you now? If Love were a god, as you say, I'd surrender under his standard and never leave you. But he's a blind imp of little worth, and you persist. Think well on what is best for you to do; and I'll carry out your commands as best I can."

P: "Let's go to her house, gain entrance, and find out where my beloved is."

A: "So this is the undertaking, and this is your plan? The gate is locked, and the walls are high. We're without keys or wings. No man in the house is your friend. How are we to get in? I don't understand."

P: "We can enter through the window that faces the garden."

A: "That was walled up out of suspicion."

P: "Then I'm lost. Help me."

A: "There's a cart driver who sells wine, and he's a very good friend of mine. If you like this idea, I can get him to take you hidden in his cart within their enclosed vineyard. Without him even knowing, I'll put the plan into action. He must pass by Angelo's house, and since it won't be possible to leave the city, he'll stay inside that courtyard because they're on familiar terms. During the night at an appointed hour, you'll go to Genevera's room. If she's there, you can weep and beg an audience with her; if she's not there, you'll be able to leave by the same way you entered.

"If by the grace of your innocence, she permits you to stay with her, you should take the attachments for the rope ladder with you. In that case, at midnight I'll bring the rope ladder to the granary road, where, I believe, there's a window from which you can descend. It's much better to keep a risk secret than display one's guilt openly. But it's also too much to ask that another pay the price of your faults."

P: "Acate, whatever the risk, I accept this plan."

Acate called for Faustino, the cart driver, and distracted him long enough for me to slip into the deepest part of his cart. Everything went according to plan. Angelo warmly welcomed Faustino, who parked his cart near the horse stables.

Book 2. Chapter 32.

Peregrino gets himself smuggled onto Angelo's property by hiding in Faustino's wine cart. Astanna discovers him and eventually convinces Genevera to hear him out.

The hour that drains warmth from one's limbs had arrived when I emerged from the cart. I was on higher alert than the guards who watched over the bodies of Thessaly. But Faustino, who had settled into a mound of hay to sleep that night, noticed me and called out: "Leave my cart be, my friend."

Ever so quietly I responded: "Have no fear, Faustino. I only wanted to nose around to discover if you had a good wine in there!"

Without another word and fleeter than a deer, I bolted to Genevera's room, where, as usual, there was a bright lamp burning. A crack in the wall there satisfied my desirous glance. I was like a puppy at the doorway, considering the possibilities. If I knocked, she wouldn't open; if I just stayed, she wouldn't realize I was there; if I went back the way I had come, Faustino would report me. What could I do? Lord of Love under whose command the universe endures, help me!

Out of desperation, I entreated: "My Lady, have pity, since I am wrongly condemned."

I heard Astanna say to her: "Genevera, it's Peregrino."

Genevera: "Where is that traitor?"

Astanna: "He's here at the door."

G: "Who brought him?"

A: "Love impelled him."

G: "So you believe he loves me?"

A: "These aren't the kinds of dangers that are faced for fun. Just think: he'd face the death penalty if anyone in the house found out."

G: "Well, that was not a sure thing when he was found in Lionora's bedroom!"

A: "That was a mistake, but this time it's done out of overwhelming love."

G: "Make him come back another time."

A: "It'd be better if you found out how he got in here, so that if we make an enemy of him, we'll know how to prevent him from harming our life or our honour."

G: "You can ask him that."

A: "He won't confess that to me."

G: "That is what he usually does."

A: "Hear him out for your own satisfaction."

G: "Listen to the one who stains the innocent through his betrayals?"

A: "What does it hurt to listen to him, when the whole world is full of deceptions?"

G: "Sure, what does it hurt sick people to drink cold water?"

A: "You are only increasing his passion and slighting virtue."

G: "That applies to those who lend an ear to his senseless babbling."

A: "It'll serve you right, girl, if you allow him to sell you black for white."

G: "How can you deny I have been betrayed?"

A: "It might not be his fault."

G: "But whose then? Was it not his belt?"

A: "Maybe it was taken from him and sold to another."

G: "Do you think I misunderstood the words of the servant?"

A: "Reason demands that you not trust such a flighty woman."

G: "She did not believe she was hurting anyone."

A: "One can hardly be pardoned who has divulged another person's secret."

G: "Who do you think it was?"

A: "The one who can tell you is right out there. Enough! What do you want to do about him?"

G: "He can go his merry way."

A: "As you wish. But let me tell you: it was far easier for him to go to Syria and endure slavery for two years for you than it is for you to take ten steps to learn the truth from him. He won't harm you, tell you lies, or accost you. The door's locked; the room's secure; and he's a modest man, humbled before you. Don't be so haughty, since that's a mean disposition."

Genevera was moved by those words, and I saw her get up slowly from her bed wearing only a pure white shirt and come toward me. When she was near enough, I whispered humbly …

Book 2. Chapter 33.

Peregrino begs Genevera's mercy, and she continues to accuse him. Contemplating her beauty, Peregrino is overwhelmed and faints, injuring his arm.

Peregrino: "O Lady, O faith, O conscience! O the countless risks I've undertaken on your behalf, is this my reward? O my lady, you've been duped into considering me your enemy. I beg you by that light of your flashing eyes, listen to a few words. My lady, have pity on my direly painful case; remember your humane pity! Have respect for my long service, and be moved a bit by my suffering. You know how I've been bound to you to command not just my will, but my life.

"Ah, the misfortunes I've accumulated out of too much love! What're you waiting for, cruel one? Every hesitation is detestable. What do you believe you can accomplish through such harshness? My death is due to you in the end. It's not in your power to break off our love. Even though you enchained me, you can't undo those bonds."

She came much closer to me, and with this great generosity of hers, welcomed me in this way: "Go away from here, you wretch with your dissembling face, speaker of lies and composer of pains, bowel of betrayals, lowlife of vices, sacrifice to Persephone, holocaust for Cerberus, and deflowerer of another's virtues! That fire that once burned in me has consumed itself, leaving only ashes. O wicked one, I put out your ardour with my love, which I sacrificed from my life to make you worthier. However, now that I have proof of your betrayals, my mind is made up."

P: "Lady, don't deny me what you would concede even to an enemy, that is a calm audience. Don't believe that some misinterpreted sign is worth more than true service."

Reasoning in this way, I contemplated her unadorned beauty, the natural harmonies of her face without any artifice. Her hair was a brilliantly resplendent golden hue and cascaded in disordered order over her white shoulders, as if she were standing in for Apollo. Her eyes shone so brightly that whenever her eye met another, it was like gazing into a mirror that always rendered your semblance even more pleasing and gracious. That diva, that shining star of a lady, was endowed with every grace. Love and favour coexisted in her. She exuded the perfume of balsam. Those tender, pale limbs of hers, made in the divine grottos from gold and nectar, emanated a fragrance from heaven. I was enthralled by her divine composition, just as Apelles of Kos had been when he painted so wondrously the face of Venus.

I, who couldn't bear to suffer any more, wept continuously, and attributed my bad luck to a cruel and malicious false accusation. Complaining in this way, strained by such great pain, and wearied by so much speech, my body collapsed to the ground out of exhaustion, and the impact dislocated one of my arms.

In the face of so many displays of feminine constancy, I lost my patience and began to say …

Book 2. Chapter 34.

Peregrino unleashes a furious tirade against his lady, and Genevera retorts tersely.

Peregrino: "Ah, prey of the Minotaur, food for Boursiris, fodder for elephants, may Mother Nature devour you in her maw! While you live, may the Furies never leave you in peace; may the three sisters who spin the thread of your life prolong it to your continual misery! May I someday chance to see you blind, deaf, dumb, and begging, decrepit and infirm without human or divine assistance! May your life make you wander as an exile and vagabond in the countries of others; and may your pronouncement, which you judge pious, come to consume you! What poisonous snake could act so cruelly toward just blood?

"Ruthless Love, why do you put up with this? His arrow, which once wounded you, should've been poisoned, so that you perished! Jove, how do you bear to see such impiety? O that you had been prey to the Giants! And you, strumpet Venus, if only Vulcan's net had burned you, so he could see you cremated. Mercury, if only your enemies had beheaded you. And you other gods of the earth and stars, rivers, fonts, fauna, satyrs, dryads, and nymphs of the forests and mountains … may ruin take all of you, so I might find comfort in your misery! Your power is false, lying, and illusory. And you, Saturn, escapee from heaven, if there's any vigour left in you, send down another chaos. Eridanus, glorious river, why didn't you drown Jove like his son, Phaeton?

"I wish heaven's fire would incinerate the entire face of the earth, so no part of it could be found habitable! I wish heaven, earth, men, gods, and everything elemental and pure would clash with one another unto death so the last human vestige would disappear. May Charon, Cerberus, Rhadamanthus and Minos, fierce dogs, tear your reign to pieces. Vulcan, may your furnace burn you up. Pallas Athena, may you be ruined along with your river, Hippocrene, from which sprang the winged horse Pegasus, and the Muses. Moving and fixed stars, superior bodies, extracted potentials, aerial and infernal spirits, may you all be without peace and rest. Cursed be the plant that ever flowers again; and desecrated be the soil that ever produces grain again! Blasted water and you, fierce Neptune, may I be able to see you in such misery that neither you nor anyone else can come to your aid! May all the signs of the zodiac come to ruin, and may the universe remain forevermore without order. Root that never germinated in soil, but rather in an infested womb, cursed fruit, why did you enchain me?"

During this lament, I heard my enemy say: "Whether you are kind or nasty, your complaints will not help you at all."

"Help me, lady," I answered, "and allow me to burn up in this flame. I'm already condemned to death by a thousand sentences, and yet I die again. Satisfy me, my lady, and then leave me to die scorched."

After I said these words, I kissed and embraced the door, and behind it, I heard her mutter under her breath, "How insane! Through threats he seeks mercy."

I immediately retorted: "Lady, I blame and hurt myself because I was born into such dire circumstances."

Genevera: "This is the fruit harvested by the man who plants his seeds poorly."

Book 2. Chapter 35.

Peregrino continues to plead with Genevera.

Peregrino: "O God, lady, which of the world's laws is so corrupted, barbarous, or bleak that it permits punishment before passing the sentence? Where's your dignity, purity, gratitude, your weighty judgment, or your reasonableness, that you condemn me before listening to me? I still haven't heard your accusation, yet you deprive me of a chance to defend myself. Listen first. Then it is in your power to grant me life or death. I'm conquered and bound by your powers. Whatever sentence you pronounce, I'll accept it quietly and contentedly. But first, kindly grant me an audience, through which your splendour and generosity can shine, as much as my sinfulness, and you can understand my extenuating circumstances.

"Lady, firm constancy is worthy of praise, but persistent stubbornness has always rightly been condemned, because it proceeds from ignorance or malice: both are damaging and hateful. I'm not asking anything more of you than that you have enough patience to permit us to clear up the matters besieging our minds.

"Our opinions aren't so divine that they can't err in human judgment. Take the chaste Hebrew woman Susanna, thanklessly accused and publicly paraded to be burned at the stake. By adhering to the purity of truth, she merited salvation; and the false accusers got their just deserts. These precipitous judgments of yours are the ruin of a good and holy life. Your sex, too credulous, and curious to hear evil, goes against God, the world, and every pure conscience. Don't try to pervert such great love. After all, one who knows how to love ardently will also know how to hate cruelly. I've always been faithful to you; and you know from experience that I've always been prompt in serving you. Why, without reason, do you wrongfully cast me away? What afflicts you to listen to your own tales with such sweet patience, and to mine so disparagingly?

"I am still yours, and I want to die yours. Well, say something to this creature barely still alive whom you control more than yourself."

Book 2. Chapter 36.

Genevera responds to Peregrino.

Genevera: "Peregrino, if I thought you were now abstaining from lies and dissimulations, which I have always avoided, then I would be swayed by your entreaties. But because you make a habit of them, relishing nothing more than your next deception, it is more prudent for me to keep some distance from you.

"I am not unaware that people seek what is most natural and convenient for them, and in this they posit a model to imitate, and to veer from that would be sacrilege. Boxers must practise militaristic discipline; scholars pursue rigorous literary studies; poets a sweet, lofty style; and historians vast knowledge. Deceivers, however, find their pleasure in cultivating the cleverness of Ulysses and the deceptiveness of Aeneas or Antenor. I know you have been born, nourished, and educated in the ways of these last ones, since you have repeatedly displayed wickedness in your indecisiveness, wandering, railing, pleading, suffering, and crying. I should have had enough after your first bitter offence without letting them multiply, because every inexcusable wrong redounds on me.

"I would surely be out of my head if I put any faith in what you say. Listening to your words causes me not scant sorrow at the memory of evil done and time wasted. Therefore, if any spark of our first love should remain in you, I beg you to leave me be in whatever peace your disloyal love has left me. If your love does not suffice to grant me such a boon, then I beg and implore that the spark you have for the woman you so eagerly gave the first memento of our love to can prompt in you some compassion for me. Do not seek my death with even sneakier and more secretive means, because if that is what you wish, all you need to do is to speak freely. I am already seeking to hasten my death, since neither God, nor the world or my cruel fate, wishes me to carry on with any honour or happiness."

I heard her spiteful words, and I sat there in no less anguish and shame than did Priam when he suddenly learned that the spawn of the faux horse would provoke his last scream of life on earth.

Finally, rather exasperated, I answered her in this way …

Book 2. Chapter 37.

Peregrino and Genevera continue arguing to the point of exhaustion. Astanna leaves Peregrino in the bedroom adjoining Genevera's room. Later that night, Peregrino enters her room through a door left ajar and considers killing her with his knife. Seeing her divine light reflected in the blade, however, his trembling hand drops the knife, and he returns to the adjoining room.

Peregrino: "Lady, since God and nature have bestowed on you exceptionally high intelligence, and everything between us up to this point has been shared, why're you so terse that you don't allow me to understand the reason for your outrage? We have exchanged a torrent of useless words. It would've been so much better to spend that time in something more satisfying, like gratifying the needs of our love, except that you – through some concoction – are trying to break our bonds of love. If this is what you wanted, you could've fulfilled your desire with far fewer words, that is, if you did not have another objective: namely, insulting me. Change your attitude – because you've wandered very far from the truth! I offer myself up even unto death because a just conscience doesn't feel fear. Any false rumour can quickly be stifled; and impending actions can easily be inferred from what has occurred. Consider if I have ever betrayed you, or acted in any way worthy of the slightest blame. And if I've always been faithful to you, why now when I'm secure in your love would I do anything to annoy you?

"Lady, it isn't possible to go through life without suffering bites from the tongues of vipers and the wicked barking of pestilent minds. For this reason, you must not trust what others say, but rather the actions I've undertaken in adapting to the context and circumstances. What heartless or completely senseless man would expose himself to so many dangers as I have with the goal of losing what he's strived to serve for so long? If you persist in your stubbornness, it must mean you've fallen in love with another or you're extraordinarily ungrateful, which must offend your peerless generosity.

"Lady, true love is patient. A meek, discreet, and serene temperament isn't broken by passion or fury, because nothing in this world can perturb its true conviction, nothing can roil its soul more, than when it causes a man to lose his honour and life. Therefore, go back to the way you were, temper this ferocity, moderate your stubbornness, embrace meekness, remember that forgiveness is the most appropriate response for your sex, and listen willingly to what cannot cause offence.

"Even if I had offended you, what would you do? You could only complain of being served honourably and adoringly! You're delicate – and still so young – why such doggedness in refusing to listen? If you believe a liar, why not believe a denier? If you put your faith in a trickster, why're you so inflexible toward a truthful man? You must believe, lady, that true love doesn't know how to lie. I won't deny whatever you ask of me, not just deeds but also the mere thought of them, because I live with this one aim: to serve and obey you.

"Because you're too credulous, you try to compensate with reticence where there's no need. This biting envy, this foxlike fraudulence, is always disposed in an evil nature to do the worst thing, commit a thousand deceptions, and dissipate our love, but you go on blindly sleeping. You must be careful, not flighty. Do you want false reports to scatter on the wind what we've worked for many years to preserve? Even if you perceived a threat to honour, would it merit the fury you've unleashed, which comes more from appetite than from reason?

"If you're determined to leave me, find some other more honest and appropriate way. I know your sex, given its mutability, doesn't endure anything for long. Answer your begging lover, then, if you please. Note how sad your victory is when it has no rationale. That you win this debate disturbs me very little. What pains me is that against all that is just, an attitude like this can take root in a young breast. You believe too easily, consent to liars, and withdraw into your own head, which are clear indications of a heedless person.

"Perhaps you believe you can prolong this conversation so long that the coming of a new day will force you to depart from me without an answer.

Parting will only fool you. I'd sooner suffer every violent death, because I trust in divine justice, which is always fair and favours the innocent, not permitting the innocent to be wrongfully cast out. Sooner or later, you'll weep for my absence because you disdained my presence.

"Cruel one! What have I gained by suffering so much to love you? What good does it do me to stretch out my arms in supplication? Wretched man, if only I'd never been born, or my mother's milk was poison to me, then I wouldn't have to suffer this split! Others are happy and carefree in love, but in loving, my heart feeds only on unhappiness and misery!

"Lady, why are you so cruel even to yourself? You pervert the order of your most gracious nature, which seems born to love. Tell me: by refusing me, what do you believe you'll gain? Remember that the greatest happiness doesn't rest in worldly things, but in having a good friend. O splendour of beauty, O morning star, O shining sun, O crown among ladies! Why do you cast away your faithful one?"

After I said these words, she left me without excusing herself.

I, who sought nothing but death at this point, closed my weep-wearied eyes and, out of mental anguish and physical exhaustion, I fell into a deep sleep, assuming that some man of the house would find me lying there and kill me. Without moving, I awaited the shadows of death.

Then at some point I stirred. I heard someone coming toward me, thinking it must be my beatifying lady. But another silently opened the door to the adjoining bedroom and ushered me toward it. The intense sun was long spent, such that a canopy of darkness covered Genevera's chaste bed and the ground below, so I couldn't see my sleeping goddess. For my safety, Astanna hid me in the other room. Out of fear of waking Genevera, she left the near door between the two bedrooms cracked and wisely locked the door to the hallway.

I stayed there, deep in thought and regret, until I lost my patience. Sick in body, anxious of mind, and without wise counsel, my love turned to offended contempt. I took out my flashing knife. It was the hour of sweet rest, and I believed my lady was resting her limbs without suspicion. I snuck into her room intending to bathe my wicked hand in her purest blood.

After parting the curtains around her chaste bed, I saw my well-formed lady sleeping formidably.[5] Her heavenly face gave off so much light that it

---

5   As Caviceo has done on previous occasions (i.e., in 2.33, when he described Genevera's hair as cascading in "disordered order"), his play on words here is "formosa donna formosamente dormire." Attractive lady attractively sleeping? Beautiful lady sleeping beautifully? I considered various possibilities before opting for this less exact solution, which hopefully nevertheless conveys the disturbingly light tone that contrasts coldly with what Peregrino intends to do.

reflected off the knife blade, sparking such splendour all around that the sun could offer nothing brighter. Frightened and terrified by such divinity, my soul shrunk back weak and trembling, and I almost fell to the ground like a dead man. I wanted so badly to force my knife to carry out the punishment due her, and I would've done so, had the knife not fallen from my quaking hand. Fearing Genevera might wake, I fled her room without a sound. Then my spirits changed for the better, and I settled back in my designated room.

Book 2. Chapter 38.

The next morning, Peregrino overhears a conversation between Astanna and Genevera. He contemplates Genevera's beauty in the light of dawn. They notice him, and Peregrino insists that Genevera listen to him again.

The herald of the first light of day had already announced dewy aurora, and the lovely birds were already singing their sweet songs and well-tuned harmonies, when I heard my lady ask in a humble voice: "Astanna, how was our friend left?"

Wise and ready, she replied, "Sad, I believe."

Genevera: "Why?"

Astanna: "I heard him wandering around muttering to himself."

G: "The sin was his, so the punishment should be, too."

A: "You could've at least heard him out."

G: "Clear actions have no need for proofs."

A: "Since this is your wish, the time has come then to obey your mother. You're entirely free of Peregrino and have satisfied every debt to him. So, if you never intended to speak of that love again, why did you bother to write him the letter or offer him an audience? Why did you expose him to more dangers and subject yourself to potential scandal for no reason? Sometimes knowing too much isn't knowing. At this point, you should change course."

G: "Astanna, since I seem not to understand faithfully anything under heaven, you would do better to drape your subtle veils of meaning elsewhere."

A: "You'll always be rich in Fortune."

G: "For me this is not about God in heaven or Fortune on earth, but rather that pity and discretion are dead."

A: "Then see to living."

G: "Sure, whoever can!"

A: "You listen to opinion more than truth, which you could've learned at once."

G: "His betrayal shamed me."

A: "Let the one who commits it be ashamed, not the one who suffers it."

G: "I cannot imagine how he entered this place."

A: "Me neither. You should've asked him that."

G: "If he tries that again, he will pay with his life."

A: "And that'll be because of you."

G: "The fault is his."

A: "From what I can gather from your words, which indicate your innermost thoughts, your love was tepid."

G: "What point is there in pining for what cannot be hoped for?"

A: "Then the marriage that has been arranged for you has discouraged you?"

G: "It is already a done deal."

A: "You're sure quick to believe what amounts to complete nonsense!"

They continued with this back and forth, while Genevera emerged from her bed's enclosure wearing a white silk damask slip finished with fine gold thread. I thought I saw Jove in all his majesty.

Wretched me! As I contemplated her great beauty, I rued everything. I contemplated her divine tresses, which were parted in three sections. Her bangs in front draped to her nose; a second section cascaded over her heavenly back; and the third twined atop to give her a crown of such brightness that she would've outshone the sun. Her white neck, the deep blush of her cheeks, and her vermilion lips stoked such a fire in me that the entire ocean could not have extinguished it.

At that moment I said to myself: 'O heavenly and omnipotent God, what do you have on high that's more beautiful than this? I never want to adore another human body. O happy, propitious, and fortunate day, arise and see the one you bless. The heavenly consistory is poorer. Jove weeps; Mars is wounded; Mercury laments; Hercules becomes impatient. The entire kingdom of heaven cries out in complaint.'

In this state, I stood there slack-jawed, and Astanna began to laugh. Genevera inquired the reason. With a conspiratorial grin, Astanna said: "The sun looks upon the sun," and with her eyes she indicated where I was.

Almost in view, I sensed Genevera was quite perturbed. In my direction, she said: "One cannot speak of loyalty with traitors! If you do not desist with your deviousness, you will easily and justifiably bring about your death."

Then, without being invited, I begged her to sit down and listen to all I had to say. She locked her door and settled herself on a seat. These words slipped from my mouth …

Book 2. Chapter 39.

Peregrino and Genevera reconcile when both finally understand what happened to the belt. They eat, then nap. Genevera has a dream and asks Peregrino what it might portend. He expounds on dream theories and offers an interpretation.[6]

Peregrino: "When I compare our once fortunate state to our present calamitous ruin, I feel my insides racked to the marrow. O Fortune, how blind and unstable you are that you exalt the wicked and bring down the good! If you ever sat in judgment of your own honour and actions, you'd flee out of shame. How many innocent spirits and excellent men have you stained and destroyed with your inconstancy and lack of consideration? How many wicked and villainous ones have you exalted on high?

"Don't you see, cruel lady, how my innocence has never sinned, yet you wrongly deprive me? You count the lashes and unbearable sufferings you're determined to mete out to me, but in your ignorance, you never cease to persecute me. Quell your ire for once, and be mindful of your condition. When you're wretched, people shun you; when you're respected, the envy this causes anguishes you. Thus, you find yourself at turns wretched and anxious. Why then, heedless of yourself as you are, are you the cause of so many wrongs? Permit me, please, while preserving your honour, to be able to enjoy in peace this heavenly good of Love, which advances every other man."

Genevera: "Peregrino, you men do not rave deliriously any less than girls when you ascribe every blame and praise for your actions to Fortune, which does not hold sway among prudent people. Moreover, all those men who spoke of generation and corruption and human things never made mention of this matter. It seems too convenient that those who wish to excuse their own mistakes blame some unknown, violent principle in order to demonstrate that they have not wilfully committed a sin. You need to recognize that everything has its own determinate reason. Our beginning, middle, and end depend on this."

P: "Then heaven has determined that there's only suffering with you?"

G: "Peregrino, prime matter is prepared to receive equally two contraries, when they are natural to it. Do you not believe that from one

---

6 From the lovers' perspective, Peregrino's interpretation of the dream will come true. For instance, the garden is Genevera's bedroom or house; the adoring snake that betrays her will be Astanna; the ship representing the change of place will be Genevera's transfer to the convent, etc.

same cause can proceed two contrary effects, which operate in the same subject?"

P: "No, I don't think so."

G: "Let this example convince you: God is One and the greatest Good, from Whom proceeds all we have, both what is good and evil. Those are two contraries with one Cause. Here is another: Rain can cause the growth of plants but also their ruin, though it is still merely rain. Fortune is mentioned only when one speaks outside the bounds of reason. Therefore, it shall not be a point of discussion between us."

P: "Lady, from what I can tell, you're philosophical."

G: "And from what I understand, Peregrino, you are a traitor! If you only conducted your life according to virtue and modesty, you would have no reason to go about condemning Fortune or anything else. You can certainly regret your depraved conscience and the lack of respect you show for another's honour. I pray God this is the first and last praise you and your house can vaunt: to have tricked a girl who loved you as much as her honour.

"If you had loved perfectly and faithfully observed what you promised, you would not find yourself in such anguish (though I believe you are putting on a show), and I will soon be free of what will ultimately bring about my life's end. You are part of that crowd of vow-breakers who, when you have run out excuses and tears, chalk the rest up to Fortune, which in your imbecility you worship as a celestial goddess, though Fortune is but a dream. You believe you can settle your vast shortcomings with your filthy chatter. Your death, whenever it should come, will mark a true sacrifice to God and the world in purging this earth of one more of those monsters who make up the corruption of the universe!

"Now see the face he sets after all his betrayals, feigned tears, double-talk, and childish whimpering! But wait – perhaps this good-for-nothing is feigning unbearable pain just to set up some greater deception. Witness the broken promise you made in a sacred place before the altar and God, in whose presence you committed yourself to me. What is more, if you have lied to God, I know full well you cannot be truthful with me. There is no greater infamy than the damnation that comes from conversing with you! Therefore, it would behoove you not to corrupt another's purity, because ultimately life will not be long for you."

P: "O gift from heaven, O thing most desired, O happiness greater than what anyone could ever wish for! It would be grand to hear and see myself slain by your hand and in your presence. What are you waiting for? Why do you tarry? Why the delay? I am guilty, evil, and a traitor. Dear Lady, here is my knife together with my flesh. Please, out of the pity that reigns and governs heaven, I beg you, for every past and future consolation, relieve me of this unhappy life, since this seems to be the only thing that will please you!

"If this is not what you want, because it will stain your pure white hand with the blood of a poor man, may you find the time and place to repay your debt to comfort me with that pity that is fitting to your divine face and this never-before-seen purity. See, lady, I am entirely consumed; I burn and am failing. Why are you so cruel? Greater compassion is shown between enemies than you show me. Don't you know how much dignity is in mercy, which accords with God? Remember: you are a woman, actually a goddess, and my lady and only mistress. Let your generosity triumph now; flee from malice."

G: "What have I done, O Peregrino, to earn the way you betrayed me?"

P: "In what way?"

G: "Since you did it, you must already know!"

P: "If you do not tell me, how am I to know? Believe me, lady, a hearth that holds smoke is no place to live!"

G: "An open room is not safe from thieves. One must be faithful, discreet, and careful to preserve another's belongings. Was there nothing else for you to give your preferred betrothed Lionora than the belt that symbolized the beginning of our love? You sent it some days ago through Gasparina, her servant girl. I saw it, and I heard the words you asked her to relay. The belt's deliverer lives. I know nothing else about it, save that you did not regift it because you cannot afford something else, but only to deprive me of happiness!"

P: "My lady, since memory can sometimes play tricks on us, it is all the more crucial for forgetful ones to listen patiently. You should recall when Love joined us we spoke of the belt, and you wanted to see its updated embellishment. You took it in your hands, then tossed it on the bed. We continued talking when Astanna came in to warn us of your mother's arrival. Anastasia entered, talked with you, and mused to herself about your comings and goings. It would have been easy for her to snatch the belt you denied to her you possessed. She then carried out this deception in order to find a legitimate way to break our love because she has in mind another match for you.

"You know that what many people bandy about is not false in every detail. Only after I asked you about going to Reggio Emilia did she bring it up with you. You know what you promised me, and if you consider it well, you'll see I have been betrayed by you and not you by me. Now it must be clear to you that I am not at fault. If only you had made this clear to me in your letters, then this matter wouldn't have dragged on so long.

"Nevertheless, it's exceedingly unbecoming when you wish to break off a friendship without cause and rescind your promise of love. You must be more considerate, especially in matters involving risks, suffering, and threats against honour."

G: "Peregrino, all-consuming passions often supersede virtue. I was abruptly assailed by my mother (as I explained to you in detail) about the marriage prospect, and because I refused it, I am where you find me. If worse does not befall me, I can be content.

"After I saw the belt in Gasparina's hands, I became so upset I tried to forget what it originally signified. So, please, forgive me! Do not ascribe any malice to what I have said nor any desire to incite a quarrel with you, since I am more convinced than ever you are my better. Your dissatisfaction with me pains me more than my sufferings, so let us put an end to this, given that you remain faithful. May the world do what it will, because I hold it as nothing."

Then with a happy face and just a few more words, she imparted to me a greater sweetness than I had ever experienced when she looked at me and said: "O my Peregrino, how bittersweet the first taste of our love has been! We must be careful that the present sweetness does not lead to more bitterness."

Then I: "Lady, I'm relieved this misunderstanding has been clarified."

She got up and began to walk toward the garden. With her penetrating glances and enticing tongue, she murmured certain phrases that would've stripped Jove of his kingdom and Plutus his domain.

After my lady rejoined her family, Astanna fortified me with the true comfort and armour of Venus, which was an exquisite meal, which Jove's cup-bearer couldn't have arrayed any better. I recounted to Astanna all the toils and sufferings I had endured, and she told me many things that greatly consoled me. Once Genevera and I had eaten, we each returned to our places.

Genevera passed a good part of the day teasing me, playing games, laughing, and conversing. Because we had not slept much, our eyes were overcome, and we decided to rest awhile. She settled into her bed, and I took a chair, so we were separated in this way in her room.

Not much time had passed when I heard Genevera talking in her sleep, saying with a broken and trembling voice: 'Peregrino, help me!' She seemed so anxious and afraid that, had Astanna not roused her then, she would've been left more dead than alive.

Genevera got up from her sleep all bewildered, surprised, and confused – and even more tired than before. With great effort she came to me and said: "I dreamed I was in a garden in its first bloom enjoying myself barefoot on the fresh grass when I happened to brush against a snake, which had been resting its head on its tail like a puppy. It caressed me so affectionately that it almost seemed to be asking me for help. So, I tried to be brave and, taking pity on it, I picked it up in both my hands. It was afraid and half dead from the cold, so I tucked it inside my robe, which was lined in fur, to warm it. As soon as it regained its warmth, it started to feel around and lick at my flesh. It laid its head where my heart was and indulgently wrapped its tail about my waist, so I was unable to move. I thought it wanted to pick a fragrant rose from among the thorns, when it bit me with its atrocious teeth! I collapsed in intense pain.

"Then after some time, I saw a ship coming toward me, which was sailing rough seas. I cannot remember what happened next. But, oh my, the sweetness of the revived serpent turned to such great bitterness! Peregrino, your faithful reassurance would be a great comfort to me now."

Peregrino: "Lady, your spirit must stand firm and strong. Do not be frightened by the figments in dreams, which can confuse images from one's daily routine with nocturnal visions signifying precisely the opposite meaning. In fact, seeing oneself tormented, insulted, or mistreated in a dream is often a sign of future happiness. Seeing fire or something red can be a sign of anger; seeing water designates phlegm. Weeping or appearing dead is an indication of impending wealth. Satisfying one's stomach with sweets or indulging in pleasures can lead to sadness of the spirit and listlessness of the body. Let's forget about these false imaginings, please, sweet Genevera, and focus on what's real, which can bring about actual happiness for both of us here together."

G: "Peregrino, the bite was such that it seemed to portend death to me more than life. Hercules, a noble and prudent astrologer, always paid attention to his dreams, because what he dreamed would always subsequently happen. The Pharaoh, Egypt's most powerful king, asked every augur, fortune teller, diviner, and soothsayer of renown at the time for a clear interpretation of his dreams, which he eventually received from Daniel, an honest seer sent from heaven. Thus, you see, dreams can have some foundation and not just be vain figments. Please tell me more, then, because an attack one knows is coming can be planned for and thereby wreak less damage."

P: "My lady, to completely dismiss a dream would entail denying something sensed; this is why every dreamer occasionally understands some truth from a vision. Even though what we comprehend isn't actually how things are, some are nevertheless quite famous. Examples of this sort are either entirely true or in some large part. These are commonly termed dreams, divinations, or prophecies. The first come from angels, the second from spirits, and the third from God."

G: "Peregrino, drawing out your explanations only wastes time before you must leave without giving me an answer. If you love me, enlighten me about whatever you know concerning what will happen to me in the future, so we can prudently prepare for it. After all, one cannot prepare for what one cannot clearly understand. Fear not – tell me boldly and faithfully what you sense about this dream."

P: "Lady, there are different kinds of dreams."

G: "You are crafting your response to the questioner rather than getting at the question, which causes me to fear some dreadful outcome. If you persist in your ambiguity, I shall be left to conclude that you are poor at satisfying me."

P: "Lady, sometimes we fear without reason. This is caused by a melancholic humour, which, because it can't discern what appears to it, yields to the imagination, which wanders here and there according to its whim without any determination or understanding of the things that appear to it. My lady, you're still agitated and moved by past anguish, so it's no wonder you're troubled.

"The cause of dreams can be considered in two ways: either as demonstrative and signifying a future event that will occur to us, as was the case with Pharaoh, who could prepare for a future shortage of grain; or as a dream that's merely a figment of the imagination. Here it's necessary to consider both interior and exterior causes. There are two interior causes: one is of the soul, when something pondered in detail and anticipated for a long time appears to the fantasy during sleep. The other is of the body, since the body can prompt movement from an interior disposition that directly matches it, such as when a person dreams of being in water or ice or snow. This comes from one's frigid humours, which predominate in our bodies during the night. If we're considering people of little experience, those dreamers can sometimes by entertained or frightened, even when nothing really happens at all.

"However, in response to your urgent request, I'll expound for you briefly what's relevant to your latest dream. Here's its meaning: the green garden is a place of sadness; the adoring and biting snake is a person close to you who will betray you; the ship that you saw represents a change of place to one that's unknown and melancholic; and the rose among thorns signifies a separation from a person you eagerly awaited. I can understand nothing more about it. You should remain optimistic, however, because all this could be caused by undigested vapours that have filled the ventricles of your brain, which may easily turn out to be empty fears."

G: "Peregrino, I have always heard it said that there is no greater truth under the heavens than what is revealed in a dream, just as is witnessed in Scripture concerning Joseph. If these things were to come about, what would happen to me?"

P: "Whatever you decide: I'll be with you always both in life and in death."

G: "Now let us put an end to this here. Maybe these dreams mean nothing."

P: "We must believe in this way because higher things are formed with such order that they may not move from that order to our understanding, even after long suffering."

G: "Still, I wish I understood this dream."

Book 2. Chapter 40.

Peregrino continues to speak to Genevera about the nature of dreams. Afterwards, they agree to ask Astanna to speak with Anastasia.

Peregrino: "Lady, a dream can oppress the soul, the body, or one's fortune, according to how tired the person is while awake, corresponding to what is simulated during sleep."

Genevera: "That is difficult for me to believe, since many times I dream of things that I have never thought about."

P: "But many times you fret or rejoice without understanding its cause or origin, since we can't comprehend all our passions while we're awake. Yet our soul discourses in the same way whether we're awake or asleep. At different times, we see various actions represented, because sometimes our souls are more relaxed, other times more agitated. When the soul is greatly burdened, it presents something bad, couching it either in the present or in the future – though it represents it in a pretend way, which can give different impressions, according to the context."

G: "Where did my dream come from? What is its power?"

P: "The imaginative faculty."

G: "How?"

P: "I'll tell you. When we're awake, outside perceptions move our senses. Corresponding sense moves the imaginative power. In sleep, when a figment is imagined, that invention, which it took from outside or a remembered power, returns and moves the corresponding sense, which then descends to a particular power and moves it. In this way, we comprehend what's perceivable, although we don't participate in its externality because it signifies by means of the senses, while we don't differentiate between external and internal significances. Thus, a person experiences fear or infirmity because this is how the imagination is moved to a different state. The great diversity of dreams derives from the evaporation, which links not only to sense, but also to the imagination, where the vapour is heavy and abundant. In this way, it keeps them joined.

"The senses are perceptible in sleepers, then, and according to the disposition of said vapours, either a greater or lesser connection ensues.

When the movement of that vapour is great, then no fantasy remains. This comprises the beginning of sleep when we still have a lot of food to digest in the intestines. If the vapour finds itself constricted, then phantasms appear transformed, corrupted, and disordered, as happens with those who are sick. If the movement of vapours is minor, then the phantasms are represented in a more orderly manner, as occurs at the end of sleep to people whose diet is moderate and clean. Nature has provided them with a vast imagination and graces. If their movement is found to be short and blocked, not only does the imagination remain free, but also the corresponding sense, such that the sleeper judges things and their similitudes as they are and finds at once such freedom of the intellect. This sleeper can resolve problems, write poetry, and philosophize.

"It was a tenet of natural science that our soul has in itself so much force that through its own nature it could know and comprehend future things, especially when it's freed of the impediment of the body and returned to itself. Such an opinion would be celebrated, if it permitted the soul to receive an understanding of its participation in the Ideals. In that way, it would understand the universal causes of all the effects, which it cannot now, given the impediment of the body. When the soul finds itself free of it, then it can perceive future things.

"However, this way of understanding isn't natural to our intellect. On the contrary, everything it perceives and receives comes from an impression from superior spiritual causes, divine power, or angelic revelation, or sometimes through demonic operations. It's very clear that superior bodies influence inferior ones, and through their impressions, they effect the phantasms. Given that celestial bodies are the cause of the recognition of many future things, they're much more active in sleep than during wakefulness, because when we're awake, they're carried away and more readily dissolve in aerial movement. But because night is calmer, what we take in then is more easily retained, and this sweet, tranquil, and slow movement comes from heaven, which moves the phantasm through which we foresee future things.

"Some of these foresights come to us by virtue of the planets, such as the birth of a child, when the meanings of the imminent birth match the place; other times, the meaning concerns something else. Then there's a split.

"Another type comes from bodily humours, and it doesn't have any significance whatsoever. This occurs when a man overflows with anger, either in quantity or quality. One can see this when he dreams he sees fire, which is a clear sign of a choleric temper. If he dreams of seeing water, then phlegm predominates in his body. If melancholy is greatest, then he dreams he's in shadows or suffocating or feels the need to carry something heavy or unbearable.

"We can note the visions that come from the planets: they appear to be of two types, either true or false. The true ones portend what is to come, and the others signify the emptiness of what proceeds from the planets' weak powers. They're so weak they can't reach the place of true planetary things, but are more readily a vision of the imagination in the memory because they don't get close enough to demonstrate the truth."

G: "Still, there are some men whose dreams are truer than those of others."

P: "That's correct, particularly in people of a melancholic, frigid, and dry complexion. In these people, virtue has such dominion that they comprehend while awake as much as others in sleep."

G: "What causes us not to remember the things that appear in dreams?"

P: "Humidity, which obstructs the way of spirits and either interrupts a dream or makes it similar to death."

G: "Is everything we understand about nocturnal visions called a dream?"

P: "No, because some are phantasms, some oracles, and others visions. The first occur between wakefulness and sleep, such as seeing wounding or killing, or wandering figures, or a mix of extreme things – whether they be happy or sad. The second ones, oracles, come when one seems to see a saintly or holy or very serious person who speaks to us, but nothing concerning the future. The third, visions, come when we see in a dream in the same way we experience wakefulness, such as when speaking, embracing, or spending time with a friend in the form and likeness that he actually is. These visions are all different from a dream, which represents him in a different guise from how you know him through experience. If he will betray you, you see him as a snake. For this reason, interpretations are needed, because if it were a vision, you would've actually seen that person who could've warned you. It can also easily happen that what appeared to you will actually happen to some friend of yours, because not all dreams pertain to the person represented."

G: "Peregrino, I am shaking all over, and I do not understand what is causing it."

P: "Your soul is overwhelmed by nerves, which exceed the power of your limbs. The soul has drawn back inside its potential, and this is why you're agitated. My lady, that's enough on this subject. Perhaps we've spoken about it too much already. Let's focus on present matters. If misfortune should leave us without go-betweens, I could always make use of this little window, which looks on Violante's garden. You could drop your letters by means of a string, and I'll watch for them day and night. It's not that I believe such an extreme will be necessary, rather I only remind you of it should an urgent scenario arise.

"Now I'll say what I feel. Your mother doesn't have a lady's nature. Otherwise, she wouldn't be so resistant to comfort you and seek your honour. Perhaps she worries about the factions that divide our households. She doesn't want openly to go along with what you might desire. You know that I know that she considers me to be a more fitting match for you than any other man in our city. If her passions didn't distract her, she would've figured this out for herself long ago. My advice would be that you talk to Astanna about it, after she's fully recovered her health. I believe she can deftly convince Anastasia to take the matter up with Angelo, whose will, once it is known, will allow us to proceed more securely and with less fear."

My lady showed no displeasure at this decision. Astanna came to us and was informed of our wish. She went to Anastasia and after a long silence said these words ...

Book 2. Chapter 41.

Astanna tells Anastasia that Genevera loves Peregrino. Anastasia decides to tell Angelo.

Astanna: "Anastasia, I could show you no clearer proof of my service and obedience than in caring for what is yours and in disclosing a secret you anxiously wish to know. From what I can tell – though not from anything verifiable, just from a few words dropped here and there – Genevera effusively and sincerely loves Peregrino, son of Antonio. She's so adamant and firm in her choice that she would sooner suffer a thousand deaths than accept another man. Considering that Peregrino is of high social standing, wealth, and intelligence, anyone would believe him to be the best match for Genevera in this city. The only knock against him concerns the ancient feud between your houses, a vice attributable more properly to ancestors than to innocent contemporaries who contribute to political life and behave graciously. I've respectfully related to you what my heart speaks to me. Do as you please, which may be best in consultation with Angelo."

Anastasia perceived the gravity of the matter. Centuries had passed without a thaw in relations, and now in so little time to be at this point ... Because it was a tough issue, she lingered in silence.

After quite some time had passed, she replied: "I would've been content had God and nature bestowed any other trait on Genevera than the one she currently displays, because then I'd be able to talk to her mother to daughter. Even if she came around to the best outcome, we might always doubt her loyalty, since in any case she's cut herself off from us. Still, so that you can see how I love her as her mother, I'll go speak with Angelo right away, and I'll tell you everything he says, so you can guide Genevera along the path that'll be best for her."

Anastasia entered the room she shared with her husband and began …

Book 2. Chapter 42.

Anastasia broaches with Angelo a marriage match between Genevera and Peregrino; he rejects it.

Anastasia: "Angelo dear, many times it's occurred to me how fragile women are, especially at that age when our fiery appetites dominate reason. Therefore, we must always be on guard, if we want to resist all the traps this world springs. I'm not speaking out of any cause to fear now, but only to remind you of the duty we have to uphold our honour.

"If love for our daughter doesn't bias me (no slight to any of the other girls), Genevera is the best of all in our city for her gentility. At this point, she's reached that age when it'd be a greater honour to have her as a neighbour than a daughter within our house. All our relatives marvel at our delay. So, I'm encouraging you to make arrangements for her, not just hypothetically but in action. I wouldn't want her reputation to be denigrated through any fault of ours."

Angelo listened to her words and warmly commended Anastasia's intelligence and caring, then said: "It's my duty as a father to give her a dowry, as it's the mother's responsibility to prepare the trousseau, and both parents' to find her a husband. I am prepared and ready."

Encouraged by his response, Anastasia continued: "Three days ago, I was walking along the road when I ran into my loose-tongued kinswoman Checa, who started asking me about marrying off Genevera. I told her we both wanted to see it happen, if we could just find a fitting match. Of all of the young men of our city, she recommended Peregrino, son of Antonio, who is exceedingly wealthy and available. I thanked her. Now I refer the matter to you to do as you wish."

Angelo became enraged and countered: he'd suffer a bond of marriage to anyone in the world before Peregrino, son of Antonio, given their families' all-consuming hatred.

Anastasia's tongue wasn't quick enough to reach the mark of disclosing that Genevera was already ardently in love with me, according to Astanna's good information.

Thetis's son, Achilles, did not burn so hotly for the death of his dear friend Patroclus than those words provoked Angelo. He resolved to kill Genevera before he was brought around to a better plan. He broached with Anastasia and Astanna the plan of secretly sending her somewhere else, and they agreed to his order.

Astanna returned to us, and she was even less generous in her words than usual. She began to mutter something about leaving the service of this house for good, now that she understood how poorly Angelo and Anastasia thought of her. Our hearts were pierced. We remained like Ugolino when he heard he'd be sealed up with his children in the tower that received its name for their famous fate.[7] Still, as best I could, I said to her …

Book 2. Chapter 43.

Peregrino begs Astanna for safe passage out of the house, but she refuses, fearing for her own safety. Peregrino manages to escape and tells Acate what he knows. The next morning Lionora's maid unexpectedly calls on Peregrino.

Peregrino: "Astanna, I've always known you to be faithful, discreet, humble, and very affectionate toward us. I beg you, as much I know how, not to leave me in these dire straits. Since the face of this earth is now cast in shadows, don't deny me the grace of seeing me out the door."

Without a second thought, though, she replied that she didn't want to, she could not, because she feared Genevera's brothers, who were armed on the ground floor. My lady was devastated by these cruel words and fell to the floor half-dead.

Then, mustering her strength, Genevera said to me: "Peregrino, neither Fortune nor Jove could prepare a more honest and fitting tomb for our bodies than this room, which has witnessed many times our faithful love. Now, take your knife, if you please, and let us die here together."

"Lady," I replied, "no, let us live, and rest assured I'll help you. Remember everything we talked about together." I dashed from the room and went about furtively scanning the movements within the house. I saw Astanna shuffle quietly in the dark from Anastasia's room to go to the sons to give the cue for my ruin.

I said then: 'O God, I can't defend myself, nor can I strike first, all alone as I am. Throwing myself on their mercy won't work, and threatening them will come to naught.' I returned to Genevera and told her to lock the door tight and not respond to any one. At the top of the stairs was a small space that was once used as a study, but was now in disuse. I paused there to rest, but straightaway I heard Astanna call Genevera's brothers to arms.

----

7   The allusion is to Dante's *Inferno* 33.46–75.

They stormed the stairs and bitterly demanded at the locked door for Genevera. She kept silent, which only made them believe I was inside with her. After they pried open the door, they all streamed in.

Without another thought, I flew down the stairs faster than the wind and out onto the public street. I went directly to that place around the corner where Acate was waiting for me with a ladder. I dropped to sit there on the bare ground without so much as a greeting. Through sighs and tears, I gave him to understand my desperate state.

Out of true benevolence, my Acate comfortingly encouraged me to be brave, since not even heaven picks a fight with a strong man, while it is the sign of defeat and utterly effeminate to give up at the tiniest obstacle. "What kind of rescue do you think you can give another, when you are so lacking in aid and good sense yourself?" Still, with his words and arms he embraced me and guided me to a place where we could stay and talk securely.

Acate went to an intersection where three roads met not far from Angelo's house, which gave him a vantage point to watch the gate to see if anyone passed through, but he couldn't see any movement. He came back to relay to me that there were some grim, armed men inside the gate who seemed to threaten anyone who passed by.

We went home, and I told him everything in detail. Seeing me so terrified for Genevera's death, Acate began to laugh and said: "O what a good man you are when you care more for the children of others than the parents who produced them! How have you convinced yourself that Angelo, a most serious man, would want to unleash such cruelty on his own blood without any sure information? Don't you know it's the act of a wise man to moderate the defects of his house as much through ignorance as through prudence, especially where a daughter's purity is concerned?

"I don't deny that had you been caught in their house, you would've deserved to suffer together the just punishment of death. But given that Fortune has repaid your efforts by permitting your escape, wait to learn what happens next, so you'll be able to respond according to the circumstance in the most honourable manner. Don't fall apart now. Don't give yourself away by your actions or words. Be as serious and modest as you can, so as to be above everyone's suspicion. How do you believe they'll feel, if they accuse you, then find the room empty? Don't you think Genevera will be heartened when she hears you're safe? How bold will you be in defending yourself against these accusations?"

Peregrino: "Woe is me, Acate! They'll send her away."

Acate: "That's your passion talking. You more readily entertain an evil thought than what's appropriately good. I don't know how to speak well when reason doesn't guide me. Let's wait for her letters, which will provide true insight, then we'll plan what to do next."

P: "I'm determined to die for her!"

A: "Then you should've done that when you were in the room with her."

P: "I didn't think so, for her honour's sake."

A: "Well, not for your convenience's sake either! There're many more ladies than you have lives. If you lose your life, you'll never reacquire it. God or nature couldn't concede to man a greater gift than life. So, preserve it for better times."

Greatly consoled, I went to bed and slept until the first herald of the morning woke me. I got up and talked a while with Acate, then Lionora's servant came to see me unannounced.

I was surprised by this novelty and approached her with a grateful and welcoming expression. I asked her the reason for such an unusual visit. In a rather roundabout way, she began to say ...

Book 2. Chapter 44.

Lionora's maid Gasparina confesses her role in delivering the belt and receives Peregrino's forgiveness. Peregrino asks Violante to watch for letters from Genevera. Violante finds one and passes it along to him.

Gasparina: "Peregrino, I tremble in your intimidating presence, and I'm afraid to admit the great betrayal I was ordered to do and carried out against you. However, I trust in your prudence and generosity of spirit. You know better than I the sacred value of keeping a secret, so I'll tell you everything. But I beg you to keep it locked in the secret recesses of your heart. You can repay the simplicity of what I'm about to say with the most stubborn silence. The force of love and the debt I owe my pricked conscience compel me to tell you everything. If you believe I've wronged you in any way, then with my hands crossed in prayer and on bended knee, I beg your forgiveness!"

I was dazed and at the same time deeply moved by this pitiable scene, which I had assumed was headed in a completely different direction. I graciously helped her up from the ground and comforted her, telling her to have courage, since there was nothing in my heart so hardened or blocked that prayers like this one couldn't soften it. "With a faithful heart and ready tongue, say then what you will, because I incline more toward forgiveness than offence."

Weeping, she began to speak: "I'm that foolish, simple, and credulous girl who delivered your belt to Lionora, not with the intent of hurting you, but to satisfy Anastasia, who had entreated me to do it so insistently. I didn't understand the intent or the outcome, only that it might somehow benefit you, so I delivered it willingly. But because you could easily have heard word of it through my friend, who is your servant Marietta's cousin, I wanted you to know that I didn't do it out of malice, at least not the part I had in it. In any event, I'll never say another word about it."

I understood everything, and I forgave her in her simplicity. Then turning these thoughts over in my mind, I went to my reliable source of comfort, Violante. After I told her what I'd heard, she was beside herself. Because her house was an extension of Genevera's, I made her aware of the plan that we had to send and receive letters by means of a string. She was happy to accept the role of keeping an eye out for a letter, and if any from Genevera came to her, she was to deliver them to me immediately. I added that, if she got the chance to visit Genevera's house, she should take it with her usual cordial friendship.

That very night a letter appeared in that place, and Violante brought it to me with the utmost secrecy and affection. This was the letter's tenor ...

Book 2. Chapter 45.

Peregrino and Genevera are incensed by what they perceive to be As-tanna's ingratitude and betrayal. Peregrino reads Genevera's desperate letter to him, then calls on aid from the spirits of the dead who have experience with ungrateful traitors. The ghost of Scipio Africanus appears and tells Peregrino to seek information about his lady in every corner of the earth and in the Other World.[8]

Peregrino,
No more wicked plan was ever hatched by Ulysses in Dolon's regard, or by Neoptolemus, the Greek captor of Andromache, than what was

---

8   Scipio is the hero of Rome's Second Punic War, who retired from public life to his villa in Liternum because of what he perceived as Rome's ingratitude for his distinguished military service, including Cato the Elder's accusations against him of taking bribes from foreign rulers. The epitaph that Scipio Africanus was said to have dictated for his own tomb read: "Ingrata patria ne ossa quidem habebis" ("O ungrateful country, you will not have my bones"). During the Italian Renaissance, Scipio was a familiar exemplar not only of Roman military prowess but also of the virtue of continence (see also 3.29). Cicero's articulation of the Dream of Scipio, in which Scipio must choose between Virtue and Luxury (with its subsequent allegorical representation in the visual arts), and Macrobius's Neoplatonic *Commentary on the Dream of Scipio* had created a foundation for Petrarch's exaltation of Scipio in his epic *Africa*, among his other works and letters (see Aldo S. Bernardo's *Petrarch, Scipio and the "Africa"*). Quattrocento Florentines were also especially receptive to the figure of Scipio as a moral-ethical guide, and Matteo Palmieri's *Vita civile* (*On Civic Life*, which began circulating c. 1435) is crucial in this regard and in contemporary questions of civic ingratitude. See Hans Baron, *In Search of Florentine Civic Humanism*, especially the fifth chapter (94–133).

carried out against us by that perfidious servant with Anastasia. But God, just and great, has taken the power from her cruel attack.

I am no less consoled by your safe escape than I am troubled by my ongoing suffering, which will end only with death or being sent away. If it be death, I will await you in that place where we can console ourselves without suspicion. Although we will not be able to speak physically there, understanding between our minds will prevail.[9] If I am to suffer the second option, I will not remain hidden from you long, because where there is fire, smoke makes it known.

Do not overexert yourself over it, because all of your efforts will only increase my pains. Let heaven do what it will, since perhaps it holds some greater plan. I send to God these supplicating prayers with a quiet and sorrowful heart, just as despairing Daphne and violated Thalia did, since I am no more capable nor deserving than them.

However, I do not believe I am so far from God's favour that He would neglect to mete out deserved punishments for servile ingratitude and permit us to reach our desired end, in which our thoughts find consolation. There is no more appropriate act at the harvest of the blessed life than the oblivion of trespasses. Any vindication must be reserved for other times when the mind is free from passions. The more we practise virtue, the more easily we might come to possess the joy of blessedness.

Go with God, and remember me.

I read the letter, and a cold sweat bathed my entire face. I couldn't bear the anguish, and I retreated to my room. I lost my wits and began to cry out: "O souls of our ancestors, if any of you has ever been oppressed by this ingratitude, come to me, for there's no greater help to the wretched than seeing others who've endured similar affliction!"

In that silent moment I thought I heard such a clamour of newly arriving souls to rival the battle of Astraea's offspring. One shade, more gracious and splendid than the others, called out to me, saying: "O Peregrino, you complain with good reason. A similar cause distracted many of your forebears."

Then, even though all of the blood had drained from my body, I pulled myself together and said: "O wandering soul, why have you taken pity on me such that you eagerly reply to my laments? Tell me your name, if you please."

Scipio: "I am that Scipio who, after innumerable battles and triumphant returns, denied Rome my bones, given her ingratitude."

---

9   Genevera is referring to the notion that in heaven, souls see truth, all that is, in God, as in a mirror. She, thus, anticipates that they will have no need for words to communicate after they are dead.

Peregrino: "O elect spirit, worthy of reverence and merited glory, why do you deign to speak to me?" I responded. "And if my question isn't foolish: How is it you're able to wander in this hemisphere of our earth,[10] since your high condition should merit the first seat in the highest of Jove's choirs?"

S: "To satisfy your humble prayers. Since time is short, keep your words brief. But tell me: Why did you request so insistently someone from our ranks?"

P: "So that I could have more faithful companionship. Now I'd like to know why you came to be so unworthily exiled."

S: "After many battles, the liberation of my country, the defeat of my enemies, and the many people I made my tributaries, the universal instigator of all powerful men entered the Senate with the intent of 'honouring' me with her usual prize; nor did she leave there before she had 'honourably' satisfied me."

P: "O Scipio, what cruelty! What universal plague do you mean? What's so inhuman and terrible? By God, don't deny me its name."

S: "Why, it is Ingratitude."

P: "What's its appearance, demeanour, and character?"

S: "It appears very eager and commanding. In its speech it is meek and eloquent; its attire is modest, but of many colours. It moves ponderously and behaves senselessly. It venerates piety, and always appears eager to assist the needy, but its hidden flesh is marred by a thousand splotches, representing its astute, clever, and pernicious malice,[11] without regard for anyone. No one is wise or prudent enough to guard against it, and the more a man is careful, solicitous, diligent, and faithful in service, the more easily he succumbs to Ingratitude.

"Consider Furius Camillus, Coriolanus, Pompey, and the Emperor Caesar, or among foreigners, Lichas, Theseus, and Hannibal, who are discussed throughout the world, and you will see clear examples. All of Greece up to your day is charmed by Ingratitude, and the whole of Italy weeps under its standard. Its scythe does not spare any person of merit. Consider Cato, Cicero, Seneca the moralist, and the poet Lucan; scan history and you will see Socrates, Solon, Plato, Aristotle, Miltiades, Aristides, and Phocion. All of them were burned by this fire."

---

10 Peregrino may intend the specification of "hemisphere" quite literally, since Dante allocated a mountain in earth's southern hemisphere as the place for Purgatory, the realm where the souls of the dead purge their sins before rising to heaven.

11 Fraud is the category of malicious sin usually recognized as represented by the leopard of spotted pelt in Dante's *Inferno* 1.32–3.

P: "Does anyone receive grace from Ingratitude?"

S: "Only deceivers, traitors, and wicked and cowardly men."

P: "Where's it found?"

S: "Ingratitude imbues the air, earth, oceans, and empires, great king-doms and small potentates, all places sacred and secular. It doesn't seek to germinate or plant anything, only to gather all to itself. This is what the world holds as a god; this is its glory and its praise. Without Ingratitude, life would cease; all other shortcomings proceed from this wickedness."

P: "I thank God we're free of those plagues."

S: "Read your modern histories carefully and you will see how inhu-manely its sword keeps turning. Because it is sometimes necessary for a sick body to find nourishment from something that might go against it, Peregrino, I would ask that you listen willingly to what may displease you, in order to shore up your soul with tolerance of the passions, which even when they come undeservedly can be contained only with great effort."

P: "Then please deign to hear the cause of my suffering. I dedicated my-self in everlasting service to a mortal goddess. I never neglected anything in satisfying her, even at great cost or effort. My unfortunate lady wrongly trusted her secret to a servant she had nourished with her own blood. Through various intrigues and deceptions, that servant found a way to deprive my lady of her homeland, relatives, and faculties. I can't even be sure she's still alive. Now see if I had a clear reason to complain."

S: "I have seen high Rome plunged to the nadir of misery, and shortly thereafter become the empress of the world. Heavenly influences never cease to change. Because they are not subject to your human powers, they cannot be stopped by your appetites.

"But, believe me, the power of virtue is so strong that you will be reu-nited in true harmony with your beloved lady. The Tarquins did not have such strength in our land along with their band of ingrates that they could last for long. Be comforted and persevere in your love, because everything you have asked will be repaid, and with prudence, all will come to you in time. The Scythians, a great warrior society, fought bravely when they fled as much as when they pursued. For this reason, the great Greek poet praised Aeneas for his understanding of fear, because it is not a lesser vir-tue to flee than to stand one's ground when the circumstance demands. My venerable fellow Roman saved our country by delaying and fleeing.[12] If you can conquer the enemy by fleeing in this way, it is a sign of even

---

12 He likely refers to Quintus Fabius Maximus Verrucosus, who received the sur-name Cunctator (the delayer) for his tactics during the Second Punic War, which are credited with saving Rome's forces.

greater virtue and fortitude to distance yourself from the sensual pleasures, pains, desires, and fears. Other times one can get further by standing than by running.

"I will not leave you without giving you some information concerning what delights you: before you can receive from your lady the prize you have hoped and laboured for, you must seek by earth and sea and visit the place that returned to Orpheus his beautiful lady. There you will find a woman who will tell you faithfully where to find your happiness."

Once the holy shade spoke these words, it disappeared. I felt sad not to have had any chance to thank him.

Book 2. Chapter 46.

Peregrino tells Acate everything he learned from the ghost of Scipio. Peregrino befriends a stable boy of Angelo's house and hides in the last cartload of hay delivered that day. During the night, Peregrino searches Genevera's house, but does not find her.

I shared with Acate all I had learned, then he smiled and admonished me in this way: "Expert doctors return more patients to health with caution than with reckless interventions. See how much hesitation and circumspection farmers employ before they harvest their crop. Before they ever plant a seed, they observe the course of the moon, the quality of the weather, and the condition of the soil. If it's necessary to act with such careful prudence in these issues of little consequence, how much more important is it to do so when your life and honour are at stake? The mark of great fortitude is the fear of its contrary. For my sake, please don't be annoyed at hearing one example from history.

"There was once a Franciscan who, in order to gain a reputation of true holiness, would always eat using a fetid net full of holes and scorn every normal utensil as a wasteful indulgence. His reputation for frugality grew, and he was eventually named a cardinal by the Church. Given the cardinal's sumptuous new position, his cupbearer thought he should put the net away and conform to the customs more befitting a cardinal's table. But the master didn't mind in the least. On the contrary, he said that, as his standing increased, his humility should keep pace.

"Around that time, the pope passed away, and this good cardinal was elected to his place. The servant, now head butler, set the table as usual in the pontiff's room. When the pope entered and saw the net, he laughed urbanely and said, 'Since I haven't any more fish to catch with this net, you can put it away.' The cautious servant understood that every action seeks its goal, and when it reaches it, then habits and customs must adapt.

"Now, Peregrino, Love has no more to do with you, nor you with him. If Genevera suffers against your will, it's her own fault, because she didn't heed your faithful reminders, don't you think?"

Peregrino: "Acate, a happy death befits a strong man so much better than the continuance of a base life. Mithridates, the Pontic king, preferred to risk his life rather than be ungrateful or even appear to be so. Let's see if we can learn anything about Genevera's state, since I'm very anxious for her. I fear she has been sent away to some island, become the food of ferocious beasts, or is locked in some dark prison."

Acate: "Peregrino, the poor man needs neither shame nor advice to be stubborn. Given that you care nothing for the life of a free man, you deserve to die in servitude. Strange thoughts abound in your mind when you worry so much about taking care of another's concerns, particularly when they continually keep company with misery and pain. Remember: he who refuses advice is bereft of everything else. There're many things that, after they come to pass, only leave annoyance.

"When the great Roman returned to the holy city from Epirus in Greece and considered his sad and miserable solitude in contrast with the clarity and great splendour of the city he had destroyed, he regretted that his name would be celebrated for this victory. He believed he would've merited greater praise for preserving that land, which was more beautiful than any other, than to be remembered for having destroyed it.

"Peregrino, don't seek to dishonour the doings of others under the pretext of friendship or piety. Remember what Phocion the Athenian said to the shade of Chabrias, that it is a heavy undertaking to govern another's children. What in your experience would ever make you think that Angelo were so depraved he'd want to deport or immolate his own daughter? If all ladies in love deserved decapitation, few would remain unpunished. Helen the Greek launched a conflagration that involved Asia and Europe. After a decade had passed, she returned and was accepted, honoured, and rewarded. Philip of Macedon patiently endured the dalliances of his lady. Sigismunda of Taranto was discovered *in flagrante delicto* by her father, who nonetheless treated her with great piety and commiseration.[13] All men are not Ptolemy, who served a meal to his wife of their dismembered child. Nor are they all like Queen Hecuba, the daughter of Cisseus, or Procne, Medea, or Scylla. Instead, Angelo is as his daughter is: of human blood, clement and pious.

---

13 She is probably the Sigismonda in love with Persile, whose story will be made famous by Miguel de Cervantes in the 1600s.

"Therefore, don't drive yourself insane, don't exhaust yourself with worry. Acting with less tempestuousness will lead you more readily to clarity regarding her condition. There'll be two benefits: you'll tacitly purge yourself of calumny, should any assumptions be drawn from Astanna's words, and you'll be able to come to Genevera's aid by waiting. If you persist in your demonstration, then you'll imprudently expose to all the world what is hidden, and you wouldn't want to hurt the very person who seeks to help you. Take my well-intended advice and pretend you're for the opposite of what your heart incites in you. Caesar always sought to display a calm and peaceful demeanour when he intended to launch a military campaign. I believe nothing fools another more than feigning the contrary of what one wants."

P: "Acate, it's natural for man to figure out how to embrace forbidden and contrary things. Since heaven and fortune have destined me for this, let's repay this debt to friendship, then, may God do what He wills.

"O lady, what harsh prison confines you? What unworthy place retains you? What Cerberus could impede your return? If you carry on in this life, or if you've already been released from the prison of your body, I wonder, how does your soul accompany you? What spirit does it get to enjoy through you? O my life, O repose of my heart already in repose, O tranquil port of all my suffering, O true repository of my cares! What shore or what road must I take to find you? What guide will show me the way? Soul, if you so inclined, aid me with a vision.

"Lady, if you already sit in triumph in the angelic choir, take whatever bodily form you wish to come to cheer me. If through some fault of mine you haven't yet reached Purgatory, may it not disturb you to come to me, as Gabienus did for Sextus Pompeius. But if you're still in full possession of your vital powers, Lady, remember the promise we made to each other. Days, nights, times, hours, and minutes bring me thoughts of this kind."

At wit's end from these voracious thoughts that my heart continually fed me to gnaw on, I searched all the places within the city that had any connection through family or friends to Angelo. I didn't overlook any monastery or holy temple in my search for the hidden light of such splendour. Fearing she might be in some kind of secret, private prison within her house, I began steeling myself to search Angelo's entire home to see where my lady might be. O God, what won't love attempt?

I met a stable boy for that family who delivered hay to the stables, and I got him to trust me. I buried myself in his last load of the day, and we whiled away so much time that unloading became inconvenient. In the dead of night, I got down from the cart and, heaving infinite sighs, I crept to her once happy room. I unlocked her door with a key I had swiped and entered her bedroom so stealthily that I didn't even hear myself. I found it devoid of people. I couldn't hold myself back from embracing her chaste bed a thousand times and that pillow where my lady had rested her lovely face. I bathed it in tears.

I searched every corner of the house most diligently, but found nothing. In the end, a servant loaned me enough rope to descend from a wall to the ground, leaving behind some skin from my hand.

Book 2. Chapter 47.

Peregrino consults every diviner he can find to learn Genevera's whereabouts. This book ends with his resolution to search for her to the ends of the earth. The narrator, Peregrino's ghost, promises to continue his story the following night in Caviceo's dream.

The next morning, I was overwhelmed by an anguish greater than any master contemplative could withstand. I set out to look for answers from anyone who claimed some divinatory talent through astrology, necromancy, spiritism, geomancy of the family, pyromancy, enchantments, nocturnal visions, the course of the moon, bird augury, invocations of the dead, palmistry, spells, haruspication, mystic insights through fasting, revelations, and contemplative devotions. In all of our city I found no one who could satisfy my need.

One was famous among those who worshipped the esoteric gods, named Thesalia. She possessed innate magical arts and was known throughout the world as an enchantress. She had drawn everyone to hold her in such high regard because they believed she had turned men into stones, fountains, and pools of milk; she could make statues walk, walls talk, and beasts of the field prophesy; she could foresee when the sun would arrive early. I was so desperate that my human faculties began to wane. I tried to implore the divine grace for the same favour that had already been conceded to the ancient Greek seer, who helped subdue the forces of the wind god Aeolus, calm Neptune, bring the besieged flotilla back to Aulis, predict victory after a decade of bloodshed, and safeguard all the knowledge kept from sly Ulysses and eloquent Nestor, King of Pylos, who otherwise exercised every gift of the gods – advice, assistance, mind, hand, spirit, and knife. After all, sometimes what can't be known by many wise men is conceded to a fool. I confidently girded myself for the great undertaking, resolved to search all the inhabited world to find assistance in my need. I put my plan into action by matching my clothing, name, and attitude to those of a pilgrim on the road to the birthplace of St. James the Apostle in Galicia. I asked leave of my dear mother and others close to me, and together with Acate, I departed.

Dawn was returning, and plaintive Procne took up her wearisome work again when the shade of Peregrino put an end to his story, promising me at the next nightfall, after a brief, concise, and clear epilogue, to satisfy all of my expectations. When Latona had made her appearance in both hemispheres and returned to her usual resting place, Peregrino continued his story in the way that follows.

Here ends the second book of Peregrino.

Peregrino Book 3

Book 3. Chapter 1.

Peregrino searches Italy for Genevera, consulting an astrologer on the road to Bologna, who tells him that he will see Genevera again within the year. Peregrino boards a ship in Naples; among the places he and Acate see are Troy, Byzantium, and Famagusta, Cyprus, before they meet with a master of the astrological sciences, Zacco Calogero, in Cyrene, Libya.

Weighed down by varied, nagging worries, I set off on the road toward the cultured city of Bologna. Passing Imola and Faenza, I came to Forlì. Although the way seemed obvious, I ended up trekking through mountains and over hills. I happened upon Meldola, a Roman aqueduct, Civitella, and Galeata. There I crossed the Apennines and reached Florence, the flourishing city of the Lily, where, word had it, lived an old priestess, well versed in the occult arts.

I spared no effort or expense to arrange an appointment to speak with her. I begged her aid humbly, divulging my whole story and my anxiousness to relocate Genevera. The priestess consulted an obscure star chart and foretold that before the sun shone in all twelve constellations of the zodiac, I would happily reunite with my Genevera. I thanked her, liberally dispensing words with money, as I was able.

I left for Siena, the ancient land whose insignia displays a suckling she-wolf. There I did little else but make a reservation for a consultation in Rome. When I arrived there, I shared my thoughts with a loyal friend, who reminded me that true oracles came from the East.

Furnished with this advice, I headed to Naples, where I found passage on a Spanish ship bound for Sicily. After navigating between Scylla and Charybdis, I reached Mount Ida. After contemplating that great summit of Jove, along with its admirable vista, we hoisted our sails again, leaving behind ancient Rhodes, Macedon, Thessaly, Boeotia, and great Cyprus. Thwarted by winds conveying Neptune's anger, we landed in Troas. That impetuous tempest forced us aground at the ruins of the port where Protesilaus sealed his grim fate by being the first of the Greek fleet to leap ashore.

The ancient foundations of such a renowned city beckoned us, and Acate and I decided we would explore every bit of it. We satisfied our curiosity by looking all around and encountered a grave inscribed with this epitaph:

> Hector of martial blood underground hear these words:
> God saves you. Breathe yet for your worthy country.
> Your Troy, illustrious city still inhabited,
> boasts warriors, but weaker and less worthy than you.
> Thessaly is no more. Get up and tell Achilles:
> She has fallen to the Romans.

I contemplated the ruins. Not far from that tomb jutted a marble gravestone of considerable height. Its sculpted verses read:

> I, commiserating virtue with rent hair,
> mark the grave of Ajax,
> deified for his outsized courage
> while Greek fraud prevailed.
> Thus, I am left widowed.[1]

I conjured in my mind the bust of Ajax, who in desperation over the loss of Achilles' shield consigned himself to death.

We paid our respects to those elect spirits and set sail, arriving near Hellespont. Through tears I grieved for Hero's loss. I adored the vestiges of the Tower of Love and said: "O fortunate house, you still preserve the fame of a most enduring love!" I expressed with those brief words the anguish I felt over the loss of young Leander of Abydos to a hostile sea. "O lovers, you are truly blessed to be given the grace to die in the presence of your lover. I, a wretched man, battle uncertainty, waste my strength, and follow I know not what!"

We sailed on to Byzantium, where I disembarked to visit the famous shrine to divine wisdom, the Hagia Sophia, which has become the abysmal

---

1   The notion of the widowed city would be familiar to Caviceo's readers from Dante's *Vita nuova* 30, when Dante compared Florence's grief at Beatrice's death to the prophet Jeremiah's first verse from Lamentations: "Quomodo sedet sola civitas …" ("How doth the city sit solitary …").

lair of that beast of Moslem insolence. It did not take much interaction to understand the customs and conditions of those people, followers of Venus, Bacchus, greed, violence, fraud, and deception.

Looking beyond, I noticed a Greek whom I had befriended and frequented in Rome named Theodore.[2] He received me warmly and inquired the reason for my far-flung journey. I cast my eyes down and remained silent as shame spread across my face. Theodore assumed I had either suffered an affront to my dignity or a loss of all my goods due to shipwreck, so he generously offered me everything at his disposal. I thanked him as best I could and, not without tears, informed him of my calamity.

That learned teacher laughed, saying: "Foolish is the man who tries to cut wood outside his own forest. Your well-educated Italy is the wisest queen of all true speculation. Here we make our way among servants, slaves, and people deprived of every good sense. You'd do better to seek your answers elsewhere.

"Word has it that on the island of Argos, where Ariadne left her body, there's a man who could easily discern the answer you so curiously desire to know. Once you've rested here a while, you may head that way, should you wish to persevere with this plan of yours. Far be it from me to upbraid or attempt to dissuade you from your amorous quest, since our land is just as obsessed with that passion. All the elements, together with our constitution, it seems, conspire to nourish lust. What we read in history and stories is nothing compared to what one does these days. But first you must stay with me a few days, so I can impart to you how not to stray from the truth."

I had not been long in that place before I was on familiar terms with ladies and maidens. I repeated to myself a thousand times, sighing: 'Italy mine, how provincial you are! Here women act with sweetness and abounding courtesy because among them love flourishes freely without its punishing sword.'

During that time the Sultan commanded his vassals in Byzantium to quash some uprisings in the realm of Persia. I repaid Theodore's friendship by agreeing to speak to the Sultan on his behalf, so I was welcomed onto the Sultan's trireme. The sea angrily threatened us with a thousand shipwrecks while we made the long and dangerous crossing. Nonetheless, thanks be to God, we arrived safely at the great Cypriot port of Famagusta.

I encountered a military commander from Parma who was there to defend the land. He warmly offered me a place to stay. I believe – indeed,

---

2 Vignali identifies Theodore as Theodore Gaza (d. 1475), the Greek humanist and translator of Aristotle.

I am certain – that Venus and Cupid left all their power as a last testament on that island. I talked to the commander about various matters, eventually broaching the subject of whether or not he knew a man there learned in the astronomical sciences. He told me that in Cyrene, a strongly fortified and well-defended land in Libya, there was a man, Zacco Calogero, who excelled both the ancients and moderns of the Greek school in that discipline.[3]

My desire to meet this Zacco exceeded all bounds. I hired a guide and with letters from the commander I presented myself to him. Zacco posed a series of questions to me in order to understand my infirmity and how I had endured such suffering longer than it would have taken to conquer the mountainous, hostile kingdom of Persia.

Zacco heard me out, then he intoned some appropriate words of prayer. He comforted me and begged me to take my fragile boat back to harbour, because he believed I was insufficiently prepared and could not survive such stormy winds.

He declared how this childish passion had caused the world much unhappiness, suffering, wretchedness, and ruin: "Africa and Europe offer countless examples. How many close friendships, relationships, and family ties have been reduced to hatred by this disordered passion? What incited the spilling of blood between the Romans and Sabines? Cupid's ruinous fury! What plotted destruction for the Tarquins? This venereal ire. What stained Clodius's imperial house? This universal pestilence. What sowed discord between Caesar and Pompey? This wild madness. What ruined Antony and Cleopatra? This shared insanity. What buried King Demetrius I of Macedon? This bitter sweetness, which King Syphax of Numidia also chose over loyalty. What conquered Hannibal? This inconsiderate bitterness. What stained with infamy the great intellects of Socrates, Plato, Aristotle, Xerxes, and Ptolemy of Egypt? Always this vain appetite! If you consider in detail all things, even the mediocre and small, as well as the temporal and sacred, you'll conclude that the whole world has been corrupted and laid waste by lust.

"The one who knows how to moderate such passion deserves praise and great blessings; indeed he resembles God! Rein in your lost spirit, son, and force yourself to do those tasks that are acceptable to God, honourable to the world, and satisfying to you. Quit this bitterness, which has already caused you to waste many years in pain and toil. You haven't gleaned anything but suffering, tears, sighs, trembling, and pains of the body and soul.

---

3 I have found no definitive confirmation of an astronomer and diviner Zacco (or Giacomo) Calogero.

You've used up your energies, passed up honours, degraded your house, brought infamy to your country, acquired perpetual hatred from your posterity, left your parents in poverty, and ultimately earned the wrath of God. Take back, son, your lost reason, and clothe yourself in manly virtue, not bestial behaviour. Cast out this insanity, stay with us a while longer so that, with time, you might forget this effeminate passion!"

Book 3. Chapter 2.

Peregrino refuses Zacco's advice and instead convinces him to recommend him to Fra Anselmo in Damascus. Peregrino meets with Anselmo, seeking advice for finding Genevera and revealing the prophecy that indicated he must go to the Other World for information.

Although Calogero's words penetrated more keenly than a bolt of lightning from the sky, my ardour nevertheless overwhelmed any possibility of reason.

Sweetly sermonizing in this way, Zacco let out a sigh, saying: "If it were the will of God, our brother would be here to satisfy your request, but he's currently in Damascus. A divinity shines in him that could stop the sun midway in its course."

Oh my! The sorrowful heart believes what it desires as easily as the absolved man's mind accepts a holy benediction. So, I begged Zacco to write recommendation letters for me to his fellow friar named Anselmo because I believed his blessedness could offer what might free me from so much torment. My lustful cause, Zacco's seriousness, Anselmo's true religion, very frugal life, and continual solitude, along with my bad example, made Zacco put off his task. Still, after I begged and pleaded with him many times, he wrote the letters, mentioning his good health and my travel to Damascus.

He sealed the letters and handed them to me. I thanked him and took my leave, returning to Famagusta. I stayed there some days for lack of a ship, though it wasn't long before a Florentine galley headed for Alexandria came ashore wearied by the vast sea. I gathered the funds, which the captain took, and we sailed quite smoothly to Alexandria. I joined some merchants travelling on foot to Damascus, where we arrived, exhausted, after eight days.

I noticed the condition in which Anselmo lived as he led me to his shelter at the far end of the village, which terminated at the foot of the hill where righteous Abel suffered fratricide. I gazed over the large population of that city and the sky shining over every house. A mosque there had three towers capped by three lawgivers who, according to the beliefs of that mad rabble, would determine the fates of the living and the dead at the Final Judgment.

Having sated my eyes, I decided this must truly be the place where our first parent Adam was formed. I turned to look again at the hovel where Fra Anselmo lived in contemplation, and it indicated his holiness. After I greeted him with dutiful reverence, I gave him the letters I carried, which he accepted with heartfelt tenderness. He kissed me on my cheeks, as men do, and thanked God for my welcome and unexpected visit.

I rested my body a bit and sent Acate to the Venetian consul's residence where he could wait for me until our departure.

Anselmo and I conversed together quietly while we ascended to the place where the son of Adam was buried and rests in peace. We sat down, and with brotherly affection he asked me where I came from, down to the province and city, about which he demonstrated precise knowledge because he had studied in Rome with the famous Greek teacher Cardinal Giovanni Bessarion.[4] In the course of our conversation, he inquired after the reason for my long journey.

Given the holiness of that man, I paled and went mute because my soul rued having come to where I feared I would find little success. Still, my necessity and desire made me bolder, and I tearfully expounded my life and the prompting of such a pilgrimage. I prayed to God that Fra Anselmo would not deny me advice or help in relieving my unbearable burden, and I told him what a shadowy oracle had revealed: I had to visit Persephone's realm if I wanted true knowledge concerning the whereabouts of my beloved lady.

Anselmo's reaction betrayed not a little scorn as he replied to my words ...

Book 3. Chapter 3.

Anselmo at first counsels Peregrino to desist, then shows Peregrino to the realm of the dead where Peregrino converses with an unnamed shade.

Anselmo: "You are wretched indeed if after so many opportunities you didn't once take a breath to measure your life! Are these the reasons to undertake pilgrimages? Do you seek to profane my conscience with matters that have never before touched my thoughts? Oh my, Zacco, is this what our holy love deserves? Is this what our mutual charity merits? You've scandalized both a friend and another at one time. Or maybe your request has come to me as ulterior penance for my sins!

"Peregrino, I cannot assist you with advice or favours. How can you assume that divine goodness will lend an ear to such nonsense? Why

---

4 Bessarion (1403–1472) was a Roman Catholic cardinal bishop and titular Latin Patriarch of Constantinople who attempted to unite the Greek and Latin Churches. His teachings, focused on Neoplatonism, are credited with reviving Italian interest in Greek philosophy.

ask what isn't appropriate or permitted to concede? It's a clear wrong. Therefore, stop your impious petition and do not take advantage of divine generosity, so you don't accrue more of God's wrath while hoping for blessings and grace."

Exhausted and almost at my last breath, I collapsed to the ground in pain, resolved and determined to be deprived of life. I saw Anselmo move a short distance from where I fell. He knelt on the ground, joined his hands together, and with tearful eyes raised to heaven, he offered prayers to the highest Father.

Meanwhile, I was splayed out on the bare ground and soon became overcome by a heavy slumber. The power of my intellectual soul didn't separate from me at all, though.

I heard someone say in a whisper: "Whoever listens little to good advice must abound in suffering."

The tone of the words squeezed the sensitive part of my heart such that I could not do anything under my own power. Lost, like a traveller who goes without a guide along an unfamiliar road, I turned around to see if anyone followed who might help me.

Only Anselmo remained, and I called out to him, saying: "Help me, father, since I do not trust myself."

He answered tersely: "Be silent and see while walking if there's anything to quell your madness."

I felt somewhat reassured. We came to a place marked by two imposing figures. I was frightened by them and drew closer to Anselmo, as a cub under its lactating mother. He comforted me, telling me not to fear because we had arrived at the glorious realm of great Jove.

We descended between those figures on a swift and incredible course. At their base a stream issued, which irrigated a dark shore. The Euphrates River with its black, diaphanous water did not flow swifter or deeper. Just looking at it struck terror in me. A squalid, greedy old man waited with his tiny boat to convey anyone who wished to cross to the other shore. I was stupefied. I looked at that dinghy, which seemed to me the very objectification of sadness. The oars represented tears and suffering, the crossbeams ceaseless sighs, the prow sempiternal penitence, and the stern damnation. I sensed gathering around it a vast crowd with eyes unreadable by anyone not conceded a divine grace to discern in that darkness. I threw myself into the crush of suffering shades to see if Genevera might be among them. My every effort was in vain. Eager to make the crossing, I gave a coin to the cruel boatman, begging him to bring his rickety boat closer to the shore, so I could more easily embark.

He looked deranged as he slapped the water with his oar. The boat drew close, and he railed at me: "I won't make the crossing for you now, though when it does happen, it'll pain you grievously! Go back! There's no flame burning in a living breast down below!"

I remained deaf to what he said. We boarded his boat only through Anselmo's intervention.

While I stood there, I heard a shade say: "Weren't you called Peregrino in your native land?"

Peregrino: "A presage of my sorry fate!"

Shade: "Then names fulfil the meaning they receive from heaven?"

P: "If you think about it, the son of Priam's Hector was called Scamandrius, then Astyanax; and to Tantalus his name foretold his difficult destiny."[5]

S: "What do you think you'll find among these dead rivers?"

P: "Satisfaction."

S: "What woeful place has ever offered comfort?"

P: "Sometimes a natural cause can produce an ambivalent effect, as tears can spring from joy or sorrow. Likewise, even this dreary place might contain something to point me toward my ultimate delight."

S: "Change your mind. You won't find that here."

P: "Then, what can I hope for here beyond?"

S: "Cruelty, ingratitude, and abounding greed. Now return to your nest and accept your fate; a transplanted root doesn't typically thrive."

Book 3. Chapter 4.

Anselmo identifies four shades for Peregrino, and Peregrino recognizes a few more. They pass the three-headed dog Cerberus and approach Persephone, Queen of the Underworld.

Four shades stood at the boat's bow lamenting their fate and blaming heaven and their circumstances. I asked Anselmo about these shades quaking with fear. However, he revealed nothing when he said: "Their souls, separated from their bodies, aren't well purged; they retain the memory of their bodily habits. When a soul doesn't receive forgiveness for its actions in its previous life, it complains and feels pain until the final purgation, when, after a cleansing in the Lethe River, it'll forget everything."

Peregrino: "Anselmo, don't withhold their names; their suffering may console my pains."

---

5   The son of Hector and Andromache was first called Scamandrius after Troy's River Scamander, a name with a disputed etymology, perhaps signifying "awkward/contorted man." Trojans subsequently gave him the name Astyanax, "Lord of the City." Tantalus, from which we have "tantalizing," was the name of the Phrygian king in mythology condemned to crave food and drink that always retreated from his grasp.

Anselmo: "Peregrino, their acts differ so much from yours! They have every reason to feel pain. But you … You languish because you will it on yourself. Nevertheless, so that your story can reveal it, the name of the first soul was Ferdinand, King of Naples; the second was Charles of Burgundy; the third Galeazzo Sforza; and the fourth was his son Gian Galeazzo."[6]

P: "Oh my, Anselmo!"

A: "Enough now! No more. Be silent, look, and listen."

Not far from the shore I saw a multitude of armed men arrive, who joined the sad shades to cheer and applaud. Among these I recognized Federico of Urbino, Sigismondo and Roberto Malatesta, and Alessandro and Costanzo of Pesaro.[7]

After we made the crossing, I witnessed a large, three-headed dog that barked threateningly as it guarded the threshold of Persephone's gloomy realm. It had no power to attack a passerby without a body. Anselmo gave it bread, and while it gnawed and growled, we passed without incident.

I drew nearer to Persephone, and I addressed her in supplication …

Book 3. Chapter 5.

Peregrino petitions Persephone to allow Genevera to return with him among the living, should he find her there. With Anselmo, Peregrino passes Lake Cocytus and the rivers Styx, Phlegethon, and Lethe, and approaches a great king.

Peregrino: "Supreme goddess, it should be an easy task to grant a favour petitioned and received by others in need. I beg you, since you have benefited from your mother Demeter's appeals, do not deny me your help. I ask aid from the heavenly stars among which you are gloriously arrayed; from the spirits of the underworld over which you hold the sceptre of power; from the natural elements, the nocturnal silences, the swelling Nile, and the sacred mysteries of the Egyptians of Memphis.

"O highest goddess, please do not refuse me what you have already conceded to another. If my Genevera has come down to your realms through ill luck before her time, may it not burden you to return her. Make me worthy of this grace of your connatural power, O immortal goddess! Do

---

6   Anselmo identifies King Ferdinand I of Naples (also known as Ferrante, d. 1494), Charles Duke of Burgundy (known as Charles the Bold, d. 1477), the previously mentioned Galeazzo Maria Sforza Duke of Milan (d. 1476), and this last man's son Gian Galeazzo Sforza, the sixth Duke of Milan (d. 1494).

7   Peregrino recognizes Federico Duke of Urbino, Sigismondo Malatesta, Roberto Malatesta, and Alessandro Sforza (previously mentioned in 1.31), along with Costanzo Sforza (previously mentioned in 2.24).

not withhold your restorative favours, which you already enjoyed, so I might have her back again unharmed."

The goddess inclined favourably to my plea, noting that she could allow me to extract Genevera, if I found her there. I thanked and adored the goddess.

We went back out to the place where the three Fates, Acheron's cruel daughters, perpetually overexcite the emotions of human generations. We saw there a countless number of possessed and oppressed people, just as one would expect, given their purview.

After we searched this area, we reached a marshy, filthy place, even more difficult and wearying to cross than the first. Here was that infernal bog, abounding in every wretchedness. Here was the final place for obstinate and perfidious men. Here marked the boundary beyond which every hope was lost.

I asked Anselmo where we were, and he answered: the furthest region of Egypt. I marvelled at its great expanse, the immensity of that country.

"Do not let admiration seize you," he said. "Here heaven's stars come to restore themselves, as in that other hemisphere. Now come in silence."

Continuing on our way, we came to Cocytus, the lake formed by the river Styx. Then the river Phlegethon appeared before our eyes, and, after examining it, we passed on. From this river, the infernal Lethe originates, where we leave behind the memory of our sins.

Drawing closer, we beheld a sublime throne where a king of very menacing aspect brandished a sceptre. I begged Anselmo to spare me his austere presence.

Then Anselmo said: "Peregrino, your time has not come yet. When it does – though late –it'll seem to you to come too soon. But I will clarify for you who that king is."

Book 3. Chapter 6.

Anselmo identifies King Minos, who judges the dead, and he points out how souls appear before the Fates, then drink from the river Lethe to forget their past life.

Anselmo: "Behold Minos, the one sung in legends, and he appears with his brother Rhadamanthus. Each soul that enters this realm must confess to them, recounting the habits, actions, and quarrels sustained during life. It is impossible to lie to them.

"Those who obey the good of their intellect will find a place among the most pious, reposing souls, where they will live out this life without envy, sadness, or toil. There fonts of pure, lucid, and crystalline water flow, and fields bloom with roses and other flowers. There you will find schools of philosophers, poets, scholars of history, and rulers who on earth took virtue as their god. They sing in melodies and eternal harmonies, and they indulge in perpetual, uplifting conversation. No cold annoys them, nor does heat assail them; instead, a temperate sky shines as their everlasting reward.

"Those other souls who indulged wicked habits during their lifetimes, however, will always be riled and tormented by the horrible judgment of Aeacus, and dragged to the dark region of shadowy Chaos. Among the multitude of impious and wicked men there, you can see suffering Tantalus, the entrails of Tityus, and Sisyphus with his boulder. Wild beasts lacerate some; burning flames or other tortures perpetually consume others.

"All souls – the good as well as the evil ones – appear before Lachesis, who confirms the character of each one. O how happy and blessed are those who have followed the good life! Afterwards, an angel accompanies each of these souls to Clotho, who ratifies everything. Atropos, the third sister, discerns everything in her unwavering stamina. After the souls confess everything, they run to drink from the river Lethe, forgetting their past actions and confirming the new."

Book 3. Chapter 7.

Peregrino witnesses the rituals the dead face in the afterlife, and Anselmo clarifies for Peregrino some of the symbolism.

It shocked me to hear the cries of the souls whose former evil life had earned them terrifying places in the afterlife. The others – the virtuous, happy souls – headed to a nicer realm, tranquil and simple, graced with green grass. O wondrous sight, O divine unknowable judgment, O expanse exceeding every human intellect!

Two gates appeared before me: one led to heaven, the other into the earth. An infinite number of souls lined up in front of them. Some souls were pristine; others squalid and covered in dust and stains, wearied beyond measure and very gravely burdened. Some approached, uttering complaints, cries, or murmurs; while others' faces appeared delighted while they recited good, pious, and holy words, according to the habits they had while they lived. All came before the three sister Fates, who wore crowns and sat upon thrones, wearing white garments.

First was Lachesis, whose herald proclaimed loudly: "O pilgrim souls who come here to receive your eternal robes, examine your virtue, because that alone is inviolable and free; everything else amounts to perpetual servitude. The destiny that awaits you will endure eternally." After hearing these words, each soul donned the robe matching its actions in the first life. O how difficult it is to die valiantly if one is born ugly or raised badly!

Anselmo explained to me: "You'll see the souls of some tyrants and wicked men put on strange robes, such as that of a bear, boar, serpent, or some other horrifying appearance, according to their previous behaviour. Other souls dress in splendid robes, and they will ultimately rejoice, like Orpheus, who, after being torn to pieces by the maenads, transformed into a swan. They left behind filth to follow chastity. O truly blessed souls to whom are granted oblivion of your sins!

"Peregrino, I don't want the metaphor to bewilder you, however. All these wretched mortals drank the same first drink of Lethe, that is the water that keeps our souls bound to everlasting calamities. The mortal soul bathes in a river of lust, sensuality, and vice, which first takes away its memory of all the endowments of the informed soul. The Phlegethon represents the burning passions of anger and cupidity; our sins abound in these. Cocytus stands for the cries and screams. The marshy Styx is what liars adore and what keeps our souls mired in damning worries.

"Next to the Styx, see those vultures who devour intestines? That is the torment of a wicked conscience ruminating on one's sins, which fears and trembles at the prospect of a severe but just judgment. There is Tantalus, whose hunger isn't sated by the abundance of those apples that appear to be filling his mouth: this represents the burning and voracious desire of prevailing greed, which will never be satisfied by piles of gold or silver. See those ones distracted by the rays from that wheel? They are the souls of those who led their lives without following advice or virtue, not moderating their ways to heed reason, discretion, or conscience. See how that large stone turns over and over? It stands for those who waste their time in vain. That other large boulder threatening destruction represents the penance of those who accepted tyranny as their god on earth. Now leave behind these realms and sad spectacles; let's ascend to the blessed places of the cleansed souls."

Book 3. Chapter 8.

Peregrino asks Anselmo about the nature of the soul and how it is joined to the human body, which Anselmo proceeds to elucidate through philosophical arguments. Peregrino takes issue with God for creating the human soul subject to its sinful body.

Peregrino: "Anselmo, since time permits, this place demands it, and the material presents itself, please tell me what a soul is."

Anselmo: "It is an essential form of the intellectual body, and it is capable of reason, invisible, and immortal. Others, such as Galen the great physician, asserted that our soul is a complexion, that is, a physical structure.

He was convinced by this rationale, which isn't commonplace: that all the passions are felt in the soul, which disturb, move, uplift, and cause it to change. And anything of a contrary quality cannot experience similar alterations. Thus, it initially appears to be a complexion.

"In response, one could argue that body and soul have distinct and determinate passions, which are unique and proper to them, as choler is to a choleric body. These passions assert such force that the soul, when it first perceives its impetus and movement, has no power over it whatsoever. We see how this plays out, for example, on ships lashed by violent winds. They toss about to the point that they can't be righted or governed by the sailor, however excellent and experienced at that task he might be.

"Moreover, if one were to concede that the soul is a complexion and, as a complexion, receives the passions, then every war with the body over the right path of honour would cease, though it remains opposed. Besides, it is said that things that are created by various contraries can't be substantial forms, because, with respect to a form, nothing can be its contrary, nor is it susceptible to a change of more or less, as an accidental thing is. Therefore, it cannot be a complexion."

Peregrino: "I'd like to know how souls are born. Are they already joined to the human form in the maternal womb?"

A: "It is said, according to the opinion of natural scientists, that a person is animate before embodied, and only after developing a body is born into this world. For this reason, a person is rightly called a microcosm, that is a lesser world, because in his first phase of generation he resembles rocks (hence what is said of Pyrrha, who with the help of her husband Deucalion cast pebbles over their shoulders, which turned into men); and this capacity is reserved to the first being. Subsequently, the soul becomes more like plants, trees, and herbs, in as much as it has a vegetative power to grow; then it resembles beasts when it acquires sensitive power. Finally, it conforms to the angelic nature, proper to the intellective power, which is not infused by the great God until the body is organized,[8] because such a form deserves nothing less than a material well-disposed and prepared to receive it. After all, the soul must infuse all the body, translating from God what it is possible to give to human beings, just as a queen rules and governs the body politic."

P: "O Anselmo, I'm seized by such wonder! Given that a soul is created and infused by God in this corporeal covering, why doesn't the soul

---

8   I have retained the somewhat awkward word choice of "organized" for *organizato* here because it may suggest not merely that the body is formed but also that its bodily organs are readied before God infuses the material with a soul.

display its first habits, which it received from God before it had a body, since only subsequently does the body gain the power to act, moving in the dimensions of longitude, latitude, and depth, and inclining the soul wherever it finds delight?"

A: "The soul develops its habits internally over a long time through its affections, behaviour, will, emotions, opinions, cares, memory, and intellect. But it's often said, and it's true, that wisdom, intellect, and discretion are acquired with time, and they grow, although they remain habits of the body, not the soul. You needn't marvel, then, that as part of the body, it has as much power as one does in a prison; the soul is compelled by another's commands."

P: "Anselmo, then it isn't true what you say, that the soul is the queen and ruler of our body, or that sinning, as an act that's compelled, requires penance. Since God oversees all, why does He permit such a spiritual substance to be ruled by bodily material and fall into sin? Why does He condemn us to such an unfitting prison?"

A: "Peregrino, animate things are changeable, and they're punished or rewarded according to that. The soul, which is capable of good or evil through the power of free will, can turn one way or another and work however it prefers and so powerfully that it can even save itself or others. When the soul clings to divine will, everything it experiences is for the good; when it works against Him, it's punished accordingly. Although the process derives from God, it cannot be said to be without sin, as God is. What you say would make sense only after a person were stripped of free will, since the body, not consenting to it, isn't of such strength that it can overcome it."

P: "Still, you aren't answering me about how the souls are born in His purity. Now speak of the soul, not the body."

A: "But souls aren't born; they're infused."

P: "Then one opinion of natural reason is false. It states: man is generated from man; man cannot understand himself except by the composition of his body and soul; ergo, composed in this way man comes through generation, not infusion."

Book 3. Chapter 9.

Anselmo continues his disquisition on the nature of soul and body.

Anselmo: "Listen, Peregrino, and revise your false opinion. If the soul were created, it would require the capacity to resolve itself in its preinfused matter as the body does. If this were so, how could the soul be tormented in the way you feel?"

Peregrino: "How much time intervenes between the creation of the embryo and the infusion of this soul?"

A: "For the male fetus, forty days; for the female, eighty."

P: "During this time, what does the embryo do?"

A: "It grows and becomes ready to receive the soul."

P: "Then the little thing grows without a soul?"

A: "I didn't say that. It grows due to the vigour of the vegetative power."

P: "Then part of the soul is created, and part is infused?"

A: "Your notion of plurality is improper. Although the intellective soul understands these powers as sensitive and vegetative, it is nevertheless a single soul because one power brings another: the sensitive supersedes the vegetative, and the intellective takes over the sensitive. Thus, within man, three souls seem to be in one power. But the dignity of the intellective power requires the essential form of man, and this distinguishes him from brutes. O how cruel it would be to deny the soul's immortality! Only evil and lazy people would fancy themselves benefiting by or rejoicing in that, because they'd be free to pursue their iniquity without punishment."

P: "When souls transmigrate, that is, when they separate from their bodies, where do they go? And how do they separate? Who guides them, since they'd be new and inexperienced in the afterlife?"

A: "They come to these eternal prisons along a torturous road and a thousand infractions, especially those contaminated and stained by greed, wickedness, and malice. Their lord is that angel they were given as their guardian in life. Others, I would guess, such as Pythagoras, only transmigrate from body to body to feel enjoyment or sadness, according to their merits or demerits. However, this understanding would insult divine omnipotence, because it would suggest that it were impossible for God to create more souls for created beings, which would be considered a lack of supreme justice. I believe that as they leave the body they go to the place where they are destined."

P: "These souls they carry with them, how do they become the way they are?"

A: "Through education and upbringing. Depending on how they behaved, they're allocated appropriate places, and either good or bad guardians."

P: "Do these souls ever appear among us?"

A: "Yes, the good ones."

P: "In what form?"

A: "They are in the guise of simulacra. Because they haven't been purged, they retain a great deal of the visible part of themselves. Those that are shadowy can wander about so much that they regain some of their purity. Some are even purged clean, lucid, and clear as a white swan, just as we read of the bards Homer and Thamyris, and Philomela. Others transform into lions, like Ajax. Some become an eagle out of hate and extreme fury, such as Agamemnon and Atlas, who refused to spare their adversaries, and so elected to crush their own souls. Others transform into a monkey, like Thersites out of his pusillanimity. Finally, others, like Ulysses, become destitute wretches because they chose the life of a private man over their prior ambitions."

P: "In this transformed state, can these souls understand anything that happens to us?"

A: "Some say absolutely not, but there are others who make a distinction: that is, that the damned understand nothing unless a dying soul reveals it to them, which is permitted by divine justice as a greater penance and punishment to the one who must listen. Good souls, on the other hand, are granted in their blessedness the power to contemplate the heart of God, which like a mirror reflects everything that is created and not created. Thus, it seems blessed souls understand all human things."

P: "If the soul, clothed again in its body, were to return to our world, would it be able to relay all knowledge accurately?"

A: "I don't believe so, because incomprehensible things are ineffable, and we would more likely be stupefied than comprehend its quiddity."

P: "Anselmo, I hear screams and moans, but I see nothing."

A: "The fire torments them."

P: "O Anselmo, speak of what is possible! I see no fire, nor any flame. Without light, how is this possible? Moreover, if the soul is invisible and immaterial, how do you expect to convince me that they're tortured by a fire whose nature is to be bright and perceptible through the senses? I know natural reason shines in you, and it dictates that the body can't act except by physical contact and that no material body can touch the spirit. So, how is it that those torments touch these punished souls whose temporary bodies are joined to them, if the spirit doesn't have any end? How exactly can they suffer in the fire? Besides, doesn't it seem to you likely and necessary that the actor and sufferer go together? But that can't be in the case of soul and body. Therefore, what you tell me can't be true."

A: "Peregrino, I want you to understand briefly that the fire is not the principal actor on the soul, but the work and instrument of God. Fire acts on the soul, as fantasy does on the intellect. Does it ever seem mysterious to you that you sometimes feel more suffering while you sleep than when you're awake? In that case, the soul receives no other punishment than intellectual comprehension of divine justice, and this is an unimaginable suffering. In this way, you must understand how fire doesn't shine here as in its proper sphere."

P: "If infernal punishment is nothing but intellectual comprehension, then it's nothing compared to the suffering of wretched lovers, whose pain afflicts constantly both soul and body. O how much better it would be to stay here than go back there!"

A: "Peregrino, it's easy to break down what is poorly understood. If you only considered what is eternal, as opposed to what is temporary, you would come to a different conclusion. This punishment, once it's imposed, can't be altered except through divine will. Your amorous passions are voluntary, and they come and go from one moment to the next. I forgive you because you speak as a man of appetite and not of reason."

P: "Will these souls ever be clothed again in their bodies?"

A: "Necessarily."

P: "By whose power: divine or human?"

A: "Only through the One Who created them, no one else."

P: "I thought nature had some power over this operation, according to what St. Paul said, that the resurrection of Christ, the great lawgiver and God made man, is the cause of our resurrection. Given that He is risen through human virtue, then human bodies will be resuscitated in the same way."

Book 3. Chapter 10.

Anselmo attempts to correct errors in Peregrino's understanding.

Anselmo: "O crass error! O eternal damnation for you! Your thought is verily far from any true, orthodox understanding. Listen to this brief response: Humanity through the Great Lawgiver was an organ of the Divine. Likewise, His resurrection must be ascribed to divine nature, not human."

Peregrino: "Anselmo, don't get angry. It is not a lesser virtue to teach than to learn. Listen to my reasoning. In nature there are two processes: one in creation and one in dissolution at death. What begins in one ends in the other, such that the terminus is subject to the action of nature. If the composite can dissolve, that same action has its place in its contrary, that is, in living. It follows then that nature can cause resurrection; and in the event anything were lacking in nature, then the influence of heaven would act."

A: "In what way?"

P: "In this one: under the heavens there's nothing new. What is, was, and ever will be. Through heaven's continual motion, each form returns to its place in that same quantity proper to its being. In this way, nature will power the generative resurrection."

A: "When will that be?"

P: "After the end of days, which will be precisely after a span of 36,000 years. Then, when our Cause returns, so will the effect. The superior bodies, all of them, will return to that same site, assuming that the starry sky moves one degree against the diurnal movement in one hundred years, which will make the west take the place of the east in 36,000 years. In this way, the resurrection would appear to be a natural power, not a divine one."

A: "O Peregrino, you seedbed of barrenness, desiccation, and sloth! You care so little for your own well-being, and you presume too much against divine knowledge and power. O too close follower of foolish Berosus![9] Compare that Babylonian composer of fantasies now to my clear reasoning and see your damnable error. The starry sky doesn't move from west to east, because, in that case, the year would begin in Cancer, that star of the ninth heaven, which once had its beginning in Capricorn. Therefore, the movement of the eighth sphere, that is the fixed stars, can be understood as a small circling around the origin of Aries and Libra. That movement is the forward and retrograde motions, from the origin of Aries, moving its circuit. It goes forward, then at the opposite ascension of Libra, doubles back. Sometimes Aries is in retrograde when Libra rises. The fixed stars of the eighth sphere move together in this way, according to their longitude and latitude.

"If you could ever prove that the movement at some point would end and all the lower spheres could not return to that same site (the origin of their movement), then I would accept your opinion. However, it's countered by this one: identity depends not only on efficient causes for its outcome, but also on its matter, which certainly can have another place with respect to the heavens. Through the exercise of free will, bodies can be impeded from being where they once were; through that exercise, the body could still be divided and matter dispersed.

"Listen to this corroboration: the exercise of free will is of necessity not subject to the causality of heaven. Consequently, souls do not return out of necessity to the same place they once were. Consider that nature can't act with movement or change; and neither of these can return to what it was. Thus, from the beginning to the end, nature can't bring about this resurrection.

"O how foolish it is to believe that the influence of heaven can do what one wishes! Evidence in nature contradicts this: when a lord or king is produced in the world, if it were because of the work of the heavens, it would follow that under that influence all who are born from him would be lords and kings, but that is not true. Thus, it isn't in the planets' power

---

9 Berosus, a Babylonian priest of the third century BCE, was author of the *Babyloniaca*, a Greek history on Babylonia in three books. Peregrino likely draws from the first book, which alludes to creation. Only fragments of the work are extant.

or grace but only in that of God, from Whom everything of ours proceeds according to His most just will. When you say nature can end, and consequently create, this consequence cannot hold. Crato the philosopher can crack gems, but not put them back together again.

"Now see, Peregrino, how your mind fills with a thousand errors, the end of which is none other than suffering of the mind and the death of your soul!"

Persevering in these delectable and salvific debates, we reached the fields of the sad, weeping shades.

Book 3. Chapter 11.

Anselmo explains the symbolism represented by various punishments, as well as the figuration of the Lord of Dis. Peregrino asks him about the whereabouts of amorous souls.

I felt pitying compassion, marvelling greatly, at hearing the scattered souls lament from those gloomy eternal prisons. Vultures continually devoured the entrails of some shades, causing them to suffer perpetually; others found that the foods prepared for them had no substance, and consequently, they could not eat. Still others rolled boulders around with great effort and difficulty. I shrank from such horrifying sights and asked Anselmo why they suffered so much useless toil.

"That first group of souls," he replied, "are those who during their lifetimes refused to repent their errors and were not sorry for their sins. Now the vultures gnaw their insides, akin to their consciences. As you can hear, they are moved and afflicted to the point of being driven witless. Divine justice will never change in their regard, either, since repentance means nothing to their ilk.

"The second group consists of the souls of people who made greed their god on earth, and to the extent that they enriched themselves, they were stingy to others. The third ones governed their states by means of the harshest tyranny. They insisted their subjects fear them more than love them, so they uselessly roll boulders."[10]

Dionysius, the tyrant of Sicily, was among these last shades. He was the one who in life had suspended an unsheathed sword by a thin thread above the head of his banquet guests. I also saw before me an elongated figure with two faces: one quite lively and the other pale and shadowy that frightened and shocked onlookers. Greatly moved, I asked Anselmo whose terrifying visage it was.

---

10 In Dante's fourth circle of hell (*Inf.* 7.16–35), it is the incontinently avaricious and prodigal shades that roll boulders. Here, it is the souls of the tyrants who anticipated the Machiavellian precept, articulated in the seventeenth chapter of *The Prince*, written in 1513.

He replied: "It belongs to the Lord of the infernal realm, which we call Dis. We understand the two faces to represent the death of the body when the soul separates from it, and the soul when it informs the body, which is none other than a trap, an arduous prison, and a dark tomb."

When we had our fill of this sight, we left that place of dire pain and arrived at those lauded fields where souls repose in sweetness and joy. Each one there retains memories, especially of the good deeds carried out in the world. I begged Anselmo to show me the place where amorous souls rested.

Book 3. Chapter 12.

Anselmo and Peregrino see the area reserved for amorous shades, and Peregrino recognizes many of them.

From the outskirts of a field we had a clear view of a little meadow, green with myrtles, junipers, palms, and fragrant trees, adorned with oriental gems, glassy clear fountains, and delightful gardens seemingly cultivated for every pleasure. Ladies and men participated in various activities on their way to their final resting places. Some sang or danced in harmony. Some jousted, practised sword fighting, rode on horseback, or relaxed. Others used fraud, murder, and betrayal to hasten their entrance through the adamantine gate, over which were written these words:

"O mortals, every concern of yours brings darkness to me."

Tired of searching, I asked the guardians if they would be so accommodating as to permit me to see if Genevera's soul had arrived at that place.

Those guardians remained silent as marble statues. Each one held in his hand a key. The one who sat on the right displayed a flashing iron key; the other held one of fine gold that permitted entry. The iron key served instead to lock anyone out who was less than worthy to reside there. I humbly begged them to allow me to peek inside the gate left ajar. I caught a glimpse of two shades: one weighed down by the mirrors he carried; the other resembled a gardener who cultivated his plot of edible herbs. They both displayed serious intent, and their words were circumspect, punctuated by continual extenuated sighs. Dismayed, I stopped in my tracks.

Anselmo said: "You've understood much, but now, nothing at all. The one who rules and governs the world through his appetite sparks the heart of lovers in such a way that to win love, they opt for death and this exile."

I raised my eyes and saw a seat, more like an imperial throne, empty of its lord.[11] Around it gathered groups of people whose hearts had served Love with loyalty, generosity, piety, mercy, modesty, and joy. Among

---

11 A similar symbolically empty throne appears in Francesco da Barberino's *Documenti d'Amore* and Dante's *Paradiso* 30.131.

these I recognized Alfonso King of Rhineland, King Philip, and Heloise of France.[12] The first two murmured in all seriousness to the daughter of King Wenceslaus.[13] The viper standard of Francesco followed, with the Estense lords of Ferrara, Lionello, Niccolò III, and Borso, then Federico V da Montefeltro of Urbino, Carlo, Sigismondo, and Roberto Malatesta, Guglielmo of Monferrato, Roberto Sanserverino, Alessandro and Costantino of Pesaro, Pier Maria Rosso, Cosimo de' Medici, Santo Bentivoglio, and Giacomo Antonio Marcello the Venetian.[14] Continuing to gaze for a while, we glimpsed four shades separated from the others for whom Love seems to have created that field: Carlo of Montone, Everso Count of Anguillara, Napoleone Orsini, and Carlo Malatesta.[15] Farther beyond them I heard others speak of high and serious things; and, if my sight was not deceiving me, they were Mehmed the Ottoman, Ludovico of France, Francesco Foscari with his son Philip Maria, Marco Barbarigo, the honour and glory of his country, Charles of Burgundy, and Galeazzo Visconti with his first-born son.[16]

When Anselmo saw me weighed down by serious thoughts, he turned to me with a happy expression and said: "Since time is short, we should go. But before you leave, I'll tell you more about this place that causes you to marvel more than the others."

---

12 Alfonso X (Alfonso the Wise) King of Castile, León, and Galicia, and at one point, King of Germany (d. 1284), King Philip II of Macedon (father of Alexander the Great, d. 336 BCE), and Héloïse d'Argenteuil (abbess and scholar, d. 1164).

13 Vignali offers a possible identification with Elisabeth, the daughter of Wenceslaus II King of Bohemia (d. 1305).

14 Caviceo refers to members of the Sforza family as *Vipereo* because their standard features a crowned blue viper devouring a man. Named here are the aforementioned Francesco Sforza Duke of Milan (see 1.31), Leonello d'Este Marquis of Ferrara (d. 1450), Niccolò III d'Este Marquis of Ferrara (d. 1441), Borso d'Este Duke of Ferrara (d. 1471), Federico V Lord of Urbino (d. 1322), Carlo I Malatesta Lord of Rimini, Fano, Cesena, and Pesaro (d. 1429), the aforementioned Sigismondo and Roberto Malatesta, Guglielmo VIII Duke of Monferrato (d. 1483), Roberto Sanserverino d'Aragona Count of Colorno and Caiazzo (d. 1487), the aforementioned Alessandro and Costanzo of Pesaro, and Pier Maria II de' Rossi, Cosimo de' Medici Lord of Florence (d. 1464), Santo Bentivoglio Lord of Bologna (d. 1482), and Giacomo Antonio Marcello Lord of Ravenna (and of a patrician Venetian family, d. 1463).

15 These men are Carlo Fortebracci Count of Montone (d. 1479), Everso II of Anguillara (d. 1464), Napoleone Orsini (*condottiero* and commander of the papal army, d. 1480), and Carlo Malatesta Count of Sogliano (d. 1486).

16 The first is Mehmed I the Ottoman Sultan (d. 1421). Vignali identifies the next as Louis II King of France (the one known as the Stammerer, d. 879). Francesco Foscari was the sixty-fifth Doge of Venice (d. 1457) and is accompanied by his son Filippo Foscari, the Venetian senator (d. 1478). Also mentioned are Marco Barbarigo, the seventy-third Doge of Venice (d. 1486), and the aforementioned Charles the Bold, Galeazzo Sforza, and Gian Galeazzo Sforza.

Book 3. Chapter 13.

Anselmo clarifies more symbolic aspects of this place. Peregrino encounters the spirit of Astanna, who confesses her role in Peregrino's plight and informs him where Genevera is among the living. Peregrino awakens from his vision of the afterlife to find himself with Anselmo back in Damascus.

Anselmo: "The florid meadow represents the first glances of love, which bring delight, and lovers run to pick the flowers and present them to one another to their undoing. The adamantine gate represents the hearts of ladies, which first appear attractive, but rather than tending toward mercy are hard as diamonds, driving their wretched lovers to the boundary of life. The bright oriental gems are the go-betweens of this love, who are eager to dispense encouraging words and promises, but fail to fulfil them.

"The inscription does not lie, since by following the dark path you end up falling: some lose their reputations, some their good sense, and some their time, boldly and basely wasted. Then you find yourself fooled, with no fruits to show for your labours.

"The two keys are of gold and iron. The first one permits entry and signifies tribute, generosity, and magnificence; with the other key, one is locked out with coldness, stinginess, bitterness, inhumanity, and unseemliness. The empty seat represents how love is a sleepless and imagined but typically vacant potential. Those who gather around with modesty and courtesy, and who have been virtuous in their action, have acquired honour and fame; the others have satisfied their lustful appetites, perhaps with some acclaim, but not with virtue or admiration. Although it appears to you that they continually cry out with open mouths, they nevertheless do not make any move. Instead, they lived the amorous life and have entered here wearing the rags they have earned; the others also appear in dress appropriate to their intent.

"After each shade has entered here, it's bound with so many chains that it cannot leave. Hope, jealousy, appetite, expenses, corruption, peace, wars, happy and sad glances, sweet and bitter words, new appearances, habits, lust, modesty, generous or stingy promises, fulfilled more or less, feigning and dissimulation: man is enchained with all of these bindings. The faculty of free will even seems lost to him, because this amorous flame enslaves him so. All these souls have repented their sin and wait here for some greater glory."

I looked all around again and came away burdened by an unimaginable pain. Then from a dense cloud a dark shadow descended on the infernal marsh, and a shade within cried out urgently for mercy and pity. Amazed,

I began to feel pity and asked Anselmo: "What sin, father, brought that pained soul to this place?"

He answered full of pity: "While still in her body, she habitually conducted her life with ingratitude and torment."

Peregrino: "Anselmo, by the holiness that shines in you, tell me where this soul is from and how much time has passed since she left her body on earth."

And he: "Ask her that yourself."

I marshalled my courage, but before I could utter the question, the apprehensive soul tried to flee out of dread, not unlike Dido when she first caught sight of Aeneas. But divine omnipotence, from which no one can hide, forced her to stay to increase her pain. By virtue of Anselmo's power, the shade cried out: "I am Astanna, who was the cause of your suffering!"

I wanted to exclaim, "O cruel one!" when she proceeded to sigh and speak through tears.

Astanna: "Blessed are you, Peregrino, for whom the prize for your suffering has been prepared. Cease your laments and stop pestering others who can reveal nothing to you to alleviate your pain. That traitor who imposes the law on everyone in the world and the underworld forced me to commit my impious and wicked act. I mean Avarice, from which every impiety proceeds."

After these few words, she moved toward a shadowy wood, when Anselmo called her back to answer for the state of my Genevera.

Astanna: "Every brief delay seems to me an eternal torture! If any pity is permitted in these infernal wards, I beg you, O holy soul, do not impede my fated course. Once I've satisfied your ardent desire, please give me peace. The great, venerable city that sits above the Adriatic holds and keeps your Genevera."

Then I complained: "Your answer is broad and ambiguous! Be more specific, and tell me exactly where she lives."

Astanna: "In Ravenna there's a church dedicated to St. Benedict of Mount Cassino. Now that you know, reform your life."

P: "How did she enter there?"

Astanna: "Heaven doesn't permit me to speak of these things. Go, live, and be well, since good fortune accompanies the solicitous."

As soon as she spoke these words, her pained and frightened shade disappeared. O divine Justice that does not leave unpunished even the least transgression! Through your mercy, you have brought an end to all that proceeded from her fraud and pain, and she receives perpetual torment.

Relieved after so much suffering, I sat on the grass to rest my tired limbs. Somewhere between wakefulness and sleep, I heard a voice say: "Neither sleep nor sloth befits a man of deeds."

I awoke as a drunkard hungover after a deep sleep. Stupefied by what I had seen, I looked here and there to discern if the things I saw were real. Only Anselmo remained at his place of prayer.

Book 3. Chapter 14.

Peregrino takes his leave of Anselmo, who requests that he pay a visit to the place where Paul the Hermit left his bodily remains.[17]

Night began to wane when I felt I owed Anselmo freedom from my anxieties, so I told him: "O elect soul, now that you've satisfied me through your intercessions, I'm determined with your leave and after commending myself to the divine to set off for Ravenna. I suppose it useless to attempt to put into words the accumulation of the debts I've incurred for your divine gifts. If I were to calculate what I owe you, the treasure of King Midas or power exceeding that of Octavius wouldn't suffice. If I were to try to thank you in words, streams of rhetorical eloquence from the Greek and Latin languages would amount to speechlessness. If I were to repay you in corporeal action, all of the deeds of Hercules would be nothing with respect to the good I've already received from you. Since I don't possess anything precious enough to match your dignity or my great debt, take from that part of me where every delight and suffering is reserved, as its proper seat, and do with my heart what you will."

After I spoke these words, he trembled full of ardent charity. He took my face in both of his hands, kissed me chastely, and answered: "We can choose in this life how to navigate our fragile little boat on this stormy sea and avoid the rocks with which the ocean teems. Some cliffs you can see, but many more lurk beneath the water's surface. We must seek to avoid them all, so that in time we don't foolishly lose both heaven and earth, like those who take lust as their god on earth. My son, I accompany you in pained, pious compassion.

"Consider your useless and indefensible toils, which proceed from loving indiscreetly. They aren't proper to a thoughtful person who seeks honour, and the more you veer from what's proper, the more you'll draw near to sensuality. If you consider with a calm mind what happens in the next life to those souls that follow a lustful path in this one, you'll understand there's nothing but suffering and pain. While you're still lord of yourself, prudently take control of this pirated boat of yours, which countless evil

---

17   St. Paul of Thebes (d. 342), also known as Paul the Hermit, left his bodily remains southeast of Cairo in the Eastern Desert of Egypt near the Red Sea Mountains.

spirits continually hijack, making it seem as if you aren't in control of yourself or your life. Your age no longer excuses you, when you could be a father or teacher to others. If this present contemplative solitude pleases you, I offer it to you with that heart with which I wish your salvation.

"O truly blessed and elect are those spirits in human flesh whose vast solitude of thoughts was and is the only consolation. One can certainly call himself blessed who by heaven's grace is permitted to get over his suffering in divine company. Scipio, after his memorable victories, didn't desire anything else but solitude. O venerated hermitage, O propitious life from which proceeds the knowledge of oneself, separation from vices, tranquillity of the body, peace of the soul, true acknowledgment of useful things, decline of all insidious dangers, and the eluding of one's enemies!

"Consider the orator Cicero. After the great upheaval in the Senate and the suffering he endured, he sought peace in a similar place, which he called the great gift of semi-freedom. Quintus Mucius Scaevola, a very learned man of law, didn't find a more secure path along his besieged life than to pull back. The great Augustus, after he dominated the world, learned about and became a lover of the sweetness of solitude, always mentioning that word. This is the solace for present toils, the mercy for past ones, and the true hope for future ones. Seneca the moralist, after his accomplishments, received no reward from his evil and ungrateful disciple, Nero, so he asked for nothing more than to lead a solitary life. That great Theban general Epaminondas, in whom military and literary discipline was born and went extinct, transmigrated to the blessed life in order to free himself from anguishing concerns and dedicated himself with great interest to music, especially playing the zither.

"Ulysses, that Greek who struck Troy its final woeful blow, found amidst the trials of war no greater delight than solitude. That sage of undisputed mortal wisdom, Socrates, passed his time in those works that naturally are more about leisure than toil. Helicon and Parnassus support life, and their philosophic schools and every intellect render homage to solitude.

"Solitude is our salvation and our glory, serving as the foundation of this life and the next. Solitude makes delinquents worthy of grace and draws ardour from madmen; it gives memory and intellect to imbeciles, sense to the lost, prudence to the uneducated, courage to the cowardly, and good habits and continence to the lascivious.

"If you wish to return to your native land, remember to hold onto reason – for the sake of your life, your country, and the sufferings you've already endured. If you see Zacco along your way, please assure him that I've given you good aid. It's your choice to stay or leave. I second whichever most pleases you. I'd suggest only that before you set out on your return, you visit the place where Paul the Hermit left his corporeal remains, so that you might extinguish in part your harmful passion."

Because an orator's speech doesn't avail the deaf or mute, I didn't heed all of Anselmo's healing words. Genevera's image was so firmly rooted in my heart that I couldn't think of anything else. We spoke as we walked back down to his shelter.

After I rested a while, gave him money, and thanked him again, I took my leave. I immediately returned to the consul's house, and he castigated me teasingly for adopting so readily the company of the Moors because they were amazingly inclined by their nature to disloyalty and greed. I thanked him for his affectionate reproof and paternal advice.

After resting for four days, I commended myself to the governance and protection of a successful Genovese trader of oriental gems from Cairo. We arrived on foot after eight days at his residence, which was on the via Sacra. Remembering what Anselmo had told me, I went back to the Jacobite abbey, which included the vast hermitage where St. Paul reposed, and visited it out of devotion and diligence.

Book 3. Chapter 15.

Peregrino carries out Anselmo's request to visit the holy site of St. Paul the Hermit. On the way back to Italy, the ship is damaged by winds and rising seas. They drop anchor near a deserted place.

It was one of those times when convents lacked provisions because of the frequency of Arab traffic, so it was necessary to send a ship for grains. I boarded it, and it wended its way along the Nile for three days. On the right-hand side looking toward Greater India, we passed the Sultan's salt mines, which produced salts of differing colours. We stopped there for one day, where the ruins of three hundred monastic cells of the Desert Fathers remain, but only seven retain their original form. The others languish abandoned and neglected on that land. All is desert, about sixty days' journey to India. There is no plant, tree, or herb there, or anything else to support human life except some running springs of water. When Phoebus chances to admire this land from his balcony, it is a marvel to contemplate the splendour of that plain, set off by the rocks there, which retain the lustre of the Orient. I collected enough of those precious stones to fill my pockets, which would have sufficed to finance all the pomp of a Hebrew ruler.

Some hermits welcomed me humbly and offered their charity quite liberally. There were numerous baking ovens there, which provided sustenance to any passersby, and in this way, those places could maintain themselves. After I offered prayer at the church and adored the tomb of St. Paul, the first hermit, the friars humbly bade me farewell, and I returned to Cairo.

After three days, I was back in Alexandria, where I located another Venetian ship on which I sailed to Cyprus. After we passed Rhodes, Crete, and the isthmus of Corinth, we felt almost sure of safe passage and were greatly relieved. But that ungrateful sea was crueller than the Chimaera that seized the four empresses and so forcefully cast them aground that no stories or legends remain to speak of them. Similarly, the offspring winds of Astreus, Titan, and Aurora conspired against our ship. Never before was a meaner blow delivered, not even on Saturn's son Zeus at the birth of Epaphus.

The sailors suffered exhaustion while attempting to overcome the sudden sea rise, which flooded everything. They pulled in the full sails because the ship's heavy load tipped the mast with such rage that it seemed we would all be bound for the antipodes. At last, thanks to the One Who saved Noah's ark from shipwreck, we came to a deserted place. Since the prow of our ship was damaged, we dropped anchor to repair it and restore our energy through a period of rest.

Book 3. Chapter 16.

Peregrino and Acate search for water, then stretch out to rest. The next morning, they discover that their ship has left without them.

The sun had just dipped below the horizon, and the intense heat left us dehydrated, so we eagerly sought refreshment. Our inner powers bolted like a wounded deer to find a spring that might relieve our insidious thirst. Shuffling along and talking together, Acate and I wandered away from the shore about two thousand paces, and we found what we so avidly sought. Then, out of bodily exhaustion, we laid our capes on the bare ground and stretched out.

While the warring weather gods reconciled and extended peace and calmness to our ship, Night covered us in a humid air, and we slept. The Moon offered scant display of her brilliant splendour, lulling us along with her in the darkness.

Just then, we heard the horn calling us back to the ship. Those sailors who slept prudently on the beach gathered together. The captain, determining that all were accounted for and desirous to set sail again, ordered the ship's anchor lifted to take advantage of the night's promise of smooth sailing. Wretched Peregrino and Acate were left among the woods and thorn-bushes of that deserted place.

We rested there so long that Aurora took pity on us when she saw us and announced our woeful predicament. We awoke, got to our feet, and hurried toward the ship. But all we saw was the boundless sea: no ship or man remained for us! We abandoned hope and let our sad mouths wail laments. Through tears we blamed thankless Fortune, the night, sleep, and ourselves. Like ravenous stray dogs, we wandered about running hither and yon. Thoughtless of the way to go, we were accompanied by starvation, poverty, sadness, suffering, love, jealousy, disdain, and castigation. Breathless, frightened, and exhausted, we blundered along inroads and byroads until we came to the fountain that had been the cause of our plight.

When we saw it, we railed against it: "O cruel fountain that transformed handsome Narcissus into a flower! O inhumane fountain that changed noble Acteon into prey! O fountain that drew the people away from divine law! O pitiless fountain that led faithful lovers to a harsh death! O ungrateful fountain, which Peregrino never offended, why with your gentle murmuring did you lead him gently and sweetly to sleep and to the extremity of life? O ill-fated night, O unhappy day, O cruel sleep, O too pious sun, why did you deprive me of your first signs of life? O desired lady of mine, I see now how heaven, the stars, winds, water, earth, and every elemental thing conspire to destroy our love. O how blessed is the one who already rests upon the other shore, but most blessed is the one who was never born!

"If I were certain, O lady, that a single heart beat within our two bodies, then I'd welcome suffering and death. However, I fear our long separation has caused you to forget my faithful service. O wandering spirits, if there's any pity remaining to you, go and reassure my lady that I know where she is, and I'm coming to her."

Book 3. Chapter 17.

Acate and Peregrino are chased up a tree by ferocious herding dogs, then encounter shepherds who provide them with food. They commit themselves to the service of the shepherds, who wander far and wide. In Mycenae, the two friends find and discuss a statue representing ideal feminine beauty.

Our empty stomachs rumbled for the payment due them. All we could provide were some herbs, roots, and water from the fountain as a meagre lunch and a most frugal supper. After three days passed, our eyes began to dim, given the austerity of our meals as well as an unrelenting nocturnal humidity.

Then, we heard shepherds coming toward us to graze their flocks. Preceding them, however, coursed four dogs, larger and fiercer than those King Sophytes gave to Alexander the Great. When they caught our scent, they rushed upon us, barking cruelly on the assumption that they chased wild beasts. Moreover, they redoubled their speed as the shepherds called after them. If it weren't for a large tree, which Acate and I flew up like birds to save our lives, we would have been the prey of those dogs, which together with their shepherds huddled to bark and shout at the foot of our tree. Given the shepherds' unknown, harsh, and difficult language, we could understand them no better than their dogs. Those men readied their cruel arrows and taut bows, intent on ending our lives through their subtle cleverness and keen aim. Our defences were bitter tears, sighs hotter than a burning flame, and trembling without uttering a word.

Divine virtue calmed the shepherds' feral hearts and inclined them to compassion. They put down their bows as a sign of peace, held out their hands, and with smiling faces motioned us to climb down.

Acate and I had to resort to gestures to recount our saga of misfortunes. They were moved to pity, and seeing the starvation in our pale, gaunt faces, they invited us to eat with them. We wanted nothing more and readily accepted their generous invitation, which restored our bodies. We ate a great deal, according to our need, until we finally drove our hunger away. After the meal was cleared, Acate and I considered our circumstances and offered our services to the shepherds.

That turned out to be a bitter and exhausting period of hunger, suffering, and endurance, as we wandered as far as cultured Athens, proud Thebes, pugnacious Megara, and great Mycenae. In this last locale, we dug in search of antiquities of any value. During these excavations we discovered a marble statue whose head of long tresses and lovely proportions indicated that it was doubtless a vestige of Venus or Helen.

Acate contemplated the statue with rapt wonder and excoriated heaven for denying any such beauty to our age. He bemoaned: "O glorious era, O worthy embellishment of eternal beatitude, O exalted beauty for which not only should Asia or Europe launch its ships but all the motions of the world and empyreal heaven should pause! O Trojan enriched by such a prize, you were blessed indeed in this world and must be joyful on high."

I saw Acate break out in such praise of bygone eras and scorn for our times, as if God, heaven, and nature had deprived us now of every celestial boon – in this way he made the statue second his opinion. So, I asked him to set aside every passion that could bias a judge's heart and assess the figure limb by limb. Only then, I suggested, might he find heaven not to be as stingy with its graces as he asserted.

Acate smiled then, saying: "I knew what you were going to say before you spoke! Given that you're such a fine judge of similar exemplars, look now and see if what you say doesn't veer from the desire for the true good. A lying conscience doesn't offer happiness."

Then I cried out: "Ah, we remember that bygone era, thanks more to their poets' commemoration than to heaven. Eloquent Greece hasn't been silent in boasting of its accomplishments in every way. Now you can see how God and nature bestowed on the female sex the greatest of all graces. But only in Genevera did all of them come together in plenitude.

"Greece claims its fame for Helen's beauty, Penelope's constancy, Artemisia's sincere love, Ipsicratea's fervent tolerance, Thamyris's strength,[18] Thetis's interventions, Argia's modesty, Antigone's piety, and Dido's admirable constancy. Rome extols her majesty through Lucretia's chastity, Martia's gravity, Venturia's most pious initiative, Portia's ardour, Claudia's restrained seriousness, Julia's refined elegance, Cecilia's feminine urbanity, Livia's great majesty, and the strength of the Cornelias. If you hold all these alongside the present figure, you will find that few or none of them compare to one woman in the world today."

Book 3. Chapter 18.

Peregrino and Acate continue to Alexandria and find passage on another ship, which takes them to an island off the Gargano peninsula of Italy, which they call Diomedea Island.[19]

We continued walking and grazing the sheep until we came to the city named after Alexander the Great, not very far from where the great Roman general Pompey fled battle and was defeated. I was obliged to hear Acate ramble on in praise of the golden age of yore, while critiquing our present one, first in terms of military force, then in literary inventiveness. He thought every noble thing of the world was now lost: good fortune, knowledge, customs, faith, clemency, generosity, strength, beauty, dignity, and seriousness.

I replied: "Acate, every age finds fault with its own time, bemoaning with cries, shouts, and laments its current suffering, cruelty, greed, ignorance, and foolishness. Not everyone back then was a demigod, as history likes to sing. Rather, it contains the hazy recollections of writers who favour elevated and expansive themes. Captivated by stories of the past, we revile our times while praising others, which isn't always reprehensible,

---

18 This Thamyris is Queen of the Scythians, also mentioned in Dante's *Purgatorio* 12.56. Given that all the other figures mentioned in this context are female, I think it unlikely that Thamyris here is the male bard identified by others.
19 The island of Diomedes is present-day San Domino.

since it can spur posterity to emulate virtue. But because this material deserves a rest or a time when we're more serene in spirit, I'd prefer to defer it to another occasion. And perhaps what's been laborious to us will be a delight to posterity."

It was already August when we made our way toward the seaport where a ship was docked, which had belonged to the great Venetian admiral Giacomo Marcello, who died victorious in Gallipoli, as the ill-omened tale recounts.[20] I begged the captain to permit me to accompany him to the land of the famous port.[21] He warmly accepted my entreaties.

We boarded and set sail, leaving behind the disagreeable shepherds with whom we had spent a year in captive service. It must have been an omen of my future: as soon as we left the shore, the ship began to sway and heave in such a way that the captain and navigator could hardly determine which direction to point the prow. We abandoned hope and consigned ourselves to Fortune. The winds' whims commandeered people and sails, which, mollified by divine commiseration, blew us to Diomedea Island, where the Assumption of Mary, true virgin mother and daughter, was celebrated on the eighteenth of the month. Three mountains stood there, one of which featured the Abbey of St. Mary, unlike any other in the Roman Church.

We disembarked to offer a pious sacrifice to God, and I met with the abbots, a Venetian of the regular canon of the Lateran congregation named Silvano Maroceno and the knowledgeable and eloquent Matteo Bosso of Verona.[22] They gave me everything necessary to my well-being out of their sweetness and charity.

---

20 The Venetian Giacomo Marcello (d. 1484) previously served as *capitano da Mar* (Commander of the Venetian naval forces) in the 1482 sea battle against Ferrara and Naples. The "ill-omened tale" may refer to the fact that, even though Venice emerged victorious in the battle of Gallipoli, Marcello died in May 1484 during that battle. It may also refer to what happened to his corpse thereafter. There was a dispute among his sailors about his place of burial (on the field of battle or in Venice). Ultimately, Marcello's body was transported back to Venice, where it rests in the Chiesa dei Frari. Despite his service on behalf of Venice, there is evidence, according to Giuseppe Gullino in the entry for Marcello in the *Dizionario biografico degli Italiani* 69 (2007), that Marcello died destitute. In June 1484, the Senate deliberated providing Marcello's daughter Isabella with a dowry of 2500 ducats.

21 Peregrino means (and the ship captain understands without need for clarification) Ravenna's port of Classe.

22 I can provide no more information regarding Silvano Maroceno. Matteo Bosso (d. 1502) was Prior of San Leonardo of Verona before accepting from Pope Sixtus IV the task of reforming convents in Genoa. Bosso authored at least one work, including the *De veris et salutaribus animi gaudiis*, which treats the immortality of the soul.

Book 3. Chapter 19.

Matteo Bosso counsels Peregrino to temper his love.

I admired the immensity and grandeur of the abbey, which was shaped like a pyramid. The architecture pleased me as much as the ways of the holy men there. One showed me to a room more kingly than common.

That night, given the weight of what I had endured, my languid limbs could find no rest, and I wavered between sleep and uneasy wakefulness. Then I heard voices, sort of whispering or whining, much like the whimpering that immature children make to their long-suffering mothers.

I discreetly went to Matteo and inquired about the voices.

Matteo: "You are on the island where Diomedes left his bones after his flight. The voices you hear belong to his companions, who were turned into birds and continue to cry out, remembering their fate."

Since my question had got us talking before dawn, he then asked me the reason for my pilgrimage. As soon as he realized that I suffered out of love, he comforted me with words that burned with ardent benevolence. He went on to suggest that, once I was freed from these mortal cares, I might want to dedicate myself to religious service, where I'd find peace, joy, and the blessed life. He believed I could easily acquire them once I put some distance between me and the alluring lady, something easily done with the mere inclination of the heart.

Matteo: "If you return to your homeland, you'll burn even more for her than before, and the closer you get to maturity the more these feelings will bring you shame. If you remain in this solitude, however, you'll become your own man in just a short time and cast away those useless passions, which while you entertain them will never leave you free.

"Peregrino, according to the Aristotelian doctrine I believe you've studied, our life is none other than a learning and development through good habits, although others say that our perfection or sin is resolved through knowledge, nature, or some combination of them. However, this cannot happen if we're estranged from good habits. You must not convince yourself that, partaking in pleasurable pursuits, you can eventually attain virtue and ease, since it's not only difficult but almost impossible to temper one's attachment to pleasurable acts. Habits fixed in the soul cannot readily be removed. Even though initially you'll recall some past pleasure you no longer enjoy or a prize for which you suffered that's still owed to you, if you don't keep the tempting object before your eyes, you can easily consign every passion to oblivion.

"Believe me, Peregrino, the sun burns only what it sees, according to the pronouncement of wise Avicenna. These amorous passions work the same way. They're merely a signification, but since they're located in the sensitive part, most of the time they convert into ruinous, insistent cares and unstoppable madness, especially if they're inflamed by the splendour of the beloved's eyes. At that point, it's easy to metamorphose into Ulysses' companions.

"O how many times you wretched lovers let yourselves be tortured and eviscerated through no fault of your own by womanly wiles and words! In a single moment love comforts you and jealousy torments you; desire carries you away and a lack of power immobilizes your soul to the point of desperation; and an act, glance, or word leads you to the boundary of your life. How many times among yourselves do you take offence and suffer without reason, moaning: 'I saw her, spoke to her, and smiled; I greeted her, and she didn't respond; I looked at her, and she refused to look up'? In similar trivialities you while away your days and nights restlessly. All these passions cease in her absence, but in her presence they grow to the point that you're carried to extreme misery. Given that you are prudent, what happens to you after death should be dearer to you than in life, which up to this point you've wasted, it seems to me.

"O undisciplined man, O one poorly advised, O sad mortal lot! O unhappy life, with what speed, art, and cleverness you race toward your downfall! O how much smoky darkness this lethal amorous flame brings to the blind world! Peregrino, remember Quintius Cincinnatus, who was called from his plough and appointed dictator, or Scipio, the poor man who subdued and conquered Carthage and Antioch. Channel your thoughts to better pursuits and mourn for how much your divine aspect has been cast down and pierced by sad cares. Leave the plough of concupiscence and set your sights on glory and greatness. Consider how much ruin you've brought to your public and private responsibilities; re-engage your weak and inert mind. Set your bold spirit loose on feats worthy of commendation. Think about the One against Whom you wage perpetual war; it isn't against the Macedonians, or the Arabs, or any other people of repute, but rather against the One, never born of mortal, Who rules above piety, discretion, and human reason.

"O man made in the divine image but afflicted with flagging spirits, lessen your anguish by lowering your sails so you can enter a more tranquil harbour. Understand you are the captive and prey of a woman who feels no pity. Such a vile state isn't proper to your high condition. See how base it is to commit your body and soul to the command of a woman who always lacks reason. Consider, son, the worst enslavement is born of an overly free licence to live. Thus, it isn't the action of a circumspect man to follow vain appetite and insult reason, to which every living one should conform, given that reason is God's bright celestial ray. One should always seek to conform to virtue and ennobling things, as great Cicero admonished us. Your spirit has such potential that you must attend to higher and greater things, which can bless you.

"When someone asked the philosopher Anaxagoras why he was born, he responded: in order to contemplate the sun. He didn't specify the sun for its solar light, but as the first principle that lends the splendour of intellection and virtue to all who seek it. O sweet and hard-earned rest, O rested exercise, O arena, praised by the ancients and celebrated by the moderns, to which God, nature, the world, and our innate desire call, invite, and prompt us! Whenever the fear of temporal punishment or the reward for endured suffering doesn't impel us to love higher things, we must follow our internal conscience to be contented with examples of the good among our friends as well as our enemies.

"Therefore, Peregrino, spare your life these useless sufferings now and remember to be a man, not a beast. Time is passing. Moderate what reason demands. I'm certain you'll conquer the beastly thought of turbid pleasure, which exacts a high toll from man, leaving behind a ruinous plague on soul and body. Even if you were innocent of this sin, bitter solicitude would hold you in such captive suffering that you wouldn't be able to promise anything to yourself. It wasn't pleasure but labours that made the great Hercules a god in this world. O how many ingenuous spirits flounder in this useless and mad obsession, including kings, lords, and rulers destroyed by this voracious flame? It led Antony, Nero, and Caligula to their deaths, along with the Roman patrician Catiline and Kings Sardanapalus of Assyria, Demetrius of Macedon, and Syphax of Numidia. Consider, Peregrino, this is the end for all lustful and lazy men. Do not seek to learn more about matters not fitting to the free and prudent man."

Book 3. Chapter 20.

Peregrino responds to Matteo, arguing that love is stronger in the absence of the beloved than in her presence, and he is determined to go back to Genevera.

Peregrino: "Matteo, there's a clear argument in natural science that states: when power is joined together it is much stronger than when it is dispersed; and it is all the more disturbing and overexcitable in inexperienced subjects. Since I have treasured and sealed in my soul the memory of my Genevera, for whom I have endured so many near-death experiences, whether I'm awake or asleep, every representation I call to mind is of her. Every pleasure and every pain offered to me comes in Genevera's name. When I am rapt in thought, wherever I turn my mind, I contemplate Genevera. In everything I think, say, and do, it seems to me Genevera is present. This is my constant, never diminishing impetus, like a burning blaze, a fire scorching my soul. I'm always imagining that the worst possible thing is happening to her, or she's being mistreated, or because of my long absence, she's giving her favour to other lovers. This is the knife that stabs my heart, the pain I cannot overcome through reason. O God, may I know death before I feel such a wound!

"You see, Matteo, I burn much hotter in her absence than her presence; and one love is as different from the other as the soul is from the body. I can demonstrate this through examples. How many ladies in love have you read about, heard of, or seen who have ever died in their lover's presence? But in his absence, countless ones! Therefore, this love burns much stronger from afar than in her presence, and attending to my beloved's needs consoles my soul at least in part. Even though I sometimes feel sad when deprived of certain pleasures, I find comfort and assurance in her promise of a future reward.

"Matteo, if two contrary outcomes can be posited from a single doctrine, and you assume Love's struggle is bitter and cruel, what do you suppose is the consequent peace and reconciliation that follow? Ah, this is the spice, the salt, the chain and lock of sacred love, when each person recounts the endured sufferings in trembling, sighing, weeping, kissing, laughing, and relaxing. No sweetness in the world equals this. Every other delight is nothing in comparison. Don't we see that when we exercise more than usual, we subsequently experience more relaxing rest and deeper sleep? He who hopes his love will last happily for a long time doesn't follow peace, but rather continually invents new enticements, because where peace and security make their nest, desire and sloth worm their way in, and these cause death and destruction to love. These excitements – what you call sufferings – are pleasures and great boons to lovers, just as what seems grief to some is to lovers the blessed life.

"Therefore, man enjoys rest much better in her presence than in her absence. I fear my beloved has fallen into some kind of trap, since she is far from our homeland. I've decided the lesser evil will be to leave you, once I have obtained your leave, offering you all of those ever-enduring graces that in my present poor state I can't give you to the degree you deserve. Do not assume my interaction with Genevera is sinful or wicked, but rather honest and chaste pleasure, as is appropriate to every noble spirit."

Book 3. Chapter 21.

Peregrino leaves Matteo and sails to Rimini, where he is offered lodging by Lazzarino. The next day Peregrino encounters Elisabetta Malatesta, who insists he join her for a meal and conversation.[23]

---

23 Lazzarino Lazzarini (1482–c. 1511) was a famed *condottiero* at different times in the service of Roberto Malatesta, Guido dei Rossi, Niccolò Orsini, and Cesare Borgia. Vignali identifies this Elisabetta Malatesta with the sister of Roberto Malatesta.

Matteo: "Peregrino, you cannot deny this contingency: whenever your body and spirits are distressed, your thoughts go to whatever is at hand. Isn't it the worst torture imaginable to have no hope of mercy or help from any quarter? But in the absence of the lover, these possibilities cannot be posed. Actually, you're more likely to find enjoyment and relaxation if you don't have to face the ever-changing circumstances of passions."

Peregrino: "Matteo, you're driving at the impossible. Who was ever so unlucky that in love he couldn't find mercy, so long as he was in the presence of one who loved him, too? Do you believe he must be denied the benefit of a servant, attendant, neighbour, or cousin, or of letters, made-up games, masquerades, gifts, serenades, balls, social parties, and intimate encounters? All these may offer some mercy. Don't you believe that if a man burns, a lady burns as well? Surely the ardour that overcomes one isn't lacking in the other? Of course, if they held differing opinions about each other, they'd certainly not fall under any category of love. But when we speak of true lovers, not anger, disdain, or lapses in time can take away their anticipations of mercy and consolation. So, in order to suffer less, I've decided to return to her to console her and be consoled."

Phoebus was showing his face, signifying the arrival of a new day, before Matteo had concluded our pleasant discussion and bidden me farewell. With Acate, I boarded a ship, and we sailed past the Manfredonian gulf and the dangerous mountain of Ancona. With propitious winds, we navigated the turbulent sea trenches skirting Pesaro and came to the ancient city of Rimini, which once hesitated to receive Julius Caesar's legions when ruin was sown between father and son-in-law.

Spooked by the sudden change of air, we entered the port in absolute silence. My friend Lazzarino had recently returned to his homeland of Rimini and was eager to hear news. When he spied our ship entering the port, he cleverly nosed around for information about those on board. As soon as he learned of my presence, he refused to accept that I stay anywhere but in his own home, where I was received more honourably and sumptuously than was my due. I was welcomed no less warmly than Cicero was by the Roman people when he returned from exile. I passed that evening in pleasant conversation at a dinner rich enough for a pope before retiring for a night's quiet repose.

The following day, against the wishes of my friend, I took a walk along the shoreline, because I was eager to acquaint myself with that holy land, which was to offer the consolation of my later life.[24] I had barely set foot

---

24 Peregrino, the character and narrator, does not return to Rimini. The voice of Caviceo-author seems to be intervening here, since his appointment as vicar general of Rimini will be the culmination of his ecclesiastical career.

outside my lodgings when I encountered on the road that flower of gentility, Elisabetta Malatesta, princess of true humanity. I greatly honoured her as much as I was able and was about to take my leave when she seized my arm and held me as tightly as Hercules gripped Anteus. She insisted I be her guest at lunch, where there would be entertainment, for the organization of which she was rightly celebrated. I bent to her will – then broke – agreeing she should do with me as she willed.

We directed our steps toward the gate of one of her orchard gardens about a thousand paces away. Entering, it seemed as if a Roman triumphal chariot were on parade. So many festive melodies and so much music filled the air that even the harmonies of the celestial spheres would yield to them. After we had settled there and rested a bit, she asked after me with modest familiarity and in particular about what caused my evident suffering. Ashamed, I told her in a low voice how the lord Love was to blame. The change in my facial expression caused that worthy lady to believe she had hurt me, so she sought to prudently heal my wound with consummate inventiveness and an equal dose of sweetness. She had all of her guests sit in a circle and began elegantly and eloquently to tell this tale …

Book 3. Chapter 22.

Elisabetta Malatesta tells a story of a boy who becomes a great philosopher out of love for an intelligent girl whose aim is to keep him in perpetual 'amorous expectation.'

Elisabetta: "Word has it that in France there is the most famous and celebrated school in all the world. A girl studied there, and she was in no way inferior in knowledge to Sappho. A youth of the same land was so taken with her that he burned to satisfy her every wish. Night and day he suffered, trying various ways to soften her resistance. In the end, his countless pleas and requests overcame her, and she agreed to meet briefly with him – not to commit herself to him, mind you, but to free herself from his attentions.

"The wretched lover appeared before his beloved lady, and she interrogated him about his actions, habits, and plans for life. The poorly prepared youth replied that he hadn't any other intention than to flirt with her. The prudent maiden, who had higher aims, told him it wasn't right for a nobleman to abandon virtue for lust. Therefore, she informed him, if he wished to pursue his amorous quest he must dedicate himself entirely to a philosophical education, which deifies men on earth. Should he acquire greater culture, he might then see with how much love he'd be embraced.

"That calculating youth understood what was required and expected of him, and he chose on the spot not to follow Love anymore if he couldn't be what his lady most desired. Humbly taking her leave, he threw himself with the greatest enthusiasm and care into his philosophical studies, to the point that at the end of their third year, he equalled or surpassed all the other youths in the school. Believing he had met his lady's worthy conditions, he requested to speak with her again, since he was now the most highly educated youth of the land.

"Well, that lady was the sort who believed that to fail was a shame, so to give in to him would be as good as death. Thus, she resorted to a new stratagem to deal with her young suitor, which she explained through the iron bars of a window when he presented himself in her garden. He laid out his case, requesting from her the promised reward, insisting he not be refused what he'd earned only with great toil and sweat.

"The lady responded in this way: 'Greatly beloved, every human care, mindful of itself and the initial impetus of its studies, aims to learn as much as possible in order to grow in good habits for this mortal life. I see such prudence in you that you should be able to satisfy my desire. May it not annoy you to help me understand, please, what the male nightingale does when it separates from the female after mating. I await your answer once you have consulted your books, whenever it should please you.'

"The late hour, the difficulty of the question, and his lack of familiarity with such matters made the young man's head spin. He said his goodbyes and returned home, where he ruminated a thousand times over all the books he could find about fauna until he became anxious, vexed, and pensive. He could find nowhere the precise answer to her question and wanted to die, even more so because a mere girl seemed to surpass him in his vaunted studies in natural science.

"He continued to ponder, emitting frequent sighs, when one day he encountered by chance a little old woman on the street. This bawd had spent her whole life as a procuress, as wily, filthy, and clever a one as nature could produce. Seeing the furrowed brow of the youth she had known for a long time, she inquired if his relatives were healthy and well.

"'Yes,' the young man answered.

"And she: 'So, what's the cause of your consternation?'

"'Woe is me!' wailed the youth, 'I wish I'd never been born!'

"Hearing this, the old lady was shocked and moved to motherly commiseration and begged him not to keep hidden the cause of his suffering.

"Overcome by her insistence, he told her about the riddle his beloved lady had posed and how his thoughts had led him to the verge of death.

"Then the old woman smiled and said to him: 'My son, do not despair. You won't lose your desired reward out of ignorance. It's the custom of the nightingale never to engage the female in the carnal act except on a green branch next to one that's dry. As soon as he has mated, he immediately flies away from the green branch and alights on the dry one, where he rights his tail, preens his feathers, and sings out rather raucously. From there, he rushes to some water to clean himself.

"'While I was still a young girl, I served the best naturalist of this city, and to amuse myself I'd listen at his table to disputes on this material. I still remember it, along with other topics that, between us, would better remain unsaid. Son, be strong in your determination, because not only will your philosophical answer satisfy your young beloved, it'd pass muster with the School of Philosophy, as well.'

"He thanked the old woman and went away happier and more contented than Caesar after the battle of Pharsalus. He sent word to his beloved that the time had come to expound the answer to her proposed question. The lovers set the time at their usual meeting place. They exchanged affectionate greetings and pleasantries with well-wishes for their families and other typical topics.

"Then the young man began: 'My lady, although your query was profound, difficult, and subtle, I was still able to elaborate a response in my mind, weak as it is, and bring it clearly to light. If your judgment sees any fault, may you not be too annoyed to freely let me know, so I might give it even more diligent study.' After these few words, he repeated what he had learned from the old woman.

"The young woman, unable to do otherwise, commended his study and praised the man, saying to him: 'Most beloved, I could give you no greater reward in return, nothing bigger, more generous, and more appropriate than what you will hear now, and it's this: if you've understood and absorbed well the meaning of this example, you'll take it as the finest moral lesson. May it prompt you to put aside what grieves you so. All those who mate with females on green branches signify those caught in sensual love. After their eager appetite is satisfied, they fall to the dry branch, that is, into oblivion of true love, and become sad and slothful. They think no more of the pleasure they had possessed. Consider that out of love for me you made yourself an educated and highly regarded man. While you continue to persevere in this virtuous love, you will always strive to accomplish similarly good and praiseworthy works, but if you satisfied your frothy lust, you'd forget how to live in a manner that is good and upstanding. Since I don't want what happened to the nightingale to happen to you, I wish you a long life in this amorous expectation.'"

Elisabetta concluded her prudent, wise, and incisive words with: "Therefore, Peregrino, be comforted after your ceaseless suffering, endurance, and peregrinations, which heaven has bestowed on you so that your life now offers more promise than a life of ease would have." Then she served an exquisite meal, which would've made the Roman Lucius Licinius Lucullus admit defeat.

Book 3. Chapter 23.

Peregrino enjoys the delightful company, which includes Ranieri Mi-
gliorato and Roberto Orsi.[25] Peregrino returns to the port, and his
friend Lazzarino insists on boarding the ship with him, which sails
only as far as Cervia, given foul weather.

Among Elisabetta Malatesta's guests were ladies and maidens of such elegance that lovers would have worthily hoisted their lutes to them, and
among the Riminensi senatorial ranks were two men, Ranieri Migliorato
and Roberto Orsi, so favoured by the Muses that they could compose
verse and prose off the cuff. Spending time with them was like attending
an assembly of the gods. But breathing air so close to the land that held
my lady, as well as the well-disposed wind and the urgency of my ship's
captain, prompted me to quit the banquet with nary a goodbye.

Accompanied by that affectionate group, I boarded the ship, and faithful
Lazzarino insisted on accompanying me. We moved out onto the high sea,
but the warring gods responsible for the weather delayed our progress. We
only reached the port at Cervia late that night. Love and fear in my heart
disrupted what little sleep I got, and I wasted away in fearful hope.

Book 3. Chapter 24.

When the ship departs again, it is blown off course to Trieste. Peregrino
decides to go back by way of land. He passes through Aquileia and
repairs to the imperial palace in Pordenone, where he and Lazzarino
are welcomed by Princivalle Mantica.[26]

Venus, the amorous morning star, had already begun to glimmer when it
pleased our captain to set off again toward Ravenna. Not far from that
shore I seemed to hear Jove speak with Mars, and look in trine aspect at
the sun. Venus and Mercury were in opposition, such that the prospect
of greater ruin was not felt by Aeneas or Ulysses, nor by Rome from the
perpetual dictator, Caesar. In less than an hour, Astraea's son the Boreo
wind whirled us about to where he held his throne. Our ship was tossed

---

25 Corroboration of the identities of these two poet senators from Rimini was
    unsuccessful.

26 Princivalle Mantica (d. 1506) was a native of Pordenone and friend of Caviceo's. Active
    in canonical law, he judged civil cases in Trieste, and served around 1500 as *Podestà* of
    Mantua. Caviceo remembers him in particular for his literary ambitions, which do not
    seem to have produced fruit.

with such fury that no one could guide it to harbour, nor could a miserable lover know peace before we watched Istria pass by. We ended up in Trieste.

By now, I had had my fill of Neptune's byways and determined henceforth to cling to Mother Earth. I took to the road. After paths crossing the Timavo River, I arrived at the enchanting, crumbling city of Aquileia. After three days, which even then didn't pass without the extreme threat of drowning in the overflowing waters of the Tagliamento River, I was admitted to the imperial place at Pordenone, where Princivalle Mantica, a man of high culture, received me most generously. Moreover, I didn't deny my friend any consolation pertaining to him.

Book 3. Chapter 25.

Lazzarino throws a party to take people's minds off war with Naples and the threat of pirates. Peregrino meets three beautiful ladies, Lucretia of Cortona, Bartolomea Fontana, and Florida of Prato, and they give a dance performance.[27] *Peregrino and Acate set sail again, but are*

---

27 Andrea Benedetti in his contribution to *Il Noncello* in 1956 attempted to furnish more information about this episode and the ladies mentioned in it. He noted that another writer, Giovanni Stefano Emiliano (known as Il Cimbriaco, d. 1496), also offered testimony in writing – in the preface to his version of *Attila* by Callimaco – of the gathering in Pordenone hosted by Princivalle Mantica that Caviceo describes. Concerning Lucrezia Cortona, Benedetti can only indicate that she is from the noble family De' Casali (29): "Di Lucrezia Cortona sappiamo solo che apparteneva alla nobile famiglia de' Casali, già signori di Cortona" ("Dame pordenonesi del Rinascimento in un passo del romanzo *Il Peregrino* di Giacomo Caviceo," 29). He admits that, concerning Florida Pratense, we know almost nothing ("quasi nulla sappiamo," 33). Her family rose to wealth and influence in the 1400s, perhaps through the profession of notary ("forse attraverso il notoriato," 33) and was made noble in 1447. On Bartolomea Fontana, Benedetti related a description by Count Jacopo di Porcia, who affectionately called her "La Fontanina": She was "petite, blonde-haired, with a high forehead, sparkling blue eyes, coral lips, rosy colouring, and magnificent bearing" ("bassa di statura, bionda di capelli, alta di fronte, occhi azzurri scintillanti, labbro corallino, colorito roseo incarnato, fastosa nel portamento," 29). Porcia continued, "she was brought up by a loving mother who possessed all the necessary qualities of the highest society. She knew how to use to her advantage a mature intelligence coupled with jovial attractiveness. She treated everyone well, never neglecting anyone. Her decorum served to discourage the bold, and her affability encouraged the timid, and she adapted to the company of polite minds as well as to the company of boors. Exposed to the best books, she drew from them a discerning taste; she possessed a knowing intellect capable of contributing a clever remark while tempering her natural, lively brio with modesty" ("Educata da una madre amorosa, che possedeva tutti i requisiti della più squisita società, seppe trarne il più vantaggioso profitto accoppiando un maturo senno ad una gioviale vaghezza. Eguale con tutti, non dimenticava nessuno, il suo decoro serviva di freno agli arditi, la

*seized by pirates just when they are about to reach Ravenna. Their
sea adventure continues through the Strait of Gibraltar to the port of
Lisbon. Peregrino encounters the King of Portugal.*[28]

It happened to be that time when the pope had declared a senseless war
on the King of Naples, and Roberto Sanseverino was assembling his army
to secure the roadways, since the Adriatic Sea already teemed with pirate
ships. Given the uncertainty of travel, everyone was dismayed.

So, Lazzarino, who was as capable in his leadership as he was accomplished
with weapons, organized a party to lighten the anxious mood. Seeing a gathering of maidens with their ladylike gentility – such a gift to the female sex! –
was a huge consolation. Three ladies excelled all the others, and I assumed
they must be descended from the third sphere of Venus. I asked their names
and learned the first was Lucretia, once the leading lady of Cortona, but now,
given the political instability, she had become a citizen of Pordenone; the
second was Bartolomea Fontana, who emanated balsam and every sweet essence; and the third was Florida from Prato, in whose beauty roses, lilies, and
other flowers always seem to bloom. They performed the featured dance.

As that entertaining party was winding down, we were called to answer to the needs of Federico III,[29] whose ambassador had arrived there to
negotiate the reconciliation of disputed and breakaway lands of Italy. To
honour the ambassador's presence, singing and storytelling resumed until
Mercury invited us all with his dewy air to sleep. Since we were all tired
and weary, it was time to bid farewell. The maidens curtseyed before me,
and as a prize for their virtue I crowned their heads and bid them peace.

A boat was readied to take me along the rivers to Portogruaro, where
I found transport headed toward Ravenna. We sailed under the unlucky
star of Saturn. Almost within sight of Ravenna's harbour, a Biscayne ship
appeared, and as fast as Jove's eagle, I was taken captive. Bound like a dog,
I turned my face toward the delicate land where my heart had its seat.

---

sua affabilità incoraggiava i più timidi, si adattava tanto alla compagnia dei geni gentili
che dei noiosi. Attinto ai migliori libri ne trasse un gusto discernitore; fornita di un
intelletto sagace sapeva intrecciare a un tempo una battuta arguta e temperare la vivacità
del naturale suo brio con la modestia," 29–30), suggesting that she was a muse equal to
Petrarch's Laura. Benedetti further noted that her family, one of the oldest and most
prominent in Pordenone, enjoyed longstanding imperial ties. I think we can assume
that Caviceo named these ladies in his text as a gallant compliment to them.

28 The King and Queen of Portugal are unnamed here, though Peregrino will claim to have
received rich attire from a King Pietro (Peter) of Portugal in 3.48. Caviceo likely intends
no identification with the historical monarchs of the time, given that King Alfonso V
reigned from 1432 to 1481, King John II from 1481 to 1495, and King Manuel I succeeded
him until 1521.

29 Federico, or Frederick III, the Holy Roman Emperor, died in 1493.

Seized by a deep pain within my soul, I collapsed, just like Moses when he heard the voice of the Lord. Instead of the usual refreshing liquids or smelling salts to revive me, that impious, pitiless, and cruel crowd took to beating me and drenched the *farseto* I was wearing.

Faithful Acate begged, pleaded, and cried out for their mercy as he could. They left me half-dead. Before my soul could re-inform my body, they had already sailed beyond the port of Ancona, where three other ships were waiting for us.

I was so distraught that in my frustration I called upon bright Apollo, supplicating: "O god, if you still have any memory of your beautiful laurel, lend me aid in my great suffering! O heaven, O earth, O sea, O depths, O rivers, O fountains that have already prolonged this ruthless war, temper your torments with reason! Who has ever lived more unhappily than me in this world? I envy you, spirits of the damned!"

All at once, someone interrupted my complaints, scoffing: "O unfortunate lover, chains, leg irons, and stocks secured with buffalo sinews will be your consolation now! This is the place of your perpetual torture. Here you'll leave your ardour behind. Here you'll forget your filthy madness, and you'll be transformed from a man into a wild beast. When the thought of your former life no longer offers anything but suffering and torment, you'll abandon it, too, as merely a burdensome reminder, so you can focus more intently on plying the sea, to which, with strength and agility, you'd do best to apply yourself!"

Speaking and suffering in this way, we came to the frightening jaws of Scylla and Charybdis. In an instant, we passed Sardinia, Menorca, and Mallorca, and sailed through the Strait of Gibraltar. Then, thanks be to God, we entered port in Lisbon.

The King of Portugal happened to be enjoying a stroll along the shore. Perhaps moved by some divine power, he decided to see for himself what new merchandise came in on the ships. He stepped aboard and went inside our ship. When he first caught sight of me, he compassionately said: "O unlucky one, where were you born that heaven has brought you to such misery? What awful sin did you or your ancestors commit that you are damned to this servitude? Please disclose your name, country, and business, because you've already moved me to compassion."

Then with a humble face and joined hands I bowed to him and said …

Book 3. Chapter 26.

Peregrino tells the King of Portugal of his plight.

Peregrino: "Sacred Majesty, your royal presence is heaven's great gift to me for all my endured suffering. I do not believe it is possible now for me to be harmed by any adverse celestial influences, because I am aided by your infallible stars. To satisfy your most humane petition, I shall render you an accurate account.

"I am Peregrino in name and consequence. My homeland is Modena, founded by Romans in the heart of Emilia, the best part of powerful Italy, ruled and governed by gifted Ercole, the second Estense Duke. My army has been that of Love, and I am its captive through suffering, as you see. Wretched me, I love too ardently! All the celestial passions burn inside me! Woe is me, I sweat in frozen snows and sea brine while cold winds warm my nakedness. I see no end or relief from such ardour, and even though the ocean continually washes over me, it doesn't extinguish this spark in the least.

"Lord, I loved and love a goddess whose sweet and lovely disposition would prompt the surrender of Ionians, Phrygians, Libyans, and all the Greeks. After my unspeakable suffering, I traversed the Orient, searched the realms of hell, and discovered where my lady is held captive. To rescue her, I sailed the Adriatic under the auspices of the ancient queen who reigns there until I was captured and brought here on this ship. Lord, please excuse my erring and my age, at which it would be more fitting to study the celestial theology of Trismegistus, the mystery of Orpheus with his Pythagorean secrets, and Socratic doctrine, along with Platonic majesty and keen Aristotelian erudition, and the wise precepts of great Solon, which do not accord with my present misery.

"Sacred Majesty, Love, which governs, rules, and moderates both this hemisphere and the other, does what it wills and likes, and has brought me to such a point that I cannot think of anything but my lady. Lord, I do not ask pardon of you, because I have never offended you; I do not ask mercy, because I have not served you; I cannot expect aid, because heaven opposes me; nor am I inclined to beg for my health, my life, or anything else of your Highness. Long may you live, King! May the eternal God give you peace for the comfort you've given me. May health, victory, and triumph be yours against your foes!"

Book 3. Chapter 27.

The king is moved to release him and Acate, then tells Peregrino about his own sufferings out of love, begging Peregrino to distract his jealous queen, so he can spend time with the woman he loves.

That compassionate king heard my words, punctuated by tears and deep sighs. He took my weary hand and said to me: "Peregrino, you are mine, and you will always be mine."

Then without delay he freed me and, together with Acate, took me into his service. We were ushered to the royal palace, where celebrations, games, and rejoicing marked our arrival. Our rooms were decorated in marble, and they featured more passageways than the labyrinth of Crete. The whole palace displayed art so resplendent that without tongues each piece seemed to speak.[30] I nourished my mind on this depicted artifice until the king separated himself from his attendants and came down to see me.

After we sat down, he heaved an enormous sigh and said: "Peregrino, if our sufferings have differed, the flame is nevertheless the same. I burn for love no less than you. I trust in your lengthy experience and beg you to find a way to address the cause of my fire. Please satisfy me as promptly as I have taken care of you. Use your poetic talent, or find some other way to pretend or invent some scenario whereby my desire can be fulfilled. When you do, you will find me even more prepared and disposed to offer you greater rewards.

"I love a beautiful young girl with all my heart, but my consort's jealous harping continually assails me, and my desires cannot reach their much-anticipated goal. However, I must be careful to preserve my reputation as much as my life, so that my subjects do not take me as an example to scandalize and insult others. A prince must seem to be exactly what he wishes to be seen and reputed to be. Nonetheless, any shortcoming due to ardour is quite excusable, and I trust in your efforts and secrecy so that all concerned will be protected."

I understood what the king proposed, though he might just as well have asked me to erect all the pyramids of Egypt after conquering the multitudes of Babylon. I was but a foreigner and a begging pilgrim. How was I supposed to carry out this arduous task in foreign lands without knowledge or authority when the heart of the ruling lord could not bring it about? On the other hand, I felt so perpetually in his debt that nothing I could do, not even give up my life, could repay him in the smallest way.

So, emboldened somewhat, I replied …

Book 3. Chapter 28.

Peregrino agrees to help the king and his beloved Constantia, setting in motion a plan that involves the fabrication of a waxen doll.

Peregrino: "Sacred King, it pains me not to have the words or cure that might quench your inner fire. Although a thousand years would be insufficient to repay you, I shall endeavour to satisfy your request to the

---

30 Cf. Dante's *Purgatorio* 10.28–96.

extent possible, in order to render a token of my thanks for your divine assistance. But please do not be annoyed if I speak with the queen. If I can reassure her on one count, then everything else should fall into place. Find an excuse to go riding and tell her to keep me company for a while."

This plan did not displease the king, so he ordered right away that things be arranged as we discussed. When he left the palace, the queen with a modest step approached my rooms, and I went to greet her with due signs of reverence. After we exchanged pleasantries, she had me sit down on a balcony overlooking the sea and sweetly asked me the reason for my capture.

Entering that palace seemed a propitious and blessed beginning that might lead to my great salvation. I began at the beginning of my gruelling love story, which originated in jealousy …

As soon as I said this last word, the queen, without realizing it, emitted a deep sigh, and I went on, saying: "If a person does not find a cure for jealousy, death will assuredly follow."

She smiled, then, and said: "O Peregrino, so that God may happily conduct you safe and sound back to your longed-for home, tell me how you freed yourself from such an aggravating condition. Please do not deny me this knowledge."

She moved a bit away from the servants and freely told me of all her suffering, which consisted of jealousy toward a maiden she suspected her husband lusted after.

It seemed we could speak freely, but I hesitated, saying that when I believed I had a secure repository for my secrets, then I would unload them. She did not spare any of the gods and the blessed among the angelic choirs, swearing not to breathe a word of what I was about to divulge, so my mind should be at ease.

I promised her I could sow such hatred between the king and the maiden that no friendship could be possible between them during their lives or even after their deaths. However, it was necessary that one of the lovers assist me for three or four hours each day for nine days in fabricating an effigy that would cause their everlasting hatred. "O queen, I would need the cooperation of either the king or Constantia" (for this was the name of the maiden). "One of them must mix together a certain combination of dark and white wax, myrrh, gold, incense, and specific herbs gathered during the waxing moon with Venus in the ascendant in conjunction with Jupiter. I recommend that Constantia be locked alone in a room with my recipe to make an image in the king's name, and I'll make sure the effigy's heart is transfixed with a sharp, hot knife. As long as it's pierced, the king will feel only a pernicious hatred toward her."

The queen liked my bogus promise and vowed to arrange all the conditions to best carry it out, beginning the next day. She planned to leave Constantia in the house and go hunt pigs and deer. Just as she made this decision, the king returned.

Smiling, I went up to him, and we spoke casually about his hunt. Meanwhile, the credulous queen excused herself with some ruse to retire to her room. The king wanted to know how it went, so I told him the whole story. He laughed so hard he fell to the ground, and it was easy to believe that his glee might give away what we had planned.

We brought our pleasant exchange to a close and agreed that, the next day, he should go out hunting together with the queen, then, feigning to be on the scent of some boar or indomitable bear, give her the slip, put on other clothes, and return alone to the house. Using the back door, he should then enter the room where I would already have Constantia beginning to put together the wax figure. That way, while the queen was wandering the woods with her retinue, the king would be home pursuing his own little hide-and-seek.

Book 3. Chapter 29.

Despite a rainstorm that interrupts the queen's hunting party, Peregrino's plan works, and both king and queen reward him. He and Acate set sail for Italy and see various cities along the way. In Genoa, they are arrested, together with the ship's financier, under suspicion of commerce with Genoa's enemy.

Heaven, sparing bestower of our every good, unleashed such a downpour that everyone in the queen's hunting party rushed back home. Some stumbled in the front door, some charged the back door, and still others poured through side entries in such disarray that nobody noticed the king's absence.

At the same time the queen returned, Constantia was giving the wily king a first glimpse of her sweet image.

The queen had hardly dismounted before she eagerly asked me if the figurine was turning out well. I promptly answered her, expressing confidence. The queen ascended the stairs and sat down outside the room to wait for Constantia to finish. Precisely four hours later, the maiden emerged sweetly from the room all happy, polite, and pretty, and she reverenced the queen and said to her: "My lady, I have kneaded all morning to warm the wax and incorporate the ingredients."

The queen took such delight in this nonsense that I almost could not hold back my laughter. The king and Constantia continued to apply themselves to their task for nine days. After that, they agreed to pretend to hate each other in order to satisfy the jealous queen.

When I took my leave, both the king and queen rewarded me hand-somely, entrusting me to a Genovese merchant with orders to maintain discretion. We set sail and arrived at Seville, where I had just enough time to visit great Cordoba and strong Toledo. Re-embarking, we navigated propitiously to the famed city of Cartagena, the memory of whose stories reduced me to tears and trembling.[31] Afterward, we passed Valencia, Barcelona, Marseille, Monaco, Albenga, and Savona, just reaching Genoa – a glorious earthly paradise, though inhabited by devils. We stopped to enjoy that delicate land, which is rich, powerful, and beautiful, even if it produces only ingrates. Every other monarchy and republic, citizen, resident, and neighbour carefully constructs and defends their buildings with thought and promptness. Only the Genoese always seek their own ruin.

The ship's patron was suspected of trading with the enemy Catalans. That night, during the Mass to St. George, he was arrested and bound, and Acate and I together with him. Without any public hearing or even private questioning, we were sent to Corsica and held in the carefully guarded Tower of St. Boniface.

Book 3. Chapter 30.

Peregrino and Acate are eventually released with some prisoners of war. Peregrino has a breakdown and must convalesce in a public hospital in Porto Venere for fifteen days. The two friends make their way to Pontremoli, then Parma, where Peregrino completes his recovery.

It was that frigid windy time of autumn, and a lethal dampness oozed from the tower's walls. Not even the contrivance Demetrius built to enter Rhodes could overcome this. Overwhelming dread brought me to a state of melancholy, which most of the time made me fear impossibilities, though other times I hallucinated transforming into a wild beast. All humanity fled from me. My worst humours, stoked by the cold and humidity, corrupted my memory, and I regressed to my most primitive instincts as if newly born.

It happened then, as it did with peculiar frequency, that Corsica declared war on Genoa, which responded by launching a powerful armada under the command of Tommasino Fregoso, who had earned the highest esteem on the mainland as well as on that island.[32] When he reached the

---

31   Cartagena, Spain, is *Carthago Nova*. Peregrino may be trembling at the memory of Scipio Africanus, who, according to Valerius Maximus (in *Factorum ac dictorum memorabilium libri IX*, 4.3.1), resisted the temptation of violating an Iberian princess taken as a war prize, the same incident mentioned in 1.53. Scipio's restoration of her to her father with her virtue intact fuelled Renaissance exemplary stories concerning his continence.

32   Tommasino Fregoso (Tommasino Campofregoso, Lord of Sarzana and governor of Corsica) was born between 1437 and 1443, the first son of Giano I Doge of the Republic of Genoa.

port of St. Boniface, he freed the Genoese merchant together with Acate and me. Out of pity he placed us in the care of certain monks.

Acate and I blinked at each other in wonder. Occasionally we spoke as foreigners do. Our memory was so far gone, yet an inner virtue remained, which inclined us to love even without understanding.

The prior took us out fishing as part of our rehabilitation. But the winds of Aeolus seized our boat, and we knew no peace until they had blown us clear to Porto Venere. The violent rocking, and my constitution, weakened by the damp cold and the persistent threat of shipwreck, provoked in me debilitating fear. I was taken to the public hospital unaware of where I was, and we stayed for fifteen days.

It was there that we saw Giovanni Antonio Tranchedini from Pontremoli, an excellent imperial functionary, who, out of pity, discretion, and generosity, willingly set me on a mule bound for his native city.[33] From Pontremoli, Acate and I continued on to Parma, originally settled by faithful Trojans. There I found a consummate physician, Bartolomeo Anselmi, son of that learned astronomer Giorgio Anselmi, and assisted by Ilario of Antonio Carissimi.[34] The diligent and prudent doctor put me up in his residence outside the city, which was very well suited for our recovery. He prescribed us a series of purgatives made from fruit pulp and castor oil, which put us on the road to health. Gradually and much to our own surprise, we recovered so completely that we forgot all of the endured calamities, nor did much time pass before we resumed our previous plans. We thanked them affectionately and returned to Parma.

Book 3. Chapter 31.

Peregrino reaches Berceto and Torrechiara, where he visits the castle of Pier Maria II de' Rossi.[35] Peregrino relates all that happened to him in his quest to find Genevera. Acate and Peregrino take their leave, bound for Ravenna once again.

---

33 Paola Sverzellati traces the complexities of the Tranchedini family genealogy in "Per la biografia di Nicodemo Tranchedini da Pontremoli, ambasciatore sforzesco."

34 The astronomer Giorgio Anselmi was born in Parma c. 1380 and died after 1451. Besides works on astronomy, he also expounded on mathematics, medicine, and music. Bartolomeo, his son, lived c. 1405–c. 1495. Caviceo calls him a consummate medical doctor; Niccolò Burci concurs, calling Bartolomeo "un altro Galeno" (another Galen). Cf. https:// www.comune.parma.it/dizionarioparmigiani/cms_controls/printNode.aspx?idNode=221. Ilario Carissimi, son of Antonio, was a nobleman of Parma. He may be the one mentioned in a letter of Francesco Sforza, dated 25 January 1451, http://www .lombardiabeniculturali.it/missive/documenti/4.128/.

35 This chapter, perhaps more than some others, permits Caviceo-author to describe places he knows well and people to whom he may feel indebted in his own life. The aforementioned Pier Maria II de' Rossi, Caviceo's protector and patron, died at the Castle of Torrechiara in 1482.

Apollo was entering the house of Mercury when we set off on the road toward our homeland. We crossed the Apennines and arrived at Berceto, the well-defended land of Pier Maria Rossi. Drawn by the castle's famed architecture, which lent the mountain its name of Torrechiara, we went to admire its ingenious structure with its many noteworthy tombs. The Roman Lucius Licinius Lucullus would have readily surrendered there. Taking in the view of the mountain, plain, and river, we judged that there was no more delightful place in all the world to govern.

The castle guardian, browbeaten by our insistence, promised to take us on a private tour of the place to examine its ivory church, dedicated to saints Laurence, Catherine, and Nicomedes, the meadows, gardens, and orchards, the freshwater fountain with its system of wells and cisterns, the castle's rooms and walkways of gold, its strong towers, its broad, triple-enforced walls, and its fertile valleys dedicated to fruit cultivation. The architect of that place had no less talent in design style than Orpheus, Homer, and Virgil had in their disciplines. At long last, we left the castle guardian in peace.

We then got it into our heads that out of virtue and piety we should pay our respects to the homeland of Macrobius, the spirits of two men of the Cassius family (one was Antony's general, and the other was a poet), the ashes of the great Biagio Pelacani, preserved deep in our memory as the famous glossator, as well as the monuments to the jurists Alberto Galeotti and Jacopo da Arena, and the poets Giorgio Anselmi and Basinio da Parma.[36]

We dismounted and looked all around that city. Among the memorable sights was the Church of St. John the Baptist, which is unlike any other in Italy. After we ate, restoring energy to our bodies, we got back on our mounts, crossed the valley, and in no time arrived in Reggio Emilia. The lawyer Andrea Cartari offered us warm hospitality before others realized we were there.[37]

He wanted to hear the story of my life, so I narrated the whole thing from beginning to end. He felt sorry for me and asked if I had heard our

---

36 Vignali notes that Caviceo erred in believing Macrobius's homeland to be Parma (*Il Peregrino*, xxxiv n42). Gaius Cassius Longinus Varus was a Roman consul. The other Cassius (Gaius Cassius Parmensis), among the conspirators against Julius Caesar, was said to have authored various works of literature, though of his poetry we have only one verse attributed to him by Marcus Terrentius Varro. Biagio Pelacani (d. 1416, also known as Blasius of Parma) was a famed philosopher, astrologer, and mathematician. He glossed Johannes de Sacrobosco's *De sphaera mundi*, among other works. Alberto Galeotti and Jacopo da Arena were both jurists active in the thirteenth century. Both Giorgio Anselmi the Younger (d. 1528) and Basinio da Parma (d. 1457) wrote poetic works in Latin. Anselmi would also write Caviceo's biography.

37 I found no other information about Andrea Cartari, possibly an older relative of the famed mythographer and diplomat for Duke Alfonso d'Este, Vincenzo Cartari (d. 1590).

language spoken in foreign countries. I answered him that, if memory served, in Lisbon I had met someone from the city of Ferrara in whose company I had enjoyed myself. His name was Girolamo Roverella, son of that Pietro whose sons and brothers were always successful.[38]

We ended our conversation quite late, and Acate and I set out again without anyone knowing except his relative Niccolò da Correggio, a gentleman most learned in literature who volunteered to go ahead of Acate to find out if any mention was made of us in that land.[39] He set off in silence and returned just as taciturn. He could not learn what had become of Genevera either. We left that sweet country behind, passing Bologna, Folimpopoli, Faenza, and utterly wild places before arriving at our desired land of Ravenna, which we saw through sweet tears. I sighed and addressed the city that held my lady.

Book 3. Chapter 32.

Peregrino offers prayers of gratitude upon entering Ravenna, and extols Genevera, whom he believes he will find there.

Peregrino: 'Most noble, ancient, and generous Ravenna, you have worthily hosted kings and emperors, and you remain the unconquered bastion for afflicted Italy. In honour and glory you surpassed Rome, as every celebrated history sings. May God save and preserve you in that true greatness and supreme joy your heart desires!

'If your fame, after eons, should ever be forgotten, at least you can rejoice in possessing the most glorious goddess that human generation, nature, and God could lend. Therefore, I beseech the innate gentility in you, do not disdain your faithful, long-suffering Peregrino. May he find and acquire through you alone the peace and tranquillity that the whole world denies him. If I've loved and humbly revered you, do not refuse a pious response. After all, where love is lacking, discretion easily dies.

'Genevera, I run to you, sweet soul, with a yearning heart and outstretched arms. Remember, lady, I'm the one who finds perpetual joy in languishing for you. If love has informed both our hearts, then you must burn even more for me, since you are more innocent and delicate. If such pure divinity ever did not accompany you, I'd lack the power to follow you, greatly tormented as I am. But I know that the one for whom I wander and search – and the

---

38   Girolamo Roverella was also the brother of Filasio, the archbishop under whom Caviceo served as vicar general. Girolamo was the captain of the Ducal guard of Ferrara and Lord of Monleone e Montenuovo.

39   Niccolò II Count of Correggio (d. 1508) was a *condottiero* and author of *Aurora* (1486), a pastoral drama in five acts, and a romance poem titled *Psiche*.

one I love, venerate, and adore – is doubtless entirely divine in human flesh. Through your dignity, my lady, that diaphanous body of yours receives your soul as its rightful place – not as a blind prison as it is for other mortals.

'So, with your splendour, which sees, shows, and illuminates all, look upon and accept again your faithful Peregrino, who comes to you humbly and meekly. Your grateful presence would be the reward for all his efforts if you make him worthy to enjoy that. My lady, I live to serve you always, which I consider divine freedom. Therefore, lady, you who can see my heart, know that I don't waver from the truth.'

With these and similar musings I entered the city.

Book 3. Chapter 33.

Peregrino encounters Bernardo Bembo, whose generosity he praises for funding the renovation of Dante's tomb.[40] *Peregrino happens upon a convent, where Sister Ruffina offers him work tending the grounds. During their conversation about the convent's inhabitants, Peregrino suspects that one guest may be Genevera and inquires further about a certain 'Hippolyta.'*

I wandered the streets of the vast city of Ravenna, sighing and weeping. I happened upon Bernardo Bembo, the generous Venetian who honoured Dante by erecting a marble tomb where the Florentine poet's ashes had long lain neglected. The worthy interpreter of Justinian law served as a magistrate and prefect at the time in Ravenna, and I conversed with him out of affection but without divulging to him any of my plans.

Heaven's happy fortune led me to a particular convent[41] where the promise I made to my lady in bitter sweetness might finally be fulfilled. When I entered the vestibule, I saw a woman whose name was Ruffina.

40　Bernardo Bembo (d. 1519) was a pre-eminent Venetian humanist and diplomat, the father of Cardinal Pietro Bembo. He funded the renovation and embellishment of the long-neglected tomb of Florentine poet Dante Alighieri, who died in exile in Ravenna in 1321. For the most recent treatment of this scandal, please see Guy P. Raffa, *Dante's Bones*, especially 45–59. It is tempting to wonder whether Caviceo, in his position as Vicar General of Ravenna, could have had some direct influence in keeping Dante's remains out of Florentine control. I have not (yet) found any proof that Florentine petitions to repatriate Dante's body passed directly through Caviceo's hands. However, it is not unthinkable that the Vicar General of Ravenna might be carefully informed of these attempts.

41　In this and the following chapters that take place in Ravenna, there is a proliferation of classicizing terms – *zenobio, phano, cavaliero, vestale*, etc. – which I translate with their approximate Christian or contemporary meanings – convent, church, nobleman, nun, etc. respectively.

Her habit suggested zealous devotion. She was advanced in years, with a sweet, guileless aspect. She surmised from my overgrown beard, pale and drawn face, and shabby clothes that I must be a farmer or gravedigger. She asked me charitably if I might be able to lend a hand to the convent, given that in eight days their gardener planned to leave. I am not sure why, but my desperate heart began to feel a sweetness, as if I sensed the presence of the lady who was my only consolation in the world.

I answered: "I thank you, Sister. I wish for nothing more than a fresh start. Your offer doesn't displease me in any way. Still, I would like to hear more about the work and its room, pay, and benefits."

"The room," Ruffina said, "is a little place at the end of the garden. The salary is three *bolognini* per month, plus the benefits of meals with a half-loaf of bread and wine. The work? Well, it's considerable, given the great number of us who live here."

Peregrino: "How many?"

Ruffina: "Sixty."

P: "All professed nuns?"

R: "Yes."

P: "What about servants or others?"

R: "Fifteen more."

P: "Prospective novices?"

R: "Fourteen of these, yes."

P: "Then the salary fits the job. All are patrician, these nuns?"

R: "Yes, except there's one lady who came to us three years ago who isn't planning to take vows, but simply wishes to stay with us."

P: "She must be here because of her lust."

R: "Oh no, not at all. She's proper and virtuous."

P: "Why do you say that?"

R: "She wanted to flee from the world. That's all I know."

P: "And her country and father, if you please?"

R: "I don't know."

P: "Her name?"

R: "Hippolyta."

P: "Is this her given name?"

R: "I didn't attend her baptism!"

P: "Well, what does she look like?"

R: "Nature could not have made a more perfect creature."

P: "Her face?"

R: "Clean, luminous, and without blemish."

P: "What colour?"

R: "Like an oriental gem."

P: "Her hair?"

R: "Golden, long, and wavy."
P: "Her forehead?"
R: "Serene."
P: "Her eyes?"
R: "Flashing."
P: "Her age?"
R: "Nineteen years old."
P: "Her nose?"
R: "Clean and shapely."
P: "Her mouth?"
R: "Quite pure."
P: "Teeth?"
R: "White and straight."
P: "Her gums?"
R: "Hygienic, not puffy, bloody, or unclean, not calcified, black, or filthy."
P: "Her breath?"
R: "Pleasant and healthy."
P: "Her tongue?"
R: "Without impediments or lisps."
P: "Her voice?"
R: "Sonorous and clear."
P: "Pronunciation?"
R: "Eloquent and without imprecisions."
P: "Her hands?"
R: "Whiter than snow."
P: "Her fingernails?"
R: "White and pink and well-maintained. None of the nails extends beyond her fingertips, so they don't give offence."
P: "Her feet?"
R: "Always without odour."
P: "Her clothes?"
R: "Proper, rich, and appropriate."
P: "Her gait?"
R: "Delicate, like a crane."
P: "And the way she sits?"
R: "At ease."
P: "What about how she speaks?"
R: "It's serious, but familiar and confiding."
P: "Her laugh?"
R: "Moderate and subdued."
P: "Her conversation?"

R: "Always discerning."

P: "And how does she behave with her companions?"

R: "She's never annoying or insolent, not mean, cruel, boisterous, vindictive, or disdainful."

P: "Is she humble?"

R: "More than a servant."

P: "Affectionate?"

R: "Like a child."

P: "So she's a goddess. What evil has brought her here? Maybe she's orphaned?"

R: "No, she doesn't dress in mournful black. Her clothes are colourful and sumptuous."

P: "How is it she stays here?"

R: "Our abbess is related to her."

P: "What do you mean?"

R: "The sister of her mother."

P: "So she's a native of Ravenna?"

R: "No, actually she came from afar."

P: "Venice? Padua?"

R: "No …"

P: "From where then?"

R: "Somewhere along the Po River, I believe."

P: "How do you know that?"

R: "I heard it said."

P: "She must be from Ferrara."

R: "No."

P: "Then Modena?"

R: "I think so."

P: "Who accompanied her here?"

R: "She entered late one night. Only two women were in her company."

P: "Their names, if you please?"

R: "One was Astanna, who passed away some months ago; the other is Lena, who still serves her."

P: "What kind of woman is this Lena?"

R: "Austere, harsh, and rough."

P: "How much time does she spend with her?"

R: "She never leaves her side."

P: "Then Hippolyta must be under suspicion of something?"

R: "What? No! Here no men enter, not even many ladies, except sometimes relatives."

P: "Why such strict chaperoning then?"

R: "It's to keep her company. She passes most of her time in prayerful devotions."

P: "She must be very temperate."

R: "She hardly lives."

P: "Then she is quite gaunt?"

R: "Oh no, she's graced with flesh on her bones."

P: "Oh my, she must be a saint!"

Speaking in this way, I inadvertently heaved a deep sigh, which startled Ruffina. Seeing that she was moved, I quickly said to her: "I give my greatest thanks to God, Who has brought me to this holy place. If you promise to be faithful and keep my secret, I'll reveal the most glorious mystery under the heavens, and you will surely enter paradise without penance."

Then Ruffina solemnly promised, saying she was and would remain faithful to me.

Once she reassured me, here is what I told her …

Book 3. Chapter 34.

Peregrino spins Ruffina a yarn about how he discovered a treasure of holy relics in Bethlehem. He wishes to entrust them to someone saintly and identifies Hippolyta as this person. Ruffina goes to Hippolyta to share the news.

Peregrino: "Ruffina, my uncle, a Benedictine monk, once told me many years ago about a treasure in Jerusalem so precious that no man in the world could pay its price. For the good of my soul, a desire to search for it grew in me. At some point I fervently and persistently begged God to deign to reveal his spiritual treasure to me. After many devotions, fasts, alms, abstinence, continence, and penance, I received a revelation: I must go to Bethlehem, where I would find what I sought. I made my way there and, not without great difficulty, found it all. Because I must now take an extended period to recover, I think it best to leave the treasure with a saintly person for safekeeping. If you think this Hippolyta of yours is good, then I'll accept your recommendation and entrust it to her.

"But first we must address one detail: I think it best you speak with her first and then, depending on her answer, we can determine how to proceed. I'll describe the holy relics to you now so you can inform her clearly. First of all, there's the breath of an ass and an ox that nourished Christ, Joseph's staff, which he used on walks with the virgin Mary and during Mary Magdalene's penance, the trumpet of the Holy Spirit, manna from heaven, the sermon by Moses, the shadow of the Ascension, the arm raised at the Last Judgment, the chain St. Bernard used to subdue humanity's foe, and some steps from Jacob's ladder used by souls to ascend to heaven."

Ruffina radiated an indescribable joy when she heard these details, and with a humble voice and eyes raised to heaven exclaimed: "O blessed Hippolyta, who shall become the guardian of such a treasure through divine inspiration! And even I'll merit some reward in the eternal life for being the deliverer of these things!" Then she turned to face me and said: "Poor man! For my consolation and comfort, I want to speak with Hippolyta, and I'll relate everything to you."

Her decision did not displease me, since it seemed to take away any unfounded – or perfectly well founded – suspicions.

She left me and went to another room, where she greeted Hippolyta, saying: "Thanks be to God!"

And Hippolyta replied, "Always," with dutiful meekness and bowed head.

Then Ruffina continued: "Hippolyta, my dear, no sweetness in the world exceeds what I feel, nor blessedness beyond what is yours. My heartfelt tears cannot possibly express to you the fullness of the plan that heaven's grace has prepared for you. O true and blessed Hippolyta, happy are those who find themselves in your service in life and in death!"

Book 3. Chapter 35.

Ruffina talks to Hippolyta, who questions her about the newcomer.

Hippolyta was struck with wonder. "Oh my, Ruffina! What news do you bring?"

Ruffina: "I'll tell you."

Hippolyta: "Please do not cry."

R: "I can't seem to stop."

H: "Why not?"

R: "God has touched my heart."

H: "With which hand?"

R: "I can't tell yet, but it's in your power to make it clear to me."

H: "Ruffina, be careful that some false vision has not tricked your heart. It would be wise to seek counsel from the Abbess. I am young, inexperienced, and not adept at interpreting these kinds of mysteries."

R: "I'll inform you completely."

H: "Please."

R: "After going out this morning, I entered the chapel, made a sign of the cross, and knelt before the crucifix."

H: "Either leave me in peace or get to the point. You only torture me with empty words."

R: "Right. I got up, reverenced the chapel's other altars, and shuffled my way outside. I saw coming toward me a man with a thick, black beard who told me about the sufferings he had endured in search of divine things, which he devoutly wishes to leave to this convent. But he wants to consign them into the hands of a saintly lady. Considering the condition of all the women here, it struck me you were the most elect and worthy. Whenever you wish, I'll take it upon myself to make you the guardian of such a treasure."

Then Hippolyta said: "What kind of man is he?"

R: "Quite young."

H: "His age?"

R: "About twenty-six or so."

H: "His face?"

R: "White, long, and well proportioned."

H: "Eyes?"

R: "Black, large, and sparkling."

H: "His speech?"

R: "Discreet and serious."

H: "And his voice?"

R: "Deep and sweet."

H: "His gait?"

R: "Proud and bold."

H: "How was he dressed?"

R: "As a pilgrim."

H: "How did he end up here?"

R: "By chance and fortune."

H: "How did I come up in your conversation?"

R: "In describing your virtue. Now he's placed all of his hope in you."

H: "Did he ask you many things about me?"

R: "Yes, about your name, house, homeland, the reason for your arrival, about your appearance and beauty, and your servants – both the one who died and the one who's still alive."

H: "And what did you tell him?"

R: "What I knew."

H: "You should have told our Abbess the things you heard."

R: "I wouldn't do so for all the gold in the world, for devotion is lost in too loose speech. One can certainly speak with good reason to one person but not what is irrelevant to another. So, please, keep this matter quiet, since there's no authority in hearsay."

H: "I will refrain then out of love for you."

R: "Thank you. Command me what you wish."

H: "I would like to know the name of this pilgrim, then I will let you know. Go in peace and make sure your actions do not draw the suspicions of others."

Book 3. Chapter 36.

Hippolyta, who is really Genevera, suspects that Peregrino has found her and asks to see his holy relics.

Ruffina went out, leaving Genevera in no less turmoil than Caesar must have felt when he cast the die and crossed the Rubicon. She feared some trap or new deception, which could harm her reputation or destroy her social standing.

She asked herself: 'If this man is Peregrino, how did he learn where I am? Astanna is dead, and Lena is captive here. Anastasia would never breathe a word about this, and the other sisters know nothing about me.

'Maybe Peregrino is dead. Perhaps his spirit has taken another body; and in whatever form passion possessed him while living, he must now do penance after death. But if this were true, what would become of me? What happened to so many other ladies! Was there ever a more unfortunate one? Of course, it's no great tragedy to lose what one never possessed. And yet I hope …

'Perhaps he is not dead. If it is him, then arranging things would be difficult indeed. I must speak to him, but perhaps it would be better to do so by some other means. But how? Right! Ruffina will bring him to this room. If he only recognized the burden he puts on others; a depraved life, led in this way, cannot be excused. O how difficult it is to make a decision when one is entirely ignorant of reliable information! Perhaps Fortune has changed for the better and will raise me up.'

Reasoning with herself in this way, she waited eagerly for Ruffina, who had just come back to me. Even through the confusion of her speech, Ruffina made everything clear to me. So, I wrote the following letter, which explained with the utmost discretion who the pilgrim was and what holy relics he brought.

Book 3. Chapter 37.

Peregrino's brief note obliquely describes his purpose, and Ruffina delivers it to Hippolyta-Genevera. A meeting is set for the following morning.

My Lady,
To find my rich treasure, I traversed the earth, searched through hell, crossed the sea, climbed many hills, and exhausted my body and soul beyond belief. Then auspiciously I arrived here, a poor pilgrim but with a heart content to entrust it to you. So your fame may be celebrated, I ask you care for it, and may it bring about your salvation and my contentedness.

When you make me worthy of a holy audience, I will divulge the observances necessary for keeping it secure. In my complete devotion, I await your answer, which I pray God guides in the right direction, as is proper for a holy lady.

Remain in peace, flower of sanctity.

Ruffina humbly accepted the letter I wrote and faithfully presented it to Hippolyta, whom she insistently urged to accept the divine treasure. Hippolyta read and reread the letter, easily understanding who this 'pilgrim' was, and she pretended with Ruffina to hold in awe what was to be entrusted to her. In the end, she agreed to proceed according to the faithful recommendation, but she insisted on doing so without a meeting in her room so as to avoid falling into scandal.

What she said didn't displease Ruffina, though she fretted profusely that such a desired end might not arrive at its rightful conclusion. The two women looked at each other in doubt and in silence, not knowing how to resolve the situation.

In the end, Ruffina broke the silence: "Our summer kitchen, which is currently in disuse, has a corner window that looks onto our garden. I'll show him there, and you can come to that kitchen at the appointed time and freely arrange things there."

Without another word, she moved from words to actions. Ruffina came back to me and declared that the following morning after matins I must present myself at that place in the garden, which would offer me the space to consign my treasure to Hippolyta.

We left without another word. Octavian could not have been happier to return to Egypt than I was to return to my rooms to relate everything to Acate, who told me …

Book 3. Chapter 38.

Acate reminds Peregrino of the risks involved in what he is doing. Later that night, Peregrino wanders around the convent grounds to think. He is spotted by the night watch but evades them by hiding in a crypt.

Acate: "Rarely does sunny weather not eventually bring a storm. If you don't temper your boundless excitement, it's bound to turn bitter. O how unthinking you are! The place you're going is sacred! And if you're discovered there at that hour, it'll be a capital offence, both by human and divine law. You're young and more than a little suspicious dressed as you are. You're a foreigner in a land that's on its guard. Every dog barks at the new moon. If you were captured, you'd be charged with enough crimes to make your head spin. Wanting to be their gardener wouldn't excuse you.

"As if you were the best choice for that line of work! You weren't born to hoe, to get filth on your hands and all over your clean, white, clear skin. Your delicate feet don't thrive on dirt clods; your noble digestion can't stomach slop; your fine coif won't withstand wind or rain. You've never previously spoken with this foolish woman, yet you put your life in her hands!"

Then I replied: "Acate, it takes more than a weak stick to beat down a well-locked door. It isn't a lesser vice to fear everything than to wager it all. So what if a poor vagabond, dressed like a hermit, is picked up? What could be said or done? The time and place are apt to prayer – I'd more likely receive commendation than blame. If my philosophical study doesn't fail me now, I understand that every perfected plan has its appointed hour to accord with the supreme harmony of heaven's motions. Besides, if I were appointed to work a garden outside my city for my health, it would hardly be such an unheard-of thing, since all the Roman nobility sought recreation in the countryside doing just that."

Acate: "Not for lust, but for virtue."

Peregrino: "What is love if not the height of virtue? Those Romans toiled after something corruptible, but I for the incorruptible."

We continued to speak in this way while we saw to the needs of our stomachs. After we had happily dined, we were shown to respectable rooms to rest. But that night I slept little, accompanied as I was by desire. It wasn't until close to midnight that I rested my eyes in half-sleep.

The Moon, renouncing her meeker nature, beamed a sun-like splendour through a hole in my window. In a stupor and angry at myself for still being awake so late, I got up without rousing Acate. I left the house through a back door and headed toward that sweet place of our meeting, though I could neither see nor hear much of anything. Heaven, earth, and the nearby sea all conspired to leave me in utter silence.

In front of the church door was a marble bench. I sat down there shortly before the public clock struck four in the morning. I felt cold and distressed. The night was long, and the sky clear and starry. The earth was frigid enough to seem hard as concrete. There was no shelter from the winds that blew to test their might. My light clothes offered scant protection. Going was risky, but staying was just as dangerous. I began to fear capture when – lo and behold – my fear was realized!

Not far off I glimpsed in the moonlight some armed men, and they caught sight of me. Hastening their steps with weapons at the ready they cried threateningly: "Seize, seize the traitor!"

Lacking favour or advice, I had no idea what to do. But fearing disgrace, I hid in a half-opened crypt I saw nearby. The group of guards arrived, stopped, and looked all around, but no one could make sense of it. One marvelled: "It must've been a ghost!" Another swore he had seen a man. The sisters' church reverberated even with a curse word or two – one muttering one thing, contradicted by another. Finally, someone decided to leave one guard behind to watch the grounds until daybreak to see if anyone entered or left.

Book 3. Chapter 39.

After daybreak Peregrino emerges from his hiding place, is revived by Ruffina, and reunites with Genevera.

Apollo moved from Pisces to Aries while I crouched in that dark, horrid sepulchre; nor did I emerge before the morning rays were shining. The guard had left, and the church was open. I stumbled in without any feeling in my legs. My teeth chattered like eager reapers hacking mature fodder in the fields. Ruffina, moved to pity, took me to the gardener's quarters, where she lit a good fire, and I began to regain my lost feeling.

At the appointed hour Genevera appeared on one side of the window, and I presented myself on the other. We gazed at each other, she at my beard, incongruous attire, and changed face, while I contemplated her unchanged beauty. We remained in shock and suspended, like Io, daughter of Ianachus.

Finally, not without tears in my eyes, I raised them to heaven and opened my mouth to speak these words of love ...

Book 3. Chapter 40.

Peregrino gives thanks to God and informs Genevera that he saw traitorous Astanna in the Other World.

Peregrino: "O adored by God and the face of the world, O celestial form, O splendour of the universe, O dignity of the virginal sex, O glory of the ages, O apple of my eye, O little heart burning with honest love, O sweetest comfort, O infallible hope, O one and only deliverer of all my suffering, O consoling happiness, O my lady, beloved, and mistress, O eternal blessing, may God save and preserve you! O greatest sweetness of my life, I don't know which joy more readily appears to my soul: seeing you safe and sound and in firm and constant love, or seeing that manifest traitor dead who conspired to destroy our love, hatefully threaten our lives, squander our goods, entrap us when we least expected it, and divulge all our secrets! My lady, I feared you had lost your life because of that ribald Astanna's betrayal. While I searched the Other World for you, these very eyes saw her going to perpetual punishment in hell.

"O great and exalted God, how can I render You thanks enough? Not in words, because You are the Author of wisdom; not through kingly authority, since You are the Lord of all. I cannot offer my life, because You are its Maker. But still, so as not to pass as an ingrate, I will offer my sacrifices eternally at Your holy altar. You have led me to a state of happiness: my lady is in good health, and in a most chaste place, preserved most virtuously. I am confirmed in love, and our enemy is relegated to sempiternal flames. It would take a thousand poem-reciting tongues furnished with copious commentaries to express the great desire of my heart and mind right now. I want to tell you so many things that I don't know where to begin. But I will speak briefly now about what my heart urges most and leave the rest to more leisurely occasions, since I've reached the goal of all my wearying peregrinations."

Book 3. Chapter 41.

Peregrino proposes marriage to Genevera, without the approval, blessing, or dowry her father might provide. His alternative is to end their relationship for good.

Peregrino: "I don't believe it necessary, O sole lady of mine who gives solace and health to my life, to recall and list what our divine love has been and is after all our toils, suffering, separations, and torments. If we had continued to pursue this love merely out of stubbornness or idiocy, it wouldn't have endured. It must have a more than human life, a divine one. Although our soul consists of divinity in large part, still, when it suffers over and over again, it weakens, gets tired, and consumes itself just like an act of the body (which divine Plato also seems to teach in his Law).

"Therefore, to preserve our body and soul together we must now convert our long languishing into eternal consolation. My recommendation would be: since heaven has reunited us, we endeavour never to break this bond, not even in death. I've accumulated enough holdings that we could live comfortably and honourably either in our city or abroad.

"If you were to compare my loving thought and firm decision to anyone else's, you wouldn't find another man so mindful of your wishes or faithful in advice to you. You've seen how inhumane and cruel your father's severity has been toward you, and how you've been sent away here as a derelict and unappreciated thing, which wouldn't be right even for a rebel against a king's divine majesty.

"What worse punishment could public justice bring against you if you had committed matricide or patricide? If you've been relegated here because you've loved virtuously, what would've happened to you if you had loved otherwise? And if they've acted so cruelly without any reason, what would they do if a more serious matter presented itself to them?

"Almost five years have passed now since love first bound our hearts together in equal measure and to the extent that neither of us can withdraw. Since we see heaven so favourably disposed toward us now, we shouldn't be presumptuous or audacious in going against its will. How else could you explain that I've managed to find you again in the face of so many obstacles or merited the vision of Astanna if it weren't the ultimate will of God to bring us together forever?

"Sweet lady and dear ruler of my heart, say that you agree with my faithful and loving recommendation, and do not order me to go crossing the sea or searching in strange lands or begging favours from foreign people or losing more of my life, which was born for this world only to serve you. By now you must be assured of my love. You couldn't possibly be more honoured or loved by any other man in the whole world. I don't deny you deserve a better man, however, or that you couldn't attract one, only that he wouldn't be more adoring of you.

"Up to this time, every act of mine has offered you clear evidence, so what I say cannot be a mystery to you. If it seems right to you, as it should, you can claim what is dearly and assuredly yours. Otherwise, we break this off right now, and tomorrow morning I'll be gone for good! I await your answer."

Book 3. Chapter 42.

Genevera presents Peregrino the belt that marks their commitment to love. She asks him about Astanna and begs him to ask her father, Angelo, for marriage terms in a prudent way before acting rashly.

Genevera: "Peregrino, if my memory did not retain evidence of your past deeds I might not believe you were the same man I encouraged in true good and the closest love. Something about what I see in you made me strongly doubt you were Peregrino – maybe some other who was trying to impersonate you. But your recounted memories of endured suffering out of love show me you are indeed Peregrino – happily returned and most welcome.

"So you may believe I have no further doubts in this regard, see here our belt, the cause of much of our shared burning, and which brought greedy Astanna's condemnation for carrying out Anastasia's plan of betrayal, because it was not right of her to keep it or show it to further her own honour.[42]

"Now, once again, I welcome you. Just as you are you, so am I me; and it is necessary that one mind inform our same flesh so that neither of us

---

42 Genevera's avowal that Astanna had the belt, given by Anastasia as a reward for service, will be further clarified in 3.44.

should veer from the true path. But I beg you, given that we have the time, please tell me now what you saw of Astanna's suffering soul. Then we can get into the details of what you have proposed."

I accepted the prized belt from her lovely white hands, and I felt I had reached the height of blessedness. I said: "After you were taken away, and I had overcome great perils, I travelled as far as hell without learning any news of you. I was so exhausted and frustrated that I considered returning and putting an end to my life, because I believed death would be preferable to life without you. As I was leaving hell, I saw a soul descending from the world above. I asked the guardian of that place why she was there, and he insisted I learn that for myself. I couldn't even open my mouth to ask her before she cried out: 'I am Astanna, the reason for your long erring,' and then she told me true information about you."

Genevera: "Oh my, Peregrino, how did you have the heart to enter the shadows of hell and then return?"

Peregrino: "I did it to see you."

G: "You certainly are brave!"

P: "My actions prove it."

G: "Did you do it for glory or out of love?"

P: "You're wise, so I won't answer that."

G: "But if you had died, where would my glory be?"

P: "I would've been content, and you immortalized."

G: "I beg you to recount the whole matter seriously."

P: "But time is short, and it demands we deal with other matters while Ruffina stands watch. Even our perfectly innocent speech can sometimes be misconstrued. Let's make a decision, then we'll have plenty of time to catch up."

G: "One deliberates poorly who fears too much. If I agree to what you have proposed, then death and perpetual infamy will always accompany me. If refuse, pain and suffering will always crush me. Besides, I cannot even determine what I want for myself. But you are a mindful judge of virtuous thoughts … you decide and command me. I will submit entirely to your discretion and prudence.

"You are the charioteer, and I am the chariot; you are the helmsman, and I am the boat. But please, avoid a dishonoured life and a shameful death, because it is most fitting for a magnanimous spirit to die upon the sun chariot. That is why Phaeton receives praise for his glorious death. That chariot symbolizes none other than an unconquered and long-sought virtue to which we incline with all our force because – when toils are praiseworthy and celebrated through fame – they are never worthy of reprehension.

"Before we resort to options that are less than honest and worthy, let us face our peril with something to alleviate the pain and fortify our bodies before we must resort to a rhubarb tonic.[43] If the following two courses of treatment do not work for us, then we are left only with the last resort, which we must avoid if at all possible. The first palliative would be for you to ask Angelo to marry me with certain terms demonstrating your suitability, generosity, and gratefulness. If he agrees, then we will achieve our goal with mutual satisfaction. If not, then we will follow luck and fortune. Finally, where God is lacking, Acheron can provide.

"But I do not believe Angelo is so unyielding as to persist in obstinate refusal. Nevertheless, you must negotiate very carefully so he does not discover where you are. Otherwise, if he had any indication you had come here, he would move me again or find some other way to cut me off from you so that neither Ruffina nor anyone else would have access to speak to me. As long as he is more enraged against you than concerned for me, he will prefer that no man in the world ever see me."

Her tears kept pace with her words, and she continued: "If this way also seems best to you, then think carefully, be patient, and carry out your plan. In the brief time we have, stay vigilant, and when you have a solution, get in touch with Ruffina, who can go between us at will and communicate to me any next steps."

I could do nothing more than praise her most prudent judgment and promise to do as she said. When we agreed on everything between us, I told her the entire story of my peregrinations, at the end of which I told her to persuade Ruffina that the one who came in the guise of a pilgrim was really an angel taking a human body, and to serve as proof, I showed her an ivory box, marvellously carved, which I had carried from Damascus.

When the time came, I humbly paid my respects and departed from her in body, though in spirit I was still under her power, as you shall hear.

Book 3. Chapter 43.

Peregrino confers with Acate, who tells him an exemplary tale. Peregrino eventually convinces Acate to return to Ferrara to convince Angelo to put aside familial hostilities and permit his marriage to Genevera.

I returned and told Acate everything. He smiled and said: "Peregrino, what you're experiencing is just like what happened some time ago to

---

43   Medicinal properties of rhubarb seem to be common knowledge in Italy from at least the Middle Ages, likely through writings, commentaries, and translations referencing Avicenna and other Arab doctors or herbalists through the school in Salerno. The tone of this passage suggests that a rhubarb tonic was viewed as a treatment for the gravest medical cases.

a canon and talented preacher named Don Domenico da Treviso. Once when he was in the city of Genoa, he took gravely ill because he couldn't pass urine. He continually prayed to God that He not deny him this grace. In the end, the preacher's infirmity increased, his pains multiplied, and his powers flagged. So, he prayed to God with even greater intensity that He spare his life, so that in receiving satisfaction he might satisfy others as well.

"One of Don Domenico's servants who attended him couldn't contain himself and blurted out how surprised he was at the canon's great persistence. If God didn't grant him a bit of urine, why did he think God would want to give him the great gift of life?

"You are just like him, Peregrino! You've convinced yourself that, even though Angelo has never once permitted you a single audience with Genevera, he'll now let you marry the one who is dearest to him in all the world! Nevertheless command, and I will obey you."

Peregrino: "You must return to our homeland and, through the influence of friends and well-chosen words, seize this moment to convince Angelo that from now on he should eradicate all memory of discord between us, which was sown by our ancestors but persists and festers in our day. To convince him my heart is sincere in wanting unity, peace, and tranquillity, I ask him for his daughter Genevera in marriage. If he asks where I am, tell him I've been delayed in Sicily. If he consents to our wish, let a month pass before you call me back home. If he denies us, send word quickly and quietly through one of my manservants so I have time to provide for what my heart will dictate next."

Acate: "Peregrino, this is a very serious undertaking. Angelo will take offence, then ask for time to think it over. In the meantime, he'll put Genevera under even closer surveillance. Let's take a different approach, if you're open to it: I'll try to understand through Violante what opinion Anastasia and Angelo have of you. If it's favourable, I'll express your wish. But if it's not, I'll say you died on the island of Rhodes.

"Remember the two Romans who were enemies their whole life, but when the false news reached one of the other's death, they wholeheartedly reconciled? Perhaps if Angelo hears about your death he'll be sorry, and what happened to them could happen to you. When I see him in that state of regret, I'll swear to him that you love and respect him as a son and you've always sought a way to mend your relations with him. If he inclines warmly, I'll use these terms: 'It was true that I left him there on his deathbed, but because of a lack of funds I had to return here. However, if God saved his life, would you be content to mend bridges through Genevera?' If he agrees, I'll let you know right away; if he refuses, then we'll be certain you'll never find contentment this way."

His new plan didn't displease me, and to carry out this order he set off on horseback and arrived in Ferrara three days later.

Book 3. Chapter 44.

In Ferrara, Acate confers with Violante, who confirms that Angelo awaits confirmation of Peregrino's death, so he can withdraw Genevera from the convent and marry her to the gentleman from Reggio Emilia. Meanwhile, Peregrino and Genevera discuss what she endured during their time apart.

The false report of our shipwreck on Rhodes spread throughout the city to the extent that we were largely forgotten. In secret, disguised as a refugee, Acate left his horse with a stable boy at an inn and went to Violante's house, where he found her safe and sound. She lavished him with news of all the comings and goings in the city and in Angelo's house. After Violante was assured I was still alive, Acate revealed my secret plan to her. Violante replied that Angelo wanted nothing more than to hear the true confirmation of my death so he could immediately send Genevera to marry the Reggio Emilian. Still, she encouraged Acate to pursue our new plan.

In the meantime, I spoke various times with Ruffina, thanking her, flattering her, and giving her some prayer objects from the east, in exchange for which she continued to let me visit the garden, showing eagerness for the conclusion of the previous gardener's term.

Early one morning, through Ruffina's intercession, Genevera appeared. After we were settled in our usual places and had exchanged greetings, I told her about the instructions I had given Acate and asked her: "Lady, how did you get here?"

"Oh my, Peregrino," she responded, "it is death just to think about it, let alone speak of it."

"Lady," I said, "the same fruit that's bitter and hard becomes sweet when it has ripened. Whatever perturbs you now will be pleasant to remember one day. So, please, tell me everything with a brave heart."

She continued: "You had hardly left my room when that traitor Astanna led my brothers there to deprive me of life. With voices raised in fury, they demanded I open the door. Mindful of your instruction, I hid quietly inside. My silence only bolstered the perception of my guilt; they convinced themselves you lurked in my bedroom. Finally, fearing the worst, but assured that enough time had passed to allow you to easily get out of the house, I opened the door to them. They entered without a word to me and looked all around, up and down, in every crack and crevice, under the seats and the bed, with lanterns lit and swords unsheathed in their hands, but in vain they searched and threatened death.

"Anastasia, Lena, and Astanna all sat with me in my room. They studied me; they pleaded, blamed, and scorned me. Each one menaced a different punishment for me: death, exile, or other sufferings. My brothers returned after searching the whole garden and determined to find out who was lying: my accuser Astanna or me. They interrogated me bitterly about who the man was who had been with me alone in my room just a little while ago. I told them that I had not seen any men but them.

"Astanna told me to my face: 'You're lying! Fraud, cheater …!' Anastasia did not feel comfortable with accusations flying so freely, so she sent my brothers away.

"Anastasia, Astanna, and I remained there alone, and Anastasia told me: 'O everlasting stain on this house and your city! What've you done? O traitor to yourself, false woman, O ungrateful daughter, O wicked seed, it would've been better to be a bold prostitute out in broad daylight than to sneak a young man – and an enemy no less! – into this house under the eyes of your father and brothers. You cannot deny it. Here's the evidence, here's the belt, here's a letter written in your own hand! I know you're a liar, yet you deny it with a brazen face. What you refuse to confess out of love will be bitterly punished through the evidence you've left. Say it: Is this your belt?'

"And I said, 'No. I never had such riches to create that kind of a noble adornment, and you know this better than I.'

"'Is the letter yours?'

"'Yes.'

"'To whom did you send it?'

"'Not to anyone. It was a writing exercise.'

"'And the young man you had in the house?'

"'No man in the flesh, though perhaps he was in my mind.'

"Astanna said: 'Anastasia, do you believe this?'

"And she replied, 'A locked prison and chains will reveal the truth.'

"Then with an indignant face I turned to her and said, 'Anastasia, you accrue little honour by accusing your daughter of infamy. This ribald, who has always been unfaithful, greedy, and wicked, has sold a pack of lies to you, and it would be more honourable for you to be silent than speak of this. Calm down and stop overreacting. The more you search, the less you will find.'

"This rankled Anastasia even more, and to spur Astanna more urgently against me, Anastasia gave the belt to Astanna just to spite me. They left the room and locked me in it alone for the night.

"The next day passed without a crumb of food. The next night they came into my room and put a black hooded mantle over me, like the kind worn by condemned men going to their execution. I was put on a boat. I saw nobody, and nobody saw me until I was here where you found me.

"The fasting was difficult and long. I was assigned to this room, which I was never permitted to leave while Astanna was alive. She surprised me in the end, acknowledging all her offences and asking my forgiveness. She left me the belt you have now.

"Even though my emotions toward her were bitter and powerful, I was even more overwhelmed by thoughts of you, uncertain about whether you lived or had died. Given that God has rewarded me with your presence, let us put an end to any lamentations and look forward to living happily. I think I hear the ladies coming toward the garden, so I encourage you to be consoled and move away so they do not become suspicious."

I left the garden and the church and went back to my room crying abundant tears to the point that I couldn't speak or eat.

Book 3. Chapter 45.

When Angelo hears of Peregrino's presumed death, he orders a servant named Antoniolo to take a letter to the Abbess giving instructions for what she should do next with Genevera. Acate learns of it through Violante, disguises himself, and accompanies Antoniolo, pilfering the letter en route.

While Genevera and I could interact this way, Acate was back in our homeland confirming the news that had been circulating about my presumed death. Everyone grieved my untimely death. Just then one of Angelo's servants, who was very close to Violante, told her among other things that Angelo was sending him to Ravenna with an important letter for the Abbess of Sant' Andrea. Violante realized that this must be where Genevera was being held in secret and that, because Angelo was assured of my death, he was on the verge of freeing her. Without hesitation, Violante called for Acate and told him he must immediately disguise himself and accompany Angelo's servant, whose name was Antoniolo, and discover surreptitiously the message and tenor of that letter.

Acate jumped on a horse without another word and ran into Antoniolo barely ten stadia from the city.[44] They exchanged greetings, and Acate asked him about his trip. Antoniolo indicated that he was headed to Ravenna, and Acate said he was bound for Rimini. They decided to ride

---

44 See 199n31.

together and quickly became friends. Antoniolo recounted many details about Angelo's household.

When evening fell, they filled their bellies with wines from Tasio and Crete, and Antoniolo closed his eyes, falling into a sleep so deep there wasn't any way to revive him. When Acate saw this, he furtively extracted the letter, opened it, and read it. Here is its gist …

Book 3. Chapter 46.

Acate reads Angelo's letter to the Abbess and decides to replace it with his own forgery containing a much different message.

Reverend Mother and Sister,

God has freed me from my great anxiety: Nature has ignominiously taken that persistent stalker Peregrino of Antonio. Therefore, I have decided to marry Genevera to Galeazzo of Reggio Emilia, since he is a man of honest character and intentions. In preparation, find a clever way to let Genevera know so she will accept my choice. I am sure she will on your holy recommendation. If she does not, she will need to learn how to live according to a way of life worse than death. So, while time permits, guide her where reason, virtue, and her duty demand. This will please me and be a comfort to her.

Regards.

After Acate reread and considered the letter, he understood he couldn't overcome Angelo's stubborn resistance – and if things continued it would be impossible to make Genevera's virginity spotless again – much less change his mind.

So, inspired from on high, Acate devised a new plan to revive my perishing life: he wrote another letter that went like this …

Book 3. Chapter 47.

The text of Acate's letter orders the Abbess to arrange a marriage between Peregrino and Genevera, but keep it secret.

Reverend Mother and Sister,

Although my stubborn mind was bitterly opposed to the will of Peregrino of Antonio, it was not out of any fault or shortcoming of his. Instead, it was due to certain jealousies among our ancestors whose less than virtuous examples we should not follow. Therefore, in my own conscience I have set aside every negative bias, rancour, animosity, and senseless emulation of the past attitudes toward him. I now love him as much as I unworthily hated him before. In order to preserve our good and true peace – and so it not be thought feigned or just for show – I have promised my daughter Genevera to be his perpetual bride, and I pray God will grace their union with every good success, which made Jacob the father of many tribes of Israel.

Because it is a serious matter to break a promise, you will need to be my shield and sword in this matter, which you can do for your honour and my salvation. I contracted another engagement for Genevera with a gentleman in Reggio Emilia. Since I firmly wish it to be revoked, he will hold this against me, as will his posterity in supreme enmity. Thus, it is necessary that when you receive this letter, you exercise your authority for the peace and tranquillity that is between us to follow these instructions and have her marry Peregrino of Antonio with an exchange of rings in the presence of your sisters.

You should also share my decision with Genevera and secretly send word to Peregrino, who is currently staying at the Inn of the Angel. You will receive the most precise and faithful information about him through Francesco Artusino, a gentleman of Ravenna.[45] However, I do not want you to breathe a word about this, so that in the future there are no witnesses to my broken promise. In order for this matter to progress expediently and secretly, once you have received this letter you should send the present messenger to stay on one of your farms outside the city until the marriage can be finalized. I want the sum of the dowry to be two pounds of gold, and another pound of gold for her along with her other goods. With this express condition and pact, Genevera should pass from her parents' oversight. In this, I want Peregrino to be able to vouch for all of my present and future goods. When it seems appropriate to you, you can inform me in detail through this messenger of mine.

Regards.

Book 3. Chapter 48.

After Acate places the new letter in Antoniolo's bag, the two men part ways, and Acate goes directly to inform Peregrino. As soon as Antoniolo delivers the letter to the Abbess, she makes the marriage arrangements. Francesco Artusino accompanies Peregrino, who confronts his own doubts and fears.

---

45   I have no more specific information about Francesco Artusino.

Acate's letter had a certain similitude to, indeed it was indistinguishable from, the one Angelo had written. Acate carefully lifted the seal from the original letter and placed it with such care on his replacement that it seemed to be impressed there by the hand of its maker. Acate folded up this letter and put it where he had found the other one.

The next morning the two men praised the previous night's dinner and the sleep they had enjoyed that night. They began to discuss lunch. They rode to Imola, and that evening they propitiously arrived in Faenza. It seemed like the right time for Acate to part from Antoniolo's company, telling him that it was here that their paths diverged. So, wishing each other well, they went to separate inns to get ready for the following morning's departures.

Persephone's first light had not yet shone over the earth when eager Acate was already back on his horse. He reached me that same day and informed me of everything. Even though the outcome of his efforts was not yet apparent, we were nonetheless consoled. I shaved my beard, changed clothes, and dressed in the richest robe adorned with oriental gems, which generous King Pietro of Portugal had given me. I took into my service four men of patrician rank, such that I was unrecognizable even to myself.

Antoniolo arrived the next day as anticipated, and he immediately presented himself, properly reverencing the Abbess. He delivered the reworded letter to her, which she read to her ladies and Genevera. Right away, she sent Antoniolo away from the city and summoned Francesco Artusino to accompany me to where the wedding would take place. Then she prepared a ground-floor room fitting enough to receive Octavian.

Almost immediately, Francesco came to me begging most humbly to go with him to the Abbess of Sant' Andrea. He indicated that she had secret, urgent matters to discuss. With a serious look of wonder on my face and a contented heart, I asked him repeatedly what made this visit so urgent. He insisted in all innocence that he did not know but he believed it must be due to the grace of a spiritual vision. We walked together talking about various matters.

Still my imagination ran wild. I did not trust Angelo's servant. I was also terrified that Genevera might not assent to our union out of overcautiousness. Moreover, the condition of the nuns also gave me pause; perhaps they would not want to proceed so quickly to celebrate the wedding or would want to move it to a different location. I continued turning over similar thoughts in my mind.

Francesco and I arrived at the holy place. The Abbess was waiting for us with her elect company in the vestibule. I thanked Francesco and entered the church with the Abbess, whom I reverenced.

After the two of us sat down, she said ...

Book 3. Chapter 49.

The Abbess, who is related to Angelo through his marriage to Anastasia, rejoices at the reconciliation of their family with Peregrino's and asks Peregrino to consent to marry Genevera, which he does.

Abbess: "Peregrino, even before I ever saw you I loved you. Now that I have seen and met you I revere you, because you seem to be precisely what nature produced you to be, and you worthily merit every grace you possess.

"Today divine meekness and just mercy have put an end to your suffering, and so may they direct the purity of your mind. My brother-in-law Angelo, who was once your foe, now wishes with a trusting heart to reconcile with you. He who was your enemy has become your defender and protector. If you are as well disposed toward him as he is toward you, he is content to offer in marriage his daughter Genevera. I believe she will accept you with all her heart, and in her name I promise her to you, to be confirmed in the presence of all, according to what is necessary and proper in confirmation of rites of this kind. If you agree, then we'll go to Genevera to get her consent."

After she said these words, I answered: "My lady, it is a greater virtue to love than to be loved, since the first is an act of the will, and the other imposed from another.[46] If you love me, you do so out of your innate nature inclined to virtue, which compels me to imitate you. With infinite thanks I am indebted to you and, if I have been slow to pay my respects to you, it isn't due to sinful malice, but rather because this is all so unanticipated. That fire of enmity Angelo has extinguished will now spark a flame of love in us that not even all the ocean's waves could tamp down in the least. Angelo is doing his duty as a good father and respected citizen, and he has considered what is good for himself and his daughter. With an ardent heart I accept her as my legitimate spouse from your hand."

We stood up and walked toward the room where Genevera sat chastely attended. Full of reverence she came forward. I on one side and she on the other, balanced like a well-laden ship, we marched, standing and awaiting our desired goal. I heard the voice of God's priest say to us as he looked at each of us admiringly ...

---

46 To love is an *acto volentario*, an act of the will/volition; to be loved, he says, perhaps intending another play on words, is *violentato*, a term that shares an array of possible meanings from something akin to violent imposition to violation/rape. My choice of phrasing in the translation indicates my hesitation to specify anything quite so strong.

Book 3. Chapter 50.

Peregrino and Genevera pronounce their vows; later they kiss and tease one another.

Priest: "Peregrino and Genevera, are you both free of all vows both private and public? Respond."

Peregrino and Genevera: "We are free and unencumbered."

Priest: "Are you related by blood?"

P and G: "We are neither related nor do we have many shared friends."

Priest: "Have you ever pledged yourselves to be engaged or married to another man or woman?"

P and G: "Never."

Priest: "Is it of your own free will that you are here to celebrate this present rite of holy matrimony?"

P and G: "We want it with all our heart and faith."

Priest: "You, my lady, present your finger, and Peregrino will place a ring on it."

After this was done, as was the custom, we went and sat down together. Talking with her, I playfully asked: "So, Genevera, when did you begin to have feelings for me?"

Genevera: "Your first letter sparked in me a fire I had never felt before and set me on the path to love."

Peregrino: "And when did it grow?"

G: "Your arrest bound me."

P: "When did you reach the fullness of your love?"

G: "When I feared you and Lionora were together. That brought me unbearable suffering, and if it were not for her consideration toward me I would never have had peace. Afterward, when I thought you had given the belt to Lionora, such a lethal pain grew in me that I thought I would leave this life."

P: "Oh my, you were always so harsh."

G: "Harsh? No. But self-respecting, yes."

P: "I endured so much."

G: "Yours are trifles compared to what we women go through."

P: "Why do you say that?"

G: "The soul, which perceives many things, cannot feel a particular pain, which is the one that truly destroys. You men distract yourselves by toiling and thinking about lots of things, and you act in such a way that your days and nights pass tranquilly. But we women are wretched and captive, so we are never free of this one constant burning, and we can think or speak of nothing else. Thus, the experience of love is different between men and women."

P: "So a lady loves more than a man?"

G: "Obviously."

P: "Your love is more doubtful, though."

G: "And yours less faithful."

P: "We shall take up this debate again in a few days."

G: "You will still lose it."

P: "Whoever learns never loses."

G: "Nobody can teach law to Minerva."

P: "O clear eloquence, O blessed hour, O propitious day, O my hope has attained its highest prize! In you, my lady, gentility, discretion, and cleverness have their seat. In you every good thing may be found. You're the true music and harmony of every discord. I find you correct in every way: at times concise, other times copious; sometimes dry, other times florid; at times sweet, now perhaps less charitable. The Maker of heaven, in making you, imitated that true Exemplar that is the highest perfection of all."

Speaking and teasing each other in this way and squeezing our hands sweetly, I pretended to whisper to her, but gave her quick tiny kisses instead, which made my heart so contented that I couldn't possibly express it in human language. When my keen eye happened to glimpse her divine breast, I was transformed within myself and I believed that a greater beatitude did not exist below the Primum Mobile than in what I saw.

More than once I said: "Toils are nothing compared to such a prize! Not a thousand and a thousand more sufferings, not even the worst extreme that one could receive from steely fortune – not the depths of the Cretan prison, not slavery in a country house, not time or separation or a tempest or begging in hell could keep me away from such beauty, which can't be exaggerated in lauds or diminished by vituperation. I know well that God and nature have produced you in this world solely for my salvation. If it weren't so, I would have just reason to argue with our Maker, who would've been depriving me of a necessity for existence."

I squeezed her hand and drew much closer to her saying: "You, my lady, are my refuge, the port of my salvation, my faithful hope, and that royal road to heaven."

Then my lady turned her sweet brow toward me teasingly and said: "Garrulous tongue of excessive praise, why do you eviscerate me? Have you not had enough of your languishing that you wish to weary me to death? I have always been aware of your lack of faith in my regard. And if necessary, I will not be able to do otherwise than what your merit and my will dispose. I acted so that we would not fall prey to common gossip. You think I was less generous than one who faithfully loves should be; but you should have accepted in grateful silence what my loving heart dictated, and your shameful tongue should not speak of it. Now that you possess me, you are the arbiter of my life."

Book 3. Chapter 51.

At the wedding dinner, some sisters object to consummation within the walls of the convent. Others insist that the marriage is invalid without consummation. Eventually, the latter opinion triumphs, and they prepare a bed for Peregrino and Genevera.

Peregrino: "Sweet soul, the one who serves faithfully feels no less happiness when recognized for the deeds he has accomplished than for the prizes he accumulates. With your eloquent tongue, the most accurate interpreter of your faithful heart, you articulate what nature, education, and true gentility have taught you. I thank God and Love, who have made me your possessor, my lady."

Speaking in this way, I stamped a kiss on her blushing cheek and continued, "Tell me, if you don't mind, what you thought when you realized a few days ago that I had arrived in the guise of a begging pilgrim."

Genevera: "I was beside myself, though not entirely surprised, because I knew how restless your life would be until you had full knowledge about me. I want you to know that since I was transferred here not a single day or night passed that I did not see your image before me, which showed me your state, whether happy or sad. It could not be otherwise, since our souls are joined together, and I have felt greater pain when thinking about how I exposed you immoderately to every kind of danger. The sun has set now, and it is getting late. Let us go to where dinner has been prepared."

We got up and walked hand in hand, talking all the while and stealing sweet kisses among honeyed words. The dinner was prepared no less lavishly than joyfully. Partaking in pleasant, modest conversation, we came to the anticipated and blessed hour to retire to bed. Among the sisters there were those who said it was not proper to put us together there, since that act should be reserved to celebrate in one's own home. Others expressed the contrary opinion, saying that our marriage wasn't finalized without consummation, and that they had a duty toward Angelo. When he should inquire, they wanted to be able to respond in all innocence that Genevera had not neglected to fulfil the second part of marriage after undergoing the first. This disputation caused me no less pain than Deianira's garment did to Hercules. If God didn't come to my aid, I'd certainly die.

Fortunately, the group that favoured me won out. A bed was prepared – softer than a swan's feather, whiter than newly fallen snow, and sweeter than the essences of cinnamon, benjamin, and storax trees, or rose water. The holy sisters left us alone in that room.

Book 3. Chapter 52.

Peregrino contemplates the beauty of his bride, and they prepare to consummate their marriage.

O how difficult it is to satisfy one's hunger when presented with a wide variety of foods! I was like poor Narcissus, who saw so much beauty he drowned in a fountain. I grasped her divinely blushing cheeks between my palms, kissing and nibbling her long, white, delicate neck, and filling my eyes with those fleshy, candid, and firm breasts, which presented themselves to me like rosy apples.

She whispered: "Lusty one, calm yourself!" and nudged me back a little with her divine hand. But the more distance she put between us, the more my desire swelled to look at her. She let her outer garments fall with such grace that I thought I saw Diana in the flesh. When only her last slip remained, she shone like Venus.

Then I said: "Jove, if you decide to take your revenge on brash Phoebus, who dishonoured your daughter, you need not fear that heaven's consistory will lack a sun, since right here stands an even greater splendour! O how jealous the goddess Diana would be if she saw the clarity of this light, because all those gifts that make a man feel blessed are united in the lady here before me!" I mixed kisses and clasping embraces with my words.

We moved toward that enclosed place of sweet, battling rest. My lady sought to arrange herself on that chaste bed just as Polyxena, Priam's virgin daughter, did on Achilles' burning pyre. Reverent, modest, bashful, quiet, and with eyes downcast, she flashed a look that expressed that she was less than happy about this. She dutifully lay in bed without moving and all covered up as if she were sick. I moved to her side, not touching her; I wanted to contemplate her.

Pausing there, what came to my mind was a verdant garden enclosed by bushes from which balsam, nectar, and ambrosia exuded sweetly. I was eager to enter, and with my faithful hand I modestly reached out to push open the gate. But the guard on watch humbly informed me that she was in no way disposed to such labour then. With well-chosen words, however, I found reassurance and pulled her onto my loving chest, such that you would have thought Hercules and Anteus wrestled together.

Book 3. Chapter 53.

Peregrino manages to consummate their marriage. The next day, a matron of the convent washes and dresses Genevera, and Peregrino is so taken by Genevera's increased beauty that he quickly dismisses the matron so he can be alone with his bride again.

Profound night, silence, a full stomach, and an unusual lassitude so entangled Genevera's feelings that she abandoned herself to drowsiness without the least suspicion, thus leaving me free rein. Gradually and by every means possible, I tried to push my battering ram through the closed gate. But the entrance remained stalwart as a diamond wall, impossible for this equipment to break through.

But now my lady was fully roused and quite resentful. Her wearied voice came piteously to me: "No one is so vigilant who can guard against a domestic traitor."

That did it. I marshalled all my forces and felt that gate and wall give way. The enemy rushed in in a fury and rummaged around all bloodied, as if wanting to avenge a patricide. After I made myself the lord and true possessor there, I refused to leave unless I was promised free passage to return. Bound and locked together, we irrigated the entire garden one part at a time.

The brother of Death was thus conquered, and we slept until daybreak, when Persephone no longer hid her face's rays out of fear of her prince. Then Genevera and I awoke together, and I began to work her raw garden with my steely plough to reduce it to the cultivation of better fruits. The celestial charioteer had already raised his wet horses from the ocean when we moved from deeds to words.

A matron who had once been married before taking vows had the task of caring for us. When she heard us speaking, she entered our room with a bright greeting and built a roaring fire of juniper, pine, and rosemary wood. She scrubbed Genevera's limbs with a clean, warm towel and dressed her in a candid shift, which was finely embroidered. Seeing Genevera rise to her feet with her ordered disordered hair, I seemed to glimpse the moment when divine light suddenly shines forth the splendour of its rays.

I could not contain myself. I devised a deft means to send away the serving woman so that I could check to see if a new rose budded in Genevera's cultivated garden. Oh my, yes! – one even rosier, fresher, more perfumed, and lovelier than before! I judged that tending it during the day was incomparably better than at night. I raised my eyes and said ...

Book 3. Chapter 54.

Peregrino praises Genevera and expresses his gratitude to Jove.

Peregrino: "O great Jove, whose virtue informs the universe, I offer in your holy temple my victorious arms, since I bring triumph from a great battle! This is that contended province that renders its victor glorious and immortal. This is that triumphal chariot where the divine consistory can honourably take its seat. Agamemnon's war booty was nothing compared to this, nor the theft of Colchis, nor the rape of the Sabines!

"How many times did Jove descend to earth for what is mortal or common? But, Jove, if you had tasted morsels similar to this one, there would be no mystery about why you kept coming back for more. Since you have exalted me over all other lovers, I will render you everlasting thanks, though never adequately repaying you, because the fortune you grant me is of such sublime value that neither I nor any other mortal could find one to equal it. Since I am not worthy of anything else, I will praise your holy name as a sign of my indebted gratitude forevermore."

Book 3. Chapter 55.

Peregrino concludes his panegyric, and the spouses go to the Abbess.

Peregrino: "The ancients had already sung in prose and verse of fierce Hannibal, who invaded and depopulated part of Italy, of Alexander against the Parthians, of Pyrrhus against the Thessalians, of Hercules against the Trojans, of Pompey against Mithridates, of Scipio against the Carthaginians, and of Marius against the Germans. Which battle, though, was ever greater than mine? Which province, which kingdom, or which climate was ever more endowed with so precious a prize than this one? How much more glory would the celebrated bard Homer or the historian Herodotus have gained had they only written about this lady? But the true Giver of heaven did not want to adorn the first age with so much splendour as to leave posterity impoverished. He gave talent to that age but virtue to the rest. Now see how different the ages are because of the arrival in this world of this one immortal phoenix!"

After I finished, we washed and dressed, then strolled hand in hand to meet the Abbess. After much discussion, it was determined that she would tell Angelo of all that had happened, and she wrote …

Book 3. Chapter 56.

The Abbess writes a letter to Angelo informing him she did what he had asked. Once again, Acate exchanges that letter for another he pens.

Angelo,

If ever there were a letter or true herald of Love with the strength and power to offer blessings and comfort, it was yours, which imparted good advice for both body and soul. Heaven's Creator, Who infused man with the breath of a living soul, was present in fullness and grace at the creation of your daughter Genevera. Thus, it would have been difficult to make any mistake.

You imitated the clever architect who first gazes on, studies, measures, and ruminates before he puts his hand to the work, then with the greatest discernment establishes his foundation on the strongest site, so his building will not collapse even in ceaseless rain or through the force of wind. You wanted to test the nature, quality, and condition of Peregrino of Antonio, and once you carefully discerned those, you affectionately ennobled him through marriage to Genevera, your one and only daughter. I had them consummate their marriage today, according to the strictest instructions you gave.

Although it is an unbearable anguish for me to lose such a great lady, I am not sorry to see her pass from the contemplative life to the active one in which infinite matrons, both ancient and modern, have acquired a distinguished name through virtue. The first life may seem more secure, but the second is not so uncertain if it can be ably faced, especially by a person as well born and excellently raised as our Genevera.

In order to satisfy your wish to the fullest, I was pleased that the marriage was both celebrated and consummated. Although this setting is typically reserved for other purposes, it did not disdain such a high sacrament. Our friendship and kinship could not but oblige me most firmly to this, if not to greater things.

I praise God most highly in joining this couple of equal station, a marriage the likes of which has never before been celebrated in our city. Both are prudent, wise, well mannered, and honest in words, gestures, and actions. They seem like two creatures made for the angelic choir, with such handsome faces, attractive virtues, and well-disposed intentions; Nature could not have produced any better. Therefore, I celebrate with you as you do with me. It must not be far from your honourable thoughts to send here a delegation to celebrate the new union and conduct them back to where they can live out their days, since convent life little resembles the married one.

Although our profession is more austere, our hearts are not so hard as diamonds, nor our eyes as marble, nor are our feelings so bound, that continually seeing and hearing them one of us might chance on an improper thought that might easily spark our ruin. Indeed, when it becomes known to our superiors, we will not pass without harsh punishment. Having reached an age of discretion and prudence, you are wise in all things, so please provide for our honour as well as yours.

Be in peace.

After the letter was signed and sealed, it was left unguarded in our room. Acate went in, disguised in such a way that nobody would have recognized him. He read the letter carefully and considered the new war ahead. He feared Angelo would not be swayed even by the *fait accompli*. So, he withdrew from us and wrote another letter in the Abbess's hand. The one he substituted went something like this …

Book 3. Chapter 57.

After substituting another letter with a much different message, Acate hustles back to Ferrara to advise Violante while Antoniolo returns to the city by a slower route with the forged letter for Angelo. Peregrino and Genevera spend six days and nights uninterrupted together.

Dear Angelo,

No creature should ever be so estranged from human pity as to take delight in the calamities of another. Moreover, in as much as a case is tragic and terrible, it must pain us in equal measure, because we recognize that we have no greater likelihood of enjoying a life untinged by grief when at times, in the course of nature and variable fortune, we witness death and evil events. No one is at greater risk of falling than those who are happiest to sit at the highest places of Fortune's wheel, if they do not take into account what can happen in the future. Whoever rejoices in another's misfortune inches closer to his own.

I am not writing in order to scold you, but only to remind you that it is time to put an end to the useless and tiresome rift that hurts you more than others. Even if Peregrino of Antonio were dead, what would that get you? Where do you think you can find a better husband for your daughter? Who is wealthier, more handsome, and more modest than he is? If you are seized by this evil inclination to hate those who make a point of loving and honouring you, who will ever put their trust in you? Even if he were once your worst enemy, you should forget everything after his death. Ancient and modern law imposes that much. Leave any vendetta to God, Who repays justly each of us.

You should harbour no suspicions about Genevera, even if Peregrino still lived, since she has placed her hope in that true Spouse Who promises His faithful followers eternal joy as their reward. Besides, if I had not discouraged her, she would have taken our vows two years ago; day after day she presses me and begs that I be content to accept her in our convent. That would please me more than admitting any other girl in the world, since Genevera was born with true devotion, peace, tranquillity, modesty, and holiness, together with all the graces that heaven could bestow on a mortal creature.

However, I have insisted on relinquishing my happiness so as not to take from you such a noble daughter, through whom, God willing, a royal line can issue, if it is true that the family tree's branches are similar to its root. I encourage you to soften your opinion one way or another, since I do not think I can resist her persistent entreaties much longer. You can speak of it all with Anastasia, my sister in the flesh and in God.

Be at peace.

After the letter was signed and sealed in the same way as the one by the Abbess, Acate replaced the other letter with this one without anyone realizing it. In order not to give Genevera cause for concern, I told her I was sending Acate back to our city in order to thank Angelo for his good opinion of me and, following his most prudent advice, to see to the transfer of items related to the dowry and pertaining to my own affairs. Genevera praised my plan.

I took Acate aside, and he told me what he had written and how he wanted to leave to inform Violante of everything so that she could plan for any consequences. After all, no one can prepare without knowing what the day holds. Agreeing, I ordered his departure and hired his passage on a departing boat. With favourable conditions, he sailed back to the city. The next morning Antoniolo was dispatched along the via Flaminia, a road that is hellish in winter and tedious in the summer.

After we had seen him off, too, Genevera and I picked up our usual amorous conversations until the lunch hour. After we ate, she wanted me to tell her in detail the entire course of my life from the time when I entered Love's service. For six days and six nights we retreated to a room with only one serving girl and shared many things. Sometimes we argued, but then we called a truce and made peace, according to the customs of ardent lovers. Neither Minerva nor Venus was at all tepid in either of us.

At the end of the sixth day, I went back to my room at the inn for some rest, pretending to wait for family from Rimini. My faithful manservant gave me a letter from Acate, which contained this news ...

Book 3. Chapter 58.

In Acate's long letter, Peregrino learns of Anastasia's grave illness. Meanwhile, Violante has convinced Anastasia and Angelo separately to accept a marriage between Genevera and Peregrino, if he lives. Angelo sends Violante to Ravenna to do whatever is necessary to bring Genevera back.

Peregrino,

With favourable conditions I reached our native land, and nothing was more pressing to me than to visit Violante and tell her what had happened so she could react or hold her silence according to the demands of the situation. Given her initial shock, she could neither speak nor even take in what I was saying, only vent the pain in her heart.

She eventually freed herself and said: "I fear an impending disaster. O God, warn him! The beginning of this new marriage will be a bloodbath between these two families. Either I was too eager to follow your badly conceived plans or you were too ready to pursue the ruin dictated by your own cleverness. O damnable foolishness of that Abbess, who so easily went along with what she should have considered at length!"

While Violante was carrying on like this, we heard a howling wail come from Angelo's house: "Hurry, neighbours, come to our aid whoever can! My lady is dying!"

Suddenly frightened by the uproar, Violante rushed in there. It was midday, when the house usually had few people around, except for Anastasia's one maidservant, who didn't know what to do. Violante found Anastasia overcome by phlegm and slumped on the floor as if dead. Violante sprang into action, gathering some towels and cold water to revive Anastasia.

Angelo and his sons returned home a short time later and heaped Violante with such thanks that it seemed she had given life to Anastasia. They exhorted her ardently and insistently to stay by Anastasia's bedside until her health fully returned.

When Anastasia came around, she grieved more for Genevera's absence than for her own poor health, and her laments were not without hot tears and heartfelt sighs. She sensed how inhumane it was to have sent her daughter away for such a slight reason and leave her in another's care.

She said: "Dear daughter of mine, O light of my eyes, O consolation of my old age, O comforting refuge, O divine creature in intellect as much as in body! Where are you in this moment? You are without consolation, and I am afflicted; in our desperation we go to hell together! O image of mine, born for paradise, if I do not see you before my death, then my spirit will always wander without peace to seek you wherever you are! You have a cruel mother, a callous father, pitiless brothers, and a traitorous servant; do you all see now how I am reduced to this through your faults? My present illness has its cause in the condemnation of Genevera's innocent blood!"

Anastasia's tremulous voice moved Angelo, who comforted her, saying: "These kinds of cases can usually be cured through a temperate, happy, and joyful life. God willing, you are in a state in which your fortune has no need of further sufferings on behalf of another. If there is something I can give you to bring you ease and delight, ask it, because I will never deny your wish. Rest assured that your health will return and preserve your life for me, because if nature wills otherwise, then I won't wish to live in this world any longer."

His good words with ample promises encouraged Anastasia, and she said that the return of her health would be impossible without seeing Genevera again. Angelo generously replied that, if there were no other cause to keep her away, he would immediately send for her. Greatly comforted, Anastasia endeavoured to live, although recovery was slow at her advanced age. But nothing is closer to a person at that phase of life than joy, since the receding of blood inclines one to pusillanimity.

Angelo left, and Anastasia and Violante began to speak of you and Genevera. The first thing Anastasia said was: "Now see under what evil star my daughter Genevera was born! She was the finest jewel of the city; now she suffers because of her forefathers' disputes. According to ancient law, it's always been said that a child shall be punished for a father's iniquity, and he for the child's. Scripture speaks clearly in this regard."

Violante: "This situation didn't arise out of some defect in the heavens, but only out of a lack of consideration here."

Anastasia: "I'll call her back."

V: "Not with much honour."

A: "A virtuous one doesn't absorb stains."

V: "Some believe that; others do not."

A: "One's conscience is sufficient."

V: "In as much as God is concerned, yes. But the world demands its share, too."

A: "I realize I acted cruelly."

V: "You acknowledge that too late."

A: "She gave me reason, though."

V: "Yours is the greater fault."

A: "I never offended her."

V: "One greatly offends who doesn't consent to what one should."

A: "I was not so well informed."

V: "You were all too ready to believe and act on the worst."

A: "And I have suffered for it."

V: "That is not enough."

A: "What do you want me to do?"

V: "Agree to her wish."

A: "What do you mean?"

V: "Marry her to Peregrino."

A: "Oh my, but he is dead!"

V: "You have heard wrong. He was on his deathbed, but he recovered."

A: "If that is the case, then he will free himself from suffering."
V: "Tardy advice renders little fruit."
A: "Still, better late than never."
V: "I praise your plan, so long as it holds."

This long, angry conversation moved Anastasia greatly, and she was left nearly spiritless. After weeping for a while, she said: "O You Who are stingy in bestowing graces to mothers, daughters, brides, and maidservants, for whom You leave only Your lowest sphere of heaven, lend me Your aid! O Madonna, Lady and Queen, do not leave me in pain. If through your intercession I regain my health, your altar will not be left without my perpetual sacrifices, and I will unite in marriage my beloved Genevera with Peregrino of Antonio, if he still lives. Angelo mine, if there remains any bond of love between us as there once was, grant my most pious prayer!"

It seemed to Angelo in that moment that he might cure her overwrought emotion, so he consented freely. But little by little, strength waned from Anastasia, and her sickness festered. She grieved her confinement to bed. The crowd of doctors, relatives, friends, and clients hastened to her bedside as to a funeral, and each one tried every means to nurse her back to health. Her weak, aged limbs ached during the rainy season, and an intense fever seized her.

It was during that time that Antoniolo came back from Ravenna with the letter from the Abbess. Angelo and Anastasia quietly received him, and everyone else except Violante was dismissed from the room. They unsealed, read, and pondered the letter. Anastasia believed that Genevera wished to be a nun and fell into a stupor. A great tremor began to pulse inside her. Her spirit was frightened, and her shocked heart could not find peace in her fearful breast. Her entire sick body began to churn, not unlike when the sea absorbs blasts of wind. Her turmoil was far worse on the inside than she showed outwardly.

With a raucous voice she said: "O wretched mother, O damning piety, O horrendous monster, how cruel you were! I sense the Furies – Megaera and Tisiphone – coming for me to seek Genevera's demands for revenge. The guardians of hell already sit in judgment against me. O just judges, have pity! Love was the cause. Pardon this error, which is without fault."

Violante was moved to compassion by her bitter tears and said: "Angelo and Anastasia, as I have always been devoted to your house and shown every affection to Genevera, I call upon you to hear me now. I would be remiss if I did not offer to do all I could for our friendship during this crisis. We are four sisters and two brothers who give our lives in service to you. If it is your good wish, we will go to Genevera wherever you inform us she is. We will present ourselves there in the most honourable and chaste manner, as if you were present with us. Even though the sky might thunder, the earth crumble, the ocean engulf us, the rivers overflow their banks, the city be destroyed, the mountains be flattened, and the conflagration of war destroy the universe, I will go to her in order to satisfy you."

To such an offer made with such strong emotion, Angelo was not stinting in his reply: "My Violante, given that you are the guardian of our house and we feel such affection for you, there is nothing of ours, however precious, that we would not leave freely up to you. Therefore, we continue to entrust you the care and upbringing of Genevera, whom we love above all others. So you will believe that our words accord with our hearts, know that Genevera currently resides in the convent of Sant' Andrea in Ravenna. If you wish to go, I'll provide you with the necessary letters of faith through which you will express our wish to Genevera, and do what you think best."

Violante accepted the mission, and a well-appointed ship was readied. But before Violante departed, she spoke to Angelo apart from Anastasia and said to him: "I find there are certain types of people to whom it is impossible to lie or to fail, such as the temporal and spiritual powers and lords. Thus, I wish to speak plainly with you so that I am not deceived by you, nor you by me. I go willingly in order to escort Genevera back here. Although she is your daughter, I must tell you: she is very obstinate."

Angelo: "So her actions have demonstrated."

Violante: "I fear she won't come back."

A: "I take that as a certainty."

V: "Do you believe she pursues some new folly?"

A: "That's the way of women who always trust in what is evil."

V: "It was not without reason."

A: 'What reason?"

V: "A stray dog is always fearful."

A: "We sent her away to correct her ways."

V: "I don't understand you."

A: "Reassure her."

V: "With what words?"

A: "Ones that will satisfy her."

V: "How?"

A: "I will marry her."

V: "To whom?"

A: "To a good match."

V: "Speak more clearly."

A: "Our city is full of prospects. We will agree to the one she prefers."

V: "It seems to me that Anastasia is of a different opinion."

A: "You do not understand her."

V: "In my presence she consented to him."

A: "Who?"
V: "Peregrino of Antonio."
A: "That was to give you something to chew on!"
V: "Then you accept him?"
A: "Not for all the gold in the world."
V: "You sure are stubborn when it comes to something so good."
A: "O how good can it be? He is dead."
V: "And if he lives?"
A: "Go now, and if he is alive, then Genevera can be his bride."
V: "May God will that I find him in Ravenna."
A: "Ha! I give you leave to contract it."
V: "And see to the consummation of the marriage?"
A: "Along with a dowry."
V: "Do you promise me this?"
A: "I swear it to you."
V: "Be at peace."
A: "And you."

With that sworn promise, Violante will depart tomorrow. Your task, Peregrino, will be to keep watch over the port if you wish to speak to her first. Perhaps it would not be a bad idea for you to pilfer the letter she is taking to the Abbess, given that your wish, as you can see, has already been granted.

After I read Acate's letter, I affirmed Fortune as the most powerful goddess of all, since she gets her way in every matter. Late in the evening I returned to my lady, whom I greeted with sweet kisses, because it felt as if a thousand years had passed since I had parted from her. We passed the time in joy and celebration until Violante's arrival. I kept Genevera in the dark about everything so as not to disturb her thoughts.

Book 3. Chapter 59.

Violante arrives in Ravenna, and Peregrino goes to meet her. He tells Acate to inform Genevera that her father has approved of their marriage and wishes her to return to Ferrara.

Precisely four days later, Violante reached the port of Ravenna in a boat that ably navigated the Po River. I managed things quietly behind the scenes. After I filled Violante in, I told Genevera I had to go to Ancona to satisfy a vow made to the Queen of Heaven. Then I gave strict orders to Acate, who had arrived the day before Violante, to inform Genevera of Angelo's approval of our marriage. Now Angelo's greatest wish was for her to return to Ferrara, which would offer him far greater happiness than that experienced by the Greek wives who welcomed their husbands home.

Violante was well received at the convent, and after she rested a bit, she delivered a letter to the Abbess, which read …

Book 3. Chapter 60.

Angelo's brief letter to the Abbess asks her to trust Violante.

Mother and Revered Sister,

My fellow citizen of Ferrara, Violante, a lady of the utmost chastity, is coming to you on my orders to express some secrets of my heart. Trust her with the unquestioning faith you would place in me, as if I spoke directly to you. As soon as you can, send her back to me, and give Genevera my best.

Regards.

After the Abbess read the letter and pondered it a while, Violante said …

Book 3. Chapter 61.

Violante tells the Abbess that Anastasia will not recover her health until Genevera returns to her. She also insists, for the reputation of the convent, that everyone feign that no marriage has been celebrated until a properly witnessed ceremony can take place.

Violante: "My lady, given the fragile and fleeting quality of human matters, which continually rise or fall, according to the unpredictable vacillations of Fortune, we should not think of them in any way other than as if they were never seen or known by us. Otherwise, sometime we might dream of them, and that hope could lead us unknowingly to a bad end. With this in mind in these stormy times, your brother-in-law Angelo sends you word that there may be no cure for the illness that besets his most loving wife Anastasia but the return of her beloved daughter Genevera, in whose recent nuptials I heartily rejoice.

"Peregrino of Antonio can certainly consider himself blessed through his union with such a lady, who I insist be married again, so that the rite can be witnessed and accepted in the divine presence, as well as be more esteemed in this world, since convents are typically excluded from similar vows. Doing so should also bring your sisters some comfort from ever having to speak on the matter, which can generate more scandal than honour. It is my recommendation that when Peregrino arrives, he should pretend he does not know her in our presence, and you should inform Genevera to do the same, so that others do not believe they have already consummated the union.

"In order to lend truth to the matter, I will announce that he has just returned from the island of Rhodes, where he was thought to have died tragically young. Once this ceremony is done and they have rested a while, we will set sail for our homeland as soon as possible. If you are in agreement, you should write a letter to Angelo. If you disagree, however, and think that I have exceeded my place in speaking to you so frankly, then you who reconcile all things can correct what I have said and offer another idea. I am done speaking. Be at peace."

Book 3. Chapter 62.

The Abbess accepts Violante's plan. Violante and Genevera reunite, and Genevera learns of her mother's illness and her father's wish to see his daughter married honourably. Violante asks Genevera for details about the marriage consummation. Meanwhile, Peregrino feigns returning to Italy, putting to rest the earlier false news of his death.

The Abbess realized that Violante raised valid, serious, and well-founded points, so she expressed her response in this way: "You are most welcome, and I am delighted to see you. I will do everything as you say; for your part, please set this plan in motion so their marriage can proceed on more justified grounds." With these words she left her in peace.

Violante and Genevera withdrew together. After they had exhausted countless embraces and shed tears, sighing over all of the ceaseless toils, the sufferings endured, the wretched transfer to Ravenna, and the less than honourably celebrated wedding, Genevera grieved for her mother's ill health and said: "O joyful tribulation, O unstable human destiny! Sunny weather awaits the rain, peace war, good health sickness, and every other thing anticipates its ruin. O supreme God, could You not defer her current illness to another time? Perhaps others thought she was too happy and at ease. But if this is the divine will, I want to conform mine to it entirely.

"Violante, my dear, I have missed you more than all the others. You are welcome a thousand and a thousand more times! No greater wish could heaven grant to satisfy me more. O consoling arrival! What more can my soul desire? But ... Why have you come here?"

Violante: "Your mother's illness is the reason, and also to give your father's assent to your marriage."

Genevera: "Violante, do not fret, act as if you did not find me here and leave me to vent my abounding woes. I blame a lack of paternal love. I detest his paltry consideration of me, and I upbraid his insatiable greed. I blame death for not depriving me of such parents and friends. Does it seem right to you, Violante, that this entourage celebrate and honour a wedding of this sort? Really, if you loved me, you would weep with me! Since my cruel father thinks so little of me, I will give him little satisfaction: I refuse to get married again."

V: "You are already bound."

G: "Yes, I have the rope in my hands and will decide for myself when to untie it."

V: "In what way?"

G: "Peregrino will not deny me whatever I want to do."

V: "Then you want to hurt the one who loves you in order to satisfy your haters? Then surely you should be lumped together with those flighty women from whom you previously distinguished yourself. Genevera, my dear, it's more important to focus on the outcome than the means. Matters that end well can't easily be criticized.

"Consider where you are. If you were called back to Ferrara now with festive pomp, you would only give reason for people to wonder about your absence. You and your household would not be spared infamy when word got out about your deportation. Think of Peregrino and how he agreed to marry you in simple attire outside his homeland. Your father wants you to return in such a way that you can be honoured rather than envied or pitied. Trust me on this.

"Now, tell me, how did you fare in your first assault as a new bride?"

G: "Yeah, as if you were a virgin needing instruction from me!"

V: "I ask you because I want to understand better."

G: "I survived."

V: "How did he enter?"

G: "Sleep tricked me."

V: "The attentive guard never sleeps."

G: "Peregrino had the right of passage."

V: "Had he no other way than by trickery?"

G: "I believe it was licit."

V: "So, were you well pleased with him?"

G: "I shall not speak about this."

V: "Did it take a lot of exertion?"

G: "He broke down the door and the walls."

V: "That was certainly cruel!"

G: "But he intended no harm."

V: "Do you think he was sorry about it?"

G: "Very much."

V: "How do you know?"

G: "He cried profusely."

V: "He's worthy of forgiveness then."

G: "So it seems to me, too."

V: "Is your stronghold repaired?"

G: "He leaves it its freedom."

V: "Perhaps to leave his force behind?"

G: "There is quite a bit of movement inside."

V: "Destructive, do you think?"

G: "No, I do not believe so. He definitely entered as an enemy, but he has since become more humane."

V: "Is there happy news to announce?"

G: "Time will tell."

V: "I like your answers."

G: "Here is the Abbess."

V: "What a face of an elephant she has!"

G: "Let us go to meet her."

V: "When she expresses her thoughts, she seems like a cauldron that bubbles."

G: "She is really all good."

V: "Sure, good to be left alone!"

G: "She has been a friend to me."

V: "At no risk to herself."

G: "Still, she is affectionate."

V: "In her light way."

G: "I remain obliged to her."

V: "Then she was permissive with you!"

G: "Welcome, my lady."

Abbess: "I was looking for Violante."

G: "Here she is."

A: "I have been with the sisters, and they agree to your plan. You should send for Peregrino to do what he must."

V: "He will not do it for me."

A: "You can work it out between yourselves. I am off to mid-afternoon prayer."

V: "Like Elias up to heaven!"

A: "May it be so!"

Violante and Genevera could hardly stifle the giggles, which, after the Abbess left, seemed to go on for a good year.

They sent for Acate and informed him of everything. He was tasked with finding me right away and telling me to pretend I had just disembarked a ship. Then he was to wait there with me until I was summoned.

I accepted the plan, changed clothes, and awaited the appointed hour.

Meanwhile, Acate playfully went back to Violante and said: "Violante, this good news demands I get dressed up."

Violante: "So long as it's good."

Acate: "I submit to your judgment."
V: "Then you make me the judge?"
A: "Very willingly."
V: "Then speak."
A: "Then give me something."
V: "I promise."
A: "Faith costs nothing."
V: "You don't trust me much."
A: "Much more than your pledge."
V: "I am unprotected outside of my house."
A: "And I'm stuck at a hostelry."
V: "Are you so stubborn you won't tell me anything?"
A: "Are you so stingy you won't offer me anything for my troubles?"
V: "I have only this ring, since I am a widow."
A: "Then I'll be content with that."
V: "Here, I offer and give it to you. Now speak."
A: "Peregrino has arrived safe and sound."
V: "You are fooling me."
A: "Come with me and I will show him to you."
V: "Your duty is to bring him here."

Acate gathered a group of Violante's brothers and Angelo's servants, and they came to the port where they found me. We shook hands and exchanged kisses, expressing fitting words, and they escorted me to where Violante was.

As soon as I saw her my heart squeezed so tightly I could not speak. But I hugged her as a son. We exchanged kisses in greeting, and I said to her …

Book 3. Chapter 63.

Peregrino rejoices in seeing Violante again, and Violante feigns informing Peregrino of Angelo's acceptance of a marriage between him and Genevera.

Peregrino: "My sweet Violante – who from time immemorial has relieved all my suffering, who doubtless made possible the accumulation of all my goods, and who blesses the end of all my toils – what good fortune brings you here to me? What celestial confluence has blessed me with your presence? What more pleasing, joyful, and welcome event could happen to me? Hero never greeted young Leander with more happiness, nor Lamia Demetrius, nor Iole Hercules, nor Jove Europa, than you do me. Tell me, if you please, in what state do you find my elderly mother?"
Violante: "She suffers in your absence."

Peregrino: "And how are things at home?"

V: "Excellent."

P: "Our homeland triumphs?"

V: "More than ever."

P: "What reason do you have for travelling here, if my question is not impertinent? Will you be here for some days? O God, how consoled I am to see you again, Violante! I love you like a son!"

V: "Peregrino, my dear, I nourished you on my milk. Now you must be for me what I was once for you. Believe me, if I had no regard for your situation, honour, and supreme happiness, I would not have made this trip during this malignant season. But if I must leave my old body for something that brings you good, I can be content to die. Therefore, you have good reason to love me. If you ever listened to me in the past, please lend me your ear now with the same dutifulness that I proffer my tongue.

"I have always been respectful and devoted to Angelo's house and tied to Genevera more affectionately than friend to friend, servant to mistress, or mother to daughter, because her virtue is such that she is loved not only by her friends but also by her enemies. Her father wanted her to be educated not just in manners but also in knowledge, beyond the discipline for which her aunt destines her, to be a lady of prudence and integrity, which signal her nobility. She has now achieved the apex of her status and divine intelligence, and Angelo believes it is time to recall her to Ferrara quietly, so that it seems she never left her native land for further instruction abroad where no one could teach her more. And so that this matter can be carried out most discreetly, I am here with my siblings to serve as her escort, guide, and companion.

"Now that her upbringing is complete, we have come to discuss the possibilities for marrying her. I told Angelo some time ago that I would be willing to come here to see if there might be a fitting match, and the idea did not displease him. It pained me that the jewel of our city, through a lack of eligible men, might pass to the possession of outsiders. I mentioned to him many young men, and your name came first.

"He sighed and wept at these words saying: 'If only death had not intervened, Genevera would be his future bride.' I informed him you most certainly lived. He replied happily to me that, when it could be brought about, he would arrange Genevera's engagement to you. 'And if you should see him along some road or by luck on the sea or beyond, give him my regards and assure him that I will render to him what I promised. I would also appreciate it if, as soon as it can happen, in the presence of my wife's sister they pronounce true vows of matrimony before all in attendance.'

"When I heard this I felt as if I were flying to satisfy God, myself, and all concerned. Now you know the reason for my trip."

Book 3. Chapter 64.

Peregrino consents to marry Genevera with Angelo's approval.

When I heard Violante's articulate, extemporaneous speech, I inwardly reproached my masculine state, since so much dignity appeared in the female sex.

I said: "Just as it is unbearable to listen to people who by their nature are odious, have annoying traits, or speak inanely, it is all the sweeter to hear a person who is worthy of love and most fluent in eloquence. Your speech is so spare and exact that it contains more meaning than words, which has infused my heart so efficaciously that it could not more resemble metal in its solidity. I rejoice that in our land there is such an accomplished lady who can at once be counted on for her prudence not just to deliver private messages but also to aid in the public good, just as we hear among the ancients, as attested in histories or monuments. I can easily believe in Genevera's qualities when I look on her tutor, especially since she is uniquely endowed with virtue. The man who is ennobled through that lady can do well to thank God and nature.

"If Angelo's opinion is, as you say, to marry her to me, I believe heaven could conceive of nothing greater to satisfy me, because a lady who can outdo her cannot be found in this world or even in heaven. If what you say is true, I am ready to satisfy Angelo and myself if you deem me worthy. For your efforts, I do not thank you, since you command me more than I do myself. It is vain to strive for what is already manifest."

I got up and left Violante, who went with her companions to the convent where the flower of beauty rested. Violante took Genevera by the hand and led her to where I was together with the Abbess. Everyone sat in a circle, and Violante began ...

Book 3. Chapter 65.

Violante says a few words about marriage, then asks Genevera if she accepts Peregrino in marriage.

Violante: "My Genevera, and everyone else gathered in attendance – you matrons and above all the most generous Abbess and holy sisters – after His creation of man, eternal God did not endeavour more urgently than to give to man a fitting companion who would delight him and make of two persons one flesh, which is as it should be for husband and wife, that only one will informs two bodies, and only one desire governs two hearts. It behooves wise and discerning parents to use all their cleverness to find a fitting match, so that their offspring can live together in peace and tranquillity. If at times disagreements come between spouses, they can resolve them easily so long as the spouses are not so dissimilar in their particulars.

"Genevera, Angelo has considered how to marry you to your divine equal, seeking to find you a man of the same homeland, high birth, distinguished lineage, customs, education, age, humanity, grace, gentility, affection, and benevolence, so that the marriage would be equal in dignity and sincerity. To this end, he has selected from among all the other men Peregrino, who is here present. In turn, Peregrino has investigated his ancestry and family connections, and accepts you as his perpetual and legitimate spouse with a dowry befitting your estates. If you grant him your free consent, we will celebrate with you. It is up to you to accept or refuse."

Book 3. Chapter 66.

Genevera modestly accepts her father's choice of Peregrino as her husband.

That peerlessly modest beauty sighed and with lowered eyes responded: "If strong warriors find it grave and disturbing to leave their homeland behind, what must it be for timid girls to abandon their homes and the company of those people born of their blood and raised in the light? O how difficult it is to endure a stranger's customs and ideas, and suffer this unrecognized servitude! My natural habits are solidly formed in me and cannot easily be removed. If they turned out to be dissimilar to a husband's, you would see what my life would be. However, because both God and nature have made us imperfect, it is best to obey when others compel us.

"I would have been quite happy if my father had willed me to remain with these ladies of the highest integrity to live out a life that in my opinion is paradise. But if it is my father's desire to make a different contract on my behalf, he can do with me justly what he will, since he is my creator. I continue to accept his will as mine because I believe he would not seek anything less than what is best for me. I believe that Peregrino (if luck should make him mine) is more intelligent and wiser than I. He will treat me better than what my merits deserve. I will be faithful, obedient, and reverent to him. Behold my person and my hand for you to bestow as the speaker for my father in this act."

When she finished speaking, Violante said: "My Genevera, with a free heart and express consent in words do you accept Peregrino of Antonio, here present, as your legitimate and perpetual husband, according to the Christian rite?"

G: "Yes, I do affirm, consent, and accept him."

V: "And you, Peregrino, with a clear tongue and sincere mind, do you consent to marry Genevera, here present, according to the Christian rite?"

P: "I desire nothing more. I want, accept, and take her as my legitimate bride in this life and the next."

Violante took Genevera's hand and placed it in mine, signifying our union.

Book 3. Chapter 67.

After this marriage ceremony ends, Peregrino marvels at the change in Genevera. They speak with Violante, who criticizes them for their deception.

After that wedding I was dazed. I could hardly believe Genevera was the same person I had already married. Indeed, if someone were to have suggested as much to me, I would have agreed it was not her. That gathering for the ceremony was infused with such dignity that Genevera seemed to undergo a transformation into another lady.

O God, it was a wonder! Her divine gaze could have bewitched heaven in any way she wanted. Those words of hers had such gravity and pithiness, and her articulation was so sweet and lilting, that she could have calmed the sea's wrath after it was stoked by impetuous winds. While she formulated her thoughts, heaven seemed to slow its course to listen to what she would say; and if she unleashed her tongue in lamentation and raised her eyes to heaven, no eye of the faithful could perceive any other motion of life. She was always attentive, not dim or intimidated, not sleepy, squirmy, or girlishly giddy. She did not stifle her smile or wrinkle her brow. Instead, she shone equally in every part like an oriental gem.

The time for dinner was nearing. Violante took it upon herself to assign tasks to the sisters and send her brothers off to tour some of Ravenna, especially the ancient site of Classe, the artful Basilica of San Vitale the martyr, along with the newly renovated monument and tomb dedicated to the Florentine poet Dante, as well as a thousand other sites worthy of memory.

While all of the others went about their business, my lady, Violante, and I were left alone together. O God, what a melody of words in perfect harmony passed between the three of us! I felt free to squeeze Genevera's hand and exchange sweet glances without words. I was in ecstasy until Violante quipped: "That captain who took the castle through stealth was vile."

Genevera: "It is hardly stealth when force is used openly."

Violante: "Yet I understood from you that your guard was down."

G: "One guards poorly what one wishes to see fall."

V: "He must account for the faith you've lent him."

G: "Why postpone giving what is owed?"

V: "To show your mettle."
G: "Anger is vain without the power to enforce it."
V: "Every little indulgence can offer comfort."
G: "Waiting so long is worse than death."

The others returned while Violante and Genevera were bantering in this way. Our departure was announced for the following day. Violante decided to send Antoniolo ahead with a letter informing Angelo about what happened. It had something of this tenor …

Book 3. Chapter 68.

Violante's letter to Angelo offers a version of what happened, which is only partly accurate, and informs him that the ladies will return to Ferrara by water, the men sooner by land.

Dear Angelo,

The day of my propitious and happy departure, all of heaven joined with us in hopefulness. When I arrived at the designated convent I visited the Abbess together with Genevera, who seems to want nothing more in the world than to obey you. However, the explanation for my visit riled the members of that order to the point that you would have thought I had advocated their final destruction.

One suggested that you wanted to take Genevera from their convent in order to honour some other convent with her placement there, which left them greatly ashamed. I began to swear and deny you could ever think such a thing. The more I said, though, the less they believed me. They boasted that it was not in my power or yours to remove Genevera, since she had already completed her novice year and was well into her second year of residence, which amounted to a tacit profession of their order. Even though she has not yet formally taken their habit, the substance of her behaviour through observations indicates her profession. If force were applied, they would try to resolve the situation through reason. Even if they were inclined to allow her to leave, that would still involve a dispensation from the pope, a permission rarely given. Nevertheless, if they could witness her marriage, then they would rejoice knowing you would be content for her to provide offspring.

"In the midst of these discussions we heard an announcement that Peregrino of Antonio had arrived on a Venetian galley from Rhodes, forced to our port by fierce winds. Mindful of Anastasia's vow and your permission to freely contract marriage with him on your behalf, I sent for him. When he appeared before me, I rejoiced in his good health and comforted him affectionately on your behalf, for which he was especially grateful, as if he had been crowned King of Rome.

He told me that he had always loved, honoured, and revered you, and he would like nothing more than to be bound to you through marriage, which he felt would be a great boon for him. He urged me to accept the task of finding out if it might in some way be possible. I made the reason for my visit clear to him and why I had been sent by you, believing I might readily satisfy him.

In that instant, Elisabetta Malatesta, the ruling lady of Rimini, arrived at the convent and was treated with every deference due to her power.[47] She engaged Peregrino in conversation on various topics before broaching the subject of offering Peregrino her daughter's hand in marriage, which would have appealed to the highest king. I saw in Peregrino's face that he was torn and inclined to consent to her offer.

Then I heard him say courageously: "My lady, your offer comes too late. I have just accepted Angelo's daughter, and we are about to seal the marriage here. We would be honoured if you would attend."

Before the Abbess and sisters, Genevera and Peregrino pronounced their marriage vows. I gloss over the details of how lavishly the wedding was celebrated, since that would take days to write. May it suffice you to know the cause and the effect, which, given that you are wise and considerate, will cheer you more than anything else that could be imagined in this world. And to dispel any doubt that might linger in your mind, let me be clear: not only was the marriage contracted, it was also celebrated.

God willing, we will leave here tomorrow, Genevera and I by water and Peregrino by land. He should arrive before us, though before doing so, it is his duty as your new son to pay visits to your close relative along the way. Moreover, so that you cannot accuse me of delaying, I am sending Antoniolo your servant back to you.[48]

Regards.

After she finished the letter and gave it to the messenger, I marvelled at her womanly cleverness and judged man's wits were no match. The next day we took our leave of the Abbess, paying her the greatest respects.

But before leaving, my lady spoke the following words to her and all of the sisters of the congregation …

---

47   Elisabetta Malatesta was previously mentioned in 3.21. Vignali identifies her as a sister of Roberto Malatesta.

48   The text reads "Antonello." However, this person appears to be the same servant sent by Angelo to Ravenna. This oscillation between Antonello and Antoniolo will continue in the next chapters. I have used only Antoniolo to avoid confusion.

Book 3. Chapter 69.

Genevera expresses her gratitude and admiration to the convent sisters.

Genevera: "It is the custom, most chaste ladies, that true athletes train their bodies with the greatest diligence. They never seek to ease up on their efforts if they have not achieved what they desired, persevering when life gets difficult. Even though their aims and exercises differ, the goal of true contentedness is nevertheless the same. It is not in our power to choose the path; but as long as it proceeds from the First True Principle, in His will we cannot fail. If we do all we can to obey, even if less than perfectly, we deserve commiseration.

"Most chaste ladies, I came to you as a simple observer of your place and way of life, assuming it would be more untamed than civil. But contemplating your holy customs, good example, continual reverence for God, devout vigils, prolonged abstinence, virginal continence, spare conversation, very rare visitors, austere cells, observance of time through prayer, shared charity, disdain of worldly things, harsh penance, supreme diligence in divine worship, and the disciplined patience you show in all your actions, I feel as if I am reborn, and all the rest of the world is nothing compared to your way of life! I am resolutely determined to persevere through the toils of my body and serenity of my mind to reach that glorious end toward which you also contend without defences.

"But he who rightly has every authority over me for the continuance of his line has promised and committed me to another battle that is more destructive and wearying than yours. Whatever he wills, it is fitting I accept as my true, sole objective. However, I will never be far from you in place or time or anything else, most holy ladies, because I will always be mindful of you. Even after many years have passed, I will appreciate all the more your unique and blessed way of life. Although I will be deprived of enjoying your continent bliss in body, I will always know it in my mind.

"You can trust in my most loving consort, as you do in your own soul, for anything in his power to provide. As for myself, I say nothing, since you already know I am more yours than mine.

"Most pious ladies, human weakness does not always permit us to obey to the letter as we should. If there have been occasions during my time in your care when I gave any of you material for scandal or wasted your time in vain, please blame my youth, licence, and ignorance or lack of awareness. Out of reverence for Him Who spilled His blood on the salvific cross, I beg you to forgive me with the same devoted mind that I ask it of you."

As she spoke these words, such emotional weeping spread among them that you would have thought she spoke to them about the total destruction of the faith.

Awhile after their bitter tears subsided, I said …

Book 3. Chapter 70.

Peregrino also expresses to the sisters his regret for his past life and asks them to pray for him.

Peregrino: "Holy ones of clearest faith and highest merits, just as good works are made manifest by actions, do not believe that any force but the hand of God has brought me here after so many tribulations by sea and by land to make me aware of your blessed life. Although my past life was mired in a pit of sensuality more than is fitting to any saved man, through your witness I have been made into what the evangelist writes of Nicodemus. I am now so firmly established on the right path that henceforth if I should try to free myself from my debt to you, not all of the riches of the Orient would suffice to repay you. However, that Lord Whom you serve with such vigilance will also remit my debt, because He is happier to save one sinner than a hundred just men for whom penance is not necessary. Although your appetite for pleasure is scant, and that for owning possessions even more so, there is no law against necessity. So, if sometimes my intentions seemed mysterious to you, now they will always be declared openly, and whatever is denied to you will not be conceded to anyone else in this world. Remember me in your holy prayers."

I put an end to my weak speech. The Abbess and all of the congregation wished to offer us their wishes in return.

Book 3. Chapter 71.

The Abbess thanks them and wishes them well. Peregrino begins to fear what Angelo might do when Violante and Genevera return.

Abbess: "Excellent spouses, if we did not know you possessed that rare goodness that hardly exists in the world today, we would judge your praises of us here mere flattery, since we see nothing in ourselves of what you have praised in us. Still, if some grace is upon us, it comes through the One whose living water saved the Samaritan woman.

"O how correct the ancients were when they insisted that commemorations be reserved until after our deaths! This way the one who praises would not risk adulation nor the object be overpraised. Since you have honoured us now, we pray for the grace to prove your words true so that you can commemorate us in the end. Because we know the sincerity of the love you have for us, we offer you our place, our power, and our persons; when you face danger, may our actions not fall short of our promises!"

She ended her modest speech, and everyone stood to accompany us to our room. Because the hour for my departure approached, I began to reason through what had to happen next, but I wavered. Desire held me back while reason pushed me forward; fear embraced me, and courage exhorted me.

I – who knew why Angelo had consented to our wedding – feared for Violante's life and dreaded that Genevera would be seized. But while my heart wept, my face smiled in the presence of others so as not to sadden them. I dared not speak with Violante apart from Genevera because every private dialogue prompts suspicion. Still, when Genevera turned to me, I said …

Book 3. Chapter 72.

Peregrino takes his leave of Genevera and goes to his country villa just outside Ferrara. Antoniolo arrives at Angelo's house first, and when Angelo learns of the marriage he threatens to kill Violante.

Peregrino: "Genevera, my saintly protector, I go in body but leave you my soul. Just as you have always been for me, so shall you be forevermore … in life and beyond death! If there is something I can do to satisfy you, please do not keep it from me. May you place greater value on this petition than wifely modesty. I can recognize your sincere openness to me only when you command me familiarly."

As women do, she responded to me saying, "I have received grace from God, consent from my father, and your heart from you. Go in peace and remember me."

I kissed her on her mouth, her forehead, and her eyes, and tearfully took my leave. I spurred my horse and, because I had mapped the route so carefully, I caught up with Antoniolo before reaching Bologna. When he saw me, he was ashamed and apologized for going so slowly. I realized that meeting up with him offered me a distinct benefit: I treated him with great affection so he would trust me enough to divulge faithfully what was being said about me.

We came to within four thousand paces from my native land, and I decided to rest at my well-appointed country villa. He continued along the road, promising not to mention that he saw me. Acate departed after him to render consoling news to my mother and relatives.

Angelo and Anastasia welcomed Antoniolo as soon as he arrived at Genevera's house. They immediately asked where Genevera was.

He said, "I left her in Ravenna. The rest will be made clear in this message."

Angelo and Anastasia withdrew, and Angelo became fully absorbed in reading Violante's letter. As he skimmed it, he began to roar, not unlike the lioness whose cubs have been ensnared. He stormed about the room like a Bacchante, howling: "O poorly guarded daughter! O virgin cleverly despoiled, O astuteness adopted for my downfall, O most ruinous trip by Violante! All the earth teems with traitors; it's impossible to find a single person worthy of trust! O Violante, did you have to celebrate the wedding right away instead of delaying until we could arrive?

"Peregrino, your iniquitous plan has come to fruition; you've sated your rabid lust, and frothing fury has been unleashed! Filthy violator, vilest rapist, acknowledged predator, most insidious deceiver! Now it's clear why your death was proclaimed: to bring about your traitorous plan. And cruel Violante was complicitous! Traitors, your indelible offence will not go unpunished! And if nothing can be done, I will change my will so all my heirs will seek the fiercest vendetta against you!

"O arms, O fire, O poison! Why do you delay? Repay these traitors! Arm yourselves, sons, all who can – to arms against these nefarious ones! That Sinon-like Violante will get what she deserves; and even if others get away, she will never be spared! If living near us was once a boon for her, now it will be her damnation!"

Angelo uttered similar words with such fury that he almost collapsed. But when his ire subsided somewhat, Anastasia, who pretended not to understand anything, began timidly to speak, sick as she was, like a student before an angry examiner.

Book 3. Chapter 73.

Angelo shows Anastasia the letter, and she tries to reason with him, suggesting they send their eldest son, Timoteo, to congratulate Peregrino before he returns to work things out. Peregrino learns of the plan and prepares to receive his guest in his country villa.

Anastasia: "Angelo, what just cause has provoked such rage in you? Seeing you so far gone only worsens my illness. Although this might be a capital offence, you should not go to pieces like this, because anger usually strips reason's perspective. Before you pass judgment you must keep an open mind and hear some advice from someone you trust. Do not hesitate to speak your mind with me, because what I lack in power I can make up for in faithfulness. If you were stingy in sharing your words with me, it would be a clear sign that you had little love for me, which would not accord with my enduring commitment to you. Therefore, I beg you to be generous in sharing what can guide us all."

Still grumbling, Angelo replied, "O harsh and bitter destiny, O unfaithful friendship, O too credulous hope, O deceiving love! Violante promised so insistently to bring Genevera pure and chaste back to me. O great God, how are You so slow to punish such wickedness? How long will You endure these evils? O violated faith, you only encourage every other betrayal ..."

Anastasia interrupted him, saying: "Angelo dear, you cannot deny anything to the companion of your bed. Aren't my weeping supplications strong enough to get you to open the secrets of your heart to me? If speaking disturbs you, let me at least read that letter that has sent you into such a rage."

Angelo, quite indignant, thrust it at her, saying: "Now see where our misplaced trust in Violante has led us!"

After Anastasia read the letter and considered it carefully, she said: "Angelo, my dear, you have little cause to lament. If you ordered her to go, what reason do you have to criticize her now? The sin – if indeed it is a sin – falls on you. What's the point in debating matters that cannot be helped in any way?"

Angelo: "She should've delayed."

Anastasia: "She couldn't do so, given the urgent circumstances she describes. Don't you understand she would've preferred to wait?"

Ang.: "Still she should've consulted with me first."

Ana.: "Time did not permit that."

Ang.: "It would've been better to leave it to me."

Ana.: "But then she would've transgressed your command."

Ang.: "I was too permissive."

Ana.: "She can't read the secrets of your heart."

Ang.: "But when it comes to important matters, one must await confirmation."

Ana.: "She doesn't know what you do; she only tries to serve you."

Ang.: "I detest such service!"

Ana.: "This is how an ingrate is served! Still, it's better to give and repent than to hold back and repent. Some merchandise costs great effort. You seem not to understand that."

Ang.: "That marriage is not without infamy."

Ana.: "The shame was in refusing it in the first place. Given that no judgment is reliable among angry men, it's best if you rest a while."

Ang.: "What should I do?"

Ana.: "Praise the outcome, commend her cleverness, and donate what cannot be sold because, if you repel Peregrino, you all but make Genevera a prostitute."

Ang.: "He is hers."

Ana.: "If that is the case, why did you deny her to him before?"

Ang.: "I didn't want it to be so."

Ana.: "I see how your anger is talking while your reason stays silent."

Ang.: "He stole my daughter, and you don't want me to speak of it?"

Ana.: "You want my advice? Thank him!"

Ang.: "O clever recommendation! No, I'll withhold her dowry."

Ana.: "So she'll be forced to beg! A man in love isn't after your money."

Ang.: "Anastasia, you're responsible for her upbringing, and I for her support. What shall we do?"

Ana.: "I'll send Timoteo, our first-born son, to congratulate Peregrino before he enters our city, since I believe he's arrived at his country villa. They can work out the matter to ensure our dignity will ultimately have its way."

They summoned Timoteo and told him to go to me with an honourable entourage. Antoniolo informed me on the sly about everything, and I quietly made plans to give Timoteo a royal reception. At the same time as Timoteo planned to leave the city, I rode toward him, pretending I knew nothing about his visit.

I had only gone about two thousand paces from my villa when I saw people approaching on horseback. One of Timoteo's servants came forth to inform me that Timoteo wished to visit me. I closed the space between us, and Timoteo and I greeted each other profusely. We rode our horses side by side while he spoke to me.

Book 3. Chapter 74.

Timoteo congratulates Peregrino and inquires how best to honour Genevera's return to Ferrara.

Timoteo: "Most beloved Peregrino, you know the longer a fruit takes to ripen the better it preserves its true sweetness; to the same extent, everything that comes to fruition easily is more readily subject to decay. Therefore, we must esteem a hard-won friendship more highly than one that arises spontaneously or through luck.

"Angelo has learned through various channels of the great passion that consumes you out of love for Genevera, his daughter and my sister. Although he never would have contracted this marriage when he knew you were still green, now that you display your full maturity he is content to satisfy you. All that Violante has promised you, he vows to uphold, because it proceeds from his true, sincere approval.

"Thus, he has sent me to you to learn how you wish to honour Genevera's return, not so much as his daughter, but as your bride, and what would please you most: if she entered with public pomp or a quiet reception. Whatever you decide, we shall arrange, so you can understand how sincerely I come to meet you, treating you as son and brother equally."

When he finished his generous words I answered him in this way …

Book 3. Chapter 75.

Peregrino responds to Timoteo with equal amity, and their reunion with Genevera and Violante is joyous. Timotheo hears the story of the newlyweds' love and praises Peregrino's persistence.

Peregrino: "Treasured Timoteo, if Philip of Macedon expressed thanks at hearing that his son – the one called 'the Great' for his famous actions – had defeated Demetrius to bring victory to Antioch, I am all the more grateful to see you. Had this only happened seven years ago, I would have been spared a thousand torments! However, what requires effort and eager anticipation brings greater pleasure in the end. I praise and commend Angelo's serious determination to test a man before accepting friendship with him, since once a bond takes hold, one must be ready to give soul and body to preserve it.

"I have always burned and continue to burn for Genevera, who was in my opinion born to be my lady. I feel as much joy in my heart when I think, write, or speak of her as I do of myself. Nor did I ever believe that Angelo and Anastasia wouldn't someday be convinced, since one can hope for nothing but success from people of good experience. I accept their generous offer, which could not be equalled or excelled in heaven or on earth. To uphold it I pledge, besides my powers, my own blood.

"To show our unity of family and sincere love, I would favour this plan: you and I, dressed as pilgrims, should go to meet Genevera's party and slip her back into your house during the night. Then after sunrise, accompanied by my relatives, I should go to honour Angelo and Anastasia as is proper to their age and our relationship. Nevertheless, I submit myself to your better judgment."

My decision did not displease Timoteo. We dismounted at my villa, rested, ate dinner, and arranged to ride again after sunrise.

Everything went according to plan. We got up, mounted our horses, each accompanied by two of our manservants on foot, and we went to meet the anticipated boat. Once there, we dismounted and went aboard. Genevera and Violante thought they beheld heaven in all its glory open to them. Genevera and Timoteo embraced each other, showing affection beyond measure.

On the way back when I was alone with Violante, we spoke of our impressions. Violante feared that she might have overstepped the bounds of her mandate. Still, she said: "He commanded me to do it. Perhaps he was joking, but I'm not God. I just do what I'm told, not what he might be thinking." Her mind thus wandered in different directions. But when she saw me arrive with Timoteo, she felt complete relief. I decided not to share with her the words Angelo had spoken against her.

Later, we passed the day all together speaking of the love Genevera and I shared and all we had endured, which Timoteo cherished hearing more than any story he had ever read. Every so often he turned to Genevera and said, "O how harsh you were, and bitter and ungrateful for so much love! I don't know if any patience in this world would have endured without breaking. Peregrino, we can certainly name you in the catalogue of martyrs and remember you most solemnly. What body would be so staunch, what spirit so inclined, what mind so frank as yours in the face of so many torments? I loved you before but now I bow before you as to a saint! If Anastasia hadn't spoken up for you, she would have no chance to get well."

Those words were a balm to the consoled lovers, and in that feeling we passed the day.

Book 3. Chapter 76.

The group enters Ferrara and goes unannounced to Angelo's house, where they are eventually welcomed and blessed.

We reached Ferrara after nightfall and entered the city without any pomp or displays. When we arrived at Angelo's house, I whispered to Genevera: "O house of martyrdom, nearly my grave, and now a burning furnace! Even if all the world drowned in shipwreck, I alone would burn!"

We entered without anyone realizing it. Then a servant asked, "Who are you? What do you want? Who are you calling on? Why are you being so secretive? Wait up. I will speak to the head of the household. Wait outside. What, you are still advancing? I will cry out … Angelo, a large group is here, and they force their way past me!"

Right away, people rushed from inside with many lit torches shining brighter than new snow. Angelo came toward us from his room, looked on the whole scene and who escorted me, and he was stunned. He came closer, looked at our faces, and kissed and hugged us all together.

On the verge of tears, Angelo said: "To whom am I most indebted among you? I cannot tell! You, Peregrino, have brought my Genevera home, and in you I have acquired another son. You are all most welcome.

You, Violante, have calmed my woes, may God save you! Without your help I would be as good as dead."

We went into the room where Anastasia lay in bed, and he said to her, "Here is your true happiness. Here is your desired match. Here is your sure cure!"

Out of sweetness we gathered closely around her bed. She spoke little, though she did say: "Peregrino, nothing could have indicated the sincere love you have for us more than your dropping in without any prearrangement, since that formality would feel wrong from a son toward his parents. Through your action, I feel so bound to you that it will harder for you to command me than for me to serve you.

"Genevera, I commend you, my daughter. After fretting and suffering you've found a man after our heart! Therefore, I encourage you to comfort and keep him as carefully as you sought him.

"Peregrino, behold the flame of your love and your delight. Here is the prize for which you have laboured so intensely, and here is the comfort of your life! May my dear Genevera now be yours. Protect her as your own."

I then took Anastasia's hand, thanked her, and said: "O reward exceeding every other, O generosity unmatched in the world! No other prize better matches my faith or your dignity, O dear parents! No other exchange can I give back to you than my perpetual service."

We congratulated each other for some time. Then it seemed I owed my disconsolate mother a visit, since Acate had already informed her of my arrival in Ferrara. I went home, taking leave of my new parents and my lady.

As soon as my mother saw me, she greeted me by saying …

Book 3. Chapter 77.

Peregrino returns home to his mother, Camilla, who upbraids him and rejects Genevera.

Camilla: "Peregrino, every fire burns in you except the one for your home! Everything pleases you except what's closest at hand; every pleasure delights you except what you're responsible for! You have returned just as you left. You went away in silence, and you return without a word. So these are the rewards, efforts, lovingness, reverence, obedience, and affection you show your mother! I sacrifice to save, while you spend. Some great glory it is to me to have a son who treats everyone else well, but shows only hatred toward me.

"Tell me what you have done with your life and what you have acquired through your efforts. O wretched one, Bounty has impoverished you as much in body as in spirit! Which ancient or modern ever worked so fruitlessly as you? Jason sweated less for Medea, Theseus for Ariadne and her sister, Paris for Helen, Perseus for Andromeda, Orpheus for Euridice, Alfonso for Lucrezia, and Francesco Sforza for Elisabetta, than you for her! So your effort has been great – our cost has been exorbitant, the blow to our honour intolerable, and the shame on your relatives unbearable! Your grand acquisition turns out to be a vile enemy. Do you believe a new marriage union can extinguish an ancient hatred? You're gravely mistaken. Your relationship will last only as long as it's convenient.

"All of Italy provides examples. First, consider the progeny of Aragon, Sforza, and Estense unions, even others of lesser nobility, and you'll see what we get from accepting women from other sides. Their houses harbour the most voracious plagues that only lead to utter ruin! It's impossible to gratify, control, or govern them! Those women always side with their children. They never devote themselves to anything except what can gratify their unquenchable appetite! You've determined to obey the commands of a lustful girl. But the adage isn't devoid of meaning that goes: 'Neither love nor agreement exist between mother and daughter-in-law.'

"I see you headed down a path that diverges from mine. You're of the age to head a household. Therefore, I'll take my dowry and return to my brothers to live out my days in peace and tranquillity. Banish from your thoughts any notion that I'll be submissive or subservient to your new bride. Just as you married her without my knowledge, you can enjoy her without my company!"

Her speech was not without tears and trembling, to which I responded ...

Book 3. Chapter 78.

Peregrino asks his mother's forgiveness and recommends Genevera to her. Camilla and her ladies offer a gift to Peregrino's bride. Camilla reconciles with Angelo's family.

Peregrino: "Most pious mother, how better could you show your considerable love for me than in this healthy way of correcting me? If a child is spoiled, the parent is considered even more vice-ridden. Besides, what might seem harsh scolding to others is a healing medicine and supreme comfort to me. I accept and appreciate your words even more in as much as I see and understand they come from a source of true love.

"Please pardon my departure, most clement mother, because I wasn't sure what the journey would entail. If it had been clear I'd be gone so long, you'd only have feared my death. So, I thought it better to depart abruptly rather than after prolonged discussions, since you'd always have objected. Besides, because I have such reverence for you, I would've delayed my departure, which would've only led to my death and consequently yours. Do not focus on the meagreness of some gain; look instead on my contentment and salvation, for which you've always volunteered to sacrifice your body and soul. I departed from you as your son; I return as your son and servant. Genevera shall not be your lady or overseer, but rather your handmaid and servant. My pilgrimage hasn't been a waste of time but a good and wise learning experience.

"Why do you believe ancient ladies received such high praise, mother? Not one of them can glory in having as much virtue as Genevera can. My efforts are nothing compared to the great prize I have earned. If you consider it well, the feud between our houses so festers that a mere greeting cannot be exchanged between them, much less marriage vows. Weddings tend to be celebrated among the powerful for greater financial gain, among the lesser families for their preservation. But what pettiness do you bring up? Why would you wish to bring evil on your own offspring by scattering wealth? If you leave me you go with your life and your possessions. I only want what you want. Wherever you'd like to live, I'll follow, not as a son but as your servant. Please don't deny me what you'd concede even to clear enemies, which is a clement face and the touch of your hand."

She collapsed in tears and couldn't speak, given the tenderness that surged in her heart, which verged dangerously close to depriving her of life. In order to calm her, I left her in peace. I relaxed and dined with some of my friends, but before I allowed myself to sleep, I checked on my mother again and begged her forgiveness. Then my body was so weary that sleep seized me. The sun shone brightly again among mortals before I could rouse my weary body from the sloth-inducing down.

Meanwhile, my loving and vigilant mother, who sought nothing but my honour, assembled her daughters and sisters without a word to me, and they went together to Genevera's house to present her with a jewellery box filled with oriental gems. As Camilla approached, Genevera caught sight of her at the foot of the stairs, and before my mother could set foot in the house, Genevera ran out, embraced, and kissed her.

They were just about to speak when Angelo and his other children came out to meet her, too, and they immediately realized that the apple did not fall far from the tree. They welcomingly ushered her up the stairs. When they all reached the room where Anastasia languished sick in bed, they sat down and began to talk.

Book 3. Chapter 79.

Peregrino's widowed mother makes a speech to Genevera while offering her the wedding gift.

Camilla: "Genevera, I foresaw many years ago what you might become, and now I see you have attained it. Since the death of my dear husband, I haven't known happiness until last night, when I discovered I had acquired what I never believed might have been possible. I thank you for saving my Peregrino, and I am certain you will care for him as your nobility and faithful love fittingly show.

"Because time passes swifter than the wind, I wanted to come to your house to put to rest those matters that, were it not for you, would always remain disturbingly unresolved. Our responsibilities are many, and I have reached an age at which I struggle to keep up with them. Our managers are not trustworthy; Peregrino is young; and there has been no one to take care of our draining patrimony. Lady, you alone must be manager and overseer; you shall have the authority and insight to decide, save, make changes, invest, or cut back our expenses. Our livelihood will depend on you. We will accept any rules or precepts you determine."

After she had said these few words, Camilla presented Genevera with a precious jewellery box along with two pounds of gold, saying: "Your poor mother-in-law gives these trifles to you. The rest you will take from the house yourself."

Rome could not have offered a greater ovation to Cicero upon his return than Angelo's household lavished on my mother. Genevera regarded the precious gems and after she expressed the gratitude that was due, she said ...

Book 3. Chapter 80.

Genevera thanks Peregrino's mother, and Camilla and Angelo make arrangements for the public wedding celebrations.

Genevera: "Camilla, I am certain I was born in this world only to be yours. Heaven sent me a good omen when I visited you the first time. I had a sense that you would surely come back to me as I had gone to you. From that moment your image implanted itself so firmly in my heart that I knew I must be yours. God, that just and clement Lord, according to His time, has satisfied both of us in our shared wish.

"O how indebted I am to you for this sudden reunion that means more to me than anything else you could give me in this world! I will accept wholeheartedly your most pious recommendations along with your exceedingly generous gifts. I will endeavour to carry out those duties to the best of my abilities, but only to lighten your troubles in some way, not to take over your primary authority. I would prefer death to the very thought of that! I will always be as obedient to you as to my mother of the flesh; and as a supplicating daughter I beg you to accept me."

After these loving words, Camilla proceeded to discuss with Angelo the plans for celebrating the wedding, which they wanted to set for the following Sunday to coincide with the arrival of the magnificent Duke Federico of Urbino and honour him as he marched his strong army toward Liguria. They agreed and straightaway tasked all their friends and youths of the city with inviting ladies, maidens, gentlemen, patricians, and lords of the castle to honour their banquet with their presence, an occasion the likes of which in our day had never been equalled.

Meanwhile, as I languished between wakefulness and sleep, I was informed that Timoteo and his brothers had stopped by. I leapt from bed and went to them dressed far too informally, cursing the sleep that had tricked me. We began to discuss various subjects before he mentioned the festive reconciliation our families had shared and the great generosity Camilla had shown toward Genevera. He heralded it so highly that he bested Homer's singing of Laertes' son.

Just then, Camilla returned and as soon as she saw me, she remarked: "It looks like you could use some exercise so that inertia and laziness don't get the best of you! Genevera was up three hours ago, and you're still dead to the world!"

That mention of death infused me with life. I immediately got dressed and went to Angelo's house, where he was preparing nothing short of a royal banquet. Although that day, which was Friday, is dedicated to Venus, I could scarcely talk with Genevera, given all of the family obligations.[49]

Book 3. Chapter 81.

Peregrino briefly describes the wedding attire and music.

When the joyous day arrived, Genevera dressed as a nymph and I as a hunter. Others came dressed as animals, dryads, tree nymphs, and other

---

49 Inherent in the names of Italian weekdays are their associations with the celestial spheres and the classical gods whose powers rule them. Monday/*lunedì* suggests *luna*/moon (hence, Diana); Tuesday/*martedì* is dedicated to Mars/*marte*; Wednesday/*mercoledì* to Mercury; Thursday/*giovedì* to Jove/*giove*/Jupiter; and Friday/*venerdì* to Venus/*venere*. Thus, Peregrino suggests that Friday should be dedicated to "venereal" diversions, but instead, too many wedding preparations remain.

creatures venerated by the credulous ancients. Some processed before us, others after. The party featured music on the zither, and ladies of notable beauty surrounded my lady. We all gathered in a large hall before Ioanne Zubero of Bagnacavallo,[50] a poet befriended by the Muses, and he spoke these words to mark the wedding festivities ...

Book 3. Chapter 82.

Ioanne Zubero speaks at the wedding celebration. Angelo joins the hands of Peregrino and Genevera, and a sumptuous banquet ensues.

Zubero: "Ladies and gentlemen, God and nature could provide no greater relief to man for the weighty concerns of his household and society than to join him in marriage. Through this union and in all of his successes and doubts, he has a faithful helpmate and companion with whom he can communicate freely the concepts of his heart, not just for the purpose of having children but also for their good, innocent, and virtuous upbringing. Human generation is more indebted to the married woman than to nature. Children receive merely their first spark from nature, but from their married mothers they receive their perpetual well-being. O how happy and blessed one can claim to be who is well born and brought up by her! The first spark would be of little value unless accompanied by the second.

"Moreover, in all the circumference of the universe, I don't believe there are any others who have been endowed with these effects as much as the two glorious lovers you see here before you. What lady can be found bestowed and confirmed with such outstanding birth, holy habits, and celestial virtue as the richly endowed Genevera, to whom these good and saintly arts are uniquely proper? I'm certain that the eternal, sublime God Who turns the heavens with such mysterious destiny has brought these two together today. Now heaven applauds, and the earth with all of its created entities rejoices in such a worthy, honourable, and holy union.

"Moreover, the great dignity this divine bond provides can easily be understood by its effects, that is, children, the same universal good that heaven provided to refill the earth with worshippers after the Flood. Only by pronouncing this vow is sinful copulation made licit and pleasing to God, nor is there any other way in this world to legitimate the act of generation or acquire from heaven its true fruit. Marriage is the means that

---

50 Vignali does not identify Zubero further. There is a record of a Joanni Zubero, a priest from Rimini and correspondent with Francesco Uberti, in whose humanist circles Zubero circulated. Cf. Leonardo Quaquarelli's entry for Uberti in the *Dizionario biografico degli italiani* 97 (2020).

renders us peaceful, tranquil, meek, and modest to God and the world. Through this holy sacrament, all injuries and offences to others desist, and peace and harmony reign. This divine union between Romans and Sabines ratified peace, and glorious Rome always triumphed during the time between Caesar and Pompey. O true, unbreakable, and unquestioned connection between fragile, weak human beings, there is no more solid foundation than marriage.

"Now, Peregrino, refuge of gentility, haven of virtue, and altar of unbreakable faith, you must answer freely and give express consent, invoking the name of the great incarnate God in order to receive in peace the grace of heaven and the eternal reward for your toils. And you, Genevera, innocent breast and font of beauty and chastity, you must consent to him with a sincere heart and unimpeded tongue."

Angelo drew near and placed her glorious hand in mine. I placed a sparkling topaz on her finger as a sign of eternal faithfulness. I immediately took off my disguise to signify how I had gone from hunter to the one who had taken that prey, and she was the alpha and omega of both my bodily and spiritual happiness. My act was honoured by a change in song, now accompanied by a musical melody, which couldn't have been performed more sweetly or with greater loveliness had the gods performed it.

A table appeared just then, arrayed to overflowing with myriad confections and the finest wines from Crete and Rhodes then available in Italy. Everyone ate their fill, according to their status. Ladies, maidens, and countless serving boys waited on the banqueters. They even offered some delicacies moulded in the shapes of mythical animals. Above the head of the table where Genevera sat hung a silk tapestry, woven with gold, representing all the zodiac signs and their courses through the starry heavens, which was a marvel to behold.

Book 3. Chapter 83.

Timoteo discusses with Isabella[51] *whether man or woman is more perfectly suited to love, and Federico Duke of Urbino insists that Genevera must resolve the debate.*

Timoteo and Isabella gazed with rapt attention at some nymphs dressed as the ones deified through their illicit copulation, whose place and

---

51   This *Helisabella* may be identified with Isabella d'Este Gonzaga, the Marchioness of Mantua, praised in the proem and dedication of the *Peregrino*.

fame endure.[52] I thought I heard the lady say, "See how the female sex so readily offers to love faithfully. For this reason, she deserves her place among the gods. I would very much like to know why the lady upholds that faithfulness more than man, given that love is a shared essence."

Moved by such eloquence, Timoteo responded in kind: "Isabella, listen to this answer, which I predict will satisfy you. Boreas the northern wind is frigid and dry; Notus is the southern wind that is hot and moist. They both originate at the earth's poles, both of which are always cold, yet one wind is hot and the other cold when they reach us. Man, over whom you seem to gloat because he burns with less constancy than the lady does, is born of the Boreas."

Isabella: "It is true that both winds are naturally frigid and dry. But the reason the Notus is hot and humid is because it passes through a hot zone where its frigidity is moderated before it reaches us. It is humid because it passes over many seas and waterways, which temper it. The Boreas remains the way it originated because it is not tempered by anything. But Love knows what is in our hearts and enters when it sees a receptive subject."

Timoteo: "Then the lady is more perfect than the man?"

I: "Incomparably."

T: "Why?"

I: "Take her creation, first of all, which is as different from man's as a purified element is from the earth. Since Love imprints itself on those closest to its own essence, Love accepts and preserves itself in the more temperate female body than the virile one. You cannot deny this reasoning, because, if man were sufficient unto himself, there would have been no need to provide him with a companion to guide and govern. Even if you men had a predominant humour disposed to love, you would not have the capacity to retain or moderate it, as women do, since you are composed of humid, earthly, and thick elements, while we possess the dry matter that sharpens knowledge. Love makes its nest readily with clever people."

T: "But I didn't think that woman – a variable, inconstant, and unstable creature – could preserve anything precious like Love. No man has ever been of such high intellect that he could not fall to a woman."

---

52 The language is oblique here. The *nymphe* are likely ladies of the city dressed in costume for the wedding festivities, as described in 3.81, though a specified few (the ones capturing the attention of Timoteo and Isabella) appear to be dressed as Sabines, who have their own region in central Italy and deities celebrated in Rome, including Semo Sancus and Quirinus.

I: "That is not a defect of Love, certainly not of women. Instead, it comes from a sort of unthinking arrogance in your hearts, which craves some prey even before you catch sight of it. Moreover, when your whims are not immediately satisfied, you throw a fit and make excuses for why you renounce Love, although that is not due to any fault in our nature."

Then I saw everyone present begin to take one side or the other. Federico of Urbino thought Genevera should settle this debate, since she possessed exceeding charm. Although Genevera found passing judgments to go against her natural inclination – after all, she preferred to be considered reticent rather than meddlesome – she said …

Book 3. Chapter 84.

Genevera settles the debate. Dancing and a joust follow. The entertainment goes into a third day, after which Camilla leads Genevera to their house. Genevera feels the effects of pregnancy.

Genevera: "May no one scorn the conclusion of a discourse with no possible connections to truth. But from my experience of this sentiment it seems to me that Love burns hotter in women but more constantly in men."

Everyone expressed contentment with such a wise, impromptu response. After the tables were cleared, the company rose to begin their courtly dancing. When we saw the matrons stroll and dance with such agility, modesty, and gentility, their souls appeared separated from their bodies. We heard such sweet words exchanged and saw such graceful clasps of the hand and pious glances that we would easily have said their peace and propriety resembled Dido and Aeneas joined together. Without clamour or directions, each dancer was intent on stepping the foot, working the hand, and creating a harmonious vision of movement.

During a longer period of rest, an armed joust was performed, in which Mars showed his prowess in handsomeness as well as strength. Each jouster presented himself in a different costume to celebratory fanfare. I noticed the first four men before I lost track of the rest. The first was Gaspare Sanseverino, the second Galeazzo of Correggio, the third Antonio Pio da Carpi, and the fourth Giovanni Ubaldini.[53] They seemed the flower of the jousters. That day passed in various entertainments. On the

---

53   The jousters are Gaspare Sanseverino (known as Capitan Fracassa or Il Fracassa, *condottiero* and Italian diplomat, d. 1519), Galeazzo of Correggio (a younger son of Manfredo Count of Correggio who died in 1476 and to whom Matteo Bandello dedicated one of his *novelle*, I.20), Antonio Pio da Carpi (notable *condottiero*, d. 1513), and Giovanni Ubaldini, who was, according to Vignali, of a noble Tuscan family.

third day, after much insistence and begging, my mother Camilla led Genevera to my house.

Through force of habit engrained in my soul, I kept calling for Genevera, even when she was right next to me, and I fretted whenever she wasn't near. I even spoke about it with Acate. Everything went on as before. If I cried, she did not laugh. Love possessed us with such force that we seemed to be two souls informing a single body. We couldn't seem to separate for more than an hour.

She began to feel the weight of a pregnant womb. Walking hurt her and standing annoyed her. Even the company of other ladies didn't delight her but seemed irritating and frivolous. Finally, as a last resort to comfort her, she kept me in her room, which meant I saw no one else.

Book 3. Chapter 85.

Nine months later, Genevera gives birth to a boy, who is baptized with the name Alexandro. Peregrino goes with Timoteo to his country villa to relax. Peregrino has a disturbing dream. The following day, three horsemen arrive with downcast faces; Peregrino mistakenly assumes they herald Anastasia's death.

As the ninth month approached, the much-anticipated fruit in Genevera's womb made itself felt before it was seen. It caused her intestinal cramps and stomach agonies, and during such terrible torments my beautiful lady could find no peace. Because crowds of visiting matrons came to her room, she allowed me to leave. When the course of her ninth month was complete, Genevera delivered a beautiful boy, who, after his Christian baptism, took the name Alexandro. Friends and relatives rejoiced; my mother Camilla so abounded with happiness that I feared she would expire out of sheer rapture.

Timoteo suggested that we take some country air together to relax. I took my leave of Genevera, and we returned to my villa. The following day I was alone gazing out my window without a care when a deep sleep seized me. I had a new and frightful vision. I seemed to be in a green meadow full of various flowers that gave off a sweet fragrance on the breeze, which, however, seemed exceedingly detrimental to the tenderest flowers because it blew them all to the ground before they blossomed. Shaken by this strangeness, I drew near a shady fruit-bearing tree at the base of which was the whitest swan that sang a celestial song. That loveliness enchanted me, and I sat down on the ground so as not to disturb it. I hadn't been there long, however, before another swan joined the first, singing in harmony, and I saw its white feathers turn black. That swan gave up its life still singing.

An anguish seized my heart so fiercely that I felt I would expire on the spot. But afterward, I slept a little better and saw my Genevera in her true form playing and singing a little song. She did so with such grace and dignity that she would have outshone Timotheus, the great musician of Mileto whose tunes moved Philip of Macedon's guests to take up arms. Had Orpheus, Amphion, Marsias, Thamyris, or Trezenius been there, they would've succumbed to sadness. The arts of Zoroaster and all of his followers could not ever provide enough time or power in the entire course of the zodiac over lesser matters than I felt in hearing that sweet, lovely, and heavenly song. For this reason, I tearfully exhorted God on high to take me from the earth before such a melody ended. Instead, I seemed to see one swan bite the other's ivory neck and leave a small mark. The two swans battled beak to beak and tongue to tongue, such that they seemed two winged serpents.

The dream disappeared, and I regained my spirit. But I kept going over what that vision showed me in an attempt to untie the knots in my mind. I remembered Cyrus II, the Great King of Persia, Cressus King of Libya, Alexander of Macedon, Hannibal, Caesar, Brutus, and Cassius, all of whom received premonitions of their deaths in dreams. This thought greatly frightened me to the point that my happiness turned to grief. God's providence is in itself so solid and firm that to us mortals it never changes.

Full of anxiousness, I left the room and saw three riders racing toward my villa with astounding speed. My fearful heart froze in the midst of burning; my tongue stuck to my palate; my limbs lost their vigour one by one: it was all a clear portent of my future.

The messengers dismounted and spoke first with Timoteo and Acate about the very grave and unexpected illness of my lady, who gave clear signs that she tended more toward death than regaining health. I saw Timoteo so convulse in sobs that he turned his back to me so he would not frighten me. Acate headed toward me with slow steps, a downturned face, tears welling in his eyes, and a cracking voice uttering imperfect words. I assumed the reason was Anastasia's death (but woe is me! It turned out to be my own!). In my presence, he said …

Book 3. Chapter 86.

Acate informs Peregrino that Genevera is on the verge of death and insists he return immediately to the city to be with her.

Acate: "Peregrino, because you are a very prudent man, I know that no message from me will distress you. You know we must tolerate and endure whatever occurs with equanimity. I am indebted to you, not through Fortune but through my own actions, so I have always been a faithful messenger to you of all the news I hear. Genevera languishes and suffers on the brink of death." Once he had uttered these words, he burst into tears and sat down.

In that moment, my vital powers shrivelled, causing me to collapse to the ground like a dead man. After some time I perceived Acate calling to me, "Peregrino, I beg you after all our peregrinations together, out of our shared adversity and prosperity – breathe firmly now and carry on! You must overcome this bitter pain, because there's no suffering so profound that prudence cannot moderate it, nor pain so bitter that patience cannot soothe it. Genevera is alive and waits for you. Get up, let's go. Your presence can console her, and she might go from death to life."

I raised my head at this, saying: "O vain illusions, O mortal breasts ensnared by countless errors, what I held as my solace has turned to grief!"

I got up from where I was sprawled and headed toward the city. At approximately the halfway point, I encountered Hippolyto, my brother-in-law, who came up to me and Timoteo in tears. He said, "If you've ever done something to please Genevera, come back to her quickly before she enters the realm of Minos!"

Without saying another word, he led me into their house. I went to her room, gave and received kisses from her beautiful mouth, and embraced her as she was lying there almost bereft of her soul. Both of us wept. Her face looked like a rose that had been separated days ago from its thorny branch. Anyone who saw her, even a cruel enemy, would have been moved to compassion for her. Pity was so strong in Camilla and Anastasia that they couldn't bear staying there with her any longer. When my lady looked at me, a tiny smile blossomed on her blessed lips, which was the sign that Love rewarded us as much in death as in life.

Anguished beyond the humanly imaginable, I raised by face to heaven and prayed in this way …

Book 3. Chapter 87.

Peregrino prays at Genevera's bedside for her recovery.

Peregrino: "Eternal, exalted, and sublime God Who governs and rules heaven, the world, and human motion through Providence, You did not scorn to come down among us for our salvation nor disdain losing Your life to redeem us. You extended the life of suffering King David. If You still hold any thought for human beings, please, Lord, deign to grant health to my lady's wearied body so that I can confess, thank, and adore You with my heart, voice, and works as the sole Maker, Creator, and Redeemer. If You grant me such grace, no church or sacred place dedicated to

Your name will remain without my visit, honour, adoration, and sacrifices. I know well that one tiny tear in faithful prayer is worth more to You than any treasure that human imbecility could offer You. So, within Your shrine, most clement Lord, accept my humble prayer so that when she is saved, we can praise Your holy name together."

But Hemera's daughter, whom natural philosophers called the last terror, had already seized my lady's delicate limbs with their lethal chill. All the doctors, matrons, maidens, relatives, and citizens surrounding her prayed to God to stop what was happening, even though it cannot be resisted through human suffering.

In the end, that immortal blessedness in her high wisdom turned toward us, saying ...

Book 3. Chapter 88.

Genevera tells everyone that her time has come and asks Peregrino to thank God for their son, in whom their love lives on.

Genevera: "Who has hoped and prayed so fervently to the gods as to secure the promise of just one more day of life or true happiness? Worthy of punishment is the one who holds his thought in transitory things. Now let this be the desired prize: that after battling and persevering, we bring victory back to Olympia. This is the final aim of virtue which all things must obey.

"Peregrino, it is time now to accept the misery of mortality. After all, prosperity generates emulation, emulation envy, and envy dissension and war. If pleasures are not governed by virtue, they are not merely useless but even harmful. Because it is not possible to govern virtue while living so freely, you must not wish that everything happen according to your human desire. Otherwise, man would exalt himself in happy times and despair in painful ones. Remember why parents have generated children: it is precisely because they are not immortal, but good and respected for following rules and knowledge.

"Most beloved Peregrino, parents, brothers, and matrons in attendance, you must readily dry your tears, which have always been offensive to the living as well as the dead. Remember: a more glorious end than mine was not granted to Camillus, Scipio, Caesar, Pompey, Cato of Utica, Alexander, Pyrrhus, Demetrius, Hannibal, Theseus, or the great Hercules. It is not a lesser happiness to be judged worthy of life than living a long time. Let us give thanks to the immortal God for the fame and praise He permits us to have as we leave here. If through His mercy we have brought honour to life, through human weakness we can denigrate it, which would be worse than a violent death. O how glorious it is to leave this life with dignity in my own city, in my father's house, and under the care of my most loving consort. Stop your weeping, Peregrino, and praise God, Who with the greatest joy advances our final day together and from our womb has caused to issue forth the fruit that will be the origin of a blessed posterity."

She sat up straighter in bed and continued with more courage, saying …

Book 3. Chapter 89.

Genevera places her son in Camilla's care. She addresses her own parents and brothers, Violante, and others, as her life wanes.

Genevera: "Dear son, true exemplar of your father, perpetual caretaker of my soul, you will be able to say when your age permits it that your most pious mother met an untimely death. Mother Camilla, please show that same care in raising him as you did his father, so that he is seen to be his worthy offspring. Peregrino, dear heart, soon you will be able to look on him as your image in the mirror. Do not suffer if he differs from you in terms of political inclinations or in any way; foster his soul more than his body if you want him to love wholeheartedly.

"My parents of the flesh, I give thanks to God for my honourable marriage and for the salubrious spiritual time you gave me when you transferred me to the convent. If I indulged in anything less than pleasing to you out of too much daughterly freedom, as a final gift I ask your forgiveness. Treat me as you hope to be treated by your celestial Father. Timoteo, dear brother, you have been my consoler of late; I am certain you will remain an intercessor for me. Brothers Hippolyto and Galeotto, remember me and remain in peace.

"Violante, my only refuge in so many long tribulations, I give thanks to you not as I wish I could, but only as much as I can. Please be mindful of my dear child by Peregrino: if his first tender age has tormented me so much, I fear his next phase even more. If you still care for me, keep him in your thoughts. Relatives, servants, friends, and neighbours, I leave all of you in peace. The hour draws near when my infirm flesh leaves this earth and my spirit goes to God."

Her last beauty was resplendent, like the setting sun when at its last light it manifests its splendour more visibly to mortals.

Book 3. Chapter 90.

Peregrino cries out in mourning and accuses himself of being the cause of her untimely death. He asks for punishment by death.

Death did not have so much power that it could disturb her face or terrify her heart. When the time came, Genevera remained entirely composed, rendering her body to the world and her spirit to God. Not in Sagunto nor in Troy when the enemy had exterminated and burned the entire population were laments and cries ever heard similar to the ones that rang out in that grief-stricken room. The priest who guides souls and unlocks heaven's gate stood at her chaste bedside to usher even greater honour to the heavenly kingdom through Genevera's departure. Halfway along its course across the sky the sun grew dark, obscured by a thick haze. Both hemispheres were shrouded, and heaven and earth remained simultaneously without light.

The crowd of matrons prepared Genevera's blessed room and honoured her glorified body with devout cries and sweet words. I succumbed suddenly to pain and cried out in renewed desperation: "O short-lived and deceptive human hope, O weak and sad condition, O glory of ours so fragile and transitory, O vain mortality, O brief and wretched life, O blind and unstable destiny, O cruel and envious fortune! You appear gracious but attack with fierce bitterness in the end. You promise grace but then neglect to uphold it. Who can ever trust your promises and persevere?

"Was it not enough to have to suffer for so many years? Is your wrath not appeased after all I've endured? Is your fury not yet consumed? O rival of the world, besieger of every noble spirit, enemy to every virtuous act, and fabricator of every pain and fraud! Was there no better reward more befitting your virtue? Your power is a clear tyranny, your life a feigned hypocrisy, your worth only cruelty and ingratitude. What praise can you gain by depriving a lady of life, the one who was the honour, light, and fame of the world? You are the plunderer of gentility, rescuer of the foolish and lowly, and enemy to yourself!

"You have left me disinherited of one of the greatest gifts, God's assurance of my eternal joy. Now I am a slave for sale who cannot find a buyer. Where have you led me, O wretchedness, through so many irremediable calamities? O unseen blindness! Who has ever been left blinder than I? O lady, why did you not weep for my death first, rather than leave me to endure the pain of your sad departure?

"Lady, this cannot be the bed you offer me, the resting place at the end of my toils. Without me your journey is uncertain. I will be your guide and faithful navigator. I have already crossed land, sea, and the underworld searching for you. Do not be impatient – wait a bit for me. Soon, very soon, I will join you. O model of the divine, where are you? O flashing eyes, where is your splendour? O wavy tresses, where is your shiny colour? O omnipotent tongue, where are your grace, eloquence, and serious words?

"May every man rush to kill me! Tear me apart, destroy and consume me! I am that traitor, the wife killer who deprived my homeland of its great adornment. In the end, I shall confess: three days ago, I poisoned her to death! You must believe me. O my fellow citizens, do not leave such wickedness unpunished!"

My voice stopped at my lips as if overcome by anguish. Acate, to console me, said:

Book 3. Chapter 91.

Acate tries in vain to console Peregrino. The whole city attends Gene-vera's funeral. Peregrino kisses her corpse and collapses.

Acate: "Peregrino, the prayer that has no prospect of hope is foolish and crazy. You can live according to your will, but she can never be returned to this world."

Peregrino: "I want to die."

Acate: "O horrid thought!"

P: "Much worse is the thought of living in this pain. I can only be unseeing, hateful, and contrary to God, the world, and myself from now on. My prospects: only grief, toil, and heartache."

A: "Peregrino, the desire for death to avoid the travails of life is a clear sign of cowardice. In what state of mind must an intelligent, clever, and powerful man be to impose death on himself, which even the lowliest animal manages to resist? Could eternal God give man a greater penance or more extreme suffering than death? All-powerful God discovered our first parents' betrayal and said: 'You will die.' He punished Adam and Eve in this way because there's no greater punishment. What kind of man would ever willingly seek for himself such a drastic finality?"

P: "Lycurgus of Sparta, Socrates, Plato, and Hannibal."

A: "You're wrong. Those men were all constrained by necessity to choose death, not because they wanted to."

P: "How many friends offered to die willingly for their friends?"

A: "An infinite number. But many of them did so to free themselves or exact their revenge. Neither case applies to you. If your death meant her resurrection, then your death would be quite excusable. But you could do her good by living. If someone denigrated her reputation, you could defend her if you were alive. However, by dying you would both be slandered.

"Every writer sings the praises of Andromache's pious love. But after the death of her beloved Hector, she accepted life and even another husband. Pompey, who loved Julia so ardently, united with Cornelia after Julia's burial. Cato the Censor remarried in his old age to avoid hardships. The human intellect quakes at the terror of death, which you seem so insipidly to desire."

P: "Then I must live only to witness the accumulation of more calamities?"

A: "Some people suffer whose every reason for fame dies with life. Not Genevera. If all the poets were to contend together to praise her, they still might as well remain mute because they'd never accomplish their task."

P: "Praise is dead, beauty extinct, piety lost, and the world remains blind."

A: "Heavenly virtue lives on, and through Genevera's death heaven shall be blessed. There's no reason for you to complain."

P: "I contaminate heaven, earth, and the stars wherever I turn. I need Genevera's spirit. I see the Furies on my heels; a constant pain plagues my breast and shows me where I must go. I don't believe there's more suffering in Rhadamanthus's house of Hades; at least a soul separated from the body knows more peace. Now I want to go toward that other shore where I'll fulfil my will by contemplating her sweet vision."

A: "Peregrino, such bitter lamentation only confuses everything because it suggests you don't believe anyone lives after the ashes of death. O vile and effeminate, indeed, is the one who believes what he sees, only grief and weeping! A wise man never frets in his heart over anguish or pain. Although nature concedes tears of pity, there's no reason to go on indulging them in this way. On the contrary, only an impious and wicked view opposes the will and power of God and nature.

"The arguments of the wisest philosophers would certainly be vain if they said that the body consists of contrary elements, and the soul's heavenly vigour, which comes from God, once stained by mortal cares, can't with the greatest joy be freed from the human prison of these mortal members and return, like little and invisible flames rising up toward heaven. After all, He descended from there and sacrificed His divine disposition to take on a human body! Sometimes hopeless thoughts come to us in a vision or premonition and aim to make us quake and despair. But given that we live the better part of our lives in a body with the sure hope of returning to Him, dry your tears and call on God and the world. Believe the scriptures and the efficacy of your prayers to God; there's no wisdom, knowledge, force, or anything else that can defeat the sublime and powerful God."

P: "I sense my madness and know where it comes from, but I can't control my limbs or govern my soul. I realize that no punishment, prayers, or advice can help the heart fated and entirely disposed to die. O wretched awareness, O wavering joy, O deceptive leisure, O too happy time, O human ostentation! Where have you brought me? O how much blessed judgment is given to one who from his birth takes as his bed the bare earth, a single bean to satiate his hunger, and pure water to relieve his thirst!"

A: "The one who accepts good advice is considered great, but happiest of all is the one who knows what's best for himself. Now that Genevera has breathed her last, what is left to do? Let's go and remind others of Genevera's sweet example."

P: "O sad memory, O unhappy day! I believe that Tisiphone ululated in grief along with her sisters when I was born into this wretched light. My dear mother would've shown pity on me then had she done as another did for Meleager!"

While Acate tried vainly to console me, my servants arranged the funeral solemnities, which in our city were quite rare. The whole house immediately donned mourning attire and went to the church where her glorious body was lying in repose. The entire city hastened there. Rome did not burst with larger crowds during the assemblies or when a triumphal chariot paraded through the city. Pure white tapers illuminated the church and consecrated altar. The needy received food and clothing. Court was suspended, commerce neglected, and everyone grieved for Genevera as they would for a city founder. A gold pall on a red background draped over her coffin. It lent some colour to her white face and made it seem in her death that Genevera merely slept. While I contemplated her, I began to forget all my cares.

Four military horsemen came to take her away, and I said of them: "O ingenuous spirits, O true fellow citizens of mine, in what great or small thing do you perceive I've offended you? If I did anything it was out of ignorance, and it should be overlooked. If I committed a sin knowingly, I ask your forgiveness. But if you love me, why do you do me this injury? Why do you impoverish me to make others rich? The lady Genevera couldn't have a more faithful resting place than with me. Stay here. Otherwise, she'll be alone and without anything. She must not go alone with you, which isn't proper. She's too young. Persephone did not satisfy Orpheus in the end; when he thought he had Euridice, she whisked her away. That place is untrustworthy; and you are inexperienced."

When they passed close by, I gave Genevera a kiss. The last one was even more ardent than the first. Then I fell to the ground out of heartfelt tenderness.

When Genevera's body reached her perpetual resting place, Alberto Cortese,[54] a most rigorous professor of the Justinian and Ciceronian eloquence, began his oration.

---

54 Alberto Cortese (d. 1487) descended from an illustrious family from Modena and served as orator and ambassador to Venice for the Estense dukes Borso and Ercole.

Book 3. Chapter 92.

Alberto Cortese offers a eulogy at Genevera's funeral. An epitaph is inscribed on Genevera's tomb.

Alberto Cortese: "Great citizens, we know that when acute pain pierces the soul one can suddenly be deprived of life, just as Homer sang of Hecuba and Bellerophon. Let Niobe, Artemisia, Phyllis, and the Roman emperors Otho and Nero be silent! Through their lust and crooked lives, they never learned the virtue of true patience. However, what obligation do we have to God, if our life is so imposed by nature that we must always carry on after the worst of it? What man bereft of his senses and railing against unconquered Minerva ever managed to do good? I don't accept that a prudent man should refuse God, nature, and himself. Instead, an everlasting and infallible intelligence must rule and govern all the lesser things, influenced by it.

"For this reason, the resurrection of man would be impossible without the rules of justice and the proper course of God and nature. Whoever opposes this determined law clearly rebels against God, since all merely human actions would amount to nothing. David, while his son was sick, never gave in to tears, trembling, cries, or prayers; and when his son breathed his last, he presented himself anointed, praiseworthy, and clean to his people. When he was asked why he didn't weep, as might be expected, the wise king responded that while his son lived he continued to hope he would get well. Whereas weeping for him after he died would only be vain and ruinous, since it'd sooner cause him to join his dead son than bring his son back to him. He knew that everything that begins in nature must naturally also have its end.

"Since our matter derives from four contrary qualities, it cannot endure as a created material form, as Aristotle teaches. Wise men who have accepted this view have easily tolerated the pains of death. Paullus celebrated his triumph, although he had learned of his first son's death only five days earlier and his second son's death only three days before the celebration. Even after the Athenian Pericles learned of the death of two sons, he did not alter his voice or dress; he retained the crown on his head and kept his dignity during the assemblies. Dion of Syracuse learned that his son died following a roof collapse. Nonetheless, he was not moved in any way, nor did he isolate himself from the company of friends, but merely commanded that his son's body be honoured with commendable burial. Demosthenes imitated this behaviour when he received news of his only daughter's death, just before the public games were to take place in his country. He refused to delay them; six days later, he dressed in white, as was the custom of the prince for such celebrations, and he sang her praises. While Xenophon was celebrating a sacrifice, he learned that his eldest son Gryllus had been stabbed in Mantinea and was dead. In cases like these the messengers are typically interrogated as if they came back from battle; but when Xenophon learned that his son had fought back and died like a man, he took off his crown, gave thanks to God, and swore he had never received greater pleasure than knowing the virtue of his son's death, and he harboured no bitterness.

"O Death, how glorious and exalted you are! O how worthy of our anticipation! You deserve commendation and everlasting praise! If you had cut King Cyrus's thread of life sooner, he wouldn't have met his ignominious and servile end. O how indebted we are to you, Death, for the mute shades of Croesus, Darius, Hannibal, Priam, Pompey, Caesar, Marius, Crassus, Cicero, Seneca, Lucan, and unhappy Hecuba, and among the moderns Gian Galeazzo I, and Galeazzo and Gian Galeazzo II Sforza. Good citizens, if you call to mind the extreme cases of unstable fortune they endured, I'm certain they who dwell now beyond the other shore find greater consolation than we who continue to suffer the offences of this world. Desist your bitter crying, since the immortality of the soul should be our comfort, just as poison was to Socrates who drank it, and the precipice of Etna was to Empedocles. Terobronta would not have leapt from the wall if he were not assured of immortality.[55] Wise Cato of Utica would not have suffered death willingly if he had suspected otherwise. This is that glory that the Sabine Mettius Curtius chose by leaping into a murky chasm, and that led King Codrus of Athens and Phylenus to their deaths. Our divine image would always live on if death didn't intervene. Only the soul does not fear death and lives eternally as the true image of the eternal God. Therefore, we must conclude from these ancient and modern examples that it is vain to cry in anguish over another's death, since we recognize that corporeal death liberates our better part, which is the soul. Instead, find consolation in the transmigration of that goddess Genevera. Just as she adorned the earth, she is now a splendour within that eternal firmament to which I pray God will guide you and me as well."

After he carried out his official duty at this tearful funeral, an epitaph was inscribed on Genevera's tomb, which read:

---

55 Most editions of the *Peregrino* spell the name "Terobronta," though at least one later edition (Venice, 1547) prefers "Terobonta" – this last echoed by the Martínez Moran 2014 Spanish edition, as well. I could find no further information about this classical example of voluntary death.

Reader, listen, pause, & learn.
I was once a beauty, now useless ashes.
As virgin, I burned & loved chastely.
Peregrino was my lover & husband; I am Genevera.
A cruel love seized us both.

Because it was not the custom for the husband to consign his beloved lady to the sepulchral pyre, I stayed at home cursing my fate. The next day all the noblemen and great scholars of the city came to me. Antonio Guidoni,[56] a most accomplished legal interpreter, said to me on the verge of tears …

Book 3. Chapter 93.

Antonio Guidoni tries to offer Peregrino consoling advice.

Antonio Guidoni: "Esteemed Peregrino, it is the duty of curious, keen, and excellent spirits to enjoy the company of others and share with them when they suffer calamities. If our arrival has been delayed more than usual, do not ascribe it to ill will or disdain on our part but rather only to our pity. After such recent pain, recalling Genevera will only disturb and redouble the pain that you in your great prudence will moderate with that equanimity that King Antiochus III the Great did when he lost the greater part of his kingdom of Antioch to the Romans. Because one must not proffer advice to a man of your character, I'll pass over in silence many matters. This was the determination of Clodius Albinus, who after the death of Commodus received the title of Caesar from the Gauls. But in a short book he castigated adulators, insisting that praise for accomplishments should be reserved until after we die, because to flatter Caesar in his presence would be a vice for rulers and wise men to flee like the plague.

"Peregrino, so that I not fall into this detestable perniciousness, I will pass over in silence rather than awkwardly commend your righteous life, your admirable virtue, and your purest faith, which all manifest quite clearly. To speak of your sublime condition would incur what Livy said to Phormion when he wanted to weigh in on military matters in Hannibal's presence. Your dignity does not deserve such faint praise.

"Alexander of Macedon condemned Fortune and Nature because they didn't bless Homer, though he was a worthy object of praise. I know that

---

56   Vignali (liii, n76) cites Antonio Guidoni as a professor of law at the *Studio ferrarese* and a gentleman and diplomat for the Estense court.

a man of slight intellect cannot accomplish anything worth exalting, no matter how hard he tries. But because my fellow citizens here have given me the great responsibility to say a few words in your presence, I could not recuse myself – nor should I have done so – given what the great Cato says: the necessity of obeying them will make up for any insufficiency of mine. You, most merciful Peregrino, should imitate the great King of Persia, who sought pious consonance more readily than social consequence.[57]

"Many maxims come to mind, but in order not to be verbose I will limit myself to only this one, that is, that one can rightly call himself a man who with good reason knows and can commend himself, who holds back his appetites, dominates his sensuality, and corrects in himself whatever offends others, following that great commandment of Apollo's Delphic oracle: know thyself. O precious motto worthy of eternal memory! If, most learned man, you consider this with your usual true judgment, you have no reason to lament or criticize and consume yourself. If things that are favourable sadden you, what will sinister and adverse ones do to you? You know yourself, Peregrino. Thank heaven and Genevera, who through her merits has ascribed immortality to you. What living man was ever glorified more than you through a lady?

"It was the custom among the ancients after a victory to honour the holy temples of their victorious army so that the givers of graces did not remain unacknowledged. If our magnanimous God has made you glorious through Genevera, do not be so put out that you do not give thanks to the Maker promptly and with joyful gratitude. What could you appreciate more than Genevera's passing? Although it seems you might follow her if you persist in so many aches and trembling, cries and continual tears. What could bring her into God's presence if not death? What could permit both of you to celebrate perpetual immortality if not death? What could be a more glorious manifestation of your life than death? O glorious and mysterious Death, through you we are saved; the human condition is indebted to you, and you make it eternal! Through you we are educated, illuminated, and justified.

"The elect spirits tend toward you with the highest desire while lazy and ignorant ones refuse you, Death. St. Paul cried out saying: 'I desire death in order to have everlasting life, which leads to a better end.' Socrates,

---

57 Despite the fact that Caviceo's character of Antonio Guidoni will claim in the next sentence not to wish to appear verbose, here he offers a rather fussy play on words between *affecto* (affect) and *effecto* (effect). Preferring to avoid the negative connotations in English of "affect," which are not intended in this Italian passage, I have rendered it imperfectly as "consonance" and "consequence."

who was considered wise because of the Delphic oracle, hastened with the greatest readiness to you, Death, in order to console himself among the elect shades. Jesus, the great lawgiver, through Whom every good proceeds, for our salvation approached you, Death, in joy and triumph. Its rule and action must be our instruction.

"The swan, unversed in reason, redoubles its singing when it draws close to the sweetness of death as if it were professing a prophecy and praising nature as the liberator from so many woes. Therefore, it is consecrated to Apollo, the god of divination. Trophonius and Agamedes, keepers of the Delphic temple, asked for a reward for their toils, and Apollo granted them death as the greatest benefit he could offer. King Midas, educated by Silenus, used to say that the best thing was never to be born or else to leave this world as soon as possible. The people of Marseille insisted that their pyres, grief, and banquets end after one day, so as not to disturb immortal God with their ongoing lamentations.

"Therefore, Peregrino, given the love you show Genevera, you should not rue the good she has. Instead, you can ascribe to her great praise that, while she was alive, she showed the world your glory, which is understood through the death of that lady who knows no superior or equal in this world. More virtue and graces were found in her than in all of the rest of the female sex, so in her you are immortal, and she in you. For this reason, you must be most comforted by her happy passing in order not to be ungrateful for that sacred and inviolable love she had for you in life, which will persevere with you in that perpetual eternity her soul now enjoys.

"Because of the highness and profundity of divine things and the brevity of our life, we cannot know God's name, His meaning, or His knowledge, because He exceeds all things, as St. Paul clearly shows us. When this Doctor of the People returned among us, he said, in fact, that he had heard things of such secrecy that to speak of them would not be permitted. Moreover, divine Plato admonished us on the topic, saying that wanting the knowledge of celestial things is equivalent to casting holy things to the dogs. Although he didn't speak specifically about it, he believed and firmly followed divine goodness, and he held as a constant that the Good cares for us, just as every wise ancient and modern scripture says. Because our soul is the worthy receptacle of God's grace, interceding through Genevera's most holy life, we can understand as true that she is among the sacred angelic choir, where in continual contemplation and divine vision she will live exalted. Through her example you must leave aside this weeping anguish so that God, having mercy on you, will render you worthy of that same glory.

"Finally, if there is anything else we can do to support your honour, ease, and reputation, we are ready and available to offer it to you. May God preserve you and us together. Be at peace."

Antonio Guidoni had barely finished his words when Aurelio Bellincini,[58] the true master of all knowledge who was sitting next to him,
expounded thus …

Book 3. Chapter 94.

Aurelio Bellincini speaks next.

Aurelio Bellincini: "Good Peregrino and esteemed fellow citizens, we must
not assume Fortune to be stable for long in our world. Even if in one moment she happens to favour one man beyond belief, he must tolerantly
bear the adversities that will follow. Philip of Macedon received in a single
day three messages containing happy news. First, he learned his four-horse
chariot won the race in Olympia. Second, the messenger announced to him
that his general Parmenion had scattered and defeated the Dardani. Third,
he heard that Olympia had made him a father by giving birth to a boy. This
most clement king raised his hands to heaven and said: 'O God, may you
balance such prosperity with only moderate misfortunes!' because this most
prudent king knew that Fortune always overturns the greatest successes.

"Caesar had a very powerful reason to arm against Pompey, to whom
Fortune had already shown great indulgence, though she could not put up
with any human happiness for long. These are the effects of this wretched,
puffed up, variable, and flighty Fortune, who is eager for our every downfall, preparing every glorious beginning for an unhappy end.

"O how blessed is your Genevera, who passed from corruptible to immortal, freed from the acute bite of envious Fortune, who, with mortifying
teeth, tears to pieces, corrupts, and kills people of the most adorned dignity,
similar to her. All her enemies are left without the power to harm her. No
envy, greed, ambition, lust, insidiousness, or anything else remains to attack
her. She has become worthy to join the assembly of the great God. In His
most holy and patient breast, He can see, know, and scorn your tears and
trembling. O insane suffering, O inconsiderate mind, O obstinate heart, O
blind consideration, O foolish ways of ours, which lead and incite our steps!

"If Genevera has been elected to the culmination of human dignity,
wouldn't you honour her only with celebrations? Wouldn't you provide
a great part of your wealth for that? O Peregrino, where is your prudence
and dignity? Genevera has joined the transcended spirits and is made citizen of heaven and member of the angelic consistory, so why do you cry

---

58   Aurelio Bellincini of Modena lectured in canonical law, philosophy, and theology at the
     Studio ferrarese.

and moan? Stop these complaints and give glory to God, Who in your life has given you so many graces. Remember: even the great Cato was not without blame when he indulged his pain over his brother's death more than he should have. But when he came back to reason, he remembered that he was a philosopher and he put an end to his pain.

"I know that no piety can be far from human hearts. But one must temper both kinds of responses to Fortune. Therefore, show now some consolation for Genevera's true immortality and do not disturb her true peace, which we all look forward to celebrating.

"Jesus our Ruler called Lazarus's spirit back to life, which unsettled Him, not because it was difficult for Him to reanimate that dead body, but because He had respect for human misery. He grieved for His reanimated friend, whom He saw taken from the consoling peace of eternal rest. In order to satisfy stubborn depravity among the Jews, He accepted making Lazarus once again a fighter in this world, where one must always battle but rarely triumph. All the cities, castles, fortresses, and other worldly places glory in having one of their own who makes their locale illustrious, and all their citizens celebrate the distinguished person's birthday with honours, festivities, and songs. If they applaud a great person for human actions, what must we do to mark divine actions, to which through Genevera we thankfully are closer than any other generation?

"Do not be pained, therefore. You will say to me: but my remaining time burdens me! You are wrong, however. Our last day has as its goal our anticipated victory: the rest of life is vile escape and laziness. What more glorious thing can happen to man than to die in battle? Genevera's death was armed and victorious. You will ask me: How is she victorious if she is dead? She is victorious in the eyes of heaven, the world, and virtue; she is only dead to vices and her companions. Although she was a worthy and circumspect person, adorned with virtue, modesty, constancy, and sanctity, she was not so holy that in staying in the world for one more instant she might not have been stained and contaminated. You and I together can rightly pray through her that we may also be glorified, and after we leave every heartache, we can sing that most glorious hymn *Te Deum Laudamus* to Him Who made her worthy of such grace."

In that moment a tremor grew in my heart that had no cure through medicine or comfort. But still, gathering my strength, in order not to seem ungrateful for such noble company, I replied …

Book 3. Chapter 95.

Peregrino thanks them and dismisses everyone. He admits to himself that he nevertheless feels no consolation.

Peregrino: "Most respected fellow citizens, your articulate speeches could soften the anger of Agamemnon, who out of strong pain tore out his own hair and fled from all human company to gnaw at his own heart. Your sweet words would also fittingly mollify and placate Dido the desperate queen, who at first was happy, then, after a change in Fortune, turned into a rabid dog, the laughingstock of all mortals. Your speeches would indeed be apt to commute to sweetness Caesar's ire against Quintus Ligarius. As much as I can, in response to your exhortations, I will cease my tears until it should please the elect spirits to put an end to my suffering, which will be quite soon.

"Woe is me! How much bitterness, sadness, suffering, and pain is the mortal loss of friends! Among the many examples is that of Phoenix and Chiron, who after the death of their dear disciple Achilles did not want to live any longer. And old Laertes … After losing his son Ulysses, he left his ruling palace of Utica to spend the rest of his days in the fields. Sulla, bitterly pained by the death of Caecilia Metella, his consort, changed the law he had established concerning funeral rites to render greater homage to her. Antony, distraught after Julius Caesar's unworthy death, experienced such grief that he went from happy to desiring nothing but death. Timoleon cried for his late brother for twenty years. As long as Herod lived, he shed tears of grief for his son Pacorus. Adam, the man who had no peer in wisdom, cried for one hundred years over his stabbed son and never found any delight that could sweeten his suffering except continuous crying.

"If we have these examples from our ancestors, how can we temper our own suffering? Agar didn't know how to face the death of his son Ishmael in any other way than through tears. Abraham cried bitterly at the death of his wife Sarah. Jacob refused all consolation when he lost his son Joseph. Our God, when He had human flesh, cried for His friend Lazarus, and Mary cried for her Son. St. Augustine, the greatest example of Catholic doctrine, wept bitter tears upon his mother Monica's death, and he had already lived fifty-six years.

"Not just rational creatures succumb to grief, but animals without sentiments do, too. The pelican, seeing a serpent kill its offspring, will draw its own blood by pecking its own breast.

"Alexander the Great of Macedon heaped tears upon his dear Hephaestion along with wails of grief, dedicating to him a tomb worth twelve thousand talents, then he decreed that Hephaestion be celebrated as a god. This death was so bitter that not even an enemy would be able to temper his tears when he learned about it. Quintus Caecilius Metellus, in emulation of the envied virtue of Scipius Emilianus, called Africanus after the fall of Carthage, heard of his death and spared no tears, crying out loudly that Rome had been destroyed. Solon, the living law to mortals and worthy of the name of wise man, was moved to compassion by the deaths of his friends and did not permit their sepulchres to be without grief, tears, and trembling. Marcellus, the praise and glory of the Roman Republic, grieved over the final downfall of the Syracusans. We read in the ancient fathers and the prophets that the deaths of their people were accompanied by open tears and manifest sobs, as the Scriptures attest of Samuel, David, and Jacob. Caesar didn't hold back his share of tears when he saw the head of his enemy. So, if that many good men have cried out of pain to the point of losing their life, why must I remain in even more pain? Now it will not prove true. O bitter time, O ruinous day full of misery, O most wretched and woeful hour, O cruel, bitter, and impious death, O furious death worthy of execration! Why did you take this innocent body so long before its time? O elect spirits, do not overlook me, because I am ready and willing to join you. I offer infinite thanks to you, my most respected citizens, and I reverence you. May God keep you in peace."

After I said these words, the nobles of the city left. Unconsoled, I retired for nightly rest more ready than ever to curse my unhappy destiny.

Book 3. Chapter 96.

Peregrino has a vision of Genevera, who entreats him to come to her. He tells her that he is on his way. The next day, he calls all of his household and Angelo's to his bedside.

When night was at its deepest in the midst of my lamentable sopor, I saw a light that would cause the Titan Hyperion and the Pleiades to easily yield their places. I sensed a splendour and warmth that made my body languish and my soul liquify. I raised my eyes and saw in the centre of heaven a lady of the greatest power who called me with a pious voice saying, "Peregrino, toil and suffering have been your companions your whole life long. Rise and come! I am your beloved Genevera for whom you uselessly weep." Then she disappeared.

With a quavering voice I cried through tears: "O happy lady, O blessed night, O holy vision, which has made me worthy of such grace through divine will! Wait for me, for I am coming faithfully and obediently!"

When I awoke I had all of my family and Angelo's household called to me, and I said to them ...

Book 3. Chapter 97.

Peregrino informs everyone that his own death is near and puts his affairs in order.

Peregrino: "Most pious mother, Camilla, I have my life from you. Anastasia, I have contentment from you; Violante, from you I have my well-being. I acknowledge you all and owe you so much for the benefits you've imparted to me. Indeed, I'm spoiled to the extent God has willed. Tears cannot sway divine action, nor can life be recalled through them. Save your tears for the benefit of true penance, since they cannot avail the dead. If you've loved me in body, please remember the health of my soul.

"Angelo, it remains a mystery who more than you might possess more intelligence and strength, to say nothing of consolation. The time has come, though, when consolation can be neither offered nor proffered. Now you must safeguard what I have.

"Camilla, I know well I haven't been a satisfactory son to you in any way, not because of malice or through any lack of true piety. My youthful ardour was the reason, which deprived me of free will. I beg you through your maternal efforts and sweetness to be generous and set aside every dissatisfaction if you have any toward me, so that I can leave with a lighter spirit.

"Anastasia, if I have ever angered you – and how could it have been otherwise? – pardon my excess of love. How great my love is will be shown this very day. Through Genevera's sweet memory I beg you to forgive me. Angelo, though my departure is imminent, love is eternal. May all of you be true executors of my will."

Book 3. Chapter 98.

Peregrino dictates his will. Those closest to him leave his room in tears.

Peregrino: "May Genevera and I share her alabaster mausoleum inscribed with junipers and accompanying words. May there be commemorations each year henceforth on our birthdays, our wedding day, and the anniversaries of our deaths. May a church worthy of fame be built with the name of St. Andrew the Apostle. May my house be open and charitable to pilgrims.

"I name Alexandro my only heir and Camilla his tutor and governess. For this purpose, may she be free of any interference. My household must always provide for Violante and Acate, and I order that they receive clothing and a honourable livelihood. Angelo shall oversee my goods, and in the unthinkable case of Camilla's death, I leave him as Alexandro's tutor and guardian."

After I said these words, they left my room crying and wailing, not unlike a cloud dispersed by the rising sun. Then I turned to the others and continued …

Book 3. Chapter 99.

Peregrino speaks to the others who remain, making it known how he wishes to be remembered. Peregrino dictates to Acate the text of his epitaph.

Peregrino: "Every living man naturally desires immortality, which can be acquired in two ways. One is through a wife and children in whom we pass from generation to generation, rendering man immortal in the world. The other is through the adherence to virtue, which is more certain. Among these are nobles, heroes, and people of virtuous action who have left their mark on the world. Up until now, I have made every effort to render myself such in this world that no one considers me useless, lazy, or anything other than a generous man. I call all of you here present as my witnesses and your posterity, to whom I ask you to relate an understanding of my righteous life; I didn't neglect any action – however difficult or almost impossible it might seem – to unite with Genevera in marriage. What I could do with the help of faith, I did, as is clear to every living person.

"I have wandered the earth and sea, searched the underworld, which has been permitted to few mortals, and endured with great equanimity the tempestuous events of this world. Moreover, out of my love of virtue I faced and overcame the impiety, cruelty, persecution, and ingratitude of others. Ever ready to praise and hesitant to criticize, I was prompt to give and slow to accept, inclining to overlook insults and forgive others on the spot. As my final test in this world, I lost my beloved lady before her time. Because I see no true happiness under the heavens, I'm determined to join my Genevera to enjoy true immortality. I already feel my weary body failing, lacking its natural spirits.

"You who remain here after me, be mindful of the three main precepts of the human endeavour: that is, to accumulate wealth, take care of the body, and avenge honour. Each person must pursue the first out of necessity and to uphold virtue; the second, in order to be of use to one's household and city, to which, after God, we are most indebted; and we must pursue the third through the exercise of virtue, not through fraud or tyranny, or any quarrels with others.

"In all your actions may you be imitators of the geometers more than the arithmeticians. Geometers consider the merits of each person and are always thoughtful of an equivalent proportion of the merits of the individual, thus rendering to each one, according to what is due. Arithmeticians consider how much to give, according to what is given, without respect for the present or the past, because they are focused only on number, weight, and measure. Their nature is evil, awful, ungrateful, adulterous, escapist, and detestable. May you be prudent, temperate, strong, and modest. Do not be pusillanimous, proud, arrogant, timid, ungrateful, stubborn toward advice, or unjust. See that in your time you don't put lust before happiness or let pain dominate your cares. May all of your decisions be moderated with reason so that no matter what arises, you can face it. May you not be a laughingstock or the object of gossip in public. If you become powerful, then conspiracies, betrayals, and ingratitude – both within and beyond your family – will always besiege you; if you are poor, you'll never lack for derision, slander, and mockery. But through it all may you be constant and tolerant.

"Honour God before all; revere your soul, fear punishment, make good decisions, be servants of faith, and live according to justice. If Fortune sets before you anything that seems to have no reason for coming your way, bear it with the virtue of fortitude, because it isn't in man's power or knowledge to offer reasons for all the things that happen, especially since human things are governed by superior forces from which we receive the effects without knowing the causes. Let us fix God in our mind, then, and truly believe that everything comes for our instruction or correction because we are sinners and err. When we're good, it's because we're illuminated by His grace and confirmed. So, no matter our path, we remain indebted to God.

"Acate, you know the secrets of my heart; you are the true consoler of my present life and the hope and comfort of all my posterity. I beg and exhort you out of our shared trials to take care of my son Alexandro and his grandmother Camilla. May my tomb be honourably constructed, which you should have engraved with this epitaph:

> Living I burned & sang of love's torments.
> Grateful for my lady, I accuse evil destiny,
> which took her prematurely from this world.
> I was Peregrino & she Genevera:
> equal passion brought us both to the same end.
> Read, pass on & be well.

"I go to spend the rest of eternity with my Genevera, if divine mercy makes me worthy of such grace."

Then I addressed Him with a humble heart and tears in my eyes.

Book 3. Chapter 100.

Peregrino confesses and prays to God and begs His forgiveness.

Peregrino: "O great and sublime God to Whom all of my faults have been laid bare from the time of my birth until my last hour, I beg You in your mercy to forgive my life. Pass over my vain, useless, and senseless acts, and do not consider, Lord, my lustful life, or any of the ways I wasted Your gifts, which You deigned to grant me. Do not focus on the stubbornness of my heart or my perseverance in the habit of sin or in my mistaking transitory things for divine ones. If through my foolishness I have denied You my best years, which passed as nothing more than a vain, interrupted, and fleeting insomnia, do not disdain, Lord, to accept my final prayer and come to support my weak valour. Draw me to the harbour of the quiet life, to the mercy You have pledged, to the font of piety, and to that incorruptible, abounding joy.

"Remember: You are Lord of all. Through You, the firmament of heaven, earth, and every elemental thing lives. Through You every good proceeds, and in You consists every happiness. You provide every grace and gratitude. You kill and you make live; You save and damn. Lord, I love You, adore You, confess You, and fear You. I know You to be the most exacting Judge of our evil, and Defender of our good. If You know me by my faith and works, that I have loved with my heart and adored You religiously, O joyful Lord, do not shun one who has taken You for granted, but through Your immense prudence and incomprehensible goodness, forgive my every fault!

"I recognize that the madness of lust has led me to where reason, conscience, and honesty did not will. My great sin is manifest. I regret my turpitude. I detest my ingratitude. Remember: You are Lord, and I am Your servant. You are the Creator, and I am Your creature. You are the Saviour, and I am Your redeemed. This is Your splendour, Your singular goodness, Your sublime power, and Your celestial glory. You can manifest Your forgiveness in no other way than this. Lord, nothing is hidden to Your providence. Through Your grace, accept my broken heart and deign to receive my weary little soul in Your holy kingdom where it can find consolation with all the elect.

Book 3. Chapter 101.

Peregrino speaks his final words to his friends and relatives and dies.

Peregrino: "Dear friends and others here present, the blessed time willed on High has come to heal my soul, reconcile grace, and purge my heart. I beg you, be vigilant in this blind world, so that the poison of worldly concupiscence doesn't deprive you of divine blessings.

"O how difficult it is to navigate Charybdis in challenging circumstances and not shipwreck! O how impossible the decision is to drink a bit from Circe and not be transformed! O how dangerous it is to listen to the sweet song of the Siren, and then not be able to approach her! May prudence always be with you, and love and the fear of offending God, to Whom I now happily endeavour to go. Now be with Him."

Speaking in this way, I gave up my spirit.

Book 3. Chapter 102.

This chapter closes the frame of the book, which opened with the proem and dedication. Peregrino the character has just died; here the voice of his ghost bids farewell to the author Caviceo, who has been serving as scribe and is on the verge of waking up from his third night of dream visions. The voice of the author bids farewell to Lazzarino Lazzarini and asks the late Ercole Strozzi, Marsilio Ficino, Angelo Poliziano, Giovanni Pico della Mirandola, and Filippo Berovaldo[59] to welcome the spirits of Peregrino and Genevera to the Elysian Fields.

Eager listener, before the herald of the day nudges his sun chariot toward us, go in peace. If you find in your humane heart that *Peregrino* has offered you pious, fruitful study, a rest that is free from disturbing thoughts, and a desire for a more relaxed life, may it please you to make known my sacrifices. When you should see the bust marking our ashes, say with a humble, quiet voice: "Loving shades, rest in peace."

Lazzarino, divine example in whose breast nature placed action and poetics, slow your steps a bit. After you left the Vatican, I know you reached the place where Ercole Strozzi, the poet originally from Florence, recently of Ferrara, awaits you. Tell him not to be annoyed if, with Ficino, Politian, Pico, Filippo Berovaldo, the great poet from Parma,[60] and the whole crowd of the greatest poets, he welcomes Peregrino and Genevera into the vestibule of the Elysian Fields to see and know his sacrifices. I will cross to the consolation of the pure and noble gathering of most noble ruling ladies from Tarsia, Ursina, and Radegonda, who will keep me company in good time.[61]

And to you, farewell!

The end.

---

59   Lazzarino Lazzarini of Rimini was previously mentioned in 3.21ff. The others are all distinguished intellectuals. Ercole Strozzi was a poet in Ferrara, patronized by Lucrezia Borgia. He was murdered in 1508, allegedly stabbed twenty-two times. Marsilio Ficino (d. 1499) was the founder of the Platonic Academy in Florence, a Neoplatonic priest, theologian, and author and translator of numerous Greek and Latin works. Angelo Poliziano (Agnolo Ambrogini, also known as Politian), the Florentine philologist, author, and translator, died at the age of forty by poisoning in 1494. Giovanni Pico della Mirandola, the noble philosopher from Mirandola and author of the *Oration on the Dignity of Man*, also died prematurely, at the age of thirty-one. At the end of his life, he was a zealous follower of Girolamo Savonarola. Filippo Berovaldo, the humanist commentator on numerous classical works (including *The Golden Ass* by Apuleius and Lucan's *Pharsalia*) was a professor at the University of Bologna and died in 1505.
60   Francesco del Pozzo is the one that Peregrino's spirit refers to as the "great poet from Parma." He was also known as *Il Puteolano* and died in Milan in 1490.
61   Caviceo acknowledges his own mortality and alludes to ladies mentioned in the work's proem and dedication.

Index